Luise Mühlbach, F. Jordan

Napoleon and Blücher

An historical novel

Luise Mühlbach, F. Jordan

Napoleon and Blücher
An historical novel

ISBN/EAN: 9783337349776

Printed in Europe, USA, Canada, Australia, Japan

Cover: Foto ©Andreas Hilbeck / pixelio.de

More available books at **www.hansebooks.com**

"You dare set your foot into the house of the Hohenzollerns?" asked the spectre in a hollow, menacing voice.   p. 23.

NAPOLEON AND BLÜCHER.

AN HISTORICAL NOVEL.

BY

L. MÜHLBACH,

AUTHOR OF

"DAUGHTER OF AN EMPRESS," "MARIE ANTOINETTE," "JOSEPH II. AND HIS COURT," "FREDERICK THE GREAT AND HIS FAMILY," "BERLIN AND SANS-SOUCI," ETC., ETC.

TRANSLATED FROM THE GERMAN, BY

F. JORDAN.

COMPLETE IN ONE VOLUME.

With Illustrations.

NEW YORK:

D. APPLETON AND COMPANY,

1, 3, AND 5 BOND STREET.

1892

NAPOLEON AND BLUCHER

NAPOLEON AT DRESDEN.

CHAPTER I.

FREDERICK WILLIAM AND HARDENBERG.

It was a fine, warm day in May, 1812. The world was groaning under the yoke of Napoleon's tyranny. As a consolation for the hopeless year, came the laughing spring. Fields, forests, and meadows, were clad in beautiful verdure; flowers were blooming, and birds were singing everywhere—even at Charlottenburg, which King Frederick William formerly delighted to call his "pleasure palace," but which now was his house of mourning. At Charlottenburg, Frederick William had spent many and happy spring days with **Queen Louisa; and when she was with him at this** country-seat, it was indeed a pleasure palace.

The noble and beautiful queen was also now at Charlottenburg, but the king only felt her presence—he beheld her **no more. Her merry** remarks and charming laughter had ceased, as also her sighs **and** suffering; her radiant eyes had closed forever, and her sweet lips spoke no more. She was still at Charlottenburg, but only as a corpse. The king had her mausoleum erected in the middle of the garden. Here lay her coffin, and room had been left for another, as Frederick William intended to repose one day at the side of his Louisa.

From the time that the queen's remains had been deposited there—from that day of anguish and tears—the king called Charlottenburg no longer his "pleasure palace." It was henceforth a tomb, where his happiness and love were buried. **Still, he** liked to remain there, for **it** seemed to him as though he felt the presence of the spirit of his blessed **queen, and understood better what** she **whispered to his** soul in the silent nights when she consoled him, and spoke **of** heaven and a renewed love. The bereaved husband, however, did not prefer to dwell in the magnificent abode of his ancestors, where he had formerly passed in spring so many happy days with his beloved Louisa. He had, therefore, a small house near the palace; it was into this plain and humble structure that he had retired with his grief-stricken heart. Here, in his solitude, he had already passed two springs.

The second year had nearly elapsed since the queen's death, and Frederick William's heart was still overburdened with sorrow, but yet he had learned what time teaches all mortals—he had learned to be resigned. Yes, resignation in these melancholy days was the only thing that remained to the unfortunate King of Prussia. It was a sad and difficult duty, for he had lost happiness, love, greatness, and even his royal independence

It is true, he was still called **King of** Prussia, but he was powerless. He had to bow to the despotic will of Napoleon, and scarcely a shadow of his **former** greatness had been left him. **The days of Tilsit** had not yet **brought disgrace and humili**ation enough upon him. **The** Emperor of the French had added fresh exactions, and his arrogance became daily more reckless and intolerable. In the face of such **demands it only** remained for Frederick William to submit or resist. He looked mournfully at his unhappy country; **at those whom** the last **war** had deprived of their husbands **and fathers; at his small army; at the** scanty **means at his disposal, compared with the** resources of Napoleon, and—the king submitted.

He had indeed hesitated long, and struggled strongly with his own feelings. For, by submitting to Napoleon's behests, he was to become the open enemy of the Emperor Alexander, and the King of Prussia **was, jointly with the Emperor of the French, to arm against the Emperor of Rus**sia. It was a terrible necessity **for** Frederick William to sacrifice his friend to his enemy, and at the very moment when Alexander had offered his hand for a new league, and proposed to conclude an offensive and defensive alliance with Prussia and England.

But such an alliance with distant Russia could not strengthen Prussia against neighboring France, **whose armies** were encamped near her frontiers. **The danger of** being crushed by Napoleon was **much more probable than the hope of** being supported by Russia. Russia had enough to do to **take care of herself. She** was unable to prevent France from destroying Prussia, if Napoleon desired, and the crown might fall from the head of Frederick William long before a Russian army of succor could cross the Prussian frontier. **He submitted** therefore, and accepted with one hand the alliance of France, while threatening her with the other.

On the 24th of February, 1812, the Prussian **king signed this new treaty.** As was stipulated by the first article, he entered into a defensive alliance with France against any European power with which either France or Prussia should here-

after be at war. Napoleon, the man who had broken Queen Louisa's heart, **was now** the friend and ally of King Frederick **William, and** the enemies of France were henceforth **to be the** enemies **of Prussia!**

It was this that **the** king thought of **to-day,** when, in the early part of May, he was alone, and absorbed in his reflections, at his **small** house in Charlottenburg. **It was** yet early, **for** he **had** risen before sunrise, and had been at work a long time, when he ceased for a moment and yielded to his meditations. Leaning back in his easy chair, he gazed musingly through the open glass-doors, now on the serene sky, and again on the fragrant verdure of his garden.

But this quiet relaxation was not **to last** long; the door of the **small anteroom** opened, and the **footman announced that his excellency** Minister **and Chancellor von Hardenberg requested to see his** majesty.

"Let him come in," said the **king, as he rose,** turning his grave eyes, which had **become even** gloomier than **before, toward the door, on the** threshold of which the elegant and somewhat corpulent form of the chancellor of state appeared. He bowed respectfully. His noble and prepossessing countenance was smiling and genial as usual; the king's, grave, thoughtful, and sad.

"Bad news, I suppose?" asked the king, briefly. "You come at so early an hour, something extraordinary must have happened. What is it?"

"Nothing of that kind, your majesty," said Hardenberg, with his imperturbable smile. **"Yet, it is true, we are constantly in an extraordinary** situation, so that what otherwise might appear unusual is now nothing but a very ordinary occurrence."

"A preamble!" said Frederick William, thoughtfully. "You have, then, **to tell** me something important. What is it? Take a seat and speak!" The king pointed **to a** chair, and resumed his own. Hardenberg seated himself, and looked down for a moment with an air of embarrassment.

"Any thing the matter in Berlin?" asked the king. "Perhaps, a quarrel between the citizens and the French?"

"No, your majesty," said Hardenberg, to whose thin lips came his wonted smile. "The people of Berlin keep very quiet, and bear the arrogance of the French with admirable patience. I have to report no quarrels, and, on the whole, nothing of importance; I wished only to inform your majesty that I received a courier from Dresden late last night."

The king started, and looked gloomy. "From whom?" he asked, in a hollow voice.

"From our ambassador," replied Hardenberg, carelessly. "Surprising intelligence has reached Dresden. They are expecting the Emperor Napoleon. He left Saint Cloud with the Empress Maria Louisa on the 9th of May, and no one knew any thing about the object or destination of the journey. It was generally believed that the emperor, with his consort, intended to take a pleasure-trip to Mentz, but immediately after his arrival there he informed his suite that he was on his way to a new war, and would accompany his wife only as far as Dresden, where they would meet their Austrian majesties. Couriers were sent from Mentz to Vienna, to Dresden, to King Jerome, and to all the marshals and generals. The columns of the army have commenced moving everywhere, and are now marching from all sides upon Dresden. As usual, Napoleon has again succeeded in keeping his plans secret to the very last moment, and informing the world of his intentions only when they are about to be realized."

"Yes," exclaimed the king, in a tone of intense hatred and anger—"yes, he wears a kind, hypocritical mask, and feigns friendship and pacific intentions until he has drawn into his nets those whom he intends to ruin; then he drops his mask and shows his true arrogant and ambitious face. He caressed us, and protested his friendship, until we signed the treaty of alliance, but now he will **insist on** the fulfilment of the engagements we **have entered** into. He commences a new war, as I, by virtue of the first article of our treaty, I

have to furnish him an auxiliary corps of twenty **thousand men and sixty field-pieces.**"

"Yes, your majesty, it is so," said Hardenberg, composedly. "The new French governor of Berlin, General Durutte, came to see me this morning, and demanded in the name of his emperor that the Prussian **auxiliary troops** should immediately take the field."

"Auxiliary troops!" exclaimed the king, angrily. "The Prussian victims, he ought to have said, for what else will my poor, unfortunate soldiers be but the doomed victims of his ambition and insatiable thirst for conquest? He will drive them into the jaws of death, that they may gain a piece of blood-stained land, or a new title from the ruin of the world's happiness; he does **not** care whether brave **soldiers die or not, so long as** his own ambition is served."

"Yes," said Hardenberg, solemnly, "his path leads across corpses and through rivers of blood, but the vengeance of God and man will finally overtake him, and who knows whether it may not do so during this wild Russian campaign?"

"**My evil forebodings, then, are proving true,**" **said the king, sighing;** "the expedition is directed **against Russia?**"

"**Yes, against Russia,**" **said Hardenberg, sneeringly;** "the master of the world intends to crush Russia also, because she ventured to remain an independent power, and the Emperor Alexander was so bold as to demand the fulfilment of the promises of Tilsit and Erfurt. Providence is always just in the final result, your majesty. It punishes the Emperor Alexander for suffering himself to be beguiled by the flatteries and promises of Napoleon, and the territories which he allowed Napoleon to give him at Tilsit, at the expense of Prussia, will be no precious stones in his crown."

"Not a word against Alexander!" exclaimed the king, imperiously. "However appearances may be against him, he has always proved a true friend of mine, and perhaps especially at a time when we suspected it the least. His keen eyes penetrated the future, and behind the clouds darkening our horizon he believed he could descry light and safety. He yielded, in order to lull Napoleon to sleep; he pretended to be fascinated, in order to convince him of his attachment and devotedness. He wished to be regarded as Napoleon's friend until he had armed himself, and felt strong enough to turn against the usurper. Hush! do not contradict me. I have heard all this from Alexander's own lips. On his return from Erfurt he confided the plans of his future to me and the queen, under the seal of secrecy. Louisa carried the secret into her grave, and I have preserved it in my breast. Now I may communicate it to you, for the hour of decision has come; it finds me on the side of France, and God has decreed that I should turn my arms against my friend, against Alexander! Ah, happy the queen, because she did not live to see this day and witness my new humiliation and disgrace! And was it, then, unavoidable? Was it, then, really necessary for me to enter into this hateful alliance? Was there no way of avoiding it?" And as the king put this question to himself rather than to Hardenberg, he laid his head against the back of his easy-chair, and looked gloomy and thoughtful.

"There was no way, unfortunately, of avoiding it," said Hardenberg, after a short pause. "Your majesty knows full well that we submitted to stern necessity only; to act otherwise would have been too dangerous, for the crown on the head of your majesty would have been menaced."

"It is better to lose the crown and die a freeman than live a crowned slave!" exclaimed the king, impetuously.

"No, pardon me, your majesty, for daring to contradict you," said Hardenberg, smiling; "it is better to keep the crown, and submit to necessity as long as possible, in order to be able to take future revenge on the oppressor. At times I am likewise tortured by the doubts and fears now disquieting the noble soul of your majesty. But at such hours I always repeat to myself, in order to justify our course, a few words from the letter which the Duke de Bassano addressed to our ambassador, Baron von Krusemark, as the ultimatum of the Tuileries. I have learned this letter by heart, and, if you will graciously permit me, I will repeat a few words." The king nodded assent, and Hardenberg added: "This letter read: 'My dear baron, the moment has come when we must give you our views about the fate of Prussia. I cannot conceal from you that this is a matter of life and death for your country. You know that the emperor entertained already at Tilsit very unfriendly intentions against Prussia. These intentions still remain the same, but will not be carried out at this time, on the condition that Prussia become our ally, and a faithful one. The moments are precious, and the circumstances very grave.'"[*]

"An outrageous letter!" muttered Frederick William to himself.

"Yes, an outrageous letter," repeated Hardenberg, bowing, "for it contained a serious threat, and yet, on the other hand, it offered us a sort of guaranty. Prussia was lost, in case she refused to join the alliance, for Austria had likewise acceded to it, and, by holding out against the wishes of France, Prussia would have run the risk of being crushed by two armed enemies in the north, as well as in the south, and blotted out from the list of nations. We, therefore, were obliged to submit; we had no other choice."

"But what did we gain by submitting?" asked the king, angrily. "In order to preserve my people from the horrors of war, I bowed to Napoleon's will, and accepted the disgraceful alliance. I thereby wished to secure peace to my unfortunate country, which stands so greatly in need of it. Instead of attaining this object, the alliance plunges us into the very abyss which I intended to avoid, and I am compelled to send my soldiers into the field for an unjust cause against a monarch who is my friend, and under the orders of a commander-in-chief who is my enemy, and has always shown his bitter hostility to me."

"But your majesty has at least prevented your own country from being devastated by war. It is true, you send out your army, but the war will not lay waste the fields of Prussia; it will not

---

* "Mémoires d'un Homme d'État," vol. xi., p. 324.

trample in the dust the crops of the Prussian farmer, interrupt the labors of the mechanic, or carry its terrors into our cities and villages, our houses and families. The enemy is at least far from our own country."

"You only wish to palliate the calamity," exclaimed the king. "The enemy is here, and you know it. He is dogging every step of ours; he is listening to every word of mine, and watching every movement. An inconsiderate word, an imprudent step, and the French gendarmes will rush upon me and conduct the King of Prussia as a prisoner to France, while no one can raise his **hand to prevent them. We have the enemy in Berlin, in Spandau, and in all our fortresses. Our** own soldiers we have to send into the field, and our cities and fortresses are occupied by French garrisons. An army of four hundred and eighty thousand infantry and seventy thousand cavalry cover Prussia like a cloud of locusts; Berlin, Spandau, Königsberg, and Pillau, have received French garrisons; only Upper Silesia, Colberg, and Graudenz, have remained exempt from them. The whole country, as though we were at war, is exposed to the robberies, extortions, and cruelties in which an enemy indulges: this time, however, he comes in the garb of a friend; and, as our ally, he is irritating and impoverishing the farmers, and plundering the mechanics and manufacturers. And I am not only obliged to suffer all this in silence, but I must send my own soldiers, the natural defenders of our states, into a foreign country, and command them to obey the man who has heaped the vilest insults not only on myself, but on the whole of Prussia, and has broken the heart of my beloved wife!" And the king, quite exhausted, breathless with his unusually long speech, and almost ashamed of his own tremulous excitement, buried his face in his hands and groaned aloud.

Hardenberg gazed upon him for a moment **with** an expression of profound sympathy; he **then** looked around the room with searching glances, which seemed to pierce every niche, every fold of the curtains, and every piece of furniture and sculpture. "Is your majesty sure that no one can hear and watch us here?" he asked in a low voice.

The king dropped his hands from his face, and looked at him in surprise.

"Your majesty, you yourself say that you are surrounded by spies and eavesdroppers," added Hardenberg. "Does your majesty suspect any such to be here?"

"No," said the king, with a mournful smile, "it is the last blessing of my Louisa that she has secured me this quiet asylum. The spies do not venture to penetrate here—this retreat is not desecrated by their inquisitive and lurking glances."

"Well," said Hardenberg, almost joyously, "if we need not be afraid of the eyes and ears of spies, your majesty will permit me to speak freely to you. My king, great events are maturing; while impenetrable darkness still seems to surround us, morning is gradually dawning, and the day of retribution is not distant. Europe is utterly tired of war, and this incessant bloodshed; she has practised forbearance until it is exhausted and converted into an intense indignation. Thanks to his unscrupulous machinations, Napoleon has hitherto succeeded in bringing about wars between the different nations of Europe in order to derive benefits for France alone from these fratricidal struggles. It was he who drove the Poles and Turks into a war against the Russians, the Italians against the Austrians, the Danes against the Swedes and English, and armed the princes of the Rhenish Confederation against their German countrymen and brethren. He instigated all against each other; he made them continue the struggle until they sank from loss of blood, for he knew that he would then be able to take the property of those whom he had made murder each other. And who could prevent him? The warriors, exhausted by their long and bloody work—the starving people, to whom, in their hunger and anguish, only he who brought them peace and a little bread seemed a true friend! Italy wished to deliver herself from the Austrian yoke, and after long struggles the liberty that Napoleon had promised her consisted but in entire submission to his own behests. To Poland, too, he promised deliverance, and, after the unfortunate country had risen, and spent her last strength and her best blood in the war against Russia, she became exhausted, and offered no resistance when he claimed her as his spoil, and declared the Poles, who had dreamed that they were free, to be subjects of France. The princes of the Rhenish Confederation were compelled to send their German troops to Spain, to wage war against a nation that was struggling for independence; and Napoleon in the meantime placed a French adventurer upon a throne in the middle of Germany, and erected a kingdom for him from the spoils he had taken from German princes. Holland, which had endeavored to preserve some vestiges of liberty, was suddenly deprived of her sovereign, and converted into a French province; and when Napoleon had succeeded in bringing about a war between Sweden and Russia, and instigating unfortunate Finland to resist the **latter power,** he profited by the favorable **moment, and** took Stralsund and the Island of Rügen, both of which belonged to the King of Sweden, who had been his ally up to that time. In Italy only the Pontifical states and the holy father at Rome still resisted him, after the remainder of the peninsula had awakened from its dreams of liberty under the rule of French marshals and Napoleonic princes. He instigated **Naples and** Sardinia against Rome, and when the struggle had commenced, he magnanimously hastened to the assistance of his brother-in-law Murat, arrested the pope, conveyed him as a prisoner to France, and declared Rome to be the property of that country until the pope should submit to his will. No country, no nation, escaped his intrigues—conflagrations, devastation, and death accompanied him everywhere! But the nations, as I have stated already, are at length impatient; they are wearied of fighting; or, rather, if they still fight, they intend to do so only in order to conquer peace for themselves, and bring retribution on him who was the sole cause of all this bloodshed."

"And they commenced by rushing, at his command, into the field—by entering upon another war!" exclaimed Frederick William, shrugging his shoulders with a sneer.

"Your majesty," said Hardenberg, solemnly, "they will do so now for the last time. Napoleon is digging his own grave, and, by consolidating the forces of all countries into one vast army, **he** makes friends of those whom he hitherto successfully tried to make enemies and adversaries of each other. But when the nations have once found out that they are really brethren, it only needs a voice calling upon them to unite for one grand object—that is to say, for the deliverance of Europe from the tyrant's yoke!"

"Those are Utopian dreams," said the king. "Whence should this voice come? Who would be so audacious as to utter it?"

"Whence should this voice come?" asked Hardenberg. "Your majesty, it will come from heaven, **and find an echo on the whole earth. It** will resound from the hundred thousand graves of the soldiers killed in battle, from the breasts of sorrowing widows and orphans, and, like the noise of the tempest, it will come from the lips of thousands of humiliated and disgraced men. This voice will not be that of a single man; but God, Nature, and all nations, will unite, and millions will utter that one shout of 'Liberty! Let us rise and expel the tyrant!'"

"But, then, the story of the tower of Babel will be reënacted," said Frederick William, sighing; "the nations will not understand each other; an endless confusion of languages will ensue, and, finally, the building, which they intended jointly to erect, will fall to ruins and they be dispersed."

"In order to prevent this, a chieftain must gladly place himself at their head, and direct their will," exclaimed Hardenberg. "I hope God will intrust this leadership to your majesty."

"To me?" asked the king, almost angrily. "Will you take the liberty of mocking my distress, or do you believe that I ought to be consoled in the calamities of the present by such hopes of the future?"

"No, your majesty, I am only convinced that God will one day intrust the task of retribution to Prussia, because it is she that has suffered most."

"**Let us** leave retribution to God," **said the king,** gently.

"No, your majesty," exclaimed Hardenberg, "let us now take upon ourselves the task of avenging our wrongs, and only pray to Heaven for a blessing on our efforts. And that God is with us, that He at last averts His face from the man who has so long trampled the world under foot, is shown by the new war into which Napoleon is about to enter. This expedition to Russia is the first step to his ruin!"

"Oh, you are mistaken!" exclaimed the king, almost indignantly. "It will be a new triumphal **procession for Napoleon.** Russia will succumb to **him, as we all have done. He marches upon the** position of his enemy with the armies of all his allies—half a million of warriors and thousands of cannon—while Russia stands alone; she has no force compared with his, and no allies whatever."

"She has one friend more powerful than any Napoleon has," said Hardenberg, solemnly—"*Nature.* When this ally appears, with its masses of ice and snow-storms, Napoleon is lost."

"But he will take good care not to wait for this reinforcement," exclaimed the king. "As always, he will finish the war in a few weeks, vanquish the feeble forces of Alexander with his own tremendous columns in one or two decisive battles, and then, on the ruins of the Russian empire, dictate terms of peace to the humiliated emperor. This has been the course of events ever since Bonaparte commanded, and so it will be hereafter."

"Your majesty, it will not; for, during twelve years, he has been the instructor of the world, and the nations have learned from him not only the art of war, but his special strategies. His secret consists in the rapidity of his movements. He has made Macchiavelli's words his own: 'A short and vigorous war insures victory!' He must, therefore, be opposed by a protracted and desultory war—his enemies must fight long, not with **heavy** columns, but with light battalions, now here, now **there;** they must take care not to bring on a general battle, but slowly thin the ranks of his army, and exhaust his resources and his patience. This was the course which the Spaniards pursued, and their hopes are, therefore, promising; they are carrying on a guerilla warfare, and he is obliged to renew the struggle every day without being able to defeat them in a decisive battle. Russia will adopt a similar plan. She will take pains to draw Napoleon farther and farther into the interior of the country, incessantly alluring him forward by insignificant victories, rendering him eager for a great battle. In strict obedience to the plans he has adopted, she will especially endeavor to weaken Napoleon, and cut him off from his supplies and base of operations. She will successively fight him at every important point, **with a** strong army, supported by large reserves, **tire him out, and ruin him in detail. This plan** she will adhere to until her great ally approaches from Siberia—grim Winter, covering Russia with an invulnerable defence, so that her sons may at last take the offensive, and expel the terrified enemy."

"That is a grand, but an infernal scheme!" exclaimed the king, who had risen, and was walking up and down with hasty steps. "Who conceived it?"

"No single brain; it is the result of the consultations of the most eminent Russian generals. They also have studied Macchiavelli, and found that significant axiom, 'He who knows how to resist will conquer in the end.' The Russians, therefore, will resist, and they will conquer."

"But who tells you that this is the plan which Russia will adopt?" asked the king. "Whence have you derived such accurate information?"

"Your majesty," said Hardenberg, smiling, "though we publicly act as the enemies of Russia, and are compelled to send our army against her, she secretly regards us as her ally, and knows well that we are only waiting for the favorable moment to drop the mask and become the open enemy of the usurper. We have, therefore, warm friends in Russia, who will keep us informed about every thing going on, that we may prudently use the favorable moment when we also can take up arms against Napoleon."

"No rash steps—no *coups de main*," exclaimed Frederick William, gravely and imperiously, standing in front of Hardenberg, and looking him full in the face. "I am opposed to any sort of underhand games; when you are not strong enough to attack your enemy openly and honestly, you ought to be too proud to shoot at him from an ambuscade, like a coward and bandit. The bullet may miss him, and he who fired it dies as a traitor, overwhelmed with disgrace. I have concluded this alliance with France; I am now her ally, and thereby compelled to furnish her an auxiliary corps of twenty thousand men against Russia; so long, therefore, as this campaign lasts, I must, by virtue of the pledges I have given, stand by France, and woe to the general of mine who should forget this, and disobey the orders I have given him!"

"There may be circumstances, however, your majesty," said Hardenberg, in an embarrassed tone, "circumstances—"

"There can be none," interrupted the king, "justifying us to turn traitors. A man has but one word to pledge, and that I have pledged to Napoleon. When my soldiers forsake the colors under which I have placed them, they shall be punished as deserters. No one knows the anguish with which I say this, but as a man who must keep his word, and as a commander-in-chief who, above all, must maintain discipline and subordination, I cannot speak otherwise. Tell your friends in Russia so. I am sad and dejected enough, compelled as I am to become Napoleon's ally. But I will not perjure myself!"

"Your majesty, I bow in admiration of these noble words of my king," exclaimed Hardenberg, enthusiastically; "I wish the whole world could hear them. At this hour you obtained a greater victory than Napoleon ever gained on the battle-field—a victory of duty and fidelity over your own inclinations and wishes! Far be it from me to oppose this magnanimous resolution. Our army, then, will march out side by side with the French troops, and will return, if it ever should, as an auxiliary corps of the grand army. But then, your majesty, the new day will dawn, for which

we must prepare while Napoleon is in Russia. It must be in secret—in the dead of night—but the rising sun will find us ready. The world is now united for the great work; brethren are offering their hands to brethren from the shores of the Mediterranean to those of the Atlantic and the Baltic. Their common sufferings have filled their hearts with the same love and hatred. All the nations are **uniting into one family, and in their** wrath will destroy him who is menacing all alike. Secret messengers keep the brethren in the west and north, in the south and east, well informed of what is done by their friends. Patriotic poets are arousing the nations from the lethargy that enthralled them during so many years; they make them hear the gospel of liberty, and awaken them from their indifference. In secret workshops the brethren are forging arms; in the night the sisters are at work upon uniforms, and their children are making lint for warriors to be wounded in the holy war of liberation. They are quietly preparing for it in the offices, the students' halls, and the workshops. At the first call they will fling **aside their pens and tools, take up the** sword, and hasten into the field, to deliver the fatherland. All Europe, at the present moment, is but one vast secret society, which has even in France active and influential members. Napoleon stands on a volcano, which will soon engulf him."

"Enough!" exclaimed the king, anxiously. "Say no more; I will know nothing about secret societies and conspiracies. They are perhaps an inevitable evil in these times, but still they are an evil, destroying those for whose benefit they were intended."

"May God in His mercy favor them in advancing our cause," exclaimed Hardenberg, "that from them may arise the army that is to deliver the nations from the yoke of the tyrant! I am convinced that it will be so, and that the moment will come when Prussia will be able to redeem the oath which I am sure every Prussian took when he saw the coffin of the august Queen Louisa. On the day, your majesty, when I saw it, I resolved to strive for no other object than to deliver my country. For this I will devote my whole strength—my life, if need be! Heaven heard my oath, and I shall not die before its fulfilment."

The king gazed long and mournfully upon the queen's portrait which hung over his desk, and represented her in the attire in which Frederick William had seen her for the first time. "But she died before the hour of deliverance struck," he said, gloomily, to himself. "Her heart was broken, and she did not even take hope with her into the grave. She—," he stopped suddenly, and turned his eyes toward Hardenberg. "I will communicate something to you," he said briefly and impulsively; "I will confess to you that I comprehend your oath; for I also took one when I held the queen's corpse in my arms. In the beginning the terrible blow paralyzed my soul, and I felt as though I had been hurled into a dark abyss. Suddenly I heard, as from a voice resounding in my ears, 'You must not die before you avenge her death upon him who broke her heart!' I bent over her, and, kissing her lips, swore that I would live only to obey. I have not forgotten that oath and that hour, and, you may depend on it, I shall ever remember it; but I will wait for the favorable moment, and it must not be supposed that I can allow myself to be carried away by imprudent projects."

"No one would wish that, your majesty," said Hardenberg, hastily. "On the contrary, prudence, above all, is necessary at the present time, and for this reason I would entreat you to overcome your feelings and go to Dresden, to pay your respects to the emperor."

"Never!" exclaimed Frederick William, starting up and blushing with indignation. "No, nowhere else than in battle can I meet again this man, who has destroyed my happiness, my honor, and my hopes! Do not allude to this any more. It cannot be. How can I meet him, whom I have not seen since the days of Tilsit? Who can ask me to go to Dresden, to stand there as a courtier at the door of an arrogant victor, and mingle with the crowd of his trainbearers?"

"Your majesty, the Emperor of Austria will also go to Dresden," said Hardenberg, entreatingly.

"The Emperor of Austria does so, because he is unfortunate enough to be Napoleon's father-in-law."

"Nevertheless, the Emperor Francis saw his son-in-law for the last time on the day when, after the battle of Austerlitz, he repaired as a supplicant to the bivouac-fire of Napoleon, and implored the conqueror to grant him peace. That was even worse than Tilsit, and still the Emperor of Austria comes to Dresden, to become, as your majesty said, the trainbearer of the victor."

"Why does he do so?" asked the king, shrugging his shoulders. "Because he must—because at the present time every wish of Napoleon is almost an order, even for princes. Napoleon caused his ambassador at Vienna verbally to inform the emperor that he wished to see his father-in-law at Dresden, and witness the meeting of his consort, Maria Louisa, with her parents. The Emperor Francis hastened to comply with this request, and is expected to arrive to-morrow."

"Well, Bonaparte, fortunately, expressed to me no such wish, and it will not be expected that I should go thither without being requested to do so."

"Pardon me, your majesty, our ambassador at Dresden received a similar communication from the French envoy at the court of Saxony. The Emperor Napoleon desires likewise to see your majesty at Dresden. Here is the letter from the ambassador."

The king took the paper and hastily glanced over it. He then heaved a profound sigh, and, returning it to Hardenberg, fixed his eyes once more upon the portrait of the queen. He gazed steadfastly upon it. Gradually the expression of his features became milder, and his gloomy eye more cheerful. With a wave of his hand he called Hardenberg to his side; looking again at the portrait, and saluting it with a gentle nod, he said, "She overcame her feelings, and went to Tilsit, because she believed it necessary, for the welfare of Prussia, to pacify the wrath of Napoleon. I will follow the example of my beloved Louisa. I will conquer myself, and go to Dresden. But you, Hardenberg, must accompany me."

———

CHAPTER II.

THE WHITE LADY.

GREAT commotion reigned at the palace of Baireuth. Servants hurried through the brilliantly-decorated rooms, spreading out here and there **an additional** carpet, placing everywhere vases filled with fragrant flowers, or dusting the finely-polished furniture. It was a great and important day for Baireuth. All felt it, and excitement and curiosity drove the inhabitants into the streets. No one cared to stay at home, or be absent at that historic hour which was to shed upon Baireuth a ray of her ancient glory.

The man at whose feet the world was prostrate, to whom kings and princes were bowing, before whom empires trembled and thrones passed away, who had only to stretch out his hand to establish new dynasties, and whom the world admired while it hated—Napoleon—was to arrive at Baireuth. The quartermasters had arrived already early in the morning, and ordered in the name of the emperor that the rooms at the palace should be put in readiness, because he intended to reach Baireuth in the afternoon of the 14th of May, and stop overnight.

The whole population seemed to be in the streets. The windows of the houses along the route of the emperor were open, crowded with the most distinguished ladies of the city; they were dressed in their most beautiful toilets, and held in their hands bouquets, with which they intended to salute Napoleon. But the greatest commotion, as we have remarked, reigned at the new palace, for the emperor had given express orders that apartments should be prepared for him there, and not at the old palace of the Margraves of Brandenburg. Count Munster, intendant of the palaces, had, of course, complied with these orders, and four brilliant rooms were ready for the reception of Napoleon. All the arrangements were completed, and **the** intendant, followed by the castellan, walked for the last time through the imperial rooms to satisfy himself that every thing was in good order.

"No, nothing has been left undone," said **the** count, when he stepped into the bedchamber destined for the emperor. "Every thing is as comfortable as it is splendid; the arrangement reflects a great deal of credit upon you, my dear Schluter, and will, doubtless, procure you a liberal reward from the emperor, who is said to be very munificent."

"I do not wish to accept any presents at the tyrant's hands," growled the castellan, with a gloomy face; "I do not want to stain my hands with the plunder which he brings from foreign lands, and which is accompanied with **a curse rather than a blessing.**"

"You are a fool, my dear Schluter," exclaimed the count, laughing. "You see at least that curses do not incommode the emperor, for his power and authority are constantly on the increase. He is now going to Dresden, to see at his feet all the princes of Germany; and he will then hasten northward, to gain new victories and humiliate the only man in the world who still dares to defy him, the Emperor Alexander of Russia."

"I know some one else who will not bow to him, and whom he will not humiliate," said the castellan, contemptuously shrugging his shoulders.

"Well, and who is that?" asked Count Munster, quickly.

"It is the White Lady!" exclaimed the castellan, solemnly and loudly.

Count Munster shuddered and glanced around in evident terror. "For Heaven's sake, hush!" he said, hastily. "Pray forget these foolish hallucinations, and, above all, do not venture to talk about them at the present time."

The castellan shook his head slowly. "You ought not to talk of hallucinations, count," he said, solemnly. "The White Lady is awake and walking, and she knows that the enemy of her house, the house of Brandenburg, will spend the coming night at this palace. I repeat it to your excellency, she is walking, and her eyes are filled with wrath, and there is a curse on her lips against the enemy of the Hohenzollerns. I would not be surprised if she should shout to-night into the ears of the tyrant, and, by her words, awaken him from his slumber."

"Gracious Heaven, Schluter, do not talk so audaciously!" exclaimed the count, anxiously. "If one of the attendants of the emperor over-**hear your words, you** would perish. Napoleon is said to be somewhat superstitious; he, who other-**wise is afraid of nothing in the world, is said** to **be easily terrified by ghosts, and to believe in all** sorts of omens and prophecies. He has already heard of the White Lady of Baireuth, and therefore given express orders that apartments should be prepared for him at the new palace, and not at the old one, and rooms selected in which she was not in the habit of walking.* I hope that you have punctually carried out this order, and that these rooms are exempt from the visits of the apparition?"

"Who has the power to give orders to spirits, and command them, 'So far and no farther?'" asked the castellan, almost scornfully. "She goes whither she desires, and the doors closed against her she opens by a breath. The walls disappear before her, and where you expect her least of all, there you suddenly meet her tall, majestic form in the white dress, her head covered with a black veil, under which her large angry eyes are flashing."

"Hush, Schluter!" exclaimed the count, anxiously, "I know the portrait of the White Lady, which hangs in the cabinet adjoining the audience-hall, and it is, therefore, unnecessary for you to describe her appearance to me."

"Your excellency knows that we have two portraits of the White Lady," said the castellan, laconically.

"Yes, the one with the white dress is at the hermitage; the other, representing her in a dark

dress, is here at the palace. Thank Heaven! there is but one portrait of her here, and I hope it is in the other wing of the building."

"That is to say, I saw the portrait there this afternoon, but who knows whether it is still there?"

"How so? Who knows?" **asked the count** impatiently. "What do you mean?"

"I mean, count, that it is in fact no portrait, but only the bed in which the White Lady sleeps until it pleases her to walk, and that, while **she** is walking, it will certainly not be found at its place. Did I not report to your excellency six months since that the portrait had again broken the nail and fallen? It was an entirely new nail, count, so firm and strong, that half a regiment of **French soldiers might have been hung upon it at the same time; I had had the nail made by the** blacksmith, and the **mason fixed it. I myself** hung up the portrait, and it seemed as firm as though it had grown in the wall. But that very night a noise like a thunder-clap rolling over my head awakened me, and when I opened my eyes, the White Lady stood at my bedside; **her right** hand raised menacingly, her black veil thrown back, she stared at **me with a face flashing with** anger. I uttered a cry, and shut my eyes. **When** I opened **them again, she had** disappeared. In the morning I went into the hall to look after the portrait. It was gone. Where the nail had been fixed nothing but a blood-red stain was to be seen ; the nail itself, broken into small pieces, lay on the floor. The portrait had walked to the small cabinet adjoining the hall, and was quietly leaning there against the wall as though nothing had happened."

"And I told you to let it stand there, and not try again to hang it up. The large painting is too heavy."

"If the large painting wanted to hang on the wall it would allow the smallest nail to hold it," said Schluter, shaking his head. "But the White Lady wishes to stand on her own feet, and no human power is able to prevent her."

"Schluter, I repeat to you, you are a dreamer," exclaimed the count, impatiently. "Let us speak

* Historical.—Vide Minutoli, "The White Lady," p. 17.

no more of the apparition. It makes one feel quite curious. Tell me now whether you have really removed the portrait far enough that it cannot be seen by the emperor?"

"When I was an hour ago at the cabinet adjoining the audience-hall, the portrait was still there. But who knows what may have happened since then?"

"Well, it is a fixed idea of yours," said the count, shrugging his shoulders. "I do not wish to hear any more of it. These rooms are finely arranged, and I have no fault to find with them. Now lock the entrance-door, and let us go out through the Gallery of Palms, by which the emperor will have to enter."

"Pray, your excellency, lead the way; I shall lock the door and immediately follow you," said the castellan, walking hastily through the opened rooms.

Count Munster slowly walked on, thoughtfully looking down, and shuddering inwardly at the immovable superstition of the castellan, whom his reason vainly endeavored to deride.

"And still it is folly, nothing but folly," he muttered to himself, while opening the high hall-door, and stepping into the anteroom, to which, on account of its length and narrowness, and the fresco paintings of tropical plants on the walls, the name of the "Gallery of Palms" had been given.

All was silent in this gallery; the setting sun shed its beams through the windows, covered with dark curtains, and drew trembling shining lines across the high room. The footsteps of the count resounded so loudly that he himself was frightened, and glanced anxiously around. Suddenly he started in dismay, and quickly advanced several steps. He had seen something moving at the lower end of the gallery, and it seemed to him as though he had heard approaching footsteps. Yes, he was not mistaken; now he saw it quite distinctly! A lady approached. The sun illuminated her tall form, and shed a golden light over the white dress falling down in ample folds over her feet. She approached with slow steps, quite regardless of the count, who at first looked at her in surprise, and then turned with an angry face toward the castellan, who just then entered.

"You did not comply, then, with my orders, Schluter?" exclaimed the count, vehemently. "I told you expressly to keep the rooms shut until the emperor's arrival, and not to admit any one. How could you dare disobey my instructions?"

"But, your excellency, I did obey them," answered Schluter. "Not a human being besides the footmen has been permitted to enter here, and even those I drove out two hours ago, and shut the doors."

"If that be true, how does it happen that there is a lady here in the gallery," asked Count Munster, stretching out his arm toward the lower end of the apartment.

"A lady?" asked Schluter, greatly amazed. "Where is she, your excellency?"

The count fixed his eyes searchingly on the large arched window, in the bright light of which he had distinctly seen the lady. She was gone—the gallery was empty. "You forgot to shut the lower door, and while I turned and scolded you, the lady escaped!" he exclaimed. He hastily rushed forward, and tried to open the door leading into the corridor: but this was locked. The count vainly shook the lock. "That is strange," he muttered, dropping his hand. "I know I saw her distinctly; it is impossible that I could have been mistaken. Where can she be? What has become of her? Where has she concealed herself?"

"What becomes of the last sigh of a dying person, your excellency," asked Schluter, solemnly. "Where does the soul conceal itself after escaping from the body?"

"Ah, nonsense!" ejaculated Count Munster. "It could not have been a spectre. Why, it is not a spectre's hour, and, besides, I certainly saw the lady plainly; it was a decidedly earthly figure. Her face was pale and grave, but there was nothing spectral about it. She wore a black veil thrown back from her face; the upper part of her body was covered with—"

"A dark pelisse trimmed with fur," interrupted Schluter, composedly. "Below this dark pelisse protruded a white silk dress, falling to the **ground** in full folds."

"Yes, yes, that was the costume," exclaimed the count. "But how do you know it without having seen her?"

"It is the costume of the White Lady, your excellency," said Schluter, "and it was she who just walked through the gallery. Pray, count, go with me to the other wing of the palace and look at her portrait; your excellency will then be convinced that I tell the truth."

"No, no, I do not wish to see it," replied Count Munster, whose cheeks turned pale, and who felt his heart frozen with terror. "Unlock **the door, Schluter!** The **air here is sultry and** very oppressive! Quick! quick! open the door!" The castellan obeyed, and the count rushed out into the corridor, where he opened a window and inhaled the fresh air in eager draughts.

At this moment shouts were heard at a distance, and at the same time the count's footman rushed breathlessly down the corridor. "Your excellency, the emperor is coming. He has already passed through the gate, and the people are loudly cheering him. I have run as fast as I could, in order to inform your excellency."

"I am coming," said the count, advancing rapidly. But, having proceeded a few steps, he turned again and beckoned the castellan to his side. "Schluter," he whispered to him, "if you love your life, do not say a word about what has just happened here. It must remain a secret."

"A secret!" muttered Schluter to himself, gazing after the count, who hurried away. "The White Lady will manage the affair in such a manner that he at least will hear of the secret, and the bloodthirsty tyrant will not sleep well in the palace of the Margraves of Brandenburg." He violently closed the door and stepped out into the large staircase-hall, the doors of which opened upon the street. Uttering incoherent words of indignation in an undertone, the castellan pushed open **one** of the windows and looked gloomily down **on** the street. An immense crowd were in front of the palace; all eyes were turned to the side from which the emperor was to approach.

Breathless with curiosity, the people waited for the arrival of the hero who had conquered nearly all the world.

"How those fools are gaping!" growled Schluter. "Idle and lazy as usual; they like to complain and lament, but they never think of doing any thing. If only each one would take up a single stone from the pavement and throw it as a greeting at the tyrant's iron head, all this distress and wretchedness would be at an end. **But no** one thinks of that, and I should not wonder if those fellows, instead of cursing him, should enthusiastically cheer him."

The shouts drew nearer at this moment, as the crowd rushed from the lower part of the street, their acclamations growing constantly more deaf-**ening.** French lancers galloped up to keep the people back, and several carriages, **preceded by a** plain calash, came in view. A negro, dressed in a richly-embroidered livery, sat on the box by the side of the coachman; two plainly-dressed gentlemen occupied the inside of the carriage.

"That is he!" growled Schluter. "The **Evil** One brings him hither—he is his best friend Yes, that is he, and he looks pale, grave, and incensed, as though he would like to wither by a single glance the whole miserable rabble staring at him."

"That is he!" shouted the people. "Long live Napoleon! Long live the emperor!"

Napoleon gazed coldly and impassively upon the crowd, whose cheers came to him as a sound to which he had long been accustomed, and which was by no means agreeable. It was not worth while for him to smile on these inhabitants of a small city; a cold, quick nod was a sufficient acknowledgment. "Long live Napoleon!" shouted the crowd again, when the emperor, having left the carriage, now turned again in front of the palace-gate, and gazed long and indifferently upon the spectators.

The castellan closed his window. "Ah!" he said, "he dares to enter this palace. The White Lady will bid him welcome, and know how to hasten the flight of this arrogant tyrant. Napoleon is coming! Do you hear that, White Lady?

Napoleon is coming!" He burst into laughter, and, opening the door of the corridor, took a position at the one leading into the Gallery of Palms.

Footsteps resounded on the staircase, and various persons appeared. Generals, adjutants, and lackeys hurried in and formed on both sides, as it were, in line of battle. The emperor then entered the lower end of the corridor; Count Munster walked by his side in the most respectful and submissive manner. All bowed their heads reverentially, but the emperor took no notice of them, and slowly passed the saluting officers and servants.

"I hope you have punctually fulfilled my orders, count?" he asked, in his sonorous voice. "This is the new palace, is it not?"

"It is, sire. And this man will testify that no one has set foot into the imperial rooms," said Count Munster, pointing with a smile to the castellan, who, holding his bunch of keys in his uplifted arm, stood at the entrance of the Gallery of Palms.

"Who is it?" asked Napoleon, whose eagle eye was fixed upon Schluter.

"Sire, it is the castellan of this palace, a faithful, reliable man, who has been on service here for more than thirty years. He has guarded and locked the rooms, and they open now only to your majesty's orders."

"Open," ordered the emperor, with a quick wave of his hand. The castellan obeyed, and Napoleon entered. Count Munster followed, and the attendants crowded in after them. Advancing quickly into the middle of the gallery, the emperor stood directly in front of the arched window in which Count Munster had before seen the strange apparition.

"The White Lady, then, never appears in this wing of the palace?" asked Napoleon, abruptly.

"No, sire—never," said Count Munster, solemnly. "On the whole, sire, no one here believes in the absurd old story, and I am sure no one knows of the White Lady otherwise than from hearsay."

The emperor nodded, and passed on. "Let us

soon have supper; you will be my guest," he said, turning on the threshold to Count Munster and dismissing the gentlemen of his suit.

The door closed. He was now a guest at the palace of the ancestors of the royal family of Prussia, the Margraves of Brandenburg.

————◆————

CHAPTER III.

THE emperor had long risen from the supper-table. The imperial suite had been allowed to withdraw. Alone he sat in a comfortable night-dress on the high, antiquated easy-chair, in front of the fireplace, in which, at his express order, notwithstanding the warm weather, a large fire had been kindled. He liked heat; the sun of Egypt and the desert had never been too warm for him; in the hottest summer days in France he frequently felt chilly, and called for a fire. It seemed as though the inflamed blood in his veins made the world appear cold to him; he saw the light of the sunbeams, but did not feel their warmth. He now sat close to the fire, his face bent over the large map that lay on the table. It was a map of Russia. He rapidly drew several lines across it, marking positions with the colored pins, taken from the small boxes beside him. "Yes, this is my plan," he said to himself, after a long pause. "Three of my corps must be placed on the Niemen; Davoust, Oudinot, and Ney, will command them. There, farther to the left, the cavalry reserves, under Nansouty and Montbrun, will take position. Here the old guard, under Lefèbore; there the young guard, under Mortier and Bessières, with the cavalry of the guard. At this point, farther to the south, the fourth corps, composed of the Italians and Bavarians, will operate, and the Viceroy of Italy, Eugène, will be its general-in-chief. Farther down, here at Grodno and Bialystock, I will place the Poles, Westphalians, and Saxons; the fifth, seventh, and eighth corps to be commanded by my brother Jerome. The Prussians will halt at Tilsit, and form the extreme left wing; Macdonald will be their leader; and below there, at Drochiczyn Schwartzenberg with his Austrians will form the extreme right wing. The preparations are complete, and the thunder-cloud is ready to burst over Russia if Alexander should persist in his obstinacy. Like the waves of the tempestuous ocean, my armies are rolling toward the shores of Russia. They can still be stopped by a suppliant word from Alexander. If he refuses, let his destiny be fulfilled, and let the roar of my cannon inform him that his hour has struck, and that the end of his imperial power draws nigh. It was his **own will. He himself has brought destruction** upon his head! He—"

A loud noise above his head, making the walls tremble and the windows rattle, suddenly interrupted the stillness. The emperor rose from his seat and shouted "Roustan!" The door of the adjoining room opened, and the Mameluke appeared on the threshold.

"What was it?" asked Napoleon, hastily.

"Sire, it was as if a wall fell in above us; the noise was as loud as though a cannon were fired in the palace. I rushed immediately into the corridor, but every thing there was quiet. Only the castellan of the palace appeared in the utmost haste in his night-gown, and asked whether an accident had happened in the rooms of the emperor."

"Where is the castellan now?"

"Sire, when I told him that the noise was on the upper floor, he immediately went thither in order to see what had occurred."

"Go and bring him to me," ordered Napoleon; and when Roustan had withdrawn, the emperor fixed his eyes steadfastly on the door, and his compressed lips quivered with impatience.

Finally, the door opened again; Roustan appeared, followed by the castellan, pale and trembling, behind the Mameluke, and clinging with his hands to the door to support himself.

Napoleon cast upon him one of his quick glances. "What was this noise, and why do you tremble so violently?"

"Pardon me, your majesty," faltered Schluter, "but my terror—the surprise—I am afraid I have lost my senses. I have just seen something so unheard of, so incredible, that I—"

"What have you seen?" asked Napoleon. "Speak! What was this noise?"

The castellan slowly raised his head, and stared with terrified eyes at the emperor. "Your majesty," he said, solemnly, "the White Lady made the noise!"

Napoleon started, and his brow grew clouded. "But did they not tell me that the miserable spectre never haunted this part of the palace?" he asked. "Did I not issue orders that rooms should be given me where I should not be disturbed by this apparition?"

"Your majesty, she has hitherto never entered these rooms," exclaimed **Schluter. "Never before** has the White Lady directed her steps hither, and this afternoon her portrait stood quietly in a cabinet of the other wing of the **palace.** I can take an oath that this is true."

"**What portrait** do you refer to?" asked Napoleon, impatiently.

"**The portrait of the White Lady,**" said Schluter. "I saw it this very day in the cabinet on the other side; all the doors were locked, and now I suddenly find this large painting in the room above you; it was lying on the floor as if in walking it had stumbled over something and fallen. It is the first time that the White Lady appears in this wing of the palace; her portrait has come from the other side, and Heaven alone knows how it has happened. Whenever we wished to convey the painting, with its enormous wooden frame, from one room to another, no less than six men were required to carry it, and now it is here as though it had flitted through the air: and it is lying on the floor as if struck down by lightning."

"And you think the fall of the painting produced the noise?"

"I feel convinced of it. If your majesty wishes me to do so, I will get a few men, go up-stairs to raise the painting, and let it fall again, that your majesty may judge whether it is the same noise or not."

" Ah, you do not feel much respect for your walking portrait," exclaimed the emperor, smiling. " You want to abuse it, and make experiments with it. We will suppose that the fall of the painting was the sole cause of the noise. Now, that it is on the floor, I believe it will lie still and disturb us no longer, unless it be that your portrait should fall asleep and snore. What do you know about that?"

"Your majesty," said Schluter, gravely, "the White Lady never sleeps!" •

The emperor cast a searching glance upon him, and then turned away, folded his hands, and slowly paced the room. Suddenly he stood in front of the castellan.

"What about this White Lady?" he asked, hastily. "Who was she, and what is her history?"

"Ah, sire, it is a long and melancholy history concerning the ancestors of the Margraves of Brandenburg," said Schluter, sighing.

"You know the history?"

"Yes, your majesty, I know it well."

"Tell it to me, but very briefly," said Napoleon, throwing himself on the easy-chair in front of the fireplace, and ordering Roustan, by a wave of his hand and the word "Fire!" to add fresh fuel.

"Now, tell me all about it."

"Your majesty," replied Schluter, hesitatingly, "I do not know how to narrate a story in fine words, and you must pardon me if I do not acquit myself very satisfactorily."

"Who was this White Lady?"

"Sire, her name was Cunigunda, Countess von Plassenburg. Her parents had compelled her to marry the old Count von Plassenburg, and when her husband died, after two years of unhappy wedded life, the Countess Cunigunda of Orlamunde and Plassenburg was a young widow, twenty-four years of age, heiress of the splendid Plassenburg, and mother of two children. She was a gay-spirited lady, and looked around for another husband. Her eyes fell on the Burgrave of Nuremberg, the distinguished nobleman Albert the Handsome. The whole German people called

him so; and all the girls, far and near, daughters of the nobility, as well as those of the citizens of Nuremberg, loved the fine-looking Burgrave of Nuremberg, who was the ancestor of the House of Hohenzollern. But the noble Count Albert loved only one young lady, beautiful Beatrice of Hainault, and would marry none but her. The Countess Cunigunda of Orlamunde, however, was not aware of this, and sent him a message, asking him whether he would not like to marry her. She would give him, besides her hand, the splendid Plassenburg and all her other property. Burgrave Albert the Handsome smiled when he heard the message; shrugging his shoulders, he said : ' Tell your countess I regard her as very amiable, and should like to marry her, provided four eyes were not in existence. But as it is, I cannot do so.' The burgrave referred to the eyes of his parents, who did not like the Countess of Orlamunde, and he wished to make them responsible for his refusal, so as not to offend the beautiful widow. But Cunigunda interpreted the words differently, and thought the four eyes, which the Burgrave said were in the way of their marriage, were those of her two children. She loved the handsome Burgrave so intensely, that she henceforth hated the children, because she believed them to be the sole obstacles to her marriage. The Evil One and her passion whispered into her ear, ' Go and kill your children.' So Cunigunda rose from her couch; in a long white night-dress, her head covered with a black veil, she crept to the bed of her children, and, drawing from her raven hair a long golden pin, set with precious stones (a gift which she had once received at the hands of Burgrave Albert), she pierced the heads of her children, penetrating the brain to the vertebra."

"Medea!" ejaculated Napoleon, staring into the fire. "This, then, is the history of the Medea of the Hohenzollern."

"No, sire, the name of the countess was not Medea, but Cunigunda," said Schluter, respectfully.

Napoleon smiled. "Proceed," he said.

"On the following morning there was great wailing at the Plassenburg, for the two sweet lit tle children lay dead in their bed ; not a vestige of violence was to be seen, and the physician of the countess decided that a stroke of apoplexy had killed them. The Countess of Orlamunde sent a mounted messenger to Nuremberg to Burgrave Albert the Handsome, requesting him to come and see her. And when the burgrave came she met him in a white bridal dress, and looked at him with radiant eyes; in her uplifted right hand she had the golden hair-pin, and said, 'The four eyes are no longer in existence. For your sake I have stabbed my two children with this pin, your first love-gift; the four eyes are extinguished forever. **Now, marry me!' But the burgrave recoiled** in terror, and pushed back the murderess, who was about to embrace him. He then dragged her through the rooms to the dungeon of the castle. She begged and cried, but the burgrave had no mercy upon the infanticide, and hurled her down into the dungeon. He then informed the courts of the crime that had been committed. The Countess von Orlamunde, the last member of her family, was put on trial, and sentence of death passed upon her. The Burgrave of Nuremberg sent the first executioner from the city to the Plassenburg, and the countess was beheaded in the presence of the burgrave, and in the same room in which she had murdered her children. Before putting her head on the block she glanced at the handsome burgrave, raised both her arms toward heaven, and took a fearful oath that she would avenge herself on him and his house; that, whenever one of his descendants was at the point of death, she would be present, as the burgrave himself was now present at her death; that she would never rest in her grave, but live and walk, though the burgrave had her executed, and that, as she was before him now at her last hour, she would appear to him at his last hour. After uttering these words, she put her head calmly on the block. The burgrave then had her buried at the convent of Himmelskron, and, by virtue of an old treaty, the Burgraves of Nuremberg now succeeded to the fiefs of the Counts of Orlamunde, whose line had become extinct. The Plassenburg, with Baireuth

and Burgundy, and all the possessions of the Counts of Orlamunde, therefore passed into the hands of Burgrave Albert the Handsome. He did not enjoy the inheritance a long time, for, a few years afterward, shortly after he had married the beautiful Countess Beatrice of Hainault, he died very suddenly. His wife was awakened by a loud cry he uttered. He then exclaimed, 'Cunigunda, do you come already to take me away? Woe to me! Woe to me!' All became still; the countess called for the servants and a light. **They** rushed into the room with torches. Burgrave Albert the Handsome lay in his bed dead. That, your majesty, is the history of the White Lady of Baireuth."

"This lady, then, followed the Hohenzollern from the Plassenburg to Baireuth and Berlin?" asked Napoleon. "For she **appears sometimes** at Berlin, does she not?"

"At Berlin, and all places where members of the house of Hohenzollern, the descendants of the Burgraves of Nuremberg, are about to die."

"Oh, the dear lady, then, appears only to the family of the Hohenzollern," exclaimed Napoleon, smiling. "Is it not so?"

"No, your majesty, at times she appears also to others," said Schluter; "she walks about the palace, and if there is any one in her way whom she dislikes, she tells them so, and angrily orders him away. She forgets no insult heaped upon her house, and she is terrible in her wrath."

"I have heard of it," exclaimed the emperor, gloomily. "My generals complained vehemently of the annoyances they had suffered here in 1806, owing to the movements of this lady. You were here at that time, were you not?"

"I was, sire, and so I was when General d'Espagne, in 1809, established his headquarters at this palace."

"Ah, I remember," said Napoleon to himself. "Duroc told me the horrible story at that time. Tell me what was it that befell General d'Espagne here?"

"Sire, the general had arrived late at night, and, being weary, had immediately retired. In the night terrible cries were heard in his room

The orderlies hastened into it; the general's bed, which, when he retired for the night stood at the wall, was now in the middle of the room; it was upset, and, having fainted, he lay under it. He was placed on a couch, and a doctor sent for, who bled him, and, when he awoke, gave him sedative powders. The general declared that the White Lady had appeared to him, and tried to kill him. While struggling with her, his bed was upset, **and, when about to succumb, he uttered** loud cries for assistance. He described all the particulars of the countenance, form, and dress of the apparition, and, at his express request, I had to conduct him to her portrait. As soon as he saw it, he turned pale, and almost sank to the floor, muttering, 'It is she! She looked exactly like that when she appeared to me! Her apparition, doubtless, indicated my impending death!' His officers tried to dissuade him from this belief, but he adhered to his conviction, and left the palace that very night in order to establish his headquarters at the 'Fantaisie,' the king's little villa near the city. On the following morning General d'Espagne sent a large detachment of soldiers to this palace; they had to open the floor under the direction of their officers, and take down the wallpaper, in order to see whether there were any secret trap-doors or hidden entrances.* But they found nothing, for the White Lady needs no theatrical apparatus; she goes where she pleases, and walls and locked doors open to her. General d'Espagne, however, was unable to overcome his horror. He left Baireuth on the following day, and when he rode out of the gate he said, 'I heard my own death-knell here at Baireuth. I shall soon die!'"

"And he really died shortly after, for he was killed at the battle of Aspern,"† said Napoleon to himself, staring gloomily into the fire. A pause ensued; suddenly the emperor rose. "It is all right," he said. "Go! Your story of the White Lady was quite entertaining. I hope she will keep quiet **now.** Go!—And you, too, Roustan! I will afterward call you!" Long after the two

had withdrawn, the emperor walked slowly up and down the room. He stood at length in front of the fireplace, and stared moodily into the blazing flames. His face was pale and gloomy. "Foolish stories, which no man of sense can believe! but which, nevertheless, are fulfilled now and then," he added, in a lower voice. "Was it not predicted to Josephine that she would become an empress; and that not death, but a woman, would hurl her from the throne? The prophecy was fulfilled! Poor Josephine! I had to desert you, and, at your lonely palace of Mal maison, you are perhaps praying for me at this hour, because you know I am about to brave new dangers. Poor Josephine!—you were my good angel, and, since you are no longer at my side—no matter!" the emperor interrupted himself; "I will retire to rest." He advanced several steps toward the door leading into his bedroom, where Roustan and Constant were waiting for him, but stopping said, "No, I will first arrange my plans, and fight my decisive battles with the Emperor Alexander." He returned with rapid steps to the table covered with maps, and resumed his seat in the easy-chair. The tapers were burning dimly; the flames in the fireplace flickered, shedding a dark-red lustre on the marble face of the emperor, who, bending over the map, sat motionless. Perhaps it was the heat, or the profound silence, that lulled him to sleep. His head fell back into the chair, and his eyes closed. The emperor slept, but his sleep was not calm, and his features, which when awake were so firm and motionless, were restless, and expressive of various emotions. Once he exclaimed in a tender voice, "My father! Do you at last come to me? Oh, welcome, father!" And a joyous expression overspread the countenance of the sleeper; but it soon faded away, and he appeared angry, and his lips quivered. "No, no," he said, with a faltering tongue, impeded by sleep, "no, father, you are mistaken! my luck does not resemble the changing seasons; I am not yet in autumn, when the fruits drop from the trees and winter is at hand." He paused again, and his face assumed the expression of an attentive listener. "What!"

---

* Vide Minutoli, "The White Lady," p. 17.
† Ibid., p. 17.

be then exclaimed in a loud voice, "you say my **family** will leave me, and betray me in adversity? No, that is impossible, I have lavished kindnesses on them, I——" He paused, and seemed to listen again. "Ah," he exclaimed, after a short interval, starting violently, "that is too much! All Europe is unable to overthrow me. My name is more powerful than Fate!"

Awakened, perhaps, by the loud sound of his own voice, he opened his eyes and looked around uneasily. "Ah," he said, putting his hand on his moist forehead, "what a terrible dream it was! My father stood before me, and predicted what would befall me. **He prophesied my ruin!** He cautioned me against my relatives, and the ingratitude of my marshals!* It is the second time that this is predicted to me, and just as I now saw and heard my father in my dream, the old sorceress spoke to me by the pyramids of Egypt." And the emperor, absorbed in his reflections, muttered in a hollow voice: "'You will have two wives,' said the Egyptian sorceress to me; 'your first wife you will unjustly desert. Your second wife will bear you a son, but your misfortunes will nevertheless begin with her. You will soon cease to be prosperous and powerful. All your hopes will be disappointed; you will be forcibly expelled, and cast upon a foreign soil, hemmed in by mountains and the sky. Beware of your relatives! Your own blood will revolt against you!'† Nonsense," exclaimed the emperor, quickly raising his head; "all this is folly. The palace, with its weird traditions, has infected me, and I scent ghosts in the air, and transform my dreams into prophecies. I will retire!"

For the second time he approached the door of the bedroom, but suddenly recoiled and stood with dilated eyes. In front of it appeared a tall female figure, her arms spread out before the door, as if she wished to prevent the emperor from passing out. A long white dress covered her slender form, a black veil concealed her bosom

and her erect head; but behind the transparent tissue of the veil was a pale, beautiful face, the eyes of which were flashing like swords' points. Breathless with horror, he fixed his eyes steadfastly on the apparition, that approached him now with uplifted arms. Trembling in spite of himself, he drew back, and, putting his hand on the back of the easy-chair, gazed searchingly at the approaching figure.

"You dare set your foot into the **house of** the Hohenzollerns?" asked the spectre, in a hollow, menacing voice. "You come hither to disturb the repose of the dead? Flee, audacious man—flee, for destruction is pursuing you; it will seize and destroy you! Your last hour has come! Prepare to stand before your Judge!"

"Ay, you will kill me, then, beautiful lady?" asked Napoleon, sneeringly. "You will revenge the defeats I have inflicted on the descendants of Burgrave Albert the Handsome, on the battle-fields of Jena, Eylau, and Friedland? In truth, I should have thought that beautiful Cunigunda of Orlamunde would rather welcome me as a friend, for was it not I who avenged her on the faithless house of Hohenzollern?"

"You try to mock me," said the spectre, **"for** your heart is filled with doubt, and your soul with pride. But beware, Bonaparte—beware, I tell you for the last time—your hour has come, and every step you advance is a step toward your ruin. Turn back, Bonaparte, if you intend to be saved, for ruin awaits you on the battle-fields of Russia! Turn back, for the souls of your victims cry to God for vengeance, and demand your blood for theirs—your punishment for the ruthlessly destroyed happiness of whole nations! Bonaparte, escape from the soil of Germany, and dare no longer to set foot upon it, for disgraceful defeats are in store for you! Return to France, and endeavor to conciliate those who are cursing you as a perjurer and renegade!"

"Who are they who dare call me a perjurer and renegade?" asked Napoleon, hastily.

"Who are they?" repeated the spectre, advancing a step toward the emperor and fixing her **menacing** eyes upon him. "The men to whom

---

* "Le Normand," vol. ii., p. 421.

† This prophecy is historical.—Vide "Le Normand," vol. ii., p. 487.

you once vowed eternal fidelity, and whom you called your brethren—Philadelphians!"

The emperor started in terror, and his cheeks turned livid. His features, which had hitherto had a sneering, scornful air, were now gloomy, and he stared with an expression of undisguised fear at the lady who stood before him in an imposing attitude, with her arm lifted in a menacing manner.

"The Philadelphians?" asked Napoleon, timidly. "I do not know them."

"You do!" said the spectre, solemnly. "You do know that the invisible ones are watching you, and will punish you because you have broken your oath!"

"I know of no oath!"

"Woe to you if you have forgotten it. I will repeat it to you! It was in 1789, at the forest of Fontainebleau, that you appeared at the meeting of the brethren and requested to be initiated. The Philadelphians admitted you into their league and received your oath. Shall I repeat this oath to you?"

"Do so if you can!"

"You swore that never again should a freeman obey kings, and that death to tyrants under all titles and in all governments is justifiable."

"That was the formality of the oath of every club and secret society at that time," exclaimed Napoleon, contemptuously.

"But the Philadelphians demanded still another written oath of you. It read as follows: 'I consent that my life be taken if I ever become reconciled to royalty. In order to contribute to its eradication in Europe, I will make use of fire and sword, and, when the society to which I belong asks me to do so, sacrifice even what is most precious to me.' You wrote this and affixed your **name to** it with your blood." *

"It is true, I did!" muttered Napoleon. "I was a fool, dreaming, like all the others, of the possibility of a republic."

"You were a believer, and have become a renegade," exclaimed the spectre, in a threatening

voice. "The invisible ones will judge and punish you, unless you make haste to conciliate them. You have forgotten that you stand under the yoke of the Philadelphians. The Emperor Napoleon believes that he has power to blot out with the blood of subjugated nations the words of the sacred oath which Lieutenant Bonaparte swore to the Philadelphians in the forest of Fontainebleau."

"And I *have* the power to do so!" exclaimed Napoleon, proudly. "I stretch out my arm over Europe, and she bows before me."

"But the Philadelphians will break your arm, and convert your crowns into dust, unless you make haste to conciliate them," exclaimed the spectre. "Turn back, for it is yet time. Return to France, renounce conquests: France wants no more wars; she is cursing the tyrant who refuses peace to her and to Europe. There has been bloodshed enough. Take an oath at this hour that you will renounce your ambition, and no longer pursue a career of crime and blood! Swear that you will return to France to-morrow!"

"Never!" ejaculated Napoleon, vehemently, and coloring with anger.

"Swear that you will return, or I will kill you!" cried the spectre. "I will kill you as a wolf. Swear that you will return!"

"Never!"

"Ah, you will not swear—you prefer to die, then," and at a bound she was by the Emperor's side, grasped him with iron hands, and threw him down on the easy-chair. "You prefer to die!" she repeated wildly, tearing the black veil from her head and showing her face unveiled. It was livid as that of a corpse, the bloodless lips quivering, and her red eyes flaming with rage.

"You prefer to die!" exclaimed the spectre, for the third time. "Well, die!" And her arms encircled Napoleon's breast like iron rings, her glance seemed to pierce his face, her lips opened and exhibited terrible teeth, as if ready to tear his breast. The emperor was unable to breathe; he felt his strength giving way, and, with a last effort, he uttered a shrill cry calling for help.

---

* "Le Normand," vol. ii, p. 516.

"**Sire,** sire, awake!" cried an anxious voice by **his side.** Napoleon started up, and violently pushed back the hand which touched his arm. "Who is there?" he asked, angrily.

"Sire, it is I!—Constant!" said the faithful *valet de chambre.* "I heard in the antechamber your majesty's groans and cries; I rushed in and saw you writhing on the easy-chair. A bad dream seemed to torment your majesty, and I therefore ventured to awaken you."

"And I am glad you did, Constant," said the emperor. "Ah, my friend, what a terrible dream it was! The White Lady was here; she threw **herself upon me like a tigress;** she wanted to tear me and drink my heart's blood."

"Your majesty had once before a similar dream," said Constant, smiling.

"Where—where was it?" asked Napoleon, hastily, wiping the cold sweat from his brow.

"Sire, it was at Erfurt, when the Emperor Alexander was there." *

"Yes, I remember," said the emperor, in a low voice. "It seems this bad dream returns as soon as I approach Alexander. Does Fate intend to warn me? Is he to be the wolf that will one day lacerate my breast? Ah, it was an awful dream, indeed, and even now it seems to me as really seen and heard." He glanced around the gloomy room. Every thing was in precisely the same condition as when he had entered it. The maps lay undisturbed on the table before him; the colored pins stood in long rows like little armies, and opposite each other, drawn up in line of battle. But the tapers had burned down, and the fire was nearly extinguished. Napoleon rose shudderingly from his easy-chair. "I will go to rest," he said.

Constant, taking a candlestick, preceded the emperor, and opened the door of the adjoining room. Fifteen minutes afterward Napoleon was in bed, and Constant and Roustan had withdrawn into the antechamber.

But this sleep was not to be of long duration. A loud cry, uttered by his master, awakened Con-

stant, and caused him to rush into the bedroom. The emperor had raised himself in bed. "Constant," he said, "it was no dream this time. **The** White Lady was here—I saw her distinctly—I had not fallen asleep, my eyes and all my senses were awake. I saw the tall white figure, her head covered with the black veil, at the wall there, as though she had grown from the ground. At a bound she was at my bedside, and raised her hands. I quickly seized her and called for you. She then glided from my fingers and disappeared. Like General d'Espagne, I say there must be a trap-door somewhere in this room. Call Roustan, take lights, and examine the walls and the floor."

The *valet de chambre* hastened to fetch Roustan; they took lights and made a thorough examination, but in vain. The oaken planks of the floor were firmly joined, and the dark velvet hangings glued to the walls.

"Well, then, the White Lady has fooled me in another dream," said the emperor. "Go! Let **us sleep.**" The two servants withdrew.

About an hour had elapsed, when another cry, uttered by the emperor, called Constant back into the bedroom. Seized with dismay, he halted at the door. The bed was in **the middle** of the room; the table which stood beside it was upset, and the night-lamp lay thrown on the floor.

"I hope that no accident has befallen your majesty," said Constant, rushing toward the emperor.

"No," said Napoleon. "But this accursed white spectre was here again. It wanted to treat me like General d'Espagne; to upset my bed and throttle me. I awoke just when this horrible monster of a woman pushed the bed with the strength of a giant into the middle of the room. I called for you, and she disappeared. As the White Lady apparently does not like several persons to be in the room, you and Roustan must remain here to-night."

"And, with your majesty's leave, each of us will hold a pistol in his hand, that we may fire at the apparition if it return."

---

* Constant, "Mémoires," vol. iv., p. 79.

"Ah, my friend, you know little of the power of spectres," said Napoleon, smiling. "When you have fired at them, they laugh scornfully, throw the bullet back to you and pass on entirely uninjured. That is their fashion. But you may take your pistols, and if she has still a human heart in her breast, she will feel some respect for it."

And the White Lady really seemed to have a human heart. Constant and Roustan, who sat on the floor beside the emperor's bed with cocked pistols, waited in vain for the return of **the apparition.** Every thing remained quiet; nothing stirred in the room, where the emperor, guarded **by his faithful servants,** now at last enjoyed repose.

When he rose on the following morning, his face was even paler and gloomier than usual. He who generally on being dressed conversed in an affable manner with his servants, remained silent and grave that day, and muttered only occasionally, "The accursed palace! The miserable **spectre-hole!"** *

Constant and Roustan, having finished the emperor's toilet, were about leaving the room, when he called them back by a gesture. "You will not mention any thing about what happened here last night!" he said, imperiously. "If I find out that you disobey my order, I shall be very **angry. Go!" And the emperor** went into the Gallery of Palms in order to receive the reports of his suite and give the usual audiences. With a nod and a dismal look he greeted Count Munster, who inquired, with the fawning smile of a true courtier, whether his majesty had passed an agreeable night.

"Your castellan, then, has not informed you of the horrible noise last night in the palace?" **asked** Napoleon, angrily. "You ought to get better nails, count, to hang up paintings, so that **they do not fall** down. He who wants to hang **anybody or** any thing, even though it be but a **painting, ought to have** at least a substantial gallows."

"Sire," faltered Count Munster, "I do not comprehend—this palace—"

"Is not even fit to be a gallows, for it drops those who have been hung in it," exclaimed Napoleon, vehemently. "It is an accursed place, and the air in it is as sultry and oppressive as in a rat-hole. Have the carriages brought to the door. Let us depart!" He did not deign the count another glance, and returned into the adjoining room, whither none but the grand marshal and his adjutants were permitted to follow.

Fifteen minutes afterward, the emperor, with his numerous suite, left the palace of Baireuth and set out for Plauen, where he intended to join the Empress Maria Louisa, who had stopped there overnight, and continue with her the journey to Dresden. The streets of Baireuth, which had presented so animated a spectacle the day before, were at this early hour quiet and deserted; all the windows were closed; only here and there a wondering, inquisitive face appeared behind the panes and looked at the carriages that rolled through the streets, and at the melancholy countenance of the emperor, who sat in his open **calash.** When out of the gate, he turned again, and cast an angry glance on the palace, whose high gray walls were brightened by the morning sun. "An accursed old palace!" he muttered to himself. "I shall never spend there another night." * And leaning back in a corner of the carriage he gazed in silence at the sky.

Count Munster, however, stood inside the palace of Baireuth, at the window of the Gallery of Palms, and looked anxiously after the emperor. The carriages disappeared at a bend in the road behind the green willows, and the count turned to Castellan Schluter, who was standing behind him.

"But tell me, for Heaven's sake, Schluter," exclaimed the count, "what did the emperor refer to? What happened to him last night?"

"There happened to him what will happen to all those who dare disquiet the White Lady of Baireuth or defy her power," said Schluter, solemnly.

---

* Historical.—Vide Minutoli, "The White Lady," p. 17.

* Napoleon's own words.—Vide Minutoli, p. 17.

"You really believe, then, that she appeared to him?" asked the count, in terror.

"The emperor sent for me late last night, and again this morning. Shall I tell your excellency what it was for? The portrait of the White Lady, which I had put yesterday into the cabinet adjoining the audience-hall in the other wing of the palace, had walked over to this side, and, in the room directly above the emperor, had thrown itself down with so much violence, that the noise resounded through the whole building."

"But that is altogether impossible," exclaimed Count Munster, in dismay. "Why, you told me that the portrait was standing in the other wing of the palace, and that you had carefully locked all the doors."

"But I told your excellency also that locks and bolts are unable to impede her progress, and that, when she intends to wander, the walls open to her, and that all obstructions give way. The air wafted her over to the enemy of her house, and, by the thunder of her wrath, she awakened him from his slumber."

"And that was the reason why the emperor sent for you last night?"

"Yes, I had the honor of narrating to him the history of the White Lady," said Schluter, laughing scornfully. "I did so, and told him also what happened here to General d'Espagne."

"But did you not say the emperor had sent for you again this morning?"

The castellan nodded.

"Well, what did he want again?"

"I had to describe to him the costume in which the White Lady is in the habit of walking—her dress, her veil, her countenance—in short, I had to tell him all about her appearance. I proposed at last that I would have the portrait brought to him, that he might himself look at it; but, when I did so, he cast a furious glance on me, and said in an angry voice, 'No, no, I do not want to see it! Let me alone with your doomed portrait!'* In truth, I believe the all-powerful emperor was frightened, and the White Lady had paid him a visit. In fact, he turned quite pale!" And Schluter burst into loud and scornful laughter.

Count Munster shook his head gravely, and hastened to leave the Gallery of Palms and the haunted palace.

The castellan remained there and listened until the count's footsteps died away. He then hurried to the rooms which the emperor had occupied. When he arrived at Napoleon's bedroom, he pushed the bed aside, and stooped down to the floor, at which he looked with searching eyes. "It is all right! Nothing is to be seen!" he muttered to himself. "The White Lady will yet be able often to walk here!" He burst into loud laughter and left the imperial apartments to return to his own rooms, which were situated on the ground-floor. "I will now put away my dear treasures, that no uninitiated eye may behold them," he said, carefully locking the door. "Come, my mysterious treasures! Come!" He drew from his bed a long white dress, a small cloak trimmed with fur, and a long black veil,* and while carefully folding up these articles, which he locked in a trunk standing under the bed, he sang in a loud and merry voice:

> † "Ein Kors', Ihr kennt den Namen schon,
>   Seit vierzehn Jahr und drüber,
> Spricht allen Nationen Hohn,
>   Giebt Fürsten—Nasenstüber,
> Stürzt Throne wie ein Kartenhaus
> Und treibt das Wesen gar zu Kraus,
> Nicht Bona—Malaparte!" ‡

---

* These articles, belonging to the toilet of the White Lady, were found in Schluter's trunk, when he died, in 1820.—Vide Minutoli, p. 17.

† A comic song, sung in Germany in 1812.

> ‡ A Corsican—you know his name—
>   For more than fourteen years
> Has scorned the nations, to their shame,
>   And pulled their princes' ears.
> He plays sad tricks upon his foes,
>   And, marching with his guards,
> He casts down kingdoms as he goes
>   Like houses made of cards.
> A better name for him would be
> Not *Bona*, but *Mala-parté*.

---

* Historical.—Vide Minutoli, p. 17.

CHAPTER IV.

NAPOLEON AT DRESDEN.

Joy, happiness, and love, reigned at the court of the King of Saxony. Napoleon had honored the royal house of Saxony with a visit; he had come to Dresden to spend a few days in the family circle of Frederick Augustus, whom he flatteringly called his "*cher papa.*" He had also come to embrace his father-in-law, the Emperor of Austria, before setting out for Russia, and to shake hands with his ally the King of Prussia; and, finally, to gather around him again his vassals, the princes of the Confederation of the Rhine, and, in the face of Europe, to receive the homage of kings, emperors, and princes.

Amid the ringing of bells and the light of torches, Napoleon and Maria Louisa made their entry into Dresden. The late hour of the night, when the imperial couple arrived, prevented the population from greeting them with cheers. But the good people of the Saxon capital were not to be deprived of the happiness of bidding Napoleon welcome, and seeing his beautiful young empress The court, therefore, arranged a drive in open calashes on the day after; and everywhere on the streets through which the procession passed the people stood in vast crowds. The windows of the **houses** were opened, and beautiful ladies looked **out of them. The imperial** and royal carriages made but slow headway, for thousands of excited spectators preceded them, and thousands more surrounding the carriages looked up with inquisitive eyes to the distinguished persons who, greeting and smiling, bowed to them on all sides. **But** the multitude were silent; not a cheer resounded—not a "*Vive l'empereur*"—and the praise of Napoleon, that was uttered by the lips of princes, lacked the wonted accompaniment of popular enthusiasm.

Good-natured King Frederick Augustus felt all this as a rebuke administered to himself, as a reflection on his hospitality, and he looked with an expression full of uneasiness and affection at the emperor, who was sitting beside him. But Napo-

leon's countenance was as calm and cold as it always was. Not a flash **of** inward anger was seen in those unfathomable eyes. He conversed quietly and almost smilingly **with his** consort, the Empress Maria Louisa, and did **not** even seem to notice that the people received **him in** silence.

"Well, he shall have a most gratifying compensation at the theatre to-night," said Frederick Augustus to himself. "The audience will there at least receive the great Napoleon with enthusiastic cheers; and when, on his return, he sees all Dresden glittering in the illumination that is to take place, he will have to admit, after all, that my good Saxons, like their king, love and admire him."

King Frederick Augustus was not **mistaken.** —The vast and brilliant audience, that in the evening assembled at the royal theatre, received the members of the court, on their appearance, with deafening cheers; all rose from their seats and shouted with constantly recurring enthusiasm, "Long live Napoleon! Long live the Emperor Francis! Long live our dear King Frederick Augustus!" **The band accompanied these** cheers, the ladies waved their bouquets, and the gentlemen their hats and handkerchiefs, and when this outburst subsided, hundreds of eyes were fixed on the royal box, to watch every motion of Napoleon's countenance, and admire him in the circle of his family; for this large gathering of princes and kings were now his family, and the son of the Corsican lawyer was its head. There was the Emperor Francis of Austria, who had arrived but a few hours before, to greet his beloved son-in-law, whom he had not seen since the battle of Austerlitz. The emperor was accompanied by his young consort, the Empress Ludovica. Every one knew that she hated Napoleon; that her proud heart never could forgive him the humiliations which he had inflicted on Austria, and that she had consented only with the utmost reluctance, and with bitter tears, to the marriage of her step-daughter, the Archduchess Maria Louisa, with the conqueror of Austria. And yet, notwithstanding her hatred

grief, and humiliated pride, the Empress Ludovica had likewise come to Dresden to witness the triumph of Napoleon, to be the second lady at this court, and the first in the suite of the Empress Maria Louisa. There were the King and Queen of Westphalia, sister-in-law of Napoleon and daughter of the King of Wurtemberg, who deemed himself happy that Napoleon was a relative of his. There were, besides, the Grand-Duke of Wurzburg, brother of the Emperor Francis, and now uncle of Bonaparte; the Grand-Duke of Baden, Napoleon's nephew, and the King of Saxony, the *cher papa* of Napoleon; and finally, the crowd of the petty German princes of the Confederation of **the Rhine, who had eagerly hurried to Dresden in** order to do homage to their protector, and seek after new gifts of territories and titles from the all-powerful master of Germany. But these personages formed only part of the suite; no one paid attention to them; they stood humbly and modestly in the background, and only the two emperors and empresses, the Queens of Saxony and Westphalia, and the King of Saxony, occupied front seats. The King of Saxony conducted Napoleon to the first gilded easy-chair on the right side; to him belonged the seat of honor here as everywhere. He was first in the line of emperors and kings. By his side sat Maria Louisa, sparkling with diamonds, which covered her head, neck, arms, and the golden belt around her slender waist. Her countenance was joyful, and never had she feasted her eyes on her husband with more heart-felt pride than during this evening, when, sitting beside him, she eclipsed her imperial step-mother in the magnificence of her toilet and the splendor of her rank. It was only when Napoleon had taken his seat that the Emperor and Empress of Austria, and all the other kings and princes, followed his example. The band immediately commenced the overture, and the festive cantata began. On the stage was seen the radiant temple of the sun, surrounded by the brilliantly-adorned crowd of priests and priestesses. They raised their arms, not to the temple of the **sun,** but toward Napoleon's box, and, amid their soul-stirring chorus, the high-priest

stepped forth from the temple. Advancing to the edge of the stage, he bowed to the imperial sun, and commenced singing in a powerful voice,— "The sun rises gloriously on the firmament, illuminating and heating the world; but thou, his greater brother, thou conquerest him, and he drives back his car, acknowledging that, since thou art here, the world needs no other sun." While the high-priest sang these words the temple on the stage suddenly paled, and over its entrance the following words appeared in large letters of gold: "*Di Lui men grande e men chiaro il Sole*," *

At this sight, cheers burst from all sides of the brilliantly decorated house; the audience rose from their seats and turned toward the imperial box to salute Napoleon; the Emperor of Austria, the King of Saxony, and the princes of the Confederation of the Rhine, joined in the applause. But Napoleon, to whom these cheers were addressed, did not even seem to notice them. He had suddenly risen and turned his back to the stage, regardless of the high-priest and his emphatic words. Heedless of the cheers and applause, he left his place and hastened to the Emperor Francis, who was sitting **on** the left side, close to the two empresses. "Sire," said Napoleon, "I request your majesty to exchange seats with me, and pardon me for erroneously taking the chair that was intended for you."

"No, no; it is no mistake at all," exclaimed the Emperor Francis, hastily. "It is all right as it is, and your majesty must stay there, for that easy-chair is the seat of honor."

"That is precisely the reason why it should be occupied by your majesty, the august Emperor of Austria, my beloved and revered father-in-law," said Napoleon, bowing his head lower than he had ever before done to any prince in the world. "Come, sire, permit me to conduct you to the seat that is due to you alone." With gentle violence he took the emperor's hand and conducted him to the seat at the right side of Maria Louisa.

---

* "Less great and brilliant than he is the sun." The author of this cantata, performed in honor of Napoleon, was Orlandi, an Italian; Morlacchi had composed the music.

"My dear Louisa," he said, turning to his consort, "I renounce the happiness of sitting beside you, because this seat is due to the head of our family, the father of my consort, the grandfather of my son. You may embrace the opportunity to tell our dear papa all about the little King of Rome." He greeted Maria Louisa with a beaming smile, and then repaired to the seat which the Emperor Francis had occupied, at the left side of the Empress Ludovica. The smile was still on his face; he sat down on this chair, and, turning to the empress, his mother-in-law, asked her, almost humbly, if she would grant him the happiness of sitting by her side.

Ludovica felt flattered; the gentle, suppliant voice of the emperor, his smile, and flashing eyes, exerted their wonted charm upon her. She had armed her heart against the arrogant master of the world, but, before the kind and almost humble bearing of Napoleon, her arms sank to the ground, and she who had hitherto felt nothing but hatred against him, regarded him now with mingled astonishment and admiration.

Napoleon seemed to have read the depths of her heart, for his face grew even milder, and his smile more fascinating. "Your majesty has hated me intensely, I suppose?" he asked, in a low voice. "Oh, do not deny it; I have been portrayed to you in very repulsive colors?"

Ludovica looked at him admiringly. "I must confess, sire," she said, "that not one of the portraits of your majesty which I have seen, is like you."

"Oh, I believe so," exclaimed Napoleon, hastily; "they have always painted me too dark, and the portraits shown to your majesty doubtless have been of that description; but before you, madame, the Moor would like to wash his face, and I wish you could see me painted less repulsively."

"Sire," said the empress, smiling, "did we not see but a few minutes since that your image is even more radiant than the sun?"

"Ah, those are silly *coups de théâtre*," exclaimed Napoleon. "It is no great honor, indeed, to surpass the splendor of a sun made out of paper. If the lamplighter had approached too

close to it it would have burned, while I think that I can stand in fire without running the risk of perishing. However, the fire of anger flashing from your eyes, madame, would annihilate me, and I pray you, therefore, to have mercy on me. Pray, let us be frank. Why do you hate me?" He looked at the empress with so mild and smiling an expression, that she felt confused by it, and a faint blush suffused her beautiful face.

"No," she said, in a low voice, "who tells you that? How would it be possible to hate the man to whom all Europe bows in admiration?"

"I have put my foot on the neck of Europe; I have tamed the wild horse, and it acknowledges me as its master," said Napoleon, proudly. "But is that a reason why you should hate me? Let all lie in the dust before me, but Austria shall stand erect by my side, for the Emperor of Austria is my father-in-law, and though I do not venture to say that the beautiful young Empress of Austria is my mother-in-law, I may be allowed to say that she is the mother of my consort, and that I admire and esteem her with all my heart. Austria has nothing to fear, so long as she is friendly toward me. She shall share my triumphs; and, when at last all Europe is prostrate, the Emperors of France and Austria will stand side by side, and divide the world between them."

"And one will take his Herculaneum, and the other his Pompeii," said the empress, sarcastically.

"Ah, you mean to say that the world we shall have conquered will consist only of ruined cities and dead subjects?" asked Napoleon, gloomily.

"Sire," said Ludovica, gently, "I mean that when Vesuvius shows itself to the wondering world in its whole majesty and beauty, it cannot prevent the molten lava, which rises from its crater, as a natural consequence, from rushing down its sides, and spreading everywhere death and destruction."

"Well," exclaimed Napoleon, smiling, "if your simile is correct, the molten lava will soon inundate Russia, and carry terror, death, and destruction into the empire of the arrogant czar."

"Ah, sire," said Ludovica, gravely, "Russia is

so very cold that I believe even the fires of Vesuvius would be extinguished there, the molten lava would freeze, or, flowing back, injure Vesuvius itself."

"Oh, no, madame," exclaimed Napoleon, hastily, "Vesuvius will not be extinguished, for divine fire is burning in its heart."

"And Russia will not thaw, for it is a divine frost that freezes every thing approaching her," said Ludovica, gently.

Napoleon cast on her one of his quick, angry glances. "Madame," he said, "I—"

At this moment the whole audience burst into loud and enthusiastic cheers, and shouted, "Long live the emperor! Long live the hero who conquers the world!"

Napoleon interrupted himself, and turned his eyes toward the stage. The temple of the sun was still dark, but a new brilliant light was beaming over it; in its middle was the word "Napoleon" in large flaming letters, which illumined the whole scene. At this sight the audience were unable to restrain their delight, and burst into the deafening cheers which had interrupted Napoleon's words.

The King of Saxony was evidently pleased with this outburst of enthusiasm. "Now," he thought, "the great Napoleon will forget the disagreeable scene of this morning. The people then were silent, and admired, but to-night they have recovered their speech; and when we leave the theatre, and behold the whole city in a flood of light, Napoleon will feel convinced that my subjects love him sincerely.—But what is that? The emperor rises. Does he intend already to leave the theatre?" And he hastened to Napoleon, who advanced toward him. "Let us leave, sire," he said. "Those flatteries are more than enough. You see the sun has set here."

"But he is still among us, sire," said Frederick Augustus. "And if it has grown dark on the stage, the reason is simply, that all the light now fills the streets of Dresden, to prove to the great Napoleon that there is no night where he is—that his presence turns darkness into light, and night into day."

"Ah," said Napoleon, in a tired, wearied tone, "an illumination then has been arranged?"

"Sire, my people, as well as I, cannot find words to utter to your majesty the transports with which your visit has filled our hearts, and I hope you will see this in the lights shining at every window. I request your majesty not to return directly to the palace, but first ride through the city."

Napoleon nodded assent. "Let us do so, cher papa," he said; "let us take a look at your illumination!" He offered his arm to Maria Louisa, and left the box with her. The crowd of kings, dukes, and princes, followed him in haste.

As the King of Saxony descended the staircase with his consort, Chamberlain von Planitz met him with a pale and frightened face.

"Well," asked the king, "I suppose the illumination has already commenced? It must be a splendid spectacle!"

"Your majesty," said the chamberlain, in a low voice, "the royal palace and the public buildings are brilliantly lit up, but the houses of the citizens are dark, and the streets are deserted."

"But," exclaimed the king, in dismay, "did not the police command the citizens to illuminate their houses?"

"Yes, your majesty, the police have done their duty."

"And yet—"

"And yet, sire, all the houses are dark. It is as if the whole population had conspired to disobey the order. The police have again given orders; they received everywhere the same reply, that neither oil nor candles were to be had anywhere."

"The stubborn people ought to have been told that they would be punished for this."

"The police tried this, too, your majesty, threatening that every citizen who did not obey should be fined a dollar, and all declared their readiness to pay rather than illuminate."

"That is open rebellion," said the king, sighing. "The streets, then, are dark?"

"Yes, sire."

"Then we must not take the intended ride through the city," exclaimed the king, anxiously. "Make haste, baron, countermand the ride, and—"

At this moment the first carriage rolled from the portal. "It is too late," groaned the king. "The emperor has already started. He will witness our humiliation."

"Possibly, he may drive immediately to the palace," said the queen. "He seemed tired and exhausted—"

"No, no," said the king, "he consented to see the illumination, and the outriders are instructed accordingly. I myself marked out the route. But, an expedient occurs to me. Quick, Baron von Planitz! Go to the outrider of my carriage. Tell him to follow the imperial carriage as fast as he can ride. He must overtake it, though his horse die under him. He must order the driver **to turn and pass** down Augustus Street to the **Linden, and then slowly across the square, to** the **palace.** Make haste!" The chamberlain hastened to carry out the king's orders.

"And we?" asked the queen—"shall we also follow him?"

"No, we return to the palace, and will wait for him there. The others, of course, will follow the imperial carriage, and I hope we shall soon see **the** two emperors again." Profoundly sighing, **the king** conducted his consort to the carriage, **and** drove with her toward the palace. A flood of light beamed upon them in the palace square. Huge pillars, covered with festoons of colored lamps, stood in front of the long palace bridge, and were connected with each other by brilliant girandoles. Four similar pillars were in front of the main portal of the Catholic church at the entrance of Augustus Street. Around the square altars were erected, on which naphtha was burning. On the royal palace the Austrian and French coats-of-arms displayed all their colors with heraldic accuracy. It was a dazzling spectacle, and even the king himself rejoiced at the beautiful and imposing effect. "I think," he said, pointing to the pillars, "I think this will be agreeable to him."

"Yes, but I **am afraid that** will be disagreeable to him," said the queen, pointing to the Neustadt, lying dark on the other side of **the Elbe.**

"Heaven grant that he may not **see it!**" said the king, sighing; he then leaned back and closed his eyes until they halted in front of **the** portal. "I shall remain here until the emperors arrive," he added, bowing to his consort. With anxious eyes he gazed upon the place, and listened in suspense to any distant noise. After waiting fifteen minutes, the roll of approaching wheels was heard, and now they thundered across the square and entered the palace portal. King Frederick Augustus, hat in hand, stepped up with a most submissive air to the first carriage, the door of which was just opened by lackeys in gorgeous liveries. He lifted the young empress Maria Louisa out, and then offered his hand almost timidly to Napoleon to assist him also. With a quick wave of his hand he refused assistance, and alighted. Anger was burning in his eyes.

"We left the theatre at an earlier hour than the citizens expected," said the king, timidly, "and that is the reason why the illumination has not yet generally commenced."

"Oh, no," said Napoleon, in a petulant voice; "*your* illumination is magnificent; as to the inhabitants of Dresden, it seems to me, they are the children of the sun that we saw at the theatre—their lights have gone out." And the emperor, coldly bowing to the king, and offering his arm to his consort, walked with her into the palace.

"He is not in good humor," muttered Frederick Augustus, in dismay. "Oh, he is incensed at me!"

At this moment the Emperor Francis, with his consort, met him. "A very pretty idea," said the emperor, with a laughing face, "to unite the coats-of-arms of Austria and France in such a blaze of variegated light! It gladdens one's heart to behold them. I thank your majesty for having thus exhibited my coat-of-arms. It looks admirably by the side of that of France."

CHAPTER V.

NAPOLEON'S HIGH-BORN ANCESTORS.

A NEW guest had arrived at Dresden to do homage to Napoleon—the King of Prussia, accompanied by the young crown prince, and Chancellor von Hardenberg. The two inimical friends, the Emperor of France and the King of Prussia, met for the first time at the rooms of the Queen of Saxony, and shook hands with forced kindness. They exchanged but a few words, when Napoleon withdrew, inviting the king to participate in the gala dinner and ball to take place that day. The king accepted the invitation with a bow, without replying a word, and repaired to the Marcolini palace, where quarters had been provided for him and his suite. Not a member of the royal family deemed it necessary to accompany him. He went away quietly and alone. His arrival had not been greeted, like that of Napoleon and the Emperor of Austria, with ringing of bells and cannon salutes, nor had the soldiers formed in line on both sides of the streets through which he passed on entering the city. The court had not shown any attention to him, but allowed him to make his entry into Dresden without any display whatever.

But if the court thought they might with impunity violate the rules of etiquette because Frederick William was unfortunate, the people indemnified him for this neglect, and honored him. Thousands hurried out of the gate to cheer him on his arrival, and escorted him amid the most enthusiastic acclamations to the royal palace. When he left it again, the crowd followed him to the Marcolini palace, and cheered so long in front of it that the king appeared on the balcony. It is true, the anterooms of the king were deserted; no smiling courtiers' faces, no chamberlains adorned with glittering orders, no dignitaries, no marshals, princes, or dukes, were there; but below in the street was his real anteroom—there his devoted courtiers were waiting for their royal master, looking up to his windows, and longing for his coming. The smiles with which they

greeted Frederick William were no parasites' smiles, and the love beaming from those countless eyes was faithful and true.

Beneath the residence of Napoleon the people did not stand, as usual, in silent curiosity staring at the windows, behind which from time to time the pale face of the emperor showed itself. The street was empty—those who formerly stood there were now joyously thronging in front of the King of Prussia's quarters; they had recovered their voices, and often cheered in honor **of Frederick William III.**

The anterooms of Napoleon indeed presented an animated spectacle. A brilliant crowd filled them at an early hour; there were generals and marshals, the princes of the Confederation of the Rhine, the dukes, princes, and kings of Germany, whom Napoleon had newly created—all longing for an audience, in order to wrest from Napoleon's munificence a province belonging to a neighbor, a title, or a prominent office. Germany was in the hands of Napoleon, and to bow the lower to him was to be raised the higher. In these rooms of the emperor there was the unwonted spectacle of German sovereigns soliciting instead of granting favors; and, instead of being surrounded by, were themselves **courtiers, who, in** the most submissive manner, sought the intercession of adjutants and chamberlains, to procure admission to the imperial presence and favor.

And all these courtiers gave vent to their love and admiration for Napoleon in terms of the most extravagant praise. They spoke with prophetic ecstasy of the fresh laurels that Napoleon was to bind upon his brow, and of Alexander's madness to resist a conqueror destined to make new triumphs for the glory of France and the humiliation of Russia. Yet, when two or three of those expectant gentlemen stood in some window-niche, and believed themselves beyond the reach of indiscreet ears, they dared to ask each other, in a low and anxious tone, whether all this splendor would not soon vanish as a meteor—whether one might not see the aurora of a new day dawning— whether the battles into which Napoleon was about to plunge so recklessly would not result in the downfall of him whom they publicly extolled, but secretly cursed. But, to these whispered questions the brilliant anterooms, the marshals of the empire, crowned with victory, the dukes and princes, the court of Napoleon, composed of the sovereigns of Germany, made a triumphant reply. Secret hope could hardly survive in the recollection of the greatness and invariable good fortune of Napoleon, and they who desired the humiliation of the conqueror yielded to submission. Returning to the crowd of princely courtiers, they renewed their enthusiasm, and joined in the plaudits of Napoleon's admirers.

When the emperor, with Maria Louisa, entered the room, all pressed forward, anxious to receive a glance, a smile, or a pleasant salutation. Rank and etiquette were overlooked; there was but one master, one sovereign, to whom all were doing homage. Rushing toward him, each one tried to outstrip the other; and many a high dignitary, prime minister, prince, duke, or king, was pushed aside by an inferior. Napoleon stood in the centre of the room, uttering words of condescending affability to the fortunate men nearest him.

Suddenly cheers resounded in the streets, rattling the window-panes. Napoleon looked in the direction of the windows. "What is that?" he asked, turning to the Duke de Bassano.

"Sire," said the duke, "the good people of Dresden are impatient to see their imperial majesties of France, and pay them their respects."

More deafening shouts were heard. Napoleon smiled, and hastily walking with his consort through the circle of the courtiers, stepped to the open window. He frowned as he looked down. An immense crowd had gathered below, but their faces were not turned toward the windows of the royal palace, and their cheers were not intended for the emperor. The multitude crossed the square, and in their midst drove slowly an open carriage, surrounded by the enthusiastic people. In this carriage sat the King of Prussia, to whom were given the loud greetings mistaken by Napoleon. He understood it at a glance, and, stepping back from the window with the empress, turned to Grand-Marshal Duroc, who was stand-

ing by his side. "See that the populace go home," he said, hastily, "and that they no longer disturb the peace of the city by indecent and riotous proceedings. I do not wish to hear any more yelling near the palace!"

Duroc bowed, and withdrew to instruct the police officers not to tolerate any similar conduct on the part of the citizens. The emperor meanwhile turned to Duke Augustus of Gotha, who had just succeeded in penetrating through the ranks of courtiers, with his broad shoulders and colossal form.

"Ah, you are back again, duke?" asked the emperor, kindly. "Did you attend thoroughly to your government affairs?"

"I did, sire," said the duke, nearly bowing to the ground, and then seizing the emperor's hand to press it to his lips.

"Well, I must confess that you accomplished your task with great rapidity. Was it not three days since you took leave of us to go to Gotha?"

"Yes, sire, I set out three days ago."

"And you are back already! You performed the trip and your official business in so short a time! How large is your duchy, then?"

"Sire," said the Duke of Gotha, quickly, "it is as large as your majesty commands it to be." *

Napoleon's smile was reflected in the faces of those seeking his favors.

At this moment the doors of the outer anteroom opened, and on the threshold appeared the grave and dignified form of King Frederick William. The courtiers, with an impatient expression, receded anxiously, as though afraid of contact with this unfortunate man, who had no territories, no riches, no honors to offer them, but had come as a vassal to pacify the wrath of Napoleon, and save at least a remnant of his kingdom. But the king did not come with craven heart; he did not hasten his approach to the emperor with fawning submissiveness, but slowly, with his head proudly erect, and a grave air.

Napoleon received him with a haughty nod. "Your majesty, you must have had a trouble-

---

* This reply is historical.

some drive from your quarters to the royal palace," he said harshly. "I noticed that the gaping crowd were thronging about your carriage and annoying you."

"Pardon me, sire," said the king, "the people did not annoy me. They did me the honor of bidding me welcome, and this was the more generous, as I am not one of those who are favored by Fortune. But the German people yield sometimes to generous impulses, and show thereby how little they know of the etiquette and sagacity of courtiers."

While uttering these words, the king glanced with his clear, calm eyes—in which a slightly sarcastic expression was to be seen—at the multitude of brilliantly adorned and distinguished gentlemen who tried to get as far as possible from him. Napoleon smiled. He himself despised sycophancy sufficiently to be pleased with this rebuke. But his severe look returned, and he gazed with some indignation upon the tall form of the King of Prussia. He noticed that, while himself appeared in silk stockings and buckled shoes, the king had come in long trousers and boots.

"Your majesty, doubtless, was not informed that there would be a ball after the banquet?" asked Napoleon, pointing to the king's boots.

"I was, sire, but since the death of my consort I have not danced."

"But etiquette," exclaimed Napoleon, vehemently, "etiquette is—"

"Sire," interrupted the king, in a calm and dignified tone, "etiquette is intended for parasites and people of the court, and it is very proper for them to adhere to it. But a sovereign king, I should think, has a right to disregard it, and follow the promptings of his own inclinations."

The door of the anteroom opened again, and the grand marshal appeared to announce dinner. The emperor offered his arm to Maria Louisa, preceded by the high dignitaries and the officers of his household, and followed by the swarm of princes and gentlemen of the courts. The King of Prussia, taking the place to which his rank entitled him, walked on the other side of the empress, and entered the dining-hall at the same time with Napoleon, amid the notes of the imperial band. Napoleon walked with his consort to his guests, who were waiting for him in the centre of the ball—the Emperor and Empress of Austria, and the King and Queen of Saxony.

The banquet was a distinguished one, and the French cooks of Napoleon's household had displayed all their culinary skill to satisfy the palate of even the most fastidious epicures. Napoleon, as usual, gave his guests but little time to revel in the delicacies prepared for them. Scarcely half an hour had elapsed since the commencement of the dinner, when he rose, and thereby gave the signal that the gala-dinner was at an end.

The Emperor Francis, who was almost always in good-humor, could not refrain from frowning, and, after offering his arm to his consort to conduct her to the saloon, where coffee was to be served, he muttered, "I do not know, but it seems to me that the Emperor Napoleon eats too little."

"And yet he has so hearty an appetite, that he is able to swallow and digest the territories of sovereigns," whispered the Empress Ludovica, with a sneer. "He is now as sated as an anaconda after devouring an ox."

"Yes, but we poor mortals are still hungry," said Francis, thoughtfully. "It does not do us any good that his appetite is satisfied."

"There will be a day when our hunger shall be appeased, and he starve," said the empress.

"Hush!" whispered Francis, "not a word against him! He is my son-in-law, Ludovica. And, besides, he has an appetite strong enough yet to swallow another ox."

"He will get it in Russia, I suppose?" said Ludovica, quickly.

"Yes," said Francis. "He explained his whole plan to me and Metternich for over an hour today, and proved to us that four weeks hence there would be no Russian emperor; that Russia would fall to ruins and decay. He dwelt on a great many other things, and told us of gigantic schemes, which, to tell the truth, I did not comprehend very well. Let me confess to you," he whispered, standing near the door of the reception-room, "that his words almost frightened me. His heart may be all right, but as to his head, I am afraid there is something wrong about it." *

Ludovica smiled. "Do you believe, then, my husband, that he has really a heart?" she asked. "But as to his head, the princes and nations of Europe, I hope, will soon find an opportunity to set it right."

"Hush!" said Francis again; "he is my son-in-law."

"And because he is your son-in-law, your majesty should hesitate no longer to deliver to him, or rather to his consort, the precious gift which you ordered for her, and which arrived to-day."

"It is true," exclaimed Francis. "Let us at once present the gift to Maria Louisa."

He entered the saloon and hastily approached his daughter, who **stood with Napoleon in the centre of the room, and was just handing him a** cup **of coffee, to which she herself had** added sugar and cream.†

"Louisa," said Francis, kindly nodding as he approached her, "I have a little gift for you, which I hope will be acceptable. I ordered it several months since, but when we set out from Vienna it was not ready To-day, however, it has arrived, and, as we are now in a family circle, I **may** as well present it to you. That is to say," added the emperor, bowing to Napoleon, "if your majesty permits me to do so."

"Your majesty was right in saying that we are here a family circle," said Napoleon, smiling; "and as the father is always the head and master, I have nothing to permit, but only to pray **that** your majesty may make what present your love **has** chosen for her."

"And I assure you, father," exclaimed Maria **Louisa,** smiling, "I am as anxious to know what

you have for me as I was at the time when I was a little archduchess, and when your majesty promised me a surprise. Let me, therefore, see your gift."

Francis smiled, and, walking to **the** open door of the adjoining room (where the dukes, who did not belong to the imperial family, the princes, the marshals, and courtiers, were assembled), made a sign to one of the gentlemen, who stood near the door. The latter immediately left the room, and returned after a few minutes with an oblong, narrow **something, carefully wrapped** in a piece of gold brocatel, which he presented to the emperor with a respectful bow. Francis took it hastily, and approached Maria Louisa with a solemn air. "Here, Louisa," he said, kindly, "here is my present. It will show you what, it is true, every day proves to admiring Europe, namely, **that genuine royal blood** is flowing in the veins of your husband."

Maria Louisa opened the covering with inquisitive impatience, and there appeared under it a golden box, ornamented with diamonds and pearls. "What **magnificent diamonds!**" she exclaimed. "**What skilful work!**" **said Napoleon, smil**ing.

"The box was made by Benvenuto Cellini," said Francis; "it was highly prized by my lamented father, the Emperor Leopold, who brought it from Florence to Vienna. But that is not the principal thing—the contents are more important. Here is the key, Louisa; open the box!" He handed her a golden key, and Maria Louisa applied it to the key-hole, adorned with large oriental turquoises. Around her stood the Emperor and Empress of Austria, the King and Queen of Saxony, the King of Prussia, and the Grand-duke of Wurzburg; Napoleon was close beside her. All eyes were expressive of curiosity and suspense. Nothing was there but a roll of parchment. Maria Louisa unfolded it. "A pedigree!" she exclaimed, wonderingly.

"**Yes, a** pedigree," said the Emperor Francis, **merrily,** "but a very precious and beautiful one, which you may put into the cradle of the little King of Rome, and from which he may learn his

---

* The emperor's own words.—Vide **Hormayer's "Le**bensbilder," vol. iii.

† The Empress Josephine, in her tender care for Napoleon, who frequently forgot to take his coffee, was in the habit of preparing a cup for him after dinner, and presenting it to him. Maria Louisa had adopted Josephine's habit.

letters. Sire," he then added, turning to Napoleon, "your majesty must allow me to add another jewel to your imperial crown. I mean, this pedigree. It proves irrefutably that your majesty is the descendant of a glorious old sovereign family, which ruled over Treviso during the middle ages. Signor Giacamonte, the most renowned genealogist in all Italy, devoted himself, at my request, for a whole year to this study, and succeeded in proving that the Bonaparte family is of ancient and sovereign origin."

"That is a splendid discovery," exclaimed Maria Louisa, with delight; "my little King of Rome, consequently, has a very respectable number of distinguished ancestors?"

"More than fifty!" exclaimed her father, proudly. "Look here; this is the founder of the whole family, the Duca di Buon et Malaparte; he lived in the twelfth century."

He pointed to the genealogical trunk of the beautifully painted and ornamented pedigree, of which Maria Louisa held the lower end, while the King and Queen of Saxony obligingly took hold of the upper end. The King of Prussia stood beside them and witnessed this strange scene with a scarcely perceptible smile, while the Empress Ludovica looked with undisguised scorn into the joy-excited countenance of her stepdaughter. Napoleon surveyed the faces of all present with a rapid glance, and an expression of sublime pride overspread his countenance.

"Look," exclaimed the Emperor Francis, bending over the pedigree, "there is his name! There is the founder of Napoleon's family."

At this moment Napoleon laid his hand gently on his shoulder. "Oh, no," he said, "the founder of that family stands here."

"Where, then?" asked Francis, eagerly, still bending over and looking for the name.

"If your majesty desires to see him, you must be so kind as to avert your eyes from that piece of parchment, and turn them toward me," said Napoleon, raising his voice.

Francis looked up and gazed wonderingly upon his son-in-law. Napoleon smiled; it was a triumphant smile. "I, and I alone, am the founder of Napoleon's family," he said, slowly and solemnly. "I am the ancestor of those who bear my name. The King of Rome needs no other, unless it be that your majesty should count every victory which his father gained an ancestor, and compose his pedigree from the laurels I have obtained in Europe and Africa. My son has a right to despise ancestors invisible in the darkness of by-gone centuries, whom history does not mention, while the vainest genealogy can scarcely discover that they lived and died. My grandsons and great-grandsons need not seek the name of the founder of their family on decayed parchments and confused pedigrees; they only need read the pages of history. They will also find it at night in the marshalled host of heaven, where twinkles a star which science names Napoleon. I think, sire, that star will never set; it will illuminate the path of your grandson better than the lamp flickering in the tombs of mouldering ancestors."

Maria Louisa at the first words of Napoleon withdrew her hands from the pedigree, and stood half sullen and ashamed by the side of her husband. The royal couple of Saxony hastened to roll up the pedigree as quickly as possible, and put it back into the golden box.

Napoleon offered his arm to his consort. "Come, madame," he said, "let us go to the ball-room." While he was walking away with her, the Emperor Francis turned to Ludovica, and, tapping his forehead, whispered cautiously, "I was right! There is something wrong in Napoleon's head."

———

CHAPTER VI.

NAPOLEON'S DEPARTURE FROM DRESDEN.

The brilliant court ball ended, and Napoleon retired to his cabinet. He seemed more careworn than he had ever allowed any of his attendants to notice. He was slowly walking his room, casting an occasional glance on the map marked with the positions of the various corps now near the frontiers of Russia. "Narbonne has not yet arrived," he muttered to himself. "Alexander seems really to hesitate whether to make peace or not. My four hundred thousand men, who have reached the Niemen, will frighten him, and he will submit as all the others. He will not dare to bid me defiance! He will yield! He—" Suddenly Napoleon paused and stepped hastily to the window on which he had happened to fix his eyes. A strange spectacle presented itself. The large **square directly in front** of his windows, which on the day of his arrival had been so splendidly lit up, was dark and silent; but, on the other side of the river, the Neustadt was now in a flood of light, and it seemed to him as if he heard cheers. He opened the window, and, leaning out, saw the houses illuminated—even the residences of the neighboring Palace Street. These houses, like those in the **other parts of the city,** had given previously no token of joy, and remained in darkness. The emperor shut the window angrily and rang the bell. "Tell the grand marshal I wish to see him," he said to the footman.

A few minutes afterward Duroc entered. "Duroc," exclaimed the emperor, in an angry voice, and pointing his arm at the window, "what is the meaning of that illumination? In whose honor is it?"

"**Sire,**" said Duroc, slowly, "I suppose it is in honor of the King of Prussia, who arrived to-day."

The emperor stamped on the floor, and his eyes flashed. "The inhabitants of Dresden are rebels, and ought to be brought to their senses by bomb-shells!" he shouted, in a thundering voice. "What does the King of Prussia concern them? And why do they show him **this honor?**"

"**Sire,**" said Duroc, smiling, "the people, as **the King of** Prussia said to-day, know but little of etiquette, and are not so wise as courtiers."

"'People!'" growled Napoleon. "There are no 'people;' there are only subjects, and they ought to be punished with fire and sword if they think of playing the part of 'the people.' Did I not issue orders to-day to the effect that all dem-onstrations should be prohibited? Why were my orders disobeyed?"

"Sire, they were obeyed so far as it was in our power. The police managed to prevent the populace from gathering and shouting **in the** street, but they are unable forcibly to enter the houses, because the inmates, without making any further demonstration, placed a few lights at their windows. Our agents, nevertheless, went to the proprietors of some of the houses, and asked for the reason of **this** sudden and unexpected demonstration. They replied that it was in honor of the Emperor Napoleon, the guest of their king."

"The villains! They dare to falsify!" exclaimed Napoleon. "The facts are against them. On the day when they were to illuminate in honor of my arrival, all the houses were gloomy as the grave, on account of hostility to me. The same feeling is the reason of to-day's illumination. It seems, then, that the king of Prussia is exceedingly popular in Saxony?"

"Yes, sire. The king, as I positively know, had instructed the inhabitants of the Prussian places **through which he had to pass on his jour-ney to Dresden, not to receive him in any** formal manner whatever; but, of course, he was **unable** to issue such orders in regard to the cities and villages of Saxony. Well, so soon as he crossed the Saxon frontier, he was everywhere received in the most ardent manner. All the bells were rung in the towns of Jüterbogk and Grossenhayn on his arrival, and the whole population, headed by the municipal authorities, and all the other functionaries, came to meet him on the outskirts of the towns, and cheered him in the most jubilant manner."

"And how did he receive these honors?"

"He thanked the citizens, in plain and simple words, for the disinterested respect they were good enough to pay to a German prince."

"A German prince?" repeated Napoleon, vehemently; "ah, this little King of Prussia still braves me! I was too generous at Tilsit! I must cut his wings still shorter! I will show him what the French emperor can do with a German prince, when he dares to bid me defiance!"

"Sire," said Duroc, in a suppliant voice, "I beseech your majesty not to go too far! The King of Prussia is backed by the sympathies of the whole German nation. His misfortunes cause the people to look on him as a martyr. They also believe that he participates but reluctantly in this Russian war, and this increases the love with which they regard him, for I venture to say to your majesty that this nation is opposed to the war."

"I have not appointed the German nation my secretary of war," exclaimed Napoleon, "and I have not asked my grand marshal to give me his advice. Carry out my orders, and do your duty. Tell Berthier to come to me!"

Duroc hung his head mournfully, and turned toward the door. The flaming eyes of Napoleon followed him. Just as the grand marshal opened the door, he heard the emperor calling him. "Sire?" he asked, turning, and standing at the door. There was now beaming so much love and mildness in the emperor's face, that Duroc was unable to resist, and, as if attracted by a magnetic power, returned.

"Duroc, my old friend," said Napoleon, offering him his hand, "I thank you for your good advice, for, though I did not ask it, it was well meant. I know full well that the so-called German people, as well as their princes, however they may cajole me, are opposed to this war. Oh, I know those treacherous princes! I know that those who flatter me to-day in the most abject manner, are only watching for an opportunity to avenge themselves for their sycophancy; but I have chained them to me with iron bands, and extracted their teeth, so that they are unable to bite—their teeth, that is to say, their soldiers, whom I am taking with me into this last and decisive war. For I tell you, Duroc, it will be our last campaign. On the ruins of Moscow I will compel Alexander to submit, and then peace will be restored to Europe for years to come. And who knows, it may not be necessary to go so far? Perhaps it may be sufficient for me to march my army as far as the Niemen, to awaken Alexander from his reveries, and bring him to his senses."

"Alas, sire!" said Duroc, sighing, "Alexander has loved your majesty too tenderly not to feel irritated in the highest degree."

"Is it I, then, who broke this friendship?" exclaimed Napoleon, vehemently. "Is it I who brought about this war? Have I not rather resorted to all means in order to avoid it? Have I not twice sent Lauriston to Alexander, and offered him peace in case he should fulfil my conditions: to shut his ports against British ships, to lay an embargo upon British goods, and give up commercial intercourse with England? But, emboldened by his victories over the Turks, the Emperor of Russia takes the liberty of dictating conditions to me! He asks me to give him an indemnity for confiscating the states of his brother in-law, the Prince of Oldenburg; he demands that I should not engage to reëstablish the kingdom of Poland! He wants to impose on me the terms by which peace is to be maintained! Conditions! I am the man to make them, but not to accept any! That would be a humiliation I could not submit to! You see, therefore, Duroc, I have been compelled to enter upon this war; I did not seek it, but I cannot avoid it. You see the justice of it, do you not? You know that I desired, and am still desiring peace, and that it is with a heavy heart I shed the blood of my brave soldiers."

"Sire," said Duroc, with a faint smile, "I see at least that it is too late now to speak of peace, inasmuch as an army of four hundred thousand men is waiting on the Niemen for the arrival of your majesty."

"Let Alexander speak; let him accept my terms, and it will not be too late," exclaimed Napoleon. "I am looking for Narbonne, who may arrive at any moment. He will bring us either peace or war, for he will have Alexander's final reply. As soon as he arrives he must be admitted, no matter whether I am asleep or awake. Go, now, Duroc! Tell Berthier to come to me!"

When Berthier entered, the emperor was standing at the window, and looking over to the Neustadt, which was still in a blaze of light. The marshal remained respectfully at the door, wait ing to be addressed. A long pause ensued. Suddenly Napoleon turned his pale countenance to Berthier, and exclaimed : " Berthier, you will set out immediately. Go to Berlin, and convey my order to the Duke de Belluno. Tell him that I recommend the utmost vigilance, and that it is his task to maintain order in Prussia. The population of that country are very seditious. They are constantly ready to conspire and rise in rebellion, and who knows whether Frederick William will not make common cause with the insurgents ? This ought to be prevented by all means ; war is at hand ; hence we must redouble our **firmness and** vigilance, that no revolution may annoy us in our rear. You will repeat all this to the duke, and take him my instructions."

" Sire," said Berthier, "if your majesty has no further orders, I shall set out immediately."

" You will tell the Duke de Belluno that it is my will that no Prussian general or officer shall command at Berlin, and that the French general alone must give all necessary orders. Sit down ; I will dictate to you the other instructions."

Berthier took a seat **at the** desk, and waited, pen in hand, for the emperor's words. Casting again a glance on the city honoring the King of Prussia, he dictated : " Special care is to be taken that neither at Berlin nor in its vicinity shall there **be a depot of small-arms or cannon,** which the populace might take possession of. No Prussian troops whatever shall be left at Berlin, and what few regular soldiers remain at the capital shall exclusively perform the military service at the palace. The French troops at Berlin shall not be lodged with the citizens, but take up their quarters at the barracks, and, if these should be insufficient for their accommodation, encamp in the open field. You will constantly keep some field-pieces ready for immediate use, in order to suppress any seditious movements that might take place. Every insult heaped upon a Frenchman will be punished by a court-martial according to the laws of war. Besides, it is necessary that the governor-general of Berlin should organize a secret police, that he may know what is going on, and have a vigilant eye on all dangerous attempts

at disturbing the public peace. You will inform the Duke de Belluno that the administration of the country will be entirely left **to** the king's ministers, but that the surveillance of the newspapers, as well as all other publications, and the whole organization of the police, must be in the duke's hands, that nothing may give a dangerous impulse to the people, and that they may have no opportunities of entering into a rebellion. Prussia must be kept down by all means at our command. You will tell the Duke de Belluno that I have given orders that three or four well-informed French officers should stay at Colberg and Graudenz. The right of having a Prussian garrison was reserved only to Colberg, and Potsdam is the only city through which the French troops are not allowed to pass ; but the inhabitants of Potsdam should be accustomed to see many French officers in their midst. The latter must frequently stop there overnight on the pretext of seeing the city, and, if their own curiosity should not impel them to do so, their commander should induce them to pursue the course I have indicated. The duke shall, under all circumstances, show the greatest deference to the King of Prussia, and even to affectation at festivals and on all public occasions. He shall, besides, frequently invite to his table the Prussian ministers, and what few Prussian officers will be left at Berlin, and always treat them in the most polite and obliging manner. But at all hours a vigilant eye must be had on the king as well as on the authorities and the people, and the duke ought always to be ready to put down the slightest demonstration or disorder. I have done," said Napoleon. " Go, Berthier, and comply carefully with my instructions. No confidence can be reposed in Frederick William or in his people. We have subjugated Prussia, but it may perhaps be necessary to crush her. At the slightest provocation this must be done ; if she will not be an honest ally, I will prove to her that I am an honest enemy, and, to give her this proof, put an end to her existence. Go, Berthier ; set out immediately."

Berthier withdrew, while Napoleon returned to the window with a triumphant air. " Ah, my little King of Prussia," he said, scornfully, " they kindle lights here under my eyes in honor of your **petty** majesty, but my breath can extinguish them and leave you in a profound darkness. Another such provocation, and your throne breaks down. Another—"

The door of the antechamber was hastily opened, and Roustan appeared. " Sire," he said, "his excellency Count de Narbonne requests an audience."

" Narbonne!" ejaculated Napoleon, joyously. " Come in, Narbonne, come in!" And he hastened to meet the count, who entered the cabinet, and, as an experienced cavalier of the court of Louis XVI., made his bows in strict accordance with etiquette.

" Omit these unnecessary ceremonies," said Napoleon, quivering with impatience and anxiety, " I have been looking for you a long time. What results do you bring me?"

" Sire," said the count, with his imperturbable, diplomatic smile, " I am afraid the result of my mission will be war."

" What!" exclaimed Napoleon, eagerly, and, for a moment, a faint blush tinged his cheeks. " What! The Emperor Alexander will not yield? He refuses to comply with my conditions?."

" Sire, your majesty will permit me to repeat to you the emperor's own words," said the count, with composure. " When I had laid your propositions before his majesty, and told him that if the czar should shut his ports against British ships, continue the war with England, lay an embargo on all British goods, and give up all direct and indirect commercial intercourse with England, your majesty then would make peace with Russia, the Emperor Alexander exclaimed vehemently, ' Such a peace I would accept only after having been forced into the interior of Siberia!' "*

" Ah," exclaimed Napoleon, " I will give him the pleasure of that journey. He will become acquainted with Siberia, and there I mean to dictate terms of peace, unless I prefer to leave him

there forever. **Did you bring** any other dispatches?"

" I did, sire. Here is the official reply of Minister Count Romanzoff to the letter of the Duke de Bassano, of which I was the bearer. It is nothing but a repetition of the phrases which the Russian ambassador at Paris made to us up to the day of his departure. Here is Romanzoff's letter. Will your majesty be so gracious as to read it?"

Napoleon took the paper and glanced over it. " You are right," he said, flinging the paper contemptuously on the table. " Nothing but the same phrase : ' Alexander wants peace, but is unable to fulfil my conditions.' Well, then, he shall have war! The first shot discharged at my soldiers will be answered by a thousand cannon, and they will announce to the world that Napoleon is expelling the barbarians from Europe."

" Sire," said Narbonne, smiling, " if your majesty intends to wait until the Russians fire the first gun, there will be no war, and may it be so! The Emperor Alexander has made up his mind not to take the initiative. Only when the armies of your majesty have crossed the frontier of Russia, when you have forcibly entered his **states,** will Alexander look upon the war as begun, but he will not carry it beyond the boundaries of his country : he will not meet the enemy, whom he would still like so much to call his friend, outside the frontiers of his empire."

" Ah, I knew well that Alexander is hesitating," exclaimed Napoleon, triumphantly. " He dares not attack me, and his vacillation will give me time to complete my preparations, and surround him so closely that he cannot escape. While he is still dreaming at the Kremlin of the possibility of peace, I shall be at the gates, and ask him in the thunder of my cannon whether he will submit, or bury himself beneath the ruins of his throne."

" He will choose the latter," exclaimed Narbonne, quickly.

" He will not!" said Napoleon, proudly. " He will submit! A terrible blow struck in the heart of the empire, Moscow—holy Moscow—delivers

---

* Alexander's own words.—Vide " Mémoires d'un Homme d'État," vol. xiii., p. 375.

Russia into my hands. I know Alexander; I exerted formerly great influence over him. I must dazzle his imagination by boldness and energy, and he will return to my friendship."

"Heaven grant that it may be so!" said Narbonne, sighing.

"It is so!" said Napoleon, confidently, walking with rapid steps and proud head; "yes, it is so! Fate has intrusted me with the mission of ridding Europe of the barbarians. The logic of events necessitates this war, and even family ties, such as we proposed to form at our interview at Erfurt, would not have prevented it. The barbarism of Russia is threatening the whole of Europe. Think of Suwarrow and his Tartars in Italy! Our reply ought to be, to hurl them back beyond Moscow; and when would Europe be able to do so, unless now and through me." *

"But, sire, Europe, in the madness of her hatred, would prefer to make common cause with Russia. Suppose she should offer her hand to the Tartars and Cossacks, to deliver herself from the yoke which the glory and greatness of Napoleon have imposed upon her neck? Sire, at this decisive hour you must permit me to tell you the truth: I am afraid the hatred, the cunning malice and rage of your enemies, will this time be stronger than the military skill of your majesty, and the bravery of the hundreds of thousands who have followed you with such enthusiasm. Your majesty says that Alexander is hesitating, and that may, perhaps, be true; but his people are the more resolute, and so is the emperor's suite. They are bent on having war, and with the whole strength of mortal hatred and patriotic fanaticism. The people, instigated by their venomous and impassioned priests, regard this as a holy war, commanded by God Himself. Their priests have told them that the Emperor of the French is coming with his armies to devastate Russia, to destroy the altars and images of the saints, and to dethrone the czar, in order to place himself on the throne. The Russian people, who, in their child-like innocence, believe to be true whatever their priests tell them, feel themselves profoundly wounded in their three most sacred sympathies: love for the fatherland, the church, and the czar, and they are rising to a man to save them. Sire, this war which your majesty is about to commence is no ordinary war: the enemy will not oppose you in the open field; like the Parthian, he will seemingly flee from his pursuer; he will decoy you forward, but in the thicket or ravine he will conceal himself, and when you pass by will have you at an advantage. He will never allow you to fight him in a pitched battle, but every village and cottage will be an obstacle, a rampart obstructing your route. Every peasant will regard himself a soldier, and believe it his bounden duty to fight, however sure he may be to die. Sire, the terrible scenes in Spain may be renewed in Russia, for all Russia will be a vast Saragossa; women, children, and old men, will participate in this struggle; they will die eating poisoned bread with the enemy, rather than give him wholesome food."

"You are exaggerating!" exclaimed Napoleon, sneeringly. "In truth, it is mere imagination to compare the Russian serf—the blood in whose veins is frozen by Siberian cold, and whose back is cut up and bowed by the knout—with the Spaniard, passionate and free beneath a torrid sun, and who in his rags still feels himself noble and a grandee. But these exaggerations shall not influence me! The die is cast: I cannot recede! Great Heaven! this tedious old Europe! I will bring from Russia the keys to unlock a new world. Or do you believe, you short-sighted little men, that I have undertaken, merely for the sake of Russia, this greatest expedition that military history will ever engrave upon its tablets? No; Moscow is to me but the gate of Asia! My route to India passes that way. Alexander the Great had as long a route to the Ganges as I shall have from Moscow, and yet he reached his destination. Should I shrink from what he succeeded in accomplishing? Since the days of St. Jean d'Acre I have thought of this scheme; if it had not been for the discontinuance of the siege and the plague, I should at that time have conquered one-half

* Napoleon's own words.—Vide "Souvenirs du Comte Villemain," vol. L, p. 168.

of Asia, **and** have thence returned to Europe for the thrones of Germany and Italy. Do not look at **me so** wonderingly, Narbonne. I tell you nothing **but** my real schemes. They shall be carried into effect, and then you and the world will have to acknowledge that my words **are** oracles, my actions miracles, and every day a new one! * In the **morning I set out** early and repair to the headquarters of my army. **Do not say a word,** Narbonne! I leave Dresden early in the morning. The fate of Russia is decided! Go!" He waved his hand toward the door, and turned his back to Narbonne.

The count left the imperial cabinet with a sigh. In the corridor **outside he met Berthier and Duroc,** who seemed to await him. **"Well," both of** them asked eagerly, "were your representations successful? Will the emperor, at the eleventh hour, make peace?"

Narbonne shook his head sadly. "It was all **in vain,**" he replied. "He wishes war, and you do not even dream how far he means to carry it. When listening to him, one believes him to be either a demigod, to whom temples should be built, or a lunatic, who should be sent to Bedlam!" *

---

* Napoleon's own words.—Vide Villemain, "Souvenirs," vol. I., p. 180.

* Count Louis de Narbonne's own words.—Vide "Souvenirs," vol. I.

CHAPTER VII.

THE CONSPIRATORS OF HELGOLAND.

THE storm was howling over the ocean, revealing its depths, and hurling **its foaming waves to** the sky. They dashed wildly against yonder lofty **rock that calmly overlooked the anger of the tempest. It was the rock of Helgoland. In times of old, it towered even more proudly above** the unruly element surrounding it. It was then a terror to seafaring nations, and when the ships of the rich merchants of Hamburg, Bremen, Holland, and Denmark, passed it **at as great** a distance as possible, the masters made the sign of **the** cross, and prayed God would deliver them **from this imminent danger. In** ancient days **Helgoland was ten times larger than it is now, and on this old rocky island,** which had been the last asylum of the gods of **northern paganism,** lived a warlike people, who knew no other laws than **those of their own will, no other toil** than piracy, and who submitted to no other master than the chieftain chosen from among their most colossal fellows. The pirates of Helgoland **were** desperate men, who had selected for themselves as a coat of arms a wheel and **a gallows,** which they wore embroidered on the sleeves **of** their jackets; and their last chieftain, who **especially** terrified the hearts of sea-captains passing the island, called himself: "I, by my own grace, and not that of God, Long Peter, Murderer **of** the Dutch, **Destroyer** of the Hamburgers, **Chastiser of** the Danes, and Scourge of the Bremen Ships." But Long Peter, "by his own grace, and not that of God," had at length fallen a victim to the vicissitudes of life. The women of Helgoland, revolting against his cruelty, baseness, and tyranny, surrendered the island, the seat of the ancient gods, to Admiral Paulsen, of the Danish navy. This occurred in 1684, and since then Helgoland remained under the authority of the Danish crown until 1807. The conflagration of Copenhagen melted the chains that fastened the old gray rock to Denmark, and England, that triumphantly conveyed the whole Danish fleet to her own shores, annexed Helgoland.

The island had become much smaller ever since Long Peter, its last chieftain, died. The storms had swept over it, tearing rocky masses from its shores, and flinging them far into the sea, which had undermined the foundations of Helgoland, and hidden the conquest beneath the waves. Although small, it was the beacon of Europe. In the last days of 1812 the eyes of all German patriots were fixed longingly and hopefully upon that lonely rock in the North Sea. It was British territory—the first advance which England had made to the shores of suffering Germany, and, her proud flag waving over it, made it the asylum of persecuted patriots and members of the secret leagues. To the red rock, in the midst of the sea, came no French spies; there were no traitors' ears, for the pilot at the light-house kept a good lookout, and no suspicious ship was permitted to anchor; no one was allowed to land without having given a good account of himself, and satisfying the authorities that confidence might be reposed in him. Those allowed to disembark were heartily welcomed, for, by setting foot on the rocky island, they had become members of the vast family of Napoleon's enemies—of the brethren who had united against his power—of the conspirators whose sworn duty it was to oppose Napoleon with the weapons of cunning as well as force—of intrigue creeping in the dark, or of brave and manly defiance.

In Helgoland the swarms of smugglers sheltered, who had taken upon themselves the risk of trading English goods, against which Napoleon's hatred tried to shut the entire **continent.** There came the **crowd of foreign merchants, to** purchase of English dealers the goods which Napoleon's decrees had prohibited in his own dominions, as well as in those of his allies. Every British manufacturer and wholesale dealer had his counting-house and depot at Helgoland. Vast warehouses, resembling palaces, rose on the plateau of the island, and approaching ships beheld them from afar. In these warehouses were stored all the articles which British industry was able to offer to the rest of Europe, and **which the people** of the whole continent desired the more ardently, the more rigorously they were forbidden to purchase them. Every large commercial firm of London and Manchester had branches of their business on the island; every wealthy banker had an office there, and people were justified in calling Helgoland "Little London." You would have thought yourself in the city of London, when passing through the narrow streets of the island, lined on both sides with vast warehouses, and reading on each the names of the most celebrated London firms. You would almost have fancied you were in the gigantic harbor of the Thames, when looking at the forest of masts, the animated crowds, the ships and boats, where from three to four hundred vessels cleared and entered every day.

Not only merchants and smugglers, adventurers and speculators, flocked to Helgoland, but diplomatists, politicians, and patriots found on the rocky island a refuge and convenient point, where they might meet their brethren and reunite kindred hearts. The members of the great secret league hastened from the north and the south of Europe to Helgoland, to hold meetings there, concert plans, and communicate to each other what they had succeeded in accomplishing.

On one of the last days in September, 1812, an unusual commotion prevailed on the island. It was noon, and yet more than two hundred ships had arrived and cast anchor. All the stores were open and the goods displayed; brokers and speculators elbowed themselves in busy haste through the multitude of merchants, owners of ships, smugglers, and sailors, that filled the whole upper part of the island, offering goods for sale in all languages; and among them were to be seen **the** beautiful girls of **Helgoland, dressed in their** strange costume, **and carrying in baskets and on** plates all sorts of delicacies, for which they sought purchasers.

At a distance from the throng stood three men, who paid but little attention to the merry, excited crowd. They were closely wrapped in cloaks, with their hats drawn over their foreheads, and looked steadfastly upon the sea. **Far** on the horizon there appeared another small dark speck, which gradually assumed a definite shape.

"A ship!" ejaculated one of the three men, eagerly.

"Yes, a ship," repeated his two companions. They paused, looking eagerly at the vessel, which rapidly darted across the waves, and could now be discerned by the unaided eye.

"Look," said one of the three, "she is a **man-**of-war. I see the port-holes."

"But I do not see her flag," said one of his companions.

"I do," exclaimed the third, who had hitherto looked at the ship through a large telescope "Yellow and blue, the Swedish colors."

"At length!" exclaimed the first speaker, joyously. "I hope it is he!"

"There is another ship," said the second speaker, pointing his hand to a different part of the horizon. "How she is dashing along!—her keel cuts the waves so that their foaming crests sweep like a silver chain behind her. Oh, I like that ship! it seems to me as though she brings us glad tidings, and comes for our sake, and not for commercial purposes."

"Now she unfurls her flag!" exclaimed the third speaker. "It is the union jack! Oh, you are right, she comes for our sake, and I hope some friend is on board. But we are forgetting the Swedish vessel. Where is she?"

"There! The little fish has become a whale. And see, the English ship, too, is much larger, and is dancing along like a beauty. Both are very fast, and in half an hour they will be at anchor in the harbor."

"Heaven grant that the friends for whom we are looking may be on board!" said his two companions, sighing.

"Your wish will be granted," said their friend. "God is with us and blesses our league. Has He not already for twelve days bidden the sea be calm, and not detain us or one of ours by adverse winds? Have we not all arrived to-day, as we had agreed to, from three different parts of the world? Why should the other brethren of our league not be able to do the same?"

"Yes, you are right," said the first speaker, smiling. "Heaven does seem to be with us, and it is apparently for our sake that this rock emerged from the waves as a snug little boudoir for our European rendezvous. Bonaparte may often enough cast angry glances in this direction, but the lightning of his eyes and the thunder of his words do not reach our sea-girt asylum, which God Himself has built and furnished for us. Grim Bonaparte cannot hurt us here, but we will try to hurt him, and one day he will find out what we are doing at the political boudoir of Helgoland."

"Look," exclaimed his friend, "the two ships have reached the island at the same time, and are now anchoring."

"They are lowering their boats," exclaimed the third speaker. "The passengers are going ashore."

"Let us go to the place agreed upon, and see whether they are the brethren we are looking for," said the first speaker.

"Yes, let us go," exclaimed his two companions.

Without exchanging another word, they turned and walked hastily through the busy crowds to the staircase leading from the upper part of the island to the lower shore. Here they passed through the streets of small, neat fishermen's huts, and then entered the last building. A footman in a gorgeous livery received them in the small hall, and opened with reverential politeness the door leading into the only room of the hut. The three men walked in, and locked the door carefully. One of them took off his hat and cloak, and now stood before his two companions in splendid uniform, his breast covered with orders. "Permit me, gentlemen," he said, smiling—"permit me to greet you here as guests of mine, for you are now at my house. I have bought this building for the purpose of holding the meetings of the members of our league. Up to this time we have recognized each other as friends only by the signs and passwords that had been agreed on; but now, if you please, we will drop our incognito. I am Count Munster, minister of the Elector of Hanover and the King of England."

"And I," said the second gentleman, taking off his cloak—"I have the honor of introducing myself to your excellency as the chief of the Berlin police, who was proscribed and exiled by Bonaparte. My name is Justus Gruner."

"A name that I have known a long time, though I was not acquainted with the man himself," said Count Munster, kindly offering him his hand. "Let me bid you welcome as a faithful and zealous adherent of the good cause—as a noble patriot in whom Germany confides and hopes."

"It is my turn now to unmask," said the third whose countenance had hitherto been almost entirely invisible, so closely had he muffled himself. Taking off his cloak and hat and bowing to his companions, he said, "My name is Frederick William of Brunswick."

"I had the honor to recognize your highness when you were yet in the boat, and I stood on the shore," said Count Munster, smiling and bowing respectfully.

"And why did you not tell me so?" asked the duke, eagerly.

"Because I respected your incognito, your highness," said the count.

The duke shook his head, which was covered with dark, curly hair. "No etiquette, count," he said, almost indignantly. "I am nothing but a poor soldier, who scarcely knows where to lay his head, whom grief is tormenting, and whose hunger for vengeance is not appeased."

"There will be a time when all those who are hungry, like your highness, will be satisfied," said Justus Gruner, solemnly.

"If you speak the truth, my friend," exclaimed the duke, with emphasis, "the eyes of my blind father, who died in despair, will reopen, and he will look down with blissful tears upon the delivered world. And they will blot out his last dying words, that are burning like fire in my heart. 'Oh, what a disgrace! what a disgrace!' were the last words my father uttered. I hear them night and day; they are always resounding in my ears like the death-knell of Germany; they are ever smarting in my heart like an open wound. Germany is groaning and lamenting, for Napoleon's foot is still on her neck, and, mortally wounded and blinded like my father, we are all crying, 'Oh, what a disgrace! what a disgrace!'"

"But the time will soon come when our wounds will heal," said Count Munster, gravely. "Our night is passing, the morning dawns, and the star of Bonaparte will fade forever."

"I do not think it," said the duke, sighing. "It is still shining over our heads—he is rather like a threatening meteor, and its eccentric course is over the snow-fields of Russia. But hush! footsteps are approaching." The duke was not mistaken. They heard the door of the hut violently open and close, and shortly after some one rapped at the locked door.

"The password!" shouted Count Munster, putting his hand on the key.

"*Il est temps de finir!*" replied a sonorous voice outside.

Count Munster opened the door. A gentleman of imposing stature entered the room. "Count Nugent," exclaimed Count Munster, joyously, offering both his hands to the friend whom he had known for many years. "Was it you who arrived on the last English ship?"

"Yes," said the count, saluting the other gentlemen. "But I believe there will be more guests here directly. I saw close behind me two men, wrapped in cloaks, who were also moving hither. Ah, they are passing the window at this moment."

"And now they are entering the house," said the count, listening.

Another rapping was heard, and the call for the password was answered again by the shout of "*Il est temps de finir!*"

"They are the passengers from the Swedish vessel, as I hoped they would be," said Count Munster, opening the door. Two men in cloaks entered, and bowed silently to the others.

"Gneisenau! My dear Gneisenau!" exclaimed Count Munster, tenderly embracing the gentleman who had entered last. "Then, you have really kept your word! You have come in spite of all dangers! I thank you in the name of Germany!"

"You will thank me only after having learned what new ally I have enlisted for our holy cause," said Gneisenau, smiling, and pointing to his companion, who, still closely muffled, was standing by his side silent and motionless.

"You come from Stockholm," said Count Munster, joyously, "you bring us a delegate of the crown prince of Sweden, the noble Bernadotte, do you not? My heart does not deceive me—I am sure!"

"No, your heart does not deceive you," said Gneisenau, smiling. "This gentleman is an envoy of the crown prince of Sweden, who promises us his friendship and assistance."

"No," said the stranger, slowly and solemnly. "At this hour there must be truth between us. I am not an envoy of the crown prince of Sweden, I am he himself, I am Bernadotte!" He took off his hat and cloak, and bowed to the astonished gentlemen. "I wish to prove to you, and to those whom you are representing, that I am in earnest," said Bernadotte, in the most dignified manner. "My French heart had to undergo a long and painful struggle, but the crown prince of **Sweden** conquered it. I must think **no longer of the** blood that is flowing in my veins, but remember **only** that, by the decree of the noble Swedish nation, I have been destined to become its king, and that, therefore, the interests of Sweden must **be more important and sacred to me than my** own heart. The Emperor of *the French has offered me an alliance. But Russia and Prussia are urging me to espouse their cause. **The interest** of Sweden requires me to ally myself with those who have justice, strength, and honor on their side; I shall, therefore, side with Russia, England, and Prussia. This is the reply which I made to the Russian ambassadors, and likewise **to the Prussian General Gneisenau here. But, at** the same time, I asked opportunity to complete my preparations, and until that can be done, I have requested the ambassadors to keep secret my accession to the northern alliance. It seemed to me as though this request of mine were looked upon as a proof of my vacillation, and as a want of candor, and as though doubts were entertained as to my ultimate decision. Hence I wished to manifest my true spirit by coming myself to you instead of sending a delegate. Now, you have heard my political confession. Are you content with it, and may I participate in your deliberations?" And the crown prince of Sweden, uttering the last words, turned with a winning smile to Count Munster, and sank his head as a prisoner waiting for sentence.

"I pray your royal highness, in the name of my friends present, to remain and participate in our discussions," said Count Munster. "We are now waiting for no further arrivals—all the invited guests have come. Let us take our seats. Let the conference commence. But first permit me to introduce the gentlemen to each other."

CHAPTER VIII.

THE EUROPEAN CONSPIRACY.

THE six gentlemen sat **down on** chairs placed **around the** table standing **in the** middle of the **room. Count** Munster bowed to them. "**As** it was I who invited you to attend this conference," he said, "I must **take** the liberty of addressing you first. I must justify myself for having called upon **you** in the name of Germany, **in** the name of Europe, to come hither **notwithstanding** the dangers and hardships of the journey. **Yes,** gentlemen, Germany stands in need of our **assistance.** But not only Germany—Spain, drenched in the blood of her patriots; poor, enslaved Italy; Holland, ruthlessly annexed to France; in short, all the states that are groaning under the tyrant's yoke; yea, France herself!—all are crying for deliverance from slavery. But whence is help to come when every one shuts his eyes against the despairing wail of Europe; when every one idly folds his hands and waits for some one else to be bold enough to call upon the people to take up arms? Every individual must be animated with this courage; must regard himself as chosen by Providence to commence the task of liberation. Each one must act as though it were he who is to set the world in motion, and were the head of the great and holy conspiracy by which mankind is to be delivered from the tyrant. I told myself so when I saw all Germany sinking; I repeat it to myself every day, and it is my excuse now for having ventured to invite thither men who are my superiors in every respect. But to Germany alone we shall give an account of what we have hitherto done for her liberation; for her let us deliberate as to what we further ought to do, and what plans we should pursue. The world lies prostrate, but we must raise it again; the nations are manacled, but we must be **the files** that imperceptibly cut through **the** fetters, and we must then tell the people **that** it is easy for them to gain their independence; that it is only necessary to take the **sword, and** prove by deeds that they feel themselves free—then they will be free. This is our task—the task of all generous

patriots. Every one has been conscious of this, **but** also that there should be a bond connecting **all the** members of this secret league, to which every patriot belongs. That was the idea which caused several friends and myself to unite our efforts. We did so, and this union made us feel doubly strong; we conferred as to our duties and schemes, and by doing so they became clearer to us, and better matured. We made ourselves emissaries of the sacred cause of the fatherland, and went into the world to enlist soldiers, to create a new nation, awaken the sleepers, enlighten the ignorant, bring back the faithless, undeceive the **deceived, and console the despairing. For this** purpose I have struggled for years, and so have all my friends, and so do all good and faithful patriots, without perhaps being fully conscious of it. But it is necessary, too, that those who, like us, are fully alive to their duty, should from time to time give each other an account of what they have accomplished, that they may agree upon new plans for the future. I, therefore, requested my friends Count Nugent and General Gneisenau, to come hither; I wrote to Minister von Stein, who is now at Prague, either to come himself, or send a reliable representative, and I requested another in Northern Germany to send one of his intimate friends. Four months ago I dispatched my invitations; the meeting was to take place to-day, and we have all promptly responded to the call. My friend in Northern Germany induced the noblest and most faithful soldier of the fatherland, Duke Frederick William of Brunswick, to go to Helgoland. Minister von Stein, who, in the mean time, was obliged to go to Russia, sends us a noble representative in the person of Justus Gruner, and the magnanimous crown prince of Sweden offers us, by his voluntary appearance in our midst, a new guaranty for the success of our schemes. We know now what has called us hither. Let us communicate to each other what we have hitherto done, in order to attain the object for which we are striving, and what plans we shall **adopt.** In this respect, the two noble princes now in our midst are especially able to

make valuable suggestions, and it is to them principally that we shall apply. The former question, however, concerns chiefly ourselves, who have for years been members of the league, and have jointly tried to promote its objects. In order to know what we should do, we must be informed exactly of what we have already done. To be able to conceive plans for the future, we must carefully weigh, and render ourselves perfectly familiar with, the present political situation, and communicate our observations and adventures to each other. Let us do so now. Let the gentleman who arrived last speak first. General Gneisenau, tell us, therefore, what hopes do you entertain in regard to Prussia? What are the sentiments of the king? What has Germany or Prussia to hope from the ministers of Frederick William? What is the spirit of the people and the soldiers?"

"You ask a great deal," said Gneisenau, sighing, "and I have but little to reply. I have no hopes whatever in regard to Prussia. That is the result of the observations during my present journey. Every thing is in about the same condition as it was in 1811; the same men are still ruling, **and the same state of affairs, on account of which I left the Prussian service at that time, is still** prevailing. **The king is the noblest and** best-meaning man, but his indecision and distrust in his own abilities are his own curse, as well as that of his country. When, in 1808, we heard at Königsberg the news of the events of Bayonne, the king said, ' Bonaparte will assuredly not catch me in such a manner!' and now he has delivered himself into the hands of his most relentless enemy, who, if Russia should be defeated, would dethrone him, or, if Bonaparte should not be successful, keep him as a hostage.* The friends of the French, the timid, and the cowards, are still besieging the king's ears, and enjoying his confidence to a greater extent than Hardenberg does. Hardenberg is all right, but he intends, after the fashion of diplomatists, to attain the great object slowly and cautiously, instead of

* Gneisenau's own words.—Vide "Lebensbilder," vol. i., p. 261.

struggling for it boldly, and sword in hand. He is secretly on our side; he hates Napoleon and curses the chains that are fettering Prussia; he is always planning as to the best means of breaking them, but publicly he negotiates with the diplomatists of Napoleon to bring about a marriage between the crown prince and one of Napoleon's nieces. There can be no question of an army in Prussia, for the forty thousand men whom Napoleon permitted the King of Prussia still to retain under arms, had either to accom**pany the French army to Russia, or are** at least stationed, as Napoleon's reserves, on the extreme **frontiers.** Berlin, as well as all larger cities, and the fortresses, are garrisoned by French troops, keeping down the national spirit of the population, and rendering any attempt at insurrection an utter impossibility, even though the people should intend to strike. **But they think no longer of rising. They are exhausted in their misery, and have lost their energy. They feel only that** they are suffering, but they inquire no more for the cause. And thus Prussia will perish, unless some powerful impetus from abroad, some dispensation of Providence, should arouse her from her lethargy, and restore her to the consciousness of her disgrace and her strength. I hope that **this** will occur; for only this and England's energy will be able to save us. But other hopes I **do not** entertain. I, therefore, shall leave Prussia again and accompany you to England, Count Munster, when you return thither."

"I shall set out for England this day, as soon as our conference is at an end," said Count Munster, "and you will be a most welcome and agreeable companion. It is only now that I perceive how necessary a personal interview was, and how good it is that we are here assembled. Many things, which cannot be explained **in the** longest letters, may be perfectly understood after **an interview** of fifteen minutes. I believe and hope, my friend, that your view of the present state of affairs is by far too gloomy. You are hoping for an impetus from abroad; but that will scarcely be needed to arouse the nations from their lethargy. A new spirit is animating Germany, and it is Spain, with her heroic victories, that has awakened this spirit. The immortal defence of Saragossa has passed like a magic song throughout Europe, and has told the oppressed and enslaved nations that Bonaparte is not invincible, and that a nation which will not suffer itself to be enslaved has the strength to defend itself against the most powerful tyrant. Looking upon Spain, the nations recollect these noble words of Tacitus: 'It is not the tyrants who make nations slaves, but the nations degrading themselves voluntarily to the abject position of slaves make tyrants.' And the nations will have no more tyrants, but are determined to annihilate him who has put his foot upon their neck. Tell us, Count Nugent—you who, in the service of holy liberty, have been wandering about the world for the last two years—tell us whether I am not justified in asserting that the nations are about to awake?"

"Yes, I believe so," said Count Nugent, joyously. "For the third time during two years I have finished a journey through Europe. From Vienna **I went by way of Trieste,** Corfu, and **Malta, to the British** generals in Sicily, Spain, and Portugal, thence to England, and from England I returned to Vienna under an assumed name and all sorts of disguises. During my first two journeys I saw everywhere only that the nations submitted unhesitatingly, as though Bonaparte were the scourge which God Himself had sent to chastise them, and against whom they were not allowed to revolt, although rivers of blood were spilled. But I saw no prince who had the strength or courage, or even the wish to rule as a free and independent sovereign over a free people. The princes were everywhere content with being the vassals of France; they **deemed** themselves happy to have secured by their humiliation at least a title; they were striving to obtain by base sycophancy additional territories and orders, and betraying their own country and their own people in order to serve the Emperor of France. It was a terrible, heartrending spectacle presented by Germany during these last years, and which could not but fill the heart of every patriot with shame and despair. And **yet this** period of degradation was necessary and even salutary; for it blinded Napoleon by the glaring sunshine of his power; it rendered him overbearing and reckless; he dared every thing, because he believed he would succeed in every thing, and that the world had utterly succumbed to his power. He dared all, trampled on every feeling of justice, and thereby finally goaded the nations to resist him. In 1810 he exclaimed triumphantly, 'Three years yet, and I shall be master of the world!' And when he lately took ne field against Russia, he said, 'After humiliating Russia and reducing her to **an Asiatic** power, I shall establish at Paris a universal European court and universal archives!' **He believes** himself to be the master of the world; he thinks the thunderbolts of heaven are in his hands, and his arrogance will drive him to destruction, for 'the gods first blind him whom they intend to destroy.' And Napoleon is blind, for he does not see the wrath of the nations; he is deaf, for he does not hear the imprecations which all nations, from the Mediterranean to the North Sea and the Baltic, are uttering against him. Yes, the morning is dawning, and the nations are awaking; Napoleon has already passed the zenith of his glory; his star does not now dazzle mankind; they have commenced to doubt the stability of his power. I saw a curious instance of this last year in Vienna at Metternich's saloon. When the courier who brought the news of the birth of the King of Rome, still exhausted by the rapid ride from Nancy, entered and held up Champagny's letter containing nothing but these words, '*Eh bien, le Roi de Rome est arrivé!*' every one cried, 'Is not the hand of God there? The wonderful man has the son he wished for. Whither will the madmen and demagogues direct their hopes now?' But a courageous and merry native of Vienna exclaimed in the midst of the diplomatists 'Oh! ten years hence this King of Rome will be a poor little student in this city!'* The diplomatists were silent; the former ambassador of Hanover, however, Count Har-

<hr>

denberg, brother of th‍ chancellor of state, burst into loud laughter. These words were circulated among the people, and the Viennese **say now** smilingly, though as yet in a low tone, 'The King of Rome will come as a poor student to Vienna.' And the same words are repeated more boldly by the faithful Tyrolese, the guardians of the fires of patriotism. The Italians are whetting their swords, and France herself is preparing for the possibility of a new state of affairs. The military ardor of her marshals is exhausted; like the whole country, they are longing for repose; they begin to curse him whom they have hitherto idolized; they want peace, and are determined to compel Napoleon to comply with their demands."

,,And is our friend, Baron von Stein, also of this opinion?" asked Count Munster, turning to Justus Gruner.

"Yes, he is," said Gruner. "When the Emperor Alexander invited him to come to St. Petersburg, he went thither not so much because he needed an asylum, but because se believed he could serve the cause of Germany in a more efficacious manner in Russia than anywhere else, and **was convinced that Alexander needed a** firm and energetic adviser to fan his hostility to Napoleon, and keep all pacific influences away from him. Nothing but a crushing defeat of Napoleon in Russia can deliver Germany; Stein feels convinced of it, and therefore he stands as an immovable rock by the side of Alexander, and never ceases to influence the emperor by soul-stirring and courageous advice. Here is a letter which Stein requested me to deliver to Count Munster."

Count Munster took the letter and quickly glanced over it. "Ah," he exclaimed, joyously, "Stein, too, believes the day to be at hand when Germany will and must rise; he, too, prophesies that Napoleon will speedily fall. It is, therefore, time for us to think of the future, and agree as to the steps to be taken. And now I take the liberty of asking the crown prince of Sweden what assistance he offers us, and what the nations enslaved by Napoleon may hope from him?"

"All the assistance which I and my country

are able to offer," said the crown prince, ardently. "The king has authorized me to take all necessary measures for an active campaign. Already I have chartered transports; the troops which are to participate in the campaign have been concentrated in their camps, and will soon march to the various points of embarkation. When the German powers call me—when it is sure that England entertains honest intentions toward us, and will stand faithfully by us, I shall be ready to embark with my troops and participate in the great struggle, provided that the annexation of Norway to Sweden be guaranteed."

"I am authorized to do so in the name of England," exclaimed Count Munster.

"In that case the Swedes will regard this campaign as a national affair," said Bernadotte, "and will joyously rally round the banner of their crown prince, who, on his part, longs for nothing more than to follow the footsteps of the great Gustavus Adolphus, and give Sweden fresh claims to her ancient glory and the gratitude of the nations.* I am waiting for the call of the allied powers to hasten to the point where I may do good service."

"And so am I," said the Duke of Brunswick, eagerly. "I have nothing to offer to Germany but my hatred against Napoleon, my burning thirst for vengeance, my name, and my sword."

"But those will be the dragon's teeth, from which, in due time, will spring up mail-clad warriors," exclaimed Munster—"warriors who, with the most ardent enthusiasm, will follow the hero whose audacious expedition from the forests of Bohemia to the Weser will never be forgotten by the patriots of Germany. Let us prepare every thing as secretly as possible; let us enlist soldiers for the great and holy army; its chieftains are ready; Gneisenau, Frederick William of Brunswick, the crown prince of Sweden, and, in due time, Blucher, Schwarzenberg, and Wellington, will join them."

"Yes, let us prepare for the great task of the future," exclaimed Gneisenau. "I feel now reanimated with hope, patience, and courage. I go to London, but not to brood over my fate; I go to enlist an English legion for Germany; to tell the English ministers that the British government can take no step more conducive to the liberation of the nations and the safety of Great Britain than make Germany the principal seat of war, and transfer thither Wellington, with all the troops in Spain, and those which can be spared from the islands of the United Kingdom. Let them consider me a visionary; the future will, perhaps, prove to them that I was right. Oh, a victory over Napoleon in Germany would loosen the fetters of all governments, throw the most determined efforts of many millions of people into the scales of Great Britain, and deliver us, perhaps forever, from the monster equally terrible in his strength and in his poison." *

"And I go to Vienna to influence, together with my friends, the patriotic impulses of the emperor," said Count Nugent. "I go to Austria to tell the noble Archdukes John and Charles that they ought to hold themselves in readiness, and to inform the Tyrolese that the war of liberation is at hand."

"Baron von Stein has sent me to Germany to enlist there an intellectual army, and set in motion for Germany not only swords but pens," said Justus Gruner, smiling. "Stein says the sword will only do its work when the mind has paved the way for it. The mind and the free word, these are the generals that must precede the sword, and, before raising an army of soldiers, we must raise an army of ideas and minds to take the field. And there can be no better mental chieftain than noble Baron von Stein. He has placed a worthy adjutant at his side; I refer to Ernst Moritz Arndt, whom Stein has called to St. Petersburg, and who is thence to send his patriotic songs into the world, and by his soul-stirring writings kindle the ardor of the Germans. I have brought with me some of Arndt's pamphlets that have been printed in St. Petersburg, and his

---

* Bernadotte's own words.—Vide "Mémoires d'un Homme d État," vol. xl.

* Gneisenau's own words.—Vide "Lebenstilder," vol. i., p. 274.

catechism for German soldiers, which gives instructions as to what a Christian warrior ought to be, and has been circulated, in spite of Napoleon's power, in all the German divisions of his army. To influence public opinion in Germany is the task which Stein and the Emperor Alexander have intrusted to me. I am to report about every thing that takes place in the rear of the French army, and try to obtain correct information concerning its reënforcements and the condition of the fortresses. My principal task, however, will be to direct public opinion, exasperate the people against their oppressors, and the accomplices of the latter, support isolated risings, and organize flying corps for the purpose of intercepting the couriers." *

"That is a plan strictly in accordance with the indomitable spirit of Baron von Stein. However, the influence and power of one person will not suffice to carry it into effect."

"I am, therefore, authorized to enlist agents whom the Emperor of Russia will pay," said Gruner. "Hired observers and spies must be spread all over Germany. I must everywhere have my confidants—my agents and instruments. Such I have already engaged in some forty cities. . furnish them instructions, telling them what to do, in order to participate in the liberation of Germany; they have to send me weekly reports, written of course in cipher and with chemical ink, and, on my part, I address reports to the Emperor Alexander and Baron von Stein, which I forward every week by special couriers to Russia. My agents, as well as myself, will endeavor to hold intercourse with all prominent patriots, and our noble Stein has referred me especially to the eminent gentlemen here assembled. General Scharnhorst, too, is aware of our enterprise; President von Vinke supports it in the most enthusiastic and active manner, and we find everywhere friends, assistance, and advice. Already the net-work is spread over the country; this will every day become more impenetrable—a fatal trap in which, if it please God, we shall one day catch Bonaparte."

"But beware of traitors," exclaimed Count

* Pertz, "Life of Baron von Stein," vol. III., p. 117.

Nugent, anxiously. "All your agents are not reticent, for, to tell you the truth, I have already heard of your bold scheme, and Austria is highly indignant. Count Metternich, a few days since, addressed a complaint to the Prussian cabinet about what he calls your revolutionary intrigues, and the Prussian Minister von Bülow, who is friendly to France, is greatly exasperated against Justus Gruner and his guerilla warfare. Be on your guard, sir, that, while weaving this net-work of conspiracy, you may not yourself fall into the snares of the insidious police."

"And if I do, what matters it if one dies, provided the cause he served lives?" exclaimed Justus Gruner, enthusiastically. "This sacred cause cannot die; it is strong enough to succeed, even without me. It is spreading everywhere, and will remain, though the little spider that wove it should be crushed. There is but one part of Germany in which my work still lacks the necessary points where I might secure it."

"You allude to Austria, do you not?"

"I do; there my agents are distrustfully turned away from the frontier, and I have so far been unable to enlist special and active allies. I pray you, therefore, give me the names of some reliable, honest, and faithful men to whom I may apply; for I must go to Austria."

"That is to say," exclaimed Count Nugent, "you are going to prison. Let me warn you, do not go to Austria; Metternich's spies have keen eyes, and if they catch you, you are lost."

"I must go to Austria," said Gruner, smiling; "the cause of the fatherland demands it. Dangers will not deter me, and if the Austrian police are on the lookout for me—well, I have been myself a police-officer, and may outwit them. In the first place, however, I shall go to Leipsic, to have the second volume of Arndt's excellent work, 'The Spirit of the Times,' secretly printed, and cause a printing-office to be established on the Saxon frontier for the purpose of issuing the war bulletins which I am to receive from Russia. But then I shall go to Prague and Vienna."

"And may God grant success to your enterprise!" said Count Munster. "We shall all, I am satisfied of it, help in carrying out your schemes wherever we can. We will try to liberate you if you are imprisoned, and avenge you if killed. Shall we not?"

"We shall!" exclaimed Gneisenau and Bernadotte, Nugent, and Frederick William of Brunswick; and all four offered their hands to Gruner.

"Henceforth we all act for one, and one for all," exclaimed the Duke of Brunswick, enthusiastically, "and my noble father is looking down and blessing us. Oh, may the hour of liberation soon strike! We have our hands on our swords, and wait for Germany to call us."

"We are ready, and wait for our country to call us," they said, shaking hands with determined eyes and smiling lips.

"And now, if the gentlemen have no objection, I will adjourn the conference," said Count Munster, after a pause. "We well know each other, and what we have to do. Here is the cipher in which we may write to each other whenever important communications are to be made. Justus Gruner will see to it that his agents will promptly forward the letters to us."

"I will," said Justus Gruner, "and as long as I am not in prison, or dead, you may be sure that your letters will not fall into the hands of enemies or traitors."*

"And now let us go. God save us and Germany!"

CHAPTER IX.

GEBHARD LEBERECHT BLUCHER.

It was a cold and unpleasant morning in December. The dreary sky hung like a pall over the oppressed world. How beautiful and fragrant

---

* The predictions and apprehensions of Count Nugent were fulfilled but too soon. Gruner went as far as Prague, but there he was arrested in the last days of October, at the special request of the Prussian police, deprived of his papers and his funds, and sent to an Austrian fortress. The Emperor of Russia succeeded only nine months afterward in obtaining his release.—Vide Pertz's "Life of Baron von Stein," vol. iii., p. 181.

had been the summer park of the estate of Kunzendorf! now it was bereft of its flowers, and the cold gray trees were moaning in the winter blasts. How bright had been this large room on the lower floor of the mansion of Kunzendorf, when the summer morning flung its beams into the windows, while a merry company were chatting and laughing there! But, on this day, no guests were assembled in it. It contained but two persons, an old gentleman and lady. The gentleman was sitting at the window and looking out mournfully into the cold; he seemed to count the snow-flakes slowly falling. A large military cloak enveloped his tall, powerful form; his right leg, encased in a heavy cavalry-boot, rested on a cushion; his head was leaning against the high back of the easy-chair on which he sat. His bearing and appearance indicated suffering, age, and disease; he who did not look at his countenance could not but believe that he was in the presence of a sick and decrepit old man; but when his face turned to the beholder, with its large, fiery blue eyes, high and scarcely-furrowed brow, Roman nose, and florid complexion, he thought he saw the head of a man of about fifty years. It is true, the hair which covered his temples in a few thin tufts was snow-white, and so was the mustache which shaded his mouth and hung down on both sides of it, imparting a vigorous and martial expression to the whole face, and contrasting with his bronzed cheeks and flashing eyes.

Opposite him, in the niche of the other window, sat a lady in a plain, yet elegant toilet. Small brown ringlets, threaded here and there with white, peeped forth from the lace cap, trimmed with blue ribbons, and a gray silk dress, reaching to the neck, enveloped her slender and graceful form. Her countenance, which still showed traces of former beauty, was bent over her embroidery, and her white, tapering fingers, adorned with many rings, busily plied the needle.

The old gentleman blew dense clouds of smoke from his long clay pipe, and nothing broke the silence save the parrot (in a large gilded cage on a marble pedestal in the third window-niche), attering from time to time a loud scream, or exclaiming in a sharp voice, "Good-morning!" The ticking of the bronze clock on the mantel-piece at the other end of the room could be distinctly heard. Suddenly the old gentleman struck the window-board so violently with his right hand that the panes rattled, the lady gave a start, and the parrot screeched. "Well, now it is all right," he exclaimed savagely,—"it snows so thickly that nothing can be seen at a distance of twenty yards. The roads will be blocked up again, and no one will come to us from Neisse to-day. We shall be left alone, and the time will hang as heavily with us as with a pug-dog in a bandbox. But," he exclaimed, jumping up so hastily that his long clay pipe broke on his knee and fell in small pieces on the floor, "it is all right. If the guests from Neisse do not come to me, I will go to them." While uttering these words, he fixed his lustrous eyes on the lady, and seemed to wait for a reply from her; but she remained silent, and seemed to ply her needle even more industriously. "Well," he asked at last, hesitatingly, "what do you say to it, Amelia?"

"Nothing at all, Blucher," she replied, without looking at him; "for you did not ask me about it."

"Why, that is an agreeable addition to this horrible weather, that my wife should pout!" exclaimed Blucher, casting a despairing glance at the sky. He then looked again at his wife. She was still bending over her embroidery and remained silent. He approached, and seizing both her hands with gentle violence, took the embroidery and threw it away. "Why is your attention directed to that old rag, Amelia, instead of looking at me?" he said, with ill-restrained anger. "Wife, you know I am not rude; when with you I am as gentle as a lamb; but you must not pout, Amelia, for that makes me angry. And now speak—tell me honestly—what is it? What have I done to you?"

"Nothing," she said, fixing her dark eyes upon him with a sad expression, "nothing at all!"

"Aha! you do not want to tell me," exclaimed Blucher, looking at her uneasily, "but I know it **nevertheless. Yes,** I know what ails you, and why you are in bad humor with me. Will you give me a kiss, if I guess what it is?" She nodded, and an almost imperceptible smile played around her finely-formed lips. "Now, listen," he said, drawing her to himself, and putting his hand under her chin. "You are angry because I came home from Neisse so late last night?"

"Last night?" she asked. "I believe it was at five o'clock this morning."

"Yes, I promised you to be back at five o'clock in the afternoon, because the doctor said the night air is injurious to me, and would increase my pains. But, you see, Amelia, it would not do. We went to the 'Ressource,' and there I met some old friends—"

"And there we played faro," his **wife interrupted** him, "and I lost the two hundred louis d'ors with which I desired to buy four new carriage-horses."

"Yes, it is all true," said Blucher, soothingly. "But what matters it? In the first place, I am quite well, which proves what fools the doctors are; they think they know every thing, and, in fact, know nothing. I feel no pain, and yet have inhaled the night air. And as to the two hundred louis d'ors—well, I am almost glad that I lost them, for I amused myself. Do you know who was among the gamblers? Ex-Major von Leesten!"

"Major von Leesten?" asked his wife, wonderingly. "But he never plays—he is so sensible a gentleman, that—"

"That he does not deal cards, you mean?" interrupted Blucher, smiling. "Yes, you see, I am also a sensible man, but I deal cards sometimes, and, for the rest, to tell you the truth, I seduced Major von Leesten to play last night."

"That was very wrong," said Madame von Blucher, in a tone of gentle reproach. "Leesten is poor; he has a large family—five full-grown daughters, who, of course, will not be married because they have no fortune. And now you seduce the poor man, and he will lose the last penny belonging to his family. For the most terrible consequences of this gambling passion are, that it deprives men of reflection, attachment to their family, and prudence. A man who is addicted to playing cards, loves nothing but his cards; every thing else seems unimportant to him; I see it in your case, Blucher, and it makes my heart ache. You do not love me, your time hangs heavy in my presence; the card-table is your only pleasure, and I believe, when the passion seizes you, and you have lost all your money, you would stake the remainder of your property **on a card, and your wife to boot!**"

Blucher burst into loud laughter. "Why," he **exclaimed, "what an** odd idea that is! I stake you on a card, you—"

"You suppose that no one would care about winning me?" asked Madame von Blucher, smiling.

"No, I do not think that," replied Blucher, suddenly growing serious. "Why should no one care about winning you? You are still a very pretty and charming little woman; your eyes still flash so irresistibly, your lips are still so red and **full, and—"**

"And my hair is beautifully gray," she interrupted him, laughing, "and I am so astonishingly young, scarcely fifty years of age!"

"Well, that is not so very old," said Blucher, merrily. "I have read somewhere a story about one Ulysses, who, in times gone by, was a very **famous and** shrewd captain. He set out to wage war with the barbarians, and his wife, whose name was Penelope, remained at home with his son **Telemachus. Ulysses was absent for twenty** long years, and when he returned home he found fifty suitors who were all courting his beautiful wife Penelope. Do you see, fifty suitors, one for every year of Penelope's age, for she must have **been** well-nigh fifty years old when Ulysses returned, and yet she was still beautiful, and men were gallanting about her. Why should not the same thing happen to you, as you are scarcely forty-eight? And who knows whether the wife of Ulysses was as beautiful and good as you? I am sure she was not. For it seems to me you are the dearest and best little woman, and look precisely as you did twenty years ago, when you

were foolish enough to marry that rough old soldier Blucher, who was already fifty years of age."

"Well, that was not so very foolish," said Madame von Blucher, smiling; "on the contrary, it was very well done, and but for those abominable playing-cards, nothing could be better."

"Ah, the shrewd little general has, by an adroit movement, brought us back to the old battle-ground," exclaimed Blucher. "We have arrived again at last night's faro! Now, tell me first of all—did I guess right? Were you not angry with me because I returned late?"

"Yes," said his wife, "that was the reason."

"Hurrah! Just as I thought!" shouted Blucher, jubilantly. "Now, quick, pay me for my correct guess! You know, you were to give me a kiss!—a kiss such as you used to give me twenty years ago!" He encircled his wife with his arms, and pressed a long and tender kiss on her lips.

"Well, are you pacified now?" he then asked. "I see in your eyes that you are, and now, come, I will tell you all that **occurred last night. You** see the money is gone, and what matters it! Money is destined to be spent; that is what the good Lord gave it to us for, and men made it round that it might roll away more rapidly. If it were to remain, they would have made it square, when the fingers could hold it better. And, then, why should I hold it? We have enough—more than enough; our two daughters are married to rich men; our two sons are provided for; our estate at Kunzendorf will not roll away, for it is not round and brings us lots of money, and I am sure there will be a day when I shall win very large sums. I do not mean at the gaming-table, Amelia, but on the battle-field. I shall reconquer to the king his cities and provinces. I shall take from Bonaparte all that he has stolen from Prussia; I—"

"You intended to tell me what occurred last night," interrupted his wife, who heard him, to her dismay, beginning again the philippic against Napoleon which he had repeated to her at least a hundred times.

"Yes, that is true," said Blucher breathing

deeply, "I wished to tell you about Major von Leeston. At the 'Ressource' I met yesterday in the afternoon an old friend of his, who told me how sad and unhappy Leesten was. His eldest daughter is betrothed to a young country gentleman: the two young folks would like to marry, but they have no money. If the young man had only a thousand dollars, he might rent an estate in this vicinity; but, in order to do so, he must give a thousand dollars security, and he is not possessed of that sum. Leesten's friend told me all this, and also how disheartened Leesten was. He said he had gone to all sorts of usurers, but no one would lend him any thing, because he could not furnish security, for he has nothing but his pension."

"Poor man! And could not his friends collect the amount and give it to him?"

"His friends have not any thing either! Who has any thing? Every one is poor since the accursed French are in the country, and Bonaparte—"

"You forget again your story of Major von Leesten, my friend."

"Oh, yes. His friends have not any thing either, and even if they had, Leesten would not accept presents. No, believe me, Amelia, when the poor are exceedingly proud, they would die of hunger sooner than accept alms at the hands of a good friend, or ask him for a slice of bread and butter. I know all about it, for I was poor, too, and starved when my pay was spent. And Leesten is proud also; alms and presents he would not accept, or if he did, for the sake of his daughter, his heart would burst with grief. That was what his friend told me; I pitied him, and thought I should like to call on the dear major and shake hands with him, that he might feel that I like him, and that he has friends, how poor soever he may be. Well, I went with his friend to the major. He was glad to see us and took pains to be merry, but I saw very well that he was sad; that his laughter was not genuine, and that, as soon as some one else spoke, he grew gloomy. But I did not ask what ailed him; I feigned not to see any thing, and begged him to accom-

pany us and spend a pleasant evening with a few friends. He refused at first to do so, but I succeeded in overcoming his resistance, and I am not sorry by any means that I did, for the poor major grew quite cheerful at last; he forgot his grief, drank some good wine with us,—more, perhaps, than he had drunk for a year, and then played a little faro with us for the first time in his life. Well, we were all in the best spirits, and that was the reason why I remained so long and came home so late. It was Major von Leesten's fault, and now my story is at an end!"

"No, it is not!" exclaimed Amelia. "You have not yet told me every thing, Blucher. You have not told me who won your two hundred louis d'ors for which you intended to purchase four new carriage-horses?"

"Yes, that was curious," said Blucher, composedly, stroking his long white mustache—"that was really curious. Leesten had never before handled a card; he did not know the game, and yet he won from such an old gambler as I am two hundred louis d'ors in the course of a few hours. Leesten won the money that was to pay for the carriage-horses, and you may give him thanks for being compelled to drive for six months longer with our lame old mares."

A sunbeam, as it were, illuminated Amelia's countenance; her eyes shone, and her cheeks were glowing with joy. Quickly putting her hands on Blucher's shoulders, she looked up to him with a smile. "You made him win the money, Gebhard," she said, in a voice tremulous with emotion. "Oh, do not shake your head—tell me the truth! You made Leesten win, because you wished to preserve him from the necessity of accepting alms. You made him win, that his daughter might marry?"

"Nonsense!" said Blucher, growlingly, "how could I make him win when he did not really win? He would have found it out, and, besides, I would have been a cheat."

"He did not find it out because you made him drink so much wine, and because he knows nothing about the game; and you are no cheat, because you intentionally made him win; on the contrary, you are a noble, magnanimous man whom Heaven must love. Oh, dear, dearest husband, tell me the truth; let me enjoy the happiness that I have guessed right! You did so intentionally, did you not? The cards did not bring so much good luck to Leesten, but Blucher did!"

"Hush! do not say that so loudly," exclaimed Blucher, looking anxiously around; "if any one should hear and repeat it, and Leesten should find out how the thing occurred, the fellow would return the money to me."

"Ah, now you have betrayed yourself—you have confessed that you lost the money intentionally," exclaimed Amelia, jubilantly. "Oh, thanks, thanks, my noble and generous friend!" She took his hands with passionate tenderness, and pressed them to her lips.

"But, Amelia, what are you doing?" said Blucher, withdrawing his hands in confusion. "Why, you are weeping!"

"Oh, they are tears of joy," she said, nodding to him with a blissful smile—"tears which I am weeping for my glorious, dear Blucher!"

"Oh, you are too good," said Blucher, whose face suddenly grew gloomy. "I am nothing but an old, pensioned soldier—a rusty sword flung into a corner. I am an invalid whom they believe to be childish, because he thinks he might still be useful, and the fatherland might need him. But I tell you, Amelia, if I ever should become childish it would be on account of the course pursued toward me; why, I am dismissed from the service; I am refused any thing to do; I am desired to be idle, and the king has given me this accursed estate of Kunzendorf, not as a reward, nor from love, but to get rid of me, and because he is afraid of the French. When he gave it to me last spring, he wrote that I ought to set out for Kunzendorf immediately, and live and remain there, as it behooved every nobleman, in the midst of my peasants. But his real object was to send me into exile; he did not wish me to remain in Berlin!"

"Well, he had to comply with the urgent recommendations of his ministers," said Madame von Blucher, smiling. "You know very well that all the ministers of the king, with the sole exception of Hardenberg, are friends of the French, and think that Prussia would be lost if she should not faithfully stand by France."

"They are traitors when they entertain such infamous sentiments," cried Blucher, wildly stamping with his foot; "they should hang the fellows who are so mean and cowardly as to think that Prussia would be lost if her mortal enemy did not condescend to sustain her. Ah, if the king had listened to me only once, we should have long since driven the French out of the country, and our poor soldiers would not freeze to death in Russia as auxiliaries of Bonaparte. When the danger is greatest, every thing must be risked in order to win every thing, and when a fellow tries to deceive and insult me, I do not consider much whether I had better endure him because I may be weaker than he is, but, before he suspects it, I knock him down if I can. You see, that is defending one's life; that is what the learned call philosophy. But, dearest Amelia, there is but one philosophy in life, and it is this: 'He who trusts in God and defends himself bravely will never miserably perish.' Now, the king and his ministers know only one-half of this philosophy, and that is the reason why the whole thing goes wrong. They mean to trust in God, even though, from their blind trust alone, all Prussia fall to ruins; but as for bravely defending themselves, that is what they do not understand. It is too much like old Blucher's way of doing things, and that is the reason why the learned gentlemen do not like it. Ah! Amelia, when I think of all the wretchedness of Prussia, and that I may have to die without having chastised Bonaparte—without having wrested from him, and flung into his face, the laurels of Jena, Eylau, and Friedland—ah, then I feel like sitting down and crying like a boy. But Heaven cannot be so cruel; it will not let me die before meeting Bonaparte on the field of battle, and avenging all our wrongs upon him. No, I trust I will not die before that—and, after all, I am quite young! Only seventy years of age! My grand father died in his ninetieth year, and my mother told me often enough that I looked exactly like my grandfather; I shall, therefore, reach my ninetieth year. I have still twenty years to live—twenty years, that is enough—" Just then the door opened, and a footman entered.

"Well, John," asked Blucher, "what is it? Why do you look so merry, my boy? I suppose you have good news for us, have you not?"

"I have, your excellency," said the footman. "There is an old man outside, an invalid, attended by a young fellow who, I believe, is his son. The two have come all the way from Pomerania, and want to see General von Blucher. He says he has important news for your excellency."

"Important news?" asked Blucher. "And he comes from Pomerania? John, I hope it will not be one who wants to tell me the same old story?"

"Your excellency, I believe that is what he comes for," said John, grinning.

"Amelia," exclaimed Blucher, bursting into loud laughter, "there is another fellow who wants to tell me that he took me prisoner fifty years since. I believe it is already the seventh rascal who says he was the man."

"The seventh who wants to get money from you and swindle you," said Madame von Blucher, smiling.

"No, I believe they do not exactly want to swindle me," said Blucher, "but I know they like to get a little money, and as they do not want to beg—"

"They come and lie," interrupted Amelia, smiling. "They know already that General Blucher gives a few louis d'ors to every one who comes and says, 'General, it was I who took you prisoner in Mecklenburg in 1760, and brought you to the Prussians. You, therefore, are indebted to me for all your glory and your happiness.'"

"Yes, it is true," said Blucher, laughing and smoothing his mustache. "That is what all six of them said. But one of them did take me prisoner, for the story is true, and if I turn away one of those who tell me the same thing, why, I might happen to hit precisely the man who took me, and that would be a great shame. Therefore, it is better I imagine a whole squadron had taken me at that time, and give money to every one who comes to me for it. Even though he may not be the man, why, he is at least an old hussar, and I shall never turn an old hussar without a little present from my door." *

"Well, I see you want to bid welcome to your seventh hero and conqueror," said Amelia, smiling. "Very well, I will quit the field and retire into my cabinet. Farewell, my friend, and when your hero has taken leave of you, I will await you." She nodded pleasantly to her husband, and left the room.

"Well, John," said Blucher, sitting down again on his easy-chair at the window, "now let the men come in. But first fill me a pipe. You must take a new one, for I broke the one I was smoking this morning."

John hastened to the elegant "pipe-board" which stood beside the fireplace, and took from it an oblong, plain wooden box; opening the lid, he drew a new, long clay pipe from it.

"How many pipes are in it yet?" asked Blucher, hastily. "A good lot, John?"

"No, your excellency, only seven whole pipes, and eight broken ones."

"You may ride to Neisse to-morrow, and buy a box of pipes. Now, give me one, and let the hussar and his son come in."

CHAPTER X.

RECOLLECTIONS OF MECKLENBURG.

John, the footman, opened the door of the anteroom, and shouted in a loud and solemn voice, "Your excellency, here is Hennemann, the hussar, and his son Christian!"

"Well, come in!" said Blucher, good-naturedly puffing a cloud of smoke from his pipe.

* Blucher's own words.—Vide "Life of Prince Blucher of Wahlstatt, by Varhagen von Ense," p. 8.

An old man with silver-white hair, his bent form clad in the old and faded uniform of a hussar, and holding his **old-fashioned shako in his hand**, entered the room. **He was followed by a** young man, wearing the costume of a North-German farmer, his heavy yellow hair combed backward and fastened with a large round comb; his full, vigorous form dressed in a long blue cloth coat, reaching down almost to his feet, and lined with white flannel; under it he wore trousers of dark-green velvet that descended only to **the** knees, and joined there the blue-and-red stockings in which his legs were encased; his feet were armed with thick shoes, adorned with buckles, while their soles bristled with large nails.

"Where do you come from?" asked Blucher, fixing his eyes with a kind expression on the two men.

"From Rostock, your excellency," said the old man, making a respectful obeisance.

"From Rostock?" asked Blucher, joyously. "Why, that is my native city."

"I know that very well, general," said the old hussar, who vainly tried to hide his Low-German accent. "All Rostock knows it, too, and every child there boasts of Blucher being our countryman."

"Well," said Blucher, smiling, "then you come from Rostock. Do you live there?"

"Not exactly in Rostock, your excellency. My daughter Frederica is married to a tailor in Rostock, and I was with her for four weeks. I myself live at Polchow, a nobleman's estate four miles from Rostock; I am there at the house of my eldest son."

"Is that your eldest son?" asked Blucher, pointing with his clay pipe at the young man, who stood by the side of his aged father, and was turning his hat in his hand in an embarrassed **manner.**

"No, sir, he is my youngest son, and it is just for his sake that I have come to you. Christian was a laborer in the service of our nobleman at Polchow, and he desired to marry a girl with whom he had fallen in love. But the nobleman would not permit it; he said Christian should wait some ten years until there was a house va-

cant in the village, and some of the old peasants had died. This drove him to despair; he wanted to commit suicide, and said he would die rather than be a day laborer on an estate in Mecklenburg, which is no better than being the nobleman's slave."

"Yes," cried Christian, indignantly, "that is true, general. A day laborer on an estate in Mecklenburg is a slave, that is all. The nobleman owns him. If he wants to do so, he may disable him, nay, he may kill him. Such a laborer has no rights, no will, no property, no home, no country; he is not allowed to live anywhere but in his village; he cannot settle in any other place, and is not permitted to marry unless the nobleman who owns the village gives his consent, nor can he ever be any thing else than what his father and grandfather were, that is to say, the nobleman's laborers. And I do not wish to be such and do nothing else than putting the horses to the plough. **I want** to marry Frederica, and become a free man, and if that cannot be I will commit **suicide.**"

"Ahem! he has young blood," said Blucher, well pleased and smiling, "fresh Mecklenburgian blood. I like that! But you must not abuse Mecklenburg, Christian; I love Mecklenburg, because it is my native country."

"It is a good country for noblemen who have money," said Christian, "but for day laborers who have none it is a poor country. And that was the reason why I said to the old man, ' *Vatting,* * I shall commit suicide or run away and enlist.'"

"And I then said, ' Well, my son, in that case it will be better for you to enlist,' added the old man, 'and, moreover, you shall enlist under a good general. I will show you that my life is yet good for something; I will do for your sake what I have purposed to do all my lifetime: I will go to General Blucher, tell him who I am, and ask him to reward my boy for what I did for him.'"

Blucher looked with a good-natured smile at the poor old man who stood before him in the

---

* " Vatting," Low-German for " papa."

faded and threadbare uniform of a private soldier.

"Well, my old friend," he said, "what have you done for me, then?"

The old man raised his head, and a solemn expression overspread his bronzed and furrowed countenance. "General," he said, gravely, "it was I who took you prisoner in Mecklenburg in 1760, and to me, therefore, you are indebted for all your glory and happiness."

Blucher covered his face with his hands, that the old man might not see his smile. "It is just as Amelia told me it would be," he said to himself. He then added aloud: "Well, tell me the story, that I may see whether it was really you who took me prisoner."

"It is a long story," said the old man, sighing, "and if I am to tell it, I must ask a favor of your excellency."

"Well, what is it? Speak, my old friend," said Blucher, puffing a cloud from his pipe, and satisfied that the old hussar would apply to him for money.

"I must beg leave to sit down, general," said the old man, timidly. "We have come on foot all the way from Rostock, and it is only fifteen minutes since we reached this village. We took only time enough at the tavern to change our dress; I put on my uniform, and Christian put on his Sunday coat. I am eighty years old, general, and my legs are not as strong as they used to be."

"Eighty years old!" exclaimed Blucher, jumping up, "eighty years old, and you have come on foot all the way from Rostock! Why, that is impossible! Christian, tell me, that cannot be true!"

"Yes, general, it is true. We have been on the way for three weeks past, for the old man cannot walk very fast, and we had not money enough to ride. We had to be thankful for having enough to pay for our beds at the taverns. And my father is more than eighty years of age! We have brought his certificate of birth with us."

"Eighty years of age, and he came on foot all the way from Rostock, and I allow the old man

to stand and offer him no chair!" exclaimed Blucher,—"I do not ask whether he is hungry and thirsty! John! John!" And Blucher rushed to the bell-rope and rang the bell so violently that John entered the room in great excitement. "John, quick!" shouted Blucher. "Quick, a bottle of wine, two glasses, and bread, butter, and ham; and tell them in the kitchen to prepare a good dinner for these men, and have a room with two beds made ready for them in the adjoining house. Quick, John! In five minutes the wine and the other things must be here! Run!"

John hastened out of the room, and Blucher approached the old man, who looked on, speechless and deeply moved by the kind zeal the general had displayed in his behalf.

"Come, my dear friend," said Blucher, kindly, taking him by the hand and conducting him across the room to his favorite seat at the window. "There, sit down on my easy-chair and rest."

"No, general, no; that would be disrespectful!"

"Fiddlesticks!" replied Blucher; "an octogenarian is entitled to more respect than a general's epaulets are. Now do not refuse, but sit down!" And with his vigorous arms he pressed him into the easy-chair. He then quietly took his clay pipe from the window, and sat down on a cane chair opposite the old hussar. "And now tell me the story of my arrest as a prisoner. I promise you that I will believe it all."

"General, you may believe nothing but what is true," replied the old man, solemnly.

Blucher nodded. "Commence," he said, "but no—wait a while! There is John with the wine and the bread and butter. Now eat and drink first."

"I cannot eat, for I am not hungry. But, if the general will permit me, I will drink a glass of wine."

"Come, John, two glasses!—fill them to the brim! And now, my friend, let us drink. Here's to our native country!" Blucher filled his glass with claret; his eyes flashed, and his face kindled with the fire of youth, when he, the young septuagenarian, touched with his glass that of the feeble octogenarian. "Hurrah, my old countryman," he shouted, jubilantly, "long live Mecklenburg! long live Rostock and the shore of the Baltic! Now empty your glass, my friend, and you, John, fill it again, and then put the wine and the bread and butter on the table beside the fireplace, that Christian may help himself. Eat and drink, Christian, but do not stir, or say a word, for we two old ones have to speak with each other. Now tell me the story, my old friend!"

"Well," said the old man, putting down his empty glass, "I had run away from my parents because I was just in the same difficulty as Christian: I did not wish to remain a day laborer. I also wanted to marry, and the nobleman would not let me. Well, I ran away, and enlisted in Old Fritz's army, in Colonel Belling's regiment of hussars. It was in 1760; we had a great deal to do at that time; we were every day skirmishing with the Swedes, for we were stationed in Mecklenburg, and the Swedes were so dreadfully bold as to make raids throughout Brandenburg and Mecklenburg. One day, I believe it was in August, 1760, just when we, Belling's hussars, occupied the towpath close to Friedland in Mecklenburg, another detachment of Swedish hussars approached to harass us. They were headed by a little ensign—a handsome young lad, scarcely twenty years of age, a very impertinent baby! And this young rascal rode closely to the old hussars, and commenced to crow in his sweet little voice, abusing us, and told us at last, if we were courageous enough, to come on; he had not had his breakfast, he said, and would like to swallow about a dozen of Belling's hussars. Well, the other hussars rejoiced in the pluck of the young fellow, and a handsome lad he was, with clear blue eyes and red cheeks. But his saucy taunts irritated me, and when the little ensign continued laughing, and telling us we were cowards, I became very angry, galloped up to him and shouted: 'Now, you little imp, I will kill you!'"

"Sure enough," exclaimed Blucher, in surprise, "that was what the hussar shouted. It seems to me as though I hear it still sounding in my ears. But none of the other hussars told me this; it is new, and it is true. Hennemann, could it be possible that you should really be the man who took me prisoner at that time?"

"Listen to the remainder of my story, general, and you will soon find out whether it was I or not. I galloped up to him, and while the Prussians and Swedes were fighting, I fixed my eyes on my merry little ensign; when I was quite close to him, I shot down his horse. The ensign was unable then to offer much resistance, and, besides, I was a very strong, active man. I took him by the collar and put him on my horse in front of me."

"And the ensign submitted to that without defending himself?" asked Blucher, angrily.

"By no means! On the contrary, he was as red in the face as a crawfish, and resisting struck me. I held his arms fast, but he disengaged himself with so violent a jerk that the yellow facings of his right sleeve remained in my hand."

"That is true," exclaimed Blucher.

"Yes, it is true," said the old man, calmly; "but it is true also that I got hold again of the ensign and took him to Colonel von Belling, to whom I stated that I had captured the handsome lad. The colonel liked his face and courageous bearing; he kept the Swedish ensign at his headquarters, where he appointed him cornet the next day, and made the little Ensign Blucher apply to the Swedes for permission to quit their service."

"And I got my discharge," exclaimed Blucher, quite absorbed in his reminiscences, "and became a Prussian soldier. Good, brave Colonel Belling bought me the necessary equipment, and appointed me his aide-de-camp and lieutenant. The Lord have mercy on his dear soul! Belling was an excellent man, and I am indebted to him for all I am."

"No, general," said Hennemann, "it is to me that you are indebted, for if I had not taken you prisoner at that time—"

"Sure enough," exclaimed Blucher, laughing, "if you had not taken me prisoner, I should now be a poor old pensioned Swedish veteran. But you certainly took me prisoner, I really believe you did!"

"I have the proofs that I did," said the old man solemnly. "Christian!"

"Here I am, vatting," said Christian, rising. "What do you want?"

"Give me the memorandum-book with the papers."

Christian drew from his blue coat a red morocco memorandum-book and handed it to his father. "Here, vatting," he said, "every thing is in it, the certificate of birth, the enlistment paper, the discharge, and the other thing."

"I just want to get the other thing," said the old man, opening the memorandum-book, "and here it is!" He took out a yellow piece of cloth and handed it to Blucher.

"It is a piece of my sleeve!" exclaimed Blucher, joyously, holding up the piece of cloth. "Yes, Hennemann, it was really you who took me prisoner, and I am indebted to you for being a Prussian general to-day! And I promise you that I will now pay you a good ransom. Give me your hand, old fellow; we ought to remain near each other. Fifty-two years since you took me prisoner, but now I take you prisoner in turn, and you must remain with me; you shall live at ease, and at times in the evening you must tell me of Mecklenburg, and how it looks there, and of Rostock, and—well, and when you are in good spirits, you must sing to me a Low-German song!"

"Mercy!" exclaimed the old man, in dismay; "I cannot sing, general. I am eighty years old, and old age has dried up the fountain of my song."

"Sure enough, you are eighty years old," said Blucher, puffing his pipe, "and at that age few persons are able to sing. But I should really like to hear again a merry native song. I have not heard one for fifty years, for here, you see, Hennemann, people are so stupid and ignorant as not even to understand Low-German."

"I believe that," said the old man, gravely, "and it is not so easy to understand—one must be a native of Mecklenburg to understand it."

"It is a pity that you cannot sing," said Blucher, sighing.

"But, perhaps Christian can," said old Hennemann. "Tell me, Christian, can you sing?"

"Yes, vatting," replied Christian, clearing his throat.

"'Vatting!'" exclaimed Blucher. "What does that mean?"

"Well, it means that he loves his father, and therefore calls him, in good Mecklenburg style, 'vatting.'"

"Sure enough, I remember now," exclaimed Blucher. "Vatting! mutting![*] Yes, yes; I have often used these words, 'mutting—my mutting!' Ah, it seems to me as though I behold the beautiful blue eyes of my mother when she looked at me so mildly and lovingly and said, 'You are a wild, reckless boy, Gebhard; I am afraid you will come to grief!' Then I used to beg her, 'My mutting, my mutting! I will no longer be a bad boy! I will not be naughty! Do not be angry any more, my mutting!' And she always forgave me, and interceded for me with my father, whenever he was incensed against me, and scolded me, because, instead of studying my books and going to school, I was always loitering about the fields or hunting in the woods. At last, when I was fourteen years old, and was still an incorrigible scapegrace, they sent me to the island of Rügen, to my sister, who was married to Baron von Krackwitz. But I did not stay there very long. The Swedes came to the island, and I could not withstand the desire to become a soldier; therefore, I ran away from the island and enlisted in the Swedish army. Well, I had to do so, I could not help it, for it was in my nature. Up to that time I was like a fish on dry land, moving his tail in every direction without crushing a fly; when I got into the water it was all right. If I had been kept much longer out, I would have died very soon.[†] When I was now in the water—that is to say, when I was a

---

[*] "Mutting," mamma.   [†] Blucher's own words.

soldier, I lost my mother; I never saw her again, and know only that she wept a great deal for me. And I never was able to beg her to forgive me, and tell her, 'Do not be angry, my dear mutting!' I was a dashing young soldier, and she was weeping for me at Rostock, for she believed I would come to grief. Well, I was first lieutenant in some Prussian fortress when they wrote to me that my mother was dead. Yes, she had died and I was not at her bedside; I was never able to say to her for the last time, 'Forgive me, my mutting!' But now I say so from the bottom of my heart." While uttering these words, Blucher raised his head and fixed his large eyes with a touching and childlike expression on the wintry sky.

Old Hennemann devoutly clasped his hands, and tears ran slowly down his furrowed cheeks. Christian stood at the door, and dried his eyes with his coat-sleeve.

"Thunder and lightning," suddenly exclaimed Blucher, "how foolish I am! That is the consequence of being absorbed in one's recollections. While talking about Mecklenburg I had really forgotten that I am an old boy of seventy years, and thought I was still the naughty young rascal who longed to ask his mutting to forgive him! Well, Christian, now sing us a Low-German song."

"I know but one song," said Christian, hesitatingly. "It is the spinning-song which my Frederica sang to me in the spinning-room."

"Well, sing your spinning-song," said Blucher, ooking at his pipe, which was going out.

Christian cleared his throat, and sang:

Spinn doch, spinn doch, min lütt, lewes Döchting,
Ick schenk Di ock'n poor hübsche Schoh!
Ach Gott, min lewes, lewes Mutting,
Wat helpen mi de hübschen Schoh!
Kann danzen nich, un kann nich spinnen,
Denn alle mine teigen Finger,
De dohn mi so weh,
De dohn mi so weh!

Spinn doch, spinn doch, min lütt, lewes Döchting,
Ick schenk Di ock'n schön Stück Geld.
Ach Gott, min lewes, lewes Mutting,
Ick wull, ick wihr man ut de Welt,
Kann danzen nich, un kann nich spinnen,
Denn alle mine teigen Finger,
De dohn mi so weh,
De dohn mi so weh!

Spinn doch, spinn doch, min lütt, lewes Döchting,
Ick schenk Di ock'n hübschen Mann!
Ach ja, min lewes, lewes Mutting,
Schenk min lewsten, besten Mann.
Kann danzen nu, un kann ock spinnen,
Denn alle mine teigen Finger,
De dohn nich mihr weh,
De dohn nich mihr weh! *

"A very pretty song," said Blucher, kindly, "And I believe I heard the girls sing it when I was a boy. Thank you, Christian, you have sung it very well. But, tell me now, old Hennemann, what is to become of Christian? You yourself shall remain here at Kunzendorf, and I will see to it that you are well provided for. But what about Christian?"

"He is anxious to enlist, general," said Hennemann, timidly, "and that is the reason why I brought him to your excellency. I wanted to request you to take charge of him, and make out of him as good a soldier as you are yourself."

Blucher smiled. "I have been successful," he said, "but those were good days for soldiers. Now, however, the times are very unfavorable; the Prussian soldier has nothing to do, and must quietly look on while the French are playing the mischief in Prussia."

"No, general," said Hennemann, "it seems to me the Prussian soldier has a great deal to do."

"Well, what do you think he has to do?" asked Blucher.

---

* Spin, spin, my little daughter, dear!
  A pretty pair of shoes for thee!—
Alas, my mother! let me hear
  What use are pretty shoes to me!
I cannot dance—I cannot spin;
And why these promised shoes to win!
O mother mine, I will not take
Thy kindly gift. My fingers ache!

Spin, spin, my little daughter dear!
  And a bright silver-piece is thine!—
Alas, my mother's loving care
  Makes not this shining money mine!
I cannot dance—I cannot spin;
What use such wages thus to win?
O mother dear! I cannot take
This silver, for my fingers ache.

Spin, spin, my little daughter dear!
  For thee a handsome husband waits.—
Oh, then, my mother, have no fear;
  My heart this work no longer hates.
Now can I dance, and also spin,
A handsome husband thus to win.
Thy best reward I gladly take!
No more—no more, my fingers ache

"To expel the French from Prussia, that is what he has to do," said the old man, raising his voice.

"Yes," said Blucher, smiling, "if that could be done, I should like to be counted in."

"It can be done, general; every honest man says so, and it ought to be, for the French are behaving too shamefully. They must be expelled from Germany. Well, then, my Christian wishes to assist you in doing so; he wishes to become a soldier, and help you to drive out the French."

" Alas, he must apply to some one else if he wishes to do that," said Blucher, mournfully. "I cannot help him, for they have pensioned me. I have no regiments. I—but, thunder and lightning! what is the matter with my pipe to-day? The thing will not burn." And he put his little finger into the bowl, and tried to smoke again.

"The pipe does not draw well, because it was not skilfully filled," said Christian. I know it was badly filled."

"Ay?" asked Blucher. "What do you know? John has been filling my pipes for four years past."

"John has done it very poorly," said Christian, composedly. "To fill such a clay pipe is an art with which a good many are not familiar, and when it is smoked for the first time it does not burn very well. It ought first to be smoked by some one, and John ought to have done so yesterday if the general wished to use his pipe to-day."

"Why, he knows something about a clay pipe," exclaimed Blucher, "and he is right; it always tastes better on the second day than on the first."

"That is the reason why the second day always ought to be the first for General Blucher," said Christian.

"He is right," exclaimed Blucher, laughing, "it would surely be better if the second were always the first day. Well, I know now what is to be made of Christian; he is to become my pipe-master."

"Pipe-master?" asked old Hennemann and Christian at the same time. "Pipe-master, what is that?"

"That is a man who keeps my pipes in good order," said Blucher, with a ludicrously grave air —"a man who makes the second my first day— who smokes my pipes first—puts them back into the box at night, preserves the broken ones, and fills them, however short they may be. He who does not prize a short pipe does not deserve to have a long one. A good pipe and good tobacco are things of the highest importance in life. Ah! if, in 1807, at Lübeck, I had had powder for the guns and tobacco for my men, I would have raised such clouds that the French could not have stood.* Well, Christian, you shall therefore become my pipe-master, and I hope you will faithfully perform the duties of your office."

"I shall certainly take pains to do so," said Christian, "and you may depend on it, general, that I shall preserve the broken, short pipes; I will not throw them away before it is necessary. But suppose there should be war, general, and you should take the field, what would become of me in that case?"

"Well, in that case you will accompany me," said Blucher. "What should I do in the field if I could not get a good pipe of tobacco all the time? Without that I am of no account.† But it is necessary to do good service for Prussia, and hence I need, above all, a good pipe of tobacco in the field. Well, then, tell me now plainly, will you accept the office I offer you in peace and in war, Christian?"

"Yes, general," said Christian, solemnly. "And I swear that General Blucher shall never lack a well-lighted pipe, even though I fetch a match from the French gunners to kindle it."

"That is right, Christian; you are in my service now, and may at once enter upon the duties of your office. You, Hennemann, stay here and do me the favor of living as long and being as merry as possible. Now, pipe-master, ring the bell!"

The new pipe-master rang the bell, and John entered the room

---

* Blucher's own words.—Vide "Marshal Forward," a popular biography.

† Blucher's own words.

"John!" said Blucher, "I owe a **reparation** of honor to this aged hussar. It was he who took me prisoner in 1760. He brought me the proof of it—the yellow facing of the sleeve here. Take it and fasten it to the old uniform of Blucher, the Swedish ensign, which I have always preserved; it belongs to it. You see that hussar Hennemann is an honest man, and that I owe him the ransom. He will stay here, and have nothing to do but eat and drink well, sit in the sun, and, in the evening, when it affords him pleasure, tell you stories of the Seven Years' War, in which he participated. If other hussars come and tell you they took me prisoner, you know it is not true, and need not admit them. But you must not abuse the poor old fellows for that reason, nor tell them that they are swindlers. You will give them something to eat and drink, a bed over-night, and, in the morning, when they set out, a dollar for travelling expenses. **Now take the** old man and his son to the adjoining building, **and tell** the inspector to give them a **room** where they are to live. And then," added Blucher, hesitatingly, and almost in confusion,—" you have too much to do, John; you must have an assistant. It takes you too much time to fill my pipes, and this young man, therefore, will help you. I **have** appointed Christian Hennemann my pipe-**master. Well,** do not reply—take the two men **to the building,** and be good friends—do you hear, **good friends!"**

John bowed in silence, and made a sign to **the** two Mecklenburgians to follow him. Blucher gazed after them with keen glances. "Well, I am afraid their friendship will not amount to much," he said, smiling and stroking his beard. "John does not like this pipe-master business, and will show it to Christian as soon as an opportunity offers. I do not care if they do have a good fight. It would be a little diversion, for it **is** horribly tedious here. **Ah, how long is this to** last? How long am I to sit here and wait until Prussia and **the king call upon** me to drive Napoleon out of the country? How long am I to be idle while Bonaparte is gaining one victory after **another in Russia?** I have not much time to spare for waiting, and—well," he suddenly interrupted himself, quickly stepping up to the **window** " what is that? Is not that **a** carriage driving **into the** court-yard?" Yes, it really is, just **entering the iron gate, and rolling with** great noise across the pavement. "I wonder **who that** is?" muttered Blucher, casting a piercing **glance** into the carriage, which stopped at that **moment** in front of the mansion. He uttered a cry of joy, and ran out of the room with the alacrity of a youth.

————

CHAPTER XI.

GLAD TIDINGS.

"**It** is he, it is he!" **exclaimed General Blucher,** rushing out of the front door, and hastening with outstretched arms toward the gentleman, who, **wrapped in a** Russian fur robe, alighted with his **two servants.** "My beloved Scharnhorst!" And he clasped his friend in his arms as if it were some longed-for mistress whom he was **pressing to his** bosom.

"Blucher, my dear friend, let me go, or you will choke me!" exclaimed Scharnhorst, laughing. "Come, let us go into the house."

"Yes, come, dearest, best friend!" said Blucher, and encircling Scharnhorst's neck with his arm, drew him along so hastily that, gasping for breath, the latter was scarcely able to accompany him.

On entering the sitting-room, Blucher himself divested his friend of his fur robe, and, throwing it on the floor in his haste, took off Scharnhorst's cap. "I must look at you, my friend," he exclaimed. "I must **see** the **face** of my dear Scharnhorst, and now that I see it, I must **kiss** it! To see you again does me as much good as a fountain in the desert to the pilgrim dying of thirst."

"**Well, but now you must** allow me to say a word," said Scharnhorst. "And let me look at yourself. Remember, it is nearly a year since I saw anything of you but your handwriting."

"**And that** is very illegible," said Blucher, laughing.

"It is at least not as legible and intelligible as your dear face," said Scharnhorst. "Here, on this forehead and in these eyes, I can read quickly and easily all that your excellent head thinks, and your noble heart feels. And now I read there that I am really welcome, and need not by any means apologize for not having announced my visit to you."

"Apologize!" exclaimed Blucher. "You know full well that you afford me the most heart-felt joy, and that I feel as though spring were coming **with all its blessed promises.**"

"**Well, let us not wish spring to come too early** this year. We need a good deal **of ice and** cold weather, to build a crystal palace for Bonaparte in Russia."

Blucher cast a flashing glance upon his guest. Scharnhorst," he asked, breathlessly, "you have come to bring me important **news,** have you not? Oh, pray, speak! I am sure you have come to tell me that the time has come for rising against the French!"

"No; I have simply come to see you," said Scharnhorst, smiling. "And you are in truth a cold-hearted friend to think any other motive was required than that of friendship."

"I thought it was time for Providence to bring about a change. But it was kind of you to come to me merely for my sake, and, moreover, in weather so cold as this, and at your age."

"At my age!" exclaimed Scharnhorst, smiling.

"Why, **yes,** my friend, at your age. If I am not mistaken, you must be well-nigh sixty, and at that time of life travelling in a season like this is assuredly somewhat unpleasant, and—but why do you laugh?"

"As you refer to my age, my dearest friend, I suppose you will permit me to speak of yours?"

"Why not? We are no marriageable girls on **the** lookout for husbands."

"**Well,** then, my dear General Blucher, how old are you?"

"I? I am a little over seventy."

"And I am fifty-six, and yet you think old age is weighing me down, while a wreath of snow-drops is overhanging your brow."

"**Yes, that is true,**" said Blucher, in confusion. "I had really forgotten my age."

"The reason is, that your heart is still young and fresh," exclaimed Scharnhorst, looking at him tenderly, and laying his hand on Blucher's broad shoulder. "Thank God! you are still young Blucher, with his fiery head and heroic arm—young Blucher whose eagle eye gazes into the future, and who does not despair, however disheartening the present may be."

"I am sure you have brought news," said Blucher. "I can see it in your eyes—Heaven knows whether good or bad. But you have news, **I know it.**"

"**No, my young firebrand,**" exclaimed Scharnhorst, "I bring only myself, and this **self I** should like now above all to lay at the **feet** of your respected wife."

"Yes, that is true," said Blucher; "in my joy I almost forgot that my Amelia ought to share it. Come, general, let me conduct you to my wife." He took Scharnhorst's arm and conducted him rapidly across the sitting-room **toward** the apartments of Madame von Blucher. "**Tread** softly; you know **what an** admirer of yours my wife is, and how glad she will be to see you. We will, therefore, surprise her. She doubtless did not notice your arrival, for her windows open upon the garden. She does not yet know that you are here, and how glad she will be! Hush!"

He glided to the door and rapped. "Amelia," he said, "are you there, and may I come in?"

"Of course I am here," exclaimed Madame von Blucher, "and you know well that I have already been looking for you for two hours past. Come in!"

"I have a visitor with me; do you allow me to enter with him, Amelia?"

"A visitor?" asked Madame von Blucher, opening the door. "General von Scharnhorst!" she exclaimed, hastening to him and offering him both her hands. "Welcome, general, and may Heaven reward you for the idea of visiting an old woman and her young husband in their wintry solitude. Come, general, do my room the honor of entering it." She took the general's arm and drew him in.

"Scharnhorst," said Blucher, "let me give you some good advice. Do not make love in too undisguised a manner to my wife, for she is right in saying that I am still a young man, and I may become jealous; that would be a pity! I should then have to fight a duel with my friend, and one of us would have to die; and yet we are destined to deliver Prussia, and to drive that hateful man Bonaparte out of Germany."

"See, madame, what a shrewd and self-willed intriguer he is!" exclaimed Scharnhorst. "He avails himself of the boundless adoration I feel for you to assist him in wandering into his favorite sphere of politics. Madame, the barbarian believes it to be altogether impossible that I come merely from motives of friendship, and insists that it was politics that brought me!"

"**Yes**," said Madame von Blucher, **smiling**, "Blucher loves politics; he has no other mistress."

"No," said Blucher, laughing, "I know nothing at all about politics, and believe the world would be better off if there were no politicians. They originate all our troubles. Those diplomatists are always sure to spoil what the sword has achieved. Politics have brought all these calamities upon Germany; otherwise, we should long since have risen against the French, instead of allowing our soldiers to fight for Bonaparte in Russia. I say it is absurd, and I am so angry at it that it will make me consumptive. I say all those diplomatists ought to be sent into the field against Russia in order to study new-fangled politics in Siberia. I say—"

"You will say nothing further about the matter, my friend, for there is John, who wishes to tell us that dinner is ready," Madame von Blucher interrupted her husband, who, glowing with anger, and trembling with excitement, was fighting with his arms in the air and with a terrible expression of countenance. "Come, general, let us go to the dining-room," said Madame von Blucher, giving her hand to Scharnhorst. "And you, my valorous young husband, give me your hand, too!"

"Wait a moment," Blucher replied. "I must first give vent to my anger, or it will choke me." At a bound, he rushed as a passionate boy toward the sofa, and, striking it with both fists, so that the dust rose from it in clouds, shouted: "Have I got you at length, you horrible butcher—are you at length under my scourge? Now you shall find out how Pomeranians whip their enemies, and what it is to treat people as shamefully as you have done. I will whip you—yes, until you cry, '*Pater, peccavi!*' There, take that for Jena, and this blow for compelling me to capitulate at Lübeck; and this and this for the infamies you have perpetrated upon our beautiful queen at Tilsit! This last blow take for the Russian treaty to which you compelled our king to accede, and now a few more yet! If Heaven does not strike you, Blucher must; you ought not to be left unpunished!"

"**Ah, well, that is enough, my friend**," exclaimed Amelia, hastening to him and seizing his arm, which he had **already raised again**. "**You** are very capable of destroying my sofa, and you believe that you have gained a campaign by tearing my beautiful velvet in shreds."

"Well, yes, it is enough now, and I feel better. Well, my friend," he said, turning to Scharnhorst, who had witnessed his foolish antics with a grave and mournful air, "you need not look at me in so melancholy a manner. I suppose they have told you, too, that old Blucher at times gets crazy, and strikes at the flies on the wall, and beats chairs and **sofas**, because, in his insanity, he believes them to be Napoleon.* But it is assuredly no madness that makes me act in this **manner, as stupid fools assert, but it is simply a** way in which I relieve my anger, that it **may not** break my heart. It is the same as if a man who has to fight a duel should take fencing-lessons, and practise with **the** sword, in order to hit his

---

* Owing to this peculiarity and the strange ebullitions of rage in which he indulged from time to time, Blucher was really believed to be deranged for several years previous to the outbreak of the war of liberation.

adversary. But I have satisfied my anger, and will again be as gentle as a lamb."

"Yes, as a lamb which reverses the order of things, and, instead of allowing the wolf to devour it, is quite ready to devour the wolf," said Scharnhorst, laughing.

"Let us go to dinner, generals," cried Amelia; "but on one condition! During the repast not a word must be said about my hateful rival, politics, nor will you be permitted to sprinkle Napoleon as cayenne pepper over our dishes. Blucher is too hot-blooded, and pepper does not agree with him."

"But a glass of champagne agrees with him when a dear friend is present," exclaimed Blucher. "Oh, John, come here! Accompany my wife, Scharnhorst; I have only to tell John what he is to fetch from the wine-cellar."

While Blucher gave his orders to John in a hurried and low voice, instructing him to place a substantial battery of bottles of champagne in front of the two generals, Scharnhorst preceded him with Madame von Blucher to the dining-room.

"Madame von Blucher," whispered Scharnhorst, after satisfying himself by a quick side-glance that Blucher was too far from them to overhear his words, "permit me to ask a question. Is your husband strong and healthy enough, both physically and mentally, for me to talk to him about politics? May I communicate to him some important news which I have received to-day, or would I thereby excite him too much?"

"Do you bring glad tidings?" asked Amelia.

"I believe we may consider them so; at all events, they are encouraging."

"In that case, general, you may unhesitatingly communicate them; but, pray, do so only after dinner, and when he has somewhat recovered from the excitement with which your welcome but unexpected visit has filled him. Blucher's mind is perfectly strong and healthy, but his body is feeble, and he is still affected with a disease of the stomach, which, precisely at dinner, very often gives him severe pain. Pray, therefore, no excitement and no politics at the dinner-table."

"So, here I am," said Blucher, who had followed them, and now took the general's arm; "now, children, quick, for I long to take wine again with my dear Scharnhorst."

Scharnhorst faithfully complied with the wishes of Madame von Blucher. No allusion to politics was made during the dinner, and their conversation was harmless, merry, and desultory. They left the dining-room and took coffee in the cosy sitting-room of Madame von Blucher.

"And now," said Blucher, who was sitting on the sofa by the side of Scharnhorst, while his wife sat in the easy-chair opposite them, "let us fill our pipes, or rather smoke them, for they have already been filled."

"But shall we be permitted to do so in your wife's room?" asked Scharnhorst.

"Oh, I have been accustomed to it for twenty years past," exclaimed Amelia, laughing. "When I wished to have Blucher in my room, and by my side, I could not show the door to his pipe; and therefore, as a good soldier's wife, I have accustomed myself to the odor of tobacco-smoke."

"Well," said Blucher, pointing to the two clay pipes which lay on the silver tray beside the burning wax-candle and the cup filled with paper-kindlers, "take a match and fire the cannon; luckily it makes no noise, but only smoke."

Madame von Blucher handed each of the gentlemen a clay pipe, and then held a burning paper close to the tobacco.

"Now, the guns are ready, and the battle may commence," said Blucher, puffing a cloud from his pipe.

"You see, general," said Amelia, turning to Scharnhorst with a significant glance, "madcap Blucher cannot refrain from talking all the time about battles and politics. Now, indulge him in his whim, general, and talk a little with him about these topics."

"I believe it will amount to little," growled Blucher. "If Scharnhorst had brought good news he would not have kept me so long from knowing it. No; the news is always the same; I know it already! New bulletins favorable to Napoleon—nothing else!"

Scharnhorst smiled. "Why, my friend, what is the reason of your sudden despondency? Have you, then, lost all your faith in the approach of better times?—you who used to be more courageous than any of us, you who hitherto cherished the firm belief in a change for the better, and were to us a shining beacon of honor, hope, and courage! What shall we do, and what is to become of us, when Blucher gets discouraged and **ceases to hope?**"

"Well," said Blucher, "I am not yet discouraged; I still hope for a change for the better, and know that it will surely come, for Scharnhorst still lives and paves the way for more prosperous times. Yes, certainly, there will be better times; Scharnhorst is secretly creating an army for us, and when the army has been organized, he will call me, and I shall put myself beside him at the head of the troops, and we shall then march against the French emperor with drums beating; **we shall defeat him—drive him with his routed** soldiers beyond the frontiers of Germany, so that **he never again shall dare to return to the father-**land. Providence has spared me so long for this purpose; I believe that I am chosen to chastise the insolent Napoleon for all his crimes committed against Germany and Prussia. I am destined to overthrow him, deliver my country, and victoriously reëstablish my dear king in all his former states. Napoleon must be hurled from his **throne, and I must** assist in bringing about his downfall; and before that has been accomplished I will and cannot die.* Yes, laugh at me as much as you please; I am already accustomed to that when talking in this style; but it will, nevertheless, prove true, and my prophecies will be fulfilled. You may deride me, but you cannot shake my firm belief in what I tell you."

"**But I** do not deride you," said Scharnhorst. "**I am glad** of your reliance on Heaven, which, while all were discouraged and despairing, stood as a rock in the midst of the breakers. I always **looked to** you, Blucher; the thought of you always strengthened and encouraged me, and when

I at times felt like giving way to despair, I said to myself, 'For shame, Scharnhorst! take heart and hope, for Blucher still lives, and so long as he lives there is hope!'"

"Henceforth," exclaimed Blucher, with radiant eyes, giving his hand to his friend, "henceforth no one will deny that God has made us **for each** other. What you said about me I have repeated to myself every day about you. What was my consolation when Prussia, after the treaty of Tilsit, was wholly prostrated and ruined? 'Scharnhorst still lives!' What did I say to myself when the cowardly ministers, in the beginning of the present year, had concluded the abominable alliance with France? 'Scharnhorst still lives!' And when our poor regiments had to march to Russia as Bonaparte's auxiliaries, I said to myself: 'Scharnhorst is still there to create a new army, and God is there to give victory one day to this army, which I shall command.' Oh, tell me, my friend, what are your plans? What have **you been able to accomplish in regard to the** reorganization of the army? And what about the new officers' regulations which you are having printed?"

"They have already been printed, and I have brought a copy for you," said Scharnhorst, drawing a printed book from his breast-pocket, and handing it to his friend.

Blucher gazed on it long with grave and musing eyes, read the title-page, and glanced over the contents. "Scharnhorst," he then said, solemnly, "this is a great and important work, and posterity only will appreciate its whole importance, and thank you deservedly for it. Our old military structure was utterly rotten, and the first storm, therefore, caused it to break down and fall to pieces. But Scharnhorst is an architect who knew how to find among the ruins material for a new and solid structure, and this structure will one day cause the power of Bonaparte to disappear. This book, which entirely changes the duties and relations of the officers of all arms, and transforms our whole military system, is the splendid plan of the building which you are about to erect. By the introduction of these regula

---

* Blucher's own words.—Vide his biography by Varnhagen von Ense, p. 123.

tions the antiquated system which brought upon **Prussia** the defeats of Jena and Auerstadt, is abolished; the great simplicity of the scheme, and **its** practical spirit, are the best antidotes against the prevalence of the old-fashioned notions which have proved so disastrous. You have performed a great work, Scharnhorst, and Prussia must thank you for it as long as she has an army."

"I may say at least that I have striven for a grand object," said Scharnhorst, "and I have left nothing undone in order to attain it. Many changes had to be made, and many evils eradicated, when the king, after the calamitous days **of Tilsit, placed** me at the head of the commission **which** was to reorganize the whole Prussian army. We had to work night and day, for it was incumbent upon us to arrange a new system of conscription, organize the levies, draw up new articles of war, and complete the battalions, squadrons, and batteries. It was, besides, our task to give the army an honorable position, to constitute the soldier the sacred guardian of the noblest blessings of all nations—liberty and nationality; and to give him a country for which he was to fight. The soldier, therefore, had to be a citizen; the army was no longer to consist of hirelings, but of the sons of the country, and to these had to be intrusted the sacred and inevitable duty of learning the profession of arms, and of devoting for some time their services to the fatherland. The citizens had to be transformed into soldiers, and the name of 'soldier' had, as it was among the Romans, to become a title of honor. In order to bring this about, it was necessary, too, that the distinction of birth, to which the government, in commissioning officers, had hitherto paid so much attention, should be entirely discarded. Every recruit had to know that by bravery, courage, industry, and intelligence, he might attain the highest positions, and that the private soldier might become a general."

"That is the very thing by which the aristocratic officers of the old *régime* became intensely exasperated against your new system," said Blucher. "I know what you had to suffer and contend against, how many stumbling-blocks were cast in your way, and how they charged you with being an innovator, and even a republican, trying to transfer the liberty, equality, and fraternity of the French *sans-culottes* into the Prussian army, and to put general's epaulets into the knapsack of the low-born recruit. But all these arrows glanced off from your dear head, which was as hard as a golden anvil, and they were unable to prevent Scharnhorst from becoming the armorer of German liberty!"

"But his head has received many a blow," said Scharnhorst, smiling. "However, he who wages war must expect to be wounded, and it was a terrible war upon which I entered—one against prejudice and old established customs—against the rights and privileges of **the aristocracy.** God was with me, and gave me strength to complete my work; He gave me, in Blucher, a friend who never refused me his advice, and to whose sagacity and courage I am indebted for one-half of what I have achieved. Without your aid I would often have given way; but it strengthened me to think of you, and your applause was a reward for my labors. May we soon be enabled to carry into effect the new organization of the army!"

"My friend," said Blucher, shaking **his head,** "God has forgotten us, I fear, and averted His eyes from Prussia and the whole of Germany. Napoleon is an instrument in His hands, just as the knout is an instrument of justice in the hand of the Russian executioner. And it seems as though the nations deserved much punishment, for He still holds his instrument firmly in His hands. But patience!—there will be a time when He will cast it aside, and when we shall arise from our prostration to take revenge upon our scourge."

"Who knows whether this new era will not dawn at an earlier moment than we hope and look for?" said Scharnhorst, smiling.

Blucher started, and cast a quick glance on his guest. "Scharnhorst," he said, hastily, "you have brought news, after all. I felt it as soon as I saw you, and it is no use for you to deny it any longer. You know, and want to tell me something. Well, speak out! I am prepared for every thing! What is it? Has Napoleon gained an other victory? Has he transported the Emperor Alexander to Siberia, and put the Russian crown on his head at the Kremlin? Have the Russian people prostrated themselves before him, and, like other nations, recognized him as their sovereign and emperor? You see, I am prepared for every thing; for I insist upon it, how high soever he may build his throne, he must at last descend, and it will be I who will bring him down. Now, speak out! Has he again obtained a great victory?"

"No, general," said Scharnhorst, solemnly, "**God has** obtained a victory!"

Blucher raised his head, and laid his clay pipe slowly on the table. "What do you mean, general?" he asked. "What do you mean by saying, 'God has obtained a victory?'"

"I mean to say that He has sent into the field troops whom even Napoleon is unable to defeat."

"What troops do you refer to?"

"I refer to the cold, the snow, the ice, the **howling** storm blowing from Siberia, like the angry voice of Heaven, striking down men and beasts alike."

"And these troops of God have defeated Napoleon?"

"They have, general!"

Blucher uttered a cry, and, jumping up from his chair, drew himself up to his full height. "The troops of God have defeated Napoleon!" he exclaimed, solemnly. "I have always believed in divine justice—slow sometimes, but sure. Tell me every thing, my friend, tell me every thing," he added, sinking back into the chair, quite overwhelmed by what he had heard. "Commence at the beginning, for I feel that my joy renders this old head confused, and I must gradually accustom myself to it. Tell me the whole history of **the** Russian campaign, for it is the preface I ought to read in order to be able to understand **the book.** And, then, in conclusion, tell me what the good Lord has done, and whether He will now employ His old Blucher. I feel as though an altar-taper had been suddenly lighted in my heart, and as though an organ were playing in my head. I must collect my thoughts. Speak, Scharnhorst,

for you see this surprising news may make me insane." He pressed his hands against his temples **and drew a deep breath.**

His wife hastened to him, and with her soft hand caressed his face, and looked with anxious and tender glances into his wild eyes. "Be calm, Blucher," she said. "Calm your great, heroic heart, else you shall and must not hear any thing further.—General Scharnhorst, I am sure **you** will not tell him anything as long as he is so agitated."

"I will be calm," said Blucher. "You see that I am so already, and that I sit here as still as a lamb. Scharnhorst, tell me, therefore, every thing. I am all attention."

"And while listening to him, take again your old friend, which has so often comforted you in your afflictions—put your pipe again into your mouth," said Amelia, handing it to him.

But Blucher refused it, almost indignantly. "No," he said, "one does not smoke at church, nor when the Lord speaks, and Scharnhorst is about to tell me that the Lord has spoken. While listening to such words, the heart must be devout, and the lips may bless or pray, but they must not hold a pipe. And now speak, Scharnhorst; I am quite calm and prepared for good and bad news."

———◆———

CHAPTER XII.

THE OATH.

"SPEAK," said Blucher, once more. "I am prepared for every thing. Tell me about Bonaparte in Russia."

"You know how victoriously and irresistibly Napoleon penetrated with the various columns of his army into the interior of Russia," said Scharnhorst. "Nothing seemed to have been able to withstand him—nothing powerful enough to arrest his triumphant progress. The Russian generals, as if panic-stricken, retreated farther and farther the deeper Napoleon advanced into the heart of the empire. Neither Kutusoff, nor Wittgenstein, not Barclay, dared risk the fate of Russia in a decisive battle; even the Emperor Alexander preferred to leave the army and retire to Moscow to wait for the arrival of fresh reënforcements, and render new resources available. Napoleon, in the mean time, advanced still farther, constantly in search of the enemy, whom he was unable to find anywhere, and everywhere meeting another enemy whom he was nowhere able to avoid or conquer. This latter was the Russian climate. The scorching heat, the drenching rains, bred diseases which made more havoc in the ranks of the French than the swords of living enemies would have been able to do. At the same time supplies were wanting, so that the immense host received but scanty and insufficient rations. The soldiers suffered the greatest privations, and the Russian people, incited by their czar and their priests to intense hatred and fanatical fury, escaped with their personal property and their provisions from the villages and the small towns rather than welcome the enemy and open to him their houses in compulsory hospitality. The French army, reduced by sickness, privations, and hunger, to nearly one-half of its original strength, nevertheless continued advancing; it forced an entrance into Smolensk after a bloody struggle; after taking a short rest in the ruined, burning, and entirely deserted city, it marched upon Moscow. In front of this ancient capital of the czars it met at length on the 7th of September the living enemy it had so long sought. Bagration, Kutusoff, and Barclay, occupied with their army positions in front of it in order to prevent the approaching foe from entering holy Moscow. You know the particulars of the bloody battle on the Moskwa. The Russians and the French fought on this 7th of September for eleven long hours with the most obstinate exasperation, with truly fanatical fury; whole ranks were mowed down like corn under the harvester's scythe; their generals and chieftains themselves were struck down in the unparalleled struggle; more than seventy thousand killed and wounded covered the battle-field, and yet there were no decisive results. The Russians had only been forced back, but not defeated and routed in such a manner as to stand in need of peace, in order to recover from the terrible consequences of the struggle. To be sure, Napoleon held the battle-field, and, on the 14th of September, made his entry into Moscow, but no messengers came to him from Alexander to sue for peace; no submissive envoys to meet him, as he had been accustomed to see in other conquered cities, and surrender him the keys; the streets were deserted, and no excited crowd appeared either there or at the windows of the houses to witness his entry. The city, whence the inhabitants and authorities had fled, was a vast gaping grave."

"But the grave soon gave signs of animation," exclaimed Blucher, excitedly; "the desert was transformed into a sea of fire, and the burning city gave a horrible welcome to the French. The governor of Moscow, Count Rostopchin, intended to greet the entering conqueror with an illumination, and, as he had no torches handy, he set fire to the houses. He removed the stores and supplies, compelled the inhabitants to leave, had the fire-engines concealed, ordered inflammable oils and rosin to be placed everywhere in order to intensify the fury of the conflagration, and then released the convicts that they might set fire to the city. The first house kindled was Rostopchin's own magnificent palace, close to the gates of Moscow. Well, it is true, Rostopchin acted like a barbarian; but still the man's character seems grand, and his ferocity that of the lion shaking his mane, and rushing with a roar upon his adversary. To be sure, it was no great military exploit to burn down a large city, but still it was a splendid stratagem, and, in a struggle with a hateful and infamous enemy, all ways and means are permitted and justifiable. I do not merely excuse Rostopchin, but I admire his tremendous energy, and believe, if I were a Russian, I would likewise have done something of the sort. His act compelled the enemy soon to leave, as he could not establish his winter-quarters amid smoking ruins, and to retreat instead of advancing, and obliged the Emperor Alexander to cease his vacillating course—inasmuch as, after the conflagration, further attempts at bringing about a compromise and reconciliation between the belligerents were entirely out of the question."

"No, general, Rostopchin did not bring this about," exclaimed Scharnhorst, "but it was our great friend Stein who did it. God Himself sent Minister von Stein to Russia, that he might stand as an immovable rock by the side of the mild and fickle Alexander, and that his fiery soul might strengthen the fluctuating resolutions of the czar, and inspire him with true faith in, and reliance on, the great cause of the freedom of the European nations, which was now to be decided upon the snowy fields of Russia. We owe it to Stein alone that the peace party at the Russian headquarters did not gain the emperor over to their side; we owe it to Stein that Alexander determined to pursue a manly, energetic course; that he refused to allow the diplomatists to interfere, but left the decision to the sword alone, and constantly and proudly rejected all the offers of peace which Napoleon now began to make to him. And Stein found a new ally in the climate uniting with him in his inexorable hostility to the French. Napoleon felt that he ought not to await the approach of winter at Moscow, and on the 18th of October he left the inhospitable city with the remnants of his army. But winter dogged his steps; winter attached itself as a heavy burden to the feet of his soldiers; it laid itself like lead on their paralyzed brain, and caused the horses, guns, and caissons, to stick fast in the snow and ice. Winter dissolved the French army. Men and beasts perished by cold; discipline and subordination were entirely disregarded; every one thought only of preserving his own life, of appeasing his hunger, and relieving his distress. Piles of corpses and dead horses marked the route of this terrible retreat of the French; and when, on the 9th of November, they entered Smolensk, the whole grand army consisted only of forty thousand armed men, and crowds of stragglers destitute of arms and without discipline."

"And still this cruel tyrant and heartless braggart, the great Napoleon, dared to boast of his victories, and the splendid condition of his army," exclaimed Blucher, angrily. "And he sent constantly new bulletins of pretended victories into the world, and the stupid Germans believed them to be true, the supposed successes causing them to tremble. I have read these lying bulletins, and the perusal made me ill. They dwelt on nothing but the victories, the glorious conduct, and the fine condition of the grand army."

"But now you shall read a new one, friend Blucher," exclaimed Scharnhorst; "here is the twenty-ninth bulletin, and I will communicate to you also the latest news from the grand army and the great Napoleon, which couriers from Berlin and Dresden brought me last night, and which induced me to set out so early to-day in order to reach my Blucher, and tell him of a new era. Here is the twenty-ninth bulletin, and in it Napoleon dares no longer boast of victories; he almost dares tell the truth."

"Let me read it!" exclaimed Blucher, impatiently seizing the printed sheet which Scharnhorst handed to him. Gasping with inward emotion, he began to read it, but his hands soon trembled, and the letters swam before his eyes.

"I cannot read it through," said Blucher, sighing. "There is a storm raging in my heart, and it blows out the light of my eyes. Read the remainder to me, my friend. I have read it to the engagement on the Beresina, where Napoleon says that General Victor gained another victory on the 28th of November."

"But this victory consisted only in the fact that General Victor, with his twelve thousand men, prevented the Russians from reaching the banks of the Beresina, so that two bridges could be built across it, and that the ragged wretches composing the grand army could reach the opposite side of the river. That passage of the Beresina was a terrible moment, which will never be forgotten by history—a tragedy full of horrors, wretchedness, and despair. Stein's agents have sent me Russian reports of this event, which contain the most heart-rending and revolting details. Books will be written to depict the dreadful scenes of that day; but neither historians, nor painters, nor poets, will find words or colors to portray those unparalleled horrors."

"And does he describe those scenes in his bulletin?" asked Blucher. "Read me its conclusion. Does he allude to those horrors of the Beresina?"

"No, general; he speaks only of the victory and the passage across the river, and then continues: 'On the following day, the 29th of November, we remained on the battle-field. We had to choose between two routes: the road of Minsk, and that of Wilna. The road of Minsk passes through the middle of a forest and uncultivated morasses; that of Wilna, on the contrary, passes through a very fine part of the country. The army, destitute of cavalry, but poorly provided with ammunition, and terribly exhausted by the fatigues of a fifty days' march, took with it its sick and wounded, and was anxious to reach its magazines.'"

"That is to say," exclaimed Blucher, "they died of hunger, and, as he says that they were terribly exhausted by a fifty days' march, dropped like flies. Oh, it is true, the Emperor Napoleon is very laconic in his account of that retreat, but he who knows how to penetrate the meaning of his few lines cannot fail to receive a deep impression of the wretchedness that unfortunate army had to undergo. Read on, dear Scharnhorst."

Scharnhorst continued: "'If it must be admitted that it is necessary for the army to reëstablish its discipline, to recover from its long fatigues, to remount its cavalry, artillery, and *matériel*, it is only the natural result of the events which we have just described. Repose is now, above all, indispensable to the army. The trains and horses are already arriving; the artillery has repaired its losses, but the generals, officers, and soldiers, have suffered intensely by the fatigues and privations of the march. Owing to the loss of their horses, many have lost their baggage; others have been deprived of it by Cossacks lying in ambush. They have captured a great many individuals, such as engineers, geographers, and wounded officers, who marched without the necessary precautions, and exposed themselves to the danger of being taken prisoners rather than quietly march in the midst of the convoys.'"

"And the Cossacks have spared *him!*" exclaimed Blucher, impatiently. "They did not take him prisoner! What is he doing, then, that the Cossacks cannot catch him? Tell me, Scharnhorst—the bulletin, then, does not, like its predecessors, dwell on the heroic exploits of the great emperor? He does not praise himself as he formerly used to do?"

"Oh, he does not fail to do so. Listen to the conclusion: 'During all these operations the emperor marched constantly in the midst of his guard, the marshal Duke d'Istria commanding the cavalry, and the Duke de Dantzic the infantry. His majesty was content with the excellent spirit manifested by the guard, always ready to march to points where the situation was such that its mere presence sufficed to check the enemy. Our cavalry lost so heavily, that it was difficult to collect officers enough, who were still possessed of horses, to form four companies, each of one hundred and fifty men. In these companies, generals performed the services of captains, and colonels those of non-commissioned officers. The "Sacred Legion," **commanded by the** King of Naples and General Grouchy, never lost sight of the emperor during all these operations. The health of his majesty never was better.'" *

"And he dares to proclaim that!" exclaimed Blucher, indignantly. "His army is dying of hunger and cold, and he proclaims to the world, as if in mockery, that his health never was better! It is his fault that hundreds of thousands are perishing in the most heart-rending manner, and he boasts of his extraordinary good health! He must have a stone in his breast instead of a heart; otherwise, a general whose army is perishing under his eyes cannot be in extraordinary good health. He will be punished for it, and will not always feel so well."

"He has already been punished, my friend," said Scharnhorst, solemnly. "It has pleased God to chastise the arrogant tyrant and to bow his proud head to the dust."

---

* Fain, "Manuscrit de 1812."

Blucher jumped up, and a deep pallor overspread his cheeks. "He has been punished?" he asked, breathlessly. "Napoleon in the dust! What is it? Speak quickly, Scharnhorst; speak, if you do not want me to die! What has happened?"

"He has left his army, and secretly fled from Russia!"

Blucher uttered a cry, and, without a word, rushed toward the door. Scharnhorst and Amelia hastened after him and kept him back.

"What do you wish to do?" asked Scharnhorst.

"I wish to pursue him!" exclaimed Blucher, vainly trying to disengage himself from the hands of his wife and the general. "Let me go—do not detain me! I must pursue him—I must take him prisoner! If he has fled from his army, he must return to France, and if he wants to return to France, he must pass through Germany. Let me go! He must not be permitted to escape from Germany!"

"But he has already escaped," said Scharnhorst, smiling.

"What! Passed through Germany?" asked Blucher. "And no one has tried to arrest him?"

"No one knew that he was there. He left his army on the 6th of December; attended only by Caulaincourt and his Mameluke Roustan, recognized by no one, expected by no one, he sped in fabulous haste in an unpretending sleigh through the whole of Poland and Prussia. Only after he set out was it known at the places where he stopped that he had been there. He travelled as swiftly as the storm. On the 6th of December he was at Wilna, on the 10th of December at Warsaw, and in the night of the 14th of December suddenly a plain sleigh stopped in front of the residence of M. Serra, French ambassador at Dresden: two footmen were seated on the box, and in the sleigh itself there were two gentlemen, wrapped in furred robes, and so much benumbed by the cold that they had to be lifted out. There two gentlemen were the Emperor Napoleon and Caulaincourt. Napoleon had an interview with the King of Saxony the same night, and, continuing his journey, reached Erfurt on the 15th, and—"

"And to-day is already the 17th of December," said Blucher, sighing; "he will, therefore, be beyond the Rhine. And I must allow him to escape! I am unable to detain him! Oh, that the little satisfaction had been granted me of capturing Napoleon! Well, it has been decreed that this should not be; but one thing at least is settled. Napoleon has been deserted by his former good luck; Dame Fortune, who always was seated in his triumphal car, has alighted from it, and now we may hope to see her soon restored to her old place on the top of the Brandenburg gate at Berlin. Hurrah, my friend! we are going to rise; I feel it in my bones, and the time has come when old Blucher will again be permitted to be a man, and will no longer be required to draw his nightcap over his ears."

"Yes, the time has come when Prussia needs her valiant Blucher," said Scharnhorst, tenderly laying his arm on Blucher's. "Now raise your head, general—now prepare for action, for Blucher must henceforth be ready at a moment's notice to obey the call of Prussia, and place himself at the head of her brave sons, who are so eager for the fray."

"Yes, yes, we shall have war now," exclaimed Blucher. "Soon the drums will roll, and the cannon boom—soon Blucher will no longer be a childish and decrepit old man whom wiseacres think they can mock and laugh at—soon Blucher will once more be a man who, sword in hand, will shout to his troops, 'Forward!—charge the enemy!' Great Heaven, Scharnhorst, and I have not even dressed becomingly—I still wear a miserable civilian's coat! Suppose war should break out to-day, and they should come and call me to the army? Why, Blucher would have to hang his head in shame, and acknowledge that he was not ready!—John! John!—my uniform! Come to my bedroom, John! I want to dress!—to put on my uniform!"

Fifteen minutes afterward Blucher returned to the sitting-room, where his wife was gayly chatting with Scharnhorst. He was not now the sick,

"I swear to you, Queen Louisa, that I will not sheathe this sword before I have avenged your death."

suffering old man whom we saw this morning sitting on the easy-chair at the window, but he was once more a fiery soldier and a hero. His head was proudly erect, his eyes were flashing, a proud smile was playing round his lips; his broad-shouldered form was clothed in the uniform of a Prussian general; orders were glittering on his breast, and the long rattling sword hung at his left side.

Blucher approached his wife and General Scharnhorst with dignified steps, and, giving his hands to both, said in a grave and solemn voice, "The time for delay, impatience, and folly, is past. With this uniform I have become a new man. I am no longer an impatient septuagenarian, cursing and killing flies on the wall because he has no one else on whom to vent his wrath; but I am a soldier standing composedly at his post, and waiting for the hour when he will be able to destroy his enemy. Come, my friends,—come with me!"

He drew the two with him, and walked so rapidly through the rooms that they were scarcely able to accompany him. They entered the large reception-room, opened only on festive occasions. It contained nothing but some tinselled furniture, a few tables with marble tops, and on the pillars between the windows large Venetian mirrors. Otherwise the walls were bare, except over the sofa, where hung, in a finely-carved and gilded frame, a painting, which however was covered with a large veil of black crape.

Blucher conducted the two to this painting; for a moment he stood still and gazed on it gravely and musingly, and, raising his right hand with a quick jerk, he tore down the mourning-veil.

"Queen Louisa!" exclaimed Scharnhorst, admiring the tall and beautiful lady smiling on him.

"Yes," said Blucher, solemnly, "Queen Louisa! The guardian angel of Prussia, whose heart Napoleon broke! This pride and joy of all our women had to depart without hoping even in the possibility that the calamities which ruined her might come to an end. On the day she died I covered her portrait with this veil, and swore not to look again at her adored countenance until able to draw my sword, and, with Prussia's soldiers, avenge her untimely death. The time has come! Louisa, rise again from your grave, open once more your beautiful eyes, for daylight is at hand, and our night is ended. Now, my beautiful queen, listen to the oath of your most faithful servant!" He drew his sword, and, raising it up to the painting, exclaimed: "Here is my sword! When I sheathed it last, I wept, for I was to be an invalid, and should no longer wield it; I was to sit here in idleness, and silently witness the sufferings of my fatherland. But now I shall soon be called into service, and I swear to you, Queen Louisa, that I will not sheathe this sword before I have avenged your death, before Germany and Prussia are free again, and Napoleon has received his punishment. I swear it to you, as sure as I am old Blucher, and have seen the tears which Prussia's disgrace has often wrung from your eyes. May God help me! may He in His mercy spare me until I have fulfilled my oath! Amen!"

"Amen!" repeated Scharnhorst and Amelia, looking up to the portrait.

"Amen!" said Blucher again. "And now, Amelia," he added, quickly, "come and give me a kiss, and, by this kiss, consecrate your warrior, that he may deliver Germany and overthrow Napoleon. For Napoleon must now be hurled from the throne!"

CHAPTER XIII.

THE INTERRUPTED SUPPER.

It was on the 4th of January, 1813. The brilliant official festivities with which the beginning of a new year had been celebrated, were at an end, and, the ceremonious dinner-parties being over, one was again at liberty to indulge in the enjoyment of familiar suppers, where more attention was paid to the flavor of choice wines and delicacies than to official toasts and political speeches. Marshal Augereau gave at Berlin on this day one of those pleasant little entertainments to his favored friends, to indemnify them, as it were, for the great gala dinner of a hundred covers, given by him on the 1st of January, as official representative of the Emperor Napoleon.

To-day the supper was served in the small, cozy saloon, and it was but a *petit comité* that assembled round the table in the middle of the room. This *comité* consisted only of five gentlemen, with pleasant, smiling faces, in gorgeous, profusely-embroidered uniforms, on the left sides of which many glittering orders indicated the high rank of the small company. There was, in the first place, Marshal Augereau, governor of Berlin, once so furious a republican that he threatened with death all the members of his division who would address any one with "monsieur," or "madame"— now the most ardent imperialist, and an admirer of the Emperor Napoleon. The gentleman by his side, with the short, corpulent figure and aristocratic countenance, from which a smile

never disappeared, was the chancellor of state and prime minister of King Frederick William III., Baron von Hardenberg. He was just engaged in an eager conversation with his neighbor, Count Narbonne, the faithless renegade and former adherent of the Bourbons, who had but lately deserted to Napoleon's camp, and allowed himself to be used by the emperor on various diplomatic missions. Next to him sat Prince Hatzfeld, the man on whom, in 1807, Napoleon's anger had fallen, and who would have been shot as a "traitor" if the impassioned intercession of his wife had not succeeded in softening the emperor, and thus saving her husband's life. Near him, and closing the circle, sat Count St. Marsan, Napoleon's ambassador at the court of Prussia.

These five gentlemen had already been at the table for several hours, and were now in that comfortable and agreeable mood which epicures feel when they have found the numerous courses palatable and piquant, the Hock sufficiently cold, the Burgundy sufficiently warm, the oysters fresh, and the truffles well-flavored. They had got as far as the roast; the pheasants, with their delicate sauce, filled the room with an appetizing odor, and the corks of the champagne-bottles gave loud reports, as if by way of salute fired in honor of the triumphant entry of Pleasure.

Marshal Augereau raised his glass. "I drink this in honor of our emperor!" he exclaimed, in an enthusiastic tone. The gentlemen touched each other's glasses, and the three representatives of France then emptied theirs at one draught.

Prince Hatzfeld followed their example, but Baron von Hardenberg only touched the brim of his glass with his lips, and put it down again.

"Your excellency does not drink?" asked Augereau. "Then you are not in earnest?"

"Yes, marshal, I am in earnest," said Hardenberg, smiling, "but you used a word which prevented me from emptying my glass. You said, 'In honor of our emperor!' Now, I am the devoted and, I may well say, faithful servant of my master, King Frederick William, and therefore I cannot call the great Napoleon my emperor."

"Oh, I used a wrong expression," exclaimed Augereau, hastily. "Let us fill our glasses anew, and drink this time 'the health of the great emperor Napoleon!'" He touched glasses with the chancellor of state, and then fixed his keen eyes upon the minister.

Baron von Hardenberg raised the glass to his lips, but then withdrew it again, and, bowing smilingly to Marshal Augereau, said: "Permit me, marshal, to add something to your toast. Let us drink 'the health of the great emperor, and a long and prosperous alliance with Prussia!'"

"'And a long and prosperous alliance with Prussia,'" repeated the four gentlemen, emptying their glasses, and resuming their chairs.

"We have just drunk to the success of our divulged secret," said Prince Hatzfeld, smiling. "For I suppose, your excellency," turning to Baron von Hardenberg, "this new happy alliance between Prussia and France is now not much of a secret?"

"I hope it will soon be no secret at all," said Hardenberg. "Prussia has received the proposition of France with heart-felt joy, and will hail the marriage of her crown prince Frederick William as the happiest guaranty of an indissoluble union. Only the crown prince is too young as yet to marry, and at the present time, at least, allusions to the happiness of his future should be avoided. His thoughts should belong only to God and religion, for you know, gentlemen, that the crown prince will be solemnly confirmed in the course of a few days. Only after he has pledged his soul to God will it be time for him to pledge his heart to love; only then communications will be made to him as to the brilliant future that is opening for him, and, no doubt, he will, like the king, be ready to bind even more firmly the ties uniting Prussia with France. He will be proud to receive for a consort a princess of the house of Napoleon, for such a marriage will render him a relative of the greatest prince of his century!"

"Of a prince whom Heaven loves above all others, as it lavishes upon him greater prosperity than upon others," exclaimed Prince Hatzfield, emphatically. "God's love is visibly with him, and protects His favorite. Who but he would have been able to overcome the terrible dangers of the Russian campaign, and, with an eagle's flight, return to France from the snowy deserts of Russia, without losing a single plume of his wings?"

"It is true," responded Augereau, thoughtfully. "Fortune, or, if you prefer, Providence, is with the emperor; it protects him in all dangers, and allows him to issue victoriously from all storms. In Russia he was in danger of ruining his glory and his army, but the battle of Borodino, and still more that on the banks of the Beresina, saved his laurels. The emperor travelled deserted roads, without an escort or protection, through Poland and Germany, in order to return to France. If he had been recognized, perhaps it might have entered the heads of some enthusiasts to attack and capture him on his solitary journey; but the eyes of his enemies seemed to have been blinded. The emperor was not recognized, and appeared suddenly in Paris, where the greatest excitement, consternation, and confusion, were prevailing at that moment. For Paris had just then been profoundly moved by the deplorable conspiracy of General Mallet, and the Parisians were asking each other in dismay whether General Mallet might not have been right after all in announcing that Napoleon was dead, and whether his death was not kept a secret merely from motives of policy. Suddenly Napoleon appeared in the streets of Paris. All rushed out to behold the emperor, or touch his horse, body, hands, or feet, to look into his eyes, to hear his voice, and satisfy themselves that it was really Napoleon—not an apparition. Their cheers rang, and, in their happiness at seeing him again in their midst, they pardoned him for having left their sons and brothers, fathers and husbands, as frozen corpses on the plains of Russia. Never before had Napoleon enjoyed a greater triumph as on the day of his return from the Russian campaign. Fortune is the goddess chained to the emperor's triumphal car, and the nations therefore would act very foolishly if they dared rise against him."

"Happily, they have given up all such schemes," said Hardenberg, smiling, and quietly cutting the pheasant's wing on his silver plate. "They are asking and longing only for peace in order to dress their wounds, cultivate their fields, and peaceably reap the harvest."

"And the word of the **Emperor** Napoleon is a pledge to nations that they shall be enabled to do so," **exclaimed St. Marson.** "He wants peace, **and is ready to make every sacrifice** to conclude **and maintain it.**"

"The German princes, of course, will joyously offer him their hands for that purpose," said Hardenberg, bowing his head. "In truth, I could not say at what point of Germany war could break out at this juncture. The princes of the German Confederation of the Rhine have long **since** acknowledged the Emperor of the French as their master, and themselves as his obedient vassals. Powerful Austria has allied herself with France by the ties of a marriage, and the hands of Maria Louisa and Napoleon are stretched out in blessing over the two countries. Poor Prussia **has** not only proved her fidelity as an ally of France, but is now, forgetful of all her former humiliations, ready to consent to a marriage of her future king with a Napoleonic princess. Whence, then, could come a cause for a new war between France and Germany? We shall have peace, doubtless—a long and durable peace!"

"And that will be very fortunate," said Count Narbonne, "for then it will no longer be necessary for us to allow miserable politics to poison our suppers. 'Politics,' said my great royal patron, King Louis XVI., the worthy uncle of the Emperor Napoleon, 'politics know nothing of the culinary art; they spoil all dishes, and care, therefore, ought to be taken not to allow them to enter the kitchen or the dining-room. One must not admit them even directly after eating, for they interfere with digestion; only during the morning hours should audiences be given to them, for then they may serve as Spanish pepper, imparting a flavor to one's breakfast.' That was a very sagacious remark; I feel it at this moment when you so cruelly sprinkle politics over this splendid pheasant."

"You are right," exclaimed Hardenberg, laughing, "I therefore beg your excellency's pardon; for Spanish pepper, which is very palatable in Cumberland sauce, and a few other dishes, is surely entirely out of place when mixed with French truffles."

"**Unhappy** man," exclaimed Narbonne, with ludicrous pathos, "you are again talking politics, and moreover of **the worst sort!**"

"How so?" asked Count St. **Marson.** "What displeases you in the remarks of Minister von Hardenberg?"

"Well, did you not notice that his excellency alluded to our unsuccessful efforts in Spain. Spanish pepper, he said, is surely entirely out of place when mixed with French truffles, but very palatable in English sauces. That is to say, Spain and England are good allies, and Spain and France will never be reconciled. And it is true, it is a mortal war which Spain is waging against us, and unfortunately one which offers us but few chances of success. The Spaniards contest every inch of ground with the most dogged **obstinacy,** and they have found very valuable auxiliaries in Lord Wellington and his English troops. They—"

"**Ah, my dear count,**" exclaimed Marshal Augereau, smiling, "now it is you who talk politics, and it behooves you no longer to accuse us."

"You are right, and I beg your pardon," said Narbonne; "but you see how true the old proverb proves: 'Bad examples spoil good manners.' Let us talk no longer about pepper, but truffles.

Just compare this truffle from Périgord with the Italian truffle at the *entremets*, and you will have to admit that our Périgord truffle is in every respect superior to the latter. It is more savory and piquant. There can be no doubt of it that Périgord furnishes the most palatable fruit to the world."

"What fruit do you allude to," asked Hardenberg, smiling. "Do you refer to the Périgord truffle, or to the Abbot of Périgord, the great Talleyrand?"

"I see you are lost beyond redemption," said Narbonne, sighing, while the other gentlemen burst into laughter. "Even in the face of a truffle you still dare to amuse yourself with political puns, and confound intentionally an abbot with a truffle! Oh, what a blasphemy against the finest of all fruits—I allude, of course, to the truffle—oh, it is treason committed—"

Just then the door of the saloon was hastily opened, and the first secretary of the French embassy entered the room.

"What, sir!" shouted Count St. Marsan to him, "you come to disturb me here? Some important event, then, has taken place?"

The secretary approached him hurriedly. "Yes, your excellency," he said, "highly important and urgent dispatches have arrived. They come from the army, and an aide-de-camp of Marshal Macdonald is their bearer. He has travelled night and day to reach your excellency at an earlier moment than the courier whom General von York no doubt has sent to the King of Prussia. Here are the dispatches which the aide-de-camp of the marshal has brought for you, and which he says ought immediately to be read by your excellency." He handed the count a large sealed letter, which the latter eagerly accepted and at once opened.

A profound silence now reigned in the small saloon. The faces of the boon companions at the table had grown grave, and all fixed their eyes with an anxious and searching expression upon the countenance of Count St. Marsan. He read the dispatch at first with a calm and indifferent air, but suddenly his features assumed an

expression of astonishment—nay, of anger, and a gloomy cloud covered his brow.

"All right," he then said, turning to the secretary. "Return to the legation. I will follow you in a few minutes." The secretary bowed and withdrew. The five gentlemen were again alone.

"Well," asked Marshal Augereau, "were the dispatches really important?"

Count St. Marsan made no immediate reply. He looked slowly around the circle of his companions, and fixed his eyes with a piercing expression on the countenance of Chancellor von Hardenberg. "Yes," he said, "they contain highly important news, and I wonder if his excellency the chancellor of state has not yet received them, for the dispatches concern above all the Prussian army."

"But I pledge your excellency my word of honor that I do not know what you refer to," said Hardenberg, gravely. "I have received no courier and no startling news from the Prussian army."

"Well, then," said St. Marsan, bowing, "permit me to communicate it to you. General York, commander of the Prussian troops belonging to the forces of Marshal Macdonald, has refused to obey the marshal's orders. He has gone even further than that, concluding a treaty with Russia, with the enemy of France and Prussia; and signed at Tauroggen, with the Russian General von Diebitsch, a convention by virtue of which he severs his connection with the French army, and, with the consent of Russia, declares that the Prussian corps henceforth will be neutral."

"But that is impossible," exclaimed Hardenberg, "he would not dare any thing of the kind; he would not violate in so flagrant a manner the orders given him by his king!"

"But he *did* so," said Augereau, "and if your excellency should have any doubts as to the truth of what Count St. Marsan said, here is the autograph letter in which General von York informs Marshal Macdonald of his defection; and, besides, another letter in which the commander of the cavalry, General von Massenbach, notifies Marshal Macdonald that he has acceded to York's convention, and henceforth will no longer obey the marshal's orders. Conformably to this convention, the Prussian troops have already left the positions assigned them by Marshal Macdonald, and returned to Prussian territory."

"It is true; there can be no doubt of it," said Hardenberg, with a deep sigh, and handing back to the marshal the papers which he had rapidly glanced over. He then rose from his chair and said: "This is so unparalleled and unexpected an event, that I am at the present moment almost unable to collect my thoughts. You will pardon me, therefore, for leaving you; above all, I have to inform his majesty, the king, of this important intelligence, and receive his orders in regard to it. But then I beg leave to see Count St. Marson at his residence, to confer with him as to the measures to be taken concerning this terrible event."

"I will await you at whatever hour of the night it may be," said Count St. Marsan; "I am now about to return to my residence."

"And I to the king!" exclaimed Hardenberg, taking leave.

CHAPTER XIV.

THE DEFECTION OF GENERAL YORK.

KING FREDERICK WILLIAM had just returned to his cabinet after attending to the last business, which he never neglected to perform on any day of the year; that is to say, he had repaired to the bedrooms of his children, and bidden the little sleepers "good-night" by gently kissing them. In former times he did this by the side of his wife, with a happy heart and a smiling face; it had been, as it were, the last seal both pressed, at the close of every day of their common happiness, upon the foreheads of their sleeping children. But since Louisa had left him, to bid this "good-night" had become, as it were, a sacred pilgrimage to his most precious recollections. When he passed through the silent corridors at

night, and entered the rooms of his sons and daughters, he thought of her who had left him three years before, but whom he believed he saw, with her sweet smile and loving eyes. He took pains to remind such of his children as he found awake of their dear departed parent, whispering to them, "Remember your noble mother, whose eyes behold you." And on the lips of those asleep he never failed to press two kisses—one for himself and the other for Louisa.

The king had just returned to his cabinet, and, like a dying glimmer of twilight, a faint smile was illuminating his countenance, which, since the queen's death, had grown grave and sad. He seated himself on the sofa where she had so often sat by his side, and cast a mournful glance upon the vacant place beside him. "Alone! Always alone!" he said in a low voice. "Nothing around me but intrigues, quarrels, and malice! No one who loves me! Alone!" With a quick motion he turned his head toward the side of the wall where hung over his desk the portrait of Queen Louisa, in her white dress, and a rose on her bosom. "Where are you, then, Louisa!" he exclaimed; "why did you leave me, though you had sworn to bear joy and grief with me? You are not here to share them, and—" Suddenly the king paused and turned his eyes toward the door. It seemed to him as though he heard hasty footsteps, and some one softly rapping at his door. Who, at this unusual hour, could ask for admittance? Who could dare now interrupt his solitude, when it was well understood he desired to be left alone?

The rapping was repeated, louder than before, and a timid, imploring voice asked, "Has his majesty returned to his cabinet?"

"It is Timm, my chamberlain," said the king. "What can he want of me?"

Ordering him in a loud tone to walk in, the door was immediately opened, and the chamberlain appeared on the threshold. "Pardon me, sire," he said, "but his excellency Chancellor von Hardenberg is in the anteroom, and urgently requests your majesty to grant him an immediate audience."

"Hardenberg!" exclaimed the king, anxiously. "What has happened; what—". He interrupted himself: "I will see the chancellor. Admit him at once."

The chamberlain withdrew. The king arose and advanced several steps toward the door; then, as if ashamed of his own impatience, he stopped, while his face expressed the agitation of his mind.

Hardenberg entered, and, closing the door rapidly, approached the king. "Your majesty," he said, "I beg pardon for daring to disturb you at so late an hour; but the extraordinary importance of the news I bring to you will be my excuse. I was at the supper-table of Marshal Augereau, in company with the French ambassador, Count St. Marsan, when important dispatches, just arrived from the army, were delivered to the ambassador."

"A battle has been fought, has it not? Has my corps been routed?" asked the king, breathlessly.

"No, your majesty, there has been no battle. A much more extraordinary event has taken place, General von York has concluded a convention with the Russian General Diebitsch, and signed a treaty by which the troops commanded by York separate from the French, and engage to remain neutral for two months."

"That is not true!" exclaimed the king. "A mere rumor!—an impossibility!"

"Your majesty, it is but too true. I myself have read the autograph letters in which Generals York and Massenbach inform Marshal Macdonald of their resolution not to obey his orders longer."

The king pressed his hands against his temple, and exclaimed, in a tremulous voice: "Oh, this is enough to throw one into a state of apoplexy!* It is unheard of, contrary to military law, contrary to all international obligations! It is open rebellion, revolutionary resistance to his king and commander-in-chief! A general who dares commit so terrible a crime must be tried by court-martial, and sentence of death passed upon him. I cannot pardon him!"

---

* The king's own words.—Vide Droysen's "Life of York," vol. ii., p. 56.

"Your majesty," said Hardenberg, in dismay, "it is possible that General York may have committed a crime against discipline, but, nevertheless, it is an heroic and magnanimous deed, and no Prussian court-martial will dare inflict punishment on him. We do not yet know the urgent circumstances obliging the general to make this decision; we do not yet know from what dangers he may have preserved the Prussian army by his quick and resolute step."

"But we know that he has committed an unparalleled crime against discipline!"

"A crime by which he may perhaps have saved Prussia from utter destruction! The general will be able to justify his deed."

"But it seems that he does not even deem it necessary to inform me of his proceedings," exclaimed the king, indignantly. "He appears to have made himself dictator, and as he does not recognize my military laws, he refuses also to acknowledge me as commander-in-chief, to whom he owes obedience."

"Your majesty, I believe there is his justification already," said Hardenberg, pointing at Timm the chamberlain, who reëntered the room at this moment.

"Well, what is it, Timm?" asked the king, hastily.

"Your majesty, a courier from General von York has just arrived; he is bearer of dispatches, which he is to deliver to your majesty in person."

"Who is the courier?" asked the king.

"The general's aide-de-camp, Major Thile."

"Let him come in," said the king.

The jingle of spurs, and heavy, weary footsteps were heard approaching; Major von Thile entered. His uniform was covered with dust and mud; his hair hung in wet locks upon his forehead, and there shone in his mustache the snow-flakes with which the stormy night had adorned it.

"Did you arrive now?" asked the king, eying him closely.

"I did, your majesty, and, agreeably to the orders of General von York, have had myself driven directly to the royal palace, for the general deemed it of the highest importance that I should **deliver my dispatches as soon as possible to your** majesty. Hence I rode night and day, and, my horse breaking down to-day, I was obliged to take a carriage."

"But the French courier reached Berlin earlier than you did," said the king, gruffly. "How does that happen? Have the French quicker horses or more devoted soldiers?"

"No, your majesty, their road to Berlin was **shorter** than mine, that is all. **As I could not ride** across the French camp, **I** had to take a roundabout road by way of Gumbinnen. This caused a delay of four hours."

"Give me your dispatches," said the king.

Major Thile handed him a large sealed paper. The king extended his hand to take it, but suddenly withdrew it again and started back.

"No," he said, "it does not behoove a king to receive letters from a traitorous subject—a rebellious soldier. Take this dispatch, M. Chancellor; **open and read it to me. Give** it to his excellency."

Major Thile handed Hardenberg the letter, and, while he was doing so, the eyes of the two men met. The major's eyes expressed **an** anxious question, those of Hardenberg made him a sad and painful reply, and both were unable to restrain a sigh.

"Read!" said the king, stepping into the window-niche, folding his hands on his breast, and placing **himself so that the curtains** shaded his face, and screened it from the two gentlemen.

Hardenberg unfolded the paper and read as follows:

"To his Majesty the **King:—TAUROGGEN,** December 30, 1812.—Placed in a very unfavorable position by setting out at a later day than the marshal did, and being ordered to march from Mitau to Tilsit, for the sole purpose of covering **the retreat** of the seventh division, I have **been compelled, on account of impassable** roads, and very severe **weather, to conclude** with the Russian commander, Major-General Diebitsch, the enclosed convention, which I beg leave to lay before your **majesty.** Firmly convinced that a continuation of the march would have unavoidably brought about the dissolution of the whole corps, and the loss of its entire artillery and baggage, as was the case of the retreat of the grand army, I believed it was incumbent upon me, as your majesty's faithful subject, to regard your interest, and no longer that of your ally, for whom our auxiliary corps would only have been sacrificed without being able to afford him any real assistance in the desperate predicament in which he was placed. The convention imposes no obligations whatever upon your majesty, but it preserves to you a corps that gives value to the old alliance, or a new one, if such should be concluded, and prevents your majesty from being at the mercy of an ally at whose hands you would have to receive as a gift the preservation or restoration of your states. I would willingly lay my head at the feet of your majesty if I have erred; I would die with the joyous conviction of having at least committed **no** act contrary to my duty as a faithful subject and a true **Prussian. Now or never is** the time for your majesty to extricate yourself **from the** thraldom of an ally whose intentions in regard to Prussia are veiled in impenetrable darkness, **and** justify the most serious alarm. That consideration has guided me. God grant it may be for the salvation of the country!—YORK." *

A pause ensued. The king still stood with folded arms in the window-niche, his face shaded by the curtains, and inaccessible to the anxious and searching glances of Hardenberg and the major.

"Does your majesty now command me to read the convention?" asked the minister.

"No," said the king, sternly, "what do I care for a convention drawn up by a traitor? **I would** not be at liberty to accept it even though it should secure me new provinces.—Major Thile!"

"Your majesty!" said the major, advancing a few steps with stiff, military bearing.

"Were you present at the negotiations preceding this convention? Are you familiar with the circumstances that led to it?"

---

* Droysen's "Life of York," vol. 1, p. 498.

"Yes, your majesty; General von York deigned to repose implicit confidence in me; I am perfectly **familiar** with the course of the negotiations, and was present when the convention was concluded. I observed the inward struggles of the general; I witnessed the terrible conflict that took place in his breast between his duty as a soldier and his conscience as a faithful subject of your majesty. As a soldier he was conscious of the crime he was about to commit against discipline; as a faithful subject, he felt that he ought to commit it if he wished to avoid plunging a corps of ten thousand men, belonging to your majesty alone, into utter **and irretrievable destruction.**"

"Did the negotiations last a long time? Speak! I want to know all; but, understand me well, the truth. No protestations! Speak now!"

"Yes, your majesty, the negotiations had been going on for some time; in fact, ever since the so-called 'grand army' made its appearance in miserable, ragged, and starving squads—mere crowds of woe-begone, famished beggars—while the splendid and powerful Russian forces were constantly approaching closer to our positions and the Prussian frontier. The Russian generals, Prince Wittgenstein and General Diebitsch, were sending one messenger after another to York and informing him of the dangers of his position, surrounded on all sides by Russian troops. They advised him therefore to yield, unless he wished needlessly to expose the soldiers of your majesty to inevitable destruction. They urged him, for the salvation of Prussia, to grasp the saving hand that was being held out to him, and compel Prussia to forsake an utterly ruined ally, who, in order to secure a brief respite, would assuredly not hesitate to sacrifice for his own benefit Prussia's last strength and resources. But the general was still unable to make up his mind to take a step which might be disavowed by your majesty. In the mean time, however, the news came that Memel had been taken and occupied by the Russians, and Prince Wittgenstein simultaneously sent word that he had placed a corps of fifty thousand men on the banks of the Niemen, and was ready to pursue the French army, which would now seek safety in Prussia. Prince Wittgenstein, therefore, demanded categorically whether York would leave the French army, or whether he was to be considered a part of it, and an enemy of Russia."

"And what did York reply?" asked the king, hastily.

"Your majesty, he was silent. **Even we, his** confidants, did not know what decision he had come to. Suddenly a messenger from Marshal Macdonald, who had succeeded in getting into our lines, appeared at York's headquarters. He informed the general that the French troops of the marshal were near Piktupöhnen, and brought orders that York should march to that place, where Macdonald would await him, and that the French and Prussian forces should **then be united.** Henceforth further hesitation **was out of the** question. The messengers, both of the Russian General Diebitsch and the French Marshal Macdonald, were at his headquarters, and insisted that he should make up his mind as to the course to be pursued by his corps. York either had to set out at once and force a passage through **the** Russian lines, in order to join the French marshal at Piktupöhnen, or to refuse to obey the marshal's orders, and, instead of marching upon Piktupöh**nen, join** the Russians, and proceed to Prussia. But General York had not yet made up his mind. Toward nightfall another messenger from General Diebitsch arrived at his headquarters. This messenger was Lieutenant-Colonel Clausewitz, whom Diebitsch had sent to insist again on a categorical reply. York received him sullenly, and **said** to him: 'Keep aloof from me. **I do not wish to** have any thing to do with you. **Your accursed** Cossacks have allowed a messenger from Macdonald to pass through your lines, and he has brought me orders to march upon Piktupöhnen, and there join him. All doubts are at an end. Your troops do not arrive; you are too weak; I decline continuing negotiations which would cost me **my** head.' " *

"Did the general really say so?" asked the king, quickly. "Do you tell me the truth?"

* York's own words.—Vide Droysen, vol. i. p. 456.

"Yes, your majesty, it is the whole truth. General York said so; I was present when Clausewitz came to him. I remained with Colonel Röden in the room when Clausewitz, at last, at his urgent request, received from General York permission to deliver to him at least the letters he had brought with him from Generals d'Anvray and Diebitsch. The general read them; he then fixed his piercing eyes on Clausewitz, and said: 'Clausewitz, you are a Prussian! Do you believe that General d'Anvray's letter is sincere, and that Wittgenstein's troops will be on the Niemen on the 31st of December? Can you give me your word of honor upon it?' Lieutenant-Colonel Clausewitz gave him his word of honor. York was silent, and repeatedly paced the room, absorbed in his reflections; he then gave Clausewitz his hand, and said in a firm voice, and with a sublime air, 'You have me! Tell General Diebitsch that we will hold an interview in the morning at the mill of Poscherun, and that I have made up my mind to forsake the French and their cause. I will not go to Piktupöhnen!' When he said so, we who witnessed that great moment were no longer able to restrain our transports. Forgetful alike of etiquette and discipline, Röden, Clausewitz, and myself, rushed up to the general to embrace him, thanking him with tearful eyes, and telling him that he had fulfilled the most ardent wishes of the whole corps, and that all Prussian officers would receive with heart-felt rejoicings the news that we were to be delivered from the French alliance. But York gazed on us with grave, gloomy eyes, and said, with a faint smile: 'It is all very well for you, young men, to talk in this way. But the head of your old commander is tottering on his shoulders.'* In the morning he summoned all the officers of his corps to his headquarters, and informed them in an affecting speech of the decision he had come to."

"What did he say?" asked the king. "Can you repeat his words to me?"

"I can, your majesty; for, after returning to my room, I wrote down the speech I had heard in my memorandum-book, and I believe every word of it was engraven in my memory."

"Have you your memorandum-book here?"

"I have, your majesty."

"Read!"

Major Thile drew his memorandum-book from his breast-pocket, and read as follows "'Gentlemen, the French army has been annihilated by Heaven's avenging hand; the time has come for us to recover our independence by uniting with the Russian army. Let those who share my sentiments, and are ready to sacrifice their lives for the fatherland and for liberty, follow me; those who are unwilling to do so may remain with the French. Let the issue of our cause be whatever it may, I shall always esteem and honor even those who do not share my sentiments, and who prefer to remain. If we succeed, the king may, perhaps, pardon me for what I have done; if we are unsuccessful, then I must lose my head. In that case, I pray my friends to take care of my wife and children.' Your majesty," said Major Thile, closing his memorandum-book, "that was the whole speech."

"And what did the officers reply to it?" asked the king. "Mind! the truth!—I want to know the truth!"

"And I am courageous enough to tell you the truth, although I am afraid that your majesty will be displeased. All the officers received the general's speech with unbounded transports and with tears of joy. They shook hands, they embraced, and greeted each other, as if they had suddenly returned from a foreign country to their beloved fatherland; as if their tongues had suddenly been loosened, and liberty to use the language of their country had been restored to them. No one thought of remaining with the French; every one was animated with enthusiasm at the thought that he should at length risk his life for the cause of his country and his king; every one had in his heart, and on his lips, a fervent prayer for the new sacred cause which he was to serve again, and an imprecation for that which he had been obliged to serve. When the general ex-

---

* This whole scene is historical.—Vide Droysen, vol. i, p. 467.

claimed, in a ringing voice, 'Let us then, with the assistance of Providence, enter upon and achieve the task of liberation,' all shouted 'Amen! We will die rather than serve the enemy longer!' Your majesty, I have now told you nothing but the whole truth. If the general deserves punishment, all the officers of his corps deserve it. He called upon us to part with him if we did not share his convictions. But none of us did so, for his convictions were ours, and we are ready to share his punishment, too, if your majesty should punish York for what he did, as a noble and devoted patriot!"

"Your remarks are impertinent, major," said the king, sternly. "I will not allow myself to be dazzled by your tirades. Go! You need repose. Report to me early in the morning. You will then return with dispatches to the army. Good-by!"

CHAPTER XV.

THE WARNING.

"WELL, M. Chancellor," said the king, when Thile had left the room, "tell me your opinion— the best way by which we may counteract this senseless and rash step, and succeed in preserving our country from the disastrous consequences."

"Your majesty, then, is not willing to approve of the bold act York has taken?" asked Hardenberg.

"I hope you did not indulge for a moment in such a belief," exclaimed the king. "York was perhaps justified in preserving his troops from being needlessly sacrificed; but he should have based his conduct solely on this idea, and from it have explained his action. Instead of doing so, he justifies it by political motives, and thereby compromises and endangers my own position. Now, I am myself entirely at the mercy of France, and utterly destitute of means to brave the anger of Napoleon." *

---

* The king's words.—Vide Droysen, vol. I, p. 452.

"No," said Hardenberg, "your majesty is not entirely at the mercy of France, and Napoleon's anger must no longer be allowed to terrify Prussia. You have only to raise your voice and call out your faithful subjects, and the whole nation will rise as one man; thousands will rally round their king, and you will enter with an invincible army upon the holy war of liberation. It will not be with a visible army only that you will take the field—an invisible army will accompany you—the army of minds and hearts, the grand army whose chieftain is public opinion, whose soldier is every beggar on the street, whose cannon is every word that is uttered, every love-greeting and every blessing. Oh, your majesty, this 'grand army' will pave the way for you, and will enlist everywhere new recruits, fill your military chests, clothe and feed your soldiers, and, under your colors, fight the enemy whom all Germany—all Europe hates intensely, and whose yoke every one feels weighing upon his neck. Oh, let me assure your majesty that it is only for you to be willing, and all Prussia will rally round you for the war of liberation!"

"But I must not be willing," said the king; "it is contrary to my honor and my conscience. I pledged my word to the Emperor Napoleon; I am his ally; I am deeply impressed with the sanctity of my existing treaties with France, and feel, as every man of honor would, that the obligation to maintain them inviolate is only rendered the more sacred by the disasters which have overwhelmed the imperial armies. Besides, you look at things in a light by far too partial and rose-colored. Do not confound your enthusiastic hopes with stern reality. The 'grand army of public opinion,' to which you refer, is an ally which cannot be depended upon—it is fickle, turning with every wind—it is an ally prodigal of words, but not of deeds. If my soldiers were to be clothed and fed by public opinion, they would likely go naked and die of hunger. If my military chests wait for public opinion to fill them, they would remain empty. Public opinion, by the way, has always been on my side and against Napoleon; it has, for six years past, disapproved

—nay, indignantly condemned his course toward Prussia, and still it has permitted Napoleon to halve my states; to take much more than he was entitled to by the treaty of Tilsit; to leave his troops in my states, in spite of the express stipulations of the treaties; to impose contributions on Prussia and extort their payment. Public opinion deplored it as a terrible calamity that I should be, as it were, a prisoner here in the capital of my own monarchy, and at the palace of my ancestors, and live under the cannon of Spandau, a fortress unlawfully occupied by the French. Public opinion, I say, deplored my fate, but it did not come to my assistance; it did not preserve me from the humiliations which, at Dresden, I had to endure, not only at the hands of Napoleon, but of all the German princes. Do not, therefore, allude again to your 'grand army of public opinion;' I despise it, and know its fickle and faithless character. By virtue of the existing treaties, I made my troops participate in Napoleon's campaign against Russia. More than one-half of my soldiers have been devoured by wolves on the fields of Russia; the other half are now in open insurrection. And these are the troops with whom I am to conquer!—conquer that powerful France which is able to call up fresh armies as from the ground, and into the treasury of which her unlimited resources are pouring millions! No, no; I will not plunge into so hazardous an enterprise. I will not, for the sake of a chimera, risk my last provinces, the inheritance of my children; I could joyously give up my life in order to bring about a change of our present deplorable situation, but I am not at liberty to endanger my crown—the crown of my successor. Prussia must not be blotted from the map of nations; she shall not be swallowed by France, and I am therefore obliged patiently to bear the burden of these times and submit to circumstances. Hence, I am not at liberty to pardon General York's crime, but must punish him for his conduct in accordance with the laws of war. I must give satisfaction to the Emperor of France for the unheard-of conduct of my general, and he shall have it! General von York shall be superseded in his command, cashiered, and put on his trial before a military commission. General Kleist will take command of the troops in his place."

"And will your majesty cashier likewise all the officers who received the announcement of the bold resolution of their general with enthusiastic cheers?" asked Hardenberg. "Will your majesty likewise put on trial the spirit of resistance pervading the whole Prussian corps? I beseech you again, in the name of your army and your people—in the name of the magnanimous queen whose inspiring eyes are gazing upon us from yonder portrait—take a bold and sublime stand! Risk every thing in order to win every thing! Approve York's step, place yourself at the head of the army, call upon the Prussians—the Germans —to rally round your flag! Oh, your majesty, believe me, Germany is only waiting for your warcry. Every thing is prepared, all are armed—all weapons, all hands are ready—all eyes are fixed upon your majesty! Oh, do not hesitate longer; make our night end, and the new day commence. Declare war against France—leave her to her destiny!"

The king walked with rapid steps and in visible agitation; and, whenever he passed the queen's portrait, he raised his eyes toward it with an anxious expression. Standing in front of Hardenberg, and laying his hand on his shoulder, he looked gravely into his pale, quivering face. "Hardenberg," he said at last, in an undertone, "I cannot allow General York to remain unpunished; I am not at liberty to approve his course, even—well, yes, even though I should wish to do so. As commander-in-chief of my army it is above all incumbent on me to maintain discipline. York acted without regard to his instructions, and without having received any orders from me to enter into so dangerous a course, and I ought not afterward to approve what one of my generals has done in so reckless and arbitrary a manner. That would be rendering obedience dependent on the whims and inclinations of every officer of my army. Unconditional obedience, entire subordination of the individual will—that is the bond which keeps armies together, and I cannot loosen it. **Where** sacred and necessary principles are at stake, I must not listen to the voice of my heart!"

"But still you ought to listen to the voice of prudence, your majesty," exclaimed Hardenberg, emphatically. "Now, prudence renders it necessary for you to fight at this juncture against the perfidious enemy, who never fulfilled his treaties, never kept his word, and is even now plotting mischief."

"What do you mean?" asked the king, hastily.

"I mean that your majesty is every day in danger of being arrested at the slightest symptom that may appear suspicious to the French gentlemen, and of being secretly conveyed to France. I mean that the French are anxious that you should give them such a pretext, so that they might charge you with secret machinations, send you to France, and appropriate the whole of Prussia. Little King Jerome is tired of his improvised kingdom of Westphalia. He longs for a more exalted throne, the existence of which has already been consecrated by centuries, and for a crown which need not, like his present one, be specially created for him. Napoleon has promised his brother the crown and throne of Prussia in case your majesty should give him the slightest ground for complaint. He has therefore here in Berlin a host of spies charged with watching every word, movement, and step of your majesty. Oh, believe me, you are at all hours in danger of seizure and secret removal. I am familiar with the whole plot; by means of bribery, dissimulation, and cunning, I have wormed myself into the confidence of, and gained over to my side, some of these spies. They have informed me that every day, shortly before nightfall, a closed carriage drives up to the royal palace, and waits there all the night long; that, at a short distance from it, soldiers are posted in isolated groups behind the trees, on the opera place, and the corners of the streets intersecting the Linden; that the royal palace is surrounded constantly by a number of agents of the **French police,** and that some of

these men always find means to slip into the palace, where they conceal themselves in dark corners and in the garden, or the yard, in order to watch every movement of your majesty. What should be the object of all these proceedings, but, on the first occasion, at the slightest symptom of your defection, to seize the sacred person of your majesty, to carry into effect Jerome's ambitious schemes, and transform the theatre king **into a** real king?"

Frederick William's face grew pale and gloomy; he compressed his lips as he used to do when any thing displeasing was communicated to him. "You have told me one of the absurd stories with which nurses try to frighten their children," he said, harshly. "But I do not believe it, nor shall I allow myself to be frightened and take imprudent steps. No one will dare attack **or arrest** me. I am the faithful ally of France, and **have** proved by my actions that I am animated with honest intentions toward her, and stand sincerely by the alliance which I have pledged my word to maintain."

"But suppose France should look upon this defection of General York as brought about by the secret orders of your majesty? **Suppose Napoleon,** in his incessant distrust, and Jerome, in his ardent desire for the possession of Prussia, should, notwithstanding all protestations of your majesty to the contrary, believe in an understanding between York and his king, and therein find a welcome pretext for carrying into effect their infamous schemes, seizing your majesty, and annihilating Prussia?"

"I shall give them such convincing proofs of my sentiments that it will be impossible for them to believe in an understanding between myself and York," exclaimed the king. "Enough! I adhere to my resolution. York must be removed from his command, and General Kleist will be his successor. I shall, besides, address an autograph letter to Murat, the emperor's lieutenant at the head of the army, and express to him my profound indignation at what has occurred, and inform him of the penalty which I am about to inflict on York."

"Very well," said Hardenberg, sighing, "if your majesty so resolves, it must be done; but it should be done in haste—this very hour. Count St. Marsan is waiting for me at his residence, to learn from me the decisions of your majesty before sending off his couriers to the Emperor Napoleon. It will be necessary for us to lay before him the letter which your majesty intends to write to the King of Naples, as well as the formal order in regard to the removal of General York. You ought also at once to name the courier who is to convey your **majesty's orders** and letters to the two camps in Old Prussia."

"You are right; all this must be done immediately," said the king, seizing his silver bell and ringing. The door opened, and Timm the chamberlain entered. "Go to my aide-de-camp, Major Natzmer," said the king to him. "Inform him that he is to set out immediately on a journey, and should, therefore, quickly prepare. **In four hours every thing must be done, and Major Natzmer** must then be in my anteroom. Go yourself to him, Timm, and inform him **of** my orders. This one courier will be sufficient," said the king, turning again to Hardenberg, after Timm had left the room. "Natzmer will first repair to the headquarters of the King of Naples, deliver my letter to him, show him the orders intended for Kleist and York, and then go to the Russian camp in order to deliver these orders to my generals."

"Will your majesty not write also a letter to the **Emperor** Alexander, begging him to spare your troops, whom Wittgenstein henceforth will consider enemies, and to address a word of consolation and encouragement to the emperor, whose magnanimous heart will bitterly feel this new disappointment?"

"Very well," said the king, after a brief reflection, "I will write such a letter to Alexander, and Natzmer shall himself take it after previously seeing Murat, Wittgenstein, and York."

An hour afterward the king wrote his letters, and Hardenberg drew up the decree removing York from the command of the army. The chancellor of state then left the king's cabinet to repair to the residence of the French ambassador, and inform him of the resolutions of his majesty. The king looked after him long and musingly, and, folding his hands behind him, paced his room. A profound silence reigned around him; the storm of the cold January night swept dense masses of snow against the windows, making them rattle as if spectral hands were tapping at the panes; the wax-tapers on the silver candelabra, standing on the king's desk, had burned low, and their flickering light flashed on the noble portrait of the queen. The king noticed the fitfully illuminated face gazing upon him, as it were, with a quick and repeated greeting; he could not help gently nodding, as if to return the salutation, and then approached the portrait with slow steps.

"Louisa," he said, in a loud, solemn voice, "God has counted your tears, and taken upon Himself the revenge of your wrongs. It was at Piktupöhnen where you first met Napoleon, and where the overbearing man bowed your noble head in the dust. At Piktupöhnen the Queen of Prussia **implored the emperor of the French to** spare her country, and grant her lenient terms of peace. It was France now that was waiting for Prussia at the same place, asking Prussia for assistance, and Prussia refused it. Where the disgraceful alliance commenced has been seen its bitter end. God is just; He has counted your tears, and He is preparing your revenge. It began at Piktupöhnen."

———+———

CHAPTER XVI

THE DIPLOMATIST

DURING an hour Chancellor von Hardenberg, in the cabinet of the French ambassador, Count St. Marsan, conferred in an animated and grave manner as to Prussia's new position, and the guaranties she offered to France for the sincerity of her alliance. Count St. Marsan felt entirely satisfied, after reading the letter which King Frederick William had written to the King of

Naples, and the decree removing York from his command. He cordially shook hands with the chancellor, and assured him that this disagreeable affair would not leave the least vestige of distrust; that his august emperor would also feel entirely satisfied of the sincerity of the king's sentiments.

"And you may add that this will also satisfy the emperor of the sincerity of my sentiments toward **him**," said Hardenberg, smiling. "I know that Napoleon has unfortunately often distrusted me, and has believed me to be animated **with feelings hostile** to his greatness. Henceforth, **however, his** majesty will have to admit **that I am one of his** most reliable and faithful **adherents.** It was I who prevailed upon the king to stand by France so firmly and constantly. You are aware of it, and I need not conceal it from you, that King Frederick William loves the Emperor Alexander, and would be happy, if circumstances enabled him, to renew his alliance with his friend Alexander. The Emperor of Russia has already stretched out his hand toward him, and is only waiting for Frederick William to grasp it. York's defection was carefully prepared on the part of Russia; it was to be the impulse which should cause the king to take Alexander's hand. And let me tell you, confidentially, he was not only greatly inclined to do so, but even the enthusiasm of those gentlemen of his suite, who, heretofore, had always been ardent adherents of the Emperor of the French, had cooled down since the disasters of the grand army in Russia, and they believed it to be incumbent on them to advise the king to join Russia. But I—I have obtained a victory over them all, and, by my zeal and eloquence, have succeeded in convincing Frederick William that just now a firm maintenance of the alliance with France is most advantageous both to the honor and welfare of Prussia. The king saw the force of my arguments, and the consequence was that he rejected the proposals of Russia, and declared in favor of a faithful continuance of the alliance with France, as is proved by this letter to Murat, and this decree, removing York, which I have drawn up, and which is already signed. France may now confidently count on Prussia, for you see we have passed through our ordeal, and have proved faithful."

"Yes, you have," exclaimed Count St. Marsan, "and the reward and acknowledgment due to your fidelity will soon be conferred on you. The emperor knows full well that the magnanimous and disinterested character of your excellency will not permit him to bestow upon you **any other rewards** and thanks than those of honor and of the heart. As for the latter, please let me return them to you now in the name of the emperor and of France, and perhaps you will authorize me to inform him that your excellency will consider the grand cross of the Legion of Honor as a sufficient acknowledgment."

"Great Heaven!" exclaimed Hardenberg, with a face radiant with joy, "you have **divined the** object of my most secret wishes. You have read my mind, and understood my ambition. There is but one order to wear which is a proud honor, and this order has not as yet decorated my breast."

Count St. Marsan bent closer to the ear of the chancellor. "My noble friend," he said, smiling, and in a low voice, "we **shall fasten this order to** the breast **of the chancellor of state on the day** when we sign the marriage-contract of the crown prince and a princess of the house of Napoleon."

"Yes," exclaimed Hardenberg, "let it be so. I accept this condition. I shall not claim, nor deem myself worthy of receiving, this longed-for order before the day when the Prussian crown prince will be betrothed to an imperial princess of France. To bring about this joyful event will henceforth be for me an affair of the heart, and, moreover, to such an extent that, if this honor should previously be offered me, I would refuse it, because I first wish to deserve it."

"And does your excellency believe that you will have to wait long?" asked Count St. Marsan. "Do you believe that the day when the betrothal will take place is yet remote?"

"I hope not. The crown prince will be confirmed next month, and after his confirmation it will be time to speak of his marriage. I am satisfied that all will turn out well, and conformably to our wishes, provided—"

"Well?" asked St. Marsan, when Hardenberg suddenly paused. "Pray, your excellency, confide in me, and tell me the whole truth. You may rest assured of my most heart-felt gratitude, my entire discretion, and the most unreserved confidence on my part. I beseech you, therefore, to **speak out.**"

"Well, then," said Hardenberg, in a low voice, and with an air of entire sincerity, "I was going to say that every thing would turn out conformably to your wishes, provided the king do not listen to the incessant secret entreaties and insinuations of Russia, and the new Russian party at our court. So long as *I* remain here, I am afraid of nothing; but if those gentlemen should succeed in persuading the king to leave Berlin, and repair to a city where he would be closer to Russia, then I **would really be afraid.**"

"**And your excellency believes that the king** might entertain such an intention?" asked Count **St. Marsan, in breathless suspense.**

Hardenberg shrugged his shoulders. "I do **not** want to believe it," he said, "but I am almost afraid of it. However, both you and I will be vigilant. But listen, your excellency, the clock is striking two! Two o'clock in the morning! Both of us have yet to send off couriers, and then we may well be allowed to seek an hour's sleep for **our exhausted bodies.** Good-night, then, my dear count and ally!—good-night! I hasten to the king to tell him that France will be content with the satisfaction which we offer her, and thereby I shall procure him a quiet and peaceful slumber for the present night."

"Ah, you are in truth a magician, your excellency!" said St. Marsan, gayly, "for you understand both how to take away and give sleep. So **long as I am near** you, I forget all weariness; and after you have left me I shall, thanks to your words and promises, be able to sleep more quietly than I have **done for a long** time. You have quieted my soul, and my body therefore will also find rest. Bid me good-night again, for when *you* say so I will be sure to have it."

"Good-night, then, my dear count," said Hardenberg, shaking hands with his friend, and withdrawing, with a smile, from the room.

This affectionate smile was still playing round the lips of the chancellor when he entered his carriage. But no sooner had its door closed and the carriage was moving, than an expression of gloomy hatred overspread his features. "**I hope** I have quite succeeded in misleading St. Marsan and arousing his suspicions in regard to the king," he said to himself. "As the king refuses to listen to my warnings and supplications, and does not believe it to be possible that France should dare seize him, it is time to give him some irrefutable proofs. Perhaps he may then **make up** his mind to leave Berlin. I may sign this longed-for betrothal at some other place, too, and then fasten on my breast the order for which I am longing. In truth," he added, laughing, "it is no fault of mine that dear Count St. Marsan interprets my desire in the way he does. I did not name to him the order I wish to wear. It is no fault of mine that he imagines I **wish for** the grand cross of the Legion of Honor. To be sure, I wish to obtain an order of honor, but one of a German patriot, and that I can only obtain from the gratitude of my countrymen and impartial history."

The carriage stopped in front of the royal palace, and Hardenberg hastened to the king. Silence reigned in the anteroom; a few sleepy footmen were sitting on the cane chairs beside the door, and scarcely took notice of the arrival of the chancellor, who passed them with soft, hurried steps, and entered the small reception-room. Here, too, all was still, and the two candles **on the** table, which had burned low, **shed but a dim** light in the room. The chancellor **noticed two** figures sitting on both sides of the door leading **into** the adjoining room, **and slowly** swinging **to and fro, like the pendulum of a clock.** He **softly approached the** two sleepers. "Ah," he **whispered, with a smile,** "there sleeps Timm, the chamberlain, who is to announce my arrival to the king; and here sleeps Major Natzmer, to whom I want to say a word before he sets out." He laid his hand gently on the major's shoulder. Natzmer jumped up at once and drew himself up in a stiff, military attitude. "You are very prudent in nodding a little now," said Hardenberg, kindly giving him his hand, "for I am afraid you will not find much time for it during the remainder of the night. You are ready to set out immediately, are you not?"

"I am, your excellency."

"And your dispatches, I believe, are ready, too.—My dear Timm," he then said to the chamberlain, "pray announce my arrival to his majesty."

"I believe it is unnecessary," said Timm, with the familiarity of a favorite servant. "His majesty is waiting for your excellency."

"You had better announce my arrival," said Hardenberg, smiling, "for it might be possible that I surprise the king in the same manner as I did these two gentlemen here, and that would be disagreeable."

"That is true," said Timm, hastily approaching the door. "I will immediately announce your excellency."

No sooner had he left the room, than the chancellor laid his hand on the major's arm, and bent over him. "My friend," he said, in a low, hurried voice, "I know you share my views."

"Your excellency knows that I adore you as the statesman who holds the future happiness of Prussia in his hands, and that I abhor the French, who have brought Prussia to the brink of ruin."

"Will you do something to bring her back from this brink?"

"Yes, your excellency, though it cost my life."

"That would be a high price. No; we stand in need of your life and your arm, for Prussia will soon need all her soldiers. What I ask of you is not near so valuable. Listen to me. The king sends you as a courier to Old Prussia. Repair, in the first place, to Murat's headquarters, and deliver the king's letter to him. Go to the Russian headquarters, and call upon Prince Wittgenstein. All I ask of you is to inform Prince Wittgenstein that you are the bearer of two dispatches. Tell him that one is an autograph letter from the king to the Emperor Alexander, and the other a decree removing General York from his command, and ordering him to be put on his trial before a military commission."

"What!" exclaimed Natzmer, in dismay. "Our noble York is to be removed from his command?"

"Yes; the king has resolved to remove and cashier him, because he has gone over with his corps to the Russians."

"York gone over to the Russians!" exclaimed Natzmer, joyously. "And for this wondrously bold step I am to bring him a decree superseding and cashiering him?"

"That is what the king orders you to do, and, of course, you will have to obey. But, I repeat to you, the only thing I ask of you is to inform Prince Wittgenstein what dispatches are in your hands, and what their contents are."

"But suppose the king should not tell me anything about them? Suppose their contents, therefore, should be unknown to me?"

"The king himself will communicate the contents to you, and even order you to mention everywhere on the road that you are the bearer of a decree cashiering York, the criminal general. It is of great importance to his majesty that every one, and, above all, France, should learn that he is highly incensed at York's defection, and that— Hush! I hear Timm coming! You will comply with my request?"

"I shall inform Prince Wittgenstein of the contents of my dispatches."

"In that case, I hope York will be safe! Hush!"

The door opened again, and the chamberlain entered. "Your excellency was quite right," he said; "it was well that I announced your arrival His majesty, like ourselves, had fallen asleep But now he is awaiting you." He opened the folding-doors, and Hardenberg hastened across the adjoining room to the king's cabinet, to communicate to him the result of his interview with the French ambassador.

An hour afterward Major Natzmer received

three dispatches at the hands of the king. The first was a letter to Napoleon's lieutenant at the head of the French army, the King of Naples. In this Frederick William informed Murat that he was filled with the most intense indignation at the step York had taken, and that he had commissioned Major Natzmer to deliver a royal decree to General Kleist, authorizing him to take command of the troops and arrest General York. He declared further in this letter that, as a matter of course, he refused to ratify the convention, and that the Prussian troops, commanded by General Kleist, should be, as they had been heretofore, subject to the orders of the Emperor Napoleon, and his lieutenant, the King of Naples.* The second dispatch was confidential, to the Emperor Alexander, the contents of which the king had not communicated even to his chancellor of state. The third was, the decree superseding York, and ordering Kleist to take command of the troops.

"I think," said the king, after Natzmer had withdrawn, "we have now done every thing to appease Napoleon's wrath, and avert from Prussia all evil consequences. Are you not also of this opinion, M. Chancellor?"

"It only remains to send a special envoy to Napoleon himself and assure him of your majesty's profound indignation," said Hardenberg, gloomily. "The proud emperor, perhaps, expects such a proof of the fidelity of your majesty."

The king cast a quick and searching glance on the gloomy countenance of the chancellor, and then gazed for some time musingly. "You are right," he said, after a pause: "I must send a special envoy to Paris. When it is necessary to appease a bloodthirsty tiger, no means should be left untried. I myself will write to Napoleon and assure him that I will faithfully adhere to the alliance. Prince Hatzfeld will depart with this letter for Paris early in the morning."

"Your majesty will then have done every thing to satisfy the French of the sincerity of your friendly intentions toward them, but I am afraid they do not care to be satisfied."

"You believe, then, seriously that the French are menacing me?" asked the king, with a contemptuous smile.

"I am convinced of it, your majesty."

"But what do you believe, then? What are you afraid of?"

"As I said before, I am afraid they will dare abduct the sacred person of your majesty, and I beseech you to be on your guard; never leave your palace alone and unarmed; never go into the street without being attended by an armed escort."

"Ah," said the king, with a sad smile, "do not the French always see to it that I am attended by an escort? Am I not always surrounded by their spies and eavesdroppers?"

"If your majesty is aware of this, why do you not yield to my entreaties? Why do you not leave Berlin?"

"Perhaps to go to Potsdam? Shall I be less watched there by the spies? Shall I there be less a prisoner?"

"No, your majesty ought to leave Berlin in order to deliver yourself at one blow, and thoroughly, from this intolerable espionage. Your majesty ought to make up your mind to go to Breslau. There you would be nearer your army; there your faithful subjects and followers would rally round you, and the Emperor Alexander perhaps would soon come thither. At all events, your majesty would there be secure from the French spies, and your adherents would be delivered from their anxiety for the personal safety of your majesty."

"To Breslau!" exclaimed the king, anxiously. "That is impossible!—that would be pouring oil into the fire—that would be to advance on the path into which York has entered."

"It would be another step toward the deliverance of your majesty, the salvation of the country, and the annihilation of the tyrant!" said Hardenberg, raising his voice.

The king made no reply; he stepped to the window, and, turning his back to the chancellor, looked out musingly into the night. Hardenberg looked now at him, and then on the queen's portrait.

Suddenly his features grew milder, and an indescribable, imploring expression was to be seen in his eyes. "Help me, queen," he whispered, in a fervid tone. "Direct his heart, guardian angel of Prussia; render it strong and firm, and—"

The king turned again to the chancellor and approached him. "I cannot comply with your request," said Frederick William, "for, if I should go to Breslau, it would be equivalent to a declaration of war, and we are, unfortunately, not in a position to justify that. I must not rashly plunge myself **and my country into** a danger which probably would bring about our utter ruin. But I pledge you my word that, if your apprehensions should really be verified—if I really obtain proofs that **my person and liberty are menaced, I** shall then deem it incumbent on me to escape from this danger, and remove the seat of government to a **safer** place—perhaps Breslau."

"Is your majesty in earnest?" exclaimed Hardenberg, joyously. "You really intend, after having satisfied yourself that dangers are threatening you here, to leave Berlin and place yourself beyond the reach of the French?"

"I pledge you my word of honor that such is my intention," said the king, solemnly. "And now, enough! I believe both of us need a few hours' rest. In the course of the forenoon I will write the letter which Prince Hatzfeld is to take to Paris. Good-night, M. Chancellor!"

"Drive me home as fast as your horses can run," **shouted Hardenberg** to his coachman, on entering his **carriage.**

"We **shall be** there in five minutes," muttered **the** coachman, whipping his horses into a gallop.

Precisely **five** minutes afterward the carriage stopped in front of the chancellor's residence, and a well-dressed young man, hastily pushing aside the footman, opened the coach door.

"Ah, is it you, my dear Richard?" said Hardenberg, surprised. "Why have you not yet gone **to** bed?"

"Because I could not sleep while your excellency had **not** returned," said the young man, assisting the minister in alighting. "It is nearly four o'clock; **the whole house was greatly** alarmed."

"Well, and what were you afraid of, you dear fools?" asked Hardenberg, smilingly, while ascending the staircase.

"That your enemies had found means to kidnap you, and that the French had resorted to such an outrage to get rid of their most dangerous and powerful adversary."

"Ah, you big children!" exclaimed Hardenberg, laughing. "How could you give way to such senseless apprehensions while I was supping in a friendly way at the house of the French marshal?"

"Just for that reason, your excellency," said Richard, **smiling. "We may know well how to** get into a mouse-trap, but we do not know how to get out again. A panic prevailed among your servants, and the footmen had already made up their minds to arm themselves, go to the house of Marshal Augereau, and forcibly deliver your excellency."

"I was lucky, therefore, in escaping from such ridicule," said Hardenberg, gravely. "A minister who is taken home by his servants *vi et armis*, because he takes **the liberty not to return** at an early hour—what a splendid **farce** that would be! Pray be kind enough to tell my servants that their anxiety was very foolish. The greatest cordiality prevails between myself and the French gentlemen, and never before has there been such a friendly understanding between France and Prussia. My servants should always remember that, and commit no follies."

He intentionally said this in so loud a tone that the two footmen who preceded him with lights, as well as the two servants who followed, heard and understood every word he uttered. Hardenberg knew, therefore, that all his servants, fifteen minutes afterward, would be informed of the new *entente cordiale* between Prussia and France; that all Berlin would be aware of it on the following day, and that he would thus have attained his object.

"Your excellency will not yet retire?" asked Richard, when the minister, instead of going down the corridor to his bedroom, now halted at the door of his cabinet.

"No, M. Private Secretary," said Hardenberg, smiling. "As you are still awake, and apparently not sleepy, let us hold a little business conference. Come!"

No sooner had the servants put the lights on the table and left the room, than the face of the chancellor suddenly assumed a grave air. Ordering, with an imperious wave of his hand, his private secretary to be silent, he hastened to his desk and quickly wrote a few lines. "Richard," he said, casting the pen aside, and turning his head toward the young man, who witnessed his mysterious proceedings in great surprise, "Richard, come here!"

The young man hastened to him, and when Hardenberg gave him his hand, with a kind smile, Richard stooped down and pressed a tender kiss on it.

"Ah, lips as glowing as yours are, should kiss only beautiful girls," said Hardenberg, smiling.

"But these lips like better to kiss the hand of my benefactor, my protector," exclaimed the young man, "the kind hand of the man who extricated me from poverty, distress, and despair; who caused me to be fed, educated, and instructed; and who (until I myself, by his liberal kindness, was enabled to discharge this sacred duty) secured to my poor sick mother an existence free from cares."

"Do not allude to these trifles," said Hardenburg, carelessly. "Tell me, rather, do you regard me with respect and love?"

"Indescribably, your excellency; with the tenderness of a son, with the devotedness and fidelity of an old servant."

"Will you give me a proof of it?"

"I will, your excellency, and should you demand my heart's blood, I would willingly spill it for you!"

"Listen to me, then! In five minutes you must be on horseback and ride at a gallop, night and day, until you reach the Russian camp."

"In three days," said Richard, gravely, "but the journey will kill my horse."

"I will give you two horses for him, provided you arrive sooner than Major Natzmer at the headquarters of Prince Wittgenstein, commander-in-chief of the Russian troops!"

"Has Natzmer left Berlin already?"

"Yes, about an hour since, and you know that he is considered the most dashing and reckless horseman among all our officers. He has, moreover, another advantage. He will ride through the French camp, and will thence go to the Russian army, which is in the rear of it; but you must ride around the French camp, and go by way of Gumbinnen, unnoticed by the French, to the Russian headquarters. But the main point is, that you arrive there sooner than Major Natzmer."

"I will arrive there sooner. Your excellency knows that I have often been in Königsberg and its surroundings; I know all the by-ways and short cuts, and am, moreover, a good horseman."

"I know all that. I presume, therefore, that you will be with Wittgenstein before Natzmer reaches him. But you will tell no one that it is I who sent you. It is your task to find means to speak to him alone. But wait—I will give you your credentials. Take this ring. General Wittgenstein knows it; he has often seen it on my finger, and he is familiar with my coat-of-arms. Send him this ring by his aide-de-camp, and he will admit you."

"He will admit me, should I have to shoot down the sentinels."

"As soon as you are face to face with the general, deliver to him this little note, which I have penned. Read it, and then I will direct and seal it." He handed the paper to the young man. "Read it aloud," he said.

"In one or two hours Major Natzmer will arrive at the headquarters of your excellency, and beg leave to pass through the Russian camp in order to repair to General York. If your excellency should grant his request, and allow him to reach York's headquarters, the hopes of Prussian patriots would be annihilated at one fell swoop. But if York remains at the head of his troops, so enthusiastically attached to him—if the whole nation and the whole corps may from this fact derive the hope that York acted in compliance with the secret instructions of his king, then we may hope for a speedy change in our affairs. The fate and the future of Prussia therefore lie in the hands of noble General Wittgenstein."

"Now read over the letter twice for yourself," said Hardenberg, "that you may engrave it on your memory. **For in case** you should happen to lose **the letter, or if it** should be stolen from you, you **must verbally** repeat its contents to Prince **Wittgenstein.**"

"**I shall not lose it, and no one can steal it from me, for I shall carry it in my heart. I have nothing further to do than to deliver this letter to** him?"

"You have to say yet to the general a few words which I dare not intrust to paper, but only to your memory. You will say to him: 'Every thing is ready, and the period of procrastination and hesitation is drawing to a close. In a few days the king will leave Berlin, where he was in danger of being arrested by the French, and repair to Breslau. At Breslau he will issue a manifesto to his people and call them to arms.' Hush, young man, hush! no joyous exclamations, no transports! **You** must set out! It is high **time!** Beware of the bullets of the French, and the thievish hands of the Russians! You must reach Wittgenstein sooner than Natzmer does; do not forget that!"

"I shall not. Farewell, your excellency!"

"Farewell, my young friend. For a week at least, then, I shall not see your dear face greeting me every morning in my cabinet. You must indemnify me for it."

"In what way, your excellency?"

"You must embrace me, my young friend," exclaimed Hardenberg, stretching out his arms toward the young man.

"Oh, how kind, how generous you are!" exclaimed Richard, encircling the minister with his arms, and then reverentially kissing his shoulders and his hands.

"Now, your excellency," he said, rising quickly, "now I am ready to brave all dangers. Fare-

well!" He waved his hand again to the minister, **and left the room.**

"He will outstrip Natzmer," said Hardenberg, gazing after him; "it is an arrow of love which I have discharged, and it will not miss its aim. And now let us see how it is about the other arrow of love, which *mes chers amis mes ennemis* would like to discharge at me!" He rang the bell. **Conrad,** his faithful old footman, entered the room.

"Has there no note come for me?" asked Hardenberg.

"Yes, there has, your excellency," said Conrad, in a low and anxious tone. "Two letters, your excellency."

"**Give them to me.**"

Conrad cast a searching glance over the room he then drew two tiny, neatly-folded letters from his bosom and handed them to the minister. "She herself was here," he whispered, "and seemed very sad when I told her his excellency was not at home, and at first she refused to believe what I said. Only when I swore to her it was true, she gave me the first note. She returned afterward and brought **the second letter.**"

"But why do you tell me all this in so mysterious and timid a manner? Are you afraid lest some one has concealed himself, and plays the eavesdropper?"

"Not that exactly, your excellency," whispered Conrad; "but—the walls might have ears!" He pointed furtively at the ceiling of **the room.**

"Ah, we are here under my wife's bedroom," said Hardenberg, laughing. "You are afraid lest she should be awake, **and** overhear our words through the floor of her room."

"**Madame von Hardenberg sees,** hears, and divines every thing," said Conrad, with an air of dismay.

"It is true," muttered Hardenberg to himself. "her jealousy gives her a thousand eyes, and the events of her own life have familiarized her with all sorts of cabals and intrigues. In this way she succeeded in becoming my wife and in bearing my name before the world. But, no matter! I am not afraid of her Argus eyes, nor shall she prevent me from pursuing my own path, and adorning my dreary private life with a flower or two of pleasure."

"I believe and fear, your excellency," whispered Conrad, "Madame von Hardenberg has found out that the young lady was here, and that I received these letters from her."

"What makes you believe so?"

"Madame von Hardenberg sent for me at eleven o'clock to-night, and asked me when your excellency would return, and whither you had gone. When I told her I could not inform her, because I did not know, she was pleased to box my ears and threaten that she would before long turn me out of the house."

"These are, indeed, very valid reasons for your suppositions," said Hardenberg, smiling. "But do not be alarmed. I know how to protect you from being turned out, and as to having your ears boxed, it is no insult, by the soft little hands of a lady. Any other news?"

"Yes, your excellency, the physician of the young lady was here at a late hour in the evening, in order to tell me that she had again fallen asleep, and, before doing so, had announced she would be clairvoyant at eight o'clock in the morning."

"At eight o'clock!" exclaimed Hardenberg. "Do you hear, Conrad?—I must be there at eight o'clock. That is to say, you must awaken me at seven o'clock."

"But, your excellency, you will then have slept scarcely two hours," said Conrad, sadly.

"My old friend," said Hardenberg, "shall we not have time enough for sleeping in our graves? Let us be awake here on earth as long as possible. You will awaken me at seven o'clock. And now, come and assist me in retiring."

Fifteen minutes afterward Hardenberg was in bed. A neat little table, with a night-lamp burning on a golden plate, was standing at his bed-side. Before falling asleep, the chancellor read the two notes which Conrad had delivered to him. "Protestations of love!" he whispered, smiling and folding them up. "Protestations of love—

that is to say, falsehoods. But I must confess that this arrow, which *mes chers amis mes ennemis* have discharged at me, is at least very finely feathered and very attractive. At eight o'clock in the morning, then! Well, I shall see whether I do not succeed in playing my hostile friends a little trick, and in returning the arrow to their own breast."

CHAPTER XVII.

THE CLAIRVOYANTE.

FOR some time past the inhabitants of Berlin had paid a great deal of attention to the doings of Doctor Binder, and told each other wonderful stories of the new medical system of this strange physician. He treated his patients in an entirely novel way, and performed his cures in a manner bordering strongly on the romantic and miraculous. He neither felt the pulse of his sick friends, nor did he examine their tongue; he only gazed on them for a minute with his sombre, flaming eyes, and the patients then felt as if fascinated by them. Their pain ceased, their blood burned less ardently, and an indescribable feeling pervaded their body for a moment. When the doctor perceived this, he would raise both his hands, and with the palms softly and repeatedly stroke his subject's face. Then the sufferer's cheeks colored; a wondrous, long-forgotten smile played round the lips which, for many months, had opened only to utter prayers, or sighs and complaints; the dimmed eyes began to brighten, and fixed themselves with a radiant expression on the face of the doctor, whose steadfast, piercing glances seemed to penetrate the sick one's countenance, and reach down into his soul, in order to divine, in its innermost recesses, his most secret feelings and thoughts. By and by a sweet peace pervaded the soul of the patient; his aching limbs relaxed; he folded his hands, which had hitherto moved convulsively and restively on the counterpane; the eyes, which had steadfastly rested on the face of the wonderful physician, closed gradually, and soon his long and regular breathings indicated that he had at length found the slumber which, during his sickness, he had so long sought and yearned for.

It is true, the patient awoke after a time, and his sufferings returned; the end of his slumber was often accompanied by painful convulsions, an indescribable feeling of depression, and the most profound sadness, but Dr. Binder was present; his eyes exorcised the patient's pain, his hands quieted the quivering limbs, and chased away the tears, and the sufferer fell again into a sweet and refreshing slumber. This lulling the patient to sleep, this fascinating gaze, and laying on of hands, were the only medicines which the doctor administered, and by which he succeeded in freeing them from their sufferings and diseases. People related the most wonderful cures which he had performed; they spoke of persons who had been blind ever since their birth, and whom he had caused to see —of deaf-mutes, to whom he had given the power of speech and hearing after a few days' treatment—of lame men, who suddenly, after being touched by the doctor's hands, had thrown away their crutches, and walked freely and easily.

But the public's attention was particularly riveted by the case of a young girl who had been for some time past under Dr. Binder's treatment. She had come from a distant city to seek a cure at the hands of the famous physician and pupil of Mesmer. A bad cold had brought about a paralysis of all her limbs; she was unable to move her hands and feet, and had for months lain on her bed as motionless, rigid, and dumb, as a marble statue. Her parents had, in the anguish of their heart, at length applied to Dr. Binder. The doctor received her into his house. He publicly invited all the physicians of Berlin to visit his patient, to examine her condition, and to satisfy themselves of the efficacy of his cure. He also requested the public to watch the progress of it, and to come to his house at the hours when he lulled his patient to sleep. The physicians had disdainfully refused to have any thing to do with the "quack doctor," who pretended to cure

diseases without medicines; but the public appeared the more eagerly.

And this public enjoyed the satisfaction of seeing that the motionless form of the young girl, who at first had lain on the bed as rigid as stone, very slowly commenced to move. It was seen that, a few days afterward, she raised her right hand, and, shortly after, her right foot; gradually life and motion were restored to her limbs, and at length, at a truly solemn hour, the young girl, at the doctor's loudly-uttered command, arose from her couch and paced the room with firm and steady steps. It is true she uttered a piercing cry, and fell at the feet of the doctor, her limbs quivering as though she were seized with convulsion, but gradually she grew more quiet; a peaceful expression beamed from her features, and she commenced talking in a tone of joyous enthusiasm. She spoke of the wonderful world on which she was gazing with her inward eyes, of the visions which burst on her soul, and her lips whispered strange prophecies. This condition of the patient repeatedly occurred every day, and with unfailing regularity followed every "crisis."

The young woman had become a clairvoyante; and it was a truly wonderful fact that she, who, according to the statements of her relatives, had never cared for politics or public affairs, and to whom it was entirely indifferent whether Napoleon or any other sovereign ruled Germany, suddenly, in her clairvoyant state, devoted her whole attention to political questions, and that she had, as it were, become a prophetess of the destinies of states.

It was not very strange, therefore, that this phenomenon excited even the attention of statesmen, and that they too went to see the clairvoyante in her political ecstasy, and to put to her questions on public affairs, which she answered always with truly wonderful tact, and with the most profound insight into all such questions.

Among those who took an interest in her was the chancellor of state, Minister von Hardenberg. Curiosity had at first induced him to call upon her; then her clever and piquant remarks struck him as something very strange, and at last he be came a regular visitor. Of late, at his special request, the room of the patient, during her crises and clairvoyant trances, had been shut against all other visitors, and only the chancellor and the physician were present.

The young woman, who, during her trances, regularly announced at what hour of the following day she would relapse into this condition, had predicted that she would awake from her magnetic slumber at eight o'clock in the morning, and would then be in a state of clairvoyance. This hour had not yet arrived; the clock which stood in her room on the bureau under the looking-glass indicated that about ten minutes were still wanting to the stated time. A profound silence reigned in the room of the young patient. The physician sat reading on a high-backed chair at her bedside—his book contained the history and revelations of Swedenborg, the great Swedish ghost-seer. From time to time, however, he turned his large, flashing eyes toward the young woman, and seemed to watch her slumber with searching glances.

The patient was motionless and rigid. A white, neat *negligée* enveloped her slender figure, which was stretched out on the bed without being covered with a counterpane. Her small, beautifully-shaped hands were folded on her breast, her head was thrown back sideways, and rested on a pillow of crimson velvet, which contrasted strangely with her pale face, and black hair, that overhung her marble cheeks in long tresses. The clock was striking eight. The doctor cast a quick glance on the patient, and then slowly closed his book. She began to stir and opened her lips, from which issued a long, painful sigh. At this moment there was heard the roll of a carriage on the street. The noise ceased, the carriage seemed to stop in front of the house. The clairvoyante shuddered, and joy kindled her countenance. "He is coming! he is coming!" she said, in a deep, melodious voice. "I see him ascending the staircase. He is pale and exhausted, and his eyes are dim, for he has slept but little. Government affairs have kept him awake. Oh, now I am well, for there he is!"

In fact, the door softly opened, and the chancellor cautiously entered. By a quick wave of his hand, he ordered the doctor not to meet him, and then approached the bed softly and on tiptoe.

The young woman did not change her position; her eyelashes did not quiver, nor did she open her eyes, and yet she seemed to see Hardenberg, for she said in a mournful and tremulous voice: "Well, doctor, was I not right? Just see how pale he looks, and how the sweet smile with which he formerly used to come to us is to-day very faintly playing round his lips like a little will-o'-the-wisp! But I told you already he has slept only two hours; he had to be so long minister of state as to find scarcely two hours' rest for the poor, exhausted man."

The physician cast an inquiring glance on the chancellor. Hardenberg nodded smilingly. "You are right, Frederica," he said. "I was minister of state all day long yesterday."

"No, no," she exclaimed, "not all the day. At the commencement of Marshal Augereau's supper you were merry, and succeeded in forgetting your onerous business; and had not the secretary of Count St. Marsan made his appearance and brought the dispatches, you would have finished your pheasant's wing with good appetite and in the best of spirits."

The minister's face assumed an air of astonishment, and almost of terror. "Ah," he said, "it seems you were present at that supper?"

"Certainly I was, for my soul is accompanying you all the time, and my soul is the eye of my body. I see all you do, and know all your thoughts."

"Well, then," said Hardenberg, smiling, "tell me what you saw last night. Look backward, Frederica, and tell me where I was, and what I did."

"Then you doubt my words?" she asked, reproachfully. "You want to see whether I am able to tell you the truth? You know that it makes my eyes ache to look backward, and that my spirit soars with easier flight into the future than the past!"

"Do so nevertheless, Frederica," said Hardenberg, imperiously. "I wish you to do so!" He laid his hand upon her arm, and the contact made her start as an electric shock.

"I will obey," she whispered, in an humble tone. "I see you sitting at the table of Marshal Augereau. You are in excellent spirits; you are just telling the marshal that the betrothed of the crown prince with a princess of the house of Napoleon will take place before long; Count Narbonne is complaining of the political conversations with which you are spicing the supper in too piquant a manner; dispatches arrive and disturb your mirth."

"From whom do these dispatches come?" asked Hardenberg.

"From Marshal Macdonald, who addressed them to the French ambassador, Count St. Marsan."

"Do you know their contents?"

"I am reading them. There is, in the first place, a letter from General York—"

"Hush!" interrupted Hardenburg; "we will speak of that hereafter; do not allude to it now. Tell me what else I did last night."

"After reading the dispatches, you hastened to the king to inform him of the dreadful news. Scarcely had you been with him for a few minutes, when a courier from General York arrived and delivered dispatches concerning the same subject to which the others had referred. After a protracted interview with the king, you went to the French ambassador, and informed him of the sentiments and resolutions of his majesty. The count declared himself satisfied with what you told him, and you then hastened back to the king. You there met Major Natzmer, whom the king intended to dispatch as a courier to Murat and General York. You entered the king's room and had another protracted interview with him. Thereupon you returned to your residence."

"With whom did I speak there first of all?"

The clairvoyante was silent for a moment. "I do not see it," she said, "the night is so dark."

"Open your eyes until you see!"

"Ah, I see now!" she exclaimed. "Your excellency spoke with old Conrad. He accompanied you to your bedroom and handed you two letters."

"She is right," muttered the chancellor, loudly enough to be heard by the young woman and the physician. "Yes, she is right; it is all precisely as she says." He then asked aloud: "Did I speak with any one else than Conrad?"

"No," she said; "I do not see anybody else. Conrad told you that I would open the eyes of my soul and see at eight o'clock this morning. You ordered him to awaken you at seven o'clock, and went to bed."

"What did I do before falling asleep?"

"You read the two little notes," she said, with a coy smile.

The chancellor turned his eyes toward the physician, who witnessed this scene in silent and solemn earnestness. "Doctor Binder," he said, "all that this young lady told me just now is strictly true. All my doubts are henceforth dispelled, and from this hour I am one of the believers. No; I say this is no deception, no imposition; it is a mystery of nature, which I am unable to explain, but in which I am compelled to believe. It is given to this young lady to look with the eyes of her soul into the past, as well as into the future, and to perceive and penetrate the most secret things. I believe in her, and shall henceforth allow myself to be directed and instructed by her revelations. I thank you for having brought this wonderful girl to my notice, and you may always count on my heart-felt gratitude."

"Belief in the high art of my science and doctrines is the only gratitude I am yearning for, and my only desire is not to be prevented from healing poor patients and making suffering humanity happy by my holy science."

"No one shall be allowed to prevent you from doing so as long as I am minister, I pledge you my word," said Hardenberg, gravely. "Take heart, therefore, and do not be afraid. I am your disciple, and at the same time your protector. But now grant me a request: I should like to put to our charming seer yet a few questions in re gard to last night's events. She shall, in her inspired and prophetic prescience, give me her advice and tell me what course I must pursue; but, in doing so, I shall have to allude to state secrets, and to speak of affairs which no one is allowed to know but the king and his ministers, and—"

"I pray your excellency to permit me to leave you alone with our young seer," interrupted Doctor Binder, with a polite smile. "I have to see several patients, and my presence is required at the 'Hall of Crises' below, for my two young assistants are scarcely able to restrain our female patients when the crisis sets in."

"Go, then, to your patients," said Hardenberg; "I shall stay here with our clairvoyante until she awakes."

"If your excellency needs any thing," said the doctor, approaching the door, "it will only be necessary for you to ring the bell; the nurse is in the reception-room, and will immediately call my assistants."

He bowed to Hardenberg, bent once more with a searching glance over the couch of his patient, drew with his hands a few circles over her head, and left the room with noiseless steps. The chancellor and the clairvoyante were alone.

———+———

CHAPTER XVIII.

AN ADVENTURESS.

WHEN the physician left the room, the chancellor returned to the bedside of the young woman; her position was the same, and her eyes were still closed. She did not see, therefore, the sarcastic smile with which Hardenberg looked down upon her, or the proud, triumphant expression that was beaming from his eyes. Hers were closed, and, notwithstanding her clairvoyance, she saw nothing, nor did Hardenberg's voice betray to her aught of the expression of his countenance or the character of his thoughts.

"Frederica," he said, in his soft, gentle voice,

"speak to me now, my seer; be my prophetess now, and let me see the future. Tell me what I must do in order to reconcile all these dissensions, and harmonize all these clashing interests. On which side is justice, prosperity, and peace?"

"On the side of the great man whose gigantic strength has lifted the world out of its hinges, and given it a new aspect," she said, gravely. "Stand faithfully by the alliance with France, unless you wish the crown to fall from the head of your king, and Prussia to be divided into two provinces, one annexed to the kingdom of Westphalia, and the other to the duchy of Warsaw."

"But will France then still have power to do so?" asked Hardenberg; "is not France herself on the brink of the abyss into which she has hurled all states, princes, and crowns?"

"France is as powerful to-day as she ever was," responded the seer. "New armies at the beck of Napoleon will spring from the ground, his military chests will be filled with new millions, and the invincible chieftain will lead his legions to new victories. Woe then to Prussia if she proves faithless—woe to her, if, in insensate infatuation, she turns her back upon France, and allows herself to listen to the insinuations and promises by which Russia is trying to gain her over to her side! Russia herself is weak and exhausted; she will be unable to afford Prussia any adequate support. Be on your guard! Russia has always been a perfidious ally; she has always crushed the hand of her allies in her grasp, while seemingly giving a pledge of her good faith. France alone is offering to Prussia substantial guaranties of peace; Napoleon alone must remain the protector of Prussia. Banish, therefore, the insidious thoughts that are troubling your soul; try no longer to dissuade the king from adhering to the alliance. Do not try to persuade him to approve York's defection! He is a traitor, whose head must fall; for such is the decree of the laws of war. To approve his defection is to throw down the gauntlet to France, and annihilate Prussia!"

"You have played your part to perfection!" exclaimed Hardenberg, laughing. "Please ac

Leaping into the middle of the room, as light-footed as a sylph, and fascinating as one of the Graces, she began to dance.   p. 103

cept my sincere congratulations, my dear child; the greatest actress in the world could not perform her *rôle* any better than you have done to-day, and ever since I became acquainted with you."

At the first words of the chancellor, the clairvoyante gave a violent start; a tremor pervaded her whole frame, and a deep blush suffused her cheeks for a moment; but all this quickly passed away, and now she was again as rigid and motionless as she was before.

Hardenberg's eyes were fixed on her. "You do not desire to understand me, Frederica," he said. "Well, then, I will speak somewhat more lucidly. Will you permit me to ask two additional questions?"

"You know very well that I must reply when your soul commands me to do so," said the young woman, in a perfectly calm voice, "for your soul has power over mine, and I must obey it."

"Well, then—my first question: did I really, last night, on returning to my residence, speak with no one but old Conrad? Was no one but he in my room until I went to bed? Look sharp, open the eyes of your soul as wide as you can, and then reply!"

"I see," she said, after a pause; "but I see that you were alone with Conrad, and with the thoughts of a lady who loves you."

"I am very glad that you tell me so," said Hardenberg, calmly, "for I understand from it that my enemies, who are furnishing you with correct reports as to all my doings, have yet remained ignorant of an affair in which I was engaged last night. For there really was another person with me, and your patrons would give a great deal to find out what instructions I gave to that person. Now, as to my second question; but I hope you hear my words, *ma toute belle*, and have not yet passed from an unnatural sleep into a natural one!"

"I hear you, and I am ready to answer if your soul commands me."

"Well, then," said Hardenberg, bending over her, and fixing his piercing eyes upon her countenance, "my question is this: How much do your protectors give you for playing the part which you performed before me?"

A pause ensued. Suddenly the clairvoyante opened her eyes, gazing with an indescribable expression on the face of the minister still bending over her.

"They give me nothing," she said, in a firm, sonorous voice, "but the hope of acquiring a brilliant position in the future."

"You confess, then, that you have played a considerable farce?" asked Chancellor von Hardenberg, smiling.

"I confess that I have played my part very badly, and that your eagle eye is able to penetrate every thing. I confess that I adore you for having unmasked me," she exclaimed, quickly encircling Hardenberg's neck with her arms, drawing his head down to her, and pressing a glowing kiss on his lips. Then, still keeping her arms around his neck, she raised herself from the couch, and leaned for a moment against the manly form of the chancellor.

Disengaging herself from him, she jumped from the bed to the floor, and, spreading out her arms, and throwing back her head, she exclaimed in a jubilant voice: "I am free! I need no longer play my irksome *rôle!* Oh, I am free!"

Leaping into the middle of the room, as light-footed as a sylph, and fascinating as one of the graces, she began to dance, raising her feet and moving her arms in a slow, measured manner, at the outset; but, turning more rapidly, with more passionate movement and increasing ardor, her countenance grew more glowing and animated. Her large black eyes flashed fire—an air of wild, bacchantic ecstasy pervaded her whole appearance, her cheeks were burning, her beautiful red lips were half opened, and revealed her ivory teeth, and her uplifted arms (from which the wide sleeves of her *négligée* had fallen back to the shoulders) were of the most charming contour. Concluding her dance, she glided breathless and with panting bosom toward Hardenberg, who had sunk into the easy-chair, and was looking on with wondering eyes. Bursting into loud, melodious laughter, she sat at his feet, and, pressing her glowing face against his knees, looked searchingly and suppliantly into his eyes.

"You are angry with me," she said; "oh, pardon me, but I had first to give vent to my exultation. Now I will be quite sensible."

"And what do you call sensible, then?" asked Hardenberg, who, under the power of the woman's glances, vainly tried to impart to his countenance an air of gravity and sternness.

"I call it sensible to reply honestly to the questions your excellency will put to me now," she said, in a caressing tone.

"Well, then, let us see whether you are really sensible or not," said Hardenberg. "In the first place, please rise."

She shook her head slowly. "No," she said, "I will remain at your feet until you have heard my confession and granted me absolution."

"And suppose I refuse to grant you absolution?"

"Then I shall die at your feet!"

"Ah, it is not so easy to die."

"It is easy to die when one wants to, and has such a friend as this is," she exclaimed, drawing from her hair one of the two long silver pins with which her heavy black tresses were partially fastened.

"Strange girl!" murmured Hardenberg, surprised, while she was looking up to him with radiant eyes, and a smile playing on her lips.

"Will you ask me now?" she then said, gently and almost humbly. "I am lying here at your feet as if you were my confessor, and I am longing with trembling impatience for my absolution."

"Well, then, tell me, in the first place, who you are."

"Who am I?" she asked. "A cheat, who, by intrigues, cabals, and cunning, tried to attain the object she yearned for so intensely, namely, to lie at the feet of a noble and eminent man, as she is doing now, and to tell him that she loves him. Who am I? An adventuress, who has gone out into the world to seek her fortune; to play, if possible, a prominent part; to acquire a distinguished name, and to obtain riches, power,

and influence. Who am I? A diver, who has plunged with reckless audacity into the foaming sea, to find at its bottom either pearls or a grave."

"But, my child," said Hardenberg, "do you not know that the divers, when plunging into the sea to seek pearls, always gird a safety-rope around their waist for the purpose of being drawn to the surface whenever they are in danger of drowning?"

"The man who loves me will be my safety-rope and draw me up," she said, gravely.

Hardenberg laughed. "In truth," he said, "I must admire your sincerity and naïveté. You must be very courageous to utter such truths about yourself."

"Certainly, it would have been easier to play the virtuous, forsaken, and unfortunate girl," she said, with a contemptuous smile. "It would have been less troublesome to throw myself at your feet, bathed in a flood of tears, and to say, 'Oh, have mercy upon me! Free me from this unworthy rôle which has been forced upon me! Save me from the torture of being compelled to dissimulate, to lie, and to cheat. Virtue dwells in my heart, innocence and truth are upon my lips. I have been forced to play a part that dishonors me. Have mercy upon me, save me from the snares threatening me!'" While saying so, she imparted to her features precisely the expression that was adapted to her words; she had spoken in a tremulous, suppliant voice, with folded hands and tearful eyes.

"Poor child," exclaimed Hardenberg, surprised, "you weep, you are deeply moved! Ah, now at last you show me your true face, now you cause me to see the poor, innocent, and unfortunate child that you really are!"

She shook away her tears and burst into laughter. "No," she exclaimed, "I have only proved to you that I would be able to play the virtuous and innocent girl to perfection, and that I might, perhaps, thereby succeed in touching your noble heart. But you have commanded me to tell you the truth, and I have pledged you my word to do so. I tell you, then, I am no persecuted, virtuous girl, no innocent angel; I am a woman, carrying a heaven and a hell in her bosom; I can be an angel, if happiness and love favor me; I will be a demon, if fate be hostile to me. Yes," she exclaimed, jumping up and pacing the room in great agitation, "there are hours and days when I myself believe that I am a demon, an angel hurled down from heaven, and doomed to walk the earth on account of some crime. There are hours when heavenly recollections fill my imagination, when an indescribable, blissful yearning is, as it were, enveloping me in a veil—when there are resounding in my heart the sweetest and most enchanting notes of sacred words and devout prayers, and when it seems to me as though I were sitting in **the midst of radiant** angels, surrounded by luminous clouds, at the feet of God, His breath upon my cheek, and looking down with compassionate, merciful love upon the world, lying at an unfathomable distance under my feet. And then I say to myself: 'You have reviled and slandered yourself; you are, after all, a good angel; God is with you, and prayer, love, and innocence, are in your heart.' Then it suddenly seems to me as if my heart were rent, and I heard loud, scornful laughter. I fall from my heaven; I look around and behold men, with their bitter-sweet faces, smiling on, and lying to, each other; I see all their duplicity and their infamy; I laugh at my own transports and swear never to be human with humanity, but a demon with the demons—to cheat as they cheat, to lie, and win from them as much happiness, honor, and wealth, as I can with some mimic talent, a cool and sharp mind, a pretty figure, and an ugly face."

"Ah, you are slandering yourself," exclaimed Hardenberg, smiling. "You have no ugly face."

She hastened to the looking-glass, and gazed on herself with searching glances. "Yes," she said, "I am really ugly. My mouth is too large, my lips too full, my face is angular and by no means prepossessing, my nose is vulgar, my forehead too low and too wide, these bushy eyebrows become rather a grenadier than a young lady, and these large black eyes look like a couple of sentinels, which, with sharp glances, have

to watch the rabble of nose, mouth, ear, and cheek, lest one should try to escape from disgust at the ugliness of the others. But I do not regret my want of beauty, for it is uncommon and piquant, and I can imagine that a gifted, **eminent** man, who is tired of the pretty faces of so-called virtuous women, may feel attracted by my ugliness. Beauty at least always becomes tiresome, for it treats you at once to all that it is and has, but ugliness excites your curiosity more and more from day to day, for, at certain moments, it may be transformed into beauty!"

"Your own case shows that," said Hardenberg, "for, although you call yourself ugly, there is a fascinating beauty in your whole appearance."

She gazed on him with a long and radiant look. "You are a great man, a genius, and you are, therefore, able to understand me. I will tell you my history now, that you may at last grant me the blessing of your forgiveness."

"Well, tell me your history," exclaimed Hardenberg. "Come, Frederica, sit down by my side here on the couch on which you have so often reposed as a modern Pythia, and proclaimed to me the oracles which your mysterious priest had whispered to you. Now you are no priestess uttering equivocal wisdom, but a young woman telling the truth, and making me listen to the revelations of her heart."

"A young woman," she repeated, sighing and reclining on the bed close to the easy-chair on which Hardenberg was sitting. "Am I young, then? It seems to me sometimes as though I were old—so old as no longer to have any illusions, any hopes or wishes; as though I were the 'Wandering Jew' who has been travelling through the world so many centuries, seeking perpetually for the rest which he can nowhere find. But still you are right; I am young, for I am only twenty years old."

"And who are your parents? Where do they live?"

"Who are my parents?" she asked, laughing. "My father was a holy man, a high-priest in the temple of Time. It depended on him when men were to awake or sleep, eat or work. It was his will that regulated rendezvous and weddings, parties and arrests, and he had no other master than the sun. He allowed the sun alone to guide him, and still he was no Persian!"

"But he was a watchmaker?" asked Hardenberg, smiling.

"Yes, he was a watchmaker, and, thanks to him, the whole town where he lived knew exactly what time it was. Only my mother did not know it. She believed herself to be a great lady, although she was only a poor watchmaker's wife, **but was unable to** efface the recollections of her youth. She was the daughter of a French marquis, who, after gambling away his whole fortune at the court of Louis XV., had emigrated with his young wife and daughter to Berlin, in order to seek another fortune at the court of Frederick the Great. But Frederick the Great had already become somewhat distrustful of the roving **marquises and counts whom France sent to Berlin. Marquis de Barbasson, my worthy grandfather, received, therefore, no office and no money, and a time of distress set in, such as he would pre**viously have deemed utterly unlikely to befall the descendant of his ancestors. He left Berlin with his family, to make his living somewhere else as a teacher of languages. He travelled from one place to another, and arrived at length at a small **town called** New Brandenburg. There he remained, for his feet were weary, and his poor wife was sick and tired of life. Well, Madame la Marquise de Barbasson died, and the marquis taught the young ladies of New Brandenburg how to conjugate *avoir* and *être;* his daughter assisted him, and, as she was very pretty, she taught many a young man how to conjugate *aimer.* But who would have thought of marrying the daughter of a French adventurer, who, it is true, styled himself marquis, but was as poor as a beggar! **He** was unable long to bear the privations and humiliations of his life; he fled from his creditors, **and perhaps** also from his remorse, by committing suicide; and his daughter, who was twenty years of age at that time, remained alone, and without any other inheritance than the debts of her father. One of the principal creditors of the marquis was the proprietor of the house in which father and daughter had lived for three years without paying rent, or refunding the small sums he had lent to them. This proprietor was a young watchmaker, named Hahn, an excellent young man, who had given the family of the French marquis not only his money, but his heart. He loved the young Marquise de Barbasson, unfortunate, or, if you prefer, fortunate man! for his courtship was successful. Now, after the death of the old marquis, he played the part of an importunate creditor, and told her she had the alternative of paying or marrying him. The young Marquise de Barbasson married him, and then paid the poor watchmaker in a manner which was not very pleasant to him. She never forgave him for having reduced her to the humble position of a watchmaker's wife, and found it disgusting to be obliged to call herself Hahn, after having so long borne the aristocratic name of Barbasson. However that might be, she was his wife, and I have the honor to represent in my humble person the legitimate daughter of Hahn, the watchmaker, and the Marquise de Barbasson."

"And I must confess that you are representing your mother and your father in a highly becoming manner," said Hardenberg. "You have the bearing and the *savoir vivre* of a French marquise, and from your oracular sayings I have seen that you are as familiar with the time as a watchmaker is. But I can imagine that the descent of your parents produced many a discord in your life."

"Say rather that my whole life was a discord," she exclaimed, vehemently, "and that I have lived in an unending conflict between my head and my heart, my reality and my imagination. Oh, how often, when lying in dreary loneliness, in the shade of an oak on the shore of the charming lake near the small town in which we lived—how often did I utter loud cries of anguish, and say to the billows that washed the shore with a low, murmuring sound: 'I am a French marquise, there is aristocratic blood in my veins; it is my vocation to shine at the courts of kings, and to see counts and princes at my feet!' Yet none but the waves of the lake believed my words; men treated me never as a Marquise de Barbasson, but only as little Frederica Hahn, daughter of a poor watchmaker. I felt this as a personal insult, and at many a bitter hour it seemed to me as though, like my mother, I hated my poor father because he had robbed us of our brilliant name and our nobility. My father bore my whims patiently, for he loved me, and I believe he loved nothing on earth better than his daughter. He saw that I was pining away in the wearisome loneliness of our dull life ; he knew that ambition was burning in my heart like a torrent of fire, and he wept with me and begged my pardon for being a poor watchmaker, and no nobleman. He did all he could to make amends for this wrong; he treated me not as his daughter, but as his superior; and, although we were scarcely in easy circumstances, he surrounded me with all comforts becoming an aristocratic young lady. I had my servants, my own room, a tolerably fashionable toilet, a piano, a small library ; and my father was proud of being able to have me instructed by the best and most expensive teachers, and of hearing that I was their most industrious and talented pupil. But what good did all this do me ? I remained what I was—Frederica Hahn, the watchmaker's daughter—and the blood of the Barbassons revolted against my position in life ; and the marquises and viscounts, my distinguished ancestors, appeared to my inward eye, and seemed to beckon me and call me to the proud castles which had formerly belonged to our family. But how should I get thither ?—how escape from my small native town ?—how rid myself of the burden of my name and my birth? That was the question which put my brain night and day on the rack, and to which my intellect was unable to make a satisfactory reply. An accident, however, came to my assistance."

"Ah, in truth, I am anxious to hear this," exclaimed Hardenberg, "for I am listening to you in breathless suspense, and am as eager to learn the conclusion of your history as though it were the *dénouement* of a drama. An accident, then,

furnished you with a rep., my beautiful Marquise de Barbasson ?"

"Yes, your excellency, and never shall I forget the day and the hour. It was on a beautiful day last autumn. As I was in the habit of doing every day, I had gone with my book into the forest on the shore of the lake. I lay in my favorite place under a large oak, in the dark foliage of which the birds were singing, while the waves of the lake at my feet were a sweet accompaniment. I was reading the lately published poetry of my favorite bard, Goethe, and had just finished 'The Wandering Fool.' This poem struck my heart as lightning. I dropped the book, looked up to the clouds and shouted to them: 'What are you but wandering fools! Oh, take me with you!' But the clouds did not reply to me; they passed on in silence, and my sad eyes turned to the lake extended before me like a polished mirror, and mingling with the blue mists of the horizon, and I said to the murmuring waves, as I had said to the clouds: 'Take me with you, wandering fools! I am suffocating in my captivity! I must leave this small town; it is a prison—an open grave!' At this moment, the oak above me shook its foliage; a wind drove the waves faster, until they broke on the shore; and a sheet of paper, which some wanderer might have lost, was blown toward me. I took it, and suddenly the wind was silent as though it had accomplished its mission ; the oak stirred no more, the lake was tranquil, and even the clouds seemed to pause and look on while I unfolded and read the paper."

"Oh, I imagine what it was!" exclaimed Hardenberg. "A love-letter from one of your admirers, who knew that the beautiful nymph of the lake had selected that spot for her sanctuary."

"Ah, you do not imagine very well, your excellency. It was no love-letter, but a newspaper ! It was a copy of your dear, venerable *Vossische Zeitung.** I read it at first very carelessly, but suddenly I noticed an article from Berlin, which

* The *Vossische Zeitung*, one of the oldest Berlin newspapers, is still published.

excited my liveliest attention. It alluded to the strange **cures performed by Doctor Binder, a** magnetizer. It related that many sufferers came to Berlin from distant cities to be cured by the doctor, whose whole treatment consisted of laying his hands and fixing his eyes on his patients. It dwelt especially upon the adventures of a young woman whose strange disease had riveted the attention of all Berlin, and who, in consequence of the doctor's treatment, had become a clairvoyante. It said that the truly wonderful sayings and predictions of the young woman were creating the greatest sensation, and that even ministers and distinguished functionaries were visiting Doctor Binder's 'Hall of Crises,' in order to listen and put questions to the clairvoyante."

"Ah, that was little Henrietta Meyer, who died a few months ago," said Hardenberg.

"Yes, she was so accommodating as to die and make room for me," exclaimed Frederica, smiling. "**When I had read this article about her, it** seemed to me as though a veil dropped from my eyes, and I were only now able to descry my future distinctly. I jumped up and uttered a single loud cry that sped over the lake like a stormbird, and was repeated many times by the distant echo. Thereupon I ran back to town, as if carried on the wings of the wind. The men on the streets, who saw me running past, gazed wonderingly after me. Some of them hailed and tried to speak to me, but I took no notice of them, ran on, reached at last the humble dwelling of my parents, and there I fell panting and senseless. They lifted me up, and carried me to my bed. I lay on it motionless, and with dilated eyes. No one knew my thoughts, or heard the voices whispering in my breast and ominously laughing. I stared upward, and matured my plan of operations. My poor father sat all night long at my bedside, weeping and imploring me to look at him, and tell him only by a single word, a single syllable, that I recognized him. My tongue remained silent, but my eyes were able to glance at and greet the poor man. But why tell you all the particulars of my wonderful disease? In short, all my limbs were paralyzed, and even my mind seemed affected and confused. I could eat and sleep, but I was unable to rise, and could not utter a word. The physicians of our small town tried all the remedies of their science to cure me. In vain! I remained dumb. Only once, four weeks afterward, I recovered the power of speech. It was in the night-time, and no one was with me but my poor father, who passed nearly every night at my bedside, always hoping for a moment when I might get better—when the spell would leave my tongue, and the power of speech be restored. This moment had come now; I intimated it to my father with my eyes, stared at him, and said in a slow and solemn voice, 'Doctor Binder, at Berlin, is alone able to cure me!'"

"Ah," exclaimed Hardenberg, drawing a deep breath, "I give you permission to laugh at me. I was just as foolish as your father was. Up to this time I believed in the reality of your sickness, and felt quite anxious and alarmed. The **words you uttered during that night** quiet me again, and illuminate the gloom, like a welcome miner's lamp in a deep shaft. I hope, however, that they did not exert the same effect upon your father."

"No, your excellency, fortunately they did not, and the proof of it is that I rode, a week afterward—in a comfortable carriage, and accompanied by my father—to Berlin, to place myself under the treatment of Doctor Binder."

"Did the doctor promise to cure you?"

"He gave me hopes at least that he would be able to do so, and, after accepting three months' pay in advance, received me into his house, and the cure commenced. I willingly submitted to his piercing glances and to his laying-on of hands. I was so obliging as to fall asleep, and scarcely three days elapsed when I began already to become slightly clairvoyant. The doctor was himself surprised at the rapid effect of his cure; he informed some of his distinguished patrons of the presence of a new clairvoyante at his house, and invited them to witness my next awakening. Among these patrons were some influential courtiers, Prince Hatzfeld and Field-Marshal Kalkreuth. I had been told that these gentlemen were the most zealous adherents of the French alliance, and the most ardent admirers of Napoleon. It was but natural, therefore, that when I became clairvoyant on that day, in the presence of these gentlemen, I was the enraptured prophetess of a golden future for Prussia, provided we maintained the alliance with France. The two courtiers were visibly surprised and delighted at my prophecies; and when the doctor had left the room for a moment, I heard Prince Hatzfeld say to Field-Marshal Kalkreuth, 'Ah, I wish Hardenberg were here, and heard the predictions of this wonderful girl! He believes in clairvoyance, and her words, therefore, would make a profound impression upon him!' 'We must try to have him brought hither,' said Field-Marshal Kalkreuth; 'we must try to influence the stubborn fellow in this way.'"

"That was a very clever idea," said Hardenberg, smiling; "I almost envy those gentlemen their very pretty intrigue. They then made offers to you, did they not?"

"No, I made offers to them."

"How so?"

"Listen to me. When the gentlemen left, and I was again alone with the doctor, I suddenly awoke from my trance; rising from my couch, I stepped up to him, and made him a respectful obeisance. He looked at me in dismay, and seemed paralyzed with stupefaction, for you know all my limbs were palsied, and I could only move my tongue. 'My dear doctor,' I said, very calmly, 'I hope I have proved to you now that I am possessed of considerable talent as an actress, and that I am as well versed in playing my part as you are in yours. Both of us try to obtain fame and wealth, you as a magnetizer, I as a clairvoyante, and we stand mutually in need of each other. You are the stage-manager, and possessed of a theatre that suits me, and I am the leading actress, without whom you would be unable to perform your play in a satisfactory manner. Let us, therefore, come to an understanding and make an agreement.' Eh bien, your excellency, we did come to an understanding; we did

make an agreement. With a view to a better position that soon would be accessible to me, I remained temporarily the first actress, and, thanks to my performances, I attracted an audience as distinguished as it was munificent."

"Now I comprehend every thing. You must permit me, however, another question. Are Prince Hatzfeld and Field-Marshal **Kalkreuth** aware that you are nothing but an—actress?"

"By no means, your excellency. They are so kind as to take me for a *bona fide* clairvoyante. The doctor told them that, by my spiritual connection with him, I was compelled to say, think, and do whatever he wanted and commanded me, and that, if he gave me my instructions while I was awake, I had to act and speak in my clairvoyant state in strict accordance with them. In this way it happened, your excellency, that I was used as the fox-tail with which the electrical machine is set in motion—to make an impression upon you, and to cure you of your hostility to France. The doctor became the confidant of these gentlemen, who desired to cure you. They surrounded your excellency with spies, a minute diary was kept of your movements, and this diary was brought early every morning to the doctor, who read it to me, and we agreed then **as to the** manner in which I should avail myself of the information."

"And dupe me!" exclaimed Hardenberg, laughing. "Fortunately, I did not allow myself to be thus dealt with, but penetrated the handsome little swindle at the outset; yet I made up my mind to continue playing the farce for some time, because it afforded me an opportunity to discover and foil the intentions, wishes, and schemes of my adversaries. But tell me now, my pretty young lady, what would have happened if I had not allowed you to perceive to-day that I was aware of the whole trick?"

"In that case I myself would have disclosed the intrigue to your excellency. Did I not send my young nurse twice to your house yesterday, in order to pray you to come to me, if possible last night, because I had important news to communicate to you? Did I not write to you that the doctor would not be at home during the whole evening, and that I might, therefore, communicate an important secret to you without being disturbed?"

"Unfortunately, I was not at home, and the supper at Marshal Augereau's, which you used so skilfully during your pretended trance, deprived me of an hour of important disclosures! But suppose I had come, and met you alone; what **would you have told me then?**"

"Precisely what I tell you now. I would have fallen down before you as I do now, and, clasping your knees in this manner, would have said what I say now: 'Mercy, my lord and master, mercy! I can lie and dissimulate no longer before your noble face; your eyes embarrass me; your smile overwhelms me with shame; the farce is at an end, and the truth commences. The truth, however, is that I adore you; that I will no longer unite with your adversaries against you; that I **will serve you and none but you,** and devote to **you** my whole life and every pulsation of my heart!'" She attempted to conceal her face, bathed in a flood of tears; but Hardenberg softly laid his hands upon her cheeks, and, gently raising her head, gazed at her long and smilingly.

"What talent!" he said; "in truth, I admire you! It was a charming performance. True love and passion could express themselves no better, or surpass your imitation."

She arose from her knees and looked at him with eyes flashing with anger. "You do not believe me?" she asked, almost menacingly. "You suspect me, although I have revealed my heart to you as sincerely as I have ever revealed it to Heaven itself."

"Foolish girl, how can I believe you?" he asked. "Have you not gone out into the world to plunge into adventures, and to seek your fortune? Have you not dived into the sea to find pearls? Can you wish me to play the agreeable part of your safety-rope—that is all!"

"No, no!" she exclaimed, wildly stamping with her feet; "that is a vile slander! Why should I choose precisely you for my safety-rope?—why reveal my soul to you? Do you not believe that

those gentlemen who are using me against you, who worship **and admire me, would not** be ready to assist me? **But I have** rejected their homage and their offers; I **despise and** abhor them all, **for they are your enemies. I hate** France, I detest Napoleon, for you are opposed **to** the French alliance, and you have been reviled by Napoleon; I am longing for an alliance with **Russia,** for I know this to be your wish, and I have **no** wishes but yours, no will but your will!"

"Ah!" exclaimed Hardenberg, laughing, "this is the strangest political declaration of love which woman ever made to man!"

"Great Heaven! you are laughing!" she cried angrily. "You do not believe **me,** then? How shall I be able to convince you?"

"I will show you a way to do so," said Hardenberg, suddenly growing very grave.

"**Tell me, and I** swear to you that I will try it!"

"Serve *me* in the same manner as you have hitherto served **my enemies. Become** the prophetess of my policy, as **you have been the prophetess** of the policy of my opponents. Permit me to become the prompter of the clever clairvoyante, and play now as inimitably against my adversaries as you have played for them."

Frederica Hahn burst into loud laughter. "In truth, that is a splendid idea," she said, "a revenge which your excellency has devised against the other gentlemen. Here is my hand. I swear to serve and to be faithful to you as long as I live. Do you now believe in the truth of my love?"

"Let me first see the actions inspired by this love," said Hardenberg, smiling. "I will prove to you immediately that I confide in your head, although I am not vain enough to believe in your heart. Listen to me, then! It is my most ardent desire that the king should leave Berlin, and be withdrawn from the influence of the French Prince Hatzfeld and old Field-Marshal Kalkreuth. however, insist that he remain at Berlin, and thereby manifest the adhesion of Prussia to the alliance with France. I suspect, nay, I might say, I know, that the king is in danger, and that, as soon as he utters a free and bold word, the French will use it as a pretext to seize his person and imprison him, as they have done Charles and Ferdinand of Spain. Caution, therefore, the sanguine and credulous gentlemen; point out to them the dangers menacing the king here; tell them that it is the bounden duty of his majesty to save himself for his people; shout with your inspired and enthusiastic voice: 'Go! Destruction will overwhelm you at Berlin! Save the king! Convey him to Breslau!'"

"I will play my part so skilfully that even the boldest will be filled with dismay," cried Frederica, with flaming eyes, "and that dear old Field-Marshal Kalkreuth will implore the king on his knees to leave Berlin, and go to Breslau. But, when I have played this part for you—when you have attained your object, and I have given you proofs of my fidelity and obedience—will you then believe that I love you?"

"We shall see," he said, smiling. "I am, perhaps, not as wise as Ulysses, and shall not fill my ears with wax, but listen to the song of the siren, even at the risk of perishing in the whirlpool of passion. Let us not impose upon ourselves any promises concerning the destiny of our hearts; but your position in the world is an entirely different question. As to this, I must make you promises, and swear that I shall fulfil them. You promise that you will serve me, enter into my plans, and support my policy?"

"Yes, your excellency, I swear to you that your opponents themselves shall beseech the king to leave Berlin, and renounce France."

"Well, then, on the day the king arrives safely at Breslau, you will receive from me a document securing you an annuity on which you will be able to live independently here at Berlin."

"And is that all?" she asked, in a contemptuous tone. "You promise me nothing but money to keep me from starvation?"

"No," said Hardenberg, smiling. "I promise you more than that. I promise that little Frederica Hahn, the watchmaker's daughter, shall be transformed into an aristocratic lady, and that I will procure you a husband, who will give you so

distinguished a name that the daughter of the Marquise de Barbasson need not be ashamed of it. Are you content with that, my beauty?"

"Would it be necessary for me to love and honor the husband whom your excellency will give me?" asked Frederica, after a pause.

"Suppose I reply in the affirmative?" asked Hardenberg.

"Then I answer: I prefer remaining Frederica Hahn, for then I shall at least have the right to sit at your feet and worship you, and no troublesome husband will be able to prevent my doing so."

"Well, then, my charming little fool, I shall select for you a husband who will, like a *deus ex machina*, appear only in order to confer his name upon you at the altar, and who will then disappear again. Do you consent to that?"

"Your excellency, that would be precisely such a husband as I would like to have, and as my imagination has dreamed of—a husband *sans conséquence*—not a man, but a manikin!"

"I shall, however, see to it that this manikin, besides his name, will lay at your feet another splendid wedding-gift, and a *corbeille de noce*, which will be worthy of you. You accept my offers, then, my friend?"

"No, unless you add something to them."

"What is it, Frederica?"

"Your love, your confidence, your belief in my love!" she exclaimed, sinking down at his feet.

"Ah," said Hardenberg, "let us not be so audacious as to attempt to raise the veil that may perhaps conceal a magnificent future from our eyes!" *

---

* This scene is not fictitious, but based upon the verbal statements and disclosures of the lady who played so prominent a part in it.—L. M.

CHAPTER XIX.

THE TWO DIPLOMATISTS.

THE royal family celebrated an important festival at Potsdam on the 20th of January. Crown-Prince Frederick William had been confirmed at the palace church. In the presence of the whole royal family, of all high officers and foreign ambassadors, the prince, who was now seventeen years of age, had made his confession of faith and taken an oath to the venerable and noble Counsellor Sack that he would faithfully adhere to God's Word, and worship Him in times of weal and woe. After the ceremonies at church were over, a gala-dinner was to take place at court, and invitations had been issued not only to the members of the royal family, but to the dignitaries and functionaries, as well as the ambassadors, who had come over from Berlin. This dinner, however, was suddenly postponed. The king was said to have been unexpectedly taken ill. It was asserted that the excitement which he had undergone at church had greatly affected his nerves, bringing on a bleeding at the nose, which had already lasted several hours, and which even the most energetic remedies were unable to relieve.

The ambassadors repaired to the palace in order to ascertain more about the health of the king, and the principal physician of his majesty was able at least to assure them that his majesty's condition was not by any means alarming or dangerous, but that the king needed repose, and could not, according to his intention, go to Berlin that day, but would remain at Potsdam, and, for a few days, abstain entirely both from engaging in public affairs and receiving visitors. This news did not seem to alarm any one more seriously than the French ambassador, Count St. Marsan. He left the royal palace in depressed spirits, and, entering his carriage, ordered the driver in a hurried tone to return to Berlin as fast as possible. Scarcely three hours elapsed when the carriage stopped in front of the French legation, and the footman hastened to open the coach-door. Count St. Marsan, however, did not rise from his feet,

but beckoned his valet de chambre to come to him. "Have no letters arrived for me?" he asked.

"Yes, your excellency; this was brought to the legation a few minutes since," said the valet, handing a small, neatly-folded letter to the count.

St. Marsan opened the note hastily. It contained nothing but the following words: "I have just returned from Potsdam. I am probably an hour ahead of your excellency, for I had caused three relays to be kept in readiness for me. As soon as your excellency has arrived, I pray you to inform me of it, that I may hasten to you.—H."

"To the residence of Chancellor von Hardenberg!" said the count, putting the letter into his breast-pocket, and leaning back on the cushions. The carriage rolled away, and ten minutes afterward it stopped in front of the residence of the chancellor of state. St. Marsan alighted with youthful alacrity, and, keeping pace with the footman who was to announce his arrival, hastened into the house and ascended the staircase. At the first anteroom the chancellor met him, greeting him with polite words and conducting him into his cabinet. "You have anticipated me, your excellency," he said; "my carriage was in readiness, and I only waited for a message from you to repair immediately to your residence."

"It is, then, highly important news that your excellency will be kind enough to communicate to me?" asked St. Marsan, uneasily.

"On the contrary, I hoped you would communicate important news to me. I cannot conceal from you that we are all in great suspense and excitement; and I suppose it is unnecessary for me to confess to so skilful and experienced a diplomatist as your excellency, that the king's illness and bleeding at the nose were mere fictions, and that his majesty thereby wished only to avoid meeting you."

"Indeed, that was what I suspected," exclaimed St. Marsan; "for the rest, every thing at Potsdam appeared to me very strange and inexplicable; I confess, however, that I do not comprehend what has aroused the king's indignation, and rendered my person so offensive to him?"

"What!" asked Hardenberg, with an air of astonishment. "Your excellency does not comprehend it? It seems to me, however, that this indignation is but too well-grounded. You know the fidelity and perseverance with which Prussia has adhered to the French alliance; that the king has withstood all promises of Russia, however alluring their character, and has proved by word and deed that he intends to remain faithful to his system, and never to dissolve the alliance **with France. And now, when my zeal, eloquence,** and untiring expositions of the utility of this alliance have succeeded in rendering him deaf to all promises, and attaching his heart more sincerely to France, you mortify and insult the king in so defiant a manner! Ah, count, this is to postpone the attainment of my object to a very distant period, and to take from me, perhaps forever, the order I am longing for. For how can I keep my word?—how can I obtain the king's consent to the betrothal of the crown prince with a princess of the house of Napoleon, if France treats him with so little deference and respect, and proves to him that she herself does not regard the treaties which she has concluded with Prussia as imposing any obligations upon her?"

"But your excellency drives me to despair," exclaimed Count St. Marsan, "for I confess to you again that I do not comprehend what act of ours would justify such grave reproaches."

"Well, permit me, then, to remind you of what has happened, and request a kind explanation. Your excellency, I suppose, is aware that the division of General Grénier, nineteen thousand strong, has approached by forced marches from Italy and occupied Brandenburg?"

"Yes, I am aware of that," said St. Marsan, hesitatingly; "but these troops will rest there but a few days, and continue their march."

"On the contrary," replied Hardenberg, "they are destined to remain in Brandenburg. Their commanders declare emphatically that they will be stationed in this province, and Brandenburg is

already so full of French soldiers that I do not see how quarters and sustenance are to be provided for an additional corps of nineteen thousand men. Besides, this augmentation of the French forces is contrary to the express stipulations of the existing treaties, and it is, therefore, but natural that this fact, which in itself would seem to point to a hostile intention, should have excited the serious displeasure of the king."

"But the extraordinary circumstances in which the French army has been placed ever since the disastrous campaign of Russia, I believe ought to excuse extraordinary measures," said St. Marsan, in his embarrassment. "His majesty the Emperor Napoleon, on learning how offensive to the king is this increase in the number of troops stationed in the province of Brandenburg, will assuredly hasten to explain the necessity of the measure, and, however late it may be, request his ally's consent to it."

"Ah," exclaimed Hardenberg, quickly, "you admit, then, that this reënforcement in Brandenburg is intended to be permanent? But I have **not yet laid** all my complaints before your excellency. I believe you are aware that, according to the last convention between France and Prussia, no French troops at all are to occupy Potsdam and its environs, and that they are not to stay there even for a single night?"

"Yes; I am aware of this stipulation, and believe it has hitherto been carefully observed."

"Hitherto—that is to say, until to-day! But this forenoon, at the very hour we were at church witnessing the confirmation of the prince, whom you wish to be as a new tie between France and Prussia, this stipulation was violated in as incomprehensible as mortifying a manner. Four thousand men of Grénier's division have marched this morning from Brandenburg to Potsdam, and have tried forcibly—do you understand me, your excellency?—forcibly to occupy the city. The municipal authorities vainly endeavored to assure them that this was entirely inadmissible, and it was only after a very stormy scene that they succeeded in prevailing upon the troops to leave Potsdam, and withdraw several miles from the city.* If no blood was shed, it was not owing to the disposition of your troops, but to the prudence and moderation of the Prussian authorities. Now, count, you fully comprehend the exasperation of my master, the king; and I hope you will give me the satisfactory explanation which he has commissioned me to request."

"Your excellency," said St. Marsan, greatly surprised, "I really do not comprehend why the king should be so irritated at this trifling deviation from the stipulation of the treaties. You yourself said it would be impossible to find quarters and sustenance for so large a number of troops in the province of Brandenburg. This fact involved the military commanders in difficulties, and explains why they at last thought of sending a detachment to Potsdam, where there are so much room and so many vacant barracks. We could not suppose that the king would object to this, and that the sight of the brave French soldiers would fill the ally of the Emperor of the French with feelings of displeasure and indignation. But, you see, the troops yielded to the will of the king, and left the city."

"But they remained near enough to be able to reoccupy it at the first signal."

"And does your excellency believe that the French authorities might have occasion to call troops to their assistance?" asked Count St. Marsan, casting a quick, searching glance at the chancellor.

But Hardenberg's countenance remained perfectly calm and unchanged; only the faint glimmer of a smile was playing round his thin lips. "I do not know," he said, "what motives might induce the French authorities to call troops to their assistance, as they are not in a hostile country, but in that of an ally, unless it were that they look upon every free expression of the royal will as an unfriendly demonstration, and interpret as an act of hostility, for instance, the king's determination not to reside at Berlin, but at Potsdam, or, according to his pleasure, in any other city of the kingdom."

"The king, then, intends to leave Potsdam and remove to another city?" inquired St. Marsan, quickly.

"I do not say that exactly," replied Hardenberg, smiling and hesitating: "but I should not be greatly surprised if, to avoid the quarrels between the French and Prussian authorities, and not to witness perhaps another violation of the treaties, and a repeated attempt of the French commanders to occupy Potsdam, he should remove to another city, where his majesty would be safe from such annoyances."

"The king intends to leave Potsdam," said St. Marsan to himself. He added aloud: "I do not know, however, of any city in the kingdom of Prussia where, owing to the present cordial relations between Prussia and France, there are no French authorities and French troops.—Yes, it occurs to me that, according to the treaties concluded last year, there are no French troops in the province of Silesia, except on the military road from Glogau to Dresden, and that they and their auxiliaries are expressly forbidden to pass through Breslau. Breslau, then, would be a city where the king would not run the risk of meeting French troops."

"You admit, then, that it is dangerous for the king to meet them? In that case it would truly be a very justifiable and wise step for the king to repair to Breslau."

"It is settled, then, that the king will go to Breslau?" asked St. Marsan. "Your excellency intended to be so kind as to intimate this to me?"

"It is settled, then, that the king is in danger near the French troops?" asked Hardenberg. "Your excellency intended to be so kind as to intimate this to me? Ah, it seems to me we have been playing hide and seek for half an hour, while both of us really ought to be frank and sincere."

"Well, then, let us be," exclaimed St. Marsan. "I have likewise reason to complain, and must demand explanations. What does it mean that the Prussian government has suddenly dispatched orders to all provincial authorities to recall the furloughed soldiers and proceed to another draft; that artillery-horses are bought, and a vast quantity of uniforms made?"

"It means simply, your excellency, that the King of Prussia expects to be requested by his ally, the Emperor of the French, to furnish him additional auxiliaries, and that he hastens to make the necessary preparations, to be able to comply at the earliest moment. These preparations, moreover, had to be made in so hasty a manner, because, as soon as the Russians advance farther into the interior of Prussia, of course both a conscription and the recall of the furloughed soldiers would be impossible."

"But this is not all. The king yesterday authorized the minister of finance to issue ten million dollars in treasury-notes, to be taken at par. What is this enormous sum destined for, M. Chancellor? Why does the king suddenly need so many millions?"

"You ask what the king needs so much money for? Sir, the clause ordering these treasury-notes at par would be a sufficient reply to your question. When a government is unable to procure funds in any other way than by compelling its subjects to take its treasury-notes at par, it proves that it has no credit to negotiate a loan—no property which it might render available; it proves that not only its treasury, but the resources of the country, are completely exhausted, and that it has reached a point where it must either go into hopeless bankruptcy or endeavor to maintain itself by palliatives. Prussia has come to this. Let us not examine by whose fault, or by what accumulation of expenses and obligations, this condition of affairs has been brought about; but the fact remains, and, as the king is unwilling that the state should be declared bankrupt, he resorts to a palliative, and issues ten million dollars in treasury-notes. In this manner he obtains funds, is enabled to relieve the distress of his subjects, and to procure horses and uniforms for the new regiments to join the forces of his ally, the Emperor Napoleon. Does not this account for the issue? Are you satisfied with this explanation, count?"

"I am; for I have no doubt that your excellency is sincere."

"Have we not yet proved that we are sincere?" exclaimed Hardenberg, in a tone of virtuous indignation. "Notwithstanding all allurements and promises by which Russia is trying to gain us over to her side, we are standing by France—and, please do not forget, at a time when she is overwhelmed with calamities, we give her our soldiers, and, the old ones having perished, recruit and equip new ones for her; we make all possible sacrifices—nay, we even run the risk of making the king lose the sympathies of his own subjects, who, you know, are not very favorable to a continuation of this alliance! And still France doubts the king's fidelity and my own heart-felt devotion! She entertains such doubts at a moment when I declare it to be my chief object to effect a marriage of the crown prince with an imperial princess; and when I have already succeeded so far that I believe I may almost positively promise that the king will give his consent."

"What!" exclaimed St. Marsan, surprised. "The king consents to such a marriage?"

"He will," said Hardenberg, smiling, "provided France make the first overtures, secure him important advantages, and raise the kingdom to a higher rank among the states of Europe."[*]

"Oh, the emperor will grant Prussia all this," said St. Marsan, joyously. "It is too important to his majesty, when a princess of his family ascends the throne of Prussia, that he should not willingly comply with all the wishes of his future brother, the King of Prussia."

"Then we are agreed," exclaimed Hardenberg, offering his hand to the count, "and all misunderstandings have been satisfactorily explained. Only confide in us—firmly believe that the system of the king has undergone no alteration—that no overtures, direct or indirect, have been made to Russia, and that he has rejected the offers which she has made to him. The repudiation of General York's course is a sufficient proof of all this.

---

* Beitzke, vol. i., p. 150.

Only believe our protestations, count, and entreat your emperor to dismiss the distrust he still seems to feel, and which alienates the hearts of the greatest emperor and the noblest king."

"I will inform his majesty of the very words your excellency has addressed me, and I have no doubt that the emperor on reading them will have the same gratification with which I have heard them. Thanks, therefore, your excellency! And now I will not detain you longer from enjoying your dinner. Both of us have returned from Potsdam without dining, and it is but natural that we should make up for it now. Therefore, farewell, your excellency!"

Hardenberg gave him his arm, and conducted him with kind and friendly words into the anteroom.

"Does your excellency think," said St. Marsan, on taking leave, "that I may venture to-morrow to go to Potsdam and personally inquire about his majesty's health?"

"Your excellency had better wait two or three days," said Hardenberg, after a moment's reflection. "By that time I shall have succeeded in overcoming the king's displeasure, and if the French troops in the mean time have made no further attempts to occupy Potsdam, but, on the contrary, have withdrawn still farther from the city, it will be easy for me to persuade the king that the whole occurrence was a mere misunderstanding. Have patience, then, for three days, my dear count!"

"Well, then, for three days. But then I shall see the king at Potsdam, shall I not?"

"Ah," exclaimed Hardenberg, smiling, "how can I know where it will please his majesty to be three days hence? The king is his own master, and I should think at liberty to go hither and thither as he pleases, provided he does not go to the Russian camp, and I would be able to prevent that."

"It is certain," muttered Count St. Marsan, when he was alone in his carriage, "it is certain that the king will no longer be at Potsdam three days hence, but intends to remove secretly, and establish his court at a greater distance. The moment, therefore, has come when we must act energetically. The troops have come for this very purpose, and the emperor's orders instruct us, in case the king should manifest any inclination to renew his former alliance with Russia, and to break with France, immediately to seize the king's person, in order to deprive the Prussian nation, which is hostile to us, of its leader and standard-bearer. Well, then, the orders of the emperor must be carried into execution. We must try to have the king arrested to-day. I shall immediately take the necessary steps, and send couriers to Grénier's troops." The carriage stopped, and Count St. Marsan, forgetful of his dinner, hastened into his cabinet, and sent for his private secretaries. An hour afterward two couriers left the French legation, and shortly after an elegant carriage rolled from the gateway. Two footmen, who did not wear their liveries, were seated on the high box; but no one was able to perceive who sat inside, for the silken window-curtains had been lowered.

Chancellor von Hardenberg, after the French ambassador left him, instead of going to the dining-room, returned to his cabinet. Like Count St. Marsan, he seemed to have forgotten his dinner. With his hands folded behind him, he was slowly pacing his room, and a proud smile was beaming in his face. "I hope," he said to himself, "I have succeeded in reassuring, and yet alarming the count. He believes in me and in the sincerity of my sentiments, and hence in the fidelity of Prussia to France, and this reassures him; but he understood very well the hints I dropped about the possibility of the king leaving Potsdam and going to Breslau, and this alarms him. He may, perhaps, be hot-headed enough to allow himself to be carried away by his uneasiness, and make an attempt to seize the king. If he should, I have won my game, and shall succeed in withdrawing the king from his reach by conveying him to Breslau. Well, fortunately, I have a reliable agent at the count's house, and if any thing should happen, he will take good care to let me know it immediately. I may, therefore, tranquilly wait for further developments." At this moment the door opened, and Conrad, the old valet de chambre, entered, presenting a letter on a silver tray to the chancellor of state.

"From whom?" asked Hardenberg.

"From *her!*" whispered Conrad, anxiously. "Her nurse brought the letter a few minutes ago, and she says it ought to be at once delivered to your excellency."

"Very well," said Hardenberg, beckoning to Conrad to leave the room. But Conrad did not go; he remained at the door, and cast imploring glances on his master.

"Well," inquired Hardenberg, impatiently, "do you want to tell me any thing else?"

"I do," said Conrad, timidly; "I just wished to tell you that her excellency Madame von Hardenberg has condescended again this morning to box my ears, because I refused to tell her whither his excellency the chancellor went every evening."

"Poor Conrad!" said Hardenberg, smiling, "my wife will assuredly pat your cheeks until they are insensible. There, take this little golden plaster."

He offered a gold-piece to Conrad, but the faithful servant refused to accept it. "No, your excellency, I do not wish it, for I have as much as I need, and I know that your excellency will take care of me when I am too old and feeble to work. I only intended to take the liberty to caution your excellency, so that you may be a little on your guard. Madame von Hardenberg has told her lady's-maid that she intends to follow the chancellor to-night, in order to find out whither he goes, and that she then would go in the morning to the lady and make such a fuss as to deter her from receiving your excellency any more. The lady's-maid has confided this to me, and ordered me to report it immediately, for you know that we all would willingly die for you, and that even the female servants of her excellency remain with her only because they love and adore you, and because it is a great honor to belong to the household of a master whom all Berlin loves and reveres."

"I thank you and the others for your attachment and fidelity," said Hardenberg, nodding kindly to his old servant. "Tell my wife's maid that I am especially obliged to her, and that I desire her to continue serving me faithfully. For what you all have to suffer by the displeasure of my wife, I shall take pains to indemnify you, particularly if you mention as little as possible to outsiders any thing about the state of affairs prevailing in my family, and the sufferings we all have to undergo in consequence of it. Go, Conrad; be reticent and vigilant! I shall profit by your advice, and my wife will be none the wiser." He nodded once more to Conrad, and, when the servant left the room, Hardenberg turned his eyes again toward the little note which he still held unopened in his hand. He unfolded it hastily and read. It contained only the following words: "My predictions are producing a good effect. Dear Köckeritz is greatly alarmed for the safety of his beloved king, and even old Kalkreuth was startled by the terrible prophecies of the clairvoyante. I am sure both of them will advise the king to shun the danger, and transfer the seat of government to some other place. Heaven grant that their words may be impressive, and that we may attain our object—for you, the liberty **of** Prussia; for me, the thraldom of my **heart!** For what else do I wish than to be your slave, and to lie at your feet, to narrate to you the story of my love? For you I wish to be an humble slave; for all others, Diavolezza Frederica, the watchmaker's daughter—and when shall I become a marquise?"

"It is true," said Hardenberg, smiling, and tearing the paper in small pieces; "it is true, she is a *diavolezza,* but one of the most amiable and charming sort, and perhaps ere long I shall, notwithstanding her deviltry, consider her an angel, and believe her charming comedy to be entirely true and sincere. But this is no time for thinking of such things. The grave affairs of life require our exclusive attention. Köckeritz, then, has been convinced, and even Kalkreuth has been shaken in his stupid belief in the French! Well, may we at length succeed in taking the fortress of this royal heart!—Ah, some one raps again at the door! Come in! What, Conrad, it is you again? Do you come to tell me that my wife has again boxed your ears?"

"No," said Conrad, smiling. "This time I have to announce a French soldier, who insists on seeing your excellency. He says he has found a precious ornament which you have lost, and for which he would himself get his reward."

"Well, let him come in; we shall see what he brings me," said Hardenberg.

A few minutes afterward Conrad opened the door, and a French soldier entered the room. "Now, let us see what you have found, my friend," said Hardenberg, "and what you bring back to me before I have missed it."

"Your excellency, it is a precious ornament," said the soldier; "but I must give it to you in secret."

"Withdraw, Conrad," said Hardenberg, beckoning to the servant, who had remained at the door, and was distrustfully and anxiously watching every motion of the soldier.

Conrad obeyed, but he left the door ajar, and remained close to it, ready to reënter the cabinet at the first word of his beloved master.

"Now we are alone. Speak!" said Hardenberg.

"Your excellency," whispered the soldier, advancing several steps, "the valet de chambre of Count St. Marsan—that is to say, my brother—has sent me to you. He dares not himself come, for the house of your excellency is watched by spies, and he would instantly be suspected, if he were seen entering it. I am to ask your excellency whether you will give me twenty louis d'ors for a letter from my brother which I am to deliver to you."

"This letter, then, contains highly important information?"

"Yes, your excellency; my brother says he would let you have it at so low a rate because he had so long been connected with you, and because you had always treated him in a munificent manner."

"Does your brother require me to pay that sum before I have received the letter?"

"He said he would leave that entirely to your excellency; only he thinks it would be more advantageous to you to pay the money before reading the letter."

"How so, more advantageous to me?"

"Because your excellency, after reading it, would doubtless, in your joy at having received this singular and important information, pay him a larger sum than he himself had asked."

"In that case I prefer to read the letter first," said Hardenberg, smiling, "for I must not allow your brother's generosity to surpass mine."

"Well, then, your excellency, here is the letter," said the soldier, handing a small, folded paper to the chancellor of state.

Hardenberg took it, and, as if to prevent the soldier from seeing the expression of his face while he was reading it, he stepped into the window-niche and turned his back to him. The soldier, however, fixed his lurking glances on the chancellor. He saw that a sudden shock made the whole frame of the chancellor tremble, and a triumphant smile overspread the countenance of the secret observer.

After a few minutes Hardenberg turned round again, and, carefully folding up the paper, concealed it in his bosom. "My friend," he said, "your brother was right. Twenty louis d'ors would be too low a price for this letter. We must pay more for it." He stepped to his desk, and, opening one of the drawers, took a roll from it and counted down a number of gold-pieces on the table. "Here are thirty louis d'ors," said Hardenberg, "and one for your trouble. See whether I have counted correctly. Tell your brother to continue serving me faithfully, and furnishing me with reliable reports. He may always count on my gratitude!"

Scarcely had the soldier left the room, when Hardenberg drew the paper from his bosom and glanced over it again. "At length!" he exclaimed, joyously. "The decisive moment is at hand! Now I hope to attain my object!" He rang the bell violently. "Have my carriage brought to the front door in half an hour," he said to Conrad, as soon as he entered the room

"But my own horses are tired. Send for four post-horses. A courier is immediately to set out for Potsdam, and see to it that relay horses be in readiness for me at Steglitz and Zehlendorf!"

CHAPTER XX.

THE ATTACK.

It was six o'clock in the afternoon. The gloomy January day had already yielded to a dark, cold night, enshrouding the city and vicinity of Potsdam. The king was, as usual, to go to Sans-Souci toward nightfall. There, far from the turmoil of the world, he liked to spend his mornings and evenings, retiring from intrusive eyes into the quiet of his simple domestic life. Like his august grand-uncle, Frederick II., the king laid down his crown and the splendor of his position at the gates of the small palace of Sans-Souci, and, at this country-seat, consecrated by so many historical recollections, he was not a king, but a man, a father, and a friend. At Sans-Souci his children gathered around him every evening, and, by their mirth and tender love, endeavored to dispel the clouds from the careworn brow of their father; at Sans-Souci, Frederick William received the small circle of his intimate friends—there old General von Köckeritz, Field-Marshal Kalkreuth, Count Dohna, Chancellor von Hardenberg, and the few who had remained faithful to him, were allowed to approach without ceremonial or etiquette. Foreign guests and court visitors, however, were never received at the country palace; he saw them only in the city of Potsdam, where he transacted government affairs. Thither the king repaired punctually at ten o'clock every morning, where took place the meetings of the cabinet, the consultations with the high functionaries, the audiences given to the foreign ambassadors, and the official levees, and there the king took his dinner in the midst of his family and the officers of his court. But as soon as the clock struck seven he entered his carriage

without any attendants, and drove out to Sans-Souci. This had been his invariable habit for many years; and when the inhabitants of the street leading to his country-seat heard the roll of a carriage at that hour, they said as positively as though they heard the clock striking, "It is just seven, for the king is driving to Sans-Souci."

The coachman, as was his habit, as soon as the clock struck six, would harness two horses to the plain carriage which the king always used, and generally drove up to the small side-gate a few minutes to seven o'clock. Without giving any orders, or uttering a word, the king would enter, and noisily closing the door, give thereby the signal to start. The chime of the neighboring church had just commenced playing the first part of the old hymn of " *Ueb' immer Treu und Redlichkeit*,"[*] thus indicating that it was half-past six when **the** carriage appeared at the side-gate. **The wind** was howling across the palace square and through the colonnade in front of the neighboring park, hurling the snow into the face of the driver, and lifting up the cape of his cloak around his head, as if to protect him from the cold and stormy night. **Thomas, the king's coachman,** had just removed with some difficulty the large **cape from** his face, and rubbed the snow from his eyes, when he heard the side-gate open. A dark figure emerged from it and entered the carriage, and noisily closed the door. Thomas had received his accustomed signal, and, although wondering that the king had come fifteen minutes earlier than usual, he took the reins, whipped the horses, and the carriage rolled away along the route to Sans-Souci. The snow-storm drowned the roll of the wheels, and rendered the vehicle almost invisible; besides, there was no one to take particular notice of it, for only here and there some closely-muffled person was to be seen on the street, too busy with himself—too much engaged in holding fast his fluttering cloak and protecting himself from the driving snow.

The square in front of the palace was deserted. The two sentinels were walking up and down

---

* "Practise always truth and honesty."

with slow, measured steps in front of the main portal, now looking up to the brilliantly-lighted windows of the royal sitting-room, and now contemplating the two dim lanterns which stood on the iron railing, and whose light, struggling with the storm, seemed about to be extinguished. The side-gate of the palace remained dark and lonely, but only for a short time. From the side of the market-place a carriage slowly approached, and stopped in front of the palace, precisely on the same spot which the king's carriage had previously occupied. The coachman sat as rigidly and stiffly on the box as worthy Thomas, and the storm played with his cloak, and threw the snow into his face, precisely in the same manner. A patrol marched across the palace-square, and approached the sentinels in front of the main portal; the usual words of command were heard, the guard was relieved, and the sentinels marched off, surrendering their places to their less fortunate comrades. When they passed the side of the palace where the carriage was to be seen, they said to each other: "Ah, we are off guard a few minutes too early. It cannot be quite seven o'clock, for the king's carriage is still waiting at the gate." The driver's laugh was unheard.

It was really not yet seven—the hour when the king usually left the palace. He was still in his sitting-room, and his two old friends, General von Köckeritz and Field-Marshal Kalkreuth, were with him. A pause in their conversation set in, which seemed to have been of a very grave character, for the faces of the two old gentlemen looked serious and careworn, and the king was pacing the room slowly and with a gloomy air.

"Köckeritz," he said, after a pause, standing in front of the old general, who was his most intimate friend, and looking him full in the face, "you are really in earnest, then? You believe in the prophecies of the clairvoyante?"

"I confess, your majesty, that I cannot but believe them," said Köckeritz, sighing. "Her words, her whole manner, all her gestures, bear the stamp of truthfulness to such an extent, that I would deem it a crime against nature to believe her to be an impostor; she has, moreover,

already predicted to me the most wonderful things, and in her trance read my thoughts. She has looked, as it were, into the depth of my soul, **so that I cannot doubt longer** that she really is a **prophetess."**

"And you, field-marshal—do you, too, believe in her?" asked the king.

"I do, reluctantly, and in spite of myself, but I cannot help it," said the old field-marshal, shrugging his shoulders. "This girl speaks so forcibly, with such eloquence and such fervor of expression, that one is obliged to believe in her. Your majesty knows that I have always sided with those who have deemed the alliance of Prussia with France to be indispensable for the welfare and salvation of the country, and that I entertain the highest admiration for the genius, the character, and military talents of the Emperor Napoleon; I have never concealed my conviction that Prussia is lost if your majesty renounce Napoleon, and accept the proffered hand of Russia. Still, this girl has filled me with misgivings. She cried in so **heart-rending a** tone, with so impressive an anxiety, 'Save the king—the king is in danger! Leave Berlin—leave Potsdam! —save the king!' that I felt a shudder pervading my limbs, and it seemed to me as though I saw already the hand which was raised menacingly against the sacred head of your majesty. I certainly do not believe that the Emperor Napoleon has any thing to do with this danger; but some officious man in authority, some adventurous general, might strike a blow on his own responsibility, and in the belief that he would gain the favor of his emperor, and anticipate his most secret wishes."

"And what do you believe?" asked the king, moodily. "Tell me, Köckeritz, what sort of danger do you think is menacing me?"

"I do not know, your majesty," said Köckeritz, almost timidly, "but I am sure there is danger, and I would beseech your majesty to remove the seat of government to some place where you would be safer, and where we would not be exposed to the attacks of prowling, reckless detachments of soldiers, such as we saw here to our profound regret but a few days since. Your majesty ought to go to Breslau!"

"Ah," exclaimed the king, vehemently, "Hardenberg has succeeded, then, in gaining you over to his views? You are now suddenly of opinion that I ought to remove to Breslau?"

"Your majesty, I swear to you that Chancellor von Hardenberg has not even tried to gain me over to his views, and that he assuredly would not have succeeded. I have no political motives whatever in entreating your majesty now to go to Breslau, but am actuated exclusively by my fears for your personal safety. These troops of General Grénier have greatly alarmed me; their strange expedition to Potsdam was calculated to give rise to the most serious misgivings, and when I add to this the prophecies of the clairvoyante, a profound concern for the safety of your majesty fills my heart, and I feel like imploring you on my knees to leave Potsdam and to go to Breslau!"

"Let me join in the request of General Köckeritz, your majesty," said Field-Marshal Kalkreuth, sighing; "I, who on the battle-field never knew fear, am afraid of a danger to which I am not even able to give a name."

"And, owing to these vague presentiments, I am to take a step that might endanger the peace of my country and the existence of my crown!" exclaimed the king, with unusual vehemence. "For, do not deceive yourself in regard to this point: if I go to Breslau, Napoleon, who is perpetually distrusting me, and who is well aware that my alliance with him is highly repugnant to my inclinations and my personal wishes, would deem it equivalent to an open rupture, and believe I had gone over to his enemy, the Emperor of Russia. But, what is still worse, my country, my people, will also believe this to be the case. Every one will suppose that, although I publicly branded York's defection as a crime, and removed him from the command-in-chief, I secretly connived at what he did, and that my journey to Breslau is but a continuation of York's plans. Every one will believe that our policy has undergone a change, and that the alliance with France

is at an end. It was an eyesore to the people; and if they now believe themselves to be delivered from it, the most calamitous consequences might ensue. A rising against the French will take place as soon as I merely seem to give the signal for it."

"Yes, that is true," exclaimed Kalkreuth "your majesty is right; it might, after all, be dangerous if you suddenly leave the city where you have so long resided. It might be deemed equivalent to a rupture with France, and we are, unfortunately, too weak to run so great a risk. France is the natural ally of Prussia; that is what the great Frederick said, and Napoleon is also of this opinion. By changing your system of policy, your majesty would only endanger your position, and give the Emperor Napoleon grounds for treating you as an enemy. To be sure, I know that there are fools who regard France as prostrated, and utterly unable to rise again, but you will soon see her with an army of three hundred thousand men, as brilliant as the former."

"I am entirely of your opinion," said the king, thoughtfully, "the resources of France seem inexhaustible, and—"

At this moment the door of the cabinet was softly opened, and Timm the chamberlain made his appearance. "His excellency, Chancellor von Hardenberg," he said, in a loud voice, and at the same moment Hardenberg appeared on the threshold of the royal room.

"Pardon me, your majesty," he said, quickly approaching, "for availing myself of the permission you have given me of entering your cabinet without being ceremoniously announced; but pressing affairs will excuse me."

"Has any thing occurred at Berlin?" asked the king, hastily.

"No, your majesty; Berlin is, at least for the present, perfectly quiet," said Hardenberg, laying stress on every word. "But scenes of the most intense excitement and an open insurrection might have occurred at Berlin and at Potsdam if I had not fortunately arrived here in time."

"What do you mean?" inquired the king.

"I mean," replied Hardenberg, slowly and solemnly, "I mean that your majesty is at this very moment in danger of being seized and abducted by the French."

The king gave a start, and his face colored for a moment; Köckeritz and Kalkreuth exchanged glances of terror and dismay.

"You have also seen the clairvoyante, then?" asked the king, after a pause, almost indignantly. "You too have allowed yourself to be frightened by her vaticinations?"

"No, your majesty, I do not believe in them, but only in what is true and real. Will your majesty condescend to listen to me for a moment?"

"Speak, M. Chancellor of State."

"I must confess that, imitating the example set us by the French, I have my spies and agents at the legation of Count St. Marsan, and at the residence of Marshal Augereau, governor-general of the province of Brandenburg, just as well as they have theirs at the palace of your majesty, **at my house, and everywhere** else. I pay my spies liberally, and hence they serve me faithfully. Well, three hours since I received a message from my first and most reliable spy, and this message seemed to me so important that I immediately hastened hither in order to take the necessary steps, and, if possible, ward off the blow aimed at your majesty."

"And what blow—what danger is it?"

"I have told your majesty already that you are in danger of being carried off by the French. Will your majesty permit me to read to you what my spy (who, as I stated already, is a very reliable man) writes me about it?"

"Read!" exclaimed the king.

Hardenberg bowed, and, taking a paper from his memorandum-book, read as follows: "'They **intend to seize** the king to-night. A courier has been dispatched to the troops of Grénier's division, which, since yesterday, is encamped at a short distance from Potsdam; he conveys to the troops the order to march to the outskirts of the city, and to wait there at a carefully designated point for the arrival of a carriage. They are then to surround this carriage, and take it at a full gallop along the road leading to Brandenburg. **The king will be in this** carriage—seized in a very simple manner. It has been ascertained that the **king drives at seven o'clock** every evening to Sans-Souci, and the most **minute** details of what occurs on **this occasion have been** reported. A man will, therefore, conceal himself shortly after nightfall near the door by which the king leaves the palace. He will approach the carriage a few minutes before seven, enter it, and noisily close the door as the king is in the habit of doing. The coachman will believe this to be the usual signal, and start. As soon as he has reached the deserted avenue outside the gate leading to Sans-Souci, the man sitting in the carriage will open the front window, throw a cape over the coachman's head, thus blindfolding and preventing him from uttering any cries. At the same time two agents, concealed behind the trees, will approach, stop the horses, seize the coachman, draw him from the box, tie his hands and feet, and then put him into the carriage. The horses are to be half unhitched so that neither they nor the coachman will be able to stir from the spot. In the mean time another carriage will occupy the place of the former, and wait for the king at the side-gate of the palace. As soon as his majesty has entered, it will start, take at first the route of Sans-Souci, but outside of the gate will immediately turn to the left, and drive for some time at a quick trot along the narrow road near the garden. At some distance from the city the chasseurs of Grénier's division will await it, and then form its escort. The carriage is arranged in such a manner that it cannot be opened on the inside. As soon as the king has entered it, he will, therefore, be a prisoner.'"

"And you believe in the reliability of these statements?" asked the king, when Hardenberg paused.

"I am satisfied of it, your majesty. The reports of my spy have hitherto always proved correct and reliable. It would be impossible for me to doubt his accuracy."

The king looked at his watch. "It is already a quarter past seven," he said. "Then it is not my carriage that is waiting for me at the palace-gate, but another?"

"Yes, your majesty."

"The clairvoyante was right," muttered General Köckeritz.

"If I now enter the carriage, you believe, M. Chancellor, I would be carried off?"

"That is what my spy reports, and I have additional evidence confirming his statements. At least it is entirely correct that Grénier's chasseurs are again in the immediate vicinity of Potsdam. I confess to your majesty that, owing to this danger, I have already taken the liberty, without obtaining your consent, to take most urgent steps, and that I have conferred with the commanders of the garrison of Potsdam for this purpose. These gentlemen, like myself, felt the necessity of immediate action. Couriers and spies were sent out by them in all directions, and have brought the news that the four thousand men who, two days ago, made an attempt to occupy Potsdam forcibly, are now again approaching the city in the utmost haste. Already about fifty chasseurs are stationed behind the high fence of the last garden on the road, alluded to in the letter of my spy, and seem to wait there for the carriage. Your majesty will see all my statements confirmed if you will be gracious enough to receive the report of the officer who commanded the expedition, and who has now accompanied me to the palace. The commanders of the garrison found the proofs of the insidious intentions of the French to be so startling that they are causing at this moment all their troops to form in line, and are marching them as noiselessly as possible to the neighboring park."

"Without having previously applied to me for orders?" asked the king, quickly.

"Your majesty, the pressing danger excuses this rashness. I have engaged to solicit your majesty's consent to this measure."

"The troops shall be sent to their quarters," said the king, energetically, after a moment's reflection.

"Great Heaven!" exclaimed General Köckeritz, anxiously, "what does your majesty intend to do? Will you expose yourself to the danger of—"

"Hush!" interrupted the king, sternly, seizing the bell and ringing. The chamberlain entered. "The officer who is waiting in the anteroom is to come in," ordered the king. A minute afterward the officer appeared, and remained in a military attitude at the door.

"Did you reconnoitre to-night?" inquired the king.

"I did, your majesty. A part of Grénier's division is rapidly approaching the city; fifty chasseurs are already on the garden road behind the last board fence."

"Return to the general commanding," ordered the king. "The troops are at once to leave the park and go back to their quarters. The whole affair is to be kept a secret, and all *éclat* to be avoided. Go!"

The officer saluted, and turned toward the door, but on opening it he looked back and cast an inquiring glance on the face of the chancellor. Hardenberg nodded almost imperceptibly. The officer went out and closed the door after him.*

"I do not wish this affair to be made public," said the king, "otherwise I should have to renounce France immediately and decidedly; but my circumstances forbid me to do so."

"But, your majesty, you are now exposing yourself to the danger of falling into the hands of the French," exclaimed General Köckeritz, anxiously. "If Grénier's troops enter Potsdam now, they would meet with no resistance whatever, as your majesty has withdrawn our own soldiers."

"The French troops will not enter Potsdam after seeing that their plan has failed, and that I do not arrive in the coach at the place where the chasseurs are waiting for me," said the king.

---

* When the king heard that the troops had been marched to the park, he ordered them to be dismissed to their quarters; but the apprehensions of the officers were so great that they dared to obey the royal orders only partially. They marched the troops from the park to another place, where they kept them under arms during the whole night and a part of the following day.

"Besides," exclaimed Field-Marshal Kalkreuth indignantly, "it remains to be seen whether the whole intrigue is not a mere fiction. The chancellor of state himself said that he paid his spies well. Perhaps some enterprising fellow has got up this story for the sole purpose of receiving a large reward. He could imagine that the king, after being warned, would not drive out to Sans-Souci to-night, and that the affair therefore would be buried in the darkness of this evening."

"And does your excellency believe, too, that my spy caused four thousand men to march upon Potsdam to second his intrigue?" asked Hardenberg, smiling. "Do you believe that he is able to send detachments of chasseurs whithersoever he pleases?"

"I cannot believe in this plan; it would be too audacious!" exclaimed Field-Marshal Kalkreuth. "I ask a favor of your majesty. If this report is correct, the carriage in which you are to be abducted ought now to be at the palace-gate and await your majesty. Please permit me to go down-stairs and enter it in your place. I want to see whither they will take me."

"No," said the king—"no! I wish to avoid any thing like an open rupture with France. The time for that has not come yet."

"Oh," whispered Hardenberg to himself, sadly and reproachfully, "that time will never come! My hopes are blasted."

The king paced the room silently and musingly, with his hands folded behind him. Field-Marshal Kalkreuth and General Köckeritz followed every motion in anxious suspense. Hardenberg cast down his eyes, and his features were expressive of profound grief.

"Gentlemen," said the king, "come with me! Let us go down to my carriage!"

"Your majesty, I trust, does not intend to enter it?" exclaimed Köckeritz, in dismay.

"Come with me!" said the king, almost smilingly. "Come!"

The firm, determined tone of his majesty admitted of no resistance. The three left the cabinet with him in silence, crossed the anteroom and the lighted corridor, until they arrived at the small staircase leading to the side-gate of the palace. All was silent. Not a footman met them on the way, and only a single sentinel stood at the upper end of the passage. The king, who led the way, went quickly down and across the small hall toward the door, which he opened with a jerk. The storm swept into the hall and beat into the faces of the gentlemen. It had already blown out the two lanterns in front of the door, and an impenetrable darkness reigned outside.

"Hush, now!" whispered the king. "Step out softly and place yourselves here at the wall. No one will see you. Wait now!" He quickly stepped to the carriage, scarcely visible in the darkness, and, groping for the knob of the coach door, opened it. A moment of breathless suspense ensued for those who stood at the wall, and tried to see what was to occur. The king slammed the door, and jumped back toward the gate. At the same moment the coachman whipped the horses and the carriage rapidly sped away.

"Now, let us reënter the palace," said the king, with perfect composure. "It is a stormy night! Come!" He stepped back into the hall, and the gentlemen followed. "Well," he said, smiling, and standing still, "the coachman, in the firm belief that I am in the carriage, will take the indicated route; the chasseurs will surround the carriage and capture it. Let those who got up this miserable intrigue convince themselves to their shame that it has miscarried. They will not dare complain, and the whole affair will never be revealed."

"But suppose it should really have been your majesty's carriage?" asked Kalkreuth. "The darkness was so great that it could not be recognized."

"But the darkness did not prevent me from feeling," said the king, "and my hands served me this time instead of my eyes. I felt that it was another carriage than mine. The door-knob was much larger. But now I should like to have some news about my dear old coachman, Thomas, and learn what has become of him."

"If your majesty will permit me, I will try to

ascertain if the carriage is still in the avenue outside the gate," said Kalkreuth, quickly.

"I intended to request you to do so, field-marshal," said the king. "Your coach is in readiness, is it not?"

"It is, your majesty."

"Let the servants, then, have it brought up," said the king, ascending the staircase. On arriving at the anteroom, he himself ordered the lackey in waiting **to have** the carriage of the field-marshal brought to the door.

"If **your** majesty will permit me," said General Köckeritz, "I will accompany the field-marshal."

"I ask for the same favor," said the chancellor of state, quickly.

"Accompany the field-marshal, general," said the king, turning to Köckeritz. "Take no servants with you, except Timm my chamberlain, who may render assistance to my poor Thomas. My chamberlain is reticent and faithful. Pray have your carriage stopped at the entrance of the avenue, and proceed then on foot. If you find every thing as stated in the spy's report, Timm will drive the carriage to Sans-Souci, that my good old coachman may go to bed and recover from his fright. You will tell him, however, that I wish him not to breathe a word about his adventure. You, gentlemen, will thereupon return and report to me. And you, M. Chancellor, will follow me into my cabinet."

CHAPTER XXI.

THE COURIER'S RETURN.

On reaching his cabinet, the king slowly paced his room, seemingly without noticing the presence of the chancellor. Hardenberg, who waited in silent patience, withdrew softly into a window-niche, and listened to the noise of the **carriage** rolling away at this moment. "The spies the king has sent out are driving to the avenue," said Hardenberg to himself. "They will, no doubt, find every thing as stated in the report, and yet **all** will be in vain. He will not make up his mind to enter a bold course, and while he is hesitating all of us and Prussia will perish."

While he was thus absorbed in his sombre reflections, and sadly gazing out into the dark night, he had not noticed that the king stood still at the other end of the room, and, with his arms folded on his breast, was casting searching glances on the chancellor of state. Now he crossed the room with slow steps and erect head, and stood in front of Hardenberg. "M. Chancellor," said Frederick William, in an unusually mild and gentle tone, "you are sad and discontented, are you not? You are almost despairing, and it seems to you that the King of Prussia, whom the French have again so deeply insulted and humiliated, and whom Napoleon is now threatening even with seizure, should at length revolt against such treatment, and submit no longer to it. It seems to you that, cut to the quick by so many slights, insults, and perfidies, he ought to put an end to his temporizing policy; to rise and exclaim, 'I will die rather than bear this disgrace any longer! I will die rather than endure these humiliations.' You are right; **were I, like you, so fortunate as** to be nothing but a man who had to defend only his own honor and existence, I would be allowed to risk every thing in order to win every thing. But I am the king, and, moreover, the king of an unfortunate state. I must forget my own wrongs, and remember only that I have sacred duties to fulfil toward my people, and that, so far as my own person is concerned, I am not yet allowed to possess any other courage than that of resignation. I am not allowed to stake the existence of my monarchy and the welfare of my people to obtain personal satisfaction. Until I obtain the incontestable certainty that such a course would be brought to a successful issue, I must not throw down the gauntlet to France, for failure in this case would be not only my ruin, but that of my whole people. I shall wait, therefore, M. Chancellor, for an opportunity; but **I** believe that this course requires on my part more constancy and courage than if I, as you wish me to do, should now unreservedly forsake France and render the decision of my fate dependent on the fortune of war. It is my solemn conviction that I ought not to do this, but advance only step by step, and with the utmost caution and deliberation, for— Well, what is it?" asked the king, turning to the chamberlain, who opened the door and entered the cabinet.

"Pardon me, you majesty, for disturbing you," said the chamberlain, respectfully. "But the gentleman who has just entered the anteroom assured me that he was the bearer of important news, which admitted of no delay."

"And who is the gentleman?"

"Sire, it is Major Natzmer, whom your majesty sent recently as a courier to Old Prussia."

"Natzmer?" exclaimed the king, joyously, "admit him at once!—Ah, M. Chancellor, we shall hear now how affairs are looking in my province of Prussia, and how my troops have received York's removal from his command."

"I hope Major Natzmer will bring your majesty good and joyful news," said Hardenberg, with perfect outward calmness, while his heart was throbbing with impatience for Major Natzmer, who now entered; and, while he saluted the king, Hardenberg fixed his eyes, with an anxious expression, on the countenance of the new-comer. For a moment their eyes met. There was an inquiry in those of Hardenberg; Natzmer replied by a slight motion of his eyelids, and an almost imperceptible smile.

"In the first place, report to me briefly and succinctly," said the king. "Reply to all my questions as pointedly and clearly as possible. Afterward we will expatiate on the most important points. Well, then, you saw Murat and Macdonald?"

"I did, your majesty. I met the King of Naples at Elbing, and had the honor of delivering your majesty's letter to him. He received me very kindly, and was delighted at being thus assured of your friendly feelings toward France. Marshal Macdonald, to whose headquarters I then repaired, was less kind and polite. He was still exceedingly indignant at the course of General York,

which he openly stigmatized as traitorous; but he was pacified when I informed him that I was the bearer of an order depriving York of his command, and was about to convey it to the camp of the Russians and Prussians."

"He raised no obstacles, then, but allowed you to pass over without hinderance to the Russian camp?"

"Yes, your majesty. While Macdonald continued his march, I rode to the Russian pickets, and was conducted by an officer, detailed by General Choplitz for this purpose, to the commander-in-chief, Prince Wittgenstein, who had established his headquarters at Heilsberg."

"What business had you at Wittgenstein's headquarters?"

"I wanted, in accordance with your orders, to ask his permission to pass through to General York; and, besides, I wished to ascertain where the Emperor Alexander had established his headquarters, that I might repair to them."

"Prince Wittgenstein, of course, gave you immediate permission to pass through his camp, did he not?"

"No, your majesty; he refused my request."

"How so? What reasons could he adduce? Did you tell him what you intended to do at York's headquarters?"

"Your majesty ordered me to tell every one what I was to do at General York's headquarters, and what punishment you intended to inflict upon him. I was therefore authorized and obliged to inform General Wittgenstein of the object of my mission."

"And he dared to resist you?"

"He did, your majesty. He declared that he would not permit me by any means to go to York, and that so long as he lived no one should bring to the general a dispatch by which the most generous, magnanimous, and valiant general of the Prussian army was to be deprived of his command."

"Then he really prevented you from going to York?"

"Yes, your majesty; he told me I was his prisoner, and did not permit me to leave him."

"**So that,** at this moment, General York has not, as I desire, transferred his command to General Kleist?"

"Precisely, your majesty. General York is still in command."

"And he did not receive the order removing him from his position?"

"I was unable to deliver it, and your majesty required me to **give** it to none but the general himself. I was, however, a prisoner at General Wittgenstein's. **He** asked me whether I had received other commissions; and when he heard that **I was to** deliver a letter to his majesty the emperor, he immediately had a sleigh brought to the door, detailed an officer to escort me, and we set out for the imperial headquarters."

"Let us speak of that hereafter," said the king, quickly. "Tell me first whether you have heard further news about my corps. General York, then, is still in command?"

"Yes, your majesty."

"But even though he has not received the dispatches, he must have seen the news in the newspapers. For the Berlin journals contained a copy of the order superseding him, and he must have noticed it."

"I was told by General Wittgenstein, on returning from the headquarters of the Emperor of Russia, that York had been informed by the newspapers of the severe punishment which your majesty intended to inflict upon him, and that you disavowed him and the course he had taken. Accordingly, he requested General Kleist to take command of the troops. But Kleist refused to do so, alleging that he had received no direct orders from your majesty, and that the dispatches of your majesty, addressed to him personally, would determine his course, and induce him to take command of the troops."

"General Kleist was right in making this declaration," said the king. "So long as York had not received the dispatches, he remained commander-in-chief."

"He is still at the head of the army," exclaimed Natzmer, "for I bring back the dispatches addressed to Generals York and Kleist. As I was unable to deliver them, I return them to your **majesty.**"

The king took the papers which the major presented to him, contemplating them for a moment. He turned toward Hardenberg, and **saw** that heart-felt joy was beaming from **his** face. "**Are** you glad that my orders have not been carried into effect, M. Chancellor of State?" asked the king.

"Yes, your majesty," said Hardenberg, **in a** voice tremulous with emotion, "I am glad of it, for now it seems to me as if our night is drawing to a close, and a new morning is about to dawn upon Prussia. York took the first step for this purpose, and it will be necessary for your majesty to pursue the same course. For, as York has not been deprived of his command, the French will no longer believe that you disavow the action of your brave general, and your people and all Germany will take heart, for they will see that the era of disgrace is past, and that a German king dares at length to resist the French tyrant."

"Well, we shall see," said the king. "Now, Major Natzmer, tell me about your mission to his majesty the Emperor Alexander. I told you **that** it was a state secret. **Did you keep it?**"

"I did, your majesty."

"Well, tell me the result."

"Will your majesty permit me to withdraw?" said the chancellor, approaching the door. "As you intrusted Major Natzmer with a secret mission—"

"Oh, no, your excellency, pray remain; I wish you to hear the message I sent to the emperor, and what he replied to it.—Answer my questions **now,** major. Did you carry out the commission I gave you? Did you verbally lay before the emperor the message which I dared not confide to pen and paper? Did you tell the emperor that I would offer him a defensive and offensive alliance if Alexander would engage to carry on the **war** against Napoleon to the best of his power, and cross the Vistula and the Oder without delay? Did you make this offer to Alexander in my name?"

"I did, your majesty."

The king glanced quickly at Hardenberg, and the surprised face of his chancellor of state made him smile.

"And what did the emperor reply?" asked Frederick William, turning again to the major.

"The emperor was overjoyed at the offer, and declared his readiness to grant all which you would stipulate now and hereafter. The Emperor Alexander imposed only a single condition."

"What was it?"

"He demanded that the fortress of Graudenz should be garrisoned by Russian troops, and insisted most obstinately on this point."

"Did you not tell him that I had made up my mind in regard to this point, and would renounce the proposed alliance if Graudenz, the most remote fortress of my kingdom, should be garrisoned by other than Prussian troops?"

"I stated this to the emperor."

"And then?"

"The emperor resolved to yield even this point, and to leave Graudenz to the Prussian troops."

A sunbeam seemed to light up the grave, calm face of the king, and the cloud that generally darkened his brow disappeared. "M. Chancellor," he said, turning to Hardenberg with a mild and kind smile, "are you now reconciled with your Fabius Cunctator? Will you forgive me for having hesitated until Natzmer would bring me Alexander's reply?"

"Oh, sire," exclaimed Hardenberg, "my soul bows in joyous admiration, and your greatness and mildness make me blush."

At this moment the door opened, and Köckeritz and Kalkreuth entered the cabinet.

"Ah," exclaimed the king, meeting them, "my two generals whom I sent out on a reconnoissance! Well, gentlemen, speak! Did you find my carriage?"

"We did, your majesty," said Field-Marshal Kalkreuth, sighing. "The report was but too true. A vile plot had been formed; we have the proofs, for we really found the carriage of your majesty in the avenue leading to Sans-Souci; the horses had been partially unhitched—"

"And my poor coachman?" asked the king. "Köckeritz, tell me what has become of my faithful Thomas?"

"We found him exactly in the condition stated in the spy's report," said General Köckeritz, hastily. "He lay in the interior of the carriage; his hands and feet firmly tied; his head covered with a cape, which had been closely fastened round his neck to prevent him from crying; it had, moreover, almost choked him when we arrived."

"But he has recovered from his fright?" asked the king, in a tone of sympathy.

"Yes, your majesty," said Köckeritz, "and he would not permit Timm to accompany him to Sans-Souci. He felt strong enough to return to Potsdam, and arrived here at the same time as we did."

"I suppose you have ordered him to say nothing about the whole affair?"

"Yes, your majesty, and he swore he would not mention it."

"And now, gentlemen, give me your opinion. Field-Marshal Kalkreuth, you have satisfied yourself now that the French really intended to seize and abduct me to-night?"

"I have unfortunately satisfied myself that they made such an attempt," said the field-marshal.

"And you, Köckeritz, believe so, too?"

"I do, your majesty; I am fully convinced that such an outrage was in contemplation."

"And you, M. Chancellor of State?"

"I was confident of the existence of this plot before coming hither, and every thing has confirmed it; yes, such an outrage was surely intended. The French meant to seize your sacred person."

"Will your majesty permit me also to reply to this question?" said Major Natzmer.

"What do you mean?" asked the king, surprised. "Have you not just arrived? How can you pass an opinion on what occurred before your arrival?"

"Your majesty, it is true I have just now come; but still I knew what was to occur here, and what an infamous transaction was planned," said **Major Natzmer**. "The Emperor Alexander gave me this information; he had just **received** from a perfectly reliable source the news that Marshal Augereau had been instructed to seize the person of your majesty. The emperor was greatly alarmed, and told me he would be unable to find any rest until he had heard that you were safe, and had left Berlin and Potsdam.* I myself set out **at once in** the greatest consternation, and as **I left** the emperor on the 13th of January, I **would have** arrived here much earlier if I had not **heard at** Landshut that Murat had issued an order **der to** all the authorities to have me arrested and conveyed to the French headquarters.† This compelled me to take a roundabout course, and now I rejoice the more heartily as I have arrived at the very time to caution your majesty, in the name of the Emperor Alexander, against the insidious designs of the French."

The king made no reply. He paced the room slowly and with his head bent down; the four gentlemen stood in silence on both sides of the cabinet. Suddenly standing in the middle of the room, with his countenance full of determination, he said: "Gentlemen, I will tell you a state secret. Will you pledge me your word of honor, all four of you, that you will keep it?"

"We will!" they all shouted at the same moment.

"Listen to me, then," added the king. "I shall leave Potsdam and repair to Breslau, whither the seat of government will be temporarily transferred. All the necessary preparations must be made from this hour with the utmost dispatch and prudence. To-morrow night I shall set out with the crown prince; the rest of the royal family will follow me on the next day. Troops will be stationed along the route; the hussars forming my escort, and the lifeguards following to Breslau. It is my duty to place myself beyond the reach of insidious attacks, and to render it impossible for the French to seize me. I will, therefore, go to Breslau!" While uttering these words, the king glanced successively at the faces of the four gentlemen. He saw that Field-Marshal Kalkreuth looked gloomy and abstracted, and opposite him the chancellor of state, with burning cheeks and radiant eyes.

"Well, Hardenberg," said the king, mildly, "have you nothing to say to me?"

"I am unable to say any thing," whispered Hardenberg, in a tremulous voice, "but I do what I have not done for many years past—I weep tears of joy! Our night is at an end; a new morning is dawning upon Prussia, and the sun of a new era will shed his beams upon all of us!"

---

* Droysen's "Life of York," vol. ii., p. 120.   † Ibid.

THE VOLUNTEERS.

CHAPTER XXII.

THE MANIFESTO.

THE people were moving in dense crowds through Berlin. The long and splendid street "Unter den Linden" was filled with a vast multitude, whose greeting cheers resembled the noise of the ocean's billows.

"The king has safely arrived at Breslau!" cried one of the men to another, and immediately the enthusiastic cry of "Long live the king!" burst from all those who heard it, and, like a jubilant echo, the people along the whole street repeated, "Long live the king!"

"The king has reappointed General Scharnhorst quartermaster-general, and General Blucher is with him at Breslau!" exclaimed a stentorian voice.

"Long live Scharnhorst! Long live Blucher!" shouted the crowd. "Long live our heroes!" "Down with the French!" and thousands answered in tones of intense hatred, "Down with the French!"

"They so long trampled us under foot!" cried another citizen. "Now, let us pay them for it! Come, let us go to the French ambassador and give him a few groans! We will no longer be silent!"

"Yes, we are determined to speak!" yelled the multitude, who hurried toward the gate in front of which the residence of the ambassador was situated. But suddenly they were stopped by a procession approaching from the Brandenburg gate. It was headed by three men—one of short and feeble frame, his face pale and emaciated, but lit up by large flashing blue eyes; the second was tall and broad-shouldered, his eye looking frank and bold, and his hair falling on his shoulders like a lion's mane; the third was not tall, but of a firmly-knit frame, and, with his proud head and intrepid air, looked like the embodiment of chivalry. Behind them was a line of more than two hundred youths, in light, simple attire, their cheeks glowing with excitement or exercise, and their eyes flashing with enthusiasm.

"Hurrah!" shouted the people. "Here are the Turners! Here is Father Jahn with his Turners! Long live Jahn!"

The Turners, at a beck from "Father Jahn," had taken position across the street, and thus, like a chain, prevented the citizens from passing on. The three leaders stood in front, and gazed gravely upon the approaching multitude.

"Clear the track!" cried the crowd. "We have business to attend to on the square in front of the gate!"

"Believe me, it is as I said," whispered the smallest of the three men to his neighbor. "It is a riot directed against the French ambassador!"

"Where are you going?" shouted the man with the lion's mane, pushing back those at the head of the crowd with his herculean arms.

"We are going to the French ambassador, to sing him a new German song, and accompany it with stones for his windows."

"And why do you wish to do so?" asked the tall man. "What do you care for the Frenchman on this beautiful and joyous day? Men like you have something else to do than to break the windows of the French ambassador. There will be other battles before long. I hope you have heard or read what great events have occurred; I hope you know the message which the king has sent to us from Breslau?"

"No, we know nothing about them!" replied a few voices. "Yes, we do," said others. "But we would like to hear the news again," cried another. "Pray, repeat it to us, Father Jahn!"

"I am not very well able to do so; our gymnastic performances to-day have exhausted me," replied Jahn. "I went out of the gate with my pupils at an early hour in the morning. These two gentlemen came to us and told us the news, and that is the reason why we have come back. My friend will tell you what he told me, and he knows better how to speak than I do, for he has an eloquent tongue. This is well known to all of you, for who among you is not acquainted with Frederick Schleiermacher, the great preacher?"

"Schleiermacher! Long live Schleiermacher! Let Schleiermacher repeat to us what the king said! Let him tell us what is on the large placards on the street corners. Hearing it read, we understand it better than on reading it ourselves." And many arms were stretched out toward the feeble little man who stood by the side of Jahn, lifting him up and placing him gently on the balcony fixed above the door of a neighboring house.

"That is a good pulpit," shouted the people; "Schleiermacher, address us from it!"

The little man with bright eyes and a genial countenance gazed for a moment in silence upon his auditors, who thronged around him in suspense and curiosity. He then raised his arms, commanding silence. The laughter, shouts, and yells died away; all eyes were fixed upon Schleiermacher, and the noise of the multitude seemed arrested as by a magician's wand, as the voice of the preacher resounded through the street clear and distinct. "You want me to read what has been addressed to us all," he said, "the manifesto which Minister von Hardenberg has issued to the people in the king's name. Listen, then!" He took a large folded paper from his breast-pocket, and, opening it, read as follows: "'The dangerous position in which the state has been placed by recent events requires a rapid augmentation of the troops now in arms, while our finances admit of no lavish expenditures. In consideration of the patriotism and faithful attachment to the king which have always animated the people of Prussia, and manifested themselves most strikingly in times of danger, there is but an opportunity required to give a definite direction to these sentiments, and to the desire for activity which distinguishes so many young men, that they may swell by their accession to the army the ranks of the older defenders of the country, whom they would emulate in nobly fulfilling the first of all duties incumbent upon us. For this reason his majesty has designed to order the organization of companies of volunteers, to be embodied with the regiments of infantry and cavalry already in the service, that an opportunity to enter the army in a manner suitable to their education, and their position in life, may be given to all those classes who, under the existing conscription laws, are exempt from service, and are rich enough to pay for their own outfit and horse, and that a prospect of distinguishing themselves may be held out to men who, owing to their education and intellect, might immediately do good service, and soon be appointed line and field officers.'* It is unnecessary for me to read the conclusion of the proclamation," said Schleiermacher. "You know enough, for you know now that the king calls his people; that he calls upon all the youths and men of his kingdom to rally round him, and that he requests, and does not order them to do so. The country is in danger; and not the king's order, but your own voluntary action, is to make you soldiers of the fatherland and put arms into your hands. Remember that your free will is your most precious and sacred

---

* Hardenberg issued this manifesto at Breslau, on the 3d of February; it was published at Berlin on the 5th.

possession, and that he is twice a hero whom it actuates, and is not forced into duty. No greater honor can be conferred on you than that your country calls you, **trusts in your strong arm, and** hopes in your free will to save it from destruction. Take that into consideration, and decide then whether you will stay at home or obey the call."

The two men who had been by his side at the **head of the procession, Jahn, the brave Turner,** and the chivalrous La Motte Fouqué, now ascended the balcony.

"I do not care to stay at home when my country calls me to her aid!" exclaimed M. de la Motte Fouqué, in a loud, sonorous voice. "I joyfully offer my services as a soldier. I have a wife and children, but my country is to me more precious than they are, and I enroll here my name as the first volunteer who responds to the call of his king and country."

"And I enroll my name as the **second** volunteer!" exclaimed Jahn, the Turners' father. "I **swear** here to my country that I will joyously fight for **it. Henceforth,** my blood and life belong to the fatherland.—And where are you, my boys, my Turners? Shall I march out all alone, or will you accompany me?"

"We will go with you!" cried a hundred youthful voices, and their enthusiastic shouts rent the sky. "We will march with you! We will fight for the fatherland!" And the crowd, carried away by what they saw and heard—the men with tearful eyes, the youths with flashing glances —all shouted: "We will march with you! We will fight for the fatherland!" Neighbor gave his hand to neighbor, and friend embraced friend; those who had never before seen each other understood the common feeling, and those who had never exchanged a word conversed now like old acquaintances. One grand impulse seemed to move **the** multitude—one patriotic feeling beamed from all eyes—one vow burned in all hearts: to be faithful soldiers to their country. It was no mere transitory enthusiasm, soon to disappear, and to be succeeded by a corresponding reaction—it was no momentary ardor kindled by the manifesto issued at Breslau, but the sacred fire of patriotism

burning in the heart of
sia, and **increased fro**
felt himself a soldier,
it a disgrace to rem
marched to **the war of**

The pupils of the l
and the teachers did n
appeared in the schoc
grown youths: "Farew
us! Let us march to tl
have reached their s
willing to fight, follov
of exultation, the olde
teachers, while the y
tearful eyes, as if ash
occurred in the lyceun
the courts, the count
and merchants. No
refuse the country his
selfish calculations, al
ceased. **Princes and**
ranks **of the voluntee**
blest youths; and po
thing they had to bu
not think of their futu
them after their returr
land had called them
up arms in its defenc
rors, life had lost
hearts, mothers saw tl
struggle. The affian
clasped her departing
her arms; without fe
and children, the hus
his dear ones, and his
suade him. She woul
desired to remain, a
children more devotec
to him in the hour of l

Four days had **not**
cation of the manifes
stood on the Gens
one hundred and fif
within a few days, ha
themselves, either fro
the assistance of fri

about to march to Potsdam in order to **set out with a** company of ninety volunteers, which had **been** recruited in that city for the king's **head-quarters** at Breslau.* All Berlin wished to participate in the farewell of this first company of volunteers which were sent to its king. Every one desired once more to shake hands with the courageous defenders of the country—to shout a love-greeting, a **last wish to** them, and bless the soldiers **of the** fatherland. The windows of **the** houses **on the** Gendarmes market were therefore filled with ladies and children, who greeted the **departing** volunteers with their handkerchiefs, **with wreaths** and flowers; the church bells were ringing in their honor, and the fathers of the city, **the** burgomasters, and other members **of** the municipality, adorned with their golden chains, were assembled on the market-place to conduct the young soldiers, in the name of the city, to the gate, and behind them a dense multitude filled the square. Those remaining looked gloomy, and envied their brethren, because they were to take the field at so early a day; wishing them joy, they shouted: "Prepare quarters for us; we shall soon follow you!"

The church bells were ringing, and amid their solemn peals and the deafening cheers of the many thousands who nodded to them in the streets, and from the windows of the houses, the young soldiers left the Gendarmes market, escorted by the members of the municipality. They did not, however, march directly to the Potsdam gate. They would not leave Berlin without receiving the blessing of the Church, and this was to be given by the man who read to them the manifesto four days before, and who had exhorted them to comply with the call of their country. A committee, appointed by the young volunteers, had therefore waited on Schleiermacher, and requested him to give the blessing of the Church to their grave undertaking, and he gladly granted their request. The procession marched to

Trinity church. There were waiting their mothers, sisters, and brides, greeting them with loving glances, and beckoning them to occupy the reserved places, embracing and praying hand in hand **with them** for the last time. The organ poured forth its solemn concords, and **from all** lips burst forth the anthem of "*In allen meinen Thaten lass ich den Höchsten rathen.*"* **The last** notes of the music had not yet died away, when the noble face of Schleiermacher appeared in the pulpit. His eyes were beaming as never before; his voice was never so fervent and powerful, nor had he ever spoken with such irresistible eloquence, energy, and courage, as on that day. A profound silence reigned in the vast building; every one listened eagerly to the inspiring words of the prophet **of a new and better era, and inwardly** resolved to remember the stirring exhortations which Schleiermacher now, in concluding his sermon, addressed to the young men, that they may remain pure and true in the service of so righteous a cause. The thoughts of the audience were with God; to Him their hearts had all turned. But now Schleiermacher's voice grew softer; his eyes, which had hitherto been **raised toward heaven, looked upon the wives and mothers,** who sat in long lines before him. "Rejoice in the Lord, ye mothers," he said, "blessed are you in having given birth to such sons! blessed your breasts that nourished such children! God gave them to you, and you give them to the fatherland! Rejoice in the Lord, for He will achieve great things through them! Rejoice, and do not weep!" But now they could restrain no longer their tears and sobs. The words addressed to them had touched their feelings. They felt their hearts' wounds, and wept aloud. An electric shock, as it were, pervaded the whole assembly; not an eye remained dry, not a heart **was unmoved; even Schleiermacher's voice** was tremulous when he uttered his "Amen!"

They departed from the church to the Potsdam gate, and along the road leading to Potsdam, continuing their march on the following day, after

---

* Nine thousand young men volunteered at Berlin in the first three days after the manifesto was issued, and active preparations were made to uniform and equip them at the earliest moment.

* "In all my deeds, I let the Highest counsel."

being joined by the company which La Motte Fouqué had recruited in that city. **The grief of their** separation from their dear ones **was for**-gotten as they hastened toward **the future—a** future of battles and victories.

"Now, no more tears, no more sighs! Let us sing a merry song!" said the young volunteers.

"Yes. Where is a poet who can sing us **a song** such as we need now?"

"Fouqué is here; let him sing! Yes, Fouqué is among **us!** We have **elected him** captain! He is a chivalrous soldier, and gained his spurs **in 1794, during** the war against the French. He **deserves** to be our captain!"

"But he deserves, too, to be our bard, for by his 'Undine' he has also won his laurels as a poet."

"Let us have a song, brave La Motte Fouqué!" shouted all the volunteers. "There is Father **Jahn, who will persuade him. Ask Fouqué to sing us a war-song!**"

Jahn galloped up to the poet, who **was riding** in thoughtful silence at the head of his **company;** it is true, he had heard the solicitations **of the** young men, but continued his way, smiling and muttering to himself. "Fouqué," shouted Jahn, in his stentorian voice; "do you not hear the requests of our bold youths? Give some expression to the enthusiasm burning in their hearts. Let us have a song, then, my poet!"

"**Well,**" replied Fouqué, quickly raising his head, and smiling on his friend; "I have just composed **a poem.** Listen to me, my friends!" He turned his horse, and in a loud voice commanded the volunteers to halt.

"You wish me to sing. **I will give you a song** just as it has sprung **up in my heart during the** march, and I have also composed the air. When **I have finished** repeat it with me!" And he began **to sing in** a powerful voice:

> Frisch auf zum fröhlichen Jagen,
>   Es ist schon an der Zeit!
> Es fängt schon an zu tagen,
>   Der Kampf ist nicht mehr weit!
>
> "Auf lasst die Faulen liegen,
>   Gönnt ihnen ihre Ruh;
> **Wir rücken mit Vergnügen**
>   **Dem lieben König zu.**

> "Der König hat gesprochen:
>   Wo sind **meine** Jäger nun?
> Da sind wir aufgebrochen,
>   Ein wackeres Werk zu thun.
>
> "**Wir woll'n ein Heil erbauen**
>   **Für all das deutsche Land,**
>   **Im frohen Gottvertrauen**
>   **Mit rüstig starker Hand.**
>
> "Schlaft ruhig nun, Ihr Lieben!
>   Am väterlichen Heerd,
> Derweil mit Feindeshieben
>   Wir ringen Keck bewehrt.
>
> "O Wonne die zu schützen,
>   Die uns das Liebste sind!
> Heil! Lasst Kanonen blitzen,
>   Ein frommer muth gewinnt!
>
> "Die mehrsten zieh'n einst wieder
>   Zurück in Siegerreih'n;
> Dann tönen Jubellieder
>   Dess' wird'ne Freude **sein!**
>
> "**Wie glüh'n davon die Herzen**
>   So froh und stark und weich.
> Wer fällt, der kann's verschmerzen,
>   Der hat das Himmelreich!" *

---

* **La Motte Fouqué** composed this poem on the march from **Potsdam to Breslau,** whither he conducted the first companies of **volunteers.** It was the first song of liberty published in 1813:

> Mount! mount! for **sacred freedom fight!**
>   The battle soon must be.
> The night is past, and red the **light**
>   Streams o'er the dewy lea.
>
> Up! let the coward idlers sleep!
>   Who envies them their rest?
> We march with joyful hearts to keep
>   Our honored king's request.
>
> To us he said: "My brave ones all!—
>   My chasseurs! where are they?"
> Responsive to his patriot call
>   We hastened to obey.
>
> We vowed to strike with mighty **hand**
>   As it becomes the free—
> A safeguard for our native land
>   With Heaven's grace to be.
>
> Sleep calmly, wives and children dear!
>   To God your sorrows tell,
> The hour, alas! of blood is near,
>   But all your fears dispel.
>
> Approved we hasten to the field;
>   What though the strife begins!
> 'Tis joy our loved **ones thus to shield,**
>   For pious courage wins.
>
> Returning, **all may not be found!**
>   But some, **in glory's grave,**
> Shall never hear **the songs resound**
>   Of those they died to save.
>
> Come, glowing heart! despise the pain
>   Of death; for, evermore,
> Shall he who falls, a kingdom gain
>   On heaven's eternal shore!

CHAPTER XXIII.

LEONORA PROHASKA.

OLD Sergeant Prohaska sat sad and musing in his old easy-chair near the stove; before him lay a copy of the *Vossische Zeitung*, which he had just perused. He laid it aside with a sigh; supporting his head on the leathern cushion, he puffed clouds of smoke from his short clay pipe. Close to him, **at the** small table standing in the niche **of the** only window which admitted light into the small, dark room, sat a young girl, busily engaged in drawing threads from a large piece of linen, and putting them carefully on the pile of **lint on the table. She** was scarcely eighteen years old, but her noble, pale countenance wore an expression of boldness and energy; her forehead was high, and vigorous thoughts seemed to dwell there. Large black eyes were flashing under her finely-arched eyebrows, which almost touched each other above her beautifully-chiselled, slightly-curved nose. Round her crimson lips was an expression of melancholy, and her cheeks seemed to have been bleached by grief rather than sickness. She was tall and well formed, but her whole appearance was more remarkable for the stern and heroic character it indicated than for grace and loveliness. While she was thus at work, and engaged in preparing lint, troubled thoughts seemed to pass from time to time across her face, and she raised her eyes to heaven with an angry and reproachful expression. She impulsively cast aside the linen, and jumped up. "No, father," she exclaimed, drawing a deep breath, "I cannot bear it any longer!"

"What is it that you cannot bear any longer, Leonora?" exclaimed her father, surprised.

"To sit here and prepare lint while the whole world is astir, while every heart is swelling with patriotism and warlike enthusiasm! And I cannot do any thing, I cannot join in the universal exultation—I can do nothing but prepare lint! **Father, it** is heart-rending, and I cannot bear it!"

"Must not I bear it?" asked her father in a tremulous voice. "Must not I sit still behind the stove, while all my old comrades are taking up arms and marching into the field? My right leg was buried at Jena, and I must limp about now as a miserable cripple; I cannot even take revenge for the disgrace of Jena; I cannot even pay the French for my leg by cutting off the heads of some of their accursed soldiers. I am a cripple, while others are hastening into the field! When *I* must bear that, a girl like you ought assuredly not to complain."

"Father," said Leonora, with flashing eyes, "do not despise me because I am a girl! Did you not tell me of the heroic women of Spain and the Tyrol, and of their glorious deeds? Did you not tell me that, by their intrepid patriotism, they had set a sublime example to the men, and that by their influence their country was to be saved? Was not the heroine of Saragossa a woman? Did not women and girls fight like heroes in the gorges of the Tyrol?"

"Yes, that is true," exclaimed her father, smiling, "but then they were Spanish and Tyrolese girls. They have fire in their veins, and love their country with an undying patriotism?"

"Ah, one need not be born in the South to have warm blood," exclaimed Leonora, ardently. "It is not the sun that gives love of country, and patriotic hearts may throb even under the snow."

"Have you such a heart, Leonora?" asked her father, casting on her a long and searching look.

"Father," she said, pressing her hands on her bosom, "there is something burning here like fire; and at times when I hear how all are rallying round the flag—and how the warlike enthusiasm is pervading the whole country, I feel as if the blood would burst from my heart and head. It is true I am no Spanish girl, but I am a Prussian girl!"

"Ah, I would **you were** a Prussian boy!" **sighed** her father, shaking his head. "If you were, I believe you would look well in the ranks of the volunteers; they would not likely reject the young soldier of eighteen."

"I am quite tall and strong, although I am but

a girl," exclaimed Leonora, with flashing eyes; "I have seen among the soldiers who started yesterday many volunteers who were a great deal shorter and slighter than I am."

"But, at all events, they had shorter hair and a stronger voice than you have," laughed her father.

"Oh, I can cut off my hair," she said, quickly; "and as for my voice, Kalbaum, the tailor, who accompanied the volunteers, **has** a voice no **stronger than mine,** and yet he was accepted. **And then—**"

"**Hush!**" interposed her father quickly. "I hear your mother coming. Do not speak of such things when she is present. It would alarm her. Bold thoughts must be locked up in our hearts, for, if we speak of them, it looks like braggadocio; we are only allowed to speak of bold deeds. Do not forget that, my daughter, and give me a kiss!" Leonora hastened to her father, **and encircling him with her arms,** pressed a glow**ing kiss on the lips of the old invalid.**

"**Father,**" she whispered, "**I believe you un**derstand me, and can read my **thoughts!**"

"God alone is able to read our thoughts," said her father, solemnly, "and it is only from Him that we must not conceal any thing. But what is that? Is not your mother weeping outside?" **And** old Prohaska jumped up and limped, as quickly as his wooden leg permitted, toward the **door.**

At this moment the door was noisily opened, and **a** woman appeared on the threshold. Behind her was a tall, slender, and pale boy, scarcely fourteen years of age. Both entered the room with tearful eyes and loud lamentations.

"Wife, what is the matter—what has happened?" exclaimed Old Prohaska, anxiously.

"Why do you weep, my brother?" asked Leonora, hastening to the boy, and clasping him in her arms. He laid his head on her breast and **wept aloud.**

"**What** has happened?" wailed his mother. "All our hopes are blasted; we have been rejected!"

"Rejected? Where? And by whom?" asked the invalid, in amazement.

"By the military commission!" cried his wife, drying her tears with her long apron.

"**What did you want** of the military commission? **Did you desire to** become a *vivandière*, old woman?"

"No, but **Charles wanted** to enlist, father! Yes, you must know all now. We thought we would prepare a joyous surprise for you, but the good Lord and the military commission would not let us do so. Look, old man! I perceived very well how painful it was to you, and how it was gnawing at your heart, that your wooden leg compels you to remain here at Potsdam, and prevents your marching out with the soldiers who are hurrying to the headquarters of their king at Breslau."

"Yes, it is true, it is very sad! My general, old Blucher, under whom I fought in 1806, is also at Breslau, and what will he say when he looks for his old hussars of 1806, and does not find Prohaska! He will say, 'Prohaska has become a coward—a lazy old good-for-nothing.'"

"No, father, he will not say so," exclaimed Leonora, ardently; "if he knows you, he cannot say so.—But speak, mother, tell us what makes you weep, and what has so afflicted my dear brother?"

"Both of us noticed father's secret grief, and comprehended how painful it was for him to be unable to participate in the war," said her mother. "I had not mentioned it to any one, and to God alone I had complained how grievous it is that I have no full-grown son, who, instead of his father, might serve his king at the present time. Last night, when all of you were asleep, Charles came to my bedside. 'Mother,' he said to me, 'mother, I must tell you something! I will and must enlist! It would be an eternal disgrace for me to stay at home, particularly as father is disabled, and cannot fight any more. Mother, the honor of the family is at stake; I must enlist or die!'"

"Ah, you are a true brother of mine," exclaimed Leonora, with a radiant face, drawing the boy closer to her heart.

"And what did you reply to Charles, mother?" asked the invalid.

"'You are my only son, and my heart would break if I should lose you. But you are right; it would be a disgrace for our whole family if it did not furnish a single soldier to the king and the fatherland, and if no substitute should enlist in your father's place, and revenge him on the French for crippling him at Jena. I will go with you to the military commission to-morrow, and we will pray the gentlemen to accept you, although you are still under age. We will pray them until they overlook your youth and enroll your name. But say nothing about it to father until we have been successful; then, tell him all.'"

"And you really went with him to the commission?" asked the old man, hastily.

His wife responded by nodding and sighing, and burst again into tears.

"Yes, father," exclaimed the boy, raising his head from Leonora's shoulder, and drying his eyes with an angry gesture, "we went to the military commission. We begged, implored, and wept! It was all in vain! They said they were not allowed to accept boys of fourteen; I was too young, and looked too feeble. In our despair we went to Eylert, the preacher, and begged him to intercede for me. He is always kind to me, and often praises me for my industry in preparing for confirmation. I revealed my whole heart to him; I told him I must consider myself disgraced, if now, that every one who is not a coward is taking the sword, I am compelled to go to school. I told him I should not dare to raise my eyes, and should think all the inhabitants would point with their fingers at me; the children in the streets' would deride me, and the old men would contemptuously avert their heads when I passed them."

"Ah, my beloved brother," exclaimed Leonora, enthusiastically, "hitherto I have loved you as a child, but henceforth I shall love as a hero!"

"But it was all in vain," cried Charles, sobbing aloud in his grief and anger. "Even M. Eylert could not give us any comfort. He said it was impossible for the commission to accept me, for, though they overlooked my youth and my somewhat feeble health, they could not enroll

me because I had not yet been confirmed. But as we begged so very hard, and I shed so many tears, M. Eylert had at last pity on me, and went with us once more to the military commission. But it was of no avail. I am under age and have no certificate of confirmation, and M. Eylert's intercession was fruitless.* They rejected me! Father, what am I to do now? I am doomed to remain here at Potsdam, with my tall figure, which will charge me with cowardice in the eyes of every one, while my schoolmates, who are much shorter than I am, are allowed to enlist and fight for their country. Oh, mother, why am I not your eldest child? Then I should be preserved from the disgrace of running about as a coward, or of being obliged to have my certificate of birth constantly in my pocket!"

"My brother," said Leonora, laying her strong white hand on her brother's light hair, "if I could give you the four years by which I am older than you, I would do so, though it should cost me my life, for I comprehend your grief. But I am innocent of your affliction, and I pray you, therefore, not to be angry with me. It was God's **will that I** should be older, and have your place. You must take into consideration that the **war** may last a long time; six months hence you will be confirmed, and then it will be time for you to enlist in the king's army, and fight for liberty. Besides, my dear brother, it is not even settled yet whether all these warlike preparations are really intended for France. To be sure, every one is in hope that such is the case, but as yet no one is sure of it, for the king has not declared his intentions, and he is still at peace with France."

"No, the king has declared his intentions," cried Charles, impetuously. "And that is exactly what causes my distress and my despair. It is certain now that there will be war with France. You do not know, then, what has occurred?"

"No," exclaimed father and daughter at the same time, "we do not—we have not yet seen any one. Tell us the news, Charles."

---

* Eylert, "Frederick William III.," vol. ii, p. 168.

"Well, we heard already at the office of the military commission that a courier had just arrived from Breslau, and brought a proclamation, addressed by the king to his people; they said it had immediately been sent to the printing-office, and was to be posted on all the street corners. The courier, besides, brought the news that the Emperor of Russia had arrived at Breslau, and that the first visit was to Baron von Stein, who secretly lived at Breslau."

"Hurrah!" shouted **old** Prohaska. "Prussia is safe now, for Baron von Stein is back again, and he will know how to expel Napoleon and his French from the country. Where Minister von Stein is he tolerates no French, and that is the reason why Bonaparte hates him, and has always been afraid of him. My boy, this is glorious news! Stein is back again; now we shall be all right! Have you any other news?"

"Yes, there is a great deal yet, father, but the tears burst from my eyes when I think of it, **because I am unable to participate in the struggle.**"

"Oh, what is it?" begged Leonora. "What else has happened at Breslau?"

"Well," said Charles, in a tremulous and melancholy voice, "the courier reports that many hundreds of volunteers are arriving every day, **not only from all** parts of Prussia, but the whole of Germany, and that the city is rejoicing as though a festival were to be celebrated, and not as though we were on the eve of a terrible war. Above all, there is Major von Lützow, round whose standard hosts of young men are rallying, enlisting a corps of volunteer riflemen, to whom he has given the name of 'The **Legion of Vengeance.**' They are to wear a black uniform as a sign of the sorrow and disgrace that have weighed down the fatherland since 1806, and which **they** intend to avenge before discarding it."

"Oh, that is a grand idea," exclaimed Leonora, with flashing eyes. "To march out in mourning—to rush to the battle-field like angels of death and shout, 'We are the legion of avengers, sent by Prussia to atone for her disgrace! Our uniform is black, but we intend to dye it red in the blood of the French!' And then to fight exultantly in the thickest of **the** fray for the fatherland, and for our queen, whose heart was broken by the national dishonor and wretchedness! Oh, it must be blissful, indeed, to march with that legion to avenge the tears of Queen Louisa, and—"

"But Leonora!" cried her mother, staring in amazement at the young girl who stood before her with glowing cheeks, panting bosom, and uplifted right arm, as if she had just drawn the sword—"but, Leonora! what is the matter with you? What does your impulsiveness mean? Has Charles infected you with his enthusiasm? Do you want to increase the excitement and despair of the poor boy? He cannot join the 'Legion of Vengeance;' he cannot be one of Lützow's riflemen!"

"No," said Leonora, vehemently and almost triumphantly, "*he* cannot be one of Lützow's riflemen!"

"Leonora!" cried her father, in a warning tone, "Leonora, what are you saying?"

She started and dropped her arm. "It is true," she muttered to herself, "we should not betray our thoughts; God alone must know them."

Her father limped to her, and, laying his hand on her shoulder, looked into her excited and glowing face. "Come, my daughter," he said, "let us go out into the street and read what the king says to his people. For I believe the king's proclamation must have been printed by this time. Come, Leonora!"

"No, it is unnecessary for you to go into the street for that purpose, father," said Charles, "we have brought a copy of the proclamation; the man who was to post them gave us one for you, saying it would no doubt gladden your heart. Where did you leave it, mother?"

"I put it into my pocket. Here it is!" said the mother, taking a large printed sheet from the pocket hanging under her apron. "There, father, read it."

The old man took the paper and handed it **to** Leonora. "Read it to us, my child," he said, tenderly. "I like best to hear from your lips what the king says to his people."

CHAPTER XXIV.

JOAN OF ORLEANS.

LEONORA took the paper and read as follows, with crimson cheeks, and her heart aglow with enthusiasm:

"*To my People!*—I need not state the causes of the impending war either to my faithful people or to the Germans in general. Unprejudiced Europe is fully aware of them. We succumbed to the superior strength of France. The peace which wrested from me one-half of my subjects, did not confer any blessings upon us, but inflicted deeper wounds upon us than war itself. The enemy was bent on exhausting the resources of the country; the principal fortresses remained in his hands; agriculture was paralyzed, and so were the manufactures of our cities, which had formerly reached so proud an eminence; trade was everywhere obstructed, and the sources of prosperity were thus almost entirely ruined. The country was rapidly impoverished. By the most conscientious fulfilment of the engagements I had taken upon myself, I hoped to mitigate the onerous burdens imposed upon my people, and to convince the French emperor at length that it was to his own advantage to leave Prussia in the enjoyment of her independence; but my best intentions were foiled by arrogance and perfidy; and we saw only too plainly that Napoleon's treaties, even more than his wars, would slowly and surely ruin us. The moment has come when all deceptions have ceased. Brandenburgians, Prussians, Silesians, Pomeranians, Lithuanians! you know what you have suffered for seven years past; you know what your fate would be if we should not succeed in the struggle about to begin. Remember the history of the past; remember the noble elector; the great and victorious Frederick; remember what our ancestors conquered with their blood—freedom of conscience, honor, independence, commerce, industry, and science; remember the great examples of our powerful allies, especially the Spaniards and the Portuguese. Even smaller nations, for the same blessings, entered into a desperate struggle with more powerful foes, and achieved a glorious victory. Remember the heroic Swiss and Dutch. Great sacrifices will be required of all classes, for our undertaking is a great one, and the numbers and resources of our enemies are not to be underrated. You will prefer to make these sacrifices for the fatherland and your legitimate king rather than for a foreign ruler, who, as is proved by many examples, would devote your sons and your last resources to objects entirely foreign to you. Confidence in God, courage, perseverance, and the assistance of our allies, will crown our honest exertions with victory. **But** whatever sacrifices may be required, they are not equivalent to the sacred objects for **which we make them, and for which we must fight and conquer, if we do not wish to cease being Prussians and Germans. It is the last, decisive** effort which we make for our existence, our independence, our prosperity. There is no other issue than an honorable peace or a glorious overthrow. You would not shrink even from the latter, for honor's sake. But we may confidently hope for the best. God and our firm determination will make us victorious, and we shall then obtain peace and the return of happier times.

"FREDERICK WILLIAM.

"BRESLAU, *March* 17, 1813."*

A pause ensued when Leonora ceased reading. Her father, who was standing by her side, and was supporting his hands on his crutch, heard her with a very grave face. Her mother sank down on one of the cane chairs, and listened devoutly, her hands clasped, and her eyes turned toward heaven; while her son, who was sitting by her side, leaned his arms on the table, and buried his face in his hands.

"Is that all?" asked the invalid, after a while.

---

* This proclamation was drawn up by Counsellor von Hippel, who proposed that the king should apply to his people directly, and call upon them to rise against the French. He communicated it to the chancellor of state at one of the conferences held every evening at Breslau, at Hardenberg's rooms, in presence of Gneisenau, Scharnhorst, Thile, and a few others. Hardenberg and all the rest approved it, and so did the king, when it was laid before him on the following day.—Vide Hippel's work on the "Life of Frederick William III.," p. 63.

"I should really like to hear more of it, for it sounds as sacred as a church organ. Did you read it all, Leonora?"

"No, father, there is still another manifesto. It is printed under the one I read to you. You yourself must read it, for my heart is throbbing as if about to burst. In his second manifesto the king orders a 'landwehr' and a 'landsturm' to be formed. Listen to what he says at the end of this second manifesto: 'My cause,' he says, 'is the cause of my people, and of all patriots in Europe.'"

"Yes, he is right," said old Prohaska; "the king's cause is our cause!"

"Queen Louisa died for us all," exclaimed Leonora; "we should all join the Legion of Vengeance—that is, to avenge her death!"

"And I—I cannot do any thing," wailed Charles, raising his face, which was bathed in tears, and lifting up his hands as if supplicating God to help him. "I must wait and suffer here; I am doomed to remain a boy while **my schoolfellows have become men.**"

"Hush," said his mother, "an idea strikes me; we may, after all, be somewhat useful to our country, though we are unable to furnish soldiers for it. There is a great deal to be done besides **fighting.** The king's manifesto says expressly: 'Great sacrifices will be required of all classes.' Well, then, my dear ones, let us make sacrifices for the fatherland and our king!"

"**What sacrifices** do you mean, mother?" asked the invalid. "What have we, if we cannot furnish any soldiers?"

"We have our labor," exclaimed his wife, with pride. "When there is war, and battles are fought, there are wounded soldiers, I suppose?"

"Of course, and cripples, too," said the invalid, pointing to his wooden leg.

"And the wounded are brought home and conveyed to the hospitals, are they not? Who is to attend to them, to dress their wounds, give them food, and nurse them? We women will do so! That is our task! I will nurse the first wounded brought to Potsdam. The first maimed soldier, however, whom I meet at the hospital, and whose

right leg has been amputated as that of my dear husband, we shall take to our house. You may nurse him here, **old man**; console him and show **him that he may live quite happily,** though with but one leg, and that wife and children will love their husband and father no less ardently, provided he is a true man, and has a courageous heart."

"You are right, mother," exclaimed Prohaska. "Let us take a wounded soldier into our house, and I will nurse him as a brother, teaching him how to use his wooden leg, while you are at the hospital, attending to the other sufferers. But you have not thought of the children. What are Leonora and Charles to do while we are thus engaged?"

"They can help us," said his wife, quickly. "Leonora will have a great deal to do. She will prepare lint, make nourishing soups, wash bandages, and sew shirts and clothing."

The invalid cast a quick glance on Leonora. She stood, drawn up to her full height, in the middle of the room; a proud, contemptuous smile was playing about her lips, which uttered no word in reply to her mother's plans.

"But what will Charles do?" asked Prohaska, quickly. "He cannot be as useful as his sister."

"Father!" ejaculated Leonora, somewhat reproachfully.

"Hush!" he said, almost sternly, "mother is right; it behooves you women to prepare lint, cook soups, nurse the wounded, and sew shirts for them. But war itself is the task of the men. But, my wife, before telling me what Charles is to do for our wounded, I must ask a very sad question. Where shall we find money for the expenses we shall have to incur? We are unfortunately poor, dependent on the labor of our hands. This small house and my pension of three dollars a month constitute our whole fortune, and if you were not the most skilful hairdresser in Potsdam—if I could not besides earn a few dollars by making baskets, and if Leonora were not the best seamstress in town, I should like to know how we could live and send Charles to the Lyceum. But if we are to nurse the wounded, and devote our labor to them alone, we shall unfortunately soon lack the necessaries of life."

"I have thought of all that, husband," said his wife, eagerly. "But, listen to me! Charles wants also to have his share in our sacrifices, he does not intend to be idle while all are at work to promote the welfare of the country. As he cannot enlist and fight, he must use his head. He will, therefore, publish this advertisement: As I have unfortunately been rejected by the military commission on account of my youth, and because I have not yet been confirmed, I request generous patriots to allow me to give private lessons to their children, that I may earn a sufficient sum to nurse and support a wounded soldier till his complete recovery.'"

"Yes, I will do that!" exclaimed Charles. "The citizens will learn then why I have not enlisted, and I shall, moreover, be able to earn money for the country. I shall certainly get pupils, for my teachers are pleased with me, and I am already in the first class. I can give lessons in Latin, Greek, mathematics, and history; I have good testimonials, and, for the sake of the noble object I have in view, parents will assuredly intrust their children to me, and pay me well for my trouble."

"All of you will have employment, then," said Leonora, "and your labor will benefit the country. But I also want to render myself useful to the country."

"Well, you can assist me," said her mother; "you can prepare food, wash, and sew shirts."

"However industrious I might be, mother, I could in that way earn only as much as my own support would cost," said Leonora, shaking her head. "I can be of no use to you, I am superfluous; I will go therefore to another place, where I can render myself useful and make money."

"But whither do you intend to go, and what do you wish to do?" asked her mother in amazement, while her father cast searching glances upon her.

"To Berlin, and seek a situation as saleswoman," said Leonora. "What money I earn I shall send to you, and you will spend it for your wounded soldier. You know, mother, my godfather, Rudolph Werkmeister, who is a merchant at Berlin, has often asked me to go to see him, and take such a situation at his house. I have always refused, because I did not like to leave you, but thought I would stay with you and devote my whole life to nursing you; but God has decreed otherwise. Yesterday my godfather wrote again, stating that his wife had been taken sick, and that he was greatly embarrassed because he had no one at his house on whom he could depend. He offers me a salary of eighty dollars a year. Now, I pray you, dear parents, let me go! Let me pursue my own paths, and do my duty as I understand it. Dear mother, I am sure you will not refuse your consent? You will permit **me to go this very day to Berlin, and** make money for our wounded soldiers?"

"I will, my child," said her mother, her voice trembling with emotion. "I have no diamonds and golden chains to give my country, so I give to it the most precious and beautiful jewels I have—my children. Yes, go, my Leonora; take the situation offered you, and give the money you earn to the fatherland and its soldiers."

"Oh, thanks, mother!" exclaimed Leonora, hastening to her and clasping her in her arms—"thanks, for permitting me to put my mite on the altar of the country!" She kissed her mother with fervent tenderness, and then turned toward her father. "And you, father," she said, in a low and almost timid tone—"you do not say a word—you do not give your consent."

The invalid stood leaning on his crutch, and looked thoughtfully into the noble face of his daughter. He then slowly raised his right hand and laid it on Leonora's shoulder. "I repeat what your mother said. Like her, I have no treasures to give my country except this jewel, my Leonora! Go, my daughter!—do what you believe to be your duty, and may God bless you!" Opening his arms, she threw herself into them and leaned her head on his breast.

"And now," said Prohaska, gently disengaging himself from a long and tearful embrace, "let us be calm. These are the first tears I have wept since the death of our dear Queen Louisa—the **first for your sake, my Leonora! May the Lord forgive them to a poor father who has but one** daughter! The heart will yield to its emotions, but now I must again be a soldier, who knows no tears!"

"But, husband, Leonora will not leave us immediately," said her mother. "She must remain **yet a day** with us. Alas! we discover what treasures we possessed only when we lose them. I believe I have never loved Leonora so intensely as I do at this hour, and my heart is unable to part with her so suddenly. I must first accustom myself to the separation, and engrave her image upon my soul, that I may never forget her dear features. Let her stay, then, until to-morrow!"

The invalid gravely shook his head. "No," he said; "what is to be done must be done at **once; otherwise, our hearts will grow weak, and our tears soften our resolutions. To-day I can permit Leonora to leave us; whether I shall be able to do so to-morrow, I do not know.'"

"**Futher, the stage-coach starts for Berlin in** two hours, and I shall take passage in it!" exclaimed Leonora, quickly. "You are right, what is to be done must be done now, and when we have taken a resolution, we must not hesitate to carry it into effect. I will go to my chamber and pack my trunk."

"I will go and help you," said her mother, hastening toward the door, and leaving the room **with Leonora.**

"And I will write my advertisement," said Charles. "It must be published to-morrow, that I am obliged to stay here because my country will not accept me as a soldier, and that I desire to give private lessons, the proceeds of which are **to** be devoted to the support of a wounded sol**dier."**

"And I—what shall I do?" asked the old invalid, when he was alone. "I must swallow my tears, and tell no one my thoughts. I shall quietly accustom myself to the idea that the darling of my heart, my Leonora, is to leave me, and that my old eyes are to see no more her dear face, or my ears hear her voice. Ah, when she looked at me, I felt as though it were spring in my heart, and the sun shining there; and when I heard her voice I thought it music rejoicing my soul. Now, how quiet and gloomy all around me will be in the small house—no more sunshine or music! all will be gone when Leonora is gone. And will she come back, then?—will not some bullet, some sword-blade—hush, my thoughts! I must not betray them! Be still, my heart, and weep! Be still and—" Tears choked his voice, and the strong man, overwhelmed with grief, sank into his easy-chair and sobbed aloud. After a long time he raised himself again and dried his tears. "Fie, Sergeant Prohaska!" he said aloud. "You sit here and cry like an old woman, and wring your hands in grief, instead of being glad and thanking the Lord that a substitute has been found for the invalid sergeant with the wooden leg. Thunder and lightning, Sergeant Prohaska! I advise you to behave yourself, and not be weak and foolish, while women are becoming men. Keep your head erect, turn your eyes on the enemy, and then, 'Charge them!' as old father Blucher used to say. I will go to work now," he continued, drawing a deep breath, after repeatedly pacing the small room with measured steps. "Yes, I will go to work, and that no one may discover that I have wept, I will sing a beautiful song I learned yesterday from a volunteer. Yes, I will work and sing!" He hastened to the chamber adjoining the sitting-room, and brought from it a neat half-finished basket upon which he had been at work the day before. "It must be finished to-day; I have promised it," he said, sitting down on his old easy-chair. He then commenced working assiduously, and sang in a powerful voice:

> "Nun mit Gott! Es ist beschlossen!
> Auf, Ihr wackern Streitgenossen,
>   Endlich kommt der Ehrentag!
> Besser flugs und fröhlich sterben,
> Als so langsam hin verderben,
>   Und **verslechen in** der Schmach.

> "Endlich **darf das** Herz sich regen,
> Sich die Zunge frei bewegen,
>   Alle Fesseln sind entzwei.
> Ach, da Alles schier zerstoben,
> Kam der Retterarm from oben,
>   Neugeboren sind wir, frei!

*Tag der Freiheit, Tag der Wonne!
Brüder, seht! es tanzt die Sonne,
  Wie am ersten Ostertag!
Todte sprengen ihre Grüfte,
Und durch Berg und Thal und Klüfte
  Hallt ein freudig Jauchzen nach!

*Auferstanden, auferstanden
Aus der Knechtschaft Todesbanden,
  Streiter Gottes, nun zu Hauf!
Unsre Adler! Ha sie wittern
Ihrer Raub—die Feinde zittern,
  Unsre Adler fahren auf!

"Zu den Waffen, zu den Rossen,
Auf, Ihr wackern Kampfgenossen
  Er ist da, Der Ehrentag!
Besser flugs und fröhlich sterben,
Als so langsam hin verderben,
  Und versiechen in der Schmach!" *

"Yes, it is better to die quickly and merrily than slowly pine away and perish in disgrace," repeated a sonorous voice behind him. It was Leonora, who had just entered the room, unnoticed by her father, and had listened to the last verse of his song. "Yes, the song is right," she said, enthusiastically. "But I, father, have already been pining away for a long time. The first volunteer I saw was as a dagger that pierced my soul, and ever since I have been ill and suffer-

---

* It is resolved in God's great name!
Up, comrades! to the field of fame!
  This day of glory save.
Quickly and merrily to die
Is better than the sick-bed sigh,
  And an unhonored grave.

Our heart at last resumes its life—
Our tongues now urge to holy strife;
  The broken chains we see.
When all seemed lost, a saving hand
From heaven vouchsafes to bless our land,
  And make us strong and free.

O happy day! The sun new-born
Is dancing as on Easter morn!
  See, risen brothers, see!
We come from slavery's grave unbound,
And mountains and the vales resound
  With songs of jubilee.

Ascending from Oppression's night,
Behold the dawn of Freedom's light!
  Soldiers of God, arise!
The enemy will rue this day,
For victory's eagle scents the prey
  And onward quickly flies.

To arms! to horse! my comrades brave!
And let the battle-standard wave,
  For now is honor's day.
The dying shout of bloody strife
Is better than the pining life
  That sinks by slow decay.

ing, and in my heart a voice has been continually singing the words I once heard at the theatre: 'I wish to be a man!'"

"And why do you wish to be a man?" asked her father, bowing his head, and seemingly devoting his whole attention to his work.

"Because a man is allowed to do freely and boldly what he deems right and good," replied Leonora; "because, when the fatherland calls him, he may step forth with a bold front, and reply: 'Here I am! To thee, my country, belongs my arm—my blood! For thee I am ready to fight, and if need be to die!' Father, when a man talks thus, his words are sublime—the women clasp their hands and listen devoutly to him, and the children fall on their knees and pray for him. But if a girl talk thus, it would be as mockery; the women would deride their heroic sister, and the children point at and shout after her, 'Look at the foolish girl who wants to do what is solely the task of men! Look at the crazy one, who imagines she can do men's work!' Her most sacred sentiments, her most patriotic desires and resolutions, would be mercilessly ridiculed!"

"That is the reason, my child," said her father, calmly laboring at his basket, "why she should not betray her sentiments, and confide her thoughts to God alone. Have you forgotten what Charles read to us about Joan of Orleans? She left her parents silently and secretly, and went whither God called her."

"But her father cursed and disowned her for it," said Leonora, in a tremulous voice. "Do you think her father was right, merely because she followed the voice of God, and went out to deliver her king and country?"

"No," said Prohaska, laying his basket aside and rising, "I do not; I was always indignant when that particular passage was read to us."

"And what would you have said, father?" asked Leonora, in a tone of profound emotion. "Imagine me to be Joan, the inspired maid of Orleans, and that I say: 'Father, I cannot remain any longer in this narrow dwelling. The voice of the king and the fatherland has peactrated my heart also, and has called me. I must obey it, for I feel courageous and strong enough, **and it would be cowardly to disobey.'** What would you say if I were Joan of Orleans, **and** should talk thus to you?"

"I should say, 'Kneel down, my Leonora, and receive my last blessing,'" replied Prohaska, straightening himself and approaching his daughter.

Leonora knelt down, and, raising her tearful eyes to her father, whispered: "What blessing would you give me if I were Joan of Orleans? Oh, think I am she, and give me your blessing!"

"If you were Joan of Orleans," responded the old man, solemnly, "and should kneel before me as you do now, and ask my blessing, I should, as I do now, lay my hands on your head, and say to you: 'God the Lord, who holds heaven and earth in His hand, and without whose will not a **hair falls from our head, watch over you and protect you! May He be with you on the battlefield! May He give you a brave heart, a strong** arm, and a steady eye! May He give you courage to brave death! You have chosen men's work, you have pledged your love and your life to the fatherland; go, then, and be a man; love your country like a man, fight like a man, and, if need be, die like a man!' But when your last hour has come, my daughter, think of your father, and pray to God with your last thoughts that He may soon deliver me also, and take me **away,** for I shall feel lonely on earth when you are no more, and even the victorious shouts of the returning would no longer gladden my old soldier's heart if I find you not among the conquerors. But, hush! let no tear desecrate this sacred hour of our last farewell! God has called all strong and courageous hearts—follow **His call!** It is incumbent on every one to love his country more intensely than parents, brothers, and sisters. Go, then, my daughter; do your duty, and remember that your father's blessing will be with you in life as well as in death! And now, give **me a last kiss."**

Leonora rose from her knees, and, encircling his neck with her arms, pressed a glowing kiss on his lips. **"Father,"** she said, looking at him with a beaming face, "my lips have not yet kissed any man's lips but yours, and here I swear to you— and may God have **mercy on** me at my last hour **if I do not keep my oath!—I** swear to you that I shall kiss no man until I am permitted to return to you, my father!"

"I believe you, dear Leonora," said Prohaska, solemnly.

"Leonora, my child, it is time now!" exclaimed her mother, hastily entering the room! "The postilion has already passed our house, and in a quarter of an hour the stage-coach will stop at our door. I have myself gone to the postmaster, and he granted it as a favor that the stage-coach should stop here, and thus save you the trouble of going to the post-office. This will enable you to remain with us fifteen minutes yet."

"But my trunk, mother; we have to take it to the post-office?" asked Leonora.

"Oh, it would have been too heavy for us," said Mrs. **Prohaska;** "Charles and two of his school-mates are just carrying it to the post-office. Leonora's trunk is quite heavy, father. Thank God, she is well provided, and for the first year it will be quite unnecessary for her to buy any thing."

"My dear mother would indeed have packed up all her own things and dresses for me if I had not prevented her," said Leonora, smiling.

"I should like best to pack up my own heart for you, my dear child," exclaimed her mother, deeply moved, "but, as I could not do so, I put my bridal dress into your trunk. It is a nice silk dress, and I have worn it only three times **in my** life—on my wedding-day, and on the days when my two children were baptized; **it is as good as new.** I suppose, husband, **you will** permit me to **give** it to her?"

"Of course, **but what is she to** do with it?" **asked Prohaska.**

"Why, what a question!" exclaimed Mrs. Prohaska, "she is to wear it, and look pretty when she goes to parties on Sundays. Leonora, I suppose you will know what to do with it?"

"Yes, mother, I thank you from the bottom **of**

my heart for the beautiful present, and I promise you that I shall use it only in a noble and worthy manner," said Leonora, gravely. "My mother's bridal dress shall not be worn for frivolous purposes, but it shall serve me to attain the highest and purest objects."

"Oh, I know," whispered the mother, who was scarcely able to restrain her tears, "I know that you are an excellent girl, and a good daughter, and that you will never do any thing of which your old parents would have to be ashamed. You have always been my pride and joy, and never would I consent to part with you unless every one had now to make the greatest sacrifices for the king and the fatherland. But still it is very painful, and—"

"Wife," interposed the old sergeant, "no tears now! When we are alone we shall have time enough for weeping. As long as Leonora is here, let us gaze at and rejoice in her.—I have to give you a commission yet. Go to my general, old Blucher, and tell him he ought not to be angry with me—that he must not believe me a lazy coward because I do not go to the war. Tell him that my leg had to be amputated some time after the battle, and that he ought to excuse my absence when the roll is called."

"I will assuredly repeat your words to the general, father."

"Why!" asked Mrs. Prohaska, wonderingly, "is General Blucher now at Berlin?"

"No," said her husband, carelessly, "he is at Breslau, whither all the volunteers are marching."

"But how is Leonora, then, to repeat your words to him?" asked his wife, in amazement.

"Father means that I shall tell General Blucher when he comes to Berlin?" said Leonora, quickly. "They say Blucher will come soon to expel the French from the capital, and father thinks I might then repeat those words to his old chieftain."

"Sister, sister, the stage-coach is coming," shouted Charles, rushing breathlessly into the room. "The postilion has already blown his bugle for the third time!"

"Well, then, my child, we must part," said the

old sergeant, deeply moved, and clasping Leonora in his arms. "God bless you, my daughter! Your father's thoughts will always be with you!" He disengaged himself from her arms, and pushed her gently toward her mother. The two women remained a long time locked in each other's arms. Neither of them said a word, but their tears and their last looks were more eloquent than words.

"And you forget me?" asked Charles, reproachfully. "You do not care to take leave of me?"

Leonora released herself from her mother's embrace, and encircled her brother's neck with her arms. "Farewell, darling of my heart!" she cried. "Be a good son to father and mother, and remember that you must henceforth love them for both of us. Farewell, brother, and forgive me for being born earlier than you, and thus preventing your being in my place. God decreed it thus, putting us in our own places, and we must both fill them worthily."

"Yes," said Charles, amid his tears, "certainly we will."

A carriage was rattling over the pavement, and stopped in front of the house. A bugle sounded.

"Father, mother, and brother, farewell!" exclaimed Leonora. Then, raising her arms to heaven, she added: "God in heaven, watch over them, and, if such be Thy will, let me return to them!" She hastily wrapped herself in her cloak, and, without looking at them again, rushed out of the room, and jumped into the coach.

"Farewell, farewell!" shouted father, mother, and brother, who had followed her, and were standing in front of the house.

She leaned her head out of the coach window. "Farewell," she exclaimed, "and God—" The bugle drowned her words; the carriage rolled away.

The loving relatives gazed after it until it had disappeared around the next corner, and then returned sighing into the small house. Charles hastened to his little chamber up-stairs to give vent to his grief. The parents returned to their sitting room. "Oh, how still it is here now, as still as in the grave," sighed Mrs. Prohaska, "for I miss my child, and will miss her everywhere. Oh, husband, my heart aches, and I feel as though I had lost my Leonora forever! Ah, why did we allow her to go? Why did we not keep her here, our child, our only daughter? Oh! if she should never return, if she should die! O God, have mercy on a poor mother's heart—protect my dear child!" She sank down on a chair, and, covering her face with her apron, sobbed aloud.

The old sergeant paced the room in silence. He scarcely knew that the tears, like large pearls, were running down his cheeks into his gray beard. The loud sobs of his wife aroused him. "Hush, wife; hush!" he said, standing in front of her. "It is too late now for weeping. Let us rather be glad, for Leonora is possessed of a brave heart, and has done her duty toward her country and her old invalid father. Let us, therefore, be glad, and sing!" And he commenced to sing in a tremulous voice, while the tears were still rolling from his eyes:

> "Ihr Deutsche auf in Süd und Nord!
> Hinweg gemeiner Neid!
> Wir alle reden eine Sprach'
> Und stehen all' für eine Sach'
> Im ehrenvollen Streit!

> "Und wer sich feig entzieht dem Kampf
> Für Freiheit und für Ehr',
> Wer nicht das Schwertergreift zur Stund!
> Der leb' und sterb' als schlechter Hund,
> Der sei kein Deutscher mehr!" *

CHAPTER XXV.

THE NATIONAL REPRESENTATIVES.

LEONORA PROHASKA reached Berlin at four o'clock in the afternoon. On the way, closing her eyes, she leaned back on the cushions, so that her companions paid little attention to her, whom they believed to be asleep. But Leonora heard every word, and every conversation of her fellow-travellers strengthened her soul and restored her former courage. They spoke of the enthusiasm in every city, village, and house—an enthusiasm spreading far beyond the frontiers of Prussia, and carrying all away as an irresistible torrent, drawing with it even the most cautious and timid, and filling the most desponding and disheartened with joyous hopes. One of the travellers was just returning from Breslau, and dwelt with impassioned eloquence on the bustle prevailing there; on the volunteers who were flocking in vast numbers to that city and parading every day under the king's windows; and on brave Major von Lützow, who, with his beautiful young wife, had come to Breslau, and was endeavoring to live at a miserable tavern, because no other accommodations were to be had.

"And in the bar-room," he said, "beautiful Madame von Lützow receives the names of the volunteers who wish to enlist in the Legion **of** Vengeance. Her husband is busily engaged, from dawn till late at night, in organizing his corps; in trying to procure arms, horses, and equipments for his men, and his handsome wife is his recruiting officer. She is as charming as an angel, the daughter of a wealthy count, and has, by her marriage with Major von Lützow, contrary to her parents' wishes, so much exasperated her proud father that he gave her no dower, but imposed it as a condition of his consent that Major von Lützow should marry without any. But the count's daughter joyously descended from the proud castle to the humble dwelling of the Prussian major, whom she loved on account of his bravery, and the scars which he bore on his forehead, and which he had received in 1806, in the war against the French."

"I know the lady," said the second traveller; "she is a daughter of the Danish Count von Ahlefeldt, a wonder of loveliness, grace, and refined manners. She hates the French as intensely as her husband, and it was precisely this com-

------

* Arise, ye Germans, North and South!
> And honor's path pursue.
> Since all one common language speak,
> And all one sacred object seek,
> Your jealousies subdue.

> Let him who shirks his country's call,
> To freedom and to fame,
> Both live and die a cowardly hound,
> Despised wherever may be found
> A man of German name.

mon hatred of the French that brought them together."

"How so?" asked the other. "Pray tell us all about it."

"Several years ago, the young countess, attended by her governess, made a journey to a fashionable German watering-place. Both took dinner at the *table d'hôte* of the 'Kurhaus,' where a crowd of persons from all countries were assembled. The neighbor of the young countess at the table happened to be a French officer, who managed to involve the young lady in a highly animated and interesting conversation. He told her in a very attractive manner of his campaigns and travels, and the young countess listened to him with pleasure and manifested her sympathy for him. The Frenchman dared to seize her hand and kiss it. The young countess started; a deep blush suffused her fair face, and, without reflecting, obeying only her first impulse, she took a glass of water which stood before her, and poured it over the hand which the Frenchman had dared to kiss. Several Prussian officers, seated near her had witnessed the occurrence, and, on noticing how she removed the stain of the French kiss from her hand, could not refrain from bursting into a loud cheer. One of them was Major von Lützow. After dinner he approached the countess, was introduced to her by a mutual acquaintance, and expressed his ardent thanks, in the name of all Germans, for the bold rebuke she had administered to the Frenchman. That was the beginning of her acquaintance with Major von Lützow, and the end of it was her marriage with him. * She is now at Breslau, and you have seen her."

"Yes, for I went to the major's headquarters with a friend who wished to enlist in his corps. We met there, however, only herself. She received my friend's request to enlist under her husband with so much grace, with such a look of joy—she dwelt in such soul-stirring words on the

great and holy national war about to break out, and in which every one ought to participate, that I was quite fascinated by her eloquence, and would have enlisted at once if I had not already entered a landwehr regiment."

Not a word of this conversation escaped Leonora, and she said to herself: "I must make the acquaintance of this lady. I will go to her, and she will enlist me for the German fatherland!"

The travellers continued their conversation, relating that Frederick William had not believed in the success of the first manifesto, in which he called for volunteers; and, for this reason, had not signed the manifesto which Chancellor von Hardenberg had drawn up; that four days afterward the king, who had just explained with unusual vehemence to General Scharnhorst the utter uselessness of this call, was interrupted by a strange noise in the street; and that, anxious to discover what was the cause, he stepped to the window, and General Scharnhorst followed him; that a line of at least eighty wagons had come in sight, and in them none but armed men were seated, who halted in front of the palace, and an aide-de-camp, who entered the room at that moment, informed the king that they were volunteers just arrived from Berlin; that Scharnhorst turned to him, and exclaimed triumphantly: "Will your majesty be convinced now that your people are ready to fight for you and the fatherland?" and that the king made no reply, but a flood of tears rushed from his eyes, and he smiled amidst his emotion.

At length Leonora arrived at Berlin. She stood alone beside her trunk in the court-yard of the royal post-office building. No notice was taken of her; no one manifested any sympathy for her; but she did not flinch, and her heart was free from doubt or anxiety. She sent for a hackney-coach by one of the boys playing in the court-yard, and then drove away. But she did not order the coachman to convey her to her godfather, Werkmeister, the merchant on Jäger Street. Driving first to Tauben Street, the carriage stopped in front of a large, gloomy house. She alighted, and, begging the coachman to wait

---

* I am indebted for an account of this occurrence to the Countess Ahlefeldt (formerly Madame Major von Lützow) herself, who related it to me with charming ... and grace.—L. M

for her, slipped into the house. Quickly ascending three narrow flights of stairs, she reached a silent corridor, on both sides of which were small doors, and on each a number had been painted. Knocking at the door of number *three*, a female voice inquired, "Who is there?"

"It is I, Leonora Prohaska!"

A loud cry of joy resounded; the door was hastily opened, and a young soldier in full uniform appeared on the threshold. It was now Leonora who uttered a cry, and blushing drew back. "Pardon me," she said, timidly; "there must be a mistake. I am looking for my friend, a young milliner, named Caroline Peters."

The young soldier laughed, but it was the fresh, ringing laughter of a girl. "Then you really do not recognize me, Leonora?" he exclaimed. "You really take me for what I like to be and am not—a man?"

"Great Heaven! is it you?" exclaimed Leonora. "You—"

"Hush!" whispered the other, hastily drawing her into the room, and carefully locking the door. "For mercy's sake, let no one hear us! What a scandal it would be, if it should be discovered that Volunteer Charles Petersen receives the visits of pretty girls at his room! This hotel is entirely occupied by volunteers, and none of them suspect that I am a woman, nor shall they ever find it out. But now welcome, my dear Leonora, and tell me what has brought you to Berlin. Did you receive my letter?"

"Yes, Caroline, I did," said Leonora, gravely, "and it gave me pain, for you called me cowardly, and destitute of honor, because I intended to stay at home when my country was in need of the arms of all its children, and when every one of any courage was participating in this holy struggle."

"And that is the truth, Leonora," exclaimed Caroline; "the fatherland has called us all, and those who do not listen to this call are cowards!"

"But who told you that I did not listen to it?" asked Leonora.

"What!" ejaculated Caroline, joyously. "Leonora, you, too—"

"Hush!" interrupted Leonora, "we must talk about all this afterward. I am in haste now, for there is a hackney-coach waiting for me at the door, and my trunk is on it. Tell me now quickly, Caroline, can I stay with you overnight?"

"In female dress, Leonora? That would be hardly prudent."

"No, in male attire, Caroline."

"Oh, then you are a thousand times welcome here," exclaimed Caroline, encircling her with her arms, and drawing her to her heart.

"But I have not yet my male attire," said Leonora, smiling, "nor have I money to buy it. Give me, therefore, quickly, the name of some one who buys dresses, for I will drive to him immediately with my trunk, and sell all I have brought with me."

"Come, Leonora, I will accompany you," said Caroline. "I know at the Hospital Bridge a very patriotic and kind-hearted old Jew, to whom I have also sold my wearing apparel, and who paid me a very liberal price for it, when I told him that I wanted to buy a uniform for my brother. Let us drive there, but I will remain in the carriage while you go into the store, for he might recognize me. You will also find men's clothing, which you may purchase for your brother—that is to say, for yourself."

"Come, then, and let us make haste," said Leonora, drawing her friend with her.

Fifteen minutes afterward the hackney-coach halted in front of one of the second-hand clothing-stores near the Hospital Bridge, and Leonora alighted, holding in her arms a large package of dresses, shawls, skirts, and aprons, which she had taken from her trunk during the drive. Mr. Hirsch, the dealer in second-hand clothing, who was standing in front of his store, received her with a pleasant greeting, and invited her to enter and tell him what she wanted.

Leonora put the wearing apparel on the counter, and, drawing a deep breath, said in a tone of embarrassment, "I should like to sell these things, sir."

The Jew put his spectacles slowly on his nose,

The Jew put his spectacles slowly on his nose, and then lifted up the dresses, one after another,
contemplating them with scrutinizing glances.   p. 113.

and then lifted up the dresses, one after another, contemplating them with scrutinizing glances.

"If he should not give me as much money as I need?" Leonora asked herself, anxiously—"if these things should not amount to so much that I cannot purchase a uniform?"

And old Hirsch, as if he heard the anxious question of her heart, said, shaking his head: "I cannot give very much for these few calico dresses and aprons. They are all very nice and well preserved, but of no value whatever."

"But there is also a silk dress, sir," said Leonora, in a tremulous voice—"an entirely new silk dress."

"New?" asked the Jew, shrugging his shoulders, drawing out the dress, and unfolding it with a sneer. "The dress is not new, for it is made after such an old fashion that it could be worn only at a masked ball; and the stuff is not worth any thing, either, for it is only half silk. It was just made to look at. It appears like heavy silk, but the oblique threads that make it look so heavy are all cotton. How much do you want for the whole, my pretty miss?"

"I do not know," said Leonora, in a low voice, "as much as you can give me for it."

"Yes, yes," grumbled the old man, "I am to give a great deal of money for very poor goods; that is what they all ask me to do. I will tell you, I cannot give you more than twelve dollars for the whole lot."

"Twelve dollars!" ejaculated Leonora, with such an expression of dismay that the Jew started, raising his green spectacles to his forehead, and fixing his small, twinkling eyes on Leonora.

"Twelve dollars!" repeated Leonora, and, no longer able to restrain her tears, she wrung her hands, and muttered: "It is all in vain, then! Twelve dollars are not sufficient to buy a uniform and arms."

Hirsch heard her words. "What?" he asked, hastily. "You want to sell the dresses in order to buy a uniform and arms?"

"Yes, sir," replied Leonora, "my mother and I wanted to sell our dresses, because we hoped we would get money enough to buy my brother a complete uniform—a rifle, sword, and shako; for my brother intends to enlist in Lützow's corps of riflemen."

"Your brother intends to enlist in Lützow's corps of riflemen?" asked Hirsch, quickly. "Is that no pretext, eh? Do you not tell me so merely for the purpose of extorting money from me? Can you swear to me that that is why you wish to sell the dresses?"

"I can swear it by the great God in heaven, in whom we all believe," said Leonora, solemnly. "But I can prove it to you, too."

"How so? In what way?"

"By buying a uniform for my brother here at your store. He is of the same height as I am, and has precisely the same figure: we are twins."

"And your brother intends to enlist in Lützow's corps? Why did he not himself come to select a uniform?"

"He is at Potsdam, sir, and does not know that I am here. To-morrow is his birthday, and we want to surprise him by giving him his uniform to-morrow."

"And he shall have it!" exclaimed the Jew; "yes, he shall have it! I read in your eyes that you have told me the truth, my child, and that you do not want the money for frivolous purposes, but for the great cause of the German fatherland. I have also a heart for my country, and no one shall say that we Israelites do not feel and act like true Germans—that our hearts did not suffer under the disgrace which, for long years, has weighed down all Germany, and that we will not joyfully sacrifice our blood and our life; and, what is still more, our property, for the sake of the fatherland. Who was the first man at Berlin to make a voluntary contribution to this object? It was a Jew! The president of the Jewish congregation, M. Gumpert, made the first patriotic contribution. He sent three hundred dollars to the military commission, with the request that this amount might be spent for buying equipments for poor volunteers.* Our Gumpert was the first man who made a sacrifice for the benefit

---

of the fatherland, and I do not wish to be the last. I made a mistake in appraising your things; I will do it over again, and what I can give I will give." He glanced again at the dresses; then, shaking his head, and stroking the silk dress with his long, lean hand, he said, "How could I make such a mistake, and believe this stuff to be only half silk? It is all silk, heavy silk—and two dresses of the now fashionable tight cut can easily be made out of this splendid one. For this alone I will give you twenty dollars, and as for the other things, well, I will give you twenty dollars more."

"Oh," exclaimed Leonora, radiant with joy, and giving both her hands to the old Jew—"oh, you are a noble, generous man, a true patriot! I thank you, and may the delivered land some day reward you!"

"Ah, poor Hirsch cannot deserve great rewards at the hands of the fatherland," said the old man, sighing. "I am poor, I have not even a son whom I might give to the country, and intrust with the task of avenging me. I had a son, a good, dear boy; but, in 1807, when the French arrived here, he wished to defend our property against the soldiers who broke into our house; he grew very angry with the infamous ruffians, and called them and their emperor murderers and robbers. Thereupon they mortally stabbed him—they killed him before my own eyes! He was my only child, my only joy on earth! But, hush! this is no time for lamentations. I will rejoice—yes, rejoice, for the hour of vengeance has come, and we will pay the French for what wrongs they have inflicted on us. If I were not so old and feeble, I should myself willingly fight, but now I am only able to assist in equipping soldiers. Your brother shall become a soldier, my child; we will equip him for the Legion of Vengeance. He shall avenge my son, my innocent, beloved son, upon Napoleon the tyrant, and the French rabble, who have trampled us under foot so long and so disgracefully. Yes, yes, I will give you forty dollars for your things, but I will not give you the whole amount in cash. Look at this black uniform; it is quite new, the tailor delivered

it only yesterday. Did not you tell me that your brother is of the same stature as you are?"

"Of the same stature and figure, for he is my twin-brother."

"Well, let us see if this uniform fits you."

Mr. Hirsch took out his tape-line, and measured Leonora's figure with the skill of an experienced tailor. He then applied the tape-line to the trousers and the coat of black cloth. "It fits splendidly," he exclaimed. "And here is also a nice silk vest that belongs to it. Now, listen to me! I charge you twelve dollars for the whole suit; you will, therefore, receive twenty-eight dollars in money. Now you will, in the first place, buy your brother a fine rifle, such as Lützow's riflemen need. You will pay ten dollars for it; besides a sword and a shako, which will cost together five dollars. You will then have thirteen dollars left. For this amount you will put a pair of good shirts and a new pair of boots into your brother's knapsack, and the remainder you will give him for pocket-money. Is it to be so? Is the bargain struck?"

"Yes, the bargain is struck."

"Very well. Here is your uniform, and here are the twenty-eight dollars." He counted the shining dollars on the counter, and then pushed the money and the clothing toward Leonora. "Here is our Lützow's rifleman's uniform," he exclaimed.

"And here are the dresses, sir," said Leonora, handing the wearing apparel to the old man, but, while doing so, she quickly bent over it, and pressed a kiss on the silk dress.

Old Hirsch looked at her with amazement.

"It is my mother's bridal dress, sir," said Leonora, as if apologetically. "It was our greatest treasure, and I gave it only a farewell kiss."

The Jew looked down musingly. "Listen, my child," he said; "I must not sell this dress. I shall keep it until the war is over. If your brother gets safely back, you may bring him here, and, as a greeting of welcome, I will present your mother's bridal dress to him. But in return, he must do me a favor."

"What favor?"

"Whenever he cuts down a Frenchman, he is to shout, 'Moses Hirsch is avenged!' Moses was the name of my dear, unfortunate son, and I think he will sleep more calmly in his grave when he hears that his father has sent out an avenger of his death. Will you promise me, in your brother's name, that he will not forget to shout what I tell you?"

"I promise it! Whenever my brother cuts down a Frenchman, he will shout, 'Moses Hirsch is avenged!'"

"Thank you!" said Hirsch, greatly moved. "My son will hear it, and he will smile down from heaven on his old, lonely father. And now, my dear, beautiful child, good-by! Give me the package; I will take it for you to the carriage!"

"No, no, give it back to me," exclaimed Leonora, anxiously.

But the old man did not listen to her. He took the package, and hastened with it out of his store to the hackney-coach. Charles Peterson, at this moment, looked impatiently out of the window, and shouted to her friend to make haste.

Old Hirsch uttered a cry and stared at Caroline. "Great Heaven!" he exclaimed, "you in uniform—you a volunteer?"

"Ah," said Caroline, concealing her confusion by loud laughter, "I see what astonishes you. You confound me with my sister. I know she sold her dresses to you to buy a uniform and arms for me. Yes, it is difficult to distinguish us, for we greatly resemble each other. The reason is, we are twins."

"He has a twin-sister as you have a twin-brother," said Hirsch, turning to Leonora with a strange smile. "Hush! I understand it all now. God protect the courageous twins! Coachman, start!"

"Whither?" asked the coachman.

"To M. Werkmeister's house, 23 Jäger Street," replied Leonora, nodding a last greeting to the old Jew. The carriage wheeled away.

"What do you want at M. Werkmeister's?" asked Caroline.

"To pay him my last visit as a girl," said Leo-nora. "Returning from his house, I shall divest myself of my female costume and become your comrade. Let us then go out together and buy my arms."

"But would it not be better for me to drive back to our hotel while you are Werkmeister's?" asked Caroline. "You have had the hackney-coach already above an hour, and we volunteers must be as economical as possible in order to support ourselves as long as we can, and not become a burden to the state."

"That is true," said Leonora. "I will alight here, and you will be so kind as to take my trunk and the package to your quarters." The hackney-coach halted, and Leonora, wrapping herself in her shawl, leaped out of the carriage. "Drive back to Tauben Street, now," she said, "and assist the gentleman in carrying this trunk up to his room. But previously I will pay you the whole fare. How much do I owe you?"

"From the post-office to Tauben Street, four groschen," said the coachman, composedly.

"And besides?"

"Nothing else."

"How so—nothing else? You waited a good while in Tauben Street; we then drove hither, where you waited a long while again, and now you are about to return to Tauben Street."

"Yes; but in Tauben Street we took in a volunteer," said the coachman, whipping his horses in a gentle, caressing manner. "We hackmen never take any money for driving a volunteer. Every one must do as much for the fatherland as he can. You owe me, therefore, only four groschen."

"Here they are," said Leonora, handing the money to the hackman, "and we are much obliged to you."

"Oh, you are not obliged to me at all," said the hackman, "for you see I do not drive girls for nothing—only volunteers."

"To-morrow he will drive me, too, for nothing," said Leonora, gazing after the hackney-coach. "To-morrow I will no longer be a girl! For I am going now to bid a last adieu to my outward maidenhood and my past!" And she walked with resolute steps across the Gendarmes Market toward Jäger Street.

"I must tell my dear godfather that I cannot accept his offer," she said to herself; "for, if I should not, he might perhaps write another letter to me to Potsdam, and mother would then learn prematurely that I told her a falsehood, and am not now at my godfather's house; but when he knows that I cannot come, he will not write again, and no one will discover my plans."

There was an unusual throng to-day in front of the house No. 23 on Jäger Street, where Werkmeister the merchant lived. It was not without difficulty that Leonora penetrated through the crowd to the door, where was to be seen a large placard, containing the following words: "*Gold wedding-rings exchanged for iron ones here.*" Somewhat astonished at this strange inscription, Leonora entered the house, and stepped across the hall to the open door of her godfather's sitting-room.

M. Rudolph Werkmeister, without looking attentively at her, presented her a small box containing a large number of glittering rings. "Please select one of these, and drop the gold ring into the aperture of the locked box," he said.

Leonora looked at him smilingly. "It is I, godfather," she said, offering him her hand.

"Ah, it is you, Leonora Prohaska," exclaimed M. Werkmeister, putting down the box. "You have received my letter, then, my child? You have at length made up your mind to comply with my wishes—to come to my house, and to assist my wife at the store and in the household? Well, you could not have come at a better hour, and I thank you for your kindness."

Leonora fixed her large dark eyes with an affectionate expression on the good-natured, pleasant face of the merchant, and stepping up to him laid both her hands on his shoulders. "Godfather, dear godfather," she said, greatly moved, "do not be angry with me, and forgive me for coming only to tell you I cannot accept your offer. Do not ask me why I cannot. I am not allowed to tell you the reason, but I know that,

when you learn it some day, you will certainly approve what I have done. I really am no ungrateful girl, but I cannot come to you, dear M. Werkmeister. I have greater and holier duties to fulfil—duties to which God Himself has called me!"

"That is to say, my child, you do not wish to leave your poor old parents?" asked Mr. Werkmeister, in great emotion. "You will stay with them at their small house and eat the invalid's brown bread rather than live luxuriously at the beautiful capital of Prussia? You are right, perhaps, my child. You are the only joy of your parents, and I was selfish, perhaps, in trying to rob them of you. But, in doing so, I thought more of yourself, and desired to give a better and brighter sphere to your youth. But we must all pursue the paths which God and our conscience have marked out for us."

"Yes," exclaimed Leonora, enthusiastically, "you are right. Let me, therefore, pursue my own path, and may Heaven accompany me! You are not angry with me, then, godfather? You really are not? No? Now give me your hand, godfather, and let me take leave of you with an affectionate kiss!" She threw her arms round the old man's neck, and kissed him tenderly.

"But you do not intend to leave immediately?" asked M. Werkmeister, surprised. "You have not even seen my sick wife, and talk already of taking leave?"

"Ah, I must go. I have still much to attend to, and must leave Berlin to-night. But, tell me one thing! What is the meaning of the inscription at your door, and why is there such a crowd in front of your house?"

"They are reading the placard which I have hung out," said M. Werkmeister—"the request which I addressed to all patriots."

"And what do you request of them to do, godfather?"

"I request all families, and especially all wives and affianced brides, to bring their gold weddingrings to me and receive iron ones in return; and in commemoration of these times, I have had ten thousand iron rings made, and the royal au thorities approved my scheme and intrusted me with **the** collection of the gold ones. My request **was** published in the papers of this morning, and already more than thirty gold rings have been exchanged. Look, here are the iron ones. They are very neat, are they not?—the exact shape of genuine wedding-rings; only in place of the names, the inside contains the words, '*I gave gold for iron*, 1813.' Read!"

"Oh, that is a very beautiful idea," exclaimed Leonora, contemplating the ring which he had handed her. "Such a memento will henceforth be the most precious ornament of all wives, and no gold will shine so brilliantly and be so valuable as these iron rings with which our women pledge their love to their native land. Ah, dear godfather, I would like to ask a favor of you. I am no wife, nor am I an affianced bride, and I have, therefore, no wedding-ring to give you. I have nothing but my heart, and in this heart there is no other love than that of country. Let me, therefore, offer it to the fatherland instead of gold, and give me for it an iron ring with the beautiful inscription: '*I gave gold for iron, 1813.*'"

"There is a ring, my child; your heart is pure gold; let it remain so; then you will well deserve your ring!" He placed it on her finger, and she thanked him with a blissful smile.

"And now I go, dear godfather," said Leonora. "Farewell, and do not forget me! And—"

At this moment a lady entered the room. Her dress indicated poverty, and her face was pale and sunken, but her eyes were lit up with a noble enthusiasm. "The wedding-rings are exchanged here?" she asked.

"Yes, here."

She quickly drew two from her finger, and handed them to M. Werkmeister. "Take them," she cried. "One of these rings belongs to me, the other I drew from the finger of my dear husband. Ten years have elapsed since then; I **have always** worn them, and, although I have often suffered great privations, I could never part with my only treasure. But to-day I do so joyously. Give me my **iron rings!**" She took

those handed her, and placed them on her finger. "Farewell, sir," she said. "These will be my daughter's heirloom, and I know she will rejoice over them." She had not yet crossed the threshold when another lady appeared, and another, and more followed in rapid succession. The newspapers, containing the **request, had been** read in the whole city; all the married women hastened to comply with it, and to lay down their wedding-rings on the altar of the fatherland. Leonora stood as if fascinated by the beautiful and soul-stirring scene. With radiant eyes she gazed at the ladies who came and received with joyous pride iron rings in exchange for gold ones—at the young women, who, blushing and with tearful eyes, gave up their first love-pledge— at the old matrons who came totteringly to exchange the golden reminiscences of the days of their youth for iron ornaments.* **Tears of** profound emotion fell from Leonora's eyes. She wished to embrace these women and thank them for their patriotism.

"I will also prove to the country how ardently I love it," she said to **herself. "I will also make** my sacrifices. **I must go, Caroline is waiting for** me. I must buy arms **for the soldiers whom I** intend to furnish." She shook hands with her godfather in silence. The crowd in front of the door receded before her, and allowed her to pass, filled with reverence for the women who returned from the solemn sacrifice they had made. She passed on, absorbed in her reflections. Once she raised her hand, and contemplated the iron ring on her finger. "I gave gold for iron!" she said, raising her dark eyes toward heaven. "I am now a bride, too, the bride of my country! Will it give me only iron for the gold of my love? Only a bullet or a sword-cut? No matter! I am the bride of the fatherland! I will live and die for it!" She was aroused from her musings by cheers suddenly resounding from the side of the Gendarmes **Market.** An immense crowd had assembled there, and shouted frantically, their faces beaming with joy.

* On the first day about two hundred wedding-rings were exchanged.—Vide Beltzke, vol. I.

" What is it ? "

And a hundred jubilant voices replied: " General York is coming with the Prussians ! The king has reinstated York ! The court-martial has acquitted him ! " *

" Long live noble General York ! " shouted the crowd. " York was the first man to take heart, and brave the French ! "

" York is coming to Berlin ! " shouted others, hurrying from the adjoining streets to the market-place. " York, with his Prussians, is outside the King's Gate, and to-morrow he will make his entry into Berlin ! "

" Long live the brave general ! All Berlin will meet him to-morrow, and cheer him who first drew his sword against the French ! The new era is dawning on Prussia ! "

" Yes, the new era is dawning on Prussia ! " exclaimed Leonora. " We have long walked in sadness. But morning is breaking—the morning of freedom. Now we shall boldly raise our heads. The country has called us, and we all have heard the call, and are ready to conquer or die. Hail, brave York ! The time of thraldom is past ! We shall rise from the dust, and the Germans will now reconquer the sacred right of being Germans. Oh, my heart, rejoice ! I am no longer a girl, I am one of Lützow's riflemen, and to-morrow I shall go to Breslau, and add another soldier to the Legion of Vengeance. Farewell, Leonora Prohaska, farewell ! Now you are a man, and your soul must be manly, strong, and hopeful. Long live Prussia ! "

---

* York made his entry into Berlin at the head of the Prussian troops on the 17th of March, 1813, and was received with boundless enthusiasm.

CHAPTER XXVI.

THEODORE KÖRNER.

ANOTHER corps of volunteers leaving Berlin had arrived at Breslau, and just alighted from their wagons on the large market-place, called the "Ring," and received their tickets for quarters at the city hall. Two of these volunteers, emerging from the building, descended arm in arm the steps of the front staircase. They were two young men of slight forms and strangely youthful appearance. Not the faintest down was around their fresh lips, and white and delicate were their foreheads. But no one was surprised at their tender age, for people were accustomed nowadays to see lads emulate manhood, believing that courage did not depend on years. By the side of aged men, boys who had just been confirmed were seen to enter the ranks of the volunteers, and handle their muskets with the same strength and energy as veteran soldiers. No one, therefore, particularly noticed the youthful age of the two volunteers who came forth from the city hall, and were now crossing the place arm in arm.

"Now our lot is cast," said one of them, with a smile. "We are soldiers!"

"Yes, we are soldiers," cried the other, "and we shall be brave ones, Caroline!"

"Caroline!" echoed the other, in dismay. "How imprudent! Did we not leave our female names with our wearing apparel at Berlin with the Jew, Leonora?"

"Ah, and you call me, too, by my female name," said Leonora, with a gentle smile. "No matter! it is all right enough so long as no one hears it. We have no secrets from each other, and we are, therefore, allowed to call each other by the names received at the baptismal font."

"But before the world we call ourselves differently now; I am Charles Petersen, and you—what is your name now, Leonora?"

"My name is Charles Renz," said Leonora, smiling. "That was the name of my dear teacher, to whom I am indebted for what little knowledge I have acquired, and who originally induced me to take the step I have ventured **upon. He** had **been a soldier a long time,** and loved his country and the royal family. History was his favorite study, and he told me of the heroic deeds of ancient nations in their struggles for liberty. His eyes beamed with transcendent ardor, and the words flowed from his lips like a stream of poetry. He taught me that, when the country was in danger, it was the duty of the women to take up arms in its defence, and that there was no more beautiful death than that on the field of honor. Joan of Orleans and the Maid of Saragossa were his favorite heroines, and he always called Queen Louisa the martyr of German liberty. When she died, three years ago, the first idea that struck me was, how my old teacher would bear up under this grief, and that it was incumbent upon me to comfort him. I hastened to him, and found him sad and disheartened. 'Now my hopes for Germany are gone,' he said, 'for the genius of German liberty has left us and fled to heaven. Beautiful and noble Queen Louisa might, perhaps, have still inspired the Germans to rise in arms against the tyrant; but she is dead, and liberty has died **with her.**' 'No,' I cried, 'no! liberty will blossom from her grave. Germany will rise to avenge the martyrdom of the queen; Germany's wrath will be kindled anew by the sufferings of this august victim that Napoleon's tyranny has wrung from us. Yes, the country will rise to avenge Louisa.' He gazed at me a long while, and his tears ceased to flow. After a prolonged pause he said: 'If it be as you say, if Germany take up arms, what will you do, Leonora? Will you stay at home, knit stockings, and scrape lint, or will you sacrifice your heart, your blood, your life, and be a heroine?' I exclaimed, joyously: 'I will sacrifice all to the **fatherland, and help to achieve the victory, or die on the battle-field!**' The eyes of my old teacher were radiant with delight. '**Swear it to me, Leonora,**' he cried, '**swear to me, by all that is sacred**—swear by the memory of our sainted Queen Louisa!' I laid my hand on the Bible, and swore by the memory of Queen Louisa to fight like a man and a hero. I am now about to fulfil my oath, and, as my dear old teacher has died, I have adopted his name as my inheritance, and **call myself Charles Renz.** It seems to me it is a doubly sacred duty now to be brave, for I must do honor to my teacher's name."

"**And** you will do so, I am sure," cried Caroline. "And I will do so, too, Leonora. No teacher has impelled me to love my native land. This sentiment is spontaneous; perhaps because I have nothing else to love. I am alone in the world; my dear parents are dead; I have no brothers or sisters, no lover; and inasmuch as I have nothing to love, I gave up my heart to hatred. I hate the French, and, above all, Napo**leon, who has** brought so much misery on Europe, and for ten years has spilt **rivers of blood. It is** hatred that has incited me—hatred has forced the sword into my hand, and when we go into battle, I shall **not** only call, like you, 'Long live the fatherland!' but add, 'Death to the tyrant Napoleon, the enemy of the Germans!' Yes, I **hate this Bonaparte** more intensely than I love **my own life; and, as I** could not stab him with **the needle, with which I** made caps and bonnets **for the fair ladies of Berlin, I** have cast it aside, and taken up the sword. That is my whole history—the history of the *ci-devant* milliner Caroline Peters, the future horseman Charles Petersen."

"What!" ejaculated Leonora, in amazement. "You intend to enlist in the cavalry?"

"If they will accept me. I am well versed in horsemanship, for when my father was still living I rode out with him every day. He was a much-respected farmer in the suburbs of Stralsund, and owned many horses. During the siege of Stralsund he lost every thing, and we were reduced to extreme poverty. My father died of grief, and since that time I have not again mounted a horse. But I think I still know how to manage one, and **am not afraid of doing so.**"

"**But why will you? Why not** remain in the infantry, which would be much more natural and simple?"

"Why? Shall I tell you the truth, Leonora? Let me tell you, then, confidentially; it is because long marches would incommode me. And you? Would it not be better for you to follow my example?"

"No," said Leonora, "I shall remain in the infantry, and become one of Lützow's riflemen— a member of the Legion of Vengeance.—I believe we have arrived at the house designated to us. Major von Lützow lives here; the numerous volunteers who are going in and out show that we have reached his headquarters. Now, Caroline, farewell! and let me greet you, friend Charles Petersen!"

"Leonora, farewell! and let me greet you, friend Charles Renz!" They shook hands and looked into each other's glowing faces.

"Forward now, comrade!" said Caroline, walking toward the house.

"Forward!" echoed Leonora, jubilantly.

Arm in arm they walked across the gloomy hall **to the low,** brown door, entering the room pointed out to **them as** Major von Lützow's recruiting-office. It was a large, low room; long tables, painted brown, such as are to be found in small taverns or beer-saloons, stood on both sides of the smoky whitewashed walls; low stools, of the same description, were beside them, and constituted, with the tables, the only furniture of this hall, where the citizens and mechanics had formerly taken their beer, and where now the volunteers came to take the oath of fidelity to the fatherland **and** Major von Lützow. In the middle of **this room stood** a young lady of rare beauty. A plain black dress enveloped her form, reaching to her neck and veiling her bust. Her face was very white and delicate, a complexion to be found only among the fair daughters of the North; her blond hair fell down in heavy ringlets beside her faintly-flushed cheeks; a fervent light was beaming from her large light-blue eyes.

"That is Madame von Lützow, to whom the travellers in the stage-coach alluded," said Leonora to herself; "it is the count's noble daughter, who poured a glass of water over her hand because a Frenchman had kissed it, and who descended from her father's castle to marry a poor Prussian officer, whom she loved for the scars on his forehead."

The beautiful lady approached the two young volunteers with a sweet, winning smile. "You wish to see Major von Lützow, do you not?" she inquired. "Unfortunately, he is not at home; pressing business matters prevent him from personally welcoming the young heroes who wish to join him. He has charged me with doing so in his place, and you may believe that I bid you welcome with as joyous a heart as my husband would do."

"Oh, we are so happy to be received by you," said Leonora, smiling, "for we were told at Berlin of noble and beautiful Madame von Lützow enlisting the Legion of Vengeance, and who is so true a representative of the great idea of our struggle. For our struggle is one both of vengeance **and** love. Since then we have longed to be enlisted by you, madame, and to take our oath of fidelity."

"I accept it in the name of Major von Lützow," said the lady, with a gentle smile. "Here are your numbers, and now give me your names that I may enter them in the recruiting-book." She approached the table on which the large open book was lying, and quickly noted down the names which the two volunteers gave, affixing the numbers already given. "Now, then," she said, kindly nodding to them, "you are enlisted in the sacred service of the fatherland, and I hope you will do your duty. I hope you—"

At this moment the door was opened hastily, and a young man rushed into the room.

"Theodore Körner!" ejaculated the lady, greeting him cordially.

"Yes, Madame von Lützow, it is I," exclaimed the young man, saluting the two volunteers—"it is I, and I come to you a prey to boundless despair!"

Madame von Lützow hastened to him, and looked with an expression of heart-felt sympathy into his handsome, pale face.

"Yes, indeed," she said, "your face looks like a cloud from which thunder and lightning may be expected at any moment. What is the matter? What has happened to you, my poet and hero?"

"Come, let us go," whispered Caroline to her friend.

"No, let us stay," said Leonora, in a low voice. "If it is a secret, they will bid us go; but I should like to know what ails the fine-looking young man whom Madame von Lützow calls a poet and a hero. Oh, I have never yet seen a poet, and this one is so handsome!"

"Let us sit down on this bench," whispered Caroline, "and—"

"Hush, let us listen!" said Leonora, sitting down.

"It is not that, then?" exclaimed the lady, who in the mean time had continued her conversation with the young man. "Your father has not rebuked his son for the quick resolve he had taken."

"No, no," said Theodore Körner, hastily, "on the contrary, my father approves my determination to enlist, and sends me his blessing. I received a very touching letter from him this morning."

"It is his affianced bride, then, that has driven our poet to despair, because he loves her more ardently than the fatherland," said Madame von Lützow. "It is true, I cannot blame her for it, for the woman that loves has but one country—the heart of her lover, and she is homeless as soon it turns from her. But this is precisely the grand and beautiful sacrifice—that you give up for the sake of your country all that we otherwise call the greatest and holiest blessings of life—your affianced bride; your pleasant, comfortable existence; a fine, honorable position, and a future full of a poet's fame and splendor. It is, indeed, a sacrifice, but a sacrifice for which the fatherland will thank you, and which will incite thousands to emulate your noble example."

"Would it were so!" exclaimed Körner, enthusiastically, raising his large black eyes to heaven; "would that our patriotic ardor struck all hearts like a thunderbolt, and kindled a conflagration, whose flames would shed a lustre over the remotest times! I do not deny that I felt how great was the sacrifice I made, but this very feeling filled me with enthusiasm. All the stars of my happiness were shining upon me in mild beauty, but I was not allowed to look up to them because it was the night of adversity; but now that this night is about to vanish, and a new morning is dawning, my stars, too, must fade before the sun of liberty. That was the sacred conviction which drove me away from Vienna, from my betrothed bride, and caused me to cast aside all that otherwise imparts value to life. A great era requires great hearts. I felt strong enough to go out and bare my breast to the storm. Could I do nothing but sing songs in honor of my victorious brethren? No one would have then loved and esteemed me any longer; my parents would have been ashamed of me, and my affianced bride would have contemptuously turned away from the cowardly poet. Therefore, I gave up every thing for the sake of my native land. It is true, my parents and my Emma will weep for me. May God comfort them!

I could not spare them this blow. It is not much that I risk my life; but that this life is adorned with love, friendship, and joy, and that I nevertheless risk it, is a sacrifice that can be compensated only by love of country, more sacred than any other love, and to it we should devote our life.* My noble father feels and knows this, and so does my betrothed."

"And yet, agreed though you are with yourself and your dear ones, why this despair?" asked Madame von Lützow, with a smile.

Körner looked down in confusion, and then raised his flaming eyes with a strange expression. "Ah, madame," he exclaimed, "I divine your stratagem; it is that of an angel, and, therefore, worthy of you."

"What stratagem do you mean?" she asked, with a semblance of surprise.

"The angelic stratagem by which you comforted me in my grief, without knowing its cause. When I rushed so impolitely into this room, I told you that I was in despair. And you, instead of urging me to tell you at once the cause of it, inquired for the great affairs of my life, and whether my affliction came from my parents or my affianced bride. You thereby wished to admonish me that these momentous affairs and relations of my life, not having lost their harmony, my grief was, perhaps, but a passing dissonance, and that it really might not be worth while to give way to despair on account of it. I am sure, madame, I have understood you: was not this the object of your questions?"

Madame von Lützow nodded gently. "You have understood me," she said. "I think in all our grievances we should, before giving way to vexation or despair, lay the great questions of life before us, and inquire whether that which weighs us down touches them, whether it strikes at our true happiness. Now, if this is not the case, we should bear the grievance lightly, and not consider it a misfortune. To feel greatly what is great, and to heed little what is little, is the true wisdom of life."

---

* His own words.—Vide "Theodore Körner's Works, edited by Carl Streckfuss, p. 54.

"You are right, as you always are," said Theodore Körner, reverentially bowing to the beautiful lady, "and let me penitently confess, then, that I have this time heeded greatly what is little and have considered what grieved me a great misfortune. But now that I have confessed my guilt, the guardian angel of the volunteers must have mercy upon me and come to my assistance. For something very unpleasant has really befallen me, and no philosophy can dispute it."

"Well, confess what it is," exclaimed Madame von Lützow, smiling.

"You know, madame, that our Legion of Vengeance is to be solemnly consecrated at the village of Rochau, at the foot of the Zobtenberg, on Sunday next?"

"Of course I do, and I shall accompany Lützow and the volunteers in order to witness the ceremony."

"At the village church we are all to appear for the first time in our black uniforms, to receive the preacher's blessing, and to be consecrated as soldiers of the fatherland. I myself have written a poem, adapted to the air of an anthem, for this solemn occasion, and all my comrades will sing it. After the sermon the volunteers in the church will take the oath of war upon the swords of their officers. I have been ardently yearning for this day, and now I shall probably be unable to participate in its services, for—do not laugh, madame, at my insignificant mishap—the tailor refuses to make me a uniform by that time, and in citizen's clothes, as a fashionable dandy, I really cannot appear among the brave men who will proudly walk about in their *litefkaes*. The tailor says it is impossible for him to make a uniform at so short a notice; he pretends to be overwhelmed with work, and does not know where to find hands. Now you, the helping, advising, and protecting genius of the volunteers, are my last consolation and resort. If you send for the cruel tailor, and tell him how important it is for me to participate in that ceremony, your words will render possible what now he declares impossible. Therefore, send for the tailor, madame; he fortunately lives close by, in the court-yard, in the large rear building; order him to make me a uniform, and he will have to do so, for who could withstand your words?"

"Well, I will try," said Madame von Lützow, smiling. "I will see whether my words are so impressive as to move a tailor's heart."

"And if he is unable to comply with your wishes because he lacks assistants," said Leonora, hastily rising from her seat near the door, and approaching Körner and Madame von Lützow, "I offer myself as an assistant, for I am a tailor."

"So am I," exclaimed Caroline, vividly. "I know, too, how to ply the needle, and am ready to assist in sewing a comrade's uniform."

"Ah, the volunteers whom I have just enlisted, and whose pardon I have to ask for having forgotten them," cried Madam Von Lützow, smiling.

"We have rather to ask your pardon for staying here," said Leonora. "But we are indebted to you and to the poet Theodore Körner for the most soul-stirring sentiments, and it seems to me as though we have received only now the true consecration for the future that lies before us. Now, that I know what great sacrifices one may joyously make, I feel how incumbent it was upon me to make them too, and I have no remorse at leaving my parents and my brothers. It is certainly true, as the poet said: 'A great era requires great hearts!' And therefore I will try, to the best of my power, to have a great heart, that I may be worthy of our great era."

"A great and noble heart is beaming from your eyes, my friend," said Theodore Körner, offering his hand to Leonora. "I greet you both as dear comrades of mine, and beg you to treat me as one."

"Yes, we will do so," exclaimed Caroline, shaking hands with the poet. "And we will prove it directly by going to that tailor and offering to assist him in making the uniform of our esteemed lieutenant."

"Softly, my friend!" laughed Theodore Körner, "I have not yet risen so high; I am no lieutenant."

"But you will be soon," said Caroline, ardently; "for one may easily read in your face that you are born to command, and not to obey. We volunteers are to elect our own officers. Well, then, I shall vote for Theodore Körner." *

"So shall I!" ejaculated Leonora.

"But while indulging in such dreams as to the future, we forget the grim tailor," said Theodore Körner, smiling. "Madame von Lützow, I beseech you, pity my distress, and send for him, that your eloquence may soften his heart."

"But suppose he does not comply?" asked Madame von Lützow. "It would be wrong, too, to occupy his time while so busy. You say the man lives near?"

"Scarcely fifty steps from here."

"Well, then, conduct me to him!" said Madame von Lützow, "we will pay a visit to him as Torquato Tasso once went to the Duke di Ferrara. You, my two young friends, will please accompany us, that we may present to him two willing assistants. Come!"

"Yes, madame, and may your eloquence prevail!" exclaimed Körner, opening the door, and posting himself beside it in order to allow the lady to pass out.

Graceful and smiling, she hastened through the gloomy room and approached the door, followed by the two volunteers with their rosy faces and bright eyes. When about to cross the threshold, she stood and gazed archly at Körner. "Stop," she said, "I have to impose a condition. If we are to assist a poet, he must in return pay us a poet's tribute. I shall not cross this threshold before you recite one of your new warsongs."

"Yes, a song!" cried the two volunteers.

"Well, you are silent?" asked Madame von Lützow, smiling. "Strike the chords of your lyre, and let us hear a battle-hymn!"

"No, not a battle-hymn," said Theodore Körner; "that requires the accompaniment of clashing arms and booming cannon. But to the fair patroness of the Legion of Vengeance I will communicate, although it is not completed, my hymn to the guardian angel of German liberty—Queen Louisa!" Raising his dark-blue eyes to heaven, he recited the following lines, addressed "to Queen Louisa:"

"Du Heilige! hör' Deiner Kinder Flehen,
    Es dringe mächtig auf zu deinem Licht.
Kannst wieder freundlich auf uns niedersehen,
    Verklärter Engel! länger weine nicht!
Denn Preussens Adler soll zum Kampfe wehen.
    Es drängt Dein Volk sich jubelnd zu der Pflicht.
Und Jeder wählt, und keinen siehst du leben,
Den freien Tod für ein bezwung'nes Leben.

"Wir lagen noch in feige Nacht gebettet;
    Da rief nach Dir Dein besseres Geschick,
An die unwürd'ge Zeit warst Du gekettet,
    Zur Rache mahnte Dein gebroch'ner Blick.
So hast Du uns den deutschen Muth gerettet.
    Jetzt sieh auf uns, sieh auf Dein Volk zurück,
Wie alle Herzen treu und muthig brennen!
Nun woll' uns auch die Deinen wieder nennen!

"Und wie einst, alle Kräfte zu beleben,
    Ein Heil'genbild, für den gerechten Krieg
Dem Heeresbanner schützend zugegeben,
    Als Oriflamme in die Lüfte stieg:
So soll Dein Bild auf unsern Fahnen schweben,
    Und soll uns leuchten durch die Nacht zum Sieg!
Louise sei der Schutzgeist deutscher Sache!
Louise sei das Losungswort zur Rache!" *

"Louisa shall be the guardian angel of the German cause and the battle-cry of vengeance," echoed the two volunteers.

Madame von Lützow said nothing. She stood, with her white hands clasped, as if in prayer, and her sweet face turned heavenward. Tears were

---

* Theodore Körner was elected lieutenant by his comrades on the 24th of April.

* O sainted one! now let thy children's prayer,
    As incense, rise to realms of heavenly light;
Beholding us thou canst with gladness hear,
    And tears no more may dim thy vision bright:
For Prussia's standard in the battle near
    Will nerve thy people to their ancient might.
Thy sons in crowded ranks await the strife,
Preferring a free death to slavery's life.

Enthralled in long and timid gloom we lay;
    When Heaven recalled thee, and thy fetters broke
Which bound thee to thy times' unworthy sway,
    Thy dying eyes of future vengeance spoke.
Thus didst thou save on that sad final day
    The German honor, and our courage woke.
Behold us now, as we all fear resign,
With glowing hearts, and once more call us thine!

As erst to serried legions in the field,
    A sacred symbol, as a golden flame,
Lit up the battle-standard, and revealed
    For whom the victory's just though bloody claim:
So let us, 'neath thy bannered image, wield
    A valiant sword—our "oriflamme" thy name—
The pledge of honor and the gathering cry,
To live for Prussia's glory, or to die!

glittering in her eyes; and, giving her hand to the poet, she said in a low voice: "You have paid us a tribute worthy of you. Thanks! And now come!" She quickly crossed the threshold toward the court-yard. Körner was by her side; Leonora and Caroline, the two volunteers, followed her.

"The four windows on the ground-floor yonder are those of the tailor's shop," said Körner.

Madame von Lützow nodded, and walked across the wide court-yard toward the house.

CHAPTER XXVII.

THE HEROIC TAILOR.

THE tailor and his hands were very busy. All sorts of colored cloths and pieces of uniforms were lying about. On the bench, in the middle of the room, sat four workmen, hard at work. Not a word interrupted the silence now desecrated by the noise of the opening door. He who sat on a somewhat raised seat, and was just braiding a magnificent scarlet hussar-jacket, hastily looked up. His hand, armed with his needle, had just risen and remained suspended; his eyes, which he had at first raised carelessly from his work, were fixed on the door, which framed so unusual and attractive a picture—a young lady of surpassing beauty, surrounded by three youthful soldiers, who looked very fine and imposing, too, and whose looks were turned to him with a kind and inquiring expression.

"You are M. Martin, the merchant tailor, are you not?" asked the lady, greeting the tailor with a gentle nod.

"That is my name," said M. Martin, involuntarily rising from his seat.

"Well, then, my dear sir," said the lady, advancing a few steps into the shop, "I should like to say a word to you."

"Yes, I imagine what it is," exclaimed the tailor, who fixed his eyes now upon Theodore Körner, and recognized his tormentor. "The gentle-

man has been here twice already about a uniform for Sunday. But I could not make it, if an angel descended from heaven to entreat me."

"Well, I thank you for your compliment," said Madame von Lützow, smiling. "But tell me now, sir, why can you not accommodate him?"

"Because I have more work now than I am able to finish. I was rash enough to accept so many orders, that I do not know how I shall be able to fill them; and in the excitement and confusion prevalent in the city it is impossible to get assistance at present."

"Well, if that is the only reason, we bring you fresh help. These two young volunteers are ready to work under your supervision, and finish the uniform of their comrades."

The tailor glanced toward the two young volunteers. "Lads, scarcely sixteen years old!" he said, shrugging his shoulders; "it is impossible that they can be experienced artists."

"But both affirm that they are tailors," said Madame von Lützow, "and skilled in their trade."

"Yes, sir, please give us a trial," begged Leonora."

"We are quick and skilful workmen," protested Caroline.

"Regular tailors?" asked M. Martin.

"Yes, regular tailors," replied Leonora.

"Very well. Finish this collar; the needle is still in it," said M. Martin, handing the scarlet soldier-jacket to Leonora.

The young volunteer blushed, and said in a low voice: "To be sure, sir, I must ask you to show me how to do it, for I have never yet worked on men's clothes."

"A ladies' tailor!" exclaimed M. Martin, with an expression of boundless contempt. "The other one, too?"

"Yes, I also am a ladies' tailor," said Caroline, smiling.

"And they are bold enough to offer their assistance to me!" exclaimed M. Martin, shrugging his shoulders.

"It is only necessary for you to give them proper directions, sir," said Madame von Lützow, entreatingly, "for as they know how to ply the needle they will easily understand what to do."

"And if the uniform should not fit well, or be badly made, it will be laid at my door, and M. Martin will be blamed for it. I assure you I cannot take the job; I am short of workmen of the necessary experience. No one wants to work nowadays—all heads are turned—all young men are enlisting."

"No, sir," said the lady, "all heads are turned right again—to one thing necessary at this time—to the service of the fatherland."

"Bah! my shop is my fatherland," said the tailor, contemptuously.

"That is not true," exclaimed Madame von Lützow, "you do not and cannot think so. For if you did, you would be no Prussian, no German, and no one could love and respect you. During the period of adversity and disgrace, your shop may have been a comfort to you; but now that **the sun of liberty is rising, all hearts must throb joyously; all must go out and gaze upon the new world; the shop no longer** contains the work worthy of a freeman—it is to be found only on the battle-field—deliverance of the country!"

"The lady is right!" exclaimed the tailor's three assistants, who had hitherto looked up but stealthily from their work, but now cast it aside with impetuosity. "Yes, the lady is right! It is a shame for honest men to sit here in this room **and ply the needle,** while our friends and brethren are drawing the sword and marching out to the holy war of liberation. We must also participate in the great struggle!"

"Oh, yes," cried the tailor, in grim despair, "now my last workmen are coaxed away from me! You have taken the money I offered you when you entered my service, and as honest men you must keep your word. Resume your work! You know well that we are very busy."

The men commenced their work again with morose faces, whispering to each other: "As soon as the week has expired, we shall leave the shop and enlist."

"Well, madame, what do you wish?" exclaimed the tailor, furiously. "You have come to give me a job, and at the same time you disparage my business, and seduce my workmen to leave me. I shall soon have to close my shop."

"But you will not do so, dear M. Martin, before having made a uniform for this young man," said Madame von Lützow, in an entreating tone and with a sweet smile. "I have certainly not come to disparage your honorable business, for what should we do without the skilful tailor, who makes the uniforms of our soldiers and fits them out, as it were, for the service of their country? Oh, I am sure that you have worked at them with grand reflections, since this labor is more agreeable to you than if you had to make the most gorgeous suit for a chamberlain, and it gladdens you to think: 'I am likewise working hard for the fatherland. I am in my own way a soldier of the country; for I devote to it my skill and labor.'"

"That is true," said M. Martin, in confusion, **"and that you may not believe me to be a worse man than I really am, I must tell you that I** do not take pay for these jobs, but that I have offered to make twelve uniforms for our soldiers free of charge. I have nothing else to offer; hence, I give all I can!"

"And there is no nobler gift!" exclaimed Madame von Lützow. "You are a good man; pray give me your hand and let me thank you." She offered her hand to the tailor, and he put his broad, cold hand timidly into it.

"Oh, now I fear nothing," said Madame von Lützow, joyfully; "as you are so good a patriot, you will fulfil our prayer, and make a uniform for this young man for next Sunday."

"But I have told you already that I cannot," replied M. Martin, almost tearfully—"I cannot finish it."

"And I reply: Try, sir! I am sure you will finish it. For, take into consideration, dear M. Martin, that your own reputation is at stake, and that all the brave volunteers would execrate your name if it should be your fault that their favorite and celebrated bard could not attend the Sunday's ceremony."

"How so? What bard do you allude to, madame?"

"I allude to the great poet who stands before you—Theodore Körner."

"Ah, this is Theodore Körner!" exclaimed the tailor. "The poet who wrote 'Toni,' the splendid comedy that I saw last winter at our theatre?"

"The same, my dear sir," said Madame von Lützow, **while** Körner nodded to the tailor with a pleasant smile. "And he has written many other beautiful **plays**, and magnificent songs to boot. This is the reason why, though he is only twenty-one years old, **he is famous** throughout Germany, **and** at Vienna occupied a brilliant position. He 's affianced to a dear, sweet young woman, whom he loves with all his heart, and to whom he was to be married within a month; but suddenly the battle-cry of freedom resounded throughout Germany, the King of Prussia called upon the able-bodied young men to volunteer and avenge the disgrace of Germany, and see what love of country can accomplish! The young man casts aside every thing—he gives up all, his fame, his betrothed, his position, and hastens with enthusiasm to offer his arm and his services—to exchange his poetical fame and his earthly happiness for victory or an honorable death on the battle-field."

"Oh, that is really glorious," cried the men, striking with their clinched right hands their knee, as though it were a recruiting-drum.

"Yes, it is so," said M. Martin, thoughtfully, to himself.

"Madame," whispered the poet, smiling, "you make me blush by your too kind praise."

"Is it my fault that a plain statement of the facts in the case is such praise for you?" asked Madame von Lützow. "For I have told you the truth, M. Martin, and all happened precisely as I have stated it. He has given up all to enlist. Vainly do his parents and his loved one weep for him. He hears nothing—sees nothing—for his country calls him, and he obeys. He does not desire happiness before his country is free, and sweeter than the most blissful life seems to him a glorious death for the fatherland. So he has come; the volunteers greeted him with shouts of exultation, and they believe now that Providence will cause their arms and their bravery to be successful, since an inspired bard will take the field with them, and endow them with redoubled ardor by his songs. But, before taking the field, they wish to implore God's blessing at the altar, and on Sunday next all those who are already uniformed and equipped are to take the oath of war and be consecrated. Theodore Körner has written for the occasion a pious hymn, which all the volunteers will sing, and now how can you be so cruel as to prevent him from singing his own hymn with them?"

"I?" cried the tailor, in dismay.

"**Yes, you! For, if you do not** accommodate him, he cannot be present."

M. Martin heaved a profound sigh, and cast a glance of despair around his shop. "There are still three hussar-jackets to be finished," he murmured. "If it were but a hussar-uniform that the gentleman asks for! But he does not wish to join the hussars?"

"No, my friend. I enlist in the Legion of Vengeance, and become one of Major von Lützow's volunteer riflemen. It will, therefore, be less troublesome to suit me."

"But that dress is not near as showy as the other," said the tailor, morosely. "An entirely black uniform with red trimmings on the sleeves looks sad, and—cruel."

"And that is as it ought to be, my dear sir. The black color signifies our grief, the red signifies blood."

And suddenly he commenced to sing:

* "Noch trauern wir im schwarzen Rächerkleide
    Um den gestorbnen Muth,
  Doch fragt man Euch, was dieses Roth bedeute;
    Das deutet Frankenblut!

---

* By this black uniform we ever mourn
    The public spirit dead!
  And why is then this crimson facing worn?—
    With Frenchmen's blood it 's red.

  When high above vast heaps of slaughtered foes,
    The star of peace shall shine,
  The banner white, which victory bestows,
    Raise by our own free Rhine.

"Mit Gott!—Einst geht hoch über Feindesleichen
    Der Stern des Friedens auf;
  Dann pflanzen wir ein weisses Siegeszeichen
    Am freien Rheinstrom auf."

"Then we shall raise a white symbol of our victory on the banks of the free Rhine!" echoed the volunteers, and the tailor and his assistants.

"M. Martin!" cried Madame von Lützow, laughing, "you have forgotten yourself; you have joined in the chorus!"

"Yes, it is true," he said, "I have sung these few words with them; they make my heart swell, and—I do not know what has happened to me—it seems to me the song and all you have said make another man of me, and—"

"You will make the uniform for Theodore Körner?" asked Madame von Lützow, smiling.

M. Martin was silent, and quickly raised his head and looked at his assistants, who were gazing at him inquiringly.

"You have made up your minds, then?" he asked; "When the week is up, and your jobs are finished, you intend to leave me, and volunteer?"

"Yes, we have come to that determination," replied the three, unanimously, "and nothing shall prevent us from carrying it out."

"Well, then, I must close my shop, and discontinue the tailoring business."

"But what do you intend to do, then, sir?" asked one of the journeymen, in surprise.

"I intend to enlist!" replied M. Martin. "This beautiful lady and the song have enchanted me. Hurrah! I also will enlist!"

"But my uniform?" asked Körner.

"Oh, you need not be concerned," exclaimed the tailor, in a proud tone; "it shall be made! I will work all night, and not lay aside my needle before it is done. Will you help me, journeymen?"

"Yes, sir, we will!"

"And you, too, volunteers? It is true, you are only ladies' tailors, but you know at least how to line and pad a coat. Will you take the job?"

"Yes, M. Martin, we will joyously do so," cried Leonora and Caroline.

"Well, then, we can finish two uniforms by Sunday—one for the poet, the other for myself!"

"My dear sir, I thank you from the bottom of my heart," said Madame von Lützow; and then, turning her radiant face to Körner, she asked, "Are you now satisfied?"

"Ah, I knew well that no one could resist you, and that you are our good angel," whispered the poet, pressing the hand of the lovely lady to his lips.

"But listen, M. Körner," said the tailor; "if I am to work for you so industriously, I must impose a condition, and you must promise to fulfil it."

"What is it?"

"It is that you shall not pay me for my labor."

"But, sir, it is impossible for me to—"

Madame von Lützow laid her hand softly on his shoulder. "I am sure you do not wish to offend this excellent man?" she whispered.

"It is impossible for me to take pay for a favor which I do to one of my future comrades," said M. Martin. "I suppose that is what you wanted to say, and you are right. But if you insist on indemnifying me, there is another way for you to do so."

"Pray tell me."

"You sang two verses, which sounded so bold and fresh that they touched my heart. Was that the whole song, or are there any more verses?"

"No, sir, they are the two last; three others precede them."

"Well, comrades," said M. Martin, gayly, "if you insist on my doing my last tailoring job for you, then sing me the other three."

Körner glanced inquiringly at Madame von Lützow. "I do not know," he said, hesitatingly, "if madame will permit it?"

Madame von Lützow smiled. "I not only permit, but pray you to sing," she said. "Give us the whole song, and let us all join in the refrain. Come, brave soldiers of the future! cast aside your work, form in line, and sing with us the song of the Black Riflemen!"

The three journeymen jumped up, and posted themselves beside M. Martin. The lady again withdrew to the door. On both sides stood the two young volunteers, with their blooming faces, and between these two groups stood the tall and noble form of the young poet, whose fine face beamed with courage and energy, and on whose brow genius had pressed the kiss of inspiration.

"Now, listen attentively!" said Theodore Körner, smiling. "My song is easy to sing, for who is ignorant of the song of the Rhenish wine. Let us sing it to that melody!"

And through the tailor's shop, hitherto so peaceful and silent, resounded the song of the Black Riflemen:

"In's Feld, in's Feld, die Rachegeister mahnen,
   Auf, deutsches Volk, zum Krieg!
In's Feld, in's Feld! Hoch flattern unsere Fahnen,
   Sie führen uns zum Sieg!

"Klein ist die Schaar, doch gross ist das Vertrauen
   Auf den gerechten Gott!
Wo seine Engel ihre Veste bauen,
   Sind Höllenkünste Spott.

"Gebt kein Pardon! Könnt Ihr das Schwert nicht heben,
   So würgt sie ohne Scheu!
Und hoch verkauft den letzten Tropfen Leben,
   Der Tod macht Alle frei!" *

---

* To the field! the spirits of vengeance cry;
   Rise, and your country save!
Uplift your eagle banners to the sky—
   For victory they wave!

In number small, but great our confidence
   In a just God's decree;
When His own angels build our sure defence,
   Vain is hell's strategy.

No quarter give, but strike the fatal blow,
   Dear let your life-blood be;
Ask not for mercy, and to none bestow,
   For death makes all men free.

This whole scene is based on facts, for which I am indebted to personal communications from the Countess Ahlefeldt. Theodore Körner fell in the first year of the war of liberation, before the decisive battle of Leipsic, on the 26th of August, 1813, in a skirmish which the corps of Major von Lützow had with the French near Gadebusch. Only an hour prior to his death, while lying in ambush, he wrote his immortal "Song of the Sword" in his note-book. The statement of Mr. Alison, the historian, that he was killed in the battle of Dresden, is erroneous.

Leonora Prohaska fell in an engagement on the Görde, the 16th of September, 1813. A bullet pierced her breast. When she felt that she was dying, she revealed to her comrades that she was a woman, and that her name was Leonora Prohaska, and not Charles Renz.

Caroline Peters was more fortunate. She participated in the campaigns of 1813 and 1814, was decorated with the order of the Iron Cross on account of her bra-

CHAPTER XXVIII.

THE GENERAL-IN-CHIEF OF THE SILESIAN ARMY.

GENERAL BLUCHER was more morose and dejected than he had been for a long time. From the day he heard of the king's arrival at Breslau, and immediately left his farm of Kunzendorf to repair to that city, a perpetual sunshine lit up his face, and a new spring bloomed in his heart. But now the old clouds of Kunzendorf were again lowering on his brow, and a frost seemed to have blighted all the blossoms of his hope.

He sat on the sofa, closely wrapped in his dressing-gown, drumming with his hand a quickstep on the table in front of him, while he was blowing clouds of smoke from his long pipe. Very gloomy thoughts appeared to fill Blucher's soul, for his bushy eyebrows contracted, the quickstep was more rapid, and the smoke arose in denser masses. In the violence of his inward trouble, he grimly shook his head without thinking of the fragile friend in his mouth. Its delicate form struck against the corner of the table and broke into pieces.

"So," muttered Blucher to himself, "that was just wanting to my afflictions. It is the second pipe broken to-day. Well, there will be a day when Bonaparte shall pay me these pipes that he has already cost me. That day must come, or there is no justice in Heaven. Christian! O Christian!"

The door opened. Christian Hennemann appeared on the threshold, awaiting the orders of the general.

"Another wounded pipe, Christian," said Blucher, pointing at the pieces on the floor. "Pick them up, and see if there is not a short pipe among them."

"No, your excellency," said Christian, approaching and carefully picking up the pieces, "that is no wounded pipe, but a dead one. Shall I fetch another to your excellency?"

---

very, and honorably discharged at the end of the war. She was then married to the captain of an English vessel whom she accompanied on his travels, and with whom she visited her relatives at Stettin in 1844.—L. M.

He was about to turn away, but Blucher seized the lap of his hussar-jacket. "Show me the broken pipe," he said, anxiously; "let me see if it really will not do any more."

"Well, look at it, your excellency," said the pipe-master, in a dignified tone, holding up the bowl with a very small part of the tube. "It is impossible for you to use it again. If I should fill the bowl with tobacco and light it, your excellency, it would assuredly burn your nose."

"That is true," said Blucher, mournfully; "I believe you are right. I might burn my nose, and that would be altogether unnecessary now. I burn it here at Breslau every day."

"How did you do it?" asked Christian, in dismay. "Your excellency has not yet smoked short pipes."

"Because I am myself like a short pipe," cried Blucher, with a grim smile, "or because the miserable, sneaking vermin at court—well, what does it concern you? Why do you stand and stare at me? Go, Christian, and fetch me a new pipe."

"What, a new pipe!" asked a voice by his side. "Why, Blucher, you are still in your dressing-gown!"

It was his wife who had just entered the room by the side-door and approached her husband without being noticed. She was in full toilet, her head adorned with plumes, her delicate form wrapped in a heavy dark satin dress, trimmed with costly silver lace. Her neck and ears were ornamented with jewelry in which large diamonds shone; in her hand, radiant with valuable rings, she held a huge fan, inlaid with pearls and precious stones.

"Yes, Amelia, I am still in my dressing-gown," said Blucher, gloomily gazing at his wife. "Why, you are splendidly dressed to-day! What is it for?—and whither do you design to go?"

"Whither!" exclaimed the lady, in surprise. "But, husband, do you forget, then, the festival to take place to-night?"

"Well, what is it?" asked Blucher, slowly drawing his long white mustache through his fingers.

"Blucher, to-night the great ball takes place which the city of Breslau gives at the city hall in honor of the Emperor of Russia, when both their majesties will appear."

"Well, what does that concern me?"

"It concerns you a great deal, for you have solemnly promised the burgomaster, who came personally to invite us, that you would attend the ball to-night."

"And I shall not go to it after all, Amelia," cried Blucher, striking with his hand on the table. "No, Amelia! I am no dancing-bear to turn around at a ball, and to be led by the nose."

"But, Blucher, what has happened to you?" asked his wife, wonderingly. "You were as merry and high-spirited as a young god of spring; the violets laughed when they saw you pass by, and the snow-drops rang their tiny bells in your honor, and now suddenly it is winter again! Pray, tell me, what has happened to you?"

"Nothing at all has happened to me—that is just the misfortune," cried Blucher. "It is more than a month now since I have been sitting here at Breslau, and nothing has happened. I am still what I always was—an old pensioned general, who has no command, and nothing to do but to retire to Kunzendorf and plant cabbage-heads, while others in the field are cutting off French heads. And it will be best for me to go back to Kunzendorf. I have nothing to do here; no one cares for an old fellow like me. I have hoped on from day to day, but all my hopes are gone now. Amelia, take off your tinsel, and pack up our traps. The best thing we can do will be to start this very evening and return to our miserable, accursed village!"

"Dear me! what a humor you are in!" exclaimed his wife. "Every thing will be right in the end, my husband; you must not despair; things are only taking their course a little more deliberately than my firebrand wishes. But finally all will be precisely as you want it, for without Blucher they are unable to accomplish any thing, and will, therefore, at last resort to him."

"And I tell you they will try to get along without me," cried Blucher; "I shall be a disgraced man, at whom the very chickens will laugh, if he has to sneak back to Kunzendorf instead of taking the field. Pack up, Amelia, we shall leave this day!"

"But that is impossible, Blucher! It would look like a cowardly flight, and your enemies would rejoice over it. No, you must go to the ball to-night; you—"

"General Scharnhorst!" announced a footman at this moment, and there appeared in the open door the general, dressed in his gala-uniform, and his breast decked with orders.

"I am glad you have come, general," exclaimed Amelia, hastening to him, and shaking hands with her friend. "Look at that stubborn old man, who does not wish to go to the ball! Say yourself, general, must he not go?"

"Certainly he must," said Scharnhorst, smiling, "and I come to beg of you a seat in your carriage, and to let me have the honor of appearing in the suite of General and Madame **von** Blucher. You had, therefore, better dress at once, my dear general. It is high time. **Even** their majesties have already set out."

Blucher gently shook his head, and slowly raised his eyes toward Scharnhorst, who stood in front of him. "Scharnhorst," he said, "every thing turns out **wrong, and** I wish myself dead rather than see such a state of affairs."

"What do you mean, general?" inquired Scharnhorst. "What has happened?"

Blucher cast a piercing glance on him, and seemed to read in the depths of his soul. "Is the matter settled?" he asked. "Pray, my friend, tell me the truth without circumlocution. It is better for me to know it at once than allow this incertitude longer to gnaw at my heart. Scharnhorst, I implore you, tell me the truth! Has the commander of the Silesian army been appointed?"

"No, general," said Scharnhorst, gravely.

"And you do not know whom they will appoint? The truth, my friend!"

"Well, then, the truth is, that I do not know it,

and that their majesties themselves do not know it, although every patriot thinks they ought not to doubt which of the three gentlemen who stand on the list should be appointed, for every heart echoes, 'General Blucher is the man whom we need, and who will lead us to victory.' The emperor and the king are still vacillating; precious time is lost—Napoleon is organizing new armies, and strengthening himself on all sides, while they are hesitating."

"Three, then, stand on the list," said Blucher. "I have two competitors. Who are they, general?"

"One is Field-Marshal Kalkreuth."

Blucher started, and his eyes flashed with anger. "What!" he cried. "That childish old man to command an army! He who is constantly singing hymns of praise to Napoleon and his French—he who, only the other day, showed again that he deemed a frown of Bonaparte more terrible than the peril of a German patriot! *He* command an army to vanquish Napoleon! I suppose you know what he has done? **He betrayed** to the French ambassador, Count St. Marsan, who followed our king to Breslau in order to watch him, that Minister von Stein, our noblest friend, had secretly come for the purpose of negotiating with the king in the name of the Emperor of Russia; that he was living in a garret, and that conferences of the enemies of Napoleon were held there every night." *

"Yes, that is true," said Scharnhorst, "Field-Marshal Kalkreuth did so, and it is no fault of his that Baron von Stein, with his friends, one of whom I happen to be, was not secretly seized and carried off by the French. Fortunately, dear Count St. Marsan did not believe the field-marshal who betrayed his German countryman. The French ambassador allowed himself to be deceived by the stillness that reigned in the garret, which, according to the statement Kalkreuth made to him, was inhabited by dangerous Minister von Stein." †

"Well, and this man, the head of the French

---

* Pertz's "Life of Stein," vol. III., p. 310.
† Beitzke, vol. I., p. 170.

party, they wish to appoint general-in-chief of the Silesian army," said Blucher, mournfully. "Amelia, pack up our traps; let us return to Kunzendorf."

"But Field-Marshal Kalkreuth has not yet been appointed," said Scharnhorst, smiling; "I believe his two competitors have as good—nay, better prospects than he has."

"It is true, I forgot the second competitor," grumbled Blucher. "Who is it?"

"It is Lieutenant-General Count Tauentzien, in whom the Emperor Alexander takes a great deal of interest."

"**Of course,**" said Blucher, sarcastically, "**he** is a count, and he has such a polish, and courtly manners; he knows how to flatter the sovereigns, and tell them only what is agreeable. But now, you yourself must admit, Scharnhorst, that it is best for me to set out immediately for Kunzendorf, and that I have no prospects—none whatever! The two sovereigns, the king and emperor, **alone will make the appointment,** will they **not?**"

"Of course, they alone!"

"Well, each of them has a candidate of his own. The emperor is in favor of Count Tauentzien, and the king is for Field-Marshal Kalkreuth. Who, then, is to think of and speak for me?"

"Your glory will speak for you, general," said Scharnhorst, feelingly; "the love which every **soldier** feels for you will speak, and you will speak for yourself by your noble appearance—your self-reliant bearing, your energy and strength, which do not shrink from truth. Come, let us get ready for the ball, and, my friend, do not impose any restraint upon yourself there; give the reins to your discontent; tell every one frankly and bluntly that you are dissatisfied—that you ardently desire to be appointed general-in-chief, and that you would consider it a great misfortune if another man should be preferred to you."

"**But, dear general,**" exclaimed Madame von **Blucher, in dismay, "how can you give Blucher such advice? You know how hot-headed and** rash he is! He will rave about so, **that the king** and the emperor themselves will hear him."

"Well," said Scharnhorst, smiling, "it is sometimes very well that there should be a man courageous enough to tell the kings and emperors the truth, and prove to them that mankind do not always fawn upon them with polite submissiveness."

"Scharnhorst is right," exclaimed Blucher, suddenly straightening himself; "yes, I will go to the ball, and tell them there at least what sort of men those are whom they wish to appoint, and what we may expect from them. They shall not afterward excuse themselves by saying that they were not forewarned, and that no one had called their attention to Blucher. I will do it myself—yes, thunder and lightning! I will remind them of Blucher, and they shall hear and understand me.

"Well," cried Madame von Blucher, "I beg permission to stay at home, for Blucher will have a scene, at which I do not wish to be present."

"Oh, no, there will be no scene whatever," said Blucher. "I shall make my obeisance to their majesties and then step aside, but of course I am not to keep altogether still, and—well, you know my motto, 'At them!'* Well, then, 'at them!' Let us go to the ball. You must accompany me, Amelia, there is no help for it; for it may be necessary for you to bring me back to reason. You know well that no one but you can do that."

"I am sure, madame, you will not abandon us at this critical hour?" begged Scharnhorst. "You do not desire his guardian angel to leave him?"

"Yes, I will go with you," she said, smiling, "if for no other purpose than to restrain my fiery thunderer in proper time."

"Well, it may not be of any avail," said Blucher, dryly. "By Heaven! I must unbosom myself a little to-day—I must tell them the truth, **which no one here at Breslau likes to hear.—** Well, Amelia, do me the favor to turn toward the window. I wish to take off my dressing-gown and put on my uniform coat—then I am dressed;

---

* "Immer drauf!"

only my coat is wanting; it lies on the chair yonder; wait until I have put it on, and then we shall ride to the ball. I will call John to assist me."

"Do not call any one," said Scharnhorst, "but permit me to assist you. Here is the coat."

"And here I am," cried Blucher, throwing off the dressing-gown and quickly plunging into the coat which Scharnhorst handed him.

"But now listen, general," said Scharnhorst, handing Blucher the sword and belt. "As you are so very amiable and kind, I will tell you good news. Gneisenau will be here to-morrow."

"What? Is he no longer in England?" asked Blucher, joyously.

"No, he is in Germany, and, as he wrote to me, will arrive to-morrow at the latest. He landed nearly a week ago from a Swedish ship at Colberg, where he was received with enthusiasm. The whole city was illuminated on the evening of his arrival, and the citizens marched in procession to his lodgings.* You see the old hatred and the old love are still alive in the people; they have not forgotten their oppressors, nor their heroes either."

"Then Gneisenau has come, too," exclaimed Blucher; "he is the petrel that heralds the storm. There will be war now, certainly; and if I am not permitted to share in it, my heart will burst like an overcharged gun. Gneisenau come! all men are coming, and Blucher is to stay at home! Well, if they do not appoint me commanding general, I will enlist as a private. For I must participate in the war that is to put an end to Bonaparte's tyranny; and, if I cannot be first dancer, I shall be one of the musicians.—Christian, have the carriage brought to the door!"

CHAPTER XXIX.

THE BALL AT THE CITY HALL OF BRESLAU.

THE large saloon of the city hall of Breslau presented an exceedingly festive and brilliant

------

spectacle. The walls were tastefully decorated with festoons and flags, exhibiting alternately the Russian and Prussian colors; between them were the Prussian eagle and the double-headed Russian eagle in richly-gilt medallions, surrounded by resplendent tapers. On the ceiling were suspended three enormous chandeliers, each adorned with fifty large wax candles, which shed **a flood of** light through the whole **ball, and reflected them**selves a hundred times in their balls and pendants of rock crystal. In the gallery, fixed on the upper half of one of the walls of the hall, and splendidly decorated with garlands and Prussian and Russian flags, sat a band of fifty musicians, who caused soul-stirring greetings to roll down into the hall, where the brilliant and numerous crowd of guests, whom the municipal authorities had invited, were moving up and down; the ladies in the most magnificent toilets, in the gorgeous splendor of diamonds and other precious stones, of flowers and laces; the gentlemen in their gold-embroidered uniforms, their breasts ornamented with orders; but among them were seen also the dark figures of Lützow's riflemen, the plain coats of the citizens, and even some of the peasantry in their becoming rural costumes. All classes were represented at this great ball, which the municipal authorities of Breslau gave in honor of the Emperor of Russia, for these representatives of all classes were to offer to Alexander the homage of the Prussian people, and to return thanks to the noble ally of the king for the assistance that he intended to lend to Prussia.

The emperor and the king, therefore, were received with boundless enthusiasm when they entered the ball arm in arm, each decorated not with his own orders, but with those of his ally. Alexander had acknowledged this flattering reception with the affability and the smiling grace peculiar to him; Frederick William, with the gravity and calmness that never left him. After the first presentations and official addresses were over, Alexander requested the presiding burgomaster to set aside the embarrassing ceremonial, and to allow every one to yield without restraint to the enjoyment of the festival. In order to give an example to the assembled guests, the emperor suggested to the managers that dancing might begin, and, offering his arm to the wife of the presiding burgomaster, he opened the ball with the *Polonaise*. After the dance he moved about the hall with the most amiable affability, always endeavoring by his kindness and politeness to cause all to forget the gulf separating them from the emperor. The king had, like him, participated in the opening of the ball; but he retired, grave, silent, and cold as ever, into the adjoining apartment which was destined for the private audience-room of the two sovereigns, and which none were permitted to enter but those whom the footmen of the king and the emperor expressly invited. As long as Alexander and Frederick William were in the large hall, they only desired to be the guests of their kind hosts, and affable and unassuming members of the party; **no sooner, however, had they crossed the threshold of their audience-room than they were again** the king and the emperor, whom no one was allowed to approach without being requested. From this audience-room a door, veiled by heavy velvet curtains, led into another apartment, where a small table, covered with the choicest cold viands, and the most exquisite and rare wines, had been set for the two sovereigns, and this small apartment led to the large supper-room that was again connected by a small room with the vast saloon. One of the long walls of this supper-room was occupied with an enormous buffet, loaded with the most select delicacies in colossal dishes of silver and porcelain, and beside which were large crystal bowls, filled with smoking punch or fragrant cardinal. In the remaining space was a number of small round tables ready for supper, at which those might take seats who desired to refresh themselves after the exhausting pleasures of the festival.

Alexander and Frederick William had retired into the audience-room, and sent for those persons whom they desired to distinguish particularly to-night. There were Majors von Lützow and Petersdorf, who had been invited to the honor of an audience which had been conferred even upon some of the volunteers, among them upon Baron la Motte Fouqué and Theodore Körner; and Alexander told them with charming enthusiasm of his sympathy for the heroic Prussian nation, and of his admiration of its glorious self-denial. He stated to Major von Lützow that, if he did not happen to be emperor, he would not allow any one to prevent him from volunteering in his Legion of Vengeance; and to Theodore Körner, in proof of the admiration he felt for his poems, he recited the first verses of his patriotic song, "*Frisch auf, mein Volk, die Flammenzeichen rauchen.*"

Frederick William contented himself with addressing a kind word, a brief salutation, to each of them, and then again moving toward the *portière*, looked at the motley crowd in the ball-room. Suddenly, while the two sovereigns were standing side by side, engaged in a familiar chat, and looking into the hall, an unusual commotion was noticed. All rushed toward the entrance of the hall, through which the two burgomasters had just stepped into the outer reception-room. Undoubtedly some one was expected, and moreover one whom all the guests were anxious to see and to welcome in the most enthusiastic manner.

The large folding-doors opened, and between the two burgomasters appeared the slender, firmly-knit form of General Blucher. Behind him was General Scharnhorst, escorting Madame von Blucher. Blucher advanced, with a winning smile on his fine, good-natured countenance, greeting the assembled guests by pleasantly nodding to the right and left. At first his polite salutations were returned in silence, but gradually there arose murmurs and whispers—the eyes which were fixed upon the hero's form grew more radiant, and soon cheers resounded **through the** whole hall—deafening **shouts of "Long live** Blucher!—Long live our hero, brave General Blucher!"

"A flourish" shouted other voices to the musicians. The presiding burgomaster nodded smilingly, and waved his white handkerchief. The musicians made a loud flourish resound, and **more** deafening and jubilant became the shouts of "Long live Blucher!—Long live our hero!" Blucher bowed, confused and almost ashamed, and with so charming an expression of surprise and joy that this called forth a new outburst of tumultuous applause and enthusiasm.

The two sovereigns stood in the open door of the audience-room, and witnessed this strange and unexpected scene, Alexander smiling and apparently well pleased, Frederick William grave and with a slight shadow on his brow.

"Ah, sir," said Alexander, in a low and quick voice, "it seems to me the guests intend to make a little demonstration in honor of your general, and to give us a gentle hint whom they would like to have appointed general-in-chief of the Silesian army."

"Indeed, it seems so," said Frederick William, morosely, "but I do not like such demonstrations, and they have no effect upon myself."

"But let us now greet the hero," exclaimed Alexander, smiling; "people ought to see that we share the general sympathy." He quickly stepped into the ballroom; the king followed him slowly and hesitatingly.

"Welcome, my dear General Blucher," said Alexander, offering his hand to the general, while the king saluted him merely with a nod. The hum and noise which hitherto filled the hall like the roar of the sea, immediately died away. Silence ensued; every one stood still as if riveted to his place; all eyes were turned in eager suspense and with breathless curiosity toward the group that stood in the middle of the hall; all tried to catch a word, a glance, in order to draw therefrom their own conclusions. And, amid this general silence, was heard the melodious voice of Alexander, who said again, "Welcome, my dear General Blucher! I am really glad to greet you, and to meet you again after so long an interval. I did not know, indeed, that you were here in Breslau; otherwise I would have called upon you."

"That would have been very gracious, and in accordance with the character of your majesty," said Blucher, loudly and firmly. "For your majesty is known never to forget those who are worthy of being remembered. All patriots have learned, with feelings of gratitude and enthusiasm, that your majesty, directly after your arrival, called upon that noble and intrepid German, Minister von Stein, who was living solitary, sick, and deserted, in his garret, and who, up to that time, only a few faithful friends and a few cowardly enemies had remembered." *

These words, uttered in a loud and powerful voice, produced various effects. The Emperor Alexander smiled and bowed his head quickly and repeatedly; King Frederick William frowned slightly, and this authorized the gentlemen of his suite, who stood behind him, Field-Marshal Kalkreuth and General Knesebeck, to frown too, and cast angry glances at Blucher. Madame von Blucher, who had modestly kept somewhat in the background, turned very pale, and leaned tremblingly upon the arm of General Scharnhorst, who smiled and whispered, "Blucher is grand! He is a true fire-king among the will-o'-the-wisps!" The two burgomasters and the host of courtiers smiled when they glanced at the emperor, and looked grave and gloomy when they turned their eyes to the clouded brow of the king. Blucher, however, did not seem to notice the impression produced by his words, and looked around as composedly as if he had made a mere courtier's reply to the emperor's gracious salutation.

"I am happy to be one of Stein's friends," said Alexander, "but I do not think it requires particular courage to profess friendship for a magnanimous man whom all Germany reveres and admires."

"No, your majesty," said Blucher, calmly, "only

* Minister von Stein had arrived sick at Breslau, and lived, as stated above, in a small garret, which Major von Lützow had surrendered to him. Only his intimate friends visited him there, and this was the reason why Count St. Marsan, whom Field-Marshal Kalkreuth had informed of Stein's arrival at Breslau, did not believe in the truth of this information. Baron von Stein, however, received secretly many proofs of love and sympathy. The king alone took no notice of him, and the members of the court, too, were prohibited from entering into any relations with Stein. There was a change for the better, however, as soon as the Emperor of Russia arrived, and at once called upon Stein. Now all hastened to visit him, and overwhelmed him with protestations of devotion, which he rejected frequently with great asperity.

a short time ago it required a great deal of courage for a German to profess friendship for Minister von Stein, for the Emperor Napoleon hates and fears him, and for this reason three-fourths of the Germans hate and fear him from humble respect for the Emperor of the French.—Is it not so ?" added Blucher, suddenly turning to Field-Marshal Kalkreuth, who stood close behind the king, "is it not as I say? Do you not admit that I am right, Field-Marshal Kalkreuth ? "

This question, which was addressed to a by-stander, with utter disregard of etiquette, caused **the** blood of the courtiers to freeze, and made Field-Marshal Kalkreuth turn purple with anger. The Emperor Alexander, however, burst into loud laughter, and, turning to the king, he whispered to him in a hurried, low voice, " You are right, sire, Blucher is a madcap, a genuine hussar, always ready to charge!" The king nodded, and as Alexander laughed, he forced himself also to smile a little. Field-Marshal Kalkreuth responded to Blucher's question only by a quick, angry glance and a gentle bow. " Well," said Alexander, turning again to Blucher, " I am satisfied, however, that you did not belong to the three-fourths of the Germans that hated and loved according to the wishes of the Emperor Napoleon, general ? "

" No, your majesty," exclaimed Blucher, " I have always belonged to his most consistent and implacable enemies, though I really owe him a great deal—nay, almost my life."

" How your life ? " asked Alexander, in amazement. " Did the emperor ever save you from peril ? "

" Yes, your majesty," said Blucher, casting a quick and fiery glance around the large circle of his audience, " the Emperor Napoleon did save me from a danger menacing my life. For, over since the disastrous days of Tilsit, I was near dying of grief at the misfortunes of Prussia ; and when our noble and august Queen Louisa died— our queen, who was so true and patriotic a German lady, and whose heart had been broken by the calamities that had befallen Prussia—I really thought a dagger had pierced my heart, and I

would have to bleed to death. But then I comforted myself by remembering that Napoleon still lived, and that I ought to live, too, in order to see the day when the tyrant would be brought to judgment, and I felt strengthened by the conviction that God had destined me to be the instrument by whom He wanted to destroy Napoleon, and that I was intended to assist in delivering Germany and avenging Queen Louisa ; and this thought, sire, kept me alive, invigorating and strengthening me ; it rendered me again so young and ardent that I am yearning for the fray like a war-horse that has heard the bugle-call."

A murmur of applause was heard, and only the feeling of awe inspired by the presence of the two sovereigns seemed to restrain a tumultuous outburst of general sympathy. Every one looked with proud and joyful glances now at the aged general, whose noble face was full of courage and determination, and again at the Emperor Alexander, who seemed to contemplate the intrepid soldier with a sort of amazement.

A brief pause ensued, when the king approached Madame von Blucher, standing by the side of Scharnhorst. " Good-evening, madame," said the king, in a loud and somewhat harsh voice ; " please tell me how old General Blucher is."

" Your majesty," said Madame von Blucher, making a profound obeisance, " according to his heart and strength, he is a youth ; according to his certificate of birth, he is seventy-one years old."

" So old ! " said the king ; " Blucher so aged a man ! But, it is true, his tongue is that of a stripling."

" Your majesty," said Blucher, quickly turning, " may it please the good God and my king to give me an opportunity to refute my certificate of birth, and to prove that I am a vigorous, courageous lad, who knows how to use his sword as well as his tongue ! "

" It is not sufficient, however, to know how to use the sword and the tongue, but one must know, too, how to restrain both," said the king, quickly turning and beckoning Field-Marshal Kalkreuth to his side, with whom he commenced chatting.

The Emperor Alexander laid his hand hastily on Blucher's shoulder, as if to soften and restrain the impending outburst of the general's anger, and, looking with a kind smile into his flushed face, he said: "restraint is not what suits you? Your motto is, 'Always forward!' And you believe it is time that all Germany, myself, and my army, should adopt this motto? Well, perhaps you are right, my dear general. At all events, it will be seen soon who are right, those who wish to procrastinate, or those who are in favor of immediate and decisive action."

He nodded pleasantly to Blucher, and then called General Scharnhorst to his side, turning, like the king, back to the audience-room. The guests who had crowded in breathless silence into the middle of the hall, dispersed again and returned to the adjoining rooms. Blucher escorted his wife to the gallery occupied by ladies, and then followed the burgomasters, who had solicited the honor of conducting him to the supper-room.

Frederick William's brow was gloomy and clouded, and he was even graver and more reticent than usual. He retired into the background of the room, addressing only now and then a few quick words to Field-Marshal Kalkreuth, who stood by his side. Alexander's countenance was serene and pleasant, and a smile played round his lips while he conversed eagerly with General Scharnhorst.

"You say, then, that Stein is of the same opinion?" asked Alexander, thoughtfully. "He thinks, too, that General Blucher should be preferred?"

"Yes, sire," said Scharnhorst, "this is the opinion of Minister von Stein, and, I may add, the opinion of every Prussian who has the happiness and greatness of the fatherland at heart. Sire, those who are in favor of a timid and vacillating policy, who would like to negotiate and compromise, who still believe in the possibility of a reconciliation with France, who still think that the pen should smoothen the rugged path before us, or unravel the knot of our difficulties— those cowardly, grovelling hearts are the real ene-

mies of our cause, and more dangerous than Napoleon with all his armies. For they are weighing down our courage, paralyzing our **arms, and** stifling our enthusiasm. But for them the king, who, in his modesty, is utterly unaware how fiery a soul, how great a heart he is possessed of, would have long since concluded an alliance with your majesty. But the king is unfortunately so modest that he distrusts himself, and subordinates his own opinion to that of his old and, as he believes, well-tried and faithful advisers. Now, these advisers are to blame for all the misfortunes of Prussia; they inveigled us into the alliance with France; they caused us to adhere to it, and would even now like to force us back into it. They would stifle the fire of patriotism because they are afraid lest it annihilate them and destroy their unworthy **efforts. For this reason** Blucher, with his heroic soul, is as much an eyesore to them as Stein, with his plans of liberation and his energetic action for constitutional reform. One wishes to create a new Prussia, the other a new state, and both these ideas are utterly distasteful to some, for they cling to the rotten old system, and new things fill them **with terror.**"

Alexander listened to the words of Scharnhorst with the liveliest attention, and looked down musingly.

"Listen, general!" he said, in a low and hurried voice, glancing around the room as if to convince himself that no one could overhear his words, "reply honestly and sincerely to the following question: Is the King of Prussia sufficiently strong to cope with France for **any** length of time?"

"No," said Scharnhorst, firmly. "The army the king could place in the field would not be able to achieve a single victory over Napoleon. But the Prussian nation is strong, and arming itself for a struggle in which it will triumph, because no army can resist the will of a united people, and because God is an ally of the nations fighting for their liberty and their princes; but he who is audacious enough to endeavor to stifle the flame of this national enthusiasm, instead of bearing it aloft like an oriflamme in the van of

the great army of liberation, would render himself guilty of a fearful sin. Prussia will conquer
with her whole people, but she will succumb if
she relies only on her army."

"It is true," said Alexander, thoughtfully,
"the Prussian nation has manifested of late a wonderful enthusiasm, and has risen as one man. It
has risen for its king and its honor, and—do you
not believe that it will fight equally well for both,
whether Tauentzien, Kalkreuth, or Blucher, be its
chieftain?"

**"No, sire," said Scharnhorst, quickly; "I
know that it** will not. The people, with their
quick and unerring instinct, know those very
well in whom they may confide, and I request
your majesty to take graciously into consideration that it is this time the people that must
render Prussia victorious. It is true, the regiments of volunteers **that have already been or-**
ganized would not disband, **even though Kal-**
kreuth or Tauentzien should be appointed gen-
eral-in-chief of the Prussian or Silesian army, but
the regiments that have not yet been organized
and equipped will hesitate and retire, unless they
know that a general will command them who has
sworn unending hatred to the Emperor Napoleon, and who will die a thousand times on the
battle-field rather than conclude peace and a new
alliance with him. Now, such a general is Blucher, the youth of seventy, a modern knight
'without fear and without reproach.' If he
stands at the **head of our army, the** Prussian
people will rally exultingly round the standards,
and the diminished regiments be replaced by new
ones that will rush into the field, because they
know that there is at their head a hero in whose
breast there is room for only two sentiments—
love of country and hatred of the French; and
who serves, without fear, his God, his king, **and**
his fatherland, impelled by this very hatred and
love, without any secondary motives—nay, **per-**
haps, even without personal ambition."

"If Blucher is really such a hero as you depict him," cried Alexander, "it would be a crime
not to place him at the head of the Silesian army.
Had you told the king all you have told me, he

would certainly not have hesitated a moment as
to the general who should be appointed commander-in-chief."

"Sire, I did tell him all that my heart and my
head prompted me, and to-day at noon I was still
convinced that the king **would** appoint General
Blucher as soon as he should have satisfied himself that he thereby would not act contrary to
the will and wishes of your majesty. But the
little scene at the hall a few minutes ago has unfortunately shaken my conviction, for the king
seemed offended at the rough and somewhat impetuous bearing of the hussar general."

"And this very bearing of the hussar general,
as you call Blucher, has impressed me very favor-
ably, for he who relies so firmly on his own
strength must feel sure of victory. I like to see,
towering above the crowd of the fawning courtiers surrounding us, men who do not bend their
backs, nor sink into the dust, before our so-called
'divine rights,' but who stand erect, and fear no
one, because they are true to themselves."

"If that is the opinion of your majesty, then I
am at liberty to confess that I share it," said a
voice behind him; and when the emperor turned,
he met the smiling gaze of the king, who had approached during the conversation with Scharnhorst, and, as he did not wish to interrupt it,
listened to its conclusion without being noticed by
the two speakers.

"What!" asked Alexander, offering his hand
to the king. "Your majesty, then, is of my
opinion — you like, too, the men who sometimes
allow us to see their brow instead of their reve-
rentially-bent back, and who tell us the truth instead of those eternal, perfumed flatteries?"

"Certainly, sire," said the king, gently bowing
his head. "It is true, the truth is sometimes
a somewhat bitter medicine, but it restores our
health, while sweet flatteries spoil our taste and
ruin our stomach."

"And we must really have a healthy stomach
to digest the hard fare of these times!" exclaimed
Alexander, smiling. "Scharnhorst thinks that
Blucher would be a good physician for our stomachs. That is your opinion, general, is it not?"

"Sire, he is at least a physician who will not resort to palliatives," said Scharnhorst, "but will immediately try to eradicate the evil by a thorough operation."

"But I have been told that a great many patients have died in consequence of operations, when they might have lived a long time if they had borne their ills with patience and resignation," said the king, growing again gloomy and thoughtful.

The emperor laid his hand on the shoulder of his royal friend. "But who would prefer a life on the sick-bed to the quick and glorious death of a hero on the field of honor?" he said, feelingly. "Not you, my august friend, I know; and even better than to me it is known to the angel who is hovering over you, and whose earthly eyes were closed in grief. But," Alexander interrupted himself, "these are thoughts that are unsuitable for a festival, and I beg your majesty's pardon for having ventured to indulge in them."

"Still, they are the thoughts that always accompany and never leave me, sire," said the king. "True, I have overcome my grief, but I will never learn to forget. At the present time I am thinking of my Louisa with redoubled longing. How her heart would have rejoiced over the renewal of an alliance which she so fervently desired, and how the noble spirit of the nation would have delighted and inspired her!"

"The noble queen, I believe, was also a warm friend of General Blucher, was she not?" asked the emperor, after a pause. "I believe she belonged to those who expected a great deal from him, and thought him a hero and a powerful enemy of Napoleon? Is it not so, sire?"

"Yes," said the king, thoughtfully, "the queen had a great regard for Blucher, and considered him a brave and faithful patriot."

"And what did she think of Field-Marshal Kalkreuth?" asked Alexander, with seeming carelessness. "Did he belong to those, too, in whom the queen confided, and from whom she expected the salvation of the fatherland?"

The king quickly looked up and met for a moment the searching gaze which the emperor fixed on him. Frederick William smiled, and inclined his head, as if he well understood the emperor's question. "No," he said, "Queen Louisa rarely approved of the views of the field-marshal, and although she felt high esteem for the general who had already shown himself a brave man under the great Frederick, she did not agree with the predilection he manifested for the Emperor Napoleon and his *invincible* armies."

"A predilection," exclaimed Alexander, smiling, "which I believe the field-marshal has not yet got rid of, notwithstanding the experience which Napoleon gained on the battle-fields of Russia."

"On the same battle-fields on which your majesty gathered new laurels," said the king, bowing **slightly.**

"And now there will spring up real laurel-woods for your majesty here in Germany!" exclaimed the emperor. "The only question for us now is, to find the right sort of gardener who knows how to cultivate them. But, I repeat, our thoughts are not suitable to this festival. Come, sire, permit me to offer you my arm as your cavalier, and to conduct you to the buffet, for how exalted soever our position may be, we must not forget that we are men, and that our stomachs sometimes need food."

He offered his arm to the king, and conducted him to the small supper-hall adjoining the audience-room. The gentlemen who were present followed them, and the chamberlains hurried to the sideboard to have supper served up to the two sovereigns.

CHAPTER XXX.

THE APPOINTMENT.

ALEXANDER took a seat by the king's side at the small table, loaded with a heavy gold service, set for them alone near the door, which was covered with a heavy *portière*, and led into the large supper-hall. The emperor and the king had just put upon their plates some of the appetizing *pâté de foie gras* which the master of ceremonies himself had served up, and were proceeding like other mortals to consume them with great relish. The cavaliers, improving the opportune moment of silence, stood about the room and partook of the viands taken from the sideboard. Suddenly this silence was interrupted by a voice which was not uttered in the room itself, but swept through it like the blast of a trumpet: "If this hesitation and vacillation continue, all is lost; and it would then be better for us to throw ourselves immediately at the feet of Bonaparte, and crave quarter, than unnecessarily spill the precious blood of the people, and at last submit. He who does not advance goes backward without noticing it, and he who is not courageous enough to attack, is vanquished even before his adversary has forced him to battle."

"Why," exclaimed Alexander, smiling, "these **are sentences that remind me of General Blucher.**"

"Your majesty is right, it is his voice," said the king; "he will give vent to his indignation, and, perhaps, at our expense. Let us not listen to him."

"On the contrary, I beg your majesty's kind permission to listen," said Alexander, pleasantly. "There is in the words of the general something **that** is as refreshing as a pure wind dispelling unhealthy vapors. Ah, hear him, sire; his tones are roaring like a hurricane."

In fact, the voice in the adjoining room had grown more violent, and the Emperor Alexander was seated in such a manner that he could distinctly hear every word uttered:

"What! you really believe **it to be possible that** they will appoint Field-Marshal Kalkreuth general-in-chief, and intrust our young and splendid **army to** him? Great Heaven! do they not know, then, that Kalkreuth, however excellent a man and brave a soldier he may be, is not fit to confront Napoleon? Is it not a matter of notoriety that the field-marshal loves and admires Bonaparte, and that he considers a rupture with France a great calamity for Prussia? How could he ever win a battle who could never look straight forward at the battle-field, but would squint sideways to see what faces Napoleon would make, and whether he would not frown at the audacity of the Prussians, who dare try to defeat the great Napoleon? We need a man with a direct look—one who fixes both his eyes on the object. We do not want any *schielwippen!* They may all go to the mischief, for one never knows what they are about! I repeat, we need a man with a straight look!"

"What is that? *schielwippen!*" inquired the emperor, smiling. "I thought I had learned the German language pretty thoroughly from my mother and my wife, both of whom have the honor of being natives of Germany, but I have never heard this word from them. Pray, sire, tell me what it means."

"I must confess that I do not understand it either," said the king, shrugging his shoulders.

"General Scharnhorst!" cried the emperor. "Pray can you tell us what *schielwippen* means?"

"Sire," said Scharnhorst, laughing, "it is a slang term for a man who squints. General Blucher likes to use the language of the people."

"Well, the Prussian people have recently used such grand and magnificent language," said Alexander, "that we may say with heart-felt conviction, '*Vox populi vox Dei!*' and that it reflects great credit on Blucher, if it is true that he speaks like the people. But, hush! what does he say now?"

"The cowards have brought all our misfortunes upon us!" thundered Blucher's powerful voice. "The hesitating men who always wish to patch up and stop the holes, instead of tearing down the old ruin and building a new house, are our curse, and have always involved Prussia in untold calamities. When I think of them I would like to have them here, to treat them as Jahn treated the other day one of the Turners at Berlin. Do you know the story?"

"No," shouted several voices, "we unfortunately do not."

"Well, I will tell it to you. Jahn went with his pupils down the Linden to the Brandenburg gate to perform the usual gymnastic exercises on the drill-grounds outside the city. On the way he happened to cast his eyes on the gate, where the Victoria formerly stood, and which the French stole and carried off to Paris. Jahn, like every honest man who looks at the gate, felt his heart swell with anger. He turned to the boy who was marching by his side and asked him, 'What stood formerly over the pillars of the gate?'—'The Victoria,' said the boy.—'Where is it now?' inquired Jahn.—'It is in Paris, where the French carried it.' Jahn asked again, 'What do you think when looking up to the vacant place on the top of the gate?'—'Well,' said the boy, with great composure, 'what should I think? I think it is a pity that the Victoria is no longer there.' And when he said so, Jahn lifted up his hand and slapped the boy's face. 'You should think that we will fetch back the Victoria, you monkey!' he shouted. That is the whole story, but I remember it whenever I see these dear tame men who merely say, 'It is a pity that we have been so unfortunate!' and whose hearts feel only a mild regret instead of the most ardent revenge. And then my hand itches, and I would like to lift it up, like Jahn, and slap their faces."

"Your Blucher is a splendid hussar," said Alexander, looking at the king. "I believe it is dangerous to stand before him when his hand is itching."

"Yes, his hand has been itching from the days of Jena," exclaimed the king, smiling. "He has been anxious to fight ever since. For this reason I gave him the estate of Kunzendorf, and sent him thither. I thought he would there quietly cure himself; but it seems it was in vain; my expectations have been disappointed. I believe his hand is incurable."

"Your majesty, therefore, had better yield to him, and allow him to fight," said Alexander, almost entreatingly. "The opportunity is excellent at the present time. If you place him at the head of the Silesian army, he will no longer slap the faces of his friends and neighbors on the right and left, but will **rush forward** and stretch out his itching hand to deal the French terrible blows."

"I am only afraid he would be too rash in his wild hussar spirit," said the king, "and spoil every thing by trying to tear down all barriers."

"A man should be placed by his side who knows how to check **his** boldness," exclaimed Alexander—"a man who does not stifle Blucher's ardor, but gives it the true direction."

"**But** where shall we find **such a one?**"

"I believe your majesty may find him close by," said Alexander, pointing to Scharnhorst, who was leaning against the *portière*.

"Ah, sire," cried the king, almost merrily, "I believe you are a magician, and understand my most secret thoughts. Scharnhorst **has a great** mind, and I owe him much. If **he would take upon himself that difficult and ungrateful part by** the side of Blucher, I believe **the general's** impetuosity would be less dangerous."

"Your majesty, please ask him whether he will or not," said Alexander.

The king called Scharnhorst to his side. "You have influence over General Blucher, **have you** not?" he asked, hastily.

"I may say, at least, your **majesty, that** General Blucher is convinced of my love **and devo**tion, and that he confides a little in me."

"**Could you** make up your mind to occupy a secondary position by his side, and, if I should appoint Blucher general-in-chief of the Silesian army, become his chief of staff?"

"Your majesty," exclaimed Scharnhorst, "I would deem it a great honor to serve under the heroic old man, and I am certain that with him I would enter upon a glorious career, particularly if your majesty should grant me a request."

"What is it? Speak!"

"If your majesty should condescend to place General Gneisenau, who will arrive to-morrow, as quartermaster-general."

The king nodded. "You have selected a noble companion," he said, smiling.

"It will be a splendid trefoil, it seems to me," cried the emperor. "Blucher, Scharnhorst, and Gneisenau! They are three well-sounding names!

But listen, sire, Blucher is still thundering. There is a way to calm this tempest."

"What is it ?" asked the king, smiling.

"Your majesty ought to be so gracious as to send for General Blucher, and tell him that you wish to confer upon him the command-in-chief of the Silesian army."

"You advise me to do so, sire ?" inquired the king. "Your majesty, in counselling this, gives up no wish?"

"Yes, I do," said Alexander, smiling. "I should wish to see General Tauentzien appointed commander-in-chief, just as your majesty probably would prefer to bestow this position on Field-Marshal Kalkreuth. Let us both, therefore, sacrifice our wishes to the great object for which I now believe Blucher to be the proper instrument."

"So let it be, your majesty," exclaimed the king. "I will send for Blucher." He beckoned to Scharnhorst to approach again. "Pray go and fetch your friend, General Blucher," said the king, rising, like the emperor, from the table.

"And I beg leave, while the general goes into the hall, to cast a glance into the next room, to see what Blucher is doing," said the emperor. "Now draw the *portière* back, General Scharnhorst, and stand there. In this way I am able to survey the whole hall."

Scharnhorst, in accordance with the emperor's order, opened the *portière* and stood in it; by his side, shaded by the curtain, stood the emperor and the king. Both gazed into the supper-hall, which presented a highly animated spectacle. At all the small tables sat the guests in attractive groups, the ladies in their rich toilets, the gentlemen in their brilliant uniforms. All were merry and loquacious; the choice delicacies had put every one in good spirits; the fiery wine had loosened all tongues. Even the eyes of the ladies were sparkling with a higher lustre, and a deeper crimson burned on their cheeks. But all those merry faces turned frequently toward the small table on one side of the hall near the *portière*. There sat General Blucher with his wife; several gentlemen were seated near him. On the

table stood one of the crystal bowls that had previously adorned the handsome sideboard, and from this bowl, filled with an amber-colored liquid, arose a delightful perfume. Blucher seemed to inhale the fragrance with pleasure, for an expression of infinite comfort beamed from his features, and whenever he emptied his glass he seized the silver ladle that lay in the bowl, and then drew his white mustache with a smile of gratification through his fingers, while his eyes surveyed the whole company with a flashing glance. Then a shadow passed across his brow. "We are highly elated to-day, because we are at length to take up arms against our foe," he said; "we are overjoyed because we are to take our revenge. And suppose every thing should again turn out wrong; suppose the cowards and the *schielwippen* should, after all, remain at the helm? Great Heaven ! the very idea maddens me ! For I know them ! I know that they will ruin every thing. At the decisive moment they are vacillating, and, in order to dishearten others, too, they exaggerate the strength of the enemy a hundred-fold, and belittle our own resources in the same proportion. Would that Heaven were to decree, 'Blucher shall command the Prussians !' Good Lord, I pledge Thee my head that I would expel Bonaparte with all his French from Germany, though I had but thirty thousand soldiers behind me !"*

"Now call him in, general," whispered Alexander. Scharnhorst stepped into the hall. The king and the emperor left the supper-hall and returned into the audience-room.

A few minutes afterward Blucher entered, followed by Scharnhorst, who remained at the door, while Blucher advanced boldly toward the two sovereigns.

"Your majesty was so gracious as to send for me," he said, bowing to the king.

"Yes," said the king, gravely. "I wish to ask you whether you belong to the vacillating cowards, or whether you are a whole man ?"

---

* Blucher's words.—Vide Varnhagen, "Life of Blucher." p. 186.

"I swear to your majesty, upon my honor, that I will hurl Bonaparte from his throne."

p. 179.

"And I," exclaimed Alexander, pathetically—'I wish to request you to confess whether you are also a *schidwippe?*"

Blucher looked at the two sovereigns with a gloomy, inquiring glance. But suddenly his face brightened, and a smile played round his lips. "Ah," he cried, "I understand! Your majesties have overheard my prattle, and have sent for me to order me to be silent. But I cannot, your majesties; I cannot! I must give vent to my wrath, my vexation, and grief! I must be allowed to scold, for if I did not I would be obliged to weep, and it would be a disgrace for Blucher to act like an old woman! Let me scold, then, your majesties; it relieves my heart a little, and my anger teaches me to forget my grief."

"You grieve, then, general?" inquired Frederick William, smiling.

"Yes, my lord and king, I do grieve intensely. I should like to lay my complaint before your majesty, and I will do so, too. I—"

"Hush!" interposed the king,—"hush, my firebrand of seventy-one years! First reply to this question: would you like to be appointed general-in-chief of the Silesian army?"

"Would I like to be appointed general-in-chief?" cried Blucher, his eyes sparkling with joy. "Your majesty, that is just as though you ask me whether I like to live any longer. For I tell your majesty I will die at once rather than let any one else have that position."

"Well, then," said the king, in a grave and dignified tone, "I appoint you general-in-chief of the Silesian army. Do you accept the position?"

Blucher uttered a cry, and his face brightened as if lit up by a sunbeam. "I accept it," he exclaimed, "and here I swear to your majesty that I shall not lay down my command before Prussia is again what she was prior to the battle of Jena, and that I shall not sheathe my sword before we have driven Napoleon beyond the Rhine, and have made him so humble that he will never again dare to cross it. I swear to your majesty, upon my honor, that I will hurl Bonaparte from his throne—that I will not rest before the crown has fallen from his head! God has spared me that I may chastise Napoleon; He has told me every night in my dreams, 'Do not despond, do not lose heart! Keep up thy courage and thy confidence, for I shall soon need thee! Thou shalt soon cut Napoleon down from his power, and throw him into the dust whence he sprang.' And I have answered, 'I am on hand, and wait only for the struggle to begin.' Now I say to your majesty what I then said, 'I am on hand, and the struggle is to begin!' I have sworn every day to chastise Bonaparte, and while I live I shall thank your majesty for giving me an opportunity. I am, then, general-in-chief of the Silesian army?"

"Yes, I appoint you, and his majesty the emperor approves my selection," said the king. "All necessary directions, instructions, and orders, you will receive to-morrow in writing. You will immediately enter upon your office, and place yourself at the head of the troops. Do you wish to prefer requests and impose conditions?"

"Yes, your majesty, I must impose two conditions. In the first place, General Scharnhorst must be my chief of staff, for Blucher is only half a man when Scharnhorst is not with him. I have the arm, he has the head; therefore we must be together."

"Your request is granted, and Scharnhorst has already accepted the position," said the king, smiling.

"Secondly, I must impose the condition that I be allowed to leave Breslau to-morrow with my Prussians, and advance toward Saxony."

"What! You intend to start at once?" cried Alexander and Frederick William, in amazement.

"Yes, at once," said Blucher, with a joyful air. "The years of waiting are past, and now comes the day of vengeance. Like a thunderstorm we must burst upon the French. Before they expect us we must expel what troops of theirs remain in Germany, dissolve the Confederation of the Rhine, and by our bold exploits stir up all Germany that she may rally round our flag, and form an enormous army before Napoleon has concentrated his newly-organized forces. That is our task, and, if it pleases God, we will fulfil it."

CHAPTER XXXI.

AFTER THE BATTLE OF BAUTZEN.

For two days the battle had been raging, and even now, in the afternoon of the 22d of May, the struggle was undecided. Blucher, who, with his Prussians, occupied the heights of Kreckwitz, near Bautzen, still hoped to achieve a victory. For two days the Prussians and Russians fought like lions along the extended line of battle; they engaged the hostile legions with undaunted courage and joyful enthusiasm, regardless of the scorching heat, hunger, thirst, and exhaustion. During these days Blucher was constantly in the midst of his troops. Where the shower of bullets was thickest, where the danger was most imminent, his voice was heard inciting the soldiers; where the enemy approached with his most formidable columns, Blucher stood with his faithful companion Gneisenau at the head of his Prussians, brandishing his sword, advancing with exulting cheers upon the enemy, and causing him to retreat.

The heights of Kreckwitz had to be held till General Barclay de Tolly, with his Russians, would arrive, and Generals York and Kleist, with their Prussians, to cover Blucher's left flank, which was threatened by Marshal Ney. The booming of cannon was incessant. The Russians stood like a wall, and when the front ranks were swept down, others took their places; the living stepped over the dying, undaunted, and remembering only one thing—that they had to take revenge for the lost battle of Lutzen.*

"Boys," shouted Blucher to his soldiers, just as the balls of the enemy struck down whole ranks, "boys, remember that we have resolved to sabre the French. They have exhausted the soil of Germany, we must fertilize it with French corpses. Remember Gross-Görschen, where they wounded our General Scharnhorst. We must chastise them for that, and capture a few French generals.* We must get at least four of their marshals in return for General Scharnhorst, for the fellows are light, and four of them do not weigh as much as one Scharnhorst. Now, tell me, shall we get those four French marshals?"

"Yes, Father Blucher, yes!" shouted the Prussians, jubilantly. "Long live Father Blucher!"

"Only a little longer, and the day is ours!" cried Gneisenau, in a ringing voice. "The legions of Marshal Ney are charging again, but General Barclay, with his Russians, has occupied the Windmill-knoll, near Gleime, and will repulse him as we shall Napoleon's columns. The heights of Kreckwitz are the Thermopylæ of the Prussians, and we will fall to a man rather than surrender!"

"Yes, that we will do!" cried the officers, enthusiastically, and the soldiers echoed their shouts.

At this moment a terrific cannonade resounded on the right wing of the Prussian troops. "There are the French!" exclaimed Blucher. "Boys, now bring in those marshals!" The cannon roared, the muskets rattled, and, as though heaven desired to participate in this struggle of the nations, the thunder rolled, and flashes of lightning darted into the clouds of battle-smoke.

But who was galloping up suddenly on a charger covered with foam, his hair fluttering in the breeze, and his face pale and terrified? It was a Prussian colonel, and still he does not join in the exultation of his countrymen. He approached Generals Blucher and Gneisenau.

"Halloo! Lieutenant-Colonel von Müffling," shouted Blucher, "are you back? Do you bring us greetings from Barclay de Tolly? Has he finished the French? Well, we are just about to recommence our work here—the last work for to-day."

"General," cried Müffling, anxiously, "the French will soon have finished Barclay de Tolly, and defeated us! For he is unable to hold out.

---

* Fought May 2, 1813. The French call this battle that of Lutzen; the Germans generally that of Gross-Görschen. Both sides claimed a victory. But the latest German historians, especially Beitzke, admit that the Germans were defeated.

* General Scharnhorst was wounded at the battle of Gross-Görschen by Blucher's side. He believed his wound was not dangerous, but he left the headquarters to be cured. He went at first to Altenburg, and then to Prague, to attend the peace congress. His wound reopened, and he died at Prague on the 28th of June, 1813.

He has only fifty thousand men, and Ney is attacking him with a much larger force. Barclay sends me for reënforcements, and if we do not strengthen his line, he cannot maintain himself on the Windmill-knoll. In a quarter of an hour it will be in Ney's hands."

"No; in a quarter of an hour Ney will be in our hands," shouted Blucher, confidently. "Ney is a marshal, and we must have him! Boys," he cried, drawing himself up in his stirrups, and looking back toward his troops—"boys, we must have Marshal Ney, must we not?"

"Yes, Father Blucher, we must have Marshal Ney!"

Heaven responded with a loud clap of thunder, the earth was shaken by the booming of the cannon, the air was rent by the cheers of the living, and the groans and imprecations of the wounded and dying. Blucher still stood with his Prussians on the heights of Kreckwitz, his face radiant with enthusiasm, his eye flashing with courage; but a warning adviser stood by his side.

"General," whispered Müffling, "we are lost if we remain here longer. We must retreat."

"Retreat!" cried Blucher, in an angry voice, and a clap of thunder burst at that moment.

Müffling pointed silently down into the plain, and over to the Windmill-knoll. "Look yonder! Napoleon is advancing directly upon our front, the Windmill-knoll is evacuated, Barclay has gone, and the Russians are routed!"

"But we still stand," cried Blucher, triumphantly, "and we shall stand in spite of Napoleon and the devil! And, then, we are not without support. The Russian artillery attached to our corps is thundering against the enemy, and York and Kleist are covering our left wing."

"But, general, listen! The Russian artillery is firing less rapidly; General Kleist is no longer able to cover our left wing, for the sovereigns have sent him to Bairuth to cover Barclay's flank; and as for York, he was unable to prevent the enemy from placing a battery near Basantwitz. I saw it when I rode hither. We are, therefore, in a triple cross-fire." And, as though the enemy intended to confirm these warning words, the cannon flashed from three sides, and hurled their balls into the ranks of the Prussians.

The flush of hoped-for victory paled in Blucher's face; Gneisenau grew grave and gloomy. The staff came nearer to their chieftain, and tried to read his thoughts in his eyes. The jubilant shouts of the soldiers were hushed; **heaven was** still thundering, and in the distance burning villages, like gigantic torches, lit up the landscape, and shed a blood-red lustre over the gray sky. Blucher looked around in silence; his lip quivered, his eyebrows contracted, and large drops of cold perspiration stood on his forehead. Gneisenau was by his side, gloomy and taciturn, like his chieftain. Behind them halted the staff-officers, mournful as their leaders, for now every one recognized the danger, and knew that, if they remained at the "Thermopylæ of Prussia," they would have to defend themselves to the last man, or lay down their arms, because, as soon as the enemy closed up the fourth side, escape would be impossible.[*]

On the other side of Blucher halted Colonel Müffling, who had brought back such **calamitous** tidings from his reconnoissance. He pointed silently to the French columns of Marshal Ney, that just commenced climbing the heights, and then pulled out his watch. "We have fifteen minutes left," he said, in a loud, solemn voice, "fifteen minutes to extricate ourselves from the noose. Afterward we shall be hemmed in. If we do not improve the time the cowards will surrender, and the brave die fighting to the last, but unfortunately without promoting in the least the welfare of the fatherland."[†]

Blucher did not reply, gazing down with a sombre eye on the enemy, coming up in increasing masses. The cannon of the French, firing from three sides, spoke a disheartening language. The Russian batteries had ceased firing, for their ammunition was exhausted.

"Gneisenau," asked Blucher at last, in a

---

* Müffling, "Aus meinem Leben," p. 42.
† Müffling's words.—Ibid., p. 42.

hollow voice, and sighing, as though a stone weighed down his breast, "Gneisenau, what do you say?"

"I must admit that Lieutenant-Colonel von Müffling is right," sighed Gneisenau. "Under the present circumstances all further bloodshed will be useless, and it is our bounden duty to preserve our men for a better opportunity. We must hasten to retreat." *

A single savage imprecation burst from Blucher's lips, but only the nearest bystanders heard it, for it was drowned by the roar of artillery and the thunder of heaven. With a quick jerk he drew his cap over his forehead, so that his eyes were shaded—those eyes which had flashed so defiantly, but which were now dim, who could say whether from the rain that was pouring down, or the smoke of battle, or from despairing tears? He slowly turned toward the gentlemen of his staff. "We must descend, therefore, from the heights," he said, in a harsh voice. "Forward! March down the turnpike toward Weissenberg. Make the enemy at least pay dearly for compelling us to retreat. Let the cavalry advance, covering our retreat, and let not a single man or standard fall into the hands of the French! Come, gentlemen, listen to what I have still to say to you."

The quarter of an hour allowed by Müffling had not yet elapsed when the Prussians commenced slowly descending the heights of Kreckwitz, and marching down the turnpike toward Weissenberg. Blucher had ridden from the position at a brisk trot, with Gneisenau and the officers of his staff, and galloped a short distance along the level valley-road; then halting suddenly, and, turning his horse, he looked up to the heights, from which the Prussians were descending in perfect order, but in gloomy silence. "This is the second time we have been obliged to retreat," said Blucher, mournfully, "the second time that Bonaparte is luckier than we are; the blockheads will now say again that Bonaparte is invincible, and that they are fools who resist him, God

being on his side, and fortune never forsaking him. But I say it is false; the good God is not on his side, but the devil is, and fortune is only lulling him to sleep, to plunge him the surer and deeper into the abyss. But it is true, nevertheless, that this is the second battle we have lost, and the second time that we are obstructed in our advance. But I swear here—and may Heaven record my oath!—that this shall be the last time that I fall back; that I will specially pay Bonaparte for my grief and anxiety for the past month, and that I will bring him as much trouble as one man can to another. What a fearful account Bonaparte has to settle with me! how much he has to pay me! But, no matter; my sword is sharp, and will surely erase one item of his indebtedness after another. From this day I will begin. Will you lend me your assistance, gentlemen?"

"Yes," replied the officers of his staff, "we will!"

"Well, then it is all right," said Blucher, nodding; "from to-day M. Napoleon had better beware of me. Hitherto, I have only hated him; now I abhor him, and the word backward exists no longer for me and my Prussians!" He quickly galloped up to his troops. "Well, boys," he cried, "the heights of Kreckwitz are of no use to us, and it is better for us, therefore, to descend from them, and leave them to Bonaparte, who may put them into his pocket, if it affords him pleasure; but henceforth let us reverse matters, and put *him* into our pocket and keep him warm; otherwise, he might feel cold again, as he did in Russia. Forward now, boys; forward! And as we are now moving, I am sure you see that we do not move backward; he who asserts that we are retreating is a blockhead. Forward!"

But whatever Blucher said—how plausibly soever he tried to represent to his troops that they were not retreating, but advancing—it was unfortunately but too true that the battle of Bautzen was lost, and that the Prussians and Russians were obliged to fall back. It is true, they did so in excellent order, but—they retreated, and Napoleon could boast of a new victory on German soil

---

* Gneisenau's words.—Ibid., p. 48.

The whole army of the allies commenced retreating about dusk on the same day, and turned again toward Silesia. The troops marched sullenly, **and** sombre too were the faces of the two sovereigns, the Emperor Alexander **and King Frederick William.** Full of hope that they would achieve a victory, they had taken the field with their troops; but now their hopes were blasted, and they were compelled to return whence they had set out.

While the troops were marching down the wide highways, the two sovereigns, preceding their forces, took a short cut to Reichenbach. They were alone; only two footmen followed them at some distance; not a vestige of their earthly greatness surrounded them. They were both silent; slowly riding along, the king looked grave, while the emperor frequently turned his eyes, with an expression of mournful emotion, upon his friend, **or** raised them heavenward with an entreating glance. Silence reigned around; only at a great distance was heard the dull rumbling of wagons, and here and there on the horizon still flickered the burning ruins of a village.

For some time they thus **rode side by side,** when the king stopped his horse. "There must be a change!" he exclaimed, in a tone of grief and despair. "We are moving eastward, but we must advance westward."

"We must all move eastward," said the emperor, in a deep, fervent tone; "from the east came our salvation; eastward, therefore, every good Christian turns his face whenever he prays for assistance and redemption."

The king, perhaps, did not hear these words, for he made no reply, but looked moody and thoughtful. Both did not notice that the sky had brightened, and that the sun in its splendor was shedding its setting beams. It was a beautiful evening. The earth, refreshed by the rain, exhaled sweet odors; the air was fresh and balmy, and the blooming fields waved as a gentle sea. The sovereigns were too much concerned with themselves to be attracted by the beauties of outward nature. Their eyes were turned inward.

"Oh," resumed the king, after a pause, "what will be the end of all this? Were not they right who cautioned me against this war, and pointed to Napoleon's luck in order to prevent me from entering upon it? Have not my troops done all that can be demanded of human strength? **Have** they not braved with heroic resolution all fatigues and privations, and behaved in battle with unsurpassed valor? Have not the Russians also manifested the noblest devotion, and the most intrepid constancy? And still our armies have been defeated in two pitched battles—and still we are retreating? What have we to hope for? What new resources have we? May we still hope for the accession of Austria to our alliance?"

He uttered these questions in an undertone and thoughtfully, as if to himself, and forgetful of the presence of another who could hear him. When the emperor, therefore, replied to him, Frederick William gave a start, and raised his head almost in surprise.

"No," said the emperor, gravely—"no, we must not count on Austria; or, if you please, *not yet.* The mission of Count Stadion ought to have proved this to us. They sent their **diplomatist** to treat with us that, in case of a victory, we might not consider Austria, too, as our enemy. Now, that we have not been victorious, Count Stadion will undoubtedly leave our headquarters, repair to those of Napoleon, and assure him of the most faithful and sincere devotion of Austria. Austria desires only negotiation—to fight with words, not with the sword."

"But, without Austria," cried the king, vehemently, "we are too weak! Oh, at times it seems to me as though no human strength were able to accomplish any thing against the surpassing genius of Napoleon, and as though God alone, who made him so great, and raised him so high, could humble him! We have done all that men could do, but it is all in vain! He has conquered!"

"But we have made him purchase his victories very dearly," said Alexander, "and if we yielded, it was at least with honor. None of our battalions were dispersed, and I believe the number of prisoners is about the same on both sides. On the whole, nothing is lost as yet, and with God's help we will soon do better."

"Yes, but only with God's help," cried the king; "we need it above all; without it we are lost."

"But God is with us," exclaimed Alexander, enthusiastically, "I know it; I have gained this firm conviction ever since the great and terrible days of Moscow and the Beresina. God sent me those days of trial and terror that I might believe—and now I do believe. Until then I was a man enthralled by worldly doubts, relying upon my own strength, and rejoicing, not without vanity, in my earthly greatness. I thought of God, I loved Him, but He did not fill my whole soul—I pursued my own path, and diverted myself. But the conflagration of Moscow illuminated my mind, and the judgment of the Lord on the ice-fields filled my heart with a fervor of faith which it had never felt until then. With the flames of the holy city the hand of God wrote on the reddened sky, 'I am the Lord thy God!' With the rivers of blood flowing from the grand army of the French, the finger of the Lord wrote on the snow-fields, 'Thou shalt have no other gods before me!' Since then there is a wonderful joy, an indescribable humility, and an immovable faith in my heart—since then I have become another man. To the deliverance of Europe from utter ruin I owe my own soul's salvation." [*]

"It is He alone who is able to deliver us," said the king, profoundly moved; "I bow my head in humility, and confess that we are nothing without Him. May He send us His support!"

"He will," exclaimed Alexander, fervently; "God will be with us, for we are engaged in a just cause!"

"Yes, it is just," responded Frederick William, with deep emotion, and, slowly raising his eyes, he whispered, "Pray for us, Louisa, that we may conquer!"

Both were silent, and, with pious emotion, they lifted their hearts to heaven. Suddenly a joyful gleam kindled the face of the king, and, offering his hand to Alexander, he said in a deeply-moved tone, "We must not despond, but courageously continue the struggle. If God, as I hope, bless our united efforts, we will profess before the whole world that the glory belongs to Him alone." [*]

"Yes," cried Alexander, putting his right hand into that of his friend. "Let us not be ashamed to declare that the glory belongs to God. And now, my friend," exclaimed the emperor, when they halted, "let us repair to our headquarters, and hold a council of war with our generals."

"Very well," replied Frederick William; "let us examine the strength of our forces, and see what ought to be done. The battle of Bautzen must not be the end of this war."

CHAPTER XXXII.

BAD NEWS.

A MOMENT of repose had interrupted the great contest. Napoleon had offered an armistice to the allies prior to the battle of Bautzen; they rejected it, full of confidence in their strength. After the battle of Bautzen, the offer was repeated, and accepted. Time was needed for levying additional troops, organizing new regiments, and concentrating new corps. But Napoleon, deceived by his victories, relying on his good luck, and on the mistakes of his enemies, was fully satisfied that this armistice was but the forerunner of peace; and that the allies, warned by the two lost battles, would be eager to accept any peace not altogether dishonorable. The negotiations were opened at Prague. France, Prussia, and Russia, sent their plenipotentiaries to that city; and Austria, having taken upon herself the part of a mediator, instructed her envoy, Minister Metternich, to participate in the congress. The armistice was from

---

the 4th of June to the 24th of July—time enough for agreeing on a peace equally advantageous to both sides—time enough, too, in case it should **not** be concluded, to concentrate the armies and bring reïnforcements from France.

So soon as the armistice was signed, Napoleon returned to Dresden, to await there the result of the negotiations. At the Marcolini Palace the emperor again established his headquarters; but no brilliant festivals were given, as previous to his expedition to Russia; the kings and princes of Germany did not gather round the powerful **conqueror.** The Emperor of Austria remained quietly but sullenly at Vienna; the King of Prussia was at Reichenbach, and was now the enemy of Napoleon, and all the princes of the German Confederation of the Rhine, who, but a year before, were humble courtiers of Napoleon, kept aloof in morose silence, or refused obedience to their former master, and raised difficulties when called upon to furnish new troops and open additional resources. None of them came to offer homage to him whom they had just feared as the most powerful ruler in the world. Only the old, feeble King of Saxony (who, at the commencement of the war had fled with his millions, and the diamonds of the Green Vault, to Plauen, in the most remote corner of his territories),* returned at the rather imperious request of Napoleon to Dresden. The emperor dined with him sometimes, but only in the most intimate family circle, and without any outward splendor; at night he went to the French theatre, which had been ordered to Dresden during the armistice. Sometimes, his favorites, the ladies Mars and Georges, and the great Talma, were allowed to sup with the emperor after the performance, and the beautiful Mars, the impassioned fervor of the gifted Georges, and the conversation of the no less genial than adroit Talma, succeeded in dispelling the emperor's discontent. But no sooner was he alone with his thoughts, his labors, his plans, than his countenance assumed its sombre expression. Thus days and weeks elapsed, and the

congress was still assembled at Prague; the end of the armistice was drawing nigh, and the plenipotentiaries had not yet been able to agree on the conditions of peace.

It was on the morning of the 28th of June. Napoleon had just finished his breakfast, and entered his map-room to conceive there the plans of future campaigns, when the door of the reception-room opened, and Minister Maret, Duke de Bassano, came in. Maret belonged to the few men in whom his master placed implicit confidence, and whose fidelity he never doubted; to those who had at all times free access to him, and were permitted to enter his apartments without being announced. Nevertheless, his arrival seemed to surprise Napoleon. Never before had the duke entered his room at so early an hour, for he knew well that the emperor, engaged in examining his maps and devising plans, did not like to be disturbed. It was undoubtedly something unusual that induced the Duke de Bassano to come to him at such a time.

Napoleon cast a quick glance on Maret's face. Standing up beside the map-table, and leaning his hand upon it, he asked, vehemently, " Well, Maret, what is it?"

" Sire, I have come only to deliver to your majesty a few letters which the courier has just brought from Paris," said the duke, handing him some sealed packages.

" Is a letter from the empress among them?" asked Napoleon, hastily.

" Yes, sire."

The emperor had already found it, and, throwing the others upon the table, he hastily opened the one from his wife and read it. His face, which until then had been so stern and gloomy, gradually assumed a milder and kindlier expression.

" Ah, dear Louisa," he said, when he had read it, " how affectionately she writes; how she is yearning for me, and how well she knows how to tell me of the King of Rome, who is constantly inquiring for his father, and every night, when he goes to bed, calls aloud, ' Dear papa emperor come back soon!'"

---

* " Lebensbilder," vol. III., p. 456.

"A call, sire, in which, I am satisfied, all France joins," said Maret, quickly.

"Ah!" exclaimed the emperor, contemptuously shrugging his shoulders, "I know well that France—that **even my marshals join** in it, not from any devotion to myself, but because they want peace. The little King of Rome, however, is longing for me, and the empress, too, is wishing for my return, without caring much whether there is war or peace. These two love me! Ah, what a happy family would we three be if a lasting peace could be established! I am tired of war; like all of you, I am yearning to return home, and to enjoy a little the fruits of our numerous victories."

"Sire," said Maret, in a low, entreating voice, "it is easy for your majesty to do so, and to restore peace to Europe."

"Do you wish also to join in the nonsense asserted by the fools?" asked Napoleon, sharply! "Always the same air—the same **strain**! You **at least, Maret, ought not to sing it, for you** alone are aware of the proposals and negotiations between me and my enemies, and should know that it does not depend on me alone to restore peace, but that I shall, perhaps, only be he who must receive it."

"Still, sire, a few concessions on the part of your majesty would be sufficient to bring about peace," Maret ventured to say.

"What do you mean?" inquired Napoleon, whose voice now assumed an angry tone. "Do you intend to intimate, by your longing for concessions, that I should submit to the disgraceful and humiliating terms on which Austria gives me hopes of her further friendship and alliance? She dares ask of me the restoration of Illyria and the territory annexed to the grand-duchy of Warsaw; she demands for Prussia the evacuation of her fortresses, the restitution of Dantzic, and the restoration of the whole sea-shore of Northern Germany. And Austria, in making these proposals to me, in her equivocal part as mediator, does not do so with the friendliness of an ally, but she dares to threaten me, to say to me, 'If France does not accept, Austria will be obliged to side with the enemies of France, and make common cause with them.' I am ready to make peace, but I shall die sword in hand rather than sign conditions forced upon me. I will negotiate, but will not allow them to dictate laws to me.'"[*]

"Sire, none would dare dictate laws to your majesty. On the contrary, Austria will be glad if you merely declare that you are ready to negotiate, and she will not have much to ask. She will be content if you restore Illyria to her; and I am convinced of it, never will the Emperor Francis ally himself seriously with the enemies of his son-in-law."

"But the Emperor Francis is not his cabinet," exclaimed Napoleon. "I might, perhaps, repose confidence in the personal attachment of my father-in-law, but this could not blind me to the policy of his cabinet. This policy never changes. Treaties of alliance and marriages may somewhat retard its course, but never deflect it. Austria never renounces what she was compelled to cede. When she is weaker than her enemy, she resorts to peace, but this is always only an armistice for her, and, in signing it, she thinks of a new war. Such has been her conduct during the long series of years during which I have been fighting and negotiating with her. When closely pressed, she always accepted peace, and offered me her hand for the conclusion of an alliance; but whenever a reverse befell me, she withdrew her hand and broke the alliance. Now believing that she sees her own interest, she immediately resumes a hostile attitude toward me. She will open the passes of Bohemia to the allies, and thereby permit them to turn the positions of the French army, attack us in the rear, and cut us off from France. In a word, Austria is unable to forget any thing! She will remain our enemy, not only so long as she has losses to make up, but so long as the power of France might threaten her with new humiliations. This instinct of jealousy is more powerful than her attachment; she will always strive to aggrandize herself and to weaken France, and if I should grant her Illyria to-day, she would, per-

---

[*] Napoleon's words.—Vide Beitzke, vol. I., p. 560.

haps, to-morrow claim the whole of Lombardy, and her former provinces in the Netherlands.* Do not deceive yourself about it, Maret, and do not think that Austria wants peace with us because the Emperor Francis is my father-in-law. I must dictate peace to them sword in hand, and then they will hasten to remind me that I am the son-in-law of the emperor, and in consideration of this relationship they will ask of me favorable terms."

"But this, it seems to me, is the very situation in which your majesty is placed now," exclaimed Maret. "Your majesty has recently achieved two new victories."

"But what victories!" said Napoleon, gloomily; "they have cost me as many soldiers **as the** enemy, and procured me no advantages. I had hoped to gain many trophies; but in the battles of Lutzen and Bautzen not a cannon, not a flag, but a few insignificant prisoners fell into our hands. After two dreadful massacres, we have obtained no results whatever—and those men have not left me a single nail to pick up. † They are no longer the soldiers of Jena, **you may be sure of it, Maret; another spirit animates them** and their commanders. The Prussians fought like lions in those battles, and their commander, General Blucher, is like a chieftain in the Iliad. He is at the same time a general and a private soldier, a madcap and a Ulysses. The army loves him, and the king confides in him. He hates me, and has an excellent memory for his defeats of Auerstadt and Lubeck, and wants to take revenge for them."

"But it is unnecessary for Russia to take revenge," said Maret.

"Yes," murmured Napoleon, gloomily. "On her snow-fields I lost my army, and perhaps also my luck. But, no matter; I shall struggle on to the end, and compel Fortune to become again my friend, that I may do without other allies. She surely owes me attachment and fidelity, for have I not again paid her a heavy tribute? was it not

necessary for **me to act like Polycrates to keep** out of bad luck? He sacrificed only a ring to the gods, while I sacrificed two friends to Fortune, and one of them my best friend—Duroc. The victory of Lutzen cost me Bessières; that of Bautzen, Duroc. It was a heavy sacrifice, Maret; my heart is still bleeding in consequence of it, and this wound will never heal."

Maret made no reply, but turned his head aside, and his face had a strange expression of uneasiness and embarrassment.

Napoleon noticed it, and slightly shrugged his shoulders. "You think that I grow sentimental, duke," he said, rudely, "and you mean that my long military experience should have rendered me insensible to such accidents. You are right; let us refer to them no more. Let us rather read what the courier has brought."

He stretched out his hand for the other letters, and took up the first one without looking at it. When he saw the superscription, his face brightened, and, fixing a quick, reproachful glance upon Maret, he said: "Fate is less rigorous than you are, Maret. It reminds me that faithful friends still remain, and that all the companions of my youth are not yet dead. There is a letter from Junot! He is one of my faithful friends!" Opening it, he read hastily, and his face darkened. "Maret," he cried, in an angry voice, "read—see what Junot dares write to me!" He handed the letter to Maret. "Read it aloud," he cried, "otherwise I shall be afraid lest my eyes deceive me, and I mistake his words. Not the commencement, but the last page is what I want to hear."

Maret read in a tremulous voice: "'I, who love your majesty with the fervor which the savage feels for the sun—I, who belong to you with body and soul—must tell you the truth; and this is: we must wage an eternal war for you, *but I will do so no more!* I want peace! I want at length to be able to rest my weary head and aching limbs in my house, in the midst of my family, to enjoy their devotion, and no longer to be a stranger to them—to enjoy what I have purchased with a treasure that is more precious than all the riches of India—with my blood, with the blood of a man

---

* Napoleon's words.—Vide "The Emperor Francis and Metternich," p. 60.

† Napoleon's words.—Constant, vol. v.

of honor, a good Frenchman, a true patriot. Well, then, I ask—I demand—the repose that I have purchased by twenty-two years of active service, and by seventeen wounds, from which my blood has welled, first for my country, and then for your glory. It is enough!—my country needs repose, and your glory is as radiant as the sun. I repeat, therefore, I want peace. I speak in the name of all your marshals and generals, in the name of your army, in the name of all France: *we demand peace; give it to us, then!—Junot, Duke d'Abrantes.'"* *

"Well!" inquired Napoleon, when Maret had read the letter, "what do you think of this impudence?"

"Sire," said Maret, in a low, tremulous voice, "your majesty knows well that the Duke d'Abrantes is very dangerously ill, and that he is said to be subject to frequent fits of insanity."

"**It is true, it is the language of a madman, but one who knows very well what he says. For he is right; he dares utter what all my marshals** are thinking, and gives utterance to their thoughts, because he imagines that my friendship for him gives him that right. The fool! I shall prove to him that I am, first and above all, the emperor, and that the emperor will, without regard to the person, punish the man who is so audacious as to threaten him. Oh, I am glad that it is Junot who has made himself the mouth-piece of my generals and marshals! I shall punish him with **inexorable rigor, and that will silence the others forever.** They will not dare that which not even Junot was permitted to do with impunity; they will obey when my first anger has crushed this traitor Junot. For he is a traitor, a—"

"Oh, sire, I implore you, do not proceed!" interposed Maret; "have mercy upon him who stands already before a higher Judge, to receive **his** sentence!"

"What do you mean?" asked Napoleon.

"I mean, sire," replied Maret, solemnly, "that I came to bring you a sad message, and that your majesty, therefore, just now did me injustice.

Sire, when you deplored the death of your lamented friend, the Duke de Frioul, I was silent and embarrassed, not because I deemed such regrets unbecoming, but because I was filled with unbounded grief at the thought that I had come to communicate a similar affliction. The courier brought me also a letter from M. Albert de Comminges, Junot's brother-in-law. He requests me therein to inform your majesty of a melancholy occurrence—the Duke d'Abrantes is dead! Here is a letter from M. de Comminges to your majesty."

The emperor made no reply, but his face, which generally seemed immovable, commenced quivering, and his lips trembled. He took the letter in silence, and, opening it with a hasty hand, began to read it. But suddenly he dropped it, and, pressing both his hands to his forehead, he groaned aloud. Then he quickly stooped down, picked up the letter and read it through. "Junot!" he then cried in a tone of profound woe—"Junot!" He crumpled the letter in his hands, and, with an expression from the depths of his heart, he repeated, "Junot! Oh, my God, Junot, too!"

At this moment his wandering eye fell upon Maret, who was gazing at him, pale and filled with profound compassion. Napoleon started and concealed the tears which came to his eyes. Before an observer he was not accustomed to show himself a man overcome by grief. He smiled, but with an indescribably mournful expression, and said in a firm voice, "Another brave soldier gone! The third victim that the war has required of me, Maret! It takes the very men who were indispensable to me, because they set so shining an example of bravery and fidelity to the whole army. That is the only reason why I complain!"

"Your majesty has a twofold right to complain," said Maret, in his calm voice; "Junot loved your majesty with the obedience of a servant, the submissiveness of a child, the enthusiasm of a pupil, the ardor of a friend. He would have gone through fire for you, and he was justified in saying that he loved your majesty with

---

* "Memoirs of the Duchess d'Abrantes," b. xvi., p. 823.

the love the savage feels for the sun. Your majesty was his sun!"

"Yes, he loved me," said Napoleon, in a low voice, dropping his head on his breast, "and I could count upon his fidelity. We had spent our youth together, had overcome together a thousand dangers, and courageously braved the vicissitudes of fate. His star had risen with mine. Will not mine sink with his? Oh, Junot, how could you leave me now, when you knew that I stood so greatly in need of you? Junot, this is the first time that you desert me, and forget your plighted faith. I am on the eve of a great and doubtful war, surrounded by enemies—and my friends are deserting me and escaping into the grave!" He paused, bowing his head lower upon his breast, and wrinkling his forehead in his grief. A sad silence ensued, which Maret dared not interrupt by a motion or a word. At length, the emperor raised his face again, resuming his usual coldness and indifference. "Maret," he said, in a firm voice, "I have no one in Illyria now, since Junot, governor of that province, has died. I must send another governor. But whom?"

"Sire," said Maret, in a timid voice, "will you not take the proposals of Austria into consideration? She demands nothing but Illyria as the price of her alliance and friendship. Fate itself seems to give us a sign to grant this demand, for it has removed the governor of Illyria."

"Fate!" cried Napoleon, shrugging his shoulders, "you only acknowledge its hints when it suits your purposes; you deny its existence when it would seem to be contrary to your wishes. Fate caused the governor of Illyria to die, because, as you yourself said, he was subject to fits of insanity; it has thereby given me an opportunity to place a sensible and prudent man in Junot's stead, a man who will not dare tell me such impudent things as you read to me from his letter. Well, then, I will obey the hint of Fate. Write immediately to Fouché. He is at Naples; tell him to set out at once and come to Dresden. I intend to appoint him governor of Illyria. Dispatch a courier with the letter. But wait! I have not yet read all the dispatches brought from Paris."

He stepped back to the table, and took one of the letters from it. "A letter from the Duke de Rovigo," he said, in a contemptuous tone, "from the police minister of Paris! He will tell me a great many stories; he will pretend to have seen many evil spirits, and, after all, not know half of what he ought to know, and what Fouché would have known if he still held that position. There, read it, Maret, and communicate the most important passages to me." He threw himself into the chair that stood in front of his desk, and, taking a penknife, commenced whittling the wooden side-arm, while Maret unfolded the dispatch and quickly glanced over its contents.

"Sire," he said, "this dispatch contains surprising news. It speaks of a new enemy who might rise against your majesty."

"Well," said Napoleon, who was just cutting a large splinter from the chair, "what new enemy is it?"

"Sire," said Maret, shrugging his shoulders, "it is Louis XVIII."

Napoleon started, and looked at his minister with a flash of anger. "What do you mean?" he asked, sternly. "Who is Louis XVIII.? Where is the country over which he rules?"

"Sire, I merely intended to designate the brother of the unfortunate King Louis XVI."

"My uncle!" said Napoleon, with a proud smile, driving his knife again into the back of the chair. "Well, what then? Whereby has the Count de Lille surprised the world with the news of his existence?"

"Sire, by a proclamation addressed to the French, and in which he implores them to return to their legitimate lord and king, making them many promises, which, however, do not contain any thing but what the French possess already by the grace of your majesty."

Napoleon shrugged his shoulders. "Savary, then, has at length seen a copy of the English newspapers which published this proclamation," he said. "I read it several weeks ago."

"No, sire, it seems that the proclamation has

not only appeared in the English newspapers, but is circulating throughout France. The Duke de Rovigo reports that secret agents of the Count de Lille are actively at work in France. They are scattering every day thousands of printed copies of the proclamation among the people. They are circulated at night in the streets, secretly pushed under the doors into the houses and rooms so that the police agents are unable to take them away. These copies, it appears, are printed on hand-presses, for their lines are often irregular and slanting, and indicate an unpractised hand, but those who receive them try to decipher them, and deliver them to the police only after having read them." *

Napoleon said nothing; he was still whittling the back of his chair, and did not once look up to his minister, who stood before him in reverential silence. "I thought I had crushed this serpent of legitimacy under my foot," he murmured at last to himself, "but it still lives, and tries **again to** rise against me. Ah, I despise it, and I have reason to do so. I alone am now the legitimate ruler of France; the fifty battles in which I have fought and conquered for France are my ancestors; the will of the French people has made me emperor, and the voice of all the sovereign princes of Europe has recognized my throne. The daughter of an emperor is my partner; and the King of Rome, the future emperor of the French, will be more of a legitimate ruler than any other prince, for the battles of his father and the ancestors of the Hapsburgs form his pedigree. Let the Count de Lille, then, flood France with copies of his proclamation, I shall in the mean time win battles for France, and with the bulletins of my victories drive his proclamations from the field. I—"

At this moment the door opened, and Roustan's black face looked in. "Sire, the Duke de Vicenza requests an audience," he said.

"Caulaincourt!" exclaimed Napoleon, surprised, rising and throwing the penknife on the floor. "Caulaincourt! Let him come in!"

---

* "Mémoires du Duc Rovigo," vol. vi., p. 351.

CHAPTER XXXIII.

THE TRAITORS.

Roustan stepped back, and the imposing form of the Duke de Vicenza appeared on the threshold. The emperor hastily met him and looked at him with a keen, piercing glance. "Caulaincourt," he exclaimed, "whence do **you** come, and what do you want here?"

"Sire," said the duke, gravely and solemnly, "I come from Prague, whither the order of your majesty had sent me, to attend the congress and to conduct the negotiations in the name of your majesty."

"These negotiations are broken off, then, as you have come without having been recalled?"

"No, they are not broken off, but I have important news to communicate to your majesty, and as I think that we are served best when serving ourselves, I have made myself the bearer of my own dispatches, to be sure that they reach your majesty in time. I have travelled post-haste, and shall return to Prague in the same manner."

"Well, then, inform me of the contents of your dispatches orally and quickly."

"Sire, I inform your majesty that the Count de Metternich is on the road to this city to convey to you the ultimatum of Austria."

A flash of anger burst from the emperor's eyes. "He dares meet me! does he not fear lest I crush him by hurling his duplicity and treachery into his face? For I know that Austria is playing a double game, negotiating at the same time with me and my enemies."

"But it is still in the power of your majesty to attach Austria to France, and secure a continued alliance with her," exclaimed the Duke de Vicenza. "This is the reason why I have hastened hither: to implore your majesty not to reject entirely, in the first outburst of your anger, the proposals of Austria, however inadmissible they may appear to be. I left Vienna simultaneously with Count Metternich, but succeeded in getting somewhat the start of him; he will be here in an hour, and I have, therefore, time enough to communicate to your majesty important news which I learned at Prague yesterday, and which is sufficiently grave to influence perhaps your resolutions."

"Speak!" commanded the emperor, throwing himself again into the chair, and taking, for want of a penknife, a pair of scissors from his desk, in order to bore the back of the chair with it. Speak!"

"In the first place, I have to inform your majesty that the **Emperor** of Austria has left Vienna for Castle Gitschin, in Bohemia, and that an **interview of** the Emperor Francis with the allied monarchs took place there on the 20th of June."

"Ah, the first step to open hostility has been taken, then," cried Napoleon.

"This interview, however, led to no results," added Caulaincourt. "The Emperor Francis, on the contrary, declared emphatically that he was still merely a mediator, and would consider the alliance with France as dissolved, if your majesty should reject the ultimatum with which he should send Metternich to Dresden."

"That is the equivocal and insidious language which the Austrian diplomacy has always used," exclaimed the emperor, shrugging his shoulders. "They want to keep on good terms with all, in order to succeed in being the friend of him who is victorious. My father-in-law, it seems, has learned by heart, and recited the lesson which Metternich taught him. Proceed, Caulaincourt."

"Next, I have to inform your majesty that a definite treaty was concluded yesterday between Austria and the allies. It was concluded at Reichenbach. Austria has solemnly engaged to declare war against you if you refuse to accept her terms, the last she would send. Besides, Prussia and Russia concluded a treaty with England, which engaged to assist both powers with money and *matériel*, and which, in return, received the promise that Hanover, England's possession in Germany, should be considerably enlarged at the end of the war, and that new territories should be added to it."

"And the short-sighted monarchs have been foolish enough to grant **this to** England!" cried Napoleon, with a **sneer**. "**In their** blind hatred against me they grant more territory in Germany to their most dangerous enemy, that England may spread still further the vast net of her egotism, and catch all Germany in it, flood the country with her manufactured goods, and drive the commerce of the continent into British hands! Ah, those gentlemen will soon perceive what a mistake they have committed in yielding to the demands of those greedy English traders. For if England gives money instead of asking it, she must have a great many substantial advantages in view, and these she can obtain only at the expense of the German sovereigns, to whom she will furnish subsidies **now**. Are you through **with your news, Caulaincourt?**"

"No, sire, I have still something to add," said the Duke of Vicenza, in a melancholy voice.

The emperor looked at him with **a piercing** glance, which seemed to fathom the depths of his soul.

"Speak!" he said, quickly.

"Your majesty knows that the crown prince **of Sweden, Bernadotte, landed with** his army at **Stralsund on the 20th of May?**"

"Yes, I do," said Napoleon, shrugging his shoulders. "**My former marshal, who acquired** in my service a name and some fame, whom I permitted to accept the dignity of crown prince of Sweden that was offered him, a Frenchman, had the meanness to turn his arms against his country, and ally himself with the enemies of France. But still it seems that his courage is failing him. A month ago he disembarked in Germany, and is idle with his troops in Mecklenburg. He allowed Hamburg to fall; he did nothing to save Brandenburg, and appears ready to embark again for Sweden. Looking the crime of treason full in the face, he was unable to bear the thought of it, and will retreat from it to the steps of the Swedish throne."

"No, sire," said Caulaincourt, gravely, "the crown prince of Sweden has made up his mind, and hesitates no longer. The Emperor Alexander sent an envoy to Bernadotte, and requested of him an interview with the monarchs of Prussia and Russia, for the purpose of concerting with them a joint plan of operations for the campaign. Bernadotte, thanks to the persuasive eloquence of the Russian envoy, eagerly accepted this invitation, and the interview is to take place on the 9th of July at Trachenberg, in Silesia. The crown prince is already on the road with a truly royal suite, and he has been solemnly assured that the sovereigns will receive him at Trachenberg with all the honors due his rank as a sovereign and legitimate prince. The envoy of the Emperor of Russia is accompanying Bernadotte on this journey, to strengthen the favorable dispositions of the crown prince, and render him at once an active and energetic member of the alliance."

"Who is this envoy whom Alexander has dispatched to Bernadotte?" asked Napoleon.

"Sire, it is Count Pozzo di Borgo."

"Ah, my Corsican countryman, and once an ardent friend," exclaimed Napoleon. "He has never forgiven me for not having assisted him, the enthusiastic republican, in becoming King of Corsica, but having left France in possession of my native country. As he was unable to become a king, M. Pozzo di Borgo entered the service of the Czar of Russia to fight against me, his countryman, with the power of his tongue, as my other countryman with the arms of the Swedes. Well, I think it will not do the allies much good to unite with traitors and apostates, and to look for assistance against me from them. I gain more moral weight by this struggle against traitors than my enemies by their support. Bernadotte's treason is my ally."

"Sire, another man has joined the traitor, a Frenchman, who wants to fight against France, against his emperor and former comrade."

"Still another! A third traitor! Who is it?"

"Sire, it is General Moreau."

"What! has Moreau returned from America?" asked Napoleon, looking up quickly.

"Yes, sire; he has left the banks of the Delaware to fight against his country, as a general of the Emperor of Russia."

The emperor looked thoughtfully, and suddenly

he raised his eyes, while a pleased expression lit up his countenance.

"My enemies assert that I have a heart of iron," he said, in a gentle voice; "they charge me with being insensible to human emotions—to compassion, friendship, and love. Well, then, I could have had Moreau and Bernadotte both killed; they were in my power, and deserved death. Moreau had entered into a conspiracy against me and the existing laws of our country —a conspiracy whose object was to assassinate me. I believe I would have been justified if I had made him feel the rigor of my laws, and expiate his murderous intent by death. Bernadotte disobeyed my orders in two battles; I would have been justified in having him tried by a court-martial, which would certainly have passed sentence of death upon him. I permitted Moreau to emigrate to America, and indulge his republican predilections there without hinderance; and Bernadotte to go to Sweden, and gratify the desires of his ambitious heart. I pardoned both because I loved them. They now reward me by allying themselves with my enemies. This is all right, however, for I have placed both under heavy obligations, and nothing is more difficult to forgive than benefits."

"Sire, as I have alluded to these traitors, I must mention still another. General Jomini, adjutant-general of Marshal Ney, has deserted his post and gone over to the camp of the allies to offer his services to the sovereigns. He has become a member of the Emperor Alexander's staff."

"Well," cried Napoleon, with the semblance of unalloyed mirth, "the world and posterity will have to pardon me now if I lose a few battles in this campaign, for those who are fighting against me are commanded by generals who have learned the art of war from me—pupils of mine. I must, therefore, allow them to gain a battle or two to prove that I am a good teacher. Besides, Jomini is not as guilty as Moreau and Bernadotte. He is a native of Switzerland, and his treason is aimed only at myself, and not at his country."

"It seems such is Jomini's excuse, too," said

Caulaincourt, "for I have been told that he treated General Moreau with surprising coolness, and when the latter offered him his hand he did not take it, but withdrew with a chilling salutation. To the Emperor Alexander, who rebuked him for it, he replied that he would gladly welcome General Moreau anywhere else than at the camp of the enemies of Moreau's own country. For if he, Jomini, **were a** native of France, he would assuredly at this hour not be at the camp of the Emperor of Russia."

"Ah!" exclaimed the emperor, "I am convinced that miserable Jomini imagines that he acted in a very noble and highly-dignified manner. A traitor who is ashamed of another traitor, and blushes for him! Ah, Caulaincourt, what a harrowing spectacle! These acts of treachery will in the end make me unhappy!* For does not Austria, too, wish to betray me? Has she not entered into an alliance with me, and does she not now wish to forsake me merely because she imagines that it would be more advantageous to her to side with my enemies? Austria is oscillating, and Metternich thinks he can preserve her equilibrium by placing Austrian **promises** as weights now into this, now into that scale. But the cabinet of Vienna deceives itself. **Count** Metternich wants his intrigues to pass for policy, while the whole object of Austria is to recover what she has lost." †

At this moment a carriage was heard to roll up to the palace and stop close under the windows of the cabinet. Maret, who, during the conversation between Napoleon and Caulaincourt, had retired into a window-niche, turned and looked out into the street.

"Sire," he then said, quickly, "Count Metternich has arrived, and already entered the palace."

"Ah, he is really coming, then!" exclaimed Napoleon, with an air of scornful triumph; "he wishes me to tear the mask from his smirking **face!** Well, I shall comply with his wishes; I, at least, shall not dissemble, nor veil my real thoughts! Austria shall learn what I think of her!"

The door opened, and Roustan entered again. "Sire," he said, "his excellency Count Metternich, minister plenipotentiary of his majesty the Emperor of Austria, requests an audience of your majesty."

Napoleon turned his head slowly toward the Dukes de Vicenza and Bassano. "Enter the cabinet of my private secretary, Fain," he said. "Leave the door ajar; I want you to hear all. Fain, if he pleases, may take notes of this interview, that he may afterward accurately testify to it. Go!"

The two gentlemen bowed in silence and withdrew. **The emperor** gazed after them until they disappeared through the door of the cabinet; then turning toward Roustan, "Let him come in," he said, with a quick nod.

A few minutes afterward the slender form, and the handsome, florid, and smiling face of Count Clement de Metternich appeared on the threshold of the imperial cabinet.

———

CHAPTER XXXIV.

NAPOLEON AND METTERNICH.

The emperor quickly met the Austrian minister, but, as if restraining himself, he stood in the middle of the room. Metternich approached, making a stiff, solemn bow, and quickly raised his head again, and turning his fine face, from which the smile did not vanish for a moment, toward the emperor, he waited in respectful silence for the latter to address him. Napoleon cast a menacing glance of hatred upon him; but Metternich did not seem to perceive his threat. He fixed his large blue eyes with perfect calmness on the face of the emperor, and awaited the commencement of the conversation.

The emperor felt that it was his province to break this silence. "Well, Metternich," he said, "you are here, then! You are welcome! But

---

* Napoleon's words.—Constant's "Mémoires," vol. v., p. 945.

† Napoleon's words.—Fain, "Manuscrit de 1813," vol. i.

answer me, without circumlocution, What do you want?"

"Sire, Austria wishes me to mediate a peace between the Prussian and Russian allies and your majesty."

"Ah, you want peace!" exclaimed Napoleon, sarcastically. "But why so late? We have lost nearly a month, and your mediation, from its long inactivity, has become almost hostile. It appears that it no longer suits your cabinet to guarantee the integrity of the French empire? Be it so; but why had you not the candor to make me acquainted with that determination at **an earlier** period? It might **have** modified my plans—perhaps prevented me from continuing the war."

"But your majesty ought graciously to remember that, for the present, there is no question of Austria and her wishes," **said Metternich, calmly**; "that Austria is merely trying **to mediate peace** between your **majesty and the sovereigns of Russia and Prussia.**"

"**Ah, that is what you call** mediating," exclaimed Napoleon, sneeringly. "When you allowed me to exhaust myself by new efforts, you doubtless little calculated on such rapid events **as have** ensued. I **have** gained, nevertheless, **two battles**; my enemies, severely weakened, **were** beginning to waken from their illusions, **when** suddenly you glided among us, and, speaking **to me of an armistice and** mediation, you spoke **to them of alliance and war.** But for your pernicious intervention, peace would have been at this moment concluded between the allies and myself. You cannot deny that, since she has assumed the office of mediator, Austria has not only ceased to **be** my ally, but is becoming my **enemy. You** were about to declare yourself so when the battle of Lutzen intervened, and, by showing you the **necessity of** augmenting your forces, made **you** desirous of gaining time. You have improved your opportunity, and now you have your two hundred **thousand men ready**, screened by the Bohe**mian hills**; Schwartzenberg commands them; at this very moment he is concentrating them in my rear; and it is because you conceive yourself in a

condition to dictate the law, that you pay this **visit.**"

"Sire, dictate!" echoed Metternich, in a tone of dismay, but with a strange smile.

"**Yes,** dictate!" repeated Napoleon, in a louder voice. "But why **do you** wish to dictate to me alone? Am I, then, no longer the same man whom you defended yesterday? If you are an honest mediator, why do you not at least treat both sides alike? Say nothing in reply, for I see through you, Metternich: your cabinet wishes to profit by my embarrassments, and augment them as much as possible, in order to recover a portion of your losses. The only difficulty you have is, whether you can gain your object without fighting, or throw yourselves boldly among the combatants; you do not know which to do, and possibly you come to seek light on the subject. Well, then, let us see! Let us treat! What do you wish?"

"**Sire,**" **said Metternich, with his** smiling calm**ness, which had not yielded for an** instant to the storm of Napoleon's **reproaches, "Austria has** no motives of self-interest. The **sole** advantage which the Emperor Francis wishes to derive from the present state of affairs is the influence which a spirit of moderation, and a respect for the rights of independent states, cannot fail to acquire from those who are animated with similar sentiments. Austria wishes not to conquer, but to preserve."

"Speak more clearly," interrupted the emperor, impatiently; "but do not forget that I am a soldier."

"Your majesty has taught Europe by upward of fifty battles never to forget that," said Metternich, **with** a pleasant nod. "Austria wishes to wound your majesty neither as a soldier nor as an emperor. She simply desires to establish a state of things which, by **a** wise distribution of power, may place the guaranty of peace under the protection of an association of independent states."

"Words, words!" cried Napoleon, impatiently. "Words having no other object than evasion, veiling your own designs! But I mean to go directly to the object. I only wish Austria to remain neutral, and I am ready to make sacrifices to her for it. My army is amply sufficient to bring back the Russians and Prussians to reason. All that I ask of you is to withdraw from the strife."

"Ah, sire," said Metternich, eagerly, "why should your majesty enter singly into the strife? Why should you not double your forces? You may do so, sire! It depends only on you to add our forces to your own. Yes, matters have come to that point that we can no longer remain neutral; we must be either for or against you."

The emperor bent on him one of those piercing glances which the eagle bends upon the clouds to which he is soaring, seeking for the sun behind them. "And which would be more desirable to you," he asked, "to be for or against me?"

"Ah, sire, the Emperor Francis wishes for nothing more ardently than that the state of affairs should enable him to be for France, whose emperor is his son-in-law."

"But my father-in-law imposes conditions! Pray, tell me what they are!" exclaimed Napoleon, striding up and down the apartment, while Metternich walked by his side, respectfully holding his hat in his hand.

"Tell me what these conditions are!" repeated Napoleon.

"Sire, they are simply these," said Metternich, in a bland tone. "During the late decade the affairs of Europe have been disturbed in a somewhat violent manner. Austria only wishes to have the equilibrium of Europe reëstablished, and all the states occupy again the same position which they held prior to these convulsions. If your majesty consents to contribute your share to this restoration, Austria in return offers to France her lasting alliance, and, in case the other powers should pursue a hostile course, her armed assistance. Austria wishes to make no conquests, to acquire no provinces, no titles—she is animated with the spirit of moderation. She demands only order, justice, and equality for all, and, moreover, only the restoration of such states as have been recognized for centuries as members of the general confederacy of European states, the reconstruction of those thrones which have existed for

ages, and whose rulers have a legitimate right to their sovereignty. I believe your majesty cannot deny that the Bourbons have a well-founded right to Spain, and that the Spaniards now, by the blood shed in their heroic struggle, have established their right to restore the throne to their legitimate rulers. You will have to admit, further, that no Christian sovereign, how powerful soever he may be, has a right to overthrow the Holy See of St. Peter, and to keep the vicegerent of God away from the capital which all Christendom has so long recognized as his own. You will have to admit, too, that both Lombardy and Illyria have long been possessions of Austria, and that Switzerland has been recognized as a confederation of republics by all the powers of Europe. If your majesty acknowledges all this, and consents to restore the state of things in accordance with those well-established rights, it only remains for us to find compensation for the three powers which have already allied themselves against you. As for Prussia, I believe a portion of Saxony would be the most suitable indemnity for her. Russia, I suppose, would be content if, after the dissolution of the duchy of Warsaw, Poland should once more fall to her share, and England demands only the possession of a few fortified places and safe harbors on the shores of Holland."

The emperor uttered a cry of anger, and, suddenly halting, cast glances on Metternich which seemed to borrow their fire from the lightning. "Are you through with your proposals, sir?" he asked, in a threatening tone.

Metternich bowed. "Yes, sire."

"Well, then," cried the emperor, stepping up to the minister, "to all this I respond only by the question: How much money has England given you to play this part?"

At this question, uttered in a menacing voice, Metternich turned pale, the smile passed from his lips, his brow darkened, and his eyes, usually so mild and pleasant, kindled with anger, and allowed the thoughts, generally concealed in the innermost recesses of the diplomatist's heart, to burst forth for a moment, and betray hatred.

"Ah," cried Napoleon, in a triumphant tone, "I have at length torn the mask from your smiling features, and I **see that a** serpent is hidden under them as under roses. It would sting, but I know how to be on my guard; I will never grant Austria the right to insult, dictate to, and humiliate me. I will **compel** her, as I have done so often, to prostrate herself in the dust before me, and ask mercy and forbearance. Do you hear what I say? I will humiliate Austria, trampling her in the dust." The emperor violently raised his clinched fist, and striking it downward struck Metternich's hat, which the minister still **held** in his hand, and caused it to fall to the **ground.**

The emperor paused and looked at Metternich, as if to request him to pick up the hat. But the latter did not make the slightest movement. His thoughts and his hatred had already retired into his bosom; his brow was serene again, and his **accustomed smile returned. He looked first at the hat, and then at the emperor, who followed** his glances, and met them sullenly and defiantly. This little incident, however, seemed to have dispelled Napoleon's anger, or at least to have appeased the first stormy waves of the sea. When he spoke again his tone was milder, and his look less scorching, returning from time to time, as it were involuntarily, to the hat lying on the floor a few steps from him. He commenced pacing the apartment again with quick steps. Metternich followed him, only with somewhat slackened pace, and thus compelled the emperor to walk a little slower.

"Now," said Napoleon, loudly, "I know what you want! Not only Illyria, but the half of Italy, the return of the pope to Rome, Poland, and the abandonment of Spain, Holland, and Switzerland! This is what you call the spirit of moderation! You are intent only on profiting by every chance; you alternately transport your alliance from one camp to the other, in order to be always a sharer in the spoil, and you speak to me of your respect for the rights of independent states! You would have Italy; Russia, Poland; Prussia, Saxony; and England, Holland and Belgium: in fine, peace is only a pretext; you are all intent on dismembering the French empire! And Austria thinks she has only to declare herself, to **crown such an enterprise! You pretend** here, with a stroke of the pen, **to make** the ramparts of Dantzic, Custrin, Glogau, Magdeburg, Wesel, Mentz, Antwerp, Alessandria, Mantua, **in** fine, all the strong places of Europe, sink **before** you, of which I did not obtain possession but by my victorious arms! And I, obedient to your policy, am to evacuate Europe, of which I still hold the half; **recall** my legions across the Rhine, the Alps, and the Pyrenees; subscribe a treaty which would be nothing but a vast capitulation; and place myself at the mercy of those of whom I am at this moment the conqueror! It is when my standards float at the mouths of the Vistula, and on the banks of the Oder; when my army is at the gates of Berlin, and Breslau; when I am at **the** head of three hundred thousand men, that Austria, **without drawing a** sword, expects to **make me subscribe such conditions!** This is an insult, and it is my father-in-law that has matured such a project; it is he that sends you on such a mission!" *

While thus speaking, the emperor was still walking, and Metternich by his side. Whenever they passed the hat lying on the floor, Napoleon cast a quick side-glance on Metternich, who appeared to take no notice of the hat, and it seemed entirely accidental that he slightly wheeled aside, and thus succeeded in passing without touching it.

"You," cried Napoleon, in a thundering voice, "have taken upon yourself the mission of insulting me, and you think I will quietly submit?"

"Sire," said Metternich, with his imperturbable calmness, "I believe you have already punished me for it!"

Now for the first time his eyes turned significantly toward his hat, and then fixed themselves steadfastly on the emperor. They did not dare to threaten, but they defied Napoleon. They

---

* This whole speech contains only Napoleon's words.—Vide Fain, "Manuscrit de 1813," vol. i.

said: "**You** have insulted me by knocking my hat out of my hand. I will not pick it up, but demand satisfaction."

Possibly Napoleon understood this language, for a smile, full of sarcasm and contempt, played around his lips, and he slightly shrugged his shoulders.

"I beg you to consider, besides," added Metternich, calmly, "that I am here only because my sovereign has commissioned and ordered me to repair to you, and that, as a faithful servant, I have repeated only what the emperor commanded me."

"Ah," cried Napoleon, with a harsh laugh, "you wish to make me believe that you are but the emperor's echo? Well, I will suppose it to be true. Then go and tell your master that I henceforth decline his mediation, and that nothing would exasperate me more than the idea that Austria, in return for her crimes and her breach of faith, should reap the best fruits and become the pacificator of Europe. Ask the Emperor Francis in what position he intends to place me in regard to my son? Tell him he is entirely mistaken if he believes a disgraced throne can be a refuge in France for his daughter and grandson.* That is my reply to the Emperor Francis. Go!"

Metternich bowed; considering the emperor's words equivalent to his dismissal, he turned and crossed the room. His way led him past his hat; he took no notice of it, but quietly walked on toward the door.

"He does not wish to take his hat," thought Napoleon.

Metternich reached the door, turned again to the emperor, and made him a last reverential bow.

"One word more, Count Metternich!" cried Napoleon. "Come, I have still something to say to you."

Metternich blandly nodded assent and returned. Napoleon commenced again pacing the room, **with** Metternich by his side. The emperor now di-

rected his steps in such a manner that he himself was near the hat. "I wish to prove to you, Metternich," said Napoleon, "that I have seen through you, and that the true reason of your coming is well known to me. You did not for an instant believe that I could accept these proposals, which would dishonor and annihilate me; **you know me too** well for that; but **they were only to be** the pretext **of the real wish that** brought you hither. To be able to ally yourself in a seemingly loyal manner with my enemies, you want to get rid of the alliance which is still connecting Austria with France. In direct contradiction to all that Austria has hitherto said to me, you wish to annul the treaty of Paris. Admit that this is the case."

The emperor, with his eyes fixed steadfastly upon Metternich, crossed the apartment. Suddenly seeming to find an obstacle in his way, he turned his eyes toward the floor. It was Metternich's hat, which his foot had already touched. As if merely to remove the obstruction, he stooped, **took** up the hat, and threw it with an indifferent **and careless motion on a** chair near the door. **He then quietly passed** on and fixed his **eyes again upon** Metternich.* "Well, reply to me—deny it if you can!"

"**Sire**," **said** Metternich, in a bland, insinuating voice, "I had already the honor of telling you **that** matters have come to that point that we can no longer remain neutral, but that we can take up arms for your majesty, only if you consent to grant us all that I have laid before you, and—"

"No," interrupted Napoleon, proudly, "do not repeat the insult! The interview is ended. I know what you desire, and I do not intend to disappoint you! I will not be a dead weight upon my friends, nor raise the slightest objection to the abandonment of the treaty that allies me with Austria, if such be the wish of the Emperor Francis. I shall to-morrow repeat this to you in

---

* Napoleon's words.—Vide Fain, "Manuscrit de 1813," vol. I.

* Vide "Mémoires de la Duchesse d'Abrantes," vol. xvi., p. 178. There is another version of this scene, according to which it was not Metternich's, but the emperor's hat that fell to the floor.—Vide Hormayr, "Lebensbilder," vol. iii., p. 460.

writing and in due form. Now we are through—farewell!" He turned his back on Count Metternich, with a quick nod, and continued his way **across the room.**

Metternich cast a .ast smiling glance on him; went with rapid, soft steps to the chair, took his hat which the emperor had picked up, hastened across the room, and went out without a word or a bow.

When Napoleon heard him close the door, "He is gone," he murmured, "the alliance is broken. I have now no ally but myself!" For a moment he looked melancholy, and then starting glanced at the small door leading into the cabinet of Baron Fain, his private secretary. He remembered that his two dukes were there, and that they could not only hear but see all. Composing his agitated face, he shouted in a merry voice, " Caulaincourt and Maret, come in!"

The door opened immediately; the **Dukes de** Bassano and Vicenza appeared on the threshold **and reëntered the room. "Well, have you heard** every thing?" asked Napoleon.

"Yes, sire."

" And Fain? has he taken notes? "

"Sire, he has written down every thing as far as it was possible, considering the rapidity of the conversation." *

"Ah, I shall read it afterward," said the emperor; "it is always good to know in what manner we shall be recognized by posterity. Now, gentlemen, since you have heard all, you understand that war is unavoidable, and that Austria will side with my enemies."

"Sire, we have heard it, and it has filled our souls with uneasiness and anxiety," said Maret.

"Perhaps, nevertheless, a compromise may still be possible," exclaimed Caulaincourt. "The armistice has not yet expired, and, in accordance with the orders of your majesty, I have already made the necessary overtures for prolonging it to the 15th of August."

"It will be prolonged, you may depend upon it," said Napoleon, "for the allies need time for completing their preparations. We shall have an armistice to that time, but then war will break out anew, and it will be terrible. I shall not indeed wage it as emperor, but as General Bonaparte." *

"Oh, sire," sighed Maret, " the whole world is longing for peace, and France, too, entertains no more ardent wish. I have received many unmistakable intimations in regard to it. Paris is not only hoping for peace, but expecting it confidently, after the two victories by which your majesty has humiliated your enemies."

"Paris is very badly informed if she thinks peace to depend upon me," replied Napoleon, indignantly. "You see how greedily Austria augments the demands of my enemies, by placing herself at their head. We were always obliged to conquer peace. Very well, we will conquer it again. The armistice will be prolonged to the 15th of August—time enough to complete, on our side, all necessary preparations, and decree a new conscription. But then, after the armistice, war—a decisive, bloody war—a war that will lead to an honorable peace! Believe me, he who has always dictated peace cannot submit to it with impunity. Courage, therefore! France wants peace, and so do I, but my cannon shall dictate the terms, and my sword write them!" †

---

* Fain, "Mémoires de 1813." Fain gives a full account of this interview, and I have strictly followed his narrative.

* Napoleon's words.

† Napoleon's words.—Vide "Mémoires du Duc de Rovigo," vol. ii.

CHAPTER XXXV.

ON THE KATZBACH.

THE armistice expired on the 15th of August, and hostilities were resumed. The state of affairs, however, was essentially different from what it was at the commencement of the armistice; for, at that time, Napoleon had just obtained two victories. During the armistice, the allies had won an important victory over him; they had gained Austria over to their side, and now, at the renewal of hostilities, Austria reënforced the allies with two hundred thousand men. For nearly fourteen years Napoleon was invariably the more powerful enemy, not only on account of his military genius, but of the numerical strength and excellent organization of his forces.

For the first time the enemy opposed him with superior forces, and this vast host struggled, moreover, with the utmost enthusiasm for the deliverance of the fatherland—with the energy of hatred and wrath against him who had so long enslaved and oppressed it. But Napoleon still possessed his grand military genius. Soon after the expiration of the armistice, he gained a new victory over the allies, that of Dresden; * and in this battle Moreau, the French general, who was fighting against his own countrymen, was struck by a French ball, which caused his death in a few

---

* The battle of Dresden lasted two days, the 26th and 27th of August. Moreau died on the 2d of September, and the battle of Culm was fought on the 29th and 30th of August.

days. But the allies took their revenge for the defeat of Dresden in the great victory of Culm, where they, also after a two days' battle, achieved a brilliant triumph over General Vandamme.

General Blucher and his Silesian army had not participated in these battles. At the time when the Russians, the Austrians, and a part of the Prussians, were fighting and yielding at Dresden, Blucher was at length to attain his object, and meet the enemy in a pitched battle. Since the **20th** of August he stood near Jauer with his army, which was ninety thousand **strong, composed** of Russians and Prussians, and **awaited** nothing more ardently than the approach of the enemy, in order to fight a general battle. Fortune seemed to favor his wishes, for Napoleon himself was advancing. On the 21st of August the scouts reported the approach of the hostile columns, who had crossed the Bober at Löwenberg. Blucher's eyes lit up with delight; he stroked his white mustache, and said : " We shall have a fight ! To-morrow we meet the French !"

But the morning of the 22d of August dawned, and the eyes of the general were still unable to descry the advancing enemy. Yet his scouts reported that the French army was advancing, and that only a detachment had set out for Dresden. "Then Bonaparte has left with this detachment," grumbled Blucher; "for if he were still with them, the French would not creep along like snails."

At length, on the 26th of August, the general's wishes seemed to be near fulfilment. The French were advancing. They approached the banks of the Katzbach, to the other side of which the Silesian army was moving. "We shall have a fight!" shouted General Blucher, exultingly; "the good God will have mercy on me after all, and treat me to a good breakfast! I have been hungering for the French so long, that I really thought I should die of starvation. I shall furnish the roast; and, that there may be something to drink, the rain is pouring down from heaven as though all the little angels on high were weeping for joy because they are to have the pleasure of seeing old Blucher at work!—Glorious hosts in heaven!" added Blucher, casting a glance at the leaden sky, "now do me only the favor to put an end to your weeping, and do not give us too much of a good thing. Pray remember that you put under water not only the enemy, but ourselves, your friends. Do not soften the soil too much, else not only the French will stick in the mud, but ourselves, your chosen lifeguard!"

But "the little angels on high" poured down their "tears of joy" in incessant torrents from early dawn. It was one of those continuous rains from a dull gray sky, giving little hope of fine weather for many days. The soil was softened, the mountain-torrents swollen, and vast masses of water foamed into the Katzbach, so that this peaceful little stream seemed a furious river. A violent norther was blowing, and driving the rain into the faces of the soldiers, drenching their uniforms, penetrating the muskets, and moistening the powder.

"Well, if the boys cannot shoot to-day, they will have to club their muskets," said Blucher, cheerfully, when he and his suite rode out of Bollwitzhof, his headquarters, to reconnoitre the position of the French.

But the wind and rain rendered a reconnoissance a matter of impossibility. The enemy was nowhere to be seen, but still the dull noise of rumbling cannon and trotting horses was heard at a distance, and the patrols reported that they had seen the foe approaching the Katzbach in heavy columns; not, however, on the other bank, but on this side. At this moment General Gneise-

nau came up at a full gallop. He had gone out toward the pickets to reconnoitre, and came back to report that the French were forming in line of battle at a short distance on the plateau near Eichholz, and that they had crossed to the right side of the Katzbach.

"Right or left," said Blucher, "it is all the same to me, provided we have them. If they have already crossed the river, well then they know the road, and will be better able to find their way back. Let us allow them to cross, until there are enough of them on this side." Then, turning with noble dignity toward his officers, he added, in an entirely changed, grave, and measured tone: "Gentlemen, the battle will commence in a few hours. Promptness and good order are of vital importance now.—The orderlies!"

The orderlies hastened to him. "You will ride to General York, who is occupying the plateau of Eichholz, and tell him to allow as many French as he thinks he can beat to march up the ascent, and then he is to charge them!" shouted Blucher to the first orderly, and, while he sped away at a furious gallop, the general turned to the second. "You will hasten to General von Sacken and tell him that it is time for attacking the French!—And we, gentlemen," he added, addressing his staff, "will place ourselves at the head of our troops. The soldiers must have their meals cooked by two o'clock; all the columns will then commence moving. When the enemy falls back, I expect, above all, the cavalry to do their duty, and to act with great courage. The foe must find out, that on retreating he cannot get out of our hands unhurt. And now, forward! The battle begins at two o'clock!" He spurred his horse, and galloped again toward the troops. With a serene face and joyful eyes he rode along the front. "Boys," he shouted, "cook your dinners quickly, do not burn your mouths, and do not eat your soup too hot; but when you have eaten it, then it is time for cooking a whipping soup for the French."

"Yes, Father Blucher, we will cook it for them!" shouted the soldiers.

"I am afraid that soup won't agree with the

French," said Blucher, with a humorous wink. "Blue-bean soup is hard to digest. But they will have to swallow it, whether they like it or or not, won't they?"

"Yes, they will!" laughed the soldiers; and Blucher galloped over to the other regiments, to fire their hearts by similar greetings.

It was two o'clock! "Boys, the fun will commence now!" shouted Blucher's powerful voice. "Now I have French soldiers enough on this side of the river. Forward!"

Forward they went, at a double-quick, directly at the French. The cannon boomed, the musketry rattled; but the rain soon silenced the latter.

"Boys," shouted Major von Othegraven to his battalion of the Brandenburg regiment, "if we cannot shoot them, we can club them!" And amid loud cheers the soldiers turned their muskets, and struck their enemies with the butts. A terrible hand-to-hand struggle ensued—howls of pain, dreadful abuse and imprecations burst from both sides; but at length they ceased on this part of the field: the Brandenburg soldiers had killed a whole French battalion with the stocks of their muskets!*

The battle raged on amid the terrible storm beating on the combatants. The wind blew violently, and the rain descended in torrents. The men sank ankle-deep in the softened soil, but "Forward!" sounded the battle-cry, and the soldiers left their shoes in the mud, rushing in their socks or bare-footed on the enemy, who fought with lion-hearted courage, here receding and there advancing.

"Father Blucher, we are doing well to-day!" shouted the soldiers to their chieftain, galloping up to the infantry.

"Yes, we are doing well," cried Blucher; "but wait, boys—we shall do still better!"

At this moment the artillery boomed from the other side. Two officers galloped up to Blucher. One was the orderly he had sent to General von Sacken.

* Beitzke, vol. II, p. 204.

"What reply did General von Sacken make?" shouted Blucher.

"'Reply to the general, "Hurrah!"'" * was all he said, your excellency."

"A splendid comrade!" cried Blucher, merrily.

"General," said the second officer, in an undertone, "I beg leave to make a communication in private."

"In private? No communications will be made in private to-day," replied Blucher, shaking his head; "my staff-officers must hear every thing." And he beckoned to his aides and officers to come closer to him.

"Your excellency then commands me to utter aloud what I have to say?"

"Well, speak directly, and, if you like, so loudly that the French will hear, too!"

"Well, then, general, I have to tell you that no time is to be lost, and that we must hasten to advance, for the Emperor Napoleon himself is coming up at the head of his troops; he is already in the rear of your excellency."

"Ah," inquired Blucher, with perfect composure, "is the Emperor Napoleon in my rear? Well, I am glad of it; then he is able to do me a great favor." He turned his eyes again toward the battle array with a defiant smile, as if confident of final victory.

The victory was not decided, although the murderous struggle had lasted already an hour. Marshal Macdonald constantly moved up fresh troops, and Blucher had sufficient reserves to meet them. Here the Prussians gave way, and there the French. From the right wing of the Prussian army orderlies informed General Blucher that General York, with his troops, had repulsed the enemy, and was advancing victoriously; messengers hastened to him from the left wing, and told him that General Langeron was about to fall back, that the Prussian cavalry were retreating, and the French cavalry approaching in dense masses, and that the Prussian batteries were in imminent danger of falling into the hands of the enemy.

Blucher uttered an oath—a single savage oath;

* Beitzke, vol. II., p. 201.

then he turned his head aside and shouted, "Hennemann! pipe-master!"

Christian Hennemann galloped up immediately. He was in full hussar-uniform, but did not belong to the ranks; he was in the suite of his general, and had to be constantly near him. On the pommel of his saddle was a long iron box, and in his mouth a short clay pipe. "General, here I am!"

"Give me a short pipe, for now we charge the enemy!"

Hennemann took the pipe from his mouth, handed it to the general, and said, with the utmost equanimity: "Here it is! It has been burning some time already, and I began to think the general had entirely forgotten the pipe and myself."

Blucher put the pipe into his mouth. At this moment a Brandenburg regiment of lancers galloped up, headed by Major von Katzeler, Blucher's former adjutant. "We are going to assist our men!" shouted Katzeler, saluting the general with his sword.

"We are moving to the relief of our comrades!" cried a captain of hussars, thundering up at the head of his regiment.

"Very well!" said Blucher. "God bless me, I must go with them! I can stand it no longer!" Drawing his sword, he galloped with the courage and ardor of a youth to the head of the column of hussars, who received him with deafening cheers. The bugles sounded, and forward sped Blucher at an impetuous gallop.

Suddenly some one shouted by his side: "General! general!" It was the pipe-master. Blucher, looking at him with eyes flashing with anger, said: "Begone! Ride to the rear!"

"God forbid!" said Hennemann, composedly; "here is my place; did not the general order me always to remain near him and hold a short pipe in readiness? Well, I am near, and the pipe is ready."

"I do not want it now, Christian; we are about to charge the enemy. To the rear, pipe-master!"

'I cannot think of it, general; no one is at liberty to desert his post, as you told me yourself," cried Hennemann. 'I am at my post, and will not allow myself to be driven from it. You will soon enough need me."

"Forward!" cried the general. And amid loud cheers the hussars rushed upon the enemy, Blucher fighting at their head, brandishing his sword with the utmost delight, forcing back the enemy, and wresting from him the advantages he had already gained. The French being driven back, Blucher suddenly commanded a halt.

"Boys!" he shouted, in a clarion voice, "this is a butchery to-day; let us stop a moment, take a drink, and fill our pipes.—Pipe-master, my pipe!"

"Did I not say that you would soon need me?" asked Hennemann, in a triumphant voice. "Here is your pipe, general!"

When the horses had taken breath, and the bold hussars a drink, and filled their pipes, the general's voice was again heard: "Forward in God's name!—we shall soon be done with the French!"

Toward dusk the battle was decided. In wild disorder fled the enemy, delayed by the softened soil, blinded by the rain, and obstructed by the Katzbach and the Neisse, with their roaring waters swelling every moment. In hot pursuit was the exultant victor, thundering with his cannon, and hurling death into the ranks of the fugitives. Field-pieces were planted on the banks of those streams, and when the French approached, they were greeted with fearful volleys. Turning in dismay, flashing swords and bayonets menaced them. Piles of dead were lying on the banks of the Katzbach; thousands of corpses were floating down the foaming waters, showing to Silesia the bloody trophies of battle, and that Blucher had at length taken revenge upon his adversary. At seven o'clock in the evening all was still. On all sides the French had fled.

Drawing his sword, he galloped with the courage and ardor of a youth at the head of the column
of hussars.

CHAPTER XXXVI.

BLUCHER AS A WRITER.

DARKNESS came, and the rain continued. The 'dear little angels in heaven," who, as Blucher said in the morning, wept for joy at the prospect of a fight, were now perhaps shedding tears of grief at the many thousands lying on the battle-field with gaping wounds, and whose last sighs were borne away on the stormy wind of the night.

Blucher rode across the field toward his head-quarters; no one was by his side but his friend, General Gneisenau, and, at some distance behind them, Christian Hennemann, holding a burning pipe in his mouth. Absorbed in deep reflections, they were riding along the dreadful road strewed with dead and wounded soldiers, and through pools of blood. Even Blucher felt exhausted after the day's work; his joy was suppressed by the incessant rain that had drenched his clothes, and by the groans of the dying, which rent his ears and filled his soul with compassion. But soon overcoming his sadness, he turned toward Gneisenau. "Well," he said, "this battle we have gained, and all the world will have to admit it; now let us think what we may put into our bulletin to tell the people **how we have gained it.** For ten years past Bonaparte has issued such high-sounding accounts of his victories that I always felt in my anger as though my heart were a bomb-shell ready to burst. Well, this time, let us also draw up such a bulletin of victory, and show that we have learned something. Let us proclaim that we have conquered, and draw up the document as soon as we arrive at Brech-telshof."

"General, you will have to decide the name of the battle," said Gneisenau. "How is it to be known in history?"

"Yes, that is true," said Blucher, thoughtfully, 'it must have a name. Well, propose one, Gneisenau!"

"We might call it the battle of Brechtelshof, because the headquarters of our brave chieftain, our Father Blucher, are at that place," said Gneisenau, in a mild tone.

"No, do not mix me up with the matter," said Blucher, hastily; "the good God has vouchsafed us a victory, let us humbly thank Him for it, and not grow overbearing.—Wait, I have it now! We shall call it, in honor of General von Sacken, the battle of the Katzbach; for, by Sacken's vigor-ous cannonade from Eichholz, on the Katzbach, and with the assistance of his brave cavalry, that drove the enemy into the river, we gained the vic-tory, and the battle ought to have that name. 'The battle of the Katzbach!'—Well, here are our quarters!"

"Now, general, you must rest," said Gneisenau, with the tenderness of a son. "You must change your dress, take food, and repose on your laurels, though there is but a straw mattress for you."

Blucher shook his head. "My clothes will dry quickest if I keep them on my body," he said, "and I must do so, for we have still a great many things to attend to; we must inform the king of our victory, take care of our wounded, arrange for the pursuit of the enemy; and, finally, write the bulletins of victory. We may take refresh-ment, but I do not care for laurels with it—laurels are bitter. But let us take a drink, and smoke a pipe.—Pipe-master!"

Fifteen minutes afterward, General Blucher en-tered with Gneisenau the small chamber called his headquarters; all the other rooms were filled with the wounded prior to the general's arrival at Brechtelshof. Pains had been taken to render this chamber as cosy and comfortable as possible, and, when Blucher entered, he was gratified in seeing a straw mattress near the wall, and on the table (beside a flickering tallow-candle placed in a bottle) a flask of wine, with a few glasses, and near it a large inkstand and several sheets of paper.

"Well," cried Blucher, cheerfully, "let us di-vide fraternally, Gneisenau; I will take the wine, and you the ink. But, first, I will give you a glass, and in return you will afterward let me have a drop of ink." Sitting down on one of the wooden stools, he quickly filled two glasses to the brim. "Gneisenau," he said, solemnly, "let us drink this in honor of those who are lying on the battle-field, and who have died like brave men! May God bid them welcome, and be a merciful Judge to them! **Let us drink also in commemoration of Queen Louisa and Scharnhorst, who** both doubtless looked down upon us from heaven to-day, and assisted us in achieving a victory. To them I am indebted for all I am. But for the angelic face of the queen the calamity of the accursed year 1807 would have driven me to despair and death; and but for Scharnhorst I should never have been appointed general-in-chief. Why, **they all considered me a bombastic old dotard of** big words and small deeds; but Scharnhorst **defended** me before the king and the emperor, and what I am now I am through him, because he, the noblest of men, believed in me. And I will not give the lie to his faith, I will still accomplish glorious things—to-day's work is only a be**ginning."**

"**But what you have done to-day is something glorious, your excellency,**" said Gneisenau. "**That we have gained the battle, thanks to your generalship and the enthusiasm of the troops, is** not the greatest advantage. A more **important** one is, that the Silesian army has been able to prove what it is, and what a chieftain is at its head. Now, all those will be silenced who constantly mistrusted and suspected us; who tried to sow the seeds of discord between the Silesian army and the headquarters of the allies; **and who** were intent on preventing your excellency from entering upon an independent **and** energetic course of action."

"It is true, they call me a mad hussar," said Blucher, shrugging his shoulders; "and Bonaparte, as I read somewhere the other day, calls me even a drunken hussar. Well, no matter! let them say what they please. **And, moreover, they** are all, to some extent, justified in making such assertions; for I cannot deny that the years of **waiting, during** which I was obliged to swallow **my grief, really made me a little mad, and with** sobriety I never intend to meet Bonaparte; **but,** for all that, it is unnecessary for me to be drunk with wine. I am still intoxicated with joy that we have at length been allowed to attack the French,

and God grant that I may never awaken from this **intoxication! Well, Gneisenau, now** let us go to **work!—you with the ink, and I with** the wine! **Draw up the necessary** instructions for the pursuit of the enemy, and, **in the** mean time, I will consider what I have to write."

Gneisenau took the pen, **and** wrote; Blucher the glass, and drank. Half an hour passed in silence; Gneisenau then laid down his pen, for he had finished the instructions; and Blucher pushed the glass aside, for the bottle was empty.

"I beg leave now to read the instructions to your excellency," said Gneisenau.

"No," said Blucher, "not now! I have myself gathered some thoughts, and if I defer writing them down, they will fly away like young swallows. Such ideas, that are to be written down, are not accustomed to have their nest in my head, and for this reason I will let them out immediately. I will write to the king and to the city of Breslau, informing him that we have gained the battle, and the city of Breslau that it ought to do something for my wounded. Give me the pen; I shall not be long about it." With extraordinary rapidity he wrote words of such a size that it would have been easy even for a short-sighted person to read them at a distance; and, although they were drawn across the paper very irregularly, the general always took pains to have broad intervals between the lines, that there might be no probability of leaving them illegible. A sheet **was soon** filled; Blucher fixed his signature, and contemplated the paper for a moment. Half an **hour** afterward two other sheets, filled with strange and uncouth characters, lay before the **old** general, and he cast the pen aside with a sigh. "It is abominable work to write letters," he said; "I cannot comprehend why you, Gneisenau, who are **so good a** soldier, at the same time know so well how to **wield** the pen. It is not my forte, although I **had a notion once to be a** *savant,* and really become a sort of writer. In those calamitous days, subsequent to 1807, despair and *ennui* sought for some relief to my mind, and made me write a book, and I believe a good one."

"A book?" asked Gneisenau, in amazement. "And you had it printed, your excellency?"

"Not I; I was no such fool as to do that. The critics and newspaper editors, who talk about every thing, and know nothing, would have pounced upon my book, and severely censured it. No, my dear Gneisenau, one must not cast pearls before swine. I keep my book in my desk, and show it only to those whom I particularly esteem. When we return home from the campaign I will let you read it; I know it will please you, and you will learn something. My work is called ' Observations on the Instruction and Tactics of Cavalry.' A splendid title, is it not? Well, you may believe me, there is a great deal in it, and many a one would be glad of having written it.* Let us say no more about it. Here are my two dispatches; there is the letter to the king, and here is my letter to the city of Breslau, and — you must do me a favor, Gneisenau. You must read what I have written, and if I have made any blunders in orthography or grammar, be so kind as to correct them."

"But, your excellency," said Gneisenau, "no one can express himself so vigorously as you, and no one knows how to put the right word in the right place as quickly as you do."

"Yes, as to the words, you are right. But the grammar! there's the rub. Men are so foolish as to refuse speaking as they please, but render life even more burdensome by all sorts of grammatical rules. I have never in my whole life paid any attention to them, but have spoken my mind freely and fearlessly. But as people really do consider him a blockhead who does not talk as they do, let us humor them, and please correct my mistakes; but, pray, do so in such a manner that it will not be found out." He handed Gneisenau the pen, and pushed the two letters toward him. "Correct what I have written," he said; "in the mean time I will read what you have written."

"And pray be so kind as to correct it, too, your

* Blucher was proud of this work, the only one he ever wrote, and always referred to it in terms of great satisfaction.—Vide Varnhagen von Ense, "Life of Prince Blucher of Wahlstatt," p. 589.

excellency," begged Gneisenau, "for possibly I may have made mistakes weighing heavier than mere infractions of grammatical rules, and I may not have succeeded in rendering your instructions in words as concise and distinct as you gave them to me."

"Well, we shall see," exclaimed Blucher, smiling, and taking up the paper.

"Very good," he said, after reading it through, "every thing is done just as I wished it, and if all our commanders act in accordance with these instructions, we shall give the enemy no time for taking a position anywhere, but completely disperse his forces without being compelled to fight another battle."

"And when the city of Breslau reads this noble and affecting plea for your wounded," **said Gneisenau,** "they will be nursed in the most careful manner, and our able-bodied soldiers will receive wagon-loads of food and refreshments. And when the king reads this dispatch, announcing our victory in language so modest and unassuming, his heart will feel satisfaction, and he will rejoice equally over the victory and the general to whom he is indebted for it."

"Have you corrected the grammatical blunders?"

"I have, your excellency; I have erased them so cautiously that no one can see that any thing has been corrected."

"Well, then, be so kind as to dispatch a courier."

"But, your excellency," said Gneisenau, "shall the courier take only these two dispatches? Have you forgotten that you promised Madame von Blucher to write to her after every battle, whether victorious or not, and that I solemnly pledged her my word to remind your excellency of it?"

"Well, it is unnecessary to remind me," cried Blucher, taking up the letter he had first written "Here is my letter to Amelia. She is a faithful wife, and I surely owed it to her to tell her first that the Lord has been kind and gracious enough toward me to let me gain the battle. But you need not correct it. My Amelia will not blame me for my grammatical blunders, and to her I freely speak my mind."

"Did you inform your wife, too, that you drew your sword yourself, and rushed into the thickest of the fray?"

"I shall take good care not to tell her any thing of the kind," exclaimed Blucher. "As far as that is concerned, I did not speak my mind to her. It is true I had promised my dear wife to be what she calls sensible, and only to command and play the distinguished general who merely looks on while others do the fighting. But it would not do—you must admit, Gneisenau, it would not do; I could not stand still like a scare-crow, while my old adjutant, Katzeler, was charging with the hussars; I had to go with them, if it cost my life. You will do me the favor, however, not to betray it to Amelia."

"Even though I should be silent, your excellency, your wife would hear of it."

"You believe Hennemann will tell her?" asked Blucher, almost in dismay. "Yes, it is true, she has ordered the pipe-master not to lose sight of me in battle, and always to remain near me with the pipe. Well, the fellow has kept his word; but he will now also fulfil what he promised my **wife,** and tell her every thing. Yes, the pipe-master will tell her that I was in the charge of the light cavalry."

"Yes," exclaimed Gneisenau, smiling, "he will betray to your wife and to history that Blucher fought and charged at the battle of the Katzbach like a young man of twenty. But for the pipe-master, history might not know it at all."

"Gneisenau, you are decidedly too sharp," cried Blucher, stroking his mustache. "Well, please forward the dispatches, and then let us try to sleep a little. We must invigorate ourselves, for we shall have plenty to do to-morrow. 'Forward, always forward!' until Bonaparte is hurled from his throne; and hurled from it he will be! Yes, as sure as there is a God in heaven!"

CHAPTER XXXVII.

THE REVOLT OF THE GENERALS.

On the morning of the 10th of October, Napoleon took leave of the King and Queen of Saxony, after delivering at Eilenburg, whither he had repaired with the royal family of Saxony, a solemn and enthusiastic address to the corps which his faithful ally, King Frederick Augustus, had added to his army, and which was to fight jointly with the French against his enemies. He then entered the carriage and rode to Duben, followed by his staff, the whole park of artillery, and all the equipages. Gloomy and taciturn, the emperor, on his arrival at the palace of Duben, retired into his apartments and spread out the maps, on which colored pins marked the various positions of the allies and his own army. "They are three to one against me," he murmured, bending over the maps and contemplating the pins. "Were none but determined and energetic generals, like Blucher, at their head, my defeat would be certain. They would then hem me in, bring on a decisive battle, and their overwhelming masses would crush me and my army. Fortunately, there is no real harmony among the allies; they will scatter their forces, post them here and there, and in the mean time I shall march to Berlin, take the city, repose there, and, with renewed strength, attack them one after another. Ah, I shall succeed in defeating them, I—"

There was a low knock at the door, and Constant, his valet de chambre, entered the room. "Sire," he said, "Marshal Marmont and the gentlemen of the staff are in the reception-room, and request your majesty graciously to grant them an audience."

An expression of surprise overspread the emperor's face, and for an instant he seemed to hesitate; but gently nodding he **said, calmly: "Open** the door. I grant **them the audience."**

Constant opened **the folding-doors, and in the** reception-room were seen the marshals and generals assembled. Their faces were pale and gloomy, and there was something solemn and constrained in their whole bearing. When Napoleon appeared on the threshold, the groups dispersed, and the gentlemen placed themselves in line, silent and noiseless, along the wall opposite the emperor, seemingly at a loss whether they or the emperor should utter the first word. Napoleon advanced a few steps. For the first time his generals, the companions of so many years and so many battles, seemed unable to bear the emperor's glance. Napoleon saw this, and a bitter smile flitted **over** his face. "Marmont," he exclaimed, **in** his ringing voice, "what do you all want? **Speak!**"

"**Sire,**" said the marshal, "we wish to take the liberty of addressing a question and a request to your majesty."

"First, the question, then!"

"Sire, we take the liberty of asking whether your majesty really intends to cross the Elbe with the army, **and** to resume the struggle on the right bank?"

"You ask very abruptly and bluntly," said Napoleon, haughtily. "I need not listen to you, but I will do so, nevertheless. I will reply to your question, not because I must, but because I choose to do so. Yes, gentlemen, I intend to transfer the whole army to the right bank of the Elbe in order to occupy Brandenburg and Berlin, then face about to the river, and make Magdeburg the support of my further operations.* This is my plan, and you, according to your duty, will assist me in carrying it into execution. I have replied to your question. Now let me hear your request."

"Sire," said Marmont, after a brief silence, "now that we have heard your gracious reply, I dare to give expression to our request, which is not only ours, but that of all the officers of the army of France. Sire, we implore you, give up this bold plan of operations; do not vainly shed the blood of thousands! The odds are too great, not only in numbers, but in warlike ardor. The enemy is struggling against us with the fanaticism of hatred, and his threefold superiority seems to secure victory to him. Our army, on

the contrary, is **exhausted and tired of war, and** the consciousness of being engaged in a struggle that apparently holds out no prospects of ultimate success, is paralyzing both its physical and moral strength. **Sire, we** implore you, **in** the name of France, make peace! Let **us return to** the Rhine! Let us at last rest from **this prolonged** war! Oh, sire, give us peace!"

"Oh, sire, give us peace!" echoed the generals, in solemn chorus.

The emperor's eyes were fixed in succession upon the faces of the bold men who dared thus to address him, and who, at this hour, confronted him in a sort of open revolt. An expression of anger flushed his face for an instant, and his features resumed their impenetrable, stony look. "You have come to hold a council of war with me," he said. "To be sure, I **have not summoned** you, but no matter. It is your unanimous opinion that we should return to the Rhine, and thence to France, avoid further battles, and make peace?"

"Sire, we pray your majesty this time to repress your military genius under the mantle **of** your imperial dignity," cried the marshal. "As soon as the general is silent, the emperor will perceive that his people and his **country need repose** and peace. France has given her wealth, her vigor, and her blood, for twenty years of victories, and she has joyfully done so; but now her wealth is exhausted, her strength and her youth are gone, for there are in France no more young men, only the aged, invalids, and children; the fighting-men lie on the battle-fields. Boys have been enrolled, and are forming the young army of your majesty. Sire, it is the last blood that France has to sacrifice: spare it! The enemy is thrice as strong as we are, and even the military genius of your majesty will be unable to achieve victories in so unequal a struggle. Listen, therefore, to reason, to necessity, and to our prayer; make peace. Sire, let us return to France!"

Another flush suffused Napoleon's face, but he controlled his anger. "You believe, then, that it depends on me only to make peace?" he asked, in a calm voice. "You think we would find no

---

* Beitzke, vol. II., p. 461.

obstacles in our way if we endeavored now to return to France?—that the enemy would leave the roads open to us, and be content with our evacuating Germany? This is a great mistake, gentlemen. I cannot make peace, for the allies would not accept it. They know their strength, and are intent on having war. You say their armies are thrice as strong as mine, and that is the reason why we could not conquer? I might reply to you **what the great Condé** replied to his generals, when he was about to attack the superior Spanish army, 'Great battles are gained with small armies.' And on the following day he gained the battle of Lens. Yes, gentlemen, the victor of Rocroy and Lens was right; great battles are gained with small armies; only we must make our dispositions correctly, and scatter the forces of our adversaries, instead of giving them an opportunity to concentrate upon **one point.** It is, **therefore, of vital importance for me to hold the line of the Elbe, for with it I possess all the strong points of Bohemia; and, besides, the for**tresses of Custrin, Stettin, and Glogau, are close to it. If I have to abandon that river, I abandon all Germany to the Rhine, with all the fortresses, and the vast *matériel* stored there. That would be to weaken us and strengthen the enemy, now on the left bank. I will, therefore, cross to the right bank of the Elbe, for thence I am able to deploy my whole army without hinderance, and **connect my line** with Davoust at Hamburg, and St. Cyr at Dresden. We shall easily take Berlin, raise the sieges of Glogau, Stettin, and Custrin, and become masters of the situation. Prussia, the hot-bed of this fermentation and revolution, will be subjugated and crushed. That will discourage the others, and they will fall back as they have so often, their plans will be disorgan**ized, and** then I shall have gained my cause; for the strength of the allies consists chiefly in the fact that they are temporarily in harmony. Let us disorganize their plans, foster their separate interests, and we gain every thing. When the Prussians see their country threatened, they will hasten to its assistance; the Russians, Swedes, and Austrians, will refuse to change and reor-

ganize their plans of operations for the sake of Prussia, and discord will prevent them from act ing. **If Germany had been united, and** acted **with one will, I could not** have taken from her a single village or fortress. Fortunately, however, the people do not act unanimously; wherever ten Germans are assembled, there are also ten separate interests at war among them, and this fact has delivered the country into my hands Let us, therefore, profit by this national peculiarity; let us stir up their separate interests, and that will be as advantageous as though we gained a battle. We shall, then, cross over to the right bank of the Elbe, make Berlin our centre, support our left on Dresden, our right on Magdeburg, and face toward the west. At all events, this will bring about an entire change of position, and it will then be my task to force my plans of oper ation upon the allies." *

"A task that would be easily accomplished by the genius of your majesty, which is so superior to that of all the generals of the allies," said the marshal; "but still this whole plan, how admirable soever it may be, is altogether too bold. If we pass over to the right bank of the Elbe, we would give up all connection with France; the allies, it would be believed, had, by skilful manœuvres, cut us off—hurled us into inevitable destruction. Moreover—your majesty will pardon me for this observation—we can no longer count upon the assistance of our German auxiliaries. They will abandon us at the very moment when we need them most. Even Bavaria is no longer a reliable ally, for, notwithstanding the benefits your majesty has conferred on her, she is about to ally herself with Austria. Sire, you said a few minutes ago that you counted upon the discord of the Germans, but this exists no more, or rather it exists only among the princes; but we have no longer to fight the latter alone—we have to struggle against the genius of Germany, which has risen against us, and for the first time the whole nation is united in hatred and wrath. Sire this national spirit is more powerful than all

---

* Beitze, vol. ii., p. 492.

princes and all armies, for it overcomes the princes, and makes new armies spring as if from the ground to defend the sacred soil of the fatherland. Those armies we shall be unable to conquer: for one-half of ours is composed of soldiers exhausted by continued wars, and longing for peace; and the other half of young, ignorant conscripts, who will yield to unwonted privations. Therefore, sire, I dare renew my prayer, and implore your majesty to give up your plan against Berlin! Let us not pass over to the right bank of the Elbe, but march toward the Rhine!"

"Is that your opinion, too, gentlemen?" asked Napoleon, turning toward the generals. "Do you, though I have condescended to explain to you at length my plan, and the motives that have caused me to adopt it, still persist in your belief that it would be better not to pass to the right bank of the Elbe, but to return to the Rhine?"

"Yes," cried the generals, unanimously, "we persist in our opinion."

Napoleon drew back a step, and a pallor overspread his face; but apparently he remained as cold and calm as ever. "My plan has been deeply calculated," he said, after a pause; "I have admitted into it, as a probable contingency, the defection of Bavaria. I am convinced that the plan of marching on Berlin is good. A retrograde movement, in the circumstances in which we are placed, is disastrous; and those who oppose my projects have undertaken a serious responsibility. However, I will think of it, and inform you of my final decision."* He saluted the generals with a careless nod and retired again into his cabinet.

The generals looked with anxious faces at one another when the door closed. "What shall we do now?" they inquired. "Wait, and not yield!" murmured the most resolute among them, and all agreed to do so.

With gloomy glances did Napoleon, after his return to his cabinet, look at the door that separated him from his mutinous generals. He felt

that now a new power had taken the field against him that might become more dangerous than all the others, and that was the revolt of his generals. He heard distinctly their last words. They had not said, "We persist in our opinion, and would like to return," but, "We must return to France." His generals, then, dared to have a will of their own, and opposed to that of their emperor. They knew it, and it did not deter them!

"Ah, the wretches," he murmured to himself, "they are blind! They will not see that we are hastening to destruction. They compel me to return as Alexander's generals compelled him to return! Woe to us! We are lost!" He sank down on the sofa; and now, when none could see him, the veil dropped from his face, the imperial mantle fell from his cowering form, and he was but a weak, grief-stricken man, who, with a pale and quivering face, was uncertain what to do. Hour after hour elapsed. He was still sitting in the corner of the sofa, rigid and motionless; only the sighs which heaved his breast from time to time, and the quiver of his eyelids, betrayed the life that was still animating him.

The court-marshal entered and announced dinner. The emperor waved his hand to him that he might withdraw, and his marshals and generals vainly awaited him. They looked at each other inquiringly and murmured, "He is reflecting! We can wait, but we cannot yield!"

At the stated hour in the afternoon, the two topographers of the emperor, Colonel Bacler d'Albe, and Colonel Duclay, entered the emperor's cabinet. As usual, they rolled the table, covered with maps and plans, before the emperor, and then took seats at the other table standing in the corner, which was also covered in like manner. They waited for the emperor, as was his habit, to speak and discuss his movements with them. But he was silent; he took up, however, a large sheet of white paper, and pen, and began to write. What did he write? The topographers were unable to see it; they sat pen in hand, and waited. But Napoleon was still silent. Hour after hour passed; not a sound of the triumphant, joyous, and proud life which used to surround

---

* Napoleon's words.—Vide Fain, "Manuscrit de 1813," vol. I.

14

the victorious emperor was to be heard in the dreary palace of Duben. The anterooms were deserted; the generals remained all day in the audience-room, and gazed with sullen faces upon the door of the imperial cabinet. But this door did not open. In the cabinet the emperor was still on his sofa, now leaning back in meditation, and now bending over the map-table, and writing slowly. Opposite him sat the two topographers, mournfully waiting for him to speak to them.* But Napoleon wrote, gazed into the air, sank back on the sofa, groaned, raised himself again, and wrote on.

This indifference and silence made a strange impression, which frightened even the generals, when the topographers, whom the emperor had at length dismissed with a quick wave of the hand, and an imperious "Go!" entered the audience-room, and told them of this extraordinary conduct. But Napoleon had written something, and it was all-important for them to know what. They wished to discover whether letters or plans had been penned by the emperor, and with what he had been occupied all day. "Let us speak with Constant," they whispered to each other. "He alone will enter the cabinet to-day. He has keen eyes, and will be able to see what the emperor has written." Constant consented to cast, at a favorable moment, a passing glance on the emperor's desk. The generals remained in the audience-room and waited.

An hour passed, when Constant, pale and sad, entered the room; he held a large, crumpled sheet of paper in his hand. "The emperor has retired," he whispered. "He called me, and when I entered the cabinet, he was still sitting on the sofa at the map-table, and engaged in writing. Suddenly he threw down the pen and seized the paper, crumpled it in his hand, and threw it on the floor. I picked it up, and may communicate it to you, for it contains no secrets." All the generals stretched out their hands. Constant handed the paper to Marshal Marmont. The sheet contained nothing but large capital letters, joined with fanciful flourishes. * The generals gazed at each other with bewildered eyes. Those capital letters, this work of a child, was the day's labor which the energetic emperor had performed! The letters, traced so carefully and elaborately, made an awful impression on the beholders—a whole history of secret despair, stifled tears of grief, and bitter imprecations, spoke from this crumpled sheet of paper. The generals turned pale, as if imminent danger was hovering over them—as if Fate had sent them its Runic letters, which they were unable to decipher. They left the room in silence, but murmured still, "We can wait, but we cannot yield."

Night had come. Silence settled on the mournful palace of Duben. The emperor lay on his field-bed, but he did not sleep; for Constant, who was in the cabinet adjoining the imperial bedchamber, heard him often sigh and utter words of anger and grief. In the middle of the night the valet heard a loud, piercing cry, and ran into the bedchamber. The emperor was in agony, writhing, and a prey to violent convulsions. He was ill with colic, which so often visited him, and the pallor of death overspread his face.

Constant hastened to bring the usual remedies, but he did not send for the doctor; for he knew that Napoleon did not like to have any importance attached to this illness. The pain at length yielded to the remedies applied. The emperor submitted to Constant's entreaties, and drank the soothing tea which he always took at these evil hours, and the efficacy of which in such cases had been discovered by the Empress Josephine. He put the teacup on the table, and looked very melancholy. Possibly he remembered how often Josephine's presence had comforted him during such hours—how her small hand had wiped the cold perspiration from his forehead—how his weary head had rested in her lap, and how her tender words had consoled and strengthened him. Possibly he remembered all this, for he murmured in a low voice, "Ah, Josephine, why are you not with me? You were my guardian angel! My

---

* Odeleben, "The Campaign in Saxony in 1813."

* Constant, "Mémoires," vol. v., p. 260.

star has set with you!" Then his head sank back on the pillow, and he closed his eyes. Perhaps his grief made him sleep.

Early on the following morning a carriage rolled into the court-yard, and Marshal Augereau requested an audience of the emperor, who had reëntered his map-cabinet.

"Augereau," said the emperor to his marshal, "you bring me bad news!"

"Only news, sire, which your majesty has already foreseen. It is the defection of Bavaria, and her accession to the alliance."

The emperor bent his head on his breast. "It must be so. All are deserting me. I must submit. Augereau," he said, aloud, "Bavaria has deserted me, but, what is still worse, my generals have done so, too. They will no longer follow me. They refuse to obey me; my plans seem too rash and dangerous. They do not wish to go to Berlin—they want peace! Do you understand, Augereau, peace at a moment when all are arming—when war is inevitable, and when it is all-important for me to extricate myself as advantageously as possible from the snare in which we shall be caught if the allies profit by their superiority, and draw together the net surrounding us."

"Sire, and I believe they have the will to do so," cried Augereau. "Nothing but the commanding military genius of your majesty is still able to conquer."

A painful smile quivered round the pale lips of the emperor. "Ah, Augereau," he said, "we are no longer the soldiers of Jena and Austerlitz. I have no longer any generals on whose obedience I may count. I shall give up my plan, I shall not pass over to the right bank of the Elbe, but, by taking this resolution, I renounce all victories and successes, and it only remains for me to succumb with honor, and to have opened as advantageous a passage as possible through Germany to France."

The marshals and generals were again assembled in the audience-room, and gazed in sullen expectation at the door of the imperial cabinet. Suddenly the emperor, pale and calm as usual, walked in, followed by Marshal Augereau. All eyes were fixed upon the emperor, whose lips were to proclaim the events of the future.

Advancing into the middle of the room, he raised his head, and sternly glanced along the line of generals. "Gentlemen," he said, in a loud voice, "I have changed my plan. We shall not pass over to the right bank of the Elbe, but turn toward Leipsic to-morrow. May those who have occasioned this movement never regret it!" *

A shout of joy burst forth when the emperor paused. The generals surrounded him, now that they had attained their object, to thank him for his magnanimity, and then they cheerfully looked at each other, shook hands, and exclaimed in voices trembling with emotion, "We shall again embrace our parents, our wives, our children, our friends!" †

"Ah, Augereau," said the emperor, mournfully, "you see I could not act otherwise; it was their will! But you, who are of my opinion that this retrograde movement is a calamity, will be able to testify in my favor if the future shows that **I am right. You will state that I was compelled to pursue a path which I knew would lead to destruction!**"

CHAPTER XXXVIII.

THE BATTLE OF LEIPSIC.

THE struggle had already been going on for two days. On the 15th and 16th of October the Austrians, Russians, Prussians, and Swedes, had fought a number of engagements with the French between Halle and Leipsic. The Austrians, or the army of Bohemia, commanded by Schwartzenberg, the general-in-chief, had been defeated by the French at Wachau on the 15th of October; but the Prussians and Russians, under Blucher, had gained a brilliant victory at Möckern on the 16th of October; and though the Swedes, under

* Napoleon's words.—Constant, vol. v., p. 269.
† Ibid.

Bernadotte, had not participated in the battle, and had, as usual, managed on that day to keep away from the carnage, they had at the same time contrived to participate in the glory of victory.

The French had not gained a single decisive battle during these two days, and yet Napoleon himself was at the head of his forces, directing their movements. Thousands of his soldiers lay on the blood-stained field of Wachau, and thousands more were mown down at Möckern. His army was melting away hour by hour, while that of his **enemies** constantly increased. Fresh reserves were moved up; the battle array of the allies grew more imposing and overwhelming, and the great, decisive battle was drawing nigh.

It was the evening of the second day, the 16th of October. Napoleon, who had his headquarters on the preceding day at Reudnitz, four miles **from Leipsic, removed them for the night into the open field, from which the city could be seen, and behind it the numerous fires of the allies gleamed through the gathering shades.** Beside the emperor's tent a large camp-fire was kindled, and near it, on a small field-stool, covered with red morocco, sat Napoleon, his gray overcoat closely buttoned up, his three-cornered hat drawn over his forehead, and his arms folded on his breast. His guards, who were encamping in the plain in wide circles around him, could distinctly see him, partially illuminated by **the camp-fire.** That bent, dark form was their only hope —**a hope** which did not look up to the stars shining above them, but which was satisfied with a mortal, who they believed could guide and protect them. And he indeed could save them from death by discontinuing the struggle, by accepting peace, though at the heaviest cost—at the sacrifice of all his possessions outside of France.

Two forms approached the camp-fire. It **was** only when they stood by the emperor's side, that e perceived them and looked up. He recognized the grave faces of Marshal Berthier and Count Daru.

"What do you want?" he asked, in a husky voice.

"Sire," said Berthier, solemnly, "we come, as envoys of all the superior officers of the army, to lay our humble requests before your majesty."

"Have you any thing to request?" asked Napoleon, sneeringly. "I thought I had fulfilled at Duben all the wishes of my generals; I gave up my plan against Berlin and the right bank of the Elbe, and marched to Leipsic, in order to take the direct road to France. Are my generals not yet satisfied?"

"Sire, who could suppose that on this road we would meet all the corps of the allies?" sighed the Prince of Neufchatel. "Even your majesty did not know it."

"I did not," replied Napoleon, "but my star forewarned me, and I conceived the plan of going to Berlin. You overcame my will; what do you still want?"

"Sire," said Berthier, almost timidly, "we want to implore your majesty to offer an armistice **and peace to** the allies. Our troops are dreadfully exhausted by these days of incessant fighting, and are, besides, discouraged by the continued victories of our enemies. **The** generals, too, are disheartened, the more so as we are unable to continue the struggle two days longer, because our ammunition begins to fail. We have recently used such a vast amount that scarcely enough remains for a single day. Sire, if we, however, continue to fight and are defeated, the road to France is open to our enemies, and your majesty cannot prevent the allies from marching directly upon Paris, for France has no soldiers to defend her when our army is routed. Let your majesty, therefore, have mercy on your country and your people; discontinue the war, and make proposals of peace!"

"Yes, sire," said Daru, "become anew the benefactor of your country, overcome your great heart for the welfare of your people and your army, whose last columns are assembled around you, and await life or death from your lips. The terrible, unforeseen **event has taken us by surprise;** we were not sufficiently prepared. We have no ambulances, no hospitals; all the elements of victory are wanting, for when the soldier knows that, after the battle, if he should be wounded **or** taken sick, he will find a good bed, careful treatment, and medical attendance, he **goes with** a feeling of some sort of security into battle; but we are destitute of these necessities. Your majesty knows full well that this is no fault of mine, but still it is so, and that we lack almost every thing. Your majesty, therefore, will be gracious enough to take a resolution which, it is true, is painful and deplorable, but under the circumstances indispensable."

Napoleon listened to the two gentlemen with calmness and attention. When Count Daru was silent, he fixed a sarcastic eye first on him, then on Berthier. "Have you any thing else to say?" he then asked. The two gentlemen bowed in silence.

"Well, then," said Napoleon, rising, and, with his arms folded, "I will reply to both of you. Berthier, you know that I do not attach to your opinion in such matters as much as a straw's value; you may, therefore, save yourself the trouble of speaking! As to you, Count Daru, it is your task to wield the pen, and not the sword; you are incapable of passing an opinion on this question. As to those who are of the same way of thinking, and whose envoys you are, tell them as my determined and final answer simply, 'They shall obey!'" *

He turned his back upon them and entered his tent. Constant and Roustan had taken pains to give it as comfortable and elegant an appearance as possible. A beautiful Turkish carpet covered the floor. On the table in the middle of the tent were placed the emperor's supper, consisting of some cold viands on silver plates and dishes. On another table was an inkstand, papers, books, and maps; and in a nook, formed by curtains and draperies, stood the emperor's field-bed. The sight of this snug little room, and the stillness surrounding him, seemed to do him good; the solitude allowed him to let the mask fall from his face, and to permit the melancholy and painful thoughts which filled his soul to reflect themselves in his features. With a sigh resembling a

---

groan he sank down on the easy-chair. "They want to crush me to earth," he murmured—"to transform the giant into a pigmy, because they are too much afraid of his strength. Their fear has at length made brave men of these allies, and they have resolved to put me on the bed of Procrustes, and to reduce me to the size of a common man, like themselves. Will it be necessary to submit to this? Must I allow them to cut off my limbs, to save my life?" He paused, and became absorbed deeper in his reflections.

Suddenly he was interrupted by approaching footsteps. The curtain of the tent was drawn back, and one of the emperor's adjutants appeared. "Sire," he said, "the Austrian General Meerfeldt, who was taken prisoner by your majesty's troops at Wachau, has just arrived under escort, and awaits your orders."

The emperor rose more quickly than usual. "Fate responds to my questions and doubts," he said to himself, hastily pacing his tent floor. "I endeavored to find an expedient, and a mediator appears between myself and my enemies. All is not yet lost, then, for Fate seems still to be my ally." He turned with a quick motion of his head toward the adjutant. "Admit General Meerfeldt. I will see him."

A few minutes afterward the Austrian general entered the tent. The emperor quickly met him, and gazed with a strange, triumphant look into the embarrassed face of the count. "I believe we are old acquaintances," said Napoleon, "for, if I am not mistaken, it was you who, in 1797, solicited the armistice of Leoben, and you participated, too, in the negotiations which terminated in the treaty of Campo-Formio."

"Yes, sire, you are right; I **had at** that time the good fortune to become acquainted with General Bonaparte," said Count Meerfeldt, with a deep bow; "he was just entering a career which has led him from victory to victory, and adorned his head with well-merited laurels."

"Yes, you were one of the signers of the treaty of Campo-Formio," exclaimed Napoleon. "But **that** was not all. Was it not you who wished to present me in the name of the emperor of

Austria, with some magnificent gifts? What was it you came to offer me then?"

"Sire," said the count, in confusion, "I had orders to repeat that which Count Cobenzl had already vainly proposed to General Bonaparte. I had orders to offer him, in the emperor's name, a principality in Germany, several millions in ready money, and a team of six white horses."

"I declined the principality in Germany because I thought that one ought either to inherit or conquer sovereignties, but never accept them as gifts, for he who accepts a gift always remains the moral vassal of the giver. I rejected the millions because I would not allow myself to be bribed; but I did accept the six horses, and with them made my entry into Germany and came to Rastadt."

"It was the first triumphal procession of your majesty in Germany, and, like Julius Cæsar, you could say, 'I came, saw, and conquered!'"

"Since then circumstances have greatly changed," said the emperor, thoughtfully; "General Bonaparte became the Emperor Napoleon, and the latter did what General Bonaparte refused to do: he accepted at the hands of the Emperor of Austria a gift more precious than principalities, for it was a beautiful young wife. Ah, general you are my prisoner, and I ought not to release you, but send you to Paris, that you might have the good fortune of kissing the hand of the Empress of France, the daughter of my enemy, and of seeing whether the little fair-haired King of Rome looks like his grandfather. But no, I will set you at liberty, I will make you my negotiator! You were one of those with whom I concluded, in the name of France, the first peace with Austria; I, therefore, commission you now to mediate my last peace; for I want to wage no more wars—I am tired of this unceasing bloodshed; I ask naught but to repose in peace, and dream of the happiness of France, after having dreamed of its glory. Go, repeat this to the emperor, your master; tell him that I desire no more conquests, but repose. Tell him that I long for nothing more ardently than peace, and that I am ready to conclude it, even before our swords have crossed."

"Sire," said Count Meerfeldt, hesitatingly, "if I repeat all this to the emperor, he will ask me what guaranties your majesty offers him, and what cessions of territory you propose to make."

"Cessions of territory!" exclaimed Napoleon. "Yes, that is it! You want to render me powerless; that is all you are fighting for; that is why the Russians and Swedes are in Germany; that is why the Germans accept subsidies at the hands of England!—all to attain a single object: to deprive me of my power, and narrow the boundaries of France. But do you think that the Russians, the Swedes, and the English, will require no indemnities for services rendered, and that they will very conveniently find them in the territories which you propose to wrest from me? What will Germany gain thereby? She will have rendered France, her natural ally, so powerless that she can never assist her, and, in return, she will have secured a footing in Germany to her three natural enemies, Russia—that is, barbarism; England—that is, foreign industry and commerce in colonial goods; Sweden—that is, navigation on the northern shores. But you will do all this rather than leave me in possession of my power, though I tell you that I wish to fight no more, but long for repose. Is it not so?"

"Sire," said Count Meerfeldt, in a low voice, "the allied sovereigns are, perhaps, familiar with the words of Cæsar, who said that laurels, if they were not to wither, should be often bathed in hostile blood, and fed every year with soil from new fields of victory. Your majesty being the modern Cæsar, the allies may be afraid lest you should adopt this maxim."

"Yes," cried Napoleon, "you are afraid of the very sleep of the lion; you fear that you will never be easy before having pared his nails and cut his mane. Well, then, after you have placed him in this predicament, what will be the consequence? Have the allied sovereigns reflected? You think only of repairing, by a single stroke, the calamities of twenty years; and, carried away by this idea, you never perceive the changes which time has made around you, and that for Austria to gain now, at the expense of France, is to lose. Tell your sovereign to take that into consideration,

Count Meerfeldt; it is neither Austria, nor France, nor Prussia, singly, that will be able to arrest on the Vistula the inundation of a half-nomadic people essentially conquering, and whose dominions extend to China. I comprehend, however, that in order to make peace, I must make sacrifices and I am ready to do so.* For the very purpose of stating this to the Emperor Francis, I set you at liberty, provided you give me your parole to serve no longer in this campaign against France."

"Sire, to fight against France has been so painful a duty that I joyfully give my word to serve no longer unless permitted to do so for France—that is to say, for your majesty."

"You may go, then, and lay my proposals before the Emperor Francis. You will tell him this: I offer to evacuate all fortresses in Germany to the Rhine, and consent to the dissolution of the Confederation of the Rhine. I am ready to restore Illyria and Spain to their former sovereigns. I further consent to the independence of Italy and Holland. If England refuses to grant peace on the seas, we will try to negotiate it, and Austria is to be the mediator."†

"Sire, these are such satisfactory promises," cried Count Meerfeldt, "that I am afraid my mere word will be insufficient to convince my master that you really intend to grant so much."

"I will give you a letter to the Emperor Francis, in which I shall make these proposals," said Napoleon, quickly. "Yes, I will write once more to the emperor. Our political alliance is broken, but between your master and me there is another bond, which is indissoluble. That is what I invoke, for I always place confidence in the regard of my father-in-law."

He went to his desk, and penned a few lines with a hasty hand, folded, sealed, and directed the letter. "Here," he said, approaching the count, "is my letter to my father-in-law. You will immediately repair to him, and deliver it into his hands. The emperor will communicate it to the other sovereigns, and they will take their resolutions accordingly. **Tell him that** I shall not attack to-morrow, but discontinue further hostilities until I have received his answer; and that I shall certainly expect him to return an answer by to-morrow. Adieu, general! When on my behalf you speak to the two emperors of an armistice, I doubt not the voice which strikes their ears will be eloquent indeed in recollections." *

"It is my last effort," murmured the emperor to himself, when Count Meerfeldt had left; "if it fail, nothing but a struggle of life and death remains to me, and, by Heaven, I will certainly fight it out! The crisis is at hand, and I cannot evade it. I will meet it with my eyes open. The laurels of Marengo and Austerlitz are not yet withered. To-morrow there will be a **cessation** of hostilities, and on the day after to-morrow peace, or war to the last!"

On the 17th of October no hostilities took place. Napoleon awaited the reply of his father-in-law. But it did not come; it was deemed unnecessary to observe the forms of courtesy toward him before whom, only a year ago, they had prostrated themselves so often in the dust.

The battle recommenced on the 18th of October. The booming of a thousand cannon was the answer of the allies. Napoleon, with only three hundred cannon, replied that he understood this answer to his peace propositions. Upward of three hundred thousand soldiers of the allies filled the plains around Leipsic. Napoleon had scarcely one hundred and twenty thousand to oppose to them, and his men were exhausted and discouraged. But he appeared on this day along the whole line, encouraging his troops by his cheerful countenance and his brief addresses. He seemed to infuse fresh courage and enthusiasm into the hearts of the French. They arose with the heroism of former days, and plunged into the thickest of the fight; the earth trembled beneath the thunder of cannon, the cheers of the victors, and the imprecations of the vanquished. The French did not yield an inch; they stood like a wall,

---

* Napoleon's words.—Fain, "Manuscrit de 1813," vol. ., pp. 412, 414.

† Ibid.

---

* Napoleon's words.—Vide Beitzke, vol. ii., p. 562.

broken here and there, but the gaps filled up again in a moment, and those who had taken the places of the fallen exhibited the **same devoted** heroism, for Napoleon was there.

And Blucher was also there. He halted opposite the enemy with his Silesian army (one-half of which he had placed under the crown prince of Sweden), composed of Russians and Prussians. Blucher, too, fired the hearts of his men by energetic words, and they fought with matchless bravery, for they fought before the eyes of their general. He shared with them every fatigue and **danger; he drank with** them, when he was **thirsty, from** one bottle; lighted his pipe from their pipes, and spoke to them, not in the condescending tone of a master, but in their own unreserved and cordial manner. Rushing onward with shouts of victory, they attacked the enemy with irresistible impetuosity, forcing the French **to fall back, step by step.**

"**Every thing is going on right, Gneisenau!**" exclaimed Blucher. "**Bonaparte cannot hold out; he must at length retreat. He is contracting the** circle of his troops **more and** more, and advancing toward Leipsic. Ah, I understand, M. Bonaparte; you want to march through Leipsic and keep open the passage across the Saale! But it won't do—it won't do! For Blucher is here, and his eyes are yet good.—A courier! Come here! Ride to General York! He is to set out this **very night** and occupy the banks of the Saale, and impede **as much** as possible the retreat of the enemy, **who** intends to fall back across the Saale.—Another courier! Ride to General Langeron! He is to return to-night to the right bank of the Partha, support General Sacken, and, as soon as the enemy begins to retreat, pursue him with the utmost energy."

"But, general," said Gneisenau, when the courier galloped off, "as yet Napoleon does not seem to think of retreating. He maintains his position and offers a bold front."

"He will not do so to-morrow," said Blucher, laconically. "If we do to-day what we can, he is annihilated. God grant that our victory may be followed up, and that they may not grow soft-

hearted again at headquarters! The Emperor of Austria never forgets that Bonaparte is his son-in-law; **nor the crown** prince of Sweden that he **is a native of France, and** he would like to spare his countrymen further bloodshed; nor the Emperor of Russia, that at Erfurt he plighted eternal fidelity to Napoleon, and kissed him as his brother. But our king, I believe, will always remember that Bonaparte humiliated and oppressed us, and that Queen Louisa died of grief and despair. He will not suffer the others to make peace too early, and cause us to shed our blood and spend our strength for nothing. We must be indemnified, and it is by no means enough for us merely to gain a victory over Bonaparte. He must surrender all that he has taken from us. Germany must have satisfaction, and I must have mine, too; for the anger I have felt for years has almost killed me. I want to be even with him, and shall not rest before he is hurled from his throne.—What is going on there? Why are they cheering yonder? Look, Gneisenau, one of the enemy's columns is advancing upon us. Do you hear the music? What does it mean?"

"It means, general," shouted an orderly, who galloped up, "that the Saxons are coming over to us. With thirty-two field-pieces, and drums beating, they have left the lines of the French, and, when these tried to prevent them, they turned their bayonets against their former comrades."

Blucher's eye lit up. "Well," he said, "now they will no longer extol Bonaparte's extraordinary luck. To-day at least he has none. The Saxons have felt at last that they are Germans, and wish to purge themselves of their disgrace. I say, Gneisenau, Bonaparte must retreat to-morrow." And what Blucher said here to Gneisenau was what Berthier said to Napoleon: "The battle is lost! We must retreat."

Night came. It is true, the French remained on the field; they did not flee, but they had no strength to continue the battle; their ammunition was exhausted, for they had discharged on this day an incredible amount of cannon-shot. Napoleon felt that he had certainly to retreat, and submit to what was inevitable. At the camp-fire, near the turf-mill, sat the emperor; his generals surrounded him, and listened in silence to his words, falling from his lips slowly and sadly. He ordered dispositions to be made for a retreat, and Berthier repeated the orders to his two adjutants, who were kneeling on the other side of the camp-fire, and writing them down. Suddenly, in the middle of a sentence, Napoleon paused, and his head dropped on his breast. The emperor had fallen asleep!

His generals, respecting this respite from sorrow and misfortune, preserved silence. The fire shed a blood-red lustre over the group; at times the flames flickered up higher, and illuminated the form of the emperor, who, with his head on his breast, his arms hanging down on both sides of the camp-stool, his body gently moving to and fro, was still wrapped in slumber. At times, when the fire blazed up, and shed a flood of light on the plain, shadows were seen emerging from the gloom, and a long line moved past. It was a portion of the imperial army already retreating toward Leipsic.

A quarter of an hour had thus elapsed when Napoleon gave a slight start, and, raising his head, cast a long look of astonishment on the persons surrounding him. His sleep had made him for an instant forget his troubles, but the sombre glances of his generals and the noise of the troops filing by, reminded him of what had happened. His eye resumed its calm expression, and, in a firm, sonorous voice he recommenced giving his orders. Suddenly a whizzing sound was in the air above him—a grenade fell to the ground close to the emperor, burrowed into the earth, and scattered the camp-fire.

"It is a cold night," said the emperor, composedly; "make up the fire again, and add fresh fuel!"

The adjutants ran to collect the firebrands, and the generals themselves hastened to pile on the fuel. But another whizzing sound rent the air, and another grenade fell into the fire, which had just blazed up again; it almost extinguished the flames, and remained in the midst of the coals.

Napoleon gazed musingly on the ball, and strange thoughts probably filled his soul at the sight of this messenger at his feet.* "It is enough," he said calmly; "no more fire may be kindled! My horse! To Leipsic! I will spend the night there." The horses were brought; attended by Berthier, Caulaincourt, and a few orderlies, the emperor rode to Leipsic, and took up his quarters at the Hotel de Prusse.

CHAPTER XXXIX.

THE NINETEENTH OF OCTOBER.

It was eight o'clock on the following morning. A dense fog covered Leipsic as with an impenetrable veil, and extended far over the landscape. No one could see as yet, in the darkness of the night, what had been done by friend or foe. At times the allies heard loud explosions, and saw flashes on the side of the French; then all was dark and silent again. Suddenly, however, a bright glare illuminated the night, for in the French camp large fires blazed, and, like a flaming serpent, stretched out far into the plain.

"Ha!" said Blucher; "Gneisenau, I was right after all: Bonaparte is retreating. Do you know the meaning of those fires? The French have placed their caissons on both sides of the road, and set them on fire, that they may serve as beacons to the retreating troops. See! they reach up to the city of Leipsic. It is as I said; the French intend to march through that city, and retreat across the Saale. Well, I think General York will await them there, and Langeron will finish them. But come, Gneisenau, the fog is clearing. Let us ride to yonder knoll; we shall be able to see better there."

With the nimbleness of a lad Blucher mounted his horse, and, no longer restraining his impatience, he galloped off. Gneisenau rode by his side, and at some distance behind him trotted the

---

* Beitzke, vol. ii., p. 615.

pipe-master, with the iron box on the pommel of his saddle.

They reached the crest of the knoll and stopped. The fog had disappeared, and they could distinctly see a field of horror and desolation as far as their eyes reached. The immense plain was covered far and wide with piles of corpses; rivulets of blood intersected the down-trodden soil; fragments of wagons, cannon, and vast heaps of horses, **lay in wild disorder, and all** around the horizon **gleamed the dying fires of upward of** twenty **villages.**

Blucher cast a mournful look on this harrow-ing spectacle. "Gneisenau," he said, "it is almost impossible for one to rejoice over this victory, for it costs too many tears—too much blood. How those poor brave men are lying there, dead or dying, and have not even a grave at which their mothers and wives may weep! May the **good God in heaven have mercy on their souls, and comfort those who are weeping for them!"** He took off his cap, and, shading his face with it, uttered a short, low prayer for the repose of the dead. With a quick jerk he then put on his cap again. "Well," he said, "we have prayed, and we will now try to find that accursed Bonaparte, who is at the bottom of all this carnage, and—"

At this moment the pipe-master galloped up to **his general.**

"Well, what do you want, Christian?"

"The morning pipe," said Christian, presenting the short pipe to his master.

Blucher stretched out his hand for it, but drew it back and cast a glance on the piles of dead which covered the battle field. "No, pipe-master," he said, solemnly, "it would be unbecoming to smoke here. We should show our respect for the dead; but hold the pipe in readiness for me, and when we ride back I will take it. **Now, get** out of my way, that I may no longer see the pipe, else— Begone, Christian!"

"No, I shall stay," said the pipe-master, coolly; "I have promised the general's wife always to stay near him, and, besides, you will soon need me, for you will not stand it long without your **pipe.** Call me, your excellency, when you want me." He moved his horse a few steps back, and was busily occupied in keeping the general's pipe lit.

Blucher and Gneisenau in the mean time were keenly looking to the side of the French camp; but not a vestige of it was to be seen. There could be no doubt now that Napoleon had commenced retreating; he had profited by the night to remove the remnants of his army toward Leipsic, that they might still be able to cross the Saale without hinderance. Blucher uttered a loud cry of joy. "He is retreating! Gneisenau, am I right now?"

"Yes, general, you are. With your sagacity you have divined Napoleon's plans better than the rest of us, and, thanks to your wise dispositions, he will find Langeron and Sacken at the gates of Leipsic, and York on the banks of the Saale."

"My dear sir, he will find us, too," exclaimed Blucher, in great glee. "We are not through yet; I know Napoleon thoroughly. You think, perhaps, that he has merely rested at Leipsic, and will evacuate the city without fighting? No, sir, then you do not know much about him. He will not yield an inch unless he must. By a battle in and around Leipsic, he intends to cover the retreat of his army, and I tell you, Gneisenau, we shall have hard work yet. Forward!"

"Yes, forward!" cried Gneisenau. "We must dispatch couriers to all the generals, and send them the glad tidings."

"Now comes the last assault," shouted Blucher. "We must take the city by storm; and this will blow Bonaparte over the Rhine, and back to France, like a bundle of rags! Forward! Pipe-master, my pipe! We will attack them!"

At ten in the morning the cannon commenced booming again around Leipsic. The city was attacked on all sides by the armies of the allies. In the south stood the commander-in-chief, Prince Schwartzenberg, with the Austrian army; in the east, the Russian General Benningsen and the crown prince of Sweden; in the north, Blucher, with the Prussians, and the Russian corps under General Sacken.

"Charge!" shouted Blucher to his troops. "General Bulow has attacked the Halle gate; we **must** hasten to his assistance, for the French are stubborn."

At this moment another volley of grape-shot was discharged from the pieces which the French had placed inside the city, and hurled death and destruction into the ranks of the assailants.

"We must reënforce Bulow," cried Blucher! "General Sacken must advance his troops! We must hurl **light** infantry against the gate! Charge! Forward!" **And,** brandishing his sword, Blucher **galloped to the side** of General Sacken, who was moving with the Russians toward the point of attack.

"Forward!" thundered Blucher to the troops. The Russians did not understand him, but they saw his countenance radiant with impatience and warlike ardor, his flashing eyes, and uplifted hand pointing the sword at the gate, and they understood his meaning.

"*Perod!*" shouted the Russians, exultingly. "Forward! *Perod!*"

The grape-shot of the enemy, and the rattling fire of the French skirmishers behind the walls, drowned their shouts. But when the artillery ceased and the smoke disappeared, they saw again the face of the old general with his young eyes, and the long white mustache. He halted on his horse in the midst of the shower of bullets fired by the skirmishers, and uttered again and again his favorite command.

"Marshal *Perod!*" shouted the Russians. "He is a little Suwarrow! Long live little Suwarrow! Long live Marshal Forward!" and, amid renewed battle-cries in honor of Blucher, and with resistless impetuosity, the Russians assaulted the gate.

While these scenes were passing outside the city, Napoleon remained within. He had sat up till daylight with Caulaincourt and Berthier, receiving reports and issuing orders; toward morning he had slept a little, and now, at ten o'clock, he dictated his last orders to the two generals. In the streets were heard the roar of artillery, the crashing of falling buildings, the wails, shrieks, and shouts of the terrified inhabitants. The **field-pieces** rattled past, regiments trotted along, and disappeared around the corners, constituting a scene of indescribable terror and destruction; but here, in the emperor's room, every thing presented a spectacle of peace and repose. Caulaincourt and Berthier sat at their desks, writing. The emperor was slowly walking up and down. He did not even listen to the noise outside; he dictated his orders in a calm, firm voice, and his face was as immovable as usual.

"Marshal Macdonald," said the emperor, concluding his instructions, "is commissioned to defend the city and the suburbs; for this purpose he will have his own corps, and those of Lauriston, Poniatowsky, and Reynier. He will **hold** the city until the corps of Marmont and Ney have evacuated it, and the rear-guard safely withdrawn. As soon as these troops have crossed the Pleisse, the bridge will be blown up." He nodded to his generals, and, striding across the room, opened the door of the antechamber. "To horse, gentlemen!" he shouted to the generals assembled there. "We must start for Erfurt!" He slowly descended the staircase and mounted his horse, the generals and adjutants following him **in** silence.

But the emperor did not turn his horse toward the side where the troops were marching along in heavy columns; he rode to the market-place, and halted in front of a large, old-fashioned house in the middle of the square. The King of Saxony and his consort lived there. "Wait!" said the emperor to his suite, alighting from his horse, and walking past the saluting sentinels into the house.

In the small sitting-room up-stairs were old King Frederick Augustus, his consort, and the Princess Augusta. The king sat with his hands folded on his knees, and his lustreless eye fixed on the windows, trembling incessantly from the roar of artillery and the rattle of musketry. The queen was near him, and whenever the volleys resounded, she groaned, and covered her face with her handkerchief, which was already moist with tears. The Princess Augusta knelt in a corner of the room, praying, while tears were rolling down her cheeks.

"Oh," murmured the queen when another rattle of musketry rent the air, "why does not a bullet strike my heart!"

"Father in heaven, and all saints, have mercy on us!" prayed the princess.

"Grant victory to the great and noble Emperor Napoleon, my God!" sighed the king. "I love him as a father, and he has always treated me with the love of a son. I have remained faithful to him when all the others betrayed him. Punish not my constancy, therefore, my Lord and God; grant victory to Napoleon, that happiness may be restored to me!"

A cry burst from the lips of the queen, and she started up from her seat. "The emperor!" she cried, looking toward the door.

Yes, in the open door that form in the gray, buttoned-up overcoat, with the small hat, and pale, stony face, was the Emperor Napoleon's. "I come to bid you farewell," he said, stepping slowly and calmly to the king.

"Farewell!" groaned Frederick Augustus, sinking back. "All is lost, then!"

"No, not all, sire," said Napoleon, solemnly. "We have lost a battle, but not our honor. The fortune of battles is fickle. After twenty years of victory, it has this time declared against me. But honor remains to me. I have, for four days, held out against an army three times as large as mine in troops, as well as in artillery, and they have not overpowered me. I have voluntarily evacuated the battle-field, not in a wild flight as did the Prussians at Jena, and the Austrians at Austerlitz. Our honor is intact. With that we must content ourselves this time."

"Oh, sire," cried the king, with tearful eyes, "how generous you are! You speak of *our* honor! But *I* have lost my honor, for my troops have committed treason—they deserted my noble, beloved ally during the battle! Oh, sire, pardon me! I am innocent of the defection of my troops!" And, rising, the king made a movement as if to kneel; but Napoleon held him in his arms, and then gently pressed him back into the easy-chair. "Sire," he said, "treason is a disease which, by this time, has become an epidemic in Germany. All those who are now fighting against me are traitors, for all of them were my allies, and, while still negotiating with me, they had already formed a league against me. Your Saxons were infected by the troops from Bavaria, Wurtemberg, and Baden."

"Alas," sighed the king, "I had a better opinion of my Saxons! They have turned traitors, and my heart will always remain inconsolable."

"But this is no time for giving way to grief," said Napoleon. "Your majesty must leave Leipsic immediately. You must not expose yourself to the dangers of a capitulation, which, unfortunately, has become unavoidable. Come, sire, intrust yourself to my protection. By my side, and in the midst of my troops, you will be safe."

"No," said the king, resolutely; "I remain! Let them kill me; I am tired of the dangers of flight! But you, sire, you must make haste! Leave us!—your precious life must not be endangered! Every minute renders the peril more imminent! Hasten to preserve yourself to your people, your consort, and your son!"

"My son!" said Napoleon, and for the first time something like an expression of pain flashed over his features. "Poor little King of Rome, from whose blond ringlets his own grandfather wants to tear the crown!" He dropped his head on his breast.

"Sire, make haste!" implored the king.— "Make haste!" echoed the queen and the princess.

At this moment there was a terrific roar of artillery. The queen buried her face in her hands; the princess had knelt again and prayed; the king leaned his head against the back of the chair, pale as a corpse, and with his eyes closed. Napoleon alone stood erect; his face was calm and inscrutable; his glances were turned toward the windows, and he seemed to listen eagerly to the thunders of war.

The door was violently opened, and General Caulaincourt appeared, pale and breathless.

"Sire," he said, "you must leave! Bernadotte has taken one of the suburbs by assault, and the forces of Blucher, Benningsen, and Schwartzenberg, are pouring in on all sides into the city, so that our troops are compelled to defend themselves from house to house."

"Sire, have mercy!—save yourself!" cried the king. "I can no longer help you, no longer support you! I have nothing left to give you—nothing but my life, and that is of no value! Save yourself, unless you want me to die at your feet!"

"Sire," exclaimed Caulaincourt, "every minute increases the danger. A quarter of an hour hence your majesty may, perhaps, be unable to get out of the captured city."

Napoleon turned with a haughty movement toward his general. "Nonsense," he said, "have I not a sword at my side? But, as you wish me to go, sire—as you are alarmed, I will leave! Farewell! May we meet in happier circumstances!"

"Sire, up there!" said the king, solemnly, pointing toward heaven. He then quickly rose from his seat, and approaching Napoleon, who had taken leave of the queen and the princess, took his arm and conducted him hastily out of the room, through the corridor, and down the staircase. At the foot he stood, and clasping the emperor in his arms, whispered, "Farewell, sire; I feel it is forever! I shall await you in heaven! Not another word now, sire! Make haste!" He turned, and slowly reascended the staircase. The emperor mounted his horse, and directed his course toward the gate of Ranstadt. Behind him rode Berthier, Caulaincourt, and a few generals; a mounted escort followed them.

The streets presented a spectacle of desolation and horror, which, the closer they approached the gate, became more heart-rending. Field-pieces, caissons, soldiers on foot and on horseback, screaming women, wounded and dying cows, sheep, and swine, entangled in an enormous mass, made it impossible to pass that way. Napoleon turned his horse, and took the road to St. Peter's gate. Slowly, and with perfect composure, he rode through Cloister and Burg Streets. Not a muscle of his face betrayed any uneasiness or embarrassment; it was grave and inscrutable as usual.

When he arrived at the inner St. Peter's gate, he found the crowd and confusion to be nearly as great as at that of Ranstadt; he did not turn his horse, but said, in a loud voice, "Clear a passage!" The generals and the mounted escort immediately rode forward, and, unsheathing their swords and spurring their horses, galloped into the midst of the crowd, driving back those who could flee, trampling under foot those who did not fall back quick enough, and removing the obstacles which obstructed their passage. In five minutes a way was cleared for the emperor—the wounded lying on both sides, and a few corpses in the middle of the street, showed how violently the cortege had penetrated the obstructing mass. The emperor took no notice of this; he was silent and indifferent, while his escort attacked the crowd, and rode on as if nothing had occurred.

At length the city lay behind him; he had passed the bridge across the Elster, and reached the mill of Lindenau, where he intended to establish his headquarters. Constant and Roustan had already reached the place with the emperor's carriages, and prepared a room for him. Napoleon rapidly stepped into it, and, greeting Constant with a nod, he said, "Only a little patience! In a week we shall be in Paris, and there you shall all have plenty of repose! We shall leave our beautiful France no more! Ah, how the Empress will rejoice, and how charming it will be for me again to embrace the little King of Rome!"

It was touching and mournful, indeed, to hear this man, usually so cold and reserved, this general who had just lost a great battle, speak of his return home and his child in so gentle and affectionate a tone, and to see how his rigid features became animated under the charm of his recollections, and how the faint glimmer of a mournful smile stole upon his lips. But it soon disappeared, and, with a sigh, the emperor drooped his head.

"Your majesty ought to try to sleep a little," said Constant, in an imploring voice.

"Yes, sleep!" exclaimed Napoleon. "To sleep is to forget!"

It was the first, the only complaint which he allowed to escape his lips, and he seemed to regret it, for, while he threw himself on the field-bed, he cast a gloomy glance on Constant, and, as if to prove how easy it was for him to forget, he fell asleep in a few minutes.

From the neighboring city resounded the artillery, indicating the final struggle of the French and the allies. The emperor's slumber was not disturbed, for the roar of battle was too familiar to him. Suddenly, however, there was a terrific explosion that shook the earth; the windows of the room were shattered to pieces, and the bed on which the emperor was reposing was pushed from the wall as if raised by invisible arms. He sprang to his feet and glanced wonderingly around. "What was that?" he inquired. "It was no discharge of artillery, it was an explosion!" He quickly left the mill and stepped out of the front door. There stood the generals, and looked in evident anxiety toward Leipsic. Here and there bright flames were bursting from the roofs of the houses; one-half of the city was wrapped in clouds of smoke, so that it was impossible to distinguish any thing.

"An explosion has taken place there," said Napoleon, pointing to that side.

At this moment several horsemen galloped rapidly toward the mill; they were headed by the King of Naples in his uniform, decked with glittering orders. A few paces from the emperor he stopped his horse and alighted.

"Murat," shouted the emperor to him, "what has happened?"

"Sire," he said, "a terrible calamity has occurred. The bridge across the Elster, the only remaining passage over the river, has been blown up!"

"And our troops?" cried the emperor.

"Sire, the rear-guard, twenty thousand strong, are still on the opposite bank, and unable to escape."

The emperor uttered a cry, half of pain, half of anger. "Ah," he exclaimed, "this, then, is the way in which my orders are carried out! My God! twenty thousand brave men are lost—hopelessly lost!" He struck both his hands against his temples.

No one dared disturb him; his generals surrounded him, silent and gloomy. Presently, some horsemen galloped up; at their head was a general, hatless and in a dripping uniform.

"Sire, there comes Marshal Macdonald," exclaimed Murat.

Napoleon hastened forward to meet the marshal, who had just jumped from his horse.

"You come out of the water, marshal?" inquired Napoleon, pointing to his wet uniform.

"Yes, sire. By swimming my horse across, I have escaped to this side of the river, and I come to inform your majesty that the troops intrusted to me have perished through no fault of mine. Sire, they were twenty thousand strong, and I come back alone. I come to lay my life at the feet of your majesty."

"God be praised that you at least have been preserved," said the emperor, offering his hand to Macdonald. "But you say the troops have perished? Is, then, that impossible for the soldiers which was possible for you? Cannot they swim across to this side of the river?"

"Sire, my escape was almost miraculous. I owe it to my horse, who carried me across in the agony of despair; I owe it to God, who, perhaps, wished to preserve a faithful and devoted servant to your majesty. But, by my side, no less faithful servants were carried away, and, standing on the other bank, I saw their corpses drifting along."

"Who were they?" asked Napoleon, abruptly, and almost in a harsh tone.

"Sire, General Dumoustier was one; but he is not the victim most to be lamented of this disastrous day."

"Who is it?" exclaimed the emperor, and, casting around a hasty, anxious glance, he seemed to count his attendants to see who was missing.

"Sire," said Macdonald, in a trembling voice, 'Prince Joseph Poniatowsky plunged with his horse into the river—"

"And he perished?" cried Napoleon.

"Yes, sire, he did not reach the opposite bank!"

The emperor buried his face in his hands, and groaned. He sat for some time motionless. At length he removed his hands from his face, which looked like marble, bloodless and cold.

"And my soldiers?" he inquired. "Did they endeavor to escape as Poniatowsky?"

"Yes, sire! Thousands threw themselves into the river, but only a few succeeded in escaping, while the others fell into the deep and muddy channel; and those who were on the opposite bank were made prisoners by the allies, who are now in possession of the city."

"Twenty thousand men lost!" sighed Napoleon, and he relapsed into gloomy thought. Presently he raised his head again and cast a flaming glance on Macdonald.

"Marshal," he said, "you will investigate this affair in the most rigorous manner; you will give me the name of him who has dared to disobey my orders. He is the murderer of twenty thousand men! He deserves death, and I shall have no mercy on him!"

"Sire, he stands already before his Supreme Judge! It was the corporal charged with applying the match as soon as our troops had all passed. He thought he saw the enemy advancing upon the bridge, and fired the train, throwing himself into the Elster. He is drowned!"

"It is good for him," said Napoleon. "God will deal more leniently with him than I should have done. To horse, gentlemen, to horse!" He walked slowly and with bowed head to his horse, and murmured, "Another Beresina! It costs me twenty thousand soldiers!"

The generals followed him, and as they saw him walking with bowed head, they whispered to one another, "Look at him now, how he is broken down! That was his very appearance when he returned from Russia! He has no strength to bear up under misfortunes!"

While the emperor and his **suite** slowly and mournfully took the road to Mark Ranstadt, the allies made their entrance into Leipsic. At the head of the procession rode the Emperor of Russia and the King of Prussia; behind them followed their brilliant staff, and then came the victorious troops, with colors flying and drums beating. The cannon still thundered, but louder were the cheers and exultant acclamations of the people, who crowded the streets by thousands, to receive the sovereigns and the victorious army. The windows of the houses were opened, and at them stood their inmates with joyful faces, holding white handkerchiefs in their hands, with which they waved their greetings. The friends—the long-yearned-for friends were there, and they received them with tears, exultation, and thanksgiving. Merry chimes rang from every steeple, and proclaimed the resurrection **of Germany.** The sovereigns rode to the great square; they halted in front of the very house of the King of Saxony, but they turned no glance upward to the windows, behind the closed blinds of which the unfortunate royal family were assembled. The victors seemed to have forgotten them.

The two monarchs alighted, for now came from the other side the crown prince of Sweden, Bernadotte, at the head of his guards, and through the other street approached the commander-in-chief of the allies, Prince Schwartzenberg. The Russian emperor and the Prussian king advanced into the middle of the square, and Bernadotte and Schwartzenberg arrived there simultaneously with them. Suddenly, deafening cheers rent the air; they drew nearer, and amid these acclamations Blucher, at the head of his staff, rode up. When he perceived the monarchs, he stopped his horse and vaulted with youthful agility from the saddle in order to meet them; but the Emperor Alexander, anticipating him, was by his side. "God bless you, heroic Blucher!" he exclaimed, affectionately embracing him. "You have fulfilled your promise made at Breslau. You have become the liberator of Germany. Your brave sword and your intrepid heart have conquered. Come, I must conduct you to the King of Prus sia!" He took Blucher's arm, and, advancing with him, he said, 'Sire, I bring you here your **hero, Blucher!"**

"You bring me Field-Marshal Blucher!" **said** the king. "God bless you, field-marshal!"

"Sire," exclaimed Blucher, "you apply to me an honorary title—"

"Which you deserve," interrupted the king. "Do not thank me, for, if you do, for conferring a title on you, how shall I thank you, who have given me by far greater honor? I know what I owe you, Blucher; your energy, courage, determination, and ardor, have gained us the most glorious victories!"

"I have only done my duty, your majesty," said Blucher. "But I think our work is not half done yet, your majesty; we are to-day in fact only at the commencement of it. It is not enough for us to drive the French from Leipsic; we must pursue them, and expel them from Germany. **For this purpose we must make haste. We have no** time to rest on our laurels and sing hymns—the main point is to pursue the enemy—pursue him incessantly and effectually."

"Again, the hot-headed madcap, whose fiery spirit believes that every thing is done too slowly," exclaimed the Emperor Alexander, smiling. "Now I ask you, as the king asked you at Breslau, 'How old are you?'—you who never need rest, like other poor mortals—myself, for instance? I confess that, after all this excitement and these long fatigues, I am longing for repose, and would not take it amiss if war and pursuit were no longer thought of. But you are always intent on going forward!"

"Sire," exclaimed the king, who in the mean time had conversed with General Sacken, "I just learn that your troops have anticipated me, and given Blucher a title that is far better than mine. At the gate of Halle they cheered, and called him 'Marshal Forward!'"

"Ah, I should like to embrace my soldiers for this excellent word," cried Alexander. "That is an honorary title, Blucher, which no prince can confer, and which only your own merit and the gratitude of the people can bestow. Yes, you are 'Marshal Forward,' and by that name history will know you; and Germany will love, praise, and **bless you. You have** earned this title by **your** deeds, and the soldiers have conferred it upon you as a token of their appreciation. Now, the soldiers are a part of the people, and the voice of the people is the voice of God. Heaven bless you, 'Marshal Forward!'"

At this moment a procession was approaching from the other side of the square, consisting of twenty-four young maidens dressed in white. All held wreaths in their hands, while the three who headed the procession carried them on silken cushions. They approached the emperor, the king, and the crown prince of Sweden, and offered them the wreaths.* The emperor took that presented to him, and pressed it with a quick and graceful movement on Blucher's head. "I represent the Muse of History," he said, "and crown 'Marshal Forward' in a becoming manner."

"And I," said the crown prince of Sweden, handing his laurel-wreath to Prince Schwartzenberg. "I present this to the commander-in-chief of all our armies, and wish him joy of having achieved a victory over which so many nations will rejoice, and which will render his name illustrious now and forever."

"Ah," cried Schwartzenberg, "I have unfortunately been unable to do much. I have only faithfully carried out my orders, and it is to them, and to the brave troops, that we are indebted for the victory."†

The king said nothing; holding his wreath, he looked at it gravely and musingly. The presentations were over, and the princes prepared to return to their quarters.

"I hope, sire, we shall all remain together to-day?" remarked Alexander, turning toward the king.

"Pray excuse me, sire," said Frederick William bowing, "I intend to go to Berlin to-night, but shall be back **in a few days.**"

---

* The emperor of Austria did not make his entry with the other monarchs, but came only in the afternoon to Leipsic, where he remained scarcely an hour. He then returned to Rötha.—Beitzke, vol. II.

† Prince Schwartzenberg's words.—Beitzke, ii., 680.

"But you, I suppose, will remain?" asked Alexander, turning toward Bernadotte.

"I shall remain, your majesty," said the crown prince of Sweden, with a polite smile. "My troops are in need of rest."

"Yes, his troops are always in need of rest," murmured Blucher to himself; "I believe—".

Just then the Emperor Alexander turned toward him. "Well, field-marshal, and you—you will stay, too, will you not? I pray you to be my guest to-day."

"Sire, I regret that I cannot accept this gracious invitation," said Blucher. "I cannot stay, and my troops, thank God! are not in need of rest. I shall start immediately in pursuit of the enemy. It is not enough for us to have gained a victory; we must also know how to profit by it. I shall march this very evening, and take up my quarters for the night at Skeuditz."

"Marshal Forward! always Marshal Forward!" exclaimed Alexander, smiling.—"Come, sire, let us hasten to dinner; otherwise he will not even permit us to dine, but compel us all to set out immediately." He took the king's arm, and went with him to the horses standing near. When he was about to vault into the saddle, he turned toward one of his adjutants. "Ah," he said, "there is another little matter which I almost forgot!—General Petrowitch, go up there." He pointed to the house of the King of Saxony. "Inform the king, in my name, that he is a prisoner.* Have a guard of thirty men placed in front of the house."

On the same evening Blucher rode, by the side of Gneisenau and attended by his staff, out of the gate of Leipsic, following his troops already on the road to Skeuditz. "Well," said Blucher, smoking his pipe, "we cannot deny that there has been an abundant shower of orders and titles to-day, and that we have all been thoroughly drenched. So I am a field-marshal now; the Emperor of Austria has conferred on me the order of Maria Theresa; and the Emperor of Russia has given me a splendid sword, which I will send as a sou-

venir to my Amelia. And you, Gneisenau, I hope you have also received your share?"

"Why, yes," said Gneisenau, "I have received titles from all the three monarchs. You are right, there was all day a perfect shower of them —orders and honors; and not a general, not a dignitary or diplomatist has been forgotten. Count Metternich, you know, has been raised by his sovereign to the rank of a prince, in acknowledgment of his diplomatic services; and Prince Schwartzenberg, already enjoying the highest Austrian honors, has received permission to add the escutcheon of the Hapsburgs to his coat-of-arms."

"These two have been in the shower of honors, but very little in the shower of balls," remarked Blucher, laconically. "I wonder what rewards will be conferred on the crown prince of Sweden?"

"He has already received the highest Prussian, Austrian, and Russian orders," replied Gneisenau, scornfully. "As I stated before, no one has been forgotten but one!"

"Who is it?" asked Blucher. "Who has been forgotten?"

"Field-marshal, one deserving the most honor —one that joyfully sacrificed property, blood, **and** life, who did not demand any reward, **and** did every thing for the sake of honor, and from love of country, and for the princes."

"What!" cried Blucher, angrily. "The monarchs have forgotten to reward such a one?"

"Yes, field-marshal, they have! This one is the people, the German people!—the noble, enthusiastic people, who joyously and generously shed their blood for the deliverance of the **fatherland**, whose mothers and wives allowed their sons and husbands exultingly to march into the field, and made themselves sisters of charity for the wounded and sick; whose men and youths did not hesitate to leave their houses, their families, their property, their business, but readily took up arms to deliver the fatherland; whose aged men became young, whose children transformed themselves into youths, to participate in the holy struggle—all these, the great, noble German people, have received no reward, and not even a promise!"

---

* Beitzke, vol. II., p. 632.

15

"But, Gneisenau, how strange you are!" said Blucher, drawing his mustache through his fingers. "The monarchs have rewarded those whom they **were** able to reward. How can they **reward the** people? What could they do?"

"They could bestow on them more liberty, more independence and honor," said Gneisenau, "by giving them the constitution which the King of Prussia promised to his people in his manifesto of the 17th of March."

"Yes, that is true," said Blucher, thoughtfully. "Well, Stein is present, and he will surely remind the king of what he ought to do. He is a patriot and a true man!"

"Yes, but he is alone," said Gneisenau, mournfully. "His voice will die away like that of the preacher in the desert. You will see, field-marshal, these promises will soon be forgotten!"

"Well," exclaimed Blucher, "we shall see. For the time being let us rejoice that we have fought the great battle of the nations, and that Napoleon's doom is sealed now. **It is all-important** for us to finish him quickly and without mercy. You know my battle-cry: 'He must be dethroned!'—Oh, pipe-master! Another pipe, this one does not burn."

As Napoleon and Blucher left Leipsic on the 19th of October, King Frederick William set out from the city for Berlin to rejoice with his people, and to thank God for the victory. All Berlin received the king with exultation, and the 20th of October was a day of universal joy. Germany was free, and this conviction transported every heart, and every one wished to greet the king. Thousands surrounded the royal palace at Berlin all day, and whenever the king appeared at the windows or on the balcony, they saluted him with cheers and waving of hats and handkerchiefs. Multitudes thronged toward the cathedral, to thank God for the glorious victory vouchsafed to them. In every house were festivities in honor of the great battle of the nations fought at Leipsic.

But during this universal exultation the king left Berlin, without his suite, attended only by **his old friend, General Köckeritz,** and rode to Charlottenburg. No n pretending equipage, d tute of escutcheons an **of the** Brandenburg g Charlottenburg witho did not, however, ente Köckeritz to fetch th open the vault of the r his cloak closer about l to conceal something, ing to the mausoleur avenue of cypress and sorbed in deep reflecti him—not a sound of tl —naught disturbed th breeze that rustled tl voice greeted the kir tions of other days, w to him, and revived t past. He had suffered **as he had been alone i** alone in his prosperity this holy hour to unde whose spirit he believe Grief for the humilia sioned her death; joy her country would, if her from the dead.

The king slowly w leum. The door was He looked around to a alone, and that no st devout pilgrimage. I that which he had bor hidden. It was the the preceding day at of victory in his hand sarcophagus in which tal of Louisa! Bend place beneath which down the wreath.* mured. "It belongs with us, and led us to

---

* Eylert, "Characteri Wilhelm III.," vol. II., p.

leave me? Why are you not with me in the days of prosperity as in the days of adversity? I have seen your beautiful eyes shed many tears, but now I cannot see them brighten with joy. I can hear no more your sweet voice, your merry laughter! I am alone!" He leaned his hands on the sarcophagus, and, pressing his head on the laurel-wreath, shed abundant tears. After a long pause, he rose and suppressed his grief. "Farewell, my Louisa," he said. "I know that you are with me, and that your love accompanies me! Farewell!" Casting a parting glance on his wife's tomb, the king left the sacred cell, and walked slowly toward the palace through the shadowy and silent avenue of the cypress-trees.

CHAPTER XL.

BLUCHER'S BIRTHDAY.

Two months had elapsed since the great battle of Leipsic, during which, to Blucher's unbounded despair, much had been spoken, much negotiated, **many schemes devised, but nothing done.** Owing **to the slowness of the allies, Napoleon had succeeded, aside from some unfortunate engagements** during the retreat, in safely returning with the remnant of his army to France; and this dilatory system of the allies seemed to be constantly adopted. The armies advanced slowly, or not at **all.** For weeks the headquarters had been at Frankfort-on-the-Main. There were the Emperor of Russia, the King of Prussia, the crown prince of Sweden, and Prince Schwartzenberg, as representative of the Emperor of Austria, besides Metternich and Hardenberg, and the whole army of diplomatists, who deemed it incumbent on them to put an end with their pens to this war which the swords of the generals had concluded by a victory. The peace party were incessantly intent on gaining the allies at headquarters over to their side, and the crown prince of **Sweden and Prince** Metternich stood at their head. Bernadotte cautioned the allies against the dangers in which an invasion of France would involve them; Metternich deemed it **more** advisable for them to conclude an advantageous peace with the angry lion Napoleon. Blucher kept murmuringly away from the headquarters, and stayed **with** his staff at Höchst, near his troops.

It was the 16th of December. The field-marshal was alone in his room, and sat on the sofa, in his comfortable military cloak, smoking his morning pipe. Before him lay a map of Germany, on which he fixed his eyes, and across which he eagerly moved his fingers from time to time, drawing lines here and there, and apparently conceiving plans of operation. The door opened, and Pipe-Master Hennemann walked in —In full gala-uniform, holding both hands behind him, he stood at the door, hoping that his field-marshal would see and ask him what he wanted. But Blucher did not look up; he was absorbed in studying his map. Christian Hennemann, therefore, ventured to interrupt him. "Field-marshal," he said, in a low and timid voice, "I—"

"Well, what do you want, Christian?" asked Blucher, lifting his eyes from the map. "What is the matter? Why do you wear your gala-uniform, and look as if you were about to go on parade? Have you become a Catholic in this Catholic country, Christian, and are you celebrating a saint's holiday?"

"Yes, field-marshal," said Christian, resolutely stepping forward, "I am celebrating the holiday of my saint, and his name is Blucher!"

"He is a queer saint," cried Blucher, laughing. "But what does it all mean, Christian?"

"It means, field-marshal, that this is your birthday, and **that you** are seventy-one years old to-day."

"**That is** true," said Blucher to himself. "My

birthday! I had given strict orders not to celebrate it, and I had forgotten it myself!"

"But no one can prevent me from celebrating it, your excellency!" exclaimed Christian. "That would be very pretty, if I could not congratulate my 'Marshal Forward' on his birthday. Long live my field-marshal! And may God spare him many years to us yet, that we may catch Bonaparte at Paris; for, if 'Marshal Forward' does not do it, no one will!"

"Yes, if they would only let me!" cried Blucher, striking with his hand on the table; "but **they will not! I am** sitting here like a pug-dog in a deal box, and Bonaparte stands outside; I can only bark—I cannot bite him, for they will not let me out."

"They will have to, your excellency," said Hennemann, quickly, "and before many pipes are smoked. But I would request your excellency to be so kind as to smoke this pipe." He drew forth his right hand, which he had held behind him, and produced a short pipe, neatly adorned with a rose-colored ribbon terminating in a rosette with two long ends. "Field-marshal," he said, "in return for all the favors you have conferred on me, a poor boy, and for having made me, a stupid peasant-lad, pipe-master of the famous Field-Marshal Blucher, I take the liberty of presenting you with this short pipe." And making a polite obeisance, he handed it to the general, who took it smilingly, and was about to reply, but Christian added, in a louder voice, "But your excellency must not think that this is a common pipe. In the first place, it is not made of clay."

"No," said Blucher, contemplating it; "the small tube is made of wood, and mounted with silver, sure enough; the bowl is carved out of wood, too, and there is another bowl inside."

"But it is no common wood, your excellency," said Christian, solemnly. "You remember that I requested a furlough immediately after the battle of Leipsic, and said I would go home, see my dear Mecklenburg again, and visit my brothers and sisters. Well, that was not my principal object; there was another reason why I wanted

to go. I have never forgotten what my General Blucher said when I first came to him, and what he told us of his *mutting*—that he still loved her. Well, I thought it would gladden the field-marshal's heart to have a little souvenir of his mother. And, therefore, I wended my way to Rastow, where my dear field-marshal's mother is buried. I went to her grave, said my prayers, and then cut off a branch from the linden which stands on her grave. Like every other son of Mecklenburg, you ought to have a souvenir of your mutting. Here it is. The tube and the bowl of the pipe I carved out of the branch cut from the linden, and, that you might know what it is, I cut these letters in the wood. Read, sir."

"Sure enough, there are letters on it," cried Blucher. "They say, ' *Souvenir of Mutting!* '"

"Yes, that it is," said Christian; "you know, with us, those who love their mother call her as you did, and therefore I offer you this souvenir."

"Christian," said Blucher, in a tremulous voice, "that was well done, and I can tell you that you give me great joy, and that I shall not forget your kindness. This shall be my gala-pipe, and I **will** smoke it on gala-days only, that is to say, when we go into battle. I thank you a thousand times, Christian, my boy, and if my dear mutting has not forgotten me, she will look down upon her boy to-day, who is seventy-one years old, and it will gladden her to know that he has now a memorial of her—and from her grave! You were on her grave, then, Christian? How does it look?"

"It was decked with flowers, your excellency, and finches and larks were chirping in **the large** linden overshadowing it. The old grave-digger told me the linden had been planted on the day when Madame von Blucher was buried, and it was quite a small twig at that time."

"Yes, that is the course of things," said Blucher, mournfully; "when I saw my mother last, she was a handsome lady, and I was a boy of sixteen. I have not felt that so many years have elapsed since then, and I feel myself still as active as a **lad.** But they tell me I am decrepit, and that there is but a step between me and the grave."

"Well, I should like to see the giant who could

cross that step," cried Christian; "a hundred thousand French corpses and Bonaparte's overturned throne lie in that step between you and the grave."

Blucher laughed. "You are a good boy, pipemaster, and in honor of you I will smoke the new pipe to-day. Fill and light it; I will—who knocks there?—Open the door, Christian."

"It is I, your excellency," said General Gneisenau, who entered the room. "You must not refuse to see me. It is true, you have forbidden any celebration, serenade, or congratulation; but you must not turn me from your door; for you know that I love you like a son, and therefore you must permit me to come and wish myself joy that Field-Marshal Blucher still lives for the welfare of Germany."

Blucher kindly shook hands with him. "Would that your were right, Gneisenau, and that I really lived for the welfare of Germany! But the gentlemen at headquarters need me no longer. I am once more a nuisance and a stumbling-block—I am, according to them, the old madcap again—the rash hussar, just because I shout, 'We must advance upon Paris!' while the *trübsalsspritzen* * are croaking all the time, 'We must make peace! If we go to France, we are lost!' Gneisenau, if this state of affairs goes on for any length of time, this will be my last birthday, for I shall die of anger. I know if we make peace, the blood shed has been in vain, and our victories in vain; and in a few years, when he has recovered from his losses, Bonaparte will commence the same game, and we shall have to pass through the same series of disastrous events. But they are destitute of courage. Bernadotte does not want us to hurt the French, and the Emperor of Austria desires to spare his dear son-in-law, and they are besieging our king and the Emperor Alexander in such a vigorous manner, that they are at a loss what to do."

"And what should we be here for?" inquired Gneisenau, smiling. "What would Field-Marshal Blucher be here for, if we do not march forward? No, the gentlemen who are so desirous of making peace are greatly mistaken if they believe that they are able to set at naught our successes, and that it depends on their will only to make peace or war. The wheel that is to crush Napoleon is in motion, and no human hand can arrest it. Let the *trübsalsspritzen*, as your excellency says, croak: public opinion in Germany and throughout Europe speaks louder, and it clamors for war, and we shall have it. For this reason your excellency ought not to despond, nor prevent us from celebrating your birthday in a worthy manner. Your whole army longs to present its congratulations to you, and the officers of York's corps, who intended to give your excellency a ball to-night, and had so confidently counted upon your consent that they had already made all arrangements, are in despair because you did not accept their invitation. General York himself is quite vexed at your refusal, and thinks you decline because you do not wish to meet him."

"I do not care if he is vexed, old curmudgeon that he is!" cried Blucher. "He must always have something to grumble at, and has often enough said very hard things about me. Let him do so again, for aught I care! I shall, nevertheless, not go to the ball. What should I do there? Merry I cannot be, for my indignation almost stifles my heart, and, instead of smiling on people, I would rather show them my fist. Ah, Gneisenau, men are mean and contemptible, after all, and those at headquarters are the most despicable! They want peace! Do you comprehend that, Gneisenau—peace! now that we are on the road to Paris, and only need make up our minds to destroy the power of our enemy! Oh, it is enough to make a fellow swear! To the gallows with all the *trübsalsspritzen !*—all the old women who are wearing uniforms, and who, in place of cocked hats, should rather put nightcaps on their heads!"

"Ah!" exclaimed Gneisenau, smiling, "should they do so, your excellency would tear off their nightcaps, and forcibly put their hats again on their heads. And as for the old women,

---

* A favorite expression of Blucher when he alluded to the timid diplomatists who advised the allies to make peace with Napoleon.

Blucher, the young hero, will in the end rout **them all, and** drive them from the field."

"**Ah,** Gneisenau, if I succeed in doing so, then I should be young again, and live to see still many a birthday," sighed Blucher. "I have conceived every thing so clearly and well—the whole plan of the campaign was already settled in my mind! Come, Gneisenau, let me show you all on the map, and then you will have to admit that Napoleon would be annihilated if we could carry this plan into execution. Come, look at the map!"

Gneisenau stood by the side of the field-marshal, and bent over the map lying on the table.

"See," said Blucher, eagerly, "**here** is Paris, here is the Rhine, and here are we; farther below—"

"But, your excellency," interrupted Gneisenau, surprised, "you have a very old and poor map; it is impossible to base any strategic plans on it."

"How so?" asked Blucher, in amazement.

"Because this map is certainly incorrect, your excellency; we have entirely new and very accurate maps now, made from the latest surveys."

"Ah, what do I care for your surveys?" cried Blucher, impatiently. "By your surveys, I suppose, you cannot displace the countries, cities, and **rivers?** Paris remains where it is, the Rhine flows where it has always flowed, and behind the Rhine lies Germany, where it has always lain?"

"Yes, but you **will** not find on this map the towns, villages, **forests,** rivers, and hills, which you will meet on your advance, and which, if not taken into consideration, might prove formidable obstacles."

"What do I care for the towns, villages, forests, rivers, and hills?" replied Blucher: "I advance all the time, and that says every thing. In the towns and villages I shall cause my troops to take up their quarters; through the forests we shall cut a road if there is none; we shall build bridges across the rivers, and run over the tops of the mountains; if the field-pieces cannot be

hauled over them, we shall take them around the base. The most important thing is, that we advance, and I am quite able to consider that on my map here.—Now, then! here is Paris. Put your finger on Paris, Gneisenau." The general obeyed, and pressed the tip of his forefinger on the spot indicated. "And here," cried Blucher, pressing his own finger on the map, "here are **we,** the Silesian **army.** Between us lies the Rhine. Put your other finger on the Rhine, Gneisenau." Gneisenau put his middle-finger on the black line marking the Rhine. "Now put your little-finger down here, between Mannheim and Kehl; there stands the army of Bohemia under Prince Schwartzenberg; and up here, where I hold my thumb, in Holland, is Bulow, with his corps. See, on this side, we have therefore completely hemmed in France; and, on the other side, where the Atlantic Ocean is—or is it no longer there on your new-fangled maps?"

"Yes, your excellency," exclaimed Gneisenau, laughing, "it is still there."

"Well, then, England posts her ships there; and in the south, on the Pyrenees, stand the Spaniards, who have sworn to revenge themselves on Bonaparte. Now we advance all at the **same** time into France. Prince Schwartzenberg penetrates with his army through Switzerland; Bulow marches through the Netherlands, after conquering them, and joins my forces; and I cross the Rhine here in three large columns with the Silesian army—the first column at Mannheim, the second at Kaub, and the third—well, now I have no finger left to—"

"Here is mine, your excellency," said Gneisenau, raising the finger marking the line of the Rhine.

But Blucher hastily pressed it down. "Do not remove that!" he cried; "**what** is to become of my whole plan if that finger should desert its position? Keep it there, then!—Well, here, where I hold my left thumb, at Coblentz, the third column will cross the Rhine. On the other bank we shall all unite, take Sarrebruck, advance by forced marches upon Metz, and—"

"Your excellency," shouted the pipe-master,

throwing open the door, "a courier from the King of Prussia, from Frankfort-on-the-Main!"

"Let **him come in!**" **cried** Blucher, hastily **throwing** off **his** military cloak, and putting on his uniform-coat. He had not yet quite done so when the courier entered the room.

"What orders do you bring from my king and master?" inquired Blucher, meeting the officer.

"Your excellency, his majesty King Frederick William III., and his majesty the Emperor Alexander, request Field-Marshal Blucher to repair immediately to Frankfort, where the monarchs **have** an important communication to make to the field-marshal. They wish your excellency to start forthwith, in order to reach Frankfort as soon as possible."

"Inform their majesties that I shall be there in two hours.—Well, Gneisenau, what do you say now?" asked Blucher, when the courier left the **room.**

"**I** say that the monarchs **have at** length discovered who alone can give them efficient assistance and valuable advice, and that they have, therefore, applied to Field-Marshal Blucher."

"And I tell you," shouted Blucher, in a thundering voice, "that the monarchs send for me to inform me that we are to face about and go home. If it were any thing else, they would have sent me **word** by an officer; but, as it is, they are afraid **lest I grow** furious, and so they intend to inform me **in** the mildest possible manner of their decision, and **wish to** pat my cheeks tenderly while telling me of it. But they mistake; I shall tell them the truth, as I would any one else, and they shall see that it is all the same to me whether they have a crown on their heads or a forage-cap; the truth must out, and they shall hear it, as sure as my name is Blucher! But I must dress for the occasion—it shall be a gala-day for me. With my orders on my breast, and the emperor's sword of honor at my side, I will appear before them and tell them the truth."

CHAPTER XLI

THE Emperor Alexander and King Frederick William were in the king's cabinet, awaiting Field-Marshal Blucher, for the **courier** had just returned and reported that the field-marshal promised to be at Frankfort within two hours.

"The two hours have just elapsed," said Alexander, glancing at the clock, "and Blucher, who is known to be a very punctual man, will undoubtedly soon be here. Ah, there is a carriage; it is he, no doubt!"

"Yes, it is he," said the king, who had stepped **to** the window, and was looking **out.** "He is alighting with the nimbleness of a youth, in spite of his seventy-one years. He is really a hero!"

"And will your majesty be so kind as to enter **into** my jest? Will you assist me in it, and confirm **my words?**"

"**Certainly, sire; but I tell you,** beforehand, our jest may render the old **firebrand** very grave, and we may happen to get a scolding."

"That is just what I am longing for," replied the emperor, smiling. "Old Blucher's scolding is wholesome, and invigorates the heart; it is a new and vital air which his words breathe upon me. It is flattering to be scolded for once like a common mortal."

"Well, if you desire that, sire," said the king, smiling, "Blucher will certainly afford you this pleasure to-day."

The door opened; a footman entered and announced Field-Marshal Blucher. The two monarchs met him. Both shook hands with him, and bade him welcome with great cordiality. This, however, instead of gladdening Blucher, filled him with distrust.

"They pat me, **because** they want to scratch me," said Blucher to himself, "but they shall not fool me!" His features assumed a defiant expression, and a dark cloud covered his brow.

"To-day is your birthday, field-marshal," said the king; "that is the reason we have sent for you; we desired to congratulate you in person

You have passed through a year of heroism, and the new one cannot bring you nobler laurels than those you have already."

"Ah, your majesty, I believe it might after all," said Blucher, quickly. "The laurels growing in France are the noblest of all; that is why I should like to gather them."

"Ah! the Emperor Napoleon will not suffer it," said Alexander. "He values them too highly, and it is not advisable for us to seek them, for he is not the man to allow us to take what belongs to him."

"But he was the very man to take a great many things that did not belong to him," cried Blucher, vehemently.

"That which did not belong to him we have taken again, and have satisfied the ends of justice," said the king, gravely.

"No, we have not satisfied the ends of justice," cried Blucher. "It is justice if we march to Paris—to take all from him whom your majesties still call the Emperor Napoleon, but who, in my eyes, is nothing but an infamous tyrant, presumptuous enough to put a crown on his head, and ascend a throne to which he has no right whatever, and who, moreover, has treated us Germans as though we were his slaves. Ay, it is justice if we take from the robber of kingdoms, the braggart winner of battles, all that he has appropriated, and send him back to Corsica. That would be justice, your majesty; and if it is not administered, it is a morbid generosity that prevents it, and which is utterly out of place in regard to him."

The emperor cast a glance full of indescribable satisfaction on the king, who responded to it with a gentle nod.

"My dear Blucher," said Alexander, kindly, "you have not yet permitted me to wish you joy of your birthday. God bless you, my dear field-marshal, and may this year bring us the peace and repose which one so much needs after the exposures of campaign life, and especially when he is seventy-one years old!"

"I do not know whether I am as old as that," said Blucher, indignantly; "I know only that I am by no means desirous of repose, but rather deem it a great misfortune just now."

The emperor seemed not to have heard him, but continued quietly: "Yes, certainly, my dear field-marshal, you need retirement; at your venerable age we should not subject ourselves to such prolonged fatigues in the field."

"Besides, I am sure you wish peace, like the rest of us," said the king, who saw that the veins on Blucher's forehead were swelling, and who wished to forestall too violent a reply. "We have reflected a long while how we might give you a pleasant surprise on your birthday, but it was difficult for us. You have already all the orders and honor we can bestow; you are blessed with riches, and we have found it difficult to make you a present worthy of the respect and love we entertain for you."

"But his majesty the king has resolved to give you something which will gladden your noble heart. Field-marshal, we give you peace as a birthday present! We have resolved to make peace with Napoleon; and to-day, on your birthday, the conditions, which, you know, have for a long time past formed the subject of secret negotiations, are to be signed. The Emperor Napoleon has declared his readiness to accept them, and, therefore, there are no further obstacles to the cessation of war."

"To-morrow our troops will set out for home," said the king. "The requirements of honor and duty have been satisfied; the welfare and prosperity of our subjects demand peace. You, my dear field-marshal, have been selected to direct the retreat of the troops. Conformably to the wishes of his majesty the Emperor Alexander, and his royal highness the crown prince of Sweden, I appoint you commander-in-chief of all the retreating troops. The generals will have strictly to comply with your orders; and, just as Prince Schwartzenberg was general-in-chief of the advance, you, field-marshal, are general-in-chief of the retreat. Confiding in your energy, sagacity, and zeal, we hope that you will conduct the retreat satisfactorily, and the men will reach their homes as soon as possible. You are now, there fore, commander-in-chief; that is your birthday gift, and we hope you will be content with it."

"No," cried Blucher, drawing a deep breath, **and** unable longer to restrain his anger, "I am not content with it—not at all; and I must say that I do not wish this appointment, which seems to me a disgrace. General-in-chief of the retreating armies! I should like to ask his majesty the Emperor of Russia why his soldiers have given me the honorary title of 'Marshal Forward,' if I am now to be 'General-in-chief Backward?' If your majesty has given me the golden-sheathed sword only for the purpose of wearing it on parade, I do not want it. Sire, here it is; I lay it down at your feet with due respect. Your majesty, you desired to give it to the general-in-chief of the retreating troops, and that I am not, and cannot be!" He hastily unbuckled his sword, and laid it on the table beside **the emperor.**

"**And why can you not?**" asked Alexander, **composedly.**

"Because I cannot disgrace my honest name by doing dishonest things," cried Blucher, vehemently.

"Blucher, you forget yourself," said the king, almost sternly; "your words are too strong."

"Yes, your majesty, I know that they are strong," exclaimed Blucher; "but the truth is **strong,** too; I must relieve myself of it; I can no longer keep it back, and, **the** truth is, that it **would be** a shame and a stupidity if we retreat without reconquering, on the left bank of the Rhine, that which we **were** obliged to cede to France. Your majesties have said that the requirements of honor and justice are satisfied. Permit me to reply that this is not so, **and cannot be,** if we retreat; for we show that we **are still** distrusting our own power, and, notwithstanding our superior army, deem ourselves too weak **to** attack the man who has been attacking us for nearly twenty years, and to whom nothing was sacred, whether treaties, or rights of property, or nationality. No, the requirements of justice are not satisfied if we face about now and consider the frontiers of France more sacred than

the French have ever considered the frontiers of Germany. Bonaparte has as yet Holland, a **piece of Germany, and** Italy, and he says he will not yield a single village which he has conquered, though the enemy stand on the heights of Paris. It would but be right for us **to** march to that city, and compel him to disgorge, not merely a village, but all that he has taken. **And** if this be not done, if the peace-croakers attain their object, a cry of disappointment and anger will burst forth throughout Europe, and the nations, lifting their hands to God, will curse the pusillanimity and weakness of their princes. They would be justified in doing so; for it was not for this that brave men, at the first call of their king, left their families; it was not for this that they sacrificed their property on the altar of the fatherland. The women did not become nurses and sisters of charity, nor did their husbands and sons shed their blood, that only one great battle might be gained over Bonaparte, and that he then might be allowed leisurely to evacuate Germany. We did not even pursue him, but marched slowly, while he safely wended his way to the Rhine. And now he is to remain quietly in France! The world is to receive no satisfaction, and the tyrant is not to be punished! If that be right and just, well—no matter! I am an old soldier, and am not versed in the tricks of diplomatists! Nor do I care to be versed in them! They know how to manage matters so insidiously that at last they convert wrong into right—falsehood into truth, and disguise their cowardice in such a manner that it looks like wisdom. The only thing I understand is, that I am no more of any use, and I **request** your majesty to give me my discharge as a birthday present—be so kind as to grant it immediately. I am much too young to become General-in-chief Backward, and it is, therefore, better for **me** to stand aside, and let others take the **command of** the retreating troops. Your **majesties will** graciously pardon me if I take the liberty of withdrawing." He **bowed with** respect and turned quickly toward the **door.**

"**But why in** such haste?" asked the king

"Pray stay; I have not yet granted your discharge."

"But your majesty, I know, will grant it, and I consider you have already done so. I beg leave to withdraw."

"But stay!" exclaimed Alexander.

"Pardon me, your majesty, I must go!"

"Why? Tell us honestly the truth, field-marshal."

"Well," said Blucher, standing at the door, "if your majesty orders me to tell the truth, I will do so. I must go, because I cannot endure it here; I must find some place where I may give vent to my rage, and, by a vast amount of swearing, relieve my heart."

"What!" cried Alexander, laughing. "Your heart is still oppressed?"

"Yes, your majesty, what I have said is as nothing," replied Blucher, in a melancholy tone; "those words were only as a few rain-drops; the whole violence of my anger, with its thunder, lightning, hail, and storm, is still in my heart, and may God have mercy on him on whom it will burst! Your majesties may see that it is high time for me to withdraw."

"Otherwise, you think, the thunder-storm might burst here?" inquired Alexander, smiling.

"I am afraid so, sire," replied Blucher, gravely.

"Perhaps it may be allayed, however," said Frederick William, approaching Blucher. "You have determined, then, not to accept the position offered you?"

"I demand at once my discharge, your majesty; my discharge!"

"You do not wish to be commander-in-chief of the retreating troops?" asked Alexander.

"My name is 'Marshal Forward!'" said Blucher, proudly.

"And it is your firm belief, field-marshal," asked the king, "that it would be neither just nor honorable for the allies now to make peace and go home?"

"Your majesty, it is—it is my earnest conviction, and I shall never be able to change it."

"Well, then," said Alexander turning toward the king, "is not your majesty, too, of the opinion that it would be advantageous for us to allow ourselves to be directed by the views and convictions of so brave and experienced a general? Do you not believe that we owe it to him, in consideration of the distinguished services which he has performed, to believe him, the brave soldier, rather than the tricky diplomatists?"

"I have no doubt of it," said the king, smiling, "and I confess that all that the field-marshal has told us has greatly modified my views, and induced me to adopt another course. If Blucher insists that, in order to satisfy the requirements of honor and justice, we should not now make peace, I believe him."

"And if he has insurmountable objections to being called Marshal Backward," exclaimed the emperor, merrily, "well, then, he must retain the name my soldiers have given him."

"But, your majesty," cried Blucher, who listened with amazement, "what means all this?"

"It means," said the king, putting his hand on Blucher's shoulder, "it means that I cannot grant you the discharge which you have requested, because I need your services more than ever."

"It means," said the emperor, putting his hand on Blucher's other shoulder, "that Marshal Forward is the very man we need at this juncture. For, in spite of all ministers, diplomatists, and peace-croakers (I thank you for that word), we have determined to carry on the war to the best of our power."

Blucher uttered a cry of joy, and lifting up his large eyes, he exclaimed: "Good Heaven, I thank Thee, with all my heart; for the day is dawning now, and we shall soon see how the sun shines in Paris!"

"You did not wish to be commander-in-chief of the retreating army," said the king, kindly; "let us appoint you, then, second general-in-chief of the advancing army."

"How so? I do not understand that," said Blucher, bewildered. "That is to say, I remain general-in-chief of my Silesian army?"

"Yes, but with enlarged power and indepen

dence, and with a greater number of troops. Your corps has suffered a great deal; on your victorious fields of Möckern and Leipsic you lost many brave soldiers. Your ranks need filling up, in order that you may act vigorously and energetically. Therefore, three new corps will be added to your forces[*]—a Prussian corps under General Kleist, a Hessian corps under the crown prince of Hesse, and a mixed corps under the Duke of Saxe-Coburg, the whole amounting to about fifty thousand fresh soldiers. With these reënforcements, added to your own eighty-five thousand men, you will be at the head of an army with which great things may be accomplished, and **with which I** believe you may gather your laurels in France."

"Moreover," said Alexander, kindly, "you will hereafter not be responsible to any other commander. We shall consider jointly with you all **operations of the war, and the whole plan of** the campaign, and lay before you all general communications. **Prince Schwartzenberg will always** keep you well instructed of the movements of the grand army, and only *request* you to inform him of those you deem it best for the Silesian army to make in coöperation with the former.[†] You will, therefore, be entirely at liberty to carry your own plans into execution, and will have only to report to Schwartzenberg and to us what you are doing. Are you now content, Blucher?"

"**Do you still** demand your discharge as a birthday present?" inquired the king.

"**You** ask me whether I am content, or demand my discharge?" cried Blucher, cheerfully. "Now that we advance, I would not take my discharge, and should your majesty give it to me, to punish me for my unseemly conduct, I would secretly accompany the army and fight in the ranks; for you ought to know that I do not advocate a vigorous prosecution of the war on account of the honor it might reflect on me, but for the rights of all Germany; and for this reason I am not only content, but I thank Heaven, my king, and the Em-

peror Alexander, from the bottom of my heart; and especially for the great confidence you place in me. This is the most flattering of all the honors you have lavished upon me, and I shall endeavor with head and arm to render myself worthy of it. I shall always remember that my king intrusted me with the sacred mission of blotting out the disgrace of Jena, and of causing our angel, Queen Louisa, who shed so many tears for us on earth, to rejoice in heaven over our deeds—and—" his words choked his utterance, his eyes grew dim; pressing his hand to them with a quivering movement, he said, in a stifled voice, "I believe—may God forgive me!—I believe I am weeping! But my tears are tears of joy; they do my heart good, and your majesties will forgive them!—Well, now I am all right again," he added, after a pause. "I request your majesties to give me instructions, and tell me what is to be done, and when we shall cross the Rhine."

Toward nightfall Blucher returned from Frankfort to Höchst. In front of his door he was met **by General Gneisenau, Colonel Müffling,** and several other gentlemen of his staff. Blucher made a very wry face, receiving them with loud grumbling. "Oh, it is all very well," he said, alighting from his carriage. "I can now communicate bad news to you. We shall lie still here, like lazy bears, during the whole winter; we shall neither advance nor retreat. The diplomatists have hatched out the idea, and I am sure they will arrange a pretty treaty of peace for us! Well, I do not care; I will try to suppress my grief, and lead a happy life. If we are inactive, we shall at least try to kill time in as pleasant a manner as possible. I shall commence diverting myself this very day, and, despite the apostles of peace, show that they have not ruffled my temper. The officers of York's corps will give a ball at Wiesbaden to-night. I will go, immediately setting out for Wiesbaden, and conveying the tidings to old York. Well, gentlemen, prepare to accompany me; and you, General Gneisenau, be so kind as to go with me to my room for a minute or two. I wish to tell you something." He saluted the officers, and stepped quickly into the house Followed by

---

[*] Varnhagen von Ense, "Biography of Prince Blucher of Wahlstatt" p. 205.

[†] Ibid.

Gneisenau, he entered the room, and carefully locked **the door.** The wrinkles now disappeared from his forehead, and an expression of happiness beamed in his face. "Gneisenau," he said, encircling the tall form of his friend in his arms, "now listen to what I have to say. What I told you about peace was not true. We are to advance—ay, to advance! and it seems to me as if I hear Bonaparte's throne giving way!"

"What, your excellency!" exclaimed Gneisenau, joyfully, "we are going to advance—to march into France?"

Blucher hastily pressed his hand on his mouth. "Hush, general!" he whispered. "At present no one must hear it; it is a secret, and we must try to conceal our movements as much as possible. We ought to do our best to mislead the enemy —that is my plan. We must make him believe that the whole offensive force of the allies is turning toward Switzerland, and that the Silesian army is to remain on the Rhine as a mere corps of observation. Napoleon will make his dispositions accordingly; he will leave but a small force on the bank of the Rhine opposite us, and on passing over to the other side we shall meet with little resistance."

"That is again a plan altogether worthy of my Ulysses," said Gneisenau, smiling. "It is all-important now for us to let every one, and above all Napoleon, know as soon as possible that we stay here."

"I will swear and rave so loudly that he will certainly hear it in Paris," said Blucher. "Let us curse the necessity imposed on us, and secretly make all necessary dispositions, inform the commanders, and issue the orders, so that we may all cross the Rhine at midnight on the 31st of December."

"What! The passage is to take place at midnight on the 31st of December?" asked Gneisenau.

"Yes, general. Let us begin the new year with a great deed, that we may end it with one."

"But will that be possible, field-marshal? Can **all our troops** be prepared at so short a notice?"

"That is your task, Gneisenau; ideas **are your** province, execution is mine. You are my head, I am your arm; and these two, I believe, ought jointly to enable us to cross the Rhine at midnight on the 31st of December, as the holy army of vengeance, which God Himself sends to Bonaparte as a New-Year's gift. But come, Gneisenau, let us ride to the ball. I must dance! Joy is in my legs, and I must allow it to get out of them. I shall ask old York to dance, and, while we two are hopping around, I must tell him what is to be done. We are to advance!"

Blucher's resolutions were carried into effect. All dispositions were made in a quiet and efficient manner; and while the field-marshal scolded vehemently at the inactivity of the winter, General Gneisenau secretly took steps to prepare for the passage of the Rhine. Napoleon's spies at Frankfort and on the Rhine heard only the grumbling of Blucher, but they did not see the preparations of Gneisenau.

On the 26th of December orders were dispatched to the commanders of the different corps of the great Silesian army, communicating the time and place of crossing the Rhine, and on the **31st** every soldier of that army stood on the bank ready for the passage. This was to be effected at three different points—Mannheim, Caub, and Coblentz. The grand, all-important moment had come; midnight was at hand.

It was a clear and beautiful night; the deep-blue sky was spangled with stars, and the air cold and bracing. None saw the black columns moving toward the Rhine. The French, on the opposite side, were asleep; they did not perceive Field-Marshal Blucher, who, at Caub, on the bank of the river, was halting on horseback by the side of his faithful Gneisenau, apparently listening in breathless suspense. Suddenly, the stillness was interrupted by the chime of a neighboring church-clock; another struck, and, like echoes, their notes resounded down the Rhine, in all cities and villages, proclaiming that the old year was past, and a new one begun.

Blucher took off his gray forage-cap, and, holding it before his face, uttered a low, fervent prayer. "And now, forward!" he said, in a resolute tone. "Let us in person convey our 'happy New-Year' to the French!—And Thou, great God, behold Thy German children, who are shaking off the thraldom of long years, and who have become again brave men! Heavenly Father, bless our undertaking! Bless the Rhine, that it may flow to the ocean again as a free German river for German freemen!—And now, boys, forward! Build your bridges, for Heaven sends us to France to punish Bonaparte, and sing him a song of the Rhine! Forward!"

———◆———

CHAPTER XLII.

NAPOLEON'S NEW-YEAR'S-DAY.

It was early on the morning of the 1st of January. Napoleon was angrily pacing his cabinet, while the police-minister, Duke de Rovigo, was standing by the emperor's desk, and waiting, as if afraid to look at his master, lest his anger burst upon his head.

"Why did you not tell me so yesterday, Savary?" asked Napoleon, with his flaming eyes on the police-minister. "Why did you not inform me, immediately after the close of the meeting of the Chamber of Deputies, of the seditious and refractory spirit of the speeches which certain members dared to deliver?"

"Sire, I had no proofs of their guilt. Speeches, it is true, had been made, but they vanish, and offer no solid grounds for convicting men of crime. As I have not the honor of being a member of the committee which your majesty has appointed to take the condition of France into consideration, I was unable to hear the speeches delivered at the meeting. I had to obtain palpable evidence. I knew, not only that the commission of the Chamber of Deputies had resolved to have an address to your majesty published, but that the opposition speaker of the committee, M. Raynouard, intended to have his speech printed and circulated, in order to prove to France that the committee of the Chamber had done every thing to give peace to the nation."

"As if that were the task of those gentlemen —as if they had to give me advice, or could influence me!" cried Napoleon, vehemently. "They have never dared raise their voices against me; but now that we are surrounded by enemies—now that it is all-important for France to startle the world by her energy and the unanimity of her will, these men dare oppose me! You allowed, then, their addresses to be sent to the printing-office, Savary?"

"Yes, sire. But I had the printing-office surrounded by my police-agents, and waited until the composition was completed and the printing commenced. Then they entered the press-room, seized the copies already printed, knocked the types into pi, and burned the manuscripts,* as well as the proofs, except this one, which I have the honor of bringing to your majesty."

The emperor, with an impetuous movement, took up the printed sheet lying on the table by the side of the duke, and glanced over it. "Savary," he said, pointing out a passage on the paper, "read this to me. Read the conclusion of Raynouard's speech. Read it aloud!" He handed the paper to the duke, and pointed out the passage.

Savary read as follows: "'Let us attempt no dissimulation—our evils are at their height; the country is menaced on the frontiers at all points; commerce is annihilated, agriculture languishes, industry is expiring; there is no Frenchman who has not, in his family or his fortune, some cruel wound to heal. The facts are notorious, and can never be sufficiently enforced. Agriculture, for the last five years, has gained nothing; it barely exists, and the fruit of its toil is annually dissipated by the treasury, which unceasingly devours every thing to satisfy the cravings of ruined and famished armies. The conscription has become, for all France, a frightful scourge, because it has always been driven to extremities in its execution. For the last three years the harvest of death has been reaped three times a year! A barbarous war, with

---

* "Mémoires d'un Homme d'État," vol. xii., p. 294.

out object, swallows up the youth torn from their education, from agriculture, commerce, and the **arts.** Have the tears of mothers and the blood of whole generations thus become the patrimony of kings? It is fit that nations should have a moment's breathing-time; the period has arrived when they should cease to tear out each other's entrails; it is time that thrones should be consolidated, and that our enemies be deprived of the plea that we are forever striving to carry into the world the torch of revolution ... To prevent the country from becoming the prey of foreigners, it is indispensable to nationalize the war; and this cannot be done unless the nation and its monarch be united by closer bonds. It has become indispensable to give a satisfactory answer to our enemies' accusations of aggrandizement: there would be real magnanimity in a formal declaration that the independence of the French people and the integrity of its territory are all that we contend for. It is for the government to propose measures which may promptly repel the enemy, and secure peace on a durable basis. Those measures would be at once efficacious, if the French people were persuaded that the government in good faith aspired only to the glory of peace, and that their blood would no longer be shed but to defend our country, and secure the protection of the laws. But these words of 'peace' and 'country' will resound in vain, if the institutions are not guaranteed which secure those blessings. It appears, therefore, to the commission, to be indispensable that, at the same time that the government proposes the most prompt and efficacious measures for the security of the country, his majesty should be supplicated to maintain entire the execution of the laws which guarantee to the French the rights of liberty and security, and to the nation the free exercise of its political rights." *

"Well," cried the emperor, impetuously, "what do you think of that? Does it not sound like the first note of the tocsin by which the people are to be called upon to rise in rebellion?"

"Sire, it is the language of treason!" replied Savary. "The conduct of the members of this committee would justify your majesty to have them shot as traitors." *

The emperor made no reply, but bowed his head on his breast, and, with his hands folded behind him, paced the room for a few moments. "Savary," he then said, "it is sufficient for u to be at war with our foreign enemies; let us not get into difficulty with our domestic adversaries. This is not the time for doing so. If we conquer our foreign enemies, the domestic ones will of themselves be silent; but if we succumb, every thing will be different. Those gentlemen have acted both foolishly and ungenerously (at a moment when it is all-important that France should **act and think** as one man), to stir up **political partisan** feeling; and it is ungrateful to **oppose** me at a time when, overwhelmed with care and work, I need my whole energy to maintain my position. Let us leave it to fate to punish the traitors. They will not have long to wait!"

"And those haughty members of the Chamber of Deputies do not even feel that they are deserving of punishment," exclaimed the duke, indignantly. "The whole committee, and M. Raynouard with them, have accompanied me to the Tuileries, and repaired to the throne-hall in order to offer your majesty their congratulations for the new year."

"Ah, it is true, to-day is New-Year's-day," said Napoleon; "I had almost forgotten it, for the cares and anxiety of the old year have, as a most faithful suite, followed me into the new year. But I am glad you remind me of it! I will go to the throne-hall and receive the congratulations of my faithful subjects, or those who call themselves so. Follow me!"

In the throne-hall were assembled, as on every New-Year's-day, the dignitaries of France and the most prominent authorities of the government; but for the first time, since the establishment of the empire, the representatives of the foreign powers and the ambassadors of the European princes failed to appear at the reception in the Tuileries.

---

* "Mémoires d'un Homme d'État," vol. xii., p. 293.

* Ibid., p. 294.

In former years they had hastened to present their congratulations; to-day not one of those representatives was present, not even the ambassador of the Emperor of Austria, Napoleon's father-in-law—not even the ambassador of the King of Naples, his brother-in-law! The troops of the Emperor Francis had invaded France; the troops of King Murat had returned to Naples, and he had informed his brother-in-law that the welfare of his own country rendered it necessary for him to forsake France. The very princes of the Confederation of the Rhine, hitherto the most sycophantic flatterers of the emperor, had likewise turned away from him; all the allies, adulators, and friends of his days of prosperity had left him, as rats desert the sinking ship. No one was in the throne-hall except the dignitaries and officers of France, and one-half of these came, perhaps, because the duties of their offices rendered it incumbent on them—because the events of the future could not be positively foreseen, and the emperor, thanks to his lucky star, might finally conquer his enemies.

The emperor entered with his usual proud and careless indifference. His quick glance swept past the ranks of the assembly, and rested for a moment on the place where the ambassadors of the foreign governments formerly stood beside the throne, and where no one was to be seen to-day. But not a feature changed; he was still calm and grave. With a gentle nod he turned toward the ministers who were on the left, and addressed each of them a few kind words; he then quickly ascended the steps of the throne. Under the canopy, he turned his eyes toward the side where were the members of the senate and the legislature.

Napoleon's eyes flashed down the silent assembly with an expression of terrible anger. When he spoke, his voice rolled like thunder through the hall, and echoed in the trembling hearts of those who were conscious of their guilt, and who hung their heads under the outburst of their sovereign's wrath. "Gentlemen of the legislature," he said, "you come to greet me. I accept your greetings, and will tell you what you ought to

hear. You have it in your power to do much good, and you have done nothing but mischief. Eleven-twelfths of you are patriotic, the rest are factious. What do you hope by putting yourselves in opposition? To gain possession of power? But what are your means? Are you the representatives of the people? I am. Four times I have been invoked by the nation, and have had the votes of four millions of men. I have a title to supreme authority, which you have not. You are nothing but the representatives of the departments. Your report is drawn up with an astute and perfidious spirit, of the effects of which you are well aware. Two battles lost in Champagne would not have done me so much mischief. I have sacrificed my passions, my pride, my ambition, to the good of France. I was in expectation that you would appreciate my motives, and not urge me to what is inconsistent with the honor of the nation. Far from that, in your report you mingle irony with reproach: you tell me that adversity has given me salutary counsels. How can you reproach me with my misfortunes? I have supported them with honor, because I have received from nature a sturdy temper; and if I had not possessed it, I would never have raised myself to the first throne in the world. Nevertheless, I have need of consolation, and I expected it from you: so far from receiving it, you have endeavored to depreciate me; but I am one of those whom you may kill, but cannot dishonor. Is it by such reproaches that you expect to restore the lustre of the throne? What is the throne? Four pieces of gilded wood, covered with a piece of velvet. The real throne has its seat in the heart of the nation. You cannot separate the two without mutual injury; for it has more need of me than I have of it. What could the nation do without a chief? When the question was, how we could repel the enemy, you demand institutions as if we had them not! Are you not content with the constitution? If you are not, you should have told me so four years ago, or postponed your demand to two years after a general peace. Is this the moment to insist on such a demand? **You** wish to imitate the Constituent Assembly, and commence a revolution? Be it **so.** You will find I will not imitate Louis XVI.: I would rather abandon the throne, I would prefer making part of the sovereign people, to being **an** enslaved king. I am sprung from the people; I know the obligations I contracted when I ascended the throne. You have done much mischief; you would have done me still more, if I had allowed your report to be printed.—You speak of abuses, of vexations. I know, as well as you, that such have existed; they arose from circumstances, and the misfortunes of the times. But was it necessary to let all Europe into our secrets? Is it fitting to wash our dirty linen in public? In what you say there is some truth and some falsehood. What, then, was your obvious duty? To have confidentially made known your grounds of complaint to me, by whom they would have been thankfully received. I do not, any more than yourselves, love those who have oppressed you. In three months we shall have peace: the enemy will be driven from our territory, or I shall be dead. We have greater resources than you imagine: our enemies have never conquered us—never will. They will be pursued over the frontier more quickly than they crossed it. Go!" *

The last words of the speech were still resounding through the hall when the deputies, with pale faces, bowing timidly and silently before the throne, turned and walked toward the door. All eyes were riveted on them, and it was felt that the men whom the emperor dismissed with such a strain of vehement invective were twenty new enemies whom Napoleon sent into the provinces, and who would bring a new hostile army—public opinion—into the field against him. Many hoped that the emperor, perceiving his blunder, would call back the deputies by some pleasant word, in order to bring about a reconciliation between him and those who, whatever the emperor might say, represented in the throne-hall the opinion of the people.

* Bucher et Roux, "Histoire Parl. de France," vol. xxix., pp. 459, 461.

But Napoleon did not call them back; standing on his throne, haughty and defiant, he looked after the disappearing deputies in anger; and only when the door of the anteroom closed, did he turn his eyes toward those who surrounded him. As if by a **magician's** wand his face resumed its former expression of august calmness. He slowly left the throne, and, dropping **here and** there a few condescending words, crossed the hall. Suddenly he noticed Baron Fontaine, the architect of the imperial palaces. "Ah," exclaimed Napoleon, quickly advancing toward him, "you are here, Fontaine? I intended to send for you to-day. Did you bring your plans with you?"

"**Yes, sire.**"

"**Well, then, come;** and you, ministers, Duke de Rovigo, Duke de Vicenza, Duke de **Bassano,** pray follow me into my cabinet."

The officers and cavaliers who remained in the hall looked after the emperor with anxious glances. "A cabinet meeting on this holiday! and at which the imperial architect has to **be** present!" they whispered. "What means this? Will the emperor commission M. de Fontaine to transform the Tuileries into a fortress, and construct ramparts and ditches? **Are we,** if all should be lost, to defend ourselves? Or will the emperor convert Paris into a fortress? Is M. de Fontaine to erect outworks and fortifications? Or will the emperor have a new Bastile built for the purpose of confining the traitorous legislature and several hundreds of these new-fangled royalists who are now springing up like mushrooms?"

But the emperor did not think of all this when, followed by the three ministers and Baron Fontaine, he entered his cabinet. An expression of affability overspread his features, and round his lips played the sunny smile which appeared so irresistible to all who had ever seen it. "Come hither, gentlemen," he said, merrily, "let us act here **as** judges. Fontaine brings us plans for a palace for the King of Rome. It is high time for me to think of building one for the heir-apparent, and this idea has engrossed my mind for a long period. If the times had not been so unfavorable, it would already have been completed. I will begin now, in order to prove to the foreign powers how great is the confidence felt by France and her emperor in their ability to withstand the attacks of the allies; for, while their armies are fighting the enemy, they are constructing a palace for their future emperor.—Now let me see your plans, Fontaine; unroll them!"

Fontaine spread out on the table the papers which he had brought with him from the anteroom. The emperor bent over them, and asked the architect to explain to him the different lines and figures. The three ministers stood beside them, grave and silent, and their furtive glances seemed to ask whether this really was not a scene intentionally contrived by the emperor—whether he really could think of building a palace for the King of Rome at a moment when France was hemmed in on all sides, and menaced by enemies, endangering the existence of the imperial throne!

But Napoleon really seemed to be quite sincere. With his magic energy he appeared to have banished all gloomy thoughts, and to be engrossed only in plans for a serene future. "See here, Caulaincourt," he said, pointing to one of the plans, "what do you think of this? It is a sort of castle or fort, and looks well, does it not?"

"Very, indeed," replied Caulaincourt. "It reminds me of the palace at Oranienbaum, which Paul I. built. The towers at the corners, the bastions, and ditches, are similar; and the interior had not only many rooms, but secret staircases, doors, and hidden passages."

"And yet Paul I. was assassinated in that palace!" cried the emperor, whose face suddenly darkened. "The doors and passages did not protect him from murderers.—Well, Maret and Savary, what do you think of it? Do you deem it best that I should build the palace for the King of Rome in the style of a fortress, like that of Oranienbaum?"

"Sire," exclaimed Savary, eagerly, "so precious a head cannot be sufficiently protected. In building a palace for the king, less attention should be paid to an attractive appearance than to safety and convenience."

"Is that your opinion, too, Maret?"

The Duke de Bassano was silent for a moment, and closely examined the plan. "No, sire," he then said, looking at the emperor, with a polite yet somewhat singular smile—"no, sire. I believe we should avoid the semblance of a fortress built for the heir-apparent, just as though he should ever need such a place of refuge against his own subjects, and in the middle of his capital! People would say your majesty intended to reconstruct for your successor the old Bastile."

"Maret is right," exclaimed the emperor. "No fortress! The confidence, love, and attachment of his people should be the only safeguard of a monarch. Ramparts did not save Paul I.; the greatest precautions, locked and guarded doors, did not protect the sultan from the scimitars of the Janizaries; every one falls when his hour has struck; it will strike for me, too, and my life will belong to him who is willing to give up his life for mine! But I shall teach my son to govern the Parisians without fortresses, and make them love him. * It is true, however, there will always be malicious men to frustrate our efforts, and sow the seeds of discord between me and my people."

"Sire," said Fontaine, anxious to turn the emperor's thoughts into a different channel, "here is another plan. The former was in the old feudal style; this would look more like a villa."

"That is the very thing I want," exclaimed the emperor, eagerly. "A villa in the grandest possible style—a palace magnificent enough to be mentioned after the Louvre, but still with all the peculiarities of a villa. For the palace of the King of Rome, after all, will be only a sort of villa in Paris; as a winter residence the Tuileries, or the Louvre, would be preferred. But, though I want the building to be large and brilliant, the total cost must not exceed ten million francs. I do not want a chimera, but something real, substantial, and practical, for myself and the king,

---

* Napoleon's words.—Vide "Memoirs of the Duchess d'Abrantes."

and not a fanciful structure merely gratifying to the architect. The completion of the Louvre will **give** glory enough to the architect. As to the **palace** of the King of Rome, he may forget his personal interest, and think only of rendering the structure as convenient as possible. It is to become a sort of Sans-Souci, where one is merry, forgets care, enjoys the sunshine in the apartments, and the shade in the garden, and may combine the simplicity of rural life with the comforts of a great city. Imagine you were building a commodious residence for a rich private citizen, a convalescent who has need of comfort, repose, and diversion. There must be, therefore, a small theatre, a small chapel, a concert-hall, a ball-room, a billiard-room, and a library; fish-ponds, and shady groves in the garden—in short, a genuine villa." [*]

"I believe your majesty will find all that you wish for united in this," said the Duke de Bassano, who had carefully examined the second plan. "It is a villa in grand style, and surely worthy of a great prince."

"Ah," said the emperor, with a profound sigh, "would it were already finished, and I could live in it with my son! I—"

At this moment the folding-doors of the cabinet were thrown open, and the usher's voice shouted, "His majesty the King of Rome!"

CHAPTER XLIII.

THE KING OF ROME.

THE emperor, with a joyful exclamation, turned toward the door. On its threshold stood a boy of remarkable beauty, such as Correggio or Murillo would have selected as a cherub model. His slender but vigorous form was clothed in sky-blue velvet, embroidered with silver, and his fairy-like feet wore shoes of the same color. His dimpled arms were bare, and a fleece of golden ringlets fell on his fair neck and shoulders. An ingenuousness, undeformed by bad training, increased the charm of his natural beauty. There was nothing affected in his blooming face; and, while a happy temper played about his lips, there was **a light in** his large blue eyes, reminding the beholder of his great father, from whom he also inherited a forehead **which, when the attractions** of his childhood had passed away, would at once assert his manly gravity and thought.

Behind the boy appeared the dignified form of Madame de Montesquiou, his governess, who seemed to take pains to keep back the boy, and, seizing his hand, hastily whispered a few words to him. But he forcibly disengaged himself, and, without noticing any one but the emperor, rushed toward him with open arms. **"Papa,"** he cried, in an imploring tone—"papa, have you not given me permission to come to you at any time?"

"Yes, sire," said the emperor, tenderly, lifting him into his arms, "and the proof of it is that you are here."

"Well, dear 'Quiou," asked the boy, in a triumphant tone, turning toward Madame de Montesquiou—"did I not tell **you so?—The** usher would not admit me, **papa, though I told** him I am the King of Rome!"

"He ran away from me," said the governess, "in the first anteroom, and so fast that I could not follow him."

"It was because I wanted to see my dear papa emperor," cried the child, fixing his eyes with an expression of indescribable tenderness on his father.

"But that was the reason, sire," said the governess, "why the usher would not immediately open the door to you. He did not know whether he was allowed to do so, and waited, therefore, until I came."

"But why did he not know that he was allowed to do so?" cried the little king, impetuously. "**Did I not tell him,** 'I *will* it, I am the King of Rome?' Pray tell me, papa emperor, do not the ushers obey you either when you say, 'I will it?'"

The emperor laughed as loudly and merrily as

---

[*] Napoleon's words.—Vide Constant, "Mémoires," vol. v. p. 184.

he had done in the days of his prosperity, and the ministers and Baron Fontaine joined heartily in his mirth; even Madame de Montesquiou could not suppress a faint smile. The boy saw it, and asked hastily, "Why do you laugh, 'Quiou? Did I say any thing ridiculous?"

"No, rather something charming," said the emperor, smiling, laying his hand on the blond head of his child, and pressing it closer to his breast. With the child still in his arms, he seated himself in an easy-chair, and, placing the little fair-haired king on his knee, gazed at him with joyful eyes. His whole countenance was changed, and beaming with mildness; even his voice assumed another tone, and seemed incapable of command or threat.

"Sire," said the emperor, "we were just speaking of you."

"Ah," cried the child, with an arch smile, "I know what it was! My papa emperor was thinking of a New-Year's present!"

"But, sire," exclaimed the governess, sharply, "it is unseemly to ask for presents."

A blush suffused the child's face, and seemed reflected on the pale cheeks of the emperor, who felt almost pained at seeing him so much ashamed of himself.

"Madame," he said, turning hastily to the governess, "I have to ask a favor of you: pray leave the King of Rome here with me for a time. I myself will take him back to you, and I promise to watch carefully over his majesty."

Madame de Montesquiou made a ceremonious obeisance; the little king kissed his hand to her, and she then left the cabinet. No sooner had the door closed than the boy, with a smile, encircled the emperor's neck with his arms, and cried, "Now we are alone, papa emperor!"

"Oh, no!" said the emperor, smiling, "did you not yet see these gentlemen?"

"No," said the child, looking round in surprise, "I saw only you, papa!"

Never had the lips of the most beautiful woman uttered words that gladdened his heart so much as these. But before his ministers he was almost ashamed of his sensitiveness, and,

therefore, he forced himself to assume a grave air. "Sire," he said, "above all, you must greet these gentlemen; they are my ministers, and very dear friends of mine."

"Ah, then they are friends of mine, too," cried the boy, with that politeness which comes from the heart. Quickly descending from his father's knee to the carpet on the floor, the little King of Rome walked several steps toward the gentlemen, and bowed so deeply to them that his blond ringlets rolled down over his face. "Pardon me, gentlemen," he said, "if I did not see and greet you! I came to my papa emperor because to-day is a holiday, and I desired to wish him a happy New-Year. I see you now, gentlemen, and, if you will permit me, I wish you all, too, a happy New-Year."

The gentlemen bowed, and looked with an expression of gentle sympathy and emotion on the lovely child, as if imploring the blessing of Heaven upon him. The emperor probably read this in their eyes, for he greeted the gentlemen with a pleasant smile, and nodded to them with the triumphant air of a happy father.

"Papa emperor," exclaimed the child, turning once more to his father, "my dear Madame 'Quiou says that France has now need of prosperity, and that I, therefore, ought to pray the good God to grant us His favor."

"Well, and did you do so?" inquired the emperor.

"Yes," replied the child, "I did, from the bottom of my heart."

"How did you pray? Let me hear, sire; it can do no harm if you pray to God once more to grant us His favor. What did you say?"

The child assumed a grave air, and knelt down. He then raised his clasped hands, and, leaning back his head, lifted up his large blue eyes. "Good God," he said aloud, "I pray to Thee for France and for my father!"

These words, uttered in so clear and melodious a voice, sounding like an angel's greeting in the solemn cabinet of the emperor, made a wonderful impression. The gentlemen averted their heads, to conceal their emotion from Napoleon.

"Good God, I pray to Thee for France and for my father."   p. 224.

But he paid no attention to them; his eyes rested on his child with an expression of profound affection; a veil seemed to overspread them, and as it perhaps prevented the emperor from seeing his kneeling child distinctly, he quickly moved his hand across his eyes. The veil disappeared, but the hand that had drawn it aside was moist.

The boy jumped up and hastened back to his father, who clasped him tenderly in his arms, and then, **as if to** apologize, turned toward his ministers. "**Well**, gentlemen," he said, gayly, "do **you** believe that the voice of the King of Rome is strong enough to reach to heaven, and bring prosperity to France and to myself?"

"Sire, I do," said the Duke de Bassano, in a trembling voice.

"And I feel convinced of it," said the Duke de Rovigo. "If any prayer can reach heaven, this must."

"It will bless France and her august emperor," said the Duke de Vicenza. "Sire, permit me to ask a favor of you. Give to France as a New-Year's present of your love, the picture of the King of Rome praying for France and his father. Your majesty, send for Isabey, and have him represent the king in this charming attitude. He will paint such a picture both with his hand and his heart, and within a month it must be circulated as a copperplate throughout France. Sire, I venture to assert that this engraving will win all hearts, and the members of the legislature cannot excite half as much hatred in the provinces as this picture will produce love."

"You are right," said the emperor, "that is an excellent idea. France shall learn that my son prays, first for it, and then for me.—Maret, see to it that Isabey come to-morrow. The plate must be ready for distribution in the course of a month.* And now," added the emperor, putting the child again on his knee, "now tell me what do you want me to give you as a New-Year's present?"

"Oh," cried the little king, smiling, "I know

something, dear papa emperor, but I dare not say what it is."

"Ah, you may," said the emperor. "I pledge you my word that I will fulfil your wish, if it be possible. Speak, then."

"Sire," asked little Napoleon, nodding toward the ministers, "sire, will these gentlemen not betray me to Madame de Montesquiou?"

"I warrant you they will not," said the emperor, gravely. "Let me hear what you want."

"Well, then, papa emperor," said the boy, leaning his head on his father's breast, and looking up to him, "I feel a great wish that I could run just once all alone into the street, and play in the mud and the gutter, as other children do." *

The emperor burst into loud laughter, in which the others did not fail to join. "Ah, you see, gentlemen," exclaimed the emperor, "this is a new rendering of Lafontaine's celebrated '*Toujours perdrix!*' The King of Rome, being able to command all that is beautiful and agreeable to his heart's content, is longing for the gutter.—Be patient, sire, I cannot immediately fulfil your wish, but I shall **have a palace for you, and in its** court-yard you shall have **a gutter, too.** Sire, look at those plans which Baron Fontaine has drawn up for a palace destined for you alone."

"What! For me alone?" asked the child, in dismay. "You will not live with me in the palace?"

"No, sire. The King of Rome must have a palace of his own, where he will reside with his court."

"Papa emperor, I thank you for your New-Year's gift," said the boy, sullenly; "I thank you, but do not accept it. I do not want a palace of my own. I thank your majesty, but prefer remaining at the Tuileries."

"But, sire, just think of it—a splendid palace belonging to you alone!"

"I do not want to live alone!"

"Well, sire, then you will request your beauti-

---

* This copperplate really appeared shortly after; it is a sweet and beautiful portrait of the little King of Rome.

* Bausset, "Mémoires sur Intérieur du Palais Impérial," vol. ii.

ful mother, the empress, to live with you. Will that be sufficient?"

The boy glanced quickly and anxiously around the room, as if to satisfy himself that neither the empress nor Madame de Montesquiou was present; he then threw both his arms round the emperor's neck, and exclaimed, "I want to be where you are, papa!"

Napoleon pressed his lips with passionate tenderness on his son's head. "Well, sire," he said, in a voice tremulous with love, "I believe your wishes will have to be complied with. As soon as your palace is completed I shall live with you. Do you accept your palace on this condition?"

"Yes, my dear papa emperor," exclaimed the prince, joyously, "now I accept it, and thank you for it."

"Well, you hear that, Fontaine," said Napoleon, turning toward his architect. "You may begin the construction of the palace; the King of Rome accepts it. I sanction this second plan. Build a magnificent villa, and it must be completed in two years. In two years—"

Suddenly the emperor paused, and his face darkened. "Ah," he said, gloomily, putting his hand on the prince's head, "ah, we purpose building you a palace, but if they conquer me you will not even possess a cabin!"* The emperor's head dropped on his breast, and a pause ensued, which the child, usually so vivacious, did not venture to interrupt.

At length Napoleon said: "Go, Fontaine, and take your plans along; I will confer further about the matter. And you, ministers, come, we have to settle some questions of importance. But, first, I must take the king back to his governess."

The boy clung with almost anxious tenderness to his father. "Ah, dear, dear papa emperor," he begged, "let me stay here! I will be quiet—oh, so very quiet! I will only sit on your knee, lean my head on your breast, and not disturb you at all."

"Well, you may stay then," said Napoleon.

---

* Napoleon's words.—Vide "Memoirs of the Duchess d'Abrantes."

"We shall see whether you really can be quiet, and not disturb us."

The little child kept his word. Sitting quietly on the emperor's knee, and leaning his little head on his father's breast, he did not interrupt in the least the important conference of Napoleon and his ministers. An hour afterward the conference was over, and the dukes were dismissed.

"Now, sire," said Napoleon, turning toward the child, "now let us play."

But the little king, who always received these words with exultation, remained silent, and when the emperor bent over him, he saw that he had fallen asleep. "Happy king!" murmured Napoleon, "happy king! who can fall asleep in the midst of state business!" Softly and cautiously drawing the boy closer to his breast, and taking pains not to disturb his slumber, he sat still and motionless, scarcely breathing, although sad thoughts oppressed his mind. It was an interesting spectacle—this lovely boy leaning his head in smiling dreams on the breast of his father, who was looking down on him with grave and tender eyes.

The emperor sat thus a long time. Strange and wonderful thoughts stole upon him—thoughts of past happiness, of past love. He thought of how long he had yearned to possess a son, and how many tears his first consort shed—how ardently he had been loved by the noble and beautiful Josephine, whom, in his pride, which demanded an heir-apparent, he had thrust into solitude. Providence had given Bonaparte all that his heart had longed for—a beautiful young wife, who loved him, and who was the daughter of an emperor; and a sweet, lovely child that was to be the heir of his imperial throne. But Providence, by giving him all, had taken all from Josephine—the heart and hand of her husband, her dignity and authority as an empress and sovereign. She was now nothing but a deserted and unhappy lady, who had only tears for her past, no joy in the present, no hopes for the future.

All this was on account of the child adored by his father, and hailed by France; and yet, despite all the mischief this little boy had done her and the fact that he was the child of another woman, Josephine loved him, and often implored the emperor to let her see and embrace the little King of Rome. He had always refused to grant this request, in order not to stir up the jealousy of his young wife, but, at this quiet hour, when he was alone with his sleeping child, Napoleon thought of Josephine with melancholy tenderness. Amid the profound silence which surrounded him, his recollections spoke to him. They pointed him to Josephine in the imperishable splendor of her love, her grace, and goodness; he thought he saw her sweet lips, which had always a smile for him; her brilliant eyes, which had ever looked tenderly on him, and which had learned to read his most secret thoughts.

"Poor Josephine!" he murmured, "poor Josephine! she loved me ardently, and many things might be different now if she were still by my side. She was my guardian angel, and with her my success has departed. She sacrificed her happiness to me and my ambition; and while formerly all hastened to offer their congratulations on this day and pay homage to the empress, she now sits lonely and deserted at Malmaison.—No," he then said aloud, "no, she shall not be lonely and deserted! I surely owe it to her to occasion her a moment of joy. She shall see my son—I myself will take him to her." He cautiously lifted up the boy in his arms and rose. The prince awoke and looked smilingly up to his father, who carried him to the sofa and laid him with tender care on the cushions. But little Napoleon jumped up, and said laughingly: "I am no longer tired. The dukes are gone now, and let us play, papa!"

"No, sire," said the emperor, "not now, I have business to attend to. But listen to me: at noon to-day I will take a ride with you, all alone—that is to be my New-Year's present."

The boy uttered a cry of joy. "All alone, papa emperor? Oh, that will be splendid!"

"But now go to Madame de Montesquiou, sire," said the emperor.—"Constant!" When the valet de chambre entered the room, he ordered Constant, "Pray conduct his majesty the King of Rome to Madame de Montesquiou, and tell her I shall call for him in a few hours in order to take a ride with him alone, without any attendants whatever.—Adieu, Sire, in a few hours we shall meet again."

But the boy stood and looked at the emperor with grave and sullen glances. "Sire," he said, "my dear Madame 'Quiou tells me often a king ought to keep his word. Now I ask you must an emperor not keep his word also?"

"Certainly, sire!"

"Well, then, your majesty, take me to Madame 'Quiou," cried the boy, joyously; "you told her you would do so. Come, papa!"

"Ah," exclaimed the emperor, smiling, "you are right—an emperor must fulfil his word, though he has pledged it only to a king. Come, sire, I will conduct you to Madame de Montesquiou. Constant, await me here!"

A few minutes afterward, the emperor returned to his cabinet. "Constant," he said, in a low voice, "I know you loved the Empress Josephine, and have not forgotten her, I suppose?"

"Sire, the empress was my benefactress; I owe to her all that I am, and she was always kind to me."

"More so than the present empress, you mean to say?" asked the emperor, casting a searching glance on his valet de chambre; and, as Constant was silent, Napoleon added, "It is true, the young empress is less condescending than my first consort. But that is, Constant, because she was brought up as the daughter of an emperor, and her feelings were restrained by the narrow limits of etiquette. Josephine forgot too much that she was an empress, Maria Louisa forgets it too little; but her heart is good and gentle, and she would never wish to grieve me. So, Constant, you have not yet forgotten the Empress Josephine?"

"Sire, none that ever knew the Empress Josephine could help remembering her. For my own part, I can never forget her."

"Ah, what a *fripon* you are, to give me such a reply! Well, I will prove to you, M. Fripon, that I have not forgotten Josephine, either. This is New-Year's-day. Would you not like to offer your congratulations to the Empress Josephine at Malmaison?"

"Sire, if so humble and low a servant as I am may dare, I should certainly be very happy to lay my congratulations at her feet."

"Go, I permit you to do so, and the empress will surely receive you very kindly."

"Particularly, sire, if I had a message from his majesty the emperor to deliver."

"Fripon, I believe you take the liberty of guessing my thoughts! Yes, I will give you a message. Hasten to the Empress Josephine, take her my greetings, but see that the empress receives you without witnesses.—Do you hear, Constant—without witnesses? Then tell her to have her carriage immediately brought to the door, and, on the pretext of being alone with her mournful New-Year's meditations, to **take a** ride without attendants. But when she is at a considerable distance from Malmaison, she is to order the coachman to drive to the little castle of La Bagatelle. She must be there precisely at four o'clock. I shall be there, and tell her majesty I shall not come alone. Now make haste, Constant! Recommend entire reticence to the empress. As to yourself, pray do not forget that, if any one shall hear of this affair, you must be held responsible. Go!"

<hr>

CHAPTER XLIV.

JOSEPHINE.

JUST as the clock struck four, the carriage of the Empress Josephine wheeled into the courtyard of the little castle of La Bagatelle. She inquired of the castellan, in a tremulous voice, whether **any** one had arrived there, and she breathed more freely when he replied in the negative. She left the carriage with youthful alacrity and **entered** the castle, followed by the castellan, who gazed in amazement at this empress without court or suite, who arrived stealthily and tremblingly, like a maiden to meet her lover for the first time. She hurried through the

well-known apartments of the castle, and entered the hall in which, during the days of her happiness, she had so often received the foreign princes and ambassadors, or the dignitaries of France. The hall was now empty; no one was there to receive the deserted empress; but bright, merry fires were burning in the fireplaces, and every thing was in readiness for the reception of distinguished guests.

"You knew, then, that I was to come?" inquired the empress of the castellan.

"Your majesty," he replied, in a low and reverential voice, "M. Constant was here, and gave orders to have the rooms in readiness. If your majesty wishes refreshments, you will find every thing served up in the dining-room."

"No, no, I thank you," cried the empress, hastily. "But tell me is my dressing-room—my former dressing-room," she corrected herself falteringly—"is that heated, too?"

"Your majesty will find all your rooms comfortable, just as though you still condescended to reside here."

"Well, then, I will go to that room. If any one comes, I shall notice it through the opened doors; it is unnecessary for you to inform me; I will go then at once to the reception-room."

The castellan withdrew, and Josephine hastened through the adjoining apartment into the dressing-room. With a long, painful sigh she glanced around the room which had so often witnessed her happiness and her triumphs. Here, surrounded by her ladies in front of this mirror, she had had her hair dressed, and the emperor had almost always made his appearance at that hour to chat with her, look at her toilet, and delight her heart by a smile, a glance, that was more transporting to her than all the homage and flattery paid her by all her other admirers. Now she was here again, but alone, and with a mournful sigh she stepped to the mirror which had so often reflected her charming portrait, radiant with happiness, and sparkling with diamonds.

And what did she see now in this mirror? A woman with a pale, grief-stricken face, features growing old, and a desponding exhaustion which only a good and pleasant life can disguise when the **vigor** of youth has faded.

"Oh, I have become old!" sighed Josephine; "the years of tears and solitude count double, for one consumes then in days the strength of many years. I have grown old because I have wept for *him*, and because I have felt his misfortunes. Oh, how will he look? Will his cheeks be even paler and his eyes gloomier than formerly? I have not seen him since his return from his disastrous campaign; if I read the history of his sufferings on his face, my grief will kill me. But no," she encouraged herself, "I will not weep, nor trouble him with my tears. I will be serene, and suppress my emotions. He will not come alone; but whom will he bring with him? I hope not the woman who is my rival—to whom I had to yield my throne!—No, I know Bonaparte's heart, I know that he would be incapable of such cruelty. She, young, beautiful, the reigning empress—I, old, sorrowful, faded, the deserted empress! I—ah, there is a carriage rolling into the court-yard! He comes!" Her whole form trembled, and, breathless, her face suffused with deep blushes, she sank into an easy-chair. "I love him still," she murmured; "my heart does not forget!" A low knocking at the small side-door leading to the inner corridor, was heard, and Constant entered. Josephine rose hastily, and with quivering lips asked, "Constant, is he there?"

"Yes, your majesty. The emperor requests you to repair to the reception-room. He will be there in a moment."

"And who is accompanying him?"

"His majesty has commissioned me to tell you that it would afford him great satisfaction to prepare a little surprise for your majesty, and that he has, therefore, fulfilled a wish which you have felt for a long time."

"Constant!" exclaimed Josephine, joyfully, "the emperor brings the King of Rome to me?"

"Yes, your majesty."

"Ah, *her* child!" cried the empress, with an emotion of jealousy, burying her face in her hands.

"The emperor requests your majesty to be so gracious as not to let the little king suspect whom he has the honor to approach," whispered Constant.

"Ah, *she* is not to suspect that her child has come to me!" murmured Josephine, while fresh tears trickled down her cheeks.

"The emperor, besides, implores your majesty not to frighten the prince by a sadness which your majesty, in the generosity and kindness of your heart, has so often overcome."

"Yes," said the empress, removing her hands from her face, and hastily drying her tears with her handkerchief, "I will not weep. It is true, I have often begged that I might see the King of **Rome—the** child for whom I have suffered so much, and to read in his face whether he is worthy of my sacrifice. The emperor is so kind as to fulfil my wish; tell him that I am profoundly grateful to him, that I will restrain my emotion and not make the prince suspect who I am. Tell him that I shall not weep when I see the child of the present empress. No, do not tell him that, Constant; it would grieve him—tell him only that I thank him, and that he shall not be displeased with me. Go! I am ready, and shall be happy to see the boy. It is not *her* child, but *his* that I am to embrace." And greeting Constant with that inimitable smile of grace and kindness peculiar to her, she walked toward the reception-room. "How my heart throbs!" she murmured; "it is as if my limbs were failing me—as if I should die." Nearly fainting, she slowly glided through the adjoining apartment, and entered the reception-room. "Courage, my heart! for it is *his* child that I am to greet." Sitting down on an easy-chair near the window, she looked in anxiety and suspense toward the large folding-doors.

At length the emperor appeared. Josephine had not seen him for nearly a year, and at first her eyes beheld only him. She read in his pallid and furrowed face the secret history of his sorrows, which he had not, perhaps, communicated to any one, but which he could not conceal from the eye of love. Unutterable sympathy and tender compassion for him filled her soul. And now she almost timidly looked upon the child that Napoleon led by the hand.

How charming was this child! How proud of him was his father! Josephine felt this, and she said almost exultingly to herself: "I have not been sacrificed in vain! This child is an ample indemnity for my tears. I am the boy's real mother, for I have suffered, sorrowed, and prayed for him!" Rejoicing in this sentiment, which seemed to restore the beauty of former days, Josephine stretched out her arms toward the child.

"Go, my son, and embrace the lady," said Napoleon, dropping the hand of the prince. He advanced, while his father stood at the table in the middle of the room, supporting his right hand on the marble slab. He looked gravely but kindly upon the empress, from whom he felt separated, by the presence of his child, as by an impassable gulf.

The little prince offered his hand to the empress with a smile, and Josephine drew him into her arms, pressing his head to her bosom. A sigh, in spite of herself, came from the depths of her heart. She slowly bent back the boy's head and gazed at him with a mournful but loving expression. Then her glance fell upon the emperor, and, with an indescribable look of love and tenderness, she said: "Sire, he is like you; God bless him for it!"

There was something so touching and heartfelt in these words—in the tone of her voice, and the glance of her eyes, that the emperor was profoundly moved, and responded only by a silent nod, not venturing to speak lest the tremor of his words should betray his emotion. Even the little king seemed to understand the excellent heart of this lady. He clung to her and said in a sweet voice, "I love you, madame, and want you to love me, too!"

"I love you, sire," cried Josephine, "and shall pray God every day to preserve you to your father—to your parents," she corrected herself with the self-abnegation of a true woman. "You will one day confer happiness on France and your people, for you undoubtedly wish to become as good, great, and wise, as your father."

"Oh, yes, my papa emperor is very good, and I love him dearly!" exclaimed the boy, looking toward his father. "But, papa, why do you not come to us? Why do you not shake hands with this dear lady, who is so good and loves me so well?"

"The emperor is generous," said Josephine, gently; "he wished me to have you a moment by yourself, sire; he has you every day, but I have never had you before."

"Why did you not come and see me?" asked the child. "You live near Paris; and, if you loved me, you would often come and see how the little King of Rome is getting on. The emperor told me you were a dear and kind-hearted lady, and that every one loved you."

"Did he tell you so, sire?" exclaimed the empress, drawing the boy into her arms. "Oh, tell the emperor that I shall always be grateful to him for it, and that these words will forever silence my grief." Her eyes glanced in gratitude to the emperor, who softly laid his finger on his mouth, to admonish her to be silent and calm.

The little prince had now, with the facility with which children pass from one subject to another, turned his attention to the large diamond brooch fastened to Josephine's golden sash. "How beautiful it is!" he exclaimed—"how it is flashing as though it were a star fallen from heaven, and fastened to your breast, because it loves you, madame, and because you are so good! And what fine ornaments you have on your watch! Ah, look here, papa emperor; see these pretty things! Come, papa, and look at them!"

"No, sire," said the emperor, with a strange and mournful smile, "let me remain here. I can see all those pretty things quite distinctly."

"They are very beautiful, are they not?" cried the child. "And if—"

"Well, sire," asked Josephine, "why do you pause? Pray speak!"

The boy had suddenly assumed a grave air, and gazed upon the ornaments of the empress.

I was just thinking—but you will be angry if I tell you what, madame."

"Certainly not, sire; tell me what you thought."

"It occurred to my mind that we met in the forest on our way a poor man who looked haggard and wretched, and begged us to give him something. But papa and I could not, for we had already distributed all our money among the unfortunate persons whom we had previously met. Why are there so many poor people, madame?— why does my papa emperor not order all men to be happy and rich?"

"Because it is impossible for him to do so, sire," said Josephine.

"And because, in order to be able to make others happy, we must ourselves be rich!" exclaimed the emperor, smiling. "Now you said yourself, sire, we could not give the poor man in the forest any thing, for we had nothing to give him."

"Yes, and I was very sorry," said the boy. "And now I was thinking if we sent for the poor man, and you, madame, gave him your watch and your diamonds, and he sold them, he would have a great deal of money, and be very rich and happy."

Josephine pressed the boy tenderly to her heart. "Sire," she said; "I promise you that I will send for your poor man and give him so much money that he will never again be wretched."

"Oh!" exclaimed the prince, encircling the lady's neck with his arms, "how good you are, madame, and how I love you!"

Josephine pressed his head to her bosom. "Oh, you may certainly love me a little," she replied, with a touching smile; "I have really deserved it of you."

"Sire," said the emperor, advancing a few steps, "now bid the lady farewell. We must go."

"Papa!" cried the boy, joyously—"papa, we must take the dear lady with us; she is so good, and I love her. Let her live with us in the Tuileries, and always stay with us. I want her to do so, and you, too, papa, do you not?"

Josephine's **eyes filled with** tears, and she looked at the emperor with an expression of unutterable woe. He immediately averted his face, perhaps to prevent Josephine from noticing his emotion. "Come, sire," he said imperiously, "it is high time; it is growing dark. Take leave of madame!"

"Oh, no; I will not take leave of her!" cried the boy, vehemently. "I say to her rather— Come with us to the Tuileries!"

"It cannot be, sire," said Josephine, smiling amidst her tears.

"Why?" cried the boy, impatiently, and throwing back his head. "Come; you may accompany the emperor, and I want you to do so!"

Napoleon, painfully moved by this scene, quickly advanced to the prince, and took his hand. "Come, sire," he said in a tone so grave that the boy dared no longer resist. Submitting to his father's will, he stepped back, and, pleasantly bowing, took leave of the empress.

"We shall meet again," said Josephine, and, turning her tearful eyes to Napoleon, she asked, "We shall meet again, sire, shall we not?"

"Yes," said Napoleon, gravely, "we shall meet again." He then took leave of her with an affectionate look, which fell as a sunbeam upon her desolate heart, and, leading the boy by the hand, turned quickly toward the door. She looked after them in silence and with clasped hands. As the door opened, the emperor turned again with a parting but melancholy glance.

Josephine was again alone. With a groan she fell on her knees, and lifting her face toward heaven, she cried, "My God, protect—preserve him! Whatever I may suffer, oh, let him be happy!"

<hr>

CHAPTER XLV.

TALLEYRAND.

For a week the emperor had scarcely left his cabinet; bending over his maps, he anxiously examined the position of his army, and that of the constantly advancing allies. Every day couriers with news of fresh disasters arrived at Paris; rumors of invading armies terrified the citizens, and disturbed the emperor's temper. It was impossible for the government to conceal the misfortunes which had befallen France from the beginning of the new year. The people knew that Blucher had crossed the Rhine, and, victoriously penetrating France, on the 16th of January had taken up his quarters at Nancy. It was publicly known that a still larger army of the allies, commanded by Prince Schwartzenberg, had advanced through Switzerland, Lorraine, and Alsace, taken the fortresses, overcome all resistance, and that both generals had sworn to appear in front of Paris by February, and conquer the capital. All Paris knew this, and longed for peace as the only way to put an end to the sufferings of the nation. The strength and the superiority of the allied army could not be concealed, and it was felt to **be impossible to expel the powerful** invaders.

Napoleon himself at length saw the necessity of peace, and, conquering his proud heart, he sent the Duke de Vicenza, his faithful friend Caulaincourt, to the headquarters of the allies, to request them to send plenipotentiaries to a peace congress. The allies accepted this proposition, but they declared that, despite the peace congress, the course of the war could not in the least be interrupted; that the operations in the field must be vigorously continued. Napoleon responded to this by decreeing a new conscription, ordering all able-bodied men in France to be enrolled in the national armies. The terrors of war were, therefore, approaching, and yet Paris was in hope that peace would be concluded; Caulaincourt was still at the headquarters of the allies, treating with them about the congress.

Early on the morning of the 23d of January, another dispatch from Caulaincourt to Maret was received at Paris, and the minister immediately repaired to the Tuileries, to communicate it to the emperor. **This** dispatch confirmed all the disastrous tidings which had arrived from day to day, and convinced Napoleon and his minister that the vast superiority of the allied armies rendered it impossible for the emperor to rid his country **of** the formidable invaders.

"Maret," said Napoleon, gloomily, "come and look at this map. What do you see here?"

"Sire, a number of colored pins extending in all directions."

"And a small number of white pins. Well, these are my troops; the colored **pins** designate the armies of my enemies. They are allied; but I—I have no longer a single ally at this hour; I stand alone, and have to meet eight different armies. See here, Maret: there is, in the first place, the grand army of the Russians, Austrians, Bavarians, and Wurtembergers, commanded by Prince Schwartzenberg, and accompanied by the allied monarchs; next, there is the grand Prussian army, with the Russian and Saxon corps, under the command of Blucher, the hussar; here stand the Swedes under Bernadotte, reënforced by Russian and English corps, and the German troops of the Confederation of the Rhine; there comes the Anglo-Batavian army; here, farther to the South, is Wellington's army, composed of English, Spaniards, and Portuguese; there, in Italy, is an Austrian corps under Bellegarde; at no great distance from it, the Neapolitan corps under the King of Naples; and, finally, here at Lyons, is another Austrian corps under Bubna. The armies of Schwartzenberg, Blucher, and Bernadotte, are about six hundred thousand strong. And now see what forces I have—I cannot call them armies! Augereau's corps is stationed near Lyons; Ney, Marmont, and Mortier, are with their corps here between the Meuse and the Seine; Sebastiani and Macdonald are with the remnants of their corps on the frontier of the Netherlands. Maret, my troops are hardly one hundred thousand; the allies, therefore, are six to one."

"Sire," said Maret, "even a military genius like that of your majesty, will be unable to cope with such odds, and it reflects no dishonor on the bravest to submit to the decrees of Fate."

"It is true," murmured Napoleon, throwing himself into his easy-chair, with his arm leaning on the desk, and his head bent forward—"it is true, I have no sufficient force to oppose them;

their armies are six times as strong as mine, and, unless fortune greatly favors me, I must yield!"

"But fortune has forsaken us, sire, and we have no strength left. Yield, therefore, sire; submit to a stern necessity; comply with the anxious demand of France; restore peace to your people—to the world! Do not endanger, without prospect of success, your precious life, which is necessary to France—your throne, threatened by foreign and domestic foes. All is at stake. Save France, save the throne! Make peace at any cost!"

While Maret was speaking, Napoleon slowly raised his head, and sent a flaming glance on his minister. Now, that Maret was silent, the emperor quickly took up an open book from his desk and handed it to Maret. "I will not answer you, duke," said Napoleon, "but Marmontel shall. Read this. Read it aloud."

Maret read: "'I know of nothing more sublime than the resolution taken by a monarch living in our times, who would be buried under the ruins of his throne rather than accept terms to which a king should not listen; he was possessed of too proud a soul to descend lower than unavoidable misfortune. He knew full well that courage may restore strength and lustre to a crown, but that cowardice and dishonor never can.'" *

"That is my reply, Maret," exclaimed Napoleon. "The example of Louis XIV. shall teach me to perish rather than humiliate myself."

"Sire," said Maret, solemnly, "Marmontel is wrong; there is something more sublime than to be buried under the ruins of a throne—a king sacrificing his own greatness to the welfare of a state that must perish with him."

"Never!" exclaimed the emperor, impetuously. "I can die beneath the ruins of my throne, but I cannot sign my own humiliation! Maret, I have made up my mind: I will continue this struggle to the last; I will conquer or die! To-morrow I set out for the army. Ah, I want to see whether

that drunken general of hussars, Blucher, shall not yield to me, notwithstanding his crazy cavalry tricks; whether Schwartzenberg, my faithless pupil, who had learned the art of war from me, will meet me in a pitched battle; and whether Bernadotte, my rebellious subject, dare look me in the face. Maret, the decisive struggle is at hand. I will take the field, save Paris, and conquer the enemy. I must call upon all the men of France to defend the sacred soil of our country, and convert every house into a castle, every village into a fortress, so that my enemies shall have to wrest every inch of ground from us at a vast sacrifice. Not another word about peace! Every thing is ready. Troops are hurrying forward from Spain to **fill up my army; in a few** days they will be here. Between the Seine and the Marne all my forces will unite and put a stop to the advance of the allies upon Paris. We shall occupy a position by which it will be easy for us to divide, disperse, and crush the enemy. Here, in the plain between these rivers, I shall march along the Aube, scatter the allied army, hurl most of my troops at one of its wings, and, by skilful manœuvres, compel the other wing to fall back. The enemy must retreat; I shall profit by it, and when I have gained a great battle over him, I can impose my own terms; I have then conquered an *honorable* peace for France—one that we can subscribe to without blushing. Ah, I see a brilliant future! It is time to begin. My eagles are ascending; they are not ravens or bats—they are soaring to the sun." As the emperor uttered these words his soul illuminated his face; he was again the conqueror, confiding in his star.

Maret looked anxiously, but admiringly, at Napoleon's face, in which great resolutions were beaming, and he read there an assurance and determination that nothing could change. "You have made up your mind, then, sire: the war is to go on, and the peace congress is not to meet?"

"On the contrary," exclaimed Napoleon, smiling, "let it meet, if the allies wish it. While Caulaincourt, Metternich, and Hardenberg, are dictating terms of peace with their pens, we shall do so with our swords, and we shall soon see which will make

* Marmontel, "Grandeur et Décadence les Romains," ch. v.

the more progress. But let us now commence with some movements of peace. We must be on good terms with Spain and Rome. Let Ferdinand return as King to Spain, and as such become my ally. I shall also open the doors of Pope Pius's prison at Fontainebleau; let him return as pope to Rome, and, as God's vicegerent, be on my side. Maret, here are already two allies. In order to conquer, but one is wanting; and it is for you, Maret, to procure it."

"Sire, what is the name of this ally?" asked the Duke de Bassano, in amazement.

"Money! money! and, for the third time, money! Procure me five millions in cash, and I can add one hundred thousand men to my army."

"Ah, sire, our chests are empty!" sighed Maret.

"But I must have money," replied Napoleon, vehemently. "Without it no war can be waged —no victory **gained.** Five millions, Maret; I **need them; I must have them!"**

Maret looked thoughtful. Suddenly his face kindled, and his whole frame shook with joy. "Sire, your majesty asks for five millions?"

"Yes, five millions, to begin with."

"Well, then, sire, I can tell you where to find them, and perhaps more."

"Where?"

"Sire, will you pledge me your imperial word not to betray that it was I who told you where to find this money?"

"Certainly, Maret."

"Listen, sire; but permit me to whisper what I do not wish even the walls to hear." He bent close to the emperor's ear.

Napoleon listened with breathless attention, and nodded repeatedly. "You really believe this to be true, Maret?" he then asked, eagerly.

"Sire, I affirm it to be true. It is a secret known only to three persons! It was betrayed to me to gain me over by an act of treachery—but that is altogether another matter; the fact is sufficient."

"And this fact is, that I shall find with my mother the millions that I need?" said the em-

peror. "Maret, if that is so, I shall have them this very day."

"Your majesty believes so? Madame Letitin—"

"My mother is avaricious, you wish to say? It is true, her extreme economy has often vexed me; to-day it gladdens my heart; for, thanks to her parsimony, I shall find with her what I need for my army. She will deny these millions to me, to be sure; but you told me where to look for them, and I pledge you my word I know how to find and take them! Hush, not another word! I shall have what I want within an hour. Go now, Maret. You will meet the Prince de Benevento in the antechamber. Send him to me. I have to address a few parting words to M. de Talleyrand."

The emperor stood in the middle of the magnificently furnished cabinet when the Prince de Benevento slowly opened the door and entered. The prince bore the emperor's piercing look with a perfectly composed air. Not a feature of his aristocratic countenance expressed any anxiety and his smile did not for an instant vanish from his lips. With a sort of careless bearing he approached the emperor, who allowed him to come near him, still watching every expression of his countenance.

"I wished to see you," he said, "in order to tell you that I shall set out for the army the day after to-morrow." Talleyrand bowed, but made no reply. "Do you desire to accompany me?" asked the emperor, vehemently.

"Sire, what should I do at the headquarters of the army?" said Talleyrand, shrugging his shoulders. "Your majesty knows well that I could be of very little service in the **army—that** I am able only to wield the pen."

"And the tongue!" **added** Napoleon. "But before leaving Paris I will give you some wholesome advice; bridle both your tongue and your pen a little better than you have done of late. I know that you will not shrink from any treachery, and that **you** are the first rat that will desert the sinking ship; but consider what you are doing. The ship is not yet in danger, and, spreading her sails, she will move proudly on her way."

"I hope she will have favorable winds and deep water," said Talleyrand, bowing carelessly.

Napoleon looked at him with hatred and rage. These equivocal words—the calm, cold tone in which they were uttered, disturbed the emperor, and his blood boiled. "I believe in the sincerity of your wish," he said, "although there are many who assert that you are a traitor. I have given you fair warning; now prove to those who are accusing you, that they are doing you injustice. No intrigues! You will be closely watched. Beware!" Talleyrand bowed again, and his face still retained its indifferent, smiling expression. "Listen now to what I have to say," added Napoleon. "Prior to my departure I desire to put an end to the dissensions with Rome and Spain. The pope will leave Fontainebleau to-morrow and return to Rome. The Infante of Spain, too, is at liberty to return to his country and ascend the throne of his ancestors. Go to-morrow to Valençay. It was you who conveyed Ferdinand thither; you must, therefore, open the doors of his prison that you locked."

"Sire, I thank your majesty for the favor which you desire to confer on me," said Talleyrand, gravely. "But it was not I who arrested the sacred person of the legitimate King of Spain; it was not I who dared to deprive him of his rights—nay, his very liberty. I acted only as the obedient servant of my master, for your majesty's orders made me the jailer of the Infante of Spain."

Napoleon approached Talleyrand, and his flaming eyes seemed to pierce his soul. "What!" he shouted, in a loud voice. "You wish to give yourself now the semblance of innocence in this affair? What! You only executed my orders, and I made you the jailer of the infante! Who was it, then, that urged me to do this? Who was it that told me it was indispensable for me to crush the head of this Spanish hydra? Who wished even to persuade me to more energetic measures than imprisonment, in order to get rid of the royal family of Spain? Who told me at

that time that it would be wiser and better for the welfare of Europe to cut the Gordian knot instead of untying it? Do you remember who did all this?"

Talleyrand made no reply. His countenance still exhibiting the same indifferent composure, he seemed scarcely to have heard the rebukes of the emperor. His head slightly bent forward, his eyes half closed, his lips compressed, he stood leaning with one hand on the back of a chair, and with the other playing with his lace-frill. This conduct greatly augmented the emperor's anger. "Will you reply to me?" thundered Napoleon, stamping the floor, and so near to Talleyrand's foot that the prince softly drew it back. "Will you reply to me?"

Talleyrand looked at the emperor with immovable calmness. **"Sire,"** he said, slowly, **"I do** not know what your majesty means."

"You do not know what I mean?" echoed Napoleon. "If you do not, listen!" Unable longer to overcome his anger, he advanced toward Talleyrand, and the prince drew back. As if beside himself, the emperor raised his clinched fists, and held them toward the prince's face, moving through the large room, while Talleyrand, looking the emperor full in the face, retreated, taking care to get nearer the door.

"I will tell you that you are a traitor," cried Napoleon, rushing forward—"a traitor who would like to deny to-day what he did yesterday, because he believes that another era is dawning, and that he must betray his master before the cock crows for the first time. You wish to deny that it was you who urged me to imprison the Spanish prince? You are impudent enough to tell me that to my face?" So saying, the emperor's clinched fist almost touched the cheek of the prince, who was still receding, and now noticed with a feeling of relief that he had reached the end of his dangerous promenade.

"Do you really dare deny your past in so barefaced a manner?" cried Napoleon, still holding his fist so close to Talleyrand's cheek that he almost felt it.

The prince softly put his hand behind his back,

and fortunately succeeded in seizing the door-knob. He opened the door with a hasty jerk so wide that the gentlemen assembled in the ante-room **enjoyed the** spectacle of Napoleon with up-lifted fists threatening his minister.

"Sire," said Talleyrand, in a calm voice, "I shall not dare say any thing; for I know of no reply to what your majesty has said." The prince pointed with a sarcastic smile to the clinched fists of the emperor, and, without complying with the re-quirements of usual ceremony, he hastened, more rapidly than his lame foot generally permitted him to do, through the antechamber, saluting the gen-tlemen as he passed with a wave of his hand and a smile. On stepping into the outer room he ac-celerated his pace, gliding down-stairs as softly as a cat, and hurrying across the hall to his car-riage.

"Home," he said aloud, "at a gallop!" When the horses started, Talleyrand leaned back, and said to himself, "This was our last adieu! I shall take good care not to meet Napoleon again, pro-vided he is stupid enough to give me time for making my dispositions."

The emperor in the mean time, half ashamed of himself, reëntered the cabinet, and locked the door. Angry as a lion in his cage, he paced to and fro with quick steps, when suddenly a gentle voice behind him said, "Sire, pray be so gracious as to listen to me!"

The emperor turned with an angry gesture, and saw the Duke de Rovigo standing near the open door of the antechamber. "Well, Savary, what do you want?" he asked in a faint voice. "Shut the door, and come here.—Speak! What do you want?"

"Sire, to implore you to be on your guard," said the duke. "Your majesty has just had a violent scene with the Prince de Benevento."

"Who told you so?"

"Sire, we could distinctly hear your majesty's voice in the antechamber; and, when the prince opened the door, the rest, like myself, saw your threatening attitude. In an **hour all** Paris will **know it.**"

"Well?"

"Sire, the Prince de Benevento is not the man **to forget an insult, and it will mortify** him doubly **that the world will hear of it.**"

"Let it mortify him!" cried Napoleon. "All of you have insinuated to me that Talleyrand is a traitor, deserving punishment. I have chastised him; that is all."

"Sire, the chastisement was either too severe, or not severe enough," said Savary, gravely. "Had it been too severe, the generous heart of your majesty would think of offering him some satis-faction; but I know Talleyrand, and am firmly con-vinced of the truth of my statement—I pronounce him a plotter of dangerous intrigues. Your ma-jesty therefore cannot chastise him too severely; and, having gone so far, you must now go still farther."

"How so? What do you mean?"

"Sire, I mean that your majesty, instead of al-lowing the Prince de Benevento to return home, ought to send him to Vincennes, and recommend him to the special care of your friend General Daumesnil."

"Ah, I ought to have him arrested!" cried Na-poleon, shrugging his shoulders. "I ought to make a martyr out of a traitor!"

"No, sire, punish a traitor, neither more nor less! I know that Talleyrand is one. He is in secret communication with the legitimists, cor-responding with the Bourbons, through other hands; at his house, meetings of malcontents and secret royalists are held every day; there the fires are kindled that will soon burst into devour-ing energy, unless your majesty extinguish them in time. You have disdained to regain Talleyrand by promises or honors. You have insulted him, and he will revenge himself, if the power of doing so be left him. Sire, I venture to remind your majesty of Machiavel, '**One** ought never to make half an enemy.' "

"It is true," murmured Napoleon to himself, thoughtfully, "nothing is more dangerous than such half enmities. Under the mask of friend-ship they betray us the more surely."

"Hence, sire, pray tear this mask from Talley-rand's treacherous face. Meet him as an open enemy. Then either his enmity will be destroyed by terror, or he will betray his intentions."

"I lack proof to convict him," said Napoleon, in a hesitating and wavering tone.

"Well, yes," exclaimed Savary, "you have no proof, but there cannot be the least doubt as to the intrigues which he is bold enough to plot. The opportunity is too favorable that he should not endeavor to embrace it. Sire, I should like to urge the example of the great police-minister of Louis XV. Whenever M. de Sartines was on the eve of a festival, or any great public ceremony, he sent for all suspicious persons to whom his attention was particularly directed, and said to them, 'I have no charge against you at present, but to-morrow it may be different. Habit you know has power over you, and you are unlikely to resist temptation. It would be incumbent upon me to treat you with extreme rigor. For your sake, as well as mine, be kind enough therefore to repair for a few days to a prison, the choice of which I leave to yourselves.' The suspected persons willingly complied with his request, and no arrests were made."

"You may be right; M. de Sartines was undoubtedly a sagacious police-minister," said the emperor, musingly. "His precaution is good for those who are afraid; but I am not! If I conquer my enemies, I thereby trample in the dust this vile serpent, too, that would sting me, and then would crawl as a worm at my feet. If I yield to my enemies, let the structure which I have built fall upon me. It will not matter then whether Talleyrand's hand, too, broke off a piece of the wall or not; it would have fallen without him. Not another word about it, Savary! My carriage—I will ride to my mother!"

On the evening of the same day, the Prince de Benevento left his palace, entered a hackney-coach, and was driven to one of the remote streets of the Faubourg St. Germain. He stopped in front of a small, mean-looking house; and, when the coach had gone, the prince knocked three times in a peculiar manner at the street door. It opened, and he cautiously entered. No one was to be seen in the lighted hall; but Talleyrand

17

seemed perfectly familiar with the locality; and, crossing, without hesitation, a long **passage, he** ascended the thickly-carpeted staircase. Here was another locked door, beside which was a bell, which the prince rang three times. The door was opened, and he walked through a long corridor. The passage widened, and the prince **was** now in a brilliant hall, decorated with paintings and gildings. The entrance through the small house was plainly but a circuitous road to one of the palaces of the Faubourg St. Germain where the royalists were plotting mischief. At the end of this hall was a *portière*, in front of which was a richly-liveried footman. Talleyrand whispered a few words; the servant bowed and opened the door. The prince now entered a saloon, furnished in the most magnificent and tasteful style, where another liveried attendant was waiting. "The Countess du Cayla?" asked the Prince de Benevento.

"She is in her cabinet. Shall I announce your highness?"

"It is unnecessary."

He quickly approached and knocked softly at the door of the cabinet. A sweet voice bade him come in. Before him stood a young lady **who** welcomed him with a charming smile, but with an air of ill-concealed amazement. "Oh, the Prince de Benevento!" she exclaimed, merrily. "You come to me to-day; but yesterday, when I went to you to bring you greetings from our august master, King Louis XVIII., you feigned not to understand whom I wished to speak of, and imposed silence."

"To-day I come to make amends for what I did yesterday, countess," said Talleyrand, with his graceful kindness. "Be good enough to inform his majesty King Louis XVIII. that he may henceforth count upon my services and my zealous devotedness. I shall assist him in opening the road to Paris, and do all I can that his majesty may soon be able to make his entrance into the capital of his kingdom."

"Then you have forsaken Napoleon openly and unreservedly!" exclaimed the Countess du Cayla, the zealous agent of the Count de Lille, whom at that time none but the royalists secretly called King Louis XVIII. "You are, then, one of us, now and forever?"

"Yes, I consider myself a member of your party," said Talleyrand, "and at heart I was always one of the most faithful and zealous servants of the king. I can prove it, for it was I who led Napoleon, step by step, frequently even in spite of his reluctance, to the brink of ruin, on which he is standing now, and I am ready to give him a last thrust to plunge him into the abyss. The emperor has been guilty of great folly to-day. He ought to have had me arrested, but he failed to do so. For this mistake I shall punish him by profiting by my liberty in the service of his majesty the king. Let us consider, therefore, countess, what we ought to do for the speedy return of King Louis XVIII. to Paris."

"Yes, let us consider that," exclaimed the countess; "and if you have no objection, prince, we shall allow the faithful friends of his majesty to participate in the consultation. Upward of one hundred friends are already assembled in the large saloon, and they are doubtless astonished at my prolonged absence. Come, prince! You will meet an old friend among your new friends."

"Who is it, countess?"

"The Duke d'Otranto!"

"What? Is he here? Has he dared to return?"

"He has, with the emperor's sister, the Princess Eliza Bacciochi; and he is believed to be with her in the south of France, in order to await the course of events. But he has secretly and in disguise come to Paris, in order, like you, to offer his services to King Louis. Late events seem to have converted him into a very zealous royalist, and he openly admits his conversion. He boasts of having said to the Princess Eliza: 'Madame, there is but one way of salvation: the emperor must be killed on the spot.'" [*]

"In truth, he is right," said Talleyrand, smiling; "that would speedily put an end to all embarrassments. Well, the emperor intends to join the army; perhaps, a hostile bullet may become our ally, and save us further trouble. If not, we shall speak of the matter hereafter. Permit me, countess, to conduct you to the saloon."

CHAPTER XLVI.

MADAME LETITIA.

PROFOUND silence reigned in the palace of "Madame Mère." It was noonday, and the male and female servants, as well as the ladies of honor of the emperor's mother, had left the palace to take elsewhere the dinner which Madame Letitia refused to give them, and for which she paid them every month a ridiculously small sum; only the two cooks, whom madame, notwithstanding her objections, had to keep, in compliance with the express orders of the emperor, were in the kitchen, but under the vigilant supervision of old Cordelia, the faithful servant who had accompanied madame from Corsica to France, and who, since then, notwithstanding all vicissitudes, had remained her companion. Cordelia not only watched the cooks and gave them what was needed for preparing the meals, but, as soon as the dishes were handed to the servant who was to carry them to the table, she hastened after him in order to prevent him from putting any thing aside. When Cordelia went with the servant, she opened, with an air of self-importance, a cupboard fixed in the wall of the corridor, near the dining-room, of which she alone possessed the key, and, as soon as the servant returned with the fragments of the dinner, she locked them in this cupboard with the wine and bread; only on Sundays did the dinner-table of Madame Mère provide any thing for the servants.

To-day, however, was not Sunday, and hence Madame Cordelia herself had placed a bottle, half filled with wine remaining from yesterday's dinner, on the table, at which no one but Madame

---

[*] "Mémoires du Duc de Rovigo," vol. vi., p. 352.

Letitia was to seat herself, one of the ladies of honor, who always dined with her, having been excused on account of indisposition. Madame Letitia was therefore alone to-day; it was unnecessary for her to submit to the restraint of etiquette, and she yielded with genuine relief to an unwonted freedom. She was in her sitting-room, busily engaged in taking from a large basket, the plebeian appearance of which contrasted strangely with the magnificent Turkish carpet on which it stood, the folded clothes which the washerwoman had just delivered. The appearance of Madame Mère herself was also in some contrast with the gorgeous surroundings amid which she moved.

The room was furnished with princely magnificence, the walls being hung with heavy satin, and curtains of the same description, adorned with gold embroideries, suspended on both sides of the high windows; the richly-carved chairs and sofas were covered with purple velvet, and the tables had marble slabs of Florentine workmanship. A chandelier of rock-crystal hung in solid gold chains from the ceiling; masterly paintings in broad, rich frames were on the silken walls; Japan vases stood on gilded consoles, and numerous costly ornaments added to the splendor of the aristocratic apartment.

Madame Letitia, standing beside the wash-basket, presented a marked contrast with all this. Her tall figure was wrapped in a light white muslin dress trimmed below with rosettes, and from which protruded a rather large foot, covered with a cotton stocking, and encased in a coarse, worn-out shoe. A sash of rose-colored silk, with faded embroidery, encircled her waist; a lace shawl, crossed over her bosom, and tied in a careless knot on her back, enveloped her neck and full shoulders. Her hair, falling down in heavy gray ringlets, was surmounted by a sort of turban, and a large bouquet of artificial roses, fastened above her forehead, was her only ornament.

There was nothing therefore imposing in the appearance of the emperor's mother; but still there was something noble about her, and that was her face. It was of imperishable beauty; its outlines were classic and of great dignity, and her eyes, which were of the deep, incomparable color which she had bequeathed to her son the emperor, possessed still the lustre of youth; her lips were fresh, and her teeth faultless; not a single wrinkle furrowed her forehead, and her finely-curved nose added to the imperious expression of her features. The whole bearing of Madame Letitia indicated a lofty and yet a gentle spirit. He who beheld only this form, with its strange dress, could not refrain from smiling; but a glance at the beautiful and dignified face filled the beholder with feelings of reverence and admiration.

Madame Letitia, as we have said, was engaged in unpacking the clothes just returned by the laundress. This was an occupation which she never intrusted to any of her attendants, but in which she could generally engage only secretly and at night, after she had dismissed them; for the emperor made it incumbent on his mother's ladies of honor to observe the strictest etiquette, and forbade her to occupy herself with affairs improper for the mother of an emperor. Hence, Madame Letitia was obliged, for the most part, to lead the life of an aristocratic lady, to embroider a little, ride out, have her companions read to her, receive visitors, and pass the day in *ennui*. Only at night, when the ladies left the palace—when etiquette permitted Madame Letitia to retire with her maid Cordelia into her bedroom—only then commenced her active life. At that time madame conversed with her confidantes about her household affairs; she decided what dishes should be prepared for the following day, and, when all were asleep and she was sure of being watched by no one, she proceeded with her faithful Cordelia to the cupboard of the corridor to examine the remnants saved from dinner, and to decide whether they might not be served up again.

On this day she was free from the restraints of etiquette. The lady on service had been taken ill; and her second lady of honor, not anticipating such an event, had obtained leave to take a trip to Versailles. Madame Letitia, therefore, was at liberty to dispose of her time as she pleased; she could fearlessly indulge in occupations entirely contrary to etiquette, and she embraced this rare opportunity in the course of the forenoon of examining the clothes, which otherwise would have had this honor only after nightfall. But the consequence was, that the usually serene forehead of Madame Letitia grew dark, because she was by no means satisfied with the performance of her laundress. Just as her busy hands took up another piece from the basket and unfolded it, the door behind her opened. She heard it, but did not turn, knowing very well that it was Cordelia who entered her room, for no one else had the right of taking **such a liberty without** being duly and formally **announced.**

"Cordelia," she exclaimed, "Cordelia, come and look at these towels of the cook; all of them are already threadbare, and it is but a year since I bought them. You ought to tell the cook very emphatically that he should be more careful and not ruin **my towels.** Do you hear, Cordelia?"

"Cordelia is not **here," said a grave, angry** voice behind her. Madame Letitia started, and a deep blush suffused her cheeks. Close behind her stood the emperor, fixing his stern eyes on his mother.

"The emperor!" she murmured, yielding to the first movement of terror, and sinking back on her chair.

"Yes, the emperor!" said Napoleon, approaching and casting angry glances on the clothes spread **out on the table.** "The emperor pays a visit to his mother, and finds to his amazement that little respect is felt here for his orders, and that it is deemed unnecessary to comply with his wishes. Ah, madame, how can the emperor expect the people to obey him everywhere and unconditionally, when his own family set an example of disobedience, and openly show that the emperor's orders are indifferent to them?"

"When have I shown indifference **to them?"** asked Madame Letitia, casting a despairing glance on the basket.

"You show it at this very hour," said the emperor, sternly, "and every thing proves that you are in the habit of disobeying my wishes. I met with no footmen in the outer antechamber; I did

not see the chamberlain of your imperial highness in the adjoining room."

"It is noonday, and they have gone to dinner."

"Ah, it is true, your imperial highness directs your court to take their meals at other houses," exclaimed the emperor, with a sarcastic smile. "You are paying board-money to the chamberlain, the valet de chambre, and the footman, so that it is unnecessary for you to feed them. But where is your waiting-lady, madame? Did I not issue orders that etiquette should be observed at my mother's palace, and that your imperial highness should always have your lady of honor with you?"

"The Duchess d'Abrantes was suddenly taken sick this morning, and had to return to her house."

"In that case the second lady of honor ought to have taken her place."

"Yesterday I gave permission to the Countess de Castries to go to a family-festival to be celebrated at Versailles, and she went early this morning."

"Every thing, then, is here just as it ought to be!" cried the emperor, indignantly, thrusting the basket with his foot. "It is in strict accordance with my wishes that your house is empty, that you are so occupied, that you are alone, and that there was no one to announce my visit?"

"But Cordelia certainly was there, and quite ready to attend to this."

"Yes, she was," cried the emperor, "and it is true she wished to do me that honor. But I would not allow her, and preferred coming to you without being announced. In truth, it would be too ludicrous if the old Sibyl had served the emperor as mistress of ceremonies."

"She formerly did him far greater and more difficult service," said Madame Letitia, in a firm and calm voice, for she had fully recovered her presence of mind, and, rising from her easy-chair, proudly bridled herself up and turned toward the emperor her face, which now had resumed its expression of noble dignity and composure.

"When I first saw your countenance," she said, calmly, "I was frightened, and greeted you in my terror as the emperor. Pardon me for it! I ought to have remembered that when the emperor crosses the threshold of this house, he ceases to be emperor, and is simply Napoleon Bonaparte, who, as it behooves a son, comes to pay his respects to his mother. Hence, I ought to have greeted you at once as my son, and if I did not, it was because I was frightened, for I am not accustomed to see any one enter here without being announced. Now, I have overcome my terror, I bid you welcome with all my heart, my dear son!" She offered her hand to Napoleon so proudly that the emperor, scarcely aware of what he did, pressed the small white hand of his mother to his lips.

A gentle smile lit up the beautiful face of Madame Letitia. "I forgive you also your vehement words, my son," she said; "and how could I be angry with you for forgetting for a moment that you are here only my son, when I myself remembered only that you are the emperor? Let us, therefore, make peace again. Napoleon, my son, I bid you welcome once more with all my heart."

"Even, my mother, if I should come to ask my dinner of you?" inquired the emperor, smiling.

Madame Letitia was silent for a moment. "Even then!" she said, after a pause. "My son will be content with what I am able to give, and he will pardon an old woman, who attaches little value to the pleasures of the table, if she has, on account of her health, but a very plain dinner."

"That is to say, we shall have the national dish of Corsica—rice dumplings baked in oil!" exclaimed the emperor, laughing.

"So it is," said madame, merrily. "Ah, I see my son has not forgotten his native Corsica; then he will also have a kind look for poor old Cordelia, who, both in good and evil days, has been the most faithful and honest servant of our house, who frequently carried Napoleon Bonaparte for whole days in her arms, and when he was sick sat at his bedside and nursed him with the tenderness of a mother. I will tell Cordelia to take this basket away, and inform the cook that we have a guest." She rang the bell; the door of the adjoining room opened immediately, and old Cordelia entered. She stood still at the door, and cast mournful glances, now on Madame Letitia, now on the emperor.

"Well, Cordelia, do you not greet my son?" asked madame. "He is not the emperor to-day, but comes incognito as my son to ask dinner of me."

"And listen, dear Delia," said the emperor, speaking to her in the voice of a child—"listen, dear old Cordelia; afterward let us go and play, and gather shells on the sea-shore. Shall we do so, 'Lia?'"

An air of unutterable happiness illuminated the face of old Cordelia when Napoleon repeated to her, in the voice of his childhood, the words which he had so often addressed to her. She rushed toward him, and, sinking down before him, seized both his hands and pressed them to her lips. "Now do with me what you like, Napoleon," she cried, in the language of her native country, while the tears were rolling down her cheeks, "I belong to you again, with every drop of my heart's blood. Trample me under foot, strike me, kick me, as you often did during your childhood—I shall never murmur. I am as a faithful dog, who allows himself to be beaten, and yet loves his master to the last!"

"Yes, she is as constant as the sea that washes the shores of our native country," said madame, with a tear in her eye. "You may count on both of us, Napoleon, and if there is power in our prayers you will always be victorious."

The emperor's face darkened. He had forgotten every thing for a moment; but he soon recollected himself. In order to be victorious and prosperous he needed not only soldiers but money, and he had come for the purpose of obtaining this from his mother. He disengaged his hands from those of old Cordelia, and motioned her to rise. She obeyed in silence, quietly took up the clothes, and carried them off in the basket.

"See that we soon have dinner," said madame to her. Cordelia turned and looked inquiringly at her mistress, who nodded to her; Cordelia nodded, too, and went out smiling.

A quarter of an hour afterward, the emperor conducted his loving mother to the dining-table, at which none other than themselves were to be seated. When they entered, the emperor's eyes glided with a strange, searching look along the paintings hanging on the walls, and rested for a moment on the landscape which, in a broad gilded frame, was directly opposite; then a faint smile flitted over his features, and he turned toward his mother to address a few pleasant words to her.

The dinner commenced, as the emperor anticipated, with Corsican rice dumplings baked in oil. He partook of them with great relish, and this favorite dish of his childhood seemed to have restored his good humor. "I believe," he said, gayly, "I am still able to read as well in your face, mother, as I could when I was a boy, and took pains to discover whether or not I **had deserved** punishment for some naughty prank. I believe I have understood your mute dialogue with Cordelia. Will you confess the truth to me if I tell you what Cordelia's glances and your nod signified?"

"Yes, if you guess it."

"Well, then, mother, did not Cordelia inquire by her glances whether she was to send to the baker for bread, and whether the remnant of yesterday's dinner should not be served again in **honor of my presence?** And did not your nod reply, 'Yes?' Was not that the meaning of it? Do I guess right?"

"Yes, my son," said madame, smiling; "I see that my haughty daughters Pauline and Eliza have made you familiar with the habits of my household."

"They have," exclaimed Napoleon. "They told me Madame Mère had every day only three loaves of white bread brought from the baker for herself and Cordelia."

"They told you the truth; all my officers and servants receive their board-money, and three loaves are sufficient for us two. Ah, my son, how happy would you have often been, when still

a lieutenant, had you had only one of the three **loaves every day!**"

"Eliza told me still other things," said Napoleon, casting a glance toward the large oil painting. "She told me you had, like all honest *bourgeoises*, your water-carrier, who furnished every day six buckets of water."

"Eliza told you the truth again. It is still the same water-carrier whom we employed when we lived in the Faubourg St. Honoré; he is a faithful and honest man; why, then, should I withdraw this little patronage from him?"

"But you pay him no more for his water, now that you are the emperor's mother, than you did when you were a' poor widow with nine children."

"God makes the water flow, and it is the same now as then. Why should I, then, pay more for it?"

"Eliza told me, also," added the emperor, dwelling with singular perseverance on the same subject, "that, instead of collecting a library, and buying the books you read, you have subscribed to the bookseller Renard's circulating library."

"There are very few books that deserve the honor of being bought," said madame, in a dignified tone.

"And is it true, too," asked the emperor, "that you have the books brought by the bookseller's clerk to you every week the year round, and that you have the same exchanged by your servants during only New-Year's week, in order thereby to avoid giving a New-Year's present to the clerk?"

"It is true," said madame, calmly. "This clerk is not poor, nor the father of a family; I avoid, therefore, giving him the money which I prefer giving to poor men."

"But, madame," cried Napoleon, angrily, "you really surpass Harpagon, and Mollère has cause to complain that he did not know you." *

"Mollère has assuredly cause to deplore that he did not live at the present time," said madame, quietly, "for if he lived now, he would have seen on the throne of France a prince who is even greater **and** more illustrious than his own

---

* Napoleon's words.—Vide Le Normand, vol. II., p. 451

Louis XIV. And he would have certainly been **glad** to make my acquaintance, as I am the mother of this great man."

"The mother of an emperor, and yet living so parsimoniously that one might believe your son suffered you to starve! And still, if I am not mistaken, you receive a million francs a year for defraying the expenses of your court. Am I right, mother?"

"Yes, my son; I receive a million francs a year."

"Ah, madame," cried the emperor, "then you must, considering your economy, lay by riches every year?"

Madame Letitia's face was serious; the emperor had touched a chord unpleasant to her ear.

"No," she said, abruptly, "I lay by no riches, for my expenses **are heavy.**"

"But your income is larger," exclaimed Napoleon. "I am satisfied that you spend far less than you receive. Whom do you economize for, madame?"

"Whom?" asked madame, in an angry voice. "I might say for myself, for my future, for that is uncertain, and one is never able to know what may happen. But, in addition to myself, I have to take care of your brother Lucien, for your majesty knows well that he is poor."

"Because he would not accept the kingdom which I offered to him."

"Because, as a king, he would not be a dependent vassal, the mere lieutenant of his brother. What, sire! Would you accept a kingdom offered to you on condition that you should never have a will of your own, but always obey that of another?"

"I would not," said the emperor, smiling; "but I am the emperor."

"You are Lucien's brother, and he is no less proud than the emperor. Let us say no more about it. He is poor; that was all I wished to say. He is unable to endow his daughters, and I have, therefore, taken this upon myself. You know now, my son, what my savings are for."

"But I am just as well your son as Lucien," said the emperor, in a bland voice; "you may

very well have laid by money for both of your sons. I am in the same predicament as my brother. I am poor, and need money. Hence I come to you, to my mother, and pray you, let me have some of your savings. I know you have money; I need it, and you would place me under the greatest obligations if you would lend me a large sum."

Madame Letitia gravely shook her head. "You are mistaken, sire," she said; "I have only as much as I need."

The emperor's forehead darkened more and more. "Madame," he cried, in a tone of irritation, "I repeat to you, it is a great favor which I ask of you!"

"And I repeat that I have no money to spare; I **had** some, but sent it recently to Lucien, who **needs it.**"

"Well, then, let us say no more about it," replied the emperor, rising, and, as if to overcome his vexation, turning toward the paintings, and closely inspecting one after another. "You have very fine paintings, madame," he said, after a pause.

"Yes, the work of great masters," replied madame, composedly. "You reproach me **with** being very parsimonious, sire; I have, however, paid very large sums to artists."

"I am especially delighted with this landscape," said the emperor, standing in front of the Swiss landscape, on which he had repeatedly cast furtive glances.

"Well, it is very fine and costly," said madame.

The emperor was silent, and looked up again attentively to the painting. He then turned toward his mother, who stood near him. "Mother," he exclaimed, "I asked money of you, and you refused it. Will you refuse my request, too, if I ask you to present me with this fine landscape?"

"On the contrary," said madame, "I am glad to **be able to** fulfil your majesty's wish. I shall have the painting conveyed to the Tuileries this very day."

"No," exclaimed the emperor, smiling, "it will

be better to take it at once with me in my carriage. You are so economical, mother, you might repent of having given me so costly a present, and might want to keep it."

"Sire," said madame, solemnly, "the emperor's mother pledges you her word that you shall receive the painting this very day."

"Madame," replied her proud son, no less solemnly, "the emperor's mother also pledged me her word that she has no money to lend me, and yet I venture to believe that she has laid by a great deal. Pardon me, therefore, if I persist in taking the painting with me.—Delia, Delia!" The door of the corridor opened, and old Cordelia looked in. "Run, Cordelia, and tell my two valets de chambre, Constant and Roustan, to come hither at once."

Cordelia disappeared, and Napoleon now turned his head slowly toward his mother. Madame Letitia became pale; large drops stood on her forehead; her eyes were flashing with angry excitement, and her lips were quivering. But overcoming her agitation she forced herself to smile, and offered her hand to the emperor. "Come, my son, let us go into my cabinet and take coffee. It is unnecessary for us to be present with the servants. Come, sire."

The emperor did not take her hand, but, slightly bowing, drew back. "Permit me to stay, madame, till my servants have taken the painting from the wall."

Madame could not suppress a sigh, and clutched a chair, as if she needed a support.

The door opened, and the two imperial valets de chambre, Constant and Roustan, entered. "Come here," cried the emperor, "take this down and carry it into my carriage." The valets hastened to take the painting carefully from the wall. The emperor's glance passed over the spot which it had covered. He saw that part of the silk hangings looked somewhat fresher and darker than the rest. "One would think the wall here were wet, and had moistened the hangings," he said, laying his hand on the dark spot. "No," he then exclaimed, "the wall is hollow here! Let us see what it means."

Madame uttered a cry, and, sinking into a chair, closed her eyes.

The emperor now hastily tore off the dark piece covering the wall, and behind it was a deep square hole, in which stood a rather large-sized iron box. "Ah! do you see, madame," cried the emperor, smiling gayly, "I discover here a secret which you yourself were ignorant of. It is evidently a box which the former proprietors of this palace concealed here during the revolution from the rapacious hands of the Jacobins."

Madame made no reply; her eyes were still closed, and she sat pale and motionless.

"The box is heavy!" added the emperor, trying to lift it up. "Constant, fetch the footmen to assist you in carrying it into my carriage.—I will take it with me, madame," he said, turning toward his mother, "I will personally examine its contents." At this moment Constant returned with four footmen, and the six men succeeded at length in lifting the iron box. "Now carry it immediately into my carriage," commanded the emperor.

Panting under their heavy load, the men left the room. The emperor looked after them until the door closed. He then turned again toward his mother, who sat motionless and with her eyes closed. "Farewell, mother," he said; "I am anxious to examine the contents of the box which I was lucky enough to find. But I must not dare now to deprive you of your beautiful painting. This hole in the wall must be covered, and your imperial highness might not at once have another picture worthy of replacing this landscape. I thank you, therefore, for your present, and take the will for the deed. Farewell, madame!" He bowed and walked slowly toward the door.[*]

Madame Letitia said nothing, and made no movement to return the emperor's salutation. As he departed, she groaned and wept. "Five millions!" she murmured, after a pause—the savings of long years has my son taken from me. Five millions!—the dower that I had laid by for Lucien's daughters—that I had econo

---

* Le Normand, "Mémoires," vol. II., p. 448.

mized for the time when these days of prosperity will end." She buried her face in her hands and sobbed aloud. At length her grief seemed somewhat calmed, and she raised her head again. "Well," she said, aloud, "I formerly supported my family of nine children on an income of less than a hundred louis d'ors a year; if need be, I can do so again, and I hope I shall have at least so much left that Lucien and his daughters will not starve. I must be even more parsimonious." *

Two days afterward, on the 25th of January, the emperor left Paris for his army, and entered upon the last struggle. He was fully aware of the dangers threatening him. Hence, prior to leaving Paris, he put his house in order. The regency by letters-patent was conferred on the Empress Maria Louisa, but with her was conjoined his brother Joseph, under the title of lieutenant-general of the empire; and Cambaceres, the arch-chancellor, was placed at the head of the council of state. The emperor then received the officers of the National Guard of Paris in the apartments of the Tuileries. The empress preceded him on entering the apartments, carrying the King of Rome in her arms. Greeting the officers, the emperor said: "Gentlemen of the National Guard of Paris, I am glad to see you assembled here. I am about to set out for the army. I intrust to you what I hold dearest in the world—my wife and my son. Let there be no political divisions; let the respect for property, the maintenance of order, and, above all, the love of France, animate every heart. I do not disguise that, in the course of the military operations to ensue, the enemy may approach in force to Paris; it will be an affair of only a few days: before they are passed I will be on their flanks and rear, and annihilate those who have dared to invade our country. Efforts will be made to cause you to waver in your allegiance and the fulfilmen of your duty; but I firmly rely on your resisting such perfidious temptations. **Farewell, and God bless us all!"** * Then, taking his son in his arms, he went through the ranks of the officers, and, presenting him to them as their future sovereign, he exclaimed, in a voice tremulous with emotion: "I intrust him to you; I intrust him to the love of my loyal city of Paris!"

The National Guard responded by protestations of fidelity and devotedness. Cries of enthusiasm rent the apartments; tears were shed, and a sense of the solemnity of the moment penetrated every mind. All shouted, "Long live the emperor! Long live the empress!" Maria Louisa, pale with emotion, her face bathed in tears, leaned her head on the emperor's shoulder; and, holding his son in his left arm, he placed his right around the trembling form of his consort. At the sight of this touching group the enthusiasm of the National Guard knew no bounds. They wept, cheered, and swore they would die to a man rather than forsake the emperor—that they would allow Paris to be laid in ruins by the artillery of the enemy rather than surrender the empress and the King of Rome.

But this enthusiasm of the National Guard met with no response beyond the Tuileries. Paris maintained an ominous silence, and, when the emperor rode through the city at night, the streets were deserted; no one had awaited him to pay him homage on his departure. Paris was asleep—its sleep that of exhaustion—and the people were dreaming, perhaps, that adversity was hastening upon them.

* Lucien, the ablest and noblest of Napoleon's brothers, lived in constant dissension with him, for he would not submit to his will. He declined the throne of Naples because the emperor imposed the condition that he should govern in precise accordance with the orders given him. He married a distinguished and beautiful Roman lady, and when Napoleon afterward offered him the throne of Tuscany on condition that he should get a divorce from his wife, Lucien refused, and preferred to live in obscurity outside of France, and to dispense with the splendor surrounding his family.

* Constant, "Mémoires," vol. vi., p. 7.

CHAPTER XLVII.

THE BATTLE OF LA ROTHIÈRE.

THE morning of the 1st of February dawned cold and gloomy; heavy gusts, driving the snow across the plain, gave to the landscape a sad and dreary aspect. Silence reigned in the camps of the hostile armies. In that of Napoleon at Brienne, and farther down the valley at the village of La Rothière, on this side of the Aube, the camp-fires of the night were flickering in the gray morning, and far away on the horizon were seen the dark outlines of the castle of Brienne. There Napoleon had passed the last night of January, and in the vicinity encamped his troops, scarcely thirty thousand strong, the remnant of that "grand army" which the emperor had so often led to victory.

In the camp of the Silesian army, too, all was quiet. It encamped beyond the Aube, on the heights of Trannes and Eclance, in the vineyards and the forests of Beaulieu; it was enjoying repose after a prolonged exposure and privation. But its commander-in-chief, Field-Marshal Blucher, seemed to have no need of rest. Scarcely had daylight dawned when he was already on horseback, and rode to the crest of the mountain, by the side of his faithful adviser and friend General Gneisenau, and followed by his pipe-master. From the crest he was able to survey the whole valley of La Rothière and Brienne, lying at a distance of scarcely four miles.

Blucher raised his right arm toward the city and heaved a deep sigh. "Gneisenau," he said, "I am deeply mortified at the defeat which Bonaparte inflicted on us two days ago. I cannot get over it, and can imagine what a hue-and-cry the distinguished gentlemen at headquarters have raised, and how the *trübsalsspritzen* are croaking again: 'Blucher is a crazy hussar who always wants to drive his head through a wall, and yet cannot get through it, and only causes us all a vast deal of trouble.' I can imagine how the peace apostles are raising their voices again, crying that war ought to cease, and we should run home because we did not gain the battle of Brienne. It is indispensable, therefore, for us, Gneisenau, to strike a good blow and get even with Napoleon. Yonder the fellow stands, with his few thousand men, showing his teeth, as if he were still the lion that needed only to shake his mane to frighten us off as flies. I will show him that I am no fly, but a man who is able at any time to cope with him and such as are with him. Gneisenau, we cannot help it; we must attack him this very day. We must silence the *trübsalsspritzen*, in order to accelerate our operations against Paris."

"You are right, field-marshal," said Gneisenau; "we must strike a decisive blow, and compel the gentlemen at headquarters to discontinue their present system of procrastination. We must show Napoleon that we have also passed through a military school, though not at Brienne."

"It makes me feel angry, Gneisenau, that we were unable to show him that at the very city of

Brienne. I had thought how well it would be for me to prove to him, at the place where he passed his examination and received his first commission, that I had also passed my examination and learned something. Well, it is no use crying about it now; we must try to get over it, and only think of the best manner in which we may be even with him. General Wrede must join us with his troops at noon to-day, when we shall be stronger than Bonaparte, Marmont, and all his marshals together."

"See!" cried Gneisenau, whose eyes were directed to the camp of the enemy, "the troops yonder have put themselves in motion; I see it quite distinctly now that the view is clearer. But they are not advancing."

"No," cried Blucher, "they are retreating; they intend to escape us; Bonaparte wishes to avoid a battle. But that will not do; I must have my battle here! How am I to get to Paris if I do not rout his forces? how am I to pull him down if the present state of affairs goes on as heretofore? A blow must be struck now; we must take revenge for Brienne to-day!"

"Wrede will be here with his troops at noon," said Gneisenau, thoughtfully; "let us, therefore, attack the enemy at twelve o'clock, and make all necessary dispositions for it. Above all, couriers should be sent to headquarters."

"Yes, Gneisenau, it is your province to attend to all that, for you know well that you are the head and I am the arm. Consider all that is necessary; I know only that Bonaparte contemplates a retreat, and that I must compel him to accept battle. I have felt sad enough for the past three days; for, say yourself, Gneisenau, is it not sheer arrogance for Bonaparte to remain here so long quietly in front of us, as though he intended to give us time for uniting our forces, and thought we were, after all, too cowardly to defeat him?"

"It is, perhaps, not arrogance, but disgust and weariness," said Gneisenau, thoughtfully. "The prince of battles seems to be exhausted, and to have lost confidence."

"A pretty fellow he is whom misfortunes at once exhaust," grumbled Blucher, "and who is courageous only as long as he is successful! But I do not object to this disposition of Bonaparte, for every thing turns out now highly advantageous to us. The Austrians, the Wurtembergers, and the Bavarians, have come up, and will coöperate with us. Gneisenau, dispatch your couriers to headquarters, that the monarchs may come. Take out your note-book; I will dictate to you what occurs to me, and what are my plans in regard to the battle.—Halloo, Christian! give me a pipe! I can think much better when smoking!"

Christian galloped up, and with a grave air handed the short pipe to his master. "Pipe-master," said Blucher, "hold a good many pipes in readiness to-day, for there will be a fight, and you know that our gunners fire more steadily when my pipe is burning well.—Well, write now, Gneisenau: 'Precisely at twelve the troops will be put in motion, and descend from Trannes into the plain. In the centre, Sacken's infantry will advance upon La Rothière in two columns. The Austrians form the left, and will march on the town of Dionville. The hereditary Prince of Wurtemberg's corps, composing the right wing, will penetrate through the forest of Beaulieu, **and** take the village of La Gibrin. Olsuwiew's infantry and Wassilchikow's cavalry, Sacken's reserves, will follow the two columns of the centre. Two divisions of Russian cuirassiers and Rajewski's corps of grenadiers will remain in reserve on the heights of Trannes. The Bavarian corps, under Wrede, will be stationed on the extreme right wing.'* Well, that is enough; close your note-book," said Blucher, blowing a large cloud of smoke from his mouth. "Every thing else will come of itself after the fight has begun. I have said what I had to say, and now commence your work, Gneisenau. Dispatch couriers quickly to the headquarters of the sovereigns, and may they arrive here in time, and not again, by their hesitation and timidity, spoil our game, coming too late from fear of coming too early! Let me tell you that I am not afraid of Bona-

---

* Beitzke, vol. iii., p. 118.

parte, with his young guard and his army of conscripts. We are twice as strong, for we have eighty thousand men, and his forces, I believe, are not forty thousand. Besides, we have allies whom Bonaparte cannot have—the good God and His angel, Queen Louisa. He has sent us to put an end to the tyranny of the robber of crowns, and Queen Louisa is looking down and praying for us and Prussia's honor. The enemy, however, whom I am afraid of, is in our own flesh and blood; he is creeping around the headquarters of the monarchs, and singing peace-hymns, and raising a hue-and-cry about the greatness of Bonaparte, representing him as invincible, and ourselves as insignificant. In that way are all our arms paralyzed! Gneisenau, should they hesitate to act in an energetic manner, and fail to be on hand in time, it would be dreadful, and I believe my rage would kill me!"

But Blucher's apprehensions were not to be verified. All the corps on which he had counted in drawing up his plan of operations arrived at the stated hour, and precisely at noon appeared the Emperor of Russia, the King of Prussia, and Prince Schwartzenberg, with their numerous and brilliant suites. The monarchs surveyed the position of the two armies from the heights of Trannes, and had Blucher explain his plan to them in his brief and energetic manner.

The Emperor Alexander then turned with a gentle smile toward Prince Schwartzenberg, commander-in-chief of the allied forces. "And what do you think of this plan of the brave field-marshal?"

"It is as well conceived as it is bold," said Schwartzenberg, "and I beg leave to intrust the command of the whole army to Field-Marshal Blucher. I renounce the privilege of directing the operations of to-day, and leave every thing to the discretion of the field-marshal."

Blucher's eyes sparkled with delight, and a glow suffused his cheeks. "Prince," he exclaimed, offering his hand to Schwartzenberg, "this is an honor for which I shall always be grateful to you. You have a generous heart, and know that I must take revenge for the disastrous affair of Brienne. I thank you, prince, for giving me an opportunity. Now I shall prove to their majesties that Bonaparte is not invincible, or, if I cannot prove it to them, I shall die! Hurrah! Let us begin!" He galloped with the impatience and ardor of a youth to the front of the troops, which put themselves rapidly in motion, and rushed like a torrent down the heights of Trannes.

Soon the artillery commenced to boom, and transmitted Blucher's battle-cry to Napoleon. The emperor, who had intended to retreat with his small army, in order to avoid a fight, now halted his troops, and formed them into line. As the allies were advancing with great impetuosity, a further retreat would have been equivalent to flight. Napoleon, therefore, accepted the battle, and his cannon soon responded. The engagement raged with murderous energy; the balls hissed in every direction; the allies rushed forward in strong columns, but the French did not fall back before them. In the midst of the fearful carnage they stood like heroes, sometimes repulsing the superior enemy with sublime valor; and when they gave way, they rallied and advanced to reconquer their positions. It was easy to see that it was Napoleon's presence that inspired the French with irresistible courage. Hour after hour vast numbers were slain on both sides, and while the earth was trembling beneath the strife, the snow fell to such a depth as to shroud the dead from view.

The contest was most furious in and around the village of La Rothière. The French held it with the utmost obstinacy, and vainly did Sacken's corps, which had been repeatedly repulsed, return to the charge; the French stood like a wall, and their cannon hurled death into the ranks of their adversaries.

Blucher witnessed this doubtful struggle for some time with growing impatience; his loud "Forward!" encouraged the troops to charge, but their assaults were in vain. "Gneisenau," he cried, "we must take the village, for La Rothière is the key of the position.—Halloo, pipemaster!" Hennemann was by his master's side. "There," said Blucher, taking the pipe from his mouth, and handing it to Christian, "take this pipe, and stay, do you hear, on this spot! I shall soon be back, and you will see to it that I then get a lighted pipe. I have to say a word or two to the French."

"You may depend on it, field-marshal, I shall stay here," said Christian, gravely; "you will find me and the pipe here."

"Very well; and now come, Gneisenau," said Blucher, galloping to the head of the assaulting columns. Turning his face, full of warlike ardor, toward his soldiers, he shouted: "You call me Marshal Forward! Now I will show you what that means!" He turned his horse, and, brandishing his sword, rushed toward the village. The soldiers followed him with deafening cheers.

Christian Hennemann looked composedly after them, **and, putting** the field-marshal's pipe into his **mouth,** he murmured, "Well, I wonder if this will burn until the field-marshal returns, or if I shall have to light another!" At this moment a bullet whizzed through the air, carrying away the pipe from his mouth, and slightly wounding him. "Well," he murmured, calmly, "the first one is gone, and a piece of my head to boot! Let us immediately dress the wound, and then light another pipe; for if he should return, and it is not ready for him—thunder and lightning!" After giving vent to his feelings, the pipe-master took **out** his little dressing-pouch, stanched the blood, applied a plaster to the wound, and wrapped a linen handkerchief around his head. "Now I am all **right** again, and will do my duty," said Christian, closing the pouch, and opening the box, which was fastened to the pommel of his saddle.

The fight was still raging. Night came, accompanied by a violent snow-storm, so as to render the muskets useless. As on the Katzbach, Blucher's soldiers had to attack the enemy with their swords and bayonets. At length the allies were successful; the French were overpowered and driven back. The soldiers, headed by Blucher, rushed exultingly into the village of La Rothière. "Forward!" shouted the field-marshal. "Forward!" repeated the soldiers. They halted in the middle of the village. The French still occupied the houses on both sides of the principal street, and, converting every building into a fortress, they fought like lions against the impetuous enemy. Blucher was in the midst of the flying bullets, but he did not notice them. The position had to be taken, and he knew that his presence inspired his soldiers to heroic efforts. The village was soon on fire, for the wind carried the flames from house to house, and the snowy plain reflected the red glare far and wide. The French rushed from the houses in hurried flight, hotly pursued by Blucher's soldiers. The battle was gained! The enemy evacuated La Rothière, and retreated in disorder to Brienne and across the Aube.

Blucher could now return to his headquarters and inform the monarchs of a victory. He rode back, thoughtfully; and Gneisenau, who was by his side, was also grave and silent.

"Gneisenau," he exclaimed, "I believe we have done very well to-day!"

"Your excellency must not say we, but I have done very well to-day," said Gneisenau, smiling. "You alone conceived the plan of battle, and directed it; for La Rothière was the key **of the** whole position, and it was Marshal Forward who took it. This time your deeds must give the name to the battle, and it must be called 'the battle of La Rothière.'"

"Well, I do not care," said Blucher. "We have gained to-day, then, the battle of La Rothière, and, what is still better, we have shown the French in their own country that Napoleon's invincibility is a myth, and that he can be beaten as well as any other general.—But what is that? See there, Gneisenau! what sentinel is posted on the road yonder?"

In fact, a dark form on horseback halted by the roadside; the flames of the burning village rose higher, **and shed** a light on the stranger. It was a man dressed in the uniform of an hussar; a white, blood-stained handkerchief was wrapped around his head and half his face; his right arm was also bandaged, and in his mouth was a clay pipe.

"It is the pipe-master!" cried Blucher, quickly galloping up.

"Yes, it is I—who should it be?" grumbled Christian.

"But, Christian," exclaimed Blucher, "how in Heaven's name do you look! And what are you doing here?"

"I am waiting for Field-Marshal Blucher. Did you not tell me that I was to wait for you here, and keep the pipe in order? Well, I did wait for you, field-marshal. And you ask, too, how I look? Just like one around whom the blue beans have been whizzing for hours past, and whose head and arm have been scratched a great deal. You kept me waiting a long time, field-marshal—more than four hours! The French have shot pipe after pipe from my mouth, and this is the last I have. If you had not come soon, it would have been smashed, too."

"No," said Blucher, smiling, "the French will not break another pipe of mine to-day, Christian, for they have taken to their heels. It is true, however, I have kept you waiting a long time. But that was the fault of the French; they resisted with the greatest obstinacy. For the rest, Christian, you had a pipe of tobacco at least during the whole time that you were waiting, and did not fare so badly after all; as for your wounds, I shall have them well attended to, my boy. You have behaved as a brave man, and stood fire as a genuine soldier ought to do. When we get home I will relate it to your old father, and he will rejoice over it. Now, give me the pipe; it will be the last that you will fill for me for some time to come, for you are disabled; your right arm is shattered, and you must be cured."

"Well," exclaimed Christian, "with my left hand I can fill your pipes. I am and must be Field-Marshal Blucher's pipe-master, and, if they do not shoot off my head, I will not give up my position!"

On the following day Blucher received at the castle of Brienne the congratulations and thanks of the allied monarchs. The Emperor Alexander embraced him, and his eyes were filled with tears of joyful emotion. "Field-marshal," he said,

"you have crowned all your former efforts by this glorious triumph. I do not know how we are to reward you for this. But I know we must admire and love you."

King Frederick William shook hands with Blucher, and a smile illuminated his features. "Blucher," he said, mildly, "you have kept your word; you have fulfilled all that you promised us at Frankfort, when I informed you of your appointment to the command-in-chief. To-day you have blotted out the disgrace of Jena. Have you any wish which I am able to fulfil. Pray let me know it, for I should like to prove to you my gratitude and love."

"I have a wish, and before it is gratified, I shall neither sleep well by night nor be calm by day. Now your majesties are quite able to grant this wish of mine, and therefore I urgently pray both of you to do so."

"Tell us what it is!" exclaimed the emperor; "I am anxious to grant it as far as I am concerned, for an heroic head like yours must not lie uneasy at night, and a childlike heart like yours must be content. Speak, then!"

"Ah, sire," said the king, smiling, and fixing a searching look on Blucher's bold face, "sire, beware of promising, for then he will leave us no rest; he will not even let us sleep at night until he has driven us to Paris.—That is your wish, Blucher, is it not?"

"It is!" exclaimed Blucher, ardently. "That is my wish; and, as your majesty has called upon me to tell you something that you could grant, and as his majesty the emperor tells me, too, that he would like to gratify me—I say, let us now set out by forced marches for Paris. Let us advance with all our armies on the capital, for then the war will soon be over. I implore your majesties, let us proceed quickly. Let us give Bonaparte no time for heading us off; but let us outstrip him moving on Paris, and, if need be, take the city by storm. When Paris falls all France is ours, and the war is over!"

"Well, what says your majesty?" asked Alexander, turning toward the king. "Shall we comply with the wish of our young madcap?"

"Sire, as far as I am concerned, I have pledged him my word," said Frederick William; "hence, I must keep it."

"And I assent with the greatest pleasure, sire," exclaimed **Alexander**; "let us march on Paris, then; but we should agree as to the best way of doing so."

"Well, we have invited our generals to hold a council of war, and I believe they are waiting for us now," said the king. "Come, therefore, sire; and you, Blucher, pray accompany us. One thing is settled: we shall march on Paris in accordance with your wish—only we have to select the routes which the various columns of the army are to take, for they are too large to move by the same road; they could not find the necessary supplies in the same section of country. We must divide them, and that is the question which we shall now discuss with our generals."

"I do not care about that," replied Blucher, merrily; "if the chief point is settled, all the rest is indifferent to me; I shall obey the orders of my king, and be content with the route selected for me and my corps. The point is—we must profit by our victory and outstrip Bonaparte! We must take Paris!"

CHAPTER XLVIII.

THE DISEASED EYES.

Upward of a month had elapsed since the victory of La Rothière, and Blucher's ardent wish had not yet been fulfilled; the allies were not in Paris. The system of procrastination had again obtained the upper hand at the headquarters of the allies. Austria hesitated to use her power in a decisive manner against Napoleon, the emperor's son-in-law; the crown prince of Sweden wished to spare France, and was still in hope that the congress, which had been in session at Chatillon since the 4th of February, would conclude a treaty of peace. Among the very attendants of the Emperor of Russia and **the** King of Prussia this peace party had its active supporters, who opposed an energetic policy, and wished the congress of Chatillon, and not the army, to put an end to the war.

Blucher once had dared openly to oppose these "peace apostles," and disregarded the instructions received from the allied monarchs to move farther back from Paris, and, instead of crossing the Seine, retreat with his army to Chaumont and Langres. This order filled the field-marshal with anger, and his generals and staff-officers shared it. Great as he was in all his actions, Blucher took the bold resolution to pay no attention to the retrograde movements of Schwartzenberg and the crown prince of Sweden, but to continue his march, even at the risk of appearing in front of Paris without support.

But it was not as a rebel that he had wished to take so daring a step; on the contrary, **before** moving, he wrote to King Frederick William, and implored him to fulfil his wish, and allow him to advance. He did not wait, however, for the king's answer, but, though he knew that the commander-in-chief, Prince Schwartzenberg, had already commenced retreating, continued to march with his Silesian army alone upon the capital of France.

The monarchs themselves were of Blucher's opinion, and gave him full power, having his army reënforced by the corps of Bulow and Winzingerode. With his forces thus increased to twice their original strength, he was able to confront Napoleon, and attack Paris even without Schwartzenberg's assistance. But the fortune of war is fickle, and he did not continue his march without experiencing this. On the 7th of March he fought a bloody battle with Napoleon and his marshals between Soissons and Craonne, and, to his profound regret, was defeated, and forced to retreat.

He took revenge at Laon, where he and his brave Silesian army gained a victory on the 9th of March. This was followed by still another. He at length silenced the "*trübsalspritzen*" and "peace apostles," who had up to this time raised their influential voices at headquarters.

All felt that a retreat, after this great victory, was entirely out of the question, and even Schwartzenberg and Bernadotte joined in Blucher's "Forward!" and marched their armies to Paris.

But the brave field-marshal himself was at this time unable to join in the movement. Since the battle of Laon he had been affected with a violent inflammation of the eyes, aggravated by a fever. Confined to his dark room, he was obliged to remain ten days at Laon, suffering not only physical but mental pain. For how could he redeem his pledge—how achieve a final victory over Napoleon—if, half-blind and doomed to the captivity of a sick-room, he could not march with his troops, and lead them in person into battle? Regardless of the warnings of his physicians, he tried to brave his sufferings, and, putting himself at the head of his troops, again advanced with them. **Finally, on the** 24th **of March, by way of Rheims, he arrived at Chalons.** But the inflammation **of his eyes had grown worse on the road, and gave him intolerable pain ; the fever sent his** blood like fire through his veins, and what neither age, nor defeat, nor disappointed hope, had been able to accomplish, was accomplished by sickness. He grew faint-hearted—his disease destroyed his enthusiasm. Longing for tranquillity, he remembered how beautiful and peaceful his dear Kunzendorf was, how kind and mild the sweet face of his Amelia, and with what soft hands she would wash his inflamed eyes, and apply the **remedies.**

During the last march from Rheims to Chalons he constantly thought of this. At length he made up his mind, and no sooner had he arrived at Chalons than he sent for Hennemann, and locked himself in his room with him.

"Christian," said Blucher, in a subdued voice, "I am going to see whether you are really a faithful fellow, and whether I may confide something **to you."**

"Very well, field-marshal, put me to the test."

"Not **so loud!**" cried Blucher, anxiously. "Let us first discover whether any one can hear us here." He opened the door, and looked into the antechamber. No one was there. He then examined **the dark alcove** adjoining the sitting-room, **which was empty, too.** "We are alone; **no one can overhear us,**" said Blucher, returning **from his reconnoissance to** the sitting-room. "Now, pipe-master, listen to me. First, however, look at my eyes, do you **hear**; look closely at them. Well, how do they look?"

"Very sore," said Christian, mournfully.

"And they have not grown better, though Voelzke, the surgeon-general, has been doctoring them every day; and, by his salves, mixtures, leeches, and blisters, causing me almost as much pain as the eyes themselves. Nay, they grow rather worse from day to day, and if I remain here longer, and allow the physicians to torment me, I shall finally lose my eyesight altogether, and when I am blind, I shall be of no account— unable to use my sword and fight Bonaparte. I am afraid the good God will not permit me to pull down Bonaparte from his throne. He knows I should then be too happy, and therefore says, ' Gotthold Leberecht Blucher, I have permitted thee to bring Bonaparte to the brink of ruin; now thine armies are close to Paris, and will, with out thee, get into the city. Go, therefore, o d boy, and have thine eyes cured!' Well, I w ll comply with God's will, and go to some place and have myself healed, where they know better how **to do it than our doctors** here. I have been told that **there are excellent** oculists at Brussels, and Brussels **is not very far from here.** I will, therefore, go there."

"**The** field-marshal intends to retreat, then ?" said Christian, laconically.

"Retreat!" cried Blucher, angrily. "Who **takes** the liberty of saying that Field-Marshal Blucher intends to retreat ? "

"**I** take that liberty," said Christian. "The field-marshal intends **to retreat** from the inflammation of his eyes."

"Why, yes ; that is an enemy from which it is no disgrace to retreat."

"A retreat is always a retreat," said Christian, with a shrug, "and if you carry out your intention you will no longer be called Marshal Forward!"

"I do not care to be called so now!" exclaimed Blucher. "The inflammation of my eyes has made me desperate; I shall lose my sight if I stay here, and then they will lead me by the nose like a blind bear. There is no use in talking any more about it; I will and must go. If you do not wish to accompany me say so, and you may stay here."

"If you go, then I will too," said Christian, with his usual calmness, "for where the field-marshal is the pipe-master must be; that is a matter of course. I have pledged my word to my father, to Madame von Blucher, and to the good God, that I would never leave my general, and it makes no difference if he is field-marshal now. If they do not shoot me, I shall stay with my field-marshal."

"Christian," said Blucher, offering him his hand, " you **are a dear** boy; your heart is in the right **place,** and it is always the best thing in a man. When we get back to Kunzendorf you shall lead a very pleasant life, for I can never forget what a faithful and excellent young fellow you have been. Then you will go with me?"

"Yes, to the end of the world, general!"

"Well, we shall not go so far as that—only to Brussels, where there are good oculists; and when they have cured me, I will see whether they still need me here, and whether every thing has then been done to my liking."

"Oh, I believe it will be then as it is now," said Christian, in a contemptuous tone. "When Marshal Forward is no longer here, things will go backward, that is sure. But we need not care, for we shall go forward to Brussels."

"Yes, to Brussels," said Blucher; "we set out to-night; but no one must know it; I will leave as quietly as possible. I cannot stand bidding them all farewell, and listening to their fine speeches; I will leave, therefore, so that no one shall discover it before I am gone."

"A secret flight!" said Christian, laconically.

"Secret flight? how stupid!" grumbled Blucher. "It is strange what ridiculous words the boy uses! How a flight? I believe I am no prisoner."

"No, but you are field-marshal."

Blucher's red eyes cast an angry glance on the bold pipe-master. "You talk as you understand it," he cried; "when I am a poor blind fellow, swallowing powders and using salves all day, I am no longer a field-marshal, and had better resign, not waiting to be deposed by a few polite **phrases.** That is the reason why I am going to leave."

"And I leave, too," said Christian; "but as the field-marshal does not wish me to say any thing about it, of course I shall not. But how are we to get away, if no one is to be informed?"

"Well, listen! I will tell you. I have already devised the whole plan of operations, and—but, hark! something seems moving in the alcove, as if a door opened."

"There is no door in the alcove," said Christian; "it was, perhaps, a mouse, and it tells no tales. Inform me, field-marshal, what I have to do."

"Well, listen, Christian!" And the field-marshal began to explain to him, in his vivacious manner, the whole plan of his departure. Christian comprehended it, and entered very seriously into the duties of quartermaster-general to his field-marshal.

"Do you remember it all now?" asked Blucher, at the conclusion of their conference. "Do you know all that you have to do?"

"I know all," said Christian. "In the first place, I am to go to General Gneisenau and inform him that the field-marshal is sick and confined to his bed to-day, and refuses to see any one. General Gneisenau will mention it, of course, to Surgeon-General Dr. Voelzke, who will come to see the field-marshal. I am to tell him that he is in so much pain from his inflamed eyes that he had ordered me to admit no one—that he is trying to sleep. Then I am to come back to you, and your excellency will give me the farewell letters to General Gneisenau, whereupon I am to pack up your things and lock the bags. When it grows dark, I am to carry them secretly into our carriage. Then it will suddenly occur to your excellency to take an airing, the sun having set, and therefore unable to hurt your eyes. I am to accompany you, and we shall not come back."

"No, we shall not come back," said Blucher, thoughtfully. "Well, every thing is settled now; run, and attend to what I told you. We shall set out at seven o'clock to-night."

Christian hastened away. Blucher looked after him with a mournful glance and a deep sigh. "The die is cast," he murmured to himself; "now I am indeed a poor old invalid, no longer of any use. God has refused to fulfil my dearest wish; He would not let me hurl Bonaparte from his stolen throne. I must face about at the gates of Paris, and creep back into obscurity. Well, let God's will be done! I have labored as long as there was daylight; now comes the night, when I can work no more. Ah, my poor sore eyes! I— but there is, after all, some one in the alcove," cried Blucher, springing to his feet. Again he heard a noise as of footsteps, and an opening door. He bounded into the alcove, but all was still; no one was there, and no door to be seen. "I was mistaken," he said. "A bad conscience is a very queer thing. Because I am about to do something secret, I am thinking that eavesdroppers are watching me and trying to forestall me."

It was seven in the evening; the sun had set. Field-Marshal Blucher, who was very sick all day, now intended to take an airing. The pipe-master had, therefore, ordered the coachman; and the field-marshal's carriage, drawn by four black horses, had just come to the door. Blucher was still in his room, but all his preparations were completed. On the table lay two letters—one addressed to the king, the other to General Gneisenau; the carpet-bags had already been conveyed into the carriage, together with the pipe-box. The invalid had only to wrap himself in his military cloak, leave the room, and enter the carriage; but he still hesitated. An anxiety, such as he had never known before, had crept over him; and, what had never before happened to him, his heart beat with fear. "That was just wanting to me,"

he murmured. "I have become a white-livered coward, whose legs are trembling, and whose heart is throbbing! What am I afraid of, then? Is that wrong which I am about to do? My heart has never acted thus even in the storm of battle. What does it mean? Bah! it is folly; no attention should be paid to it. I hope, however, that no one will meet me when I go downstairs, or at the carriage when I enter it. Let me see if there is any one in the street." He quickly stepped to the window and looked out; there was no one in the street, or near his carriage. "I will go now," said Blucher, turning again toward the room. "I—" He paused, and a blush suffused his cheeks. There, in the middle of the room, stood General Gneisenau, and gazed at him with a strange, mournful air. "Gneisenau, is it you?" asked Blucher, in a faltering voice. "How did you get in?"

"Simply by the door, your excellency," said Gneisenau, smiling. "Your pipe-master kept the door closed all day, and turned me away by informing me the field-marshal had ordered him to admit no one, because he wished to sleep; but my desire to see you brought me back again and again, and so I have come, fortunately at the opportune hour, when the Cerberus is no longer at the door, but is standing below at the carriage, waiting for the field-marshal, who intends to take an airing."

"Yes, I do," said Blucher, casting an anxious glance on the two letters lying on the table. "I do intend to take an airing; good-by, then, Gneisenau!" He turned toward the door, but Gneisenau kept him back. "Your excellency must not ride out to-night," he said; "I implore you not to do so. There is a cold wind, and you must not expose your inflamed eyes to it. You are not careful enough of your health; Surgeon-General Voelzke complains of the little attention you pay to his prescriptions, and that your eyes, instead of getting better, are growing worse and worse."

"Yes, that is true," grumbled Blucher, "they are burning like fire. I will go out, therefore; the night-wind will cool them."

He turned again toward the door, but at this mo

ment it was thrust open, and Surgeon-General Voelzke entered the room. "I am told your excellency intends to take an airing," said the physician, almost indignantly. "But I declare that I cannot permit it. You have intrusted yourself to my treatment; I am responsible to God, to the king, to the whole world—nay, to history, if I allow you to rush so recklessly to destruction; I will not suffer it; your excellency must not ride out!"

"I should like to see who is to prevent me!" cried Blucher, striding toward the door.

"The physician will prevent you," said Voelzke, standing in the doorway with his large, tall form. "The physician has the right of giving orders to kings and emperors, and Marshal Forward has to submit to his commands, too."

"I do not think of it," said Blucher; "I do not permit any one to give me orders."

"Not even your disease—your inflamed eyes?" asked Voelzke, solemnly. "Did you not obey when your fever and inflamed eyes commanded you to remain idle at Laon for ten days, although you were in a towering passion, and were bent on advancing with the army? Well, your excellency, I tell you, if you do not now obey me, and consent to desist from taking an airing—if you are determined to ride out in the cold night-air, one more powerful than I am will compel you to obey; and that one is your disease. You may ride out to-day, but to-morrow it will command you to keep your bed; the inflammation of your eyes will make you a prisoner, and you will be unable to flee from it, notwithstanding your imperious will, or your four-horsed carriage."

"Well, well," said Blucher, "you put on such solemn airs as almost to frighten me. It is true, my disease is very powerful, and this soreness of my eyes has already rendered me so desperate that—"

"That your excellency has written letters," interposed Gneisenau, pointing to the table. "But, what do I see? There is one addressed to me!"

"No, give it to me," cried Blucher, embarrassed; "now that you are here, I can tell you every thing verbally, and it is unnecessary for you to read what I have written."

He was about to seize the letter, but Gneisenau drew back a step, and, bowing deeply, said, "Your excellency has done me the honor of writing to me. Permit me, therefore, to read." He stepped quickly into the window-niche, and opened the letter.

"Well, stand back there, doctor," cried Blucher, "let me out! Do not make me angry; leave the door!"

"I do not care if you are angry, your excellency," said the surgeon-general, folding his arms, "but in order to get me out of this doorway you will have to kill me."

At this moment, Gneisenau uttered a cry of terror, and hastened toward Blucher. "What! your excellency," he exclaimed, "you intend to leave us? To set out secretly?"

"What do you say?" thundered the physician. "What did my patient intend to do?"

"He intends to forsake us—his army that worships him, his friends who idolize him, his king who hopes in him—he intends to leave us all!" said Gneisenau, mournfully. "It is written here, doctor; I may mention it to you, for you are one of our most devoted friends."

"And he intends also to leave his physician; he will go, and get blind!" exclaimed Voelzke, reproachfully.

"Well, it is precisely because I do not wish to get blind that I must move from here," said Blucher, who had now recovered his firmness, and felt relieved, since his secret had been disclosed. "What am I, a poor blind old man, to do longer in the field? I am fit for nothing. In the end I shall perhaps fare like old Kutusoff, whom they dragged along with the army. Thus would they drag me when I am no longer myself."*

"But," said the physician, "your excellency is not blind; you will be well in two weeks if you only resolve to comply with my prescriptions, use the remedies I give you, and punctually obey my

---

* Blucher's words.—Vide Varnhagen, "Prince Blucher of Wahlstatt," p. 372.

instructions. You intend to go to Brussels, where you will certainly find celebrated physicians; but **they do not know you; they will only doctor your eyes, not suspecting that the seat of** your disease is in your nerves, and that your eyes are unhealthy because your mind is suffering. And it will suffer still more when you have deserted your army, your friends—nay, I may say, your duty. The strange surroundings, the want of care, the unknown physicians, your anxiety at being ignorant of what the army is doing —all this will torture your soul, and aggravate the disease of your eyes."

"It is true, I shall be very lonely in a foreign city," said Blucher, thoughtfully; "but it is, after all, better than to stay here as a useless, blind old man. I can never again command an army or direct a battle."

"**If you** cannot command an army in person, **you can by your words," exclaimed Gneisenau; "and if you cannot direct the battle with your arms, you can do so with your spirit; for that** fires our hearts as long as you are with us, and bids defiance to the adversaries and hesitating diplomatists. If your person leaves us, your spirit does also, and with Marshal Forward we lose all prospect of marching forward. Consider this, your excellency; consider that you endanger not only the welfare of your army, but the success of the war; for when you are not present, **all** will go wrong."

"Well, you will be here, Gneisenau," said Blucher; "you are half myself; you know my thoughts just as well as I do—nay, you often know them much better! You will, therefore, carry on all just as though I were still here."

"But shall I have the power to do so?" asked Gneisenau. "Your excellency did not take into the account that when you leave the army, and give up your position as commander-in-chief, another general must be appointed in your stead. Who will receive this nomination? The senior general is Langeron, and do you consider him qualified to replace you?"

"Well, that would be a pretty thing, if **he** should become commander-in-chief!" cried

Blucher. "The confusion and wrangling that **would ensue would baffle** description; for York **and Bulow would be** even more disobedient to him than they are to me."

"But he would have to **take** command of the army until orders from headquarters arrived appointing another general-in-chief. We might have to wait a long time; for we are distant from the allied monarchs now, and they, moreover, will not hasten to make that appointment. Until this is done, Langeron will command the army, and thereby I, the quartermaster-general, as well as Colonels Muffling and Grolman, will be completely paralyzed in the discharge of our duties, or even lose our positions, which your excellency has always said we filled to your satisfaction, and in a manner conducive to the welfare of the army. If you go now, you thereby deprive three men of their places, although they feel strong enough yet to serve their country."

"It is true, I have not thought of that," said Blucher, embarrassed. "It did not occur to me that I should have a successor here, and that he might be so stupid as to be unable to appreciate my Gneisenau, and the brave Colonels Muffling and Grolman. No, no, that will not do; Langeron must not become commander-in-chief."

"If you leave us, he will surely have that position, and our brave Silesian army will then be headed by a Russian. No, field-marshal, you must not go. You have no right to quit the army so arbitrarily, and without the king's permission!"

"Well, I should like to see who would prevent me!" cried Blucher, defiantly.

"Your noble soul, your devotion to duty, and your love of country, will prevent you," said Gneisenau. "You will refuse to abandon your work before it is completed. You will not incur the disgrace of confessing to all the world that you are unable to fulfil your word—not to rest before having overthrown Napoleon, and made your entrance into Paris. Nor will you tarnish your glory on account of your eyes. You will not become a faithless father and friend to your soldiers, whom you have so often greeted as your children, and who have always confided in you; nor will you break our courage and paralyze our souls by deserting us in this manner."

"It is true, I did not think sufficiently on this matter," murmured Blucher to himself.— "Voelzke," he then cried aloud, "you pledge me your word of honor that you can cure me?"

"I swear it to your excellency by all that is sacred that, if you take care of yourself, and comply with my prescriptions, you will be cured in the course of two weeks."

"Well," said Blucher, after a short reflection, "in that case I will yield, and stay."

"Heaven be praised, your excellency!" cried Gneisenau, tenderly embracing Blucher, "you are still my noble field-marshal, who will not desert his army, his fatherland, and his friends, for the sake of his individual comfort."

"Yes, I will stay," said Blucher; "but as I have to obey the grim doctor there, and submit to his treatment thoroughly, as a matter of course I cannot work and make the necessary dispositions, but leave this to my head—to Gneisenau alone. I lend you my name for two weeks, and know that you will make good use of it. But if at the end of that time, doctor, I am not yet well, then, beware! May the Lord have mercy on your soul! for you will certainly get yourself into trouble."

"Your excellency," cried a loud voice outside, at this moment—"your excellency, are you not coming at all?" The door of the anteroom was violently thrust open, and the pipe-master appeared on the threshold. "It is past eight o'clock," he exclaimed, "and—" He paused on perceiving the two gentlemen, and was about to retire very quickly.

"Come here, pipe-master," exclaimed Blucher, "come here and look at me. Now tell me, pipe-master, have you been a chatterbox, after all, and told these two gentlemen what was the object of our airing?"

"No, your excellency; I have not uttered a word about it to any one," replied the pipe-master, solemnly. "I have been as dumb as a fish; only in secret have I complained of my distress;

and, when that did not relieve me, and I still felt as though my heart would burst, I did what I have learned to do from the field-marshal: I went to my room, closed the door, and swore in the most fearful manner! That relieved my heart, and I proceeded **to do all your** excellency charged **me** with."

"First, therefore, you had to swear?" asked Blucher, drawing his long mustache through his fingers. "You were, then, greatly dissatisfied with my departure?"

"I did not conceal it from your excellency. I told you honestly that you would no longer be called Marshal Forward if you retreated."

"Yes, retreat—that is just what he said," exclaimed Blucher, laughing, and turning again toward the two gentlemen; "and when I told him I would leave the army and set out for Brussels he remarked that it was a secret flight."

"The pipe-master is an honest man, who loves his master," said Gneisenau, kindly smiling on him. "I have often and urgently begged him today to announce me to the field-marshal; but he persisted in replying that he was not allowed to do so, and that he was ordered to admit no one."

"And I would have given my little-finger, if I could have admitted General Gneisenau, and Dr. Voelzke, too; for I knew that, as soon as they would be with the field-marshal, his departure would not be very soon. As they are here now—though I do not know how they got here so unexpectedly—I suppose, field-marshal, we shall not set out, and I may send the horses back to the stable?"

"Yes, you may," said Blucher. "But **wait,** Christian, do not go yet; I have first to say a few words to these gentlemen, and you may listen. I will stay here, then, but on one condition. Will you fulfil it?"

"Yes, your excellency," cried Gneisenau and Voelzke at the same time.

"Well, tell me, then, how did you discover that I intended to start to-day, the pipe-master having said nothing about it to you? For I shall never believe that both of you could happen to come to me at so unusual an hour, and without any reason. Reply—who told you that I was about to leave?"

"You yourself, your excellency," said Surgeon-General Voelzke.

"What, I! What nonsense is this!" cried Blucher, laughing.

"Yes, I heard it from yourself. Do you not remember that you heard a mouse rustle in your alcove?"

"To be sure, I did; I heard it twice."

"Well, then, the mouse was myself! I discovered a small secret side-door in your room, and desired to know whither it led. I therefore thrust it open, and was in your alcove; just as I entered I heard your voice, saying, 'It is settled, then, Christian, I shall set out for Brussels to-night, but no one must know a word about it!'—Your excellency, I confess my crime: I stood and listened; only when the pipe-master left your room did I softly creep away, too, and hasten to General Gneisenau to inform him of what I had heard."

"Let us examine the alcove more carefully, pipe-master," said Blucher, "and see whether there is not somewhere else a secret door. Well, you may go now, Hennemann, and send the horses back to the stable."

"Heaven be praised!" exclaimed Christian, hastening out of the room. But scarcely had he closed the door, when he thrust it open again. "Field-marshal," he said, "General von Pietrowitch, adjutant of the Emperor of Russia, wishes to see your excellency immediately."

"Come in, general," exclaimed Blucher; and, offering his hand to the officer, he asked hastily, "tell me, in the first place, general, whether you bring good or bad news?"

"I believe I bring what Marshal **Forward** would call good news," said the general, smiling. "I come as a messenger from the emperor my master, and the king your master, and am commissioned to inform you of the determination taken at headquarters, and to obtain your consent and coöperation."

"Is it a secret mission?" asked Gneisenau.

"On the contrary, the whole army will have to hear it to-night," said the general. "My first news, then, is, that the congress of Chatillon was dissolved on the 19th of March."

"Without leading to any results?" asked Blucher, breathlessly. "Without agreeing on a treaty of peace, or an armistice?"

"Nothing of the kind, your excellency. The congress has had an entirely opposite result—the speedy and energetic prosecution of the war. All the diplomatists, and the Emperor Francis with them, after the dissolution of the congress, retired southward to Dijon."

"And Schwartzenberg?" cried Blucher.

"Prince Schwartzenberg remained, and held a council of war with the monarchs yesterday near Vitry. The result of this I am commissioned to communicate to you. The resumption of the offensive against Paris has been decided upon. Prince Schwartzenberg agrees with the sovereigns that Paris is the decisive point, and that it is all-important for us to cut off Napoleon from the capital, and take the city before he is able to reach it. Prince Schwartzenberg, therefore, sends word to your excellency that from this day all his standards are turned toward Paris, and that the army of Bohemia is marching in three columns. To-night they encamp at Fère Champenoise, where the headquarters of the allies are to be. Now, Prince Schwartzenberg invites you to participate with the Silesian army in this advance, starting at once, and advancing by the road of Montmirail and La Ferté-sous-Jouarre, and then form a connection with the army of Bohemia."*

"Yes, I shall certainly do so," joyfully cried Blucher. "Hurrah! This is good news; now the word is not only with us, but everywhere, 'Forward!' Tell their majesties, and, above all, Prince Schwartzenberg, that they have made me very happy, and have performed a truly miraculous cure. I was **sick** and desponding; now, since you have come, I am again well and in good spirits. I feel no longer any pain, and my eyes will be all right again, now that they know that they are to see the city of Paris. I thought that it would come to this—that my brave brother

---

* Beitzke, vol. III., p. 481.

Schwartzenberg would at length agree with me. We shall soon now put an end to the war. Bonaparte must be dethroned, and that speedily." *

CHAPTER XLIX.

ON TO PARIS!

NAPOLEON'S courage was not yet paralyzed; he had not yet given up the struggle. His indomitable heart was still wrestling with adversity, and hoping that he would be able to overcome it. It is true, the disastrous battle of Bar-sur-Aube, where the army of Bohemia had gained a victory on the 20th of March, had greatly weighed him down; but a few days sufficed to restore his determination and energy. On the 26th, when he arrived with his army at St. Dizier, he had already devised new plans, and was again resolved to give battle to the allies. "We are still strong," he said to Caulaincourt, who had just joined him at St. Dizier. "We have upward of fifty thousand men here. I have issued orders to Marshals Marmont and Victor, as well as to all reënforcements that are on the road from Paris, to join our army. When they arrive, my forces will be eighty thousand, and the allies will not dare march on Paris, where they will find me. If I can now induce them to hesitate, and retard their operations a short time, by drawing reënforcements from the neighboring fortresses of the Meuse and the Moselle, I shall increase my army to upward of one hundred thousand, and it will then be easy for me to delay the progress of the enemy by constantly renewed attacks, and thus prolong the war."

"But I am afraid, sire, you labor under a delusion as to one point: that it is still possible for you to delay the progress of the allies by any means whatever," sighed Caulaincourt. "I have examined every thing on my trip to your majesty's headquarters; I have conversed with every prisoner fallen into the hands of our troops, and I do not believe that the army of Bohemia is in the rear of your majesty, but that it has outstripped you, and is already on the road to Paris."

Napoleon shrugged his shoulders and stepped to the door, which he opened, shouting, "The mayor of St. Dizier!" The corpulent form of the mayor, who greeted the emperor with awkward obeisances, appeared immediately. "Pray repeat your statements," said the emperor. "The enemy's troops were here yesterday, were they not?"

"They were, sire; all St. Dizier was occupied by them. It was General Winzingerode, with the soldiers of the allies. They stated that they were the vanguard of the principal army. General Winzingerode inspected all the large houses in the city, and reserved the best, adding that the Emperor of Russia and the King of Prussia would arrive here to-morrow, and take up their quarters at those houses; * but when the approach of your majesty was reported, the enemy quickly left the city."

"Very well; you may go," said Napoleon, motioning to the mayor to leave the room.—"Well, Caulaincourt, have you satisfied yourself now? Do you see now that the allies are not in our front, but still in our rear?"

"Sire, suppose it were a delusion, after all?" sighed Caulaincourt. "Suppose the allies had devised this stratagem, to mislead your majesty?—if none but Winzingerode's corps follow us, while the principal army is hastening toward Paris by different routes? Oh, I implore your majesty, do not suffer your keen eyes to be blinded by false hopes! Look around and examine the evidences that confirm my views. All the prisoners report that the armies of Bohemia and Silesia have united, and are now marching on Paris. Besides, on our way from Bar-sur-Aube to this place, we have nowhere met with large

---

* Blucher's own words.—Vide Varnhagen von Ense, Blucher," p. 375.

* This was a stratagem, resorted to by Winzingerode, in order to mislead Napoleon as to the march of the allies

columns of troops, and nothing whatever indicates the approach of the enemy in **force**."

"Well," cried Napoleon, vehemently, "if **we** have not met with the enemy's forces, it may **be** because they are in full retreat toward Lorraine, and that they are at last tired of carrying on a fruitless struggle with me." *

"Ah, your majesty still thinks that you are opposed only by the timid and desponding enemies of former times!" said Caulaincourt, sighing; "**but** this is a mistake, which will prove disastrous."

"Ah!" cried Napoleon, vehemently, "you dare tell **me** that?"

"Sire," said Caulaincourt, calmly, "it is my duty to tell you the truth, and you are in duty bound to listen to it.† Now, the truth is, that the allies are firmly determined to carry on the war to the last extremity, and that, at the best, they will leave to your majesty the frontiers of France as they were under the Bourbons. I venture, **therefore, once more to implore your majesty** to make peace; sire, peace at any cost! Perhaps it may be time yet. Send me once more to the allied monarchs! Tell them that you will now accept the ultimatum offered us at the congress of Chatillon, and that you will content your**self with** the frontiers of France, as they were **previous to** the rise of the empire. Send me **with this** declaration to the Emperor Alexander of Russia, who, at the bottom of his heart, is still your friend!"

"And whose devoted friend you are!" cried Napoleon. "Yes, you are Alexander's servant, and not mine! You are a thorough Russian!"

"No, sire, I am a Frenchman!" said Caulaincourt, proudly, looking the emperor **full in the** face, "and I believe I prove it by imploring your majesty to give peace to France and save your **crown**."

"Ah, save my crown!" exclaimed Napoleon. "Who dares, then, threaten my crown?"

"Sire, the **allies and the** Bourbons. The former have issued a proclamation, stating that they come to this country to make war on the Emperor Napo**leon, and not on France**; and the Bourbons, who **are now in France, at the** headquarters of the allies, **have** issued another proclamation, calling upon the nation to return **to its** duty and to the allegiance due to its legitimate king."

"I am neither afraid of the allies nor of the Bourbons," said Napoleon. "The French nation knows no Bourbons; it knows none but *me*, its emperor, and we two shall not break the faith we have plighted to each other. We shall conquer together. Dare no longer ask me to accept the ignominious terms of the congress of Chatillon. It is better to die beneath the ruins of my throne than be at the mercy of my enemies. The allies are in my rear, and the arrival of reënforcements will soon enable me to give them battle; I shall win, and it will be for me to dictate terms. Under the walls of Paris the grave of the Russians will be dug. My dispositions have been made, and I shall not fail." *

Caulaincourt sighed, and gazed with an air of painful astonishment on the serene face of the emperor. "Sire," he said, solemnly, "I call Heaven to witness that I have tried my best to incline your majesty to my prayers! You have refused to listen to me."

"Because I am not at liberty to do so, Caulaincourt; and, besides, I do not believe in your apprehensions. Suppose that Alexander and Frederick William should determine to continue the war, there is a third sovereign who will decide the matter—the Emperor Francis, my father-in-law, and grandfather of the King of Rome. You see, therefore, that, though the present prospects were unfavorable to me, I should at least have nothing to fear from the Bourbons; for the emperor will not permit his daughter to be robbed of her crown, nor his grandson of his rightful inheritance."

"Sire," said Caulaincourt, in a low voice, "do not rely too much on the attachment of the Em-

---

* Fain, "Manuscrit de 1814," p. 142.
† Caulaincourt's words,—"Mémoires d'un Homme d'État," vol. xii., p. 392.

* Napoleon's words.—Vide Constant, "Mémoires," vol vi., p. 48.

peror Francis. I know that, though he is your father-in-law, he has never forgotten the day when, after the battle of Austerlitz, he met you as an humble suppliant at your camp-fire, and begged you to spare him and make peace with him. I know that that recollection has greater power over him than any bonds of relationship. I know that Metternich, who is still devoted to your majesty, vainly tried a few days ago to prevail upon the Emperor Francis to intercede energetically with the other monarchs for his son-in-law and daughter, and that he unsuccessfully urged him to take into consideration the future of his grandson, the King of Rome."

"And what did the emperor reply?" asked Napoleon, quickly.

"Sire, the emperor replied, in his strong Austrian dialect, 'Do not always talk to me about the child! I have at home many children of whom I ought to think first.'"*

"That is not true; he did not say so!" cried Napoleon.

"Sire, he did; Prince Metternich told me so."

Napoleon paused a moment. A low knocking at the door interrupted his meditation. One of the adjutants entered, and reported that the emperor's equerry, Count Saint-Aignan, whom the emperor had intrusted with a mission, had returned, and requested an audience of his majesty. The emperor himself hastened to the door, and eagerly motioned to the count to approach. "Well, Saint-Aignan," he asked, "what did you find? How is the disposition of the people in the south of France?"

"Sire," said the count, mournfully, "I bring no news that will gladden your majesty's heart. Southern France is discontented; the people are complaining of the duration of the war; they desire peace at any price, and are disposed to resort to extreme measures in order to reëstablish it."

"What does that mean?" asked **the emperor.**

"I do not understand you; express yourself more distinctly."

"Well, then, sire, the people there have read the proclamation of the Bourbons, and think of reinstating them, for the purpose of putting an end to the war."

"They will not dare to do that," cried Napoleon, casting an angry glance on Saint-Aignan.

"They have already, sire," said the count. "The city of Bordeaux has declared for the Bourbons, and the Count d'Artois, as well as the Duke and Duchess d'Angoulême, have made their entrance into the city, and—"

"And have been received with enthusiasm by the population!" cried Napoleon. "Pray, finish your sentence, and tell me so. Add that the inhabitants of Bordeaux have returned to their duty, and that you, too, have discovered what your duty is, and that you intend to return to the legitimate rulers of France! Go! I permit you; I relieve you of the duties of your office! Go to the Bourbons!"

Count Saint-Aignan did not stir; pallor overspread his cheeks; his eyes, fixed on the emperor with an indescribable expression of grief, filled with tears, and his quivering lips were unable to speak.

"Sire," said the Duke de Vicenza, "your majesty does injustice to the count. You commanded him to give a reliable report of his mission; he was not at liberty, therefore, to conceal any thing, but was obliged to tell you the whole truth."

"The truth!" cried Napoleon, violently stamping, "that which you fear or desire you call the truth! You all see through the colored spectacles of your anxiety, and would compel me to do so, too; but I will not; my eyes are open, and see things as they are. Go, Count Saint-Aignan; your report is finished!" The count, with a sigh, approached the door, and, slowly walking backward, left the room. "The Bourbons!" murmured Napoleon to himself; "they shall not dare to threaten me with this spectre! There are no Bourbons! I am the Emperor of France, and it is to me alone that the French nation owes allegiance!" He looked thoughtfully, with a dark and wrinkled forehead,

---

* The Emperor Francis said: "Redt's mier nit allweil von dem Kind; bei mier z' Haus hab' ich gar vielle Kinder, an die ich z' erst denken muess."—Hormayr, "Lebensbilder," vol. i., p. 98.

but, presently lifting his head—"Oh, Caulaincourt," he exclaimed, "I will personally satisfy myself whether the army of the allies is really in our rear, or whether your fears are well grounded. Let us set out for Vitry!"

"Heaven be praised!" replied the Duke de Vicenza, joyfully. "All is not yet lost; for Vitry is on the road to Paris."

On the following morning the emperor moved with his forces toward Vitry, and took up his quarters at Marolles, a short distance from the little fortress. Here at length he was to find out the true state of affairs. He was met by inhabitants of Fère Champenoise, who had fled to Marolles, and informed him that Marshals Marmont and Mortier had suffered decisive defeats at the hands of the allies; that the divisions of General Pacthod and Aurey had been annihilated, and that the united armies of Bohemia and Silesia were in **rapid** march on Paris.

An expression of terror passed over the face **of** Napoleon, and his equanimity seemed to be shaken; but he soon overcame the effect of this news, calmly remarking, "Well, if the allies are marching on Paris, we must march too."

"Yes, on to Paris!" cried the marshals. "That is the most important point in present circumstances, and it can be defended, if the emperor hasten with his army."

"On to Paris, then!" exclaimed Napoleon. "But we must move with the speed of the wind!" He appeared to have regained his whole energy; his eyes beamed again, his face resumed its old determination, and he issued his orders in a firm and cheerful voice.

It was all-important to defend the emperor's throne at Paris, and to protect the inheritance of the King of Rome from the allies and the Bourbons. Forward, then, by forced marches! Napoleon's headquarters were soon at Montier-en-Der—much nearer the capital. On the 28th of March he reached Doulevant, when a horseman, covered with dust, pale and breathless, coming from the direction of the capital, galloped up to the head of the column. "Where is the emperor?" he cried. Having been conducted to

him, "Sire," he whispered, "I am sent by the postmaster-general, your faithful Count La Valette, **to deliver this** paper."

The emperor unfolded the paper and read. A slight tremor pervaded his frame, and his eyes grew gloomier. He cast another glance on the paper, and then, seizing it with his teeth, he tore it to pieces. None but himself was to learn the contents of that paper, which read: "The adherents of the invaders, encouraged by the defection of Bordeaux, are raising their heads; secret intrigues are helping them. The emperor's presence is necessary, if he wishes to prevent his capital from being delivered into the hands of the enemy. We must march immediately. Not a moment is to be lost." *

"Forward!" shouted the emperor. "We must hasten to Paris, and be there to-morrow!" The emperor, with the cavalry of his guard, headed the column. His countenance was still calm and impenetrable; but at times a gleam lit up his sombre eyes, as he moved on in a violent thunderstorm.

Another courier galloped up and asked for the emperor. "Announce me to him. The lieutenant-general of the empire, King Joseph, the emperor's brother, sends me."

He was conducted to Napoleon, who received him with the words, "News from my brother at Paris? Give me your dispatch!"

"Sire, I have no dispatch to deliver; dispatches may be lost, or revealed if their bearer should be arrested; but memory betrays nothing. I have ridden from Paris in fourteen hours. Here are my credentials, King Joseph's signet-ring."

"I recognize it. Speak!" By a wave of his hand Napoleon ordered the marshals to retire, and, bending his head toward his brother's messenger, he repeated calmly, "Speak!"

"Sire," whispered the messenger, "the king informs your majesty **that the** allies are near Paris; that Marshals Marmont and Mortier, though determined to defend the capital, have no hope of holding their positions. The king in

---

* Fain, "Manuscrit de 1814."

plores your majesty most urgently to leave nothing undone to hasten to the assistance of your capital." *

Having heard this message, the emperor's face was unveiled; it was quivering with anguish, and his eyes turned to heaven in despair. "Oh, if I had wings!" he cried, in an outburst of grief; "if I could be in Paris at this hour!" Then he became silent, and his head sank on his breast. His generals surrounded him, when he lifted his head again with drops of sweat on his forehead, but his face resumed its wonted calmness. "General Dejean," he cried, in a powerful voice, "ride to Paris as fast as you can. Inform my brother that I am making a forced march to the capital. Hasten then to Marmont and Mortier; tell them to resist to the last, and leave nothing untried in order to hold out but for two days. In that time I shall be in front of Paris, and it is safe! Marmont is to dispatch a courier to Prince Schwartzenberg, and inform him that I have sent an envoy to the Emperor Francis with propositions leading to peace. Schwartzenberg will hesitate, and we shall gain time. Haste, Dejean, and remember that the fate of my capital rests with you!"

When General Dejean rode off, Napoleon sought his faithful friend, the Duke de Vicenza. He was by his side before the emperor had uttered his name. "Caulaincourt," he said, in a gentle voice, "you were right. I have lost two days. I might now be in Paris. Fate is behind me, intent on crushing me, and death itself refuses to take me! At the battle of Bar-sur-Aube I did all I could to die while defending my country. I plunged into the thickest of the fight; the balls tore my clothes, and yet not one of them injured me. I am a man doomed to live †—a man that, for the welfare of his people, is to subscribe his own humiliation and disgrace! Caulaincourt, go to the Emperor Francis of Austria. Tell him I accept the ultimatum which the allies offered me at Chatillon. I sign the death-

warrant of my glory! Hasten! And now, forward! In two days we must reach Paris!"

CHAPTER L.

DEPARTURE OF MARIA LOUISA.

On the same day, and nearly at the same hour of the 29th of March, while the emperor was moving with his troops toward Paris, a scene of an entirely different description took place at the rooms of the empress, his consort, in the Tuileries. Napoleon, in his despair, wished for wings to fly to Paris; Maria Louisa, in her anguish, wished for wings to fly away from Paris; for the enemy was at its gates, and it was plain that the city must either capitulate or run the risk of an assault.

As yet Maria Louisa called the allies threatening the throne of her husband, and the inheritance of her son, her enemies, although her own father was among them. She deemed herself in duty bound to stand by her husband, to brave the vicissitudes of fortune jointly with him, and obey his will. The emperor desired that his consort and his son should not remain in the city if any danger should menace them. When the news reached the Tuileries that the allies had arrived at the walls of Paris, and it became obvious that the corps of Marmont and Mortier were not strong enough to withstand the armies of the enemy, King Joseph, the lieutenant of the emperor, summoned the regent, Maria Louisa, and the council of state, to deliberate on the grave question whether or not the empress and the King of Rome should remain, or be withdrawn to a place of safety beyond the Loire.

The decision was left with Maria Louisa; but the regent had declared it was not for her to settle this question; it was for the very purpose of advising her and guiding her steps that the emperor had associated the council of state with her. King Joseph produced a letter from Napoleon of

----

* Fain, "Manuscrit de 1814."
† Napoleon's words.—Vide Bausset's "Mémoires," vol. ii., p. 246.

a nature to indicate his wishes. It was dated Rheims, 15th of March, and read:

"In accordance with the verbal instructions which I have given, and with the spirit of all my letters, you are in no event to permit the empress and the King of Rome to fall into the hands of the enemy. I am about to manœuvre in such a manner that you may possibly be several days without hearing from me. Should the enemy advance upon Paris with such forces as to render all resistance impossible, send off in the direction of the Loire the empress, the King of Rome, the great dignitaries, the ministers, the officers of the senate, the president of the council of state, the great officers of the crown, and the treasure. Never quit my son; and keep in mind that I would rather see him in the Seine than in the hands of the enemies of France! The fate of Astyanax, a prisoner in the hands of the Greeks, has always appeared to me the most deplorable in history.

"Your brother, NAPOLEON." *

This, of course, put an end to all debate. The emperor's precise and final order, providing for the very case which had occurred, could not be disregarded, and Maria Louisa accordingly determined to leave with her son and her suite for Rambouillet. The morning of the 29th of March was fixed for the departure. The travelling-carriages, loaded with baggage, stood in the court-yard of the Tuileries; but Maria Louisa still hesitated. Her travelling-toilet was completed; her ladies were with her in the reception-room, filled with persons forming the cortege of the empress. All entered in mournful silence, and to their bows the empress responded only with a nod. Her eyes, red with weeping, were fixed on the door; she awaited in suspense the return of King Joseph, who had left the Tuileries at daybreak, and had gone to the gates of Paris to reconnoitre the enemy's position. At first the departure was to have taken place at eight in the morning; now it was past nine, and King Joseph had not yet returned.

---

* Baron de Meneval, "Marie Louise et Napoléon," vol. II., p. 280.

This unexpected delay increased the anxiety. None dared interrupt the breathless silence reigning in the apartment; only here and there some one whispered, and, whenever a door opened, all started and turned anxiously toward it, as if expecting a bearer of sad tidings. The face of the empress was pale and agitated, her form trembled; at times she turned toward her ladies, who stood behind her, and addressed to them some almost inaudible question, not waiting for a reply, but looking again toward the door, or inclining her head on her bosom.

Suddenly the door was opened, and on the threshold appeared the little King of Rome, followed by his governess, Madame de Montesquiou. The boy's face did not exhibit to-day its air of childlike mirth, which usually beamed like sunshine from his beautiful features. No smile was on his fresh lips, and his lustrous eyes were dimmed. With a sullen face and without looking at any one, the child, so intelligent for his years, stepped through the room directly toward his mother. "Mamma empress," he said, in his silvery voice, "my 'Quiou says that we are about to leave Paris, and shall no longer live at the Tuileries. Is that true, mamma?"

"Yes, my son, we must leave," said the empress, in a low voice, "but we shall return."

"We must leave?" inquired the little king. "But my papa once said to me, the word 'must' is not for me, and I do not want it either, and I pray my dear mamma not to leave Paris with me."

"But the emperor himself wishes us to leave, Napoleon," said the empress, sighing, and with some displeasure. "Your papa has ordered us to depart if the enemy should come."

"The enemy!" cried the boy; "I am not afraid of the enemy. If he comes, we do as my papa emperor always does—we beat the enemy, and then he runs away."

But these words of the brave child, which would have delighted his father's heart, seemed to make a disagreeable impression upon his mother. She murmured a few inaudible words, and slightly shrugged her shoulders.

Madame de Montesquiou took the child by the hand. "Come, sire," she said, in a low voice, "do not disturb her majesty. Come!"

"No, no," cried the boy, violently disengaging himself, "I am sure you want to carry me down to the carriage, and I tell you I will not go! Let me stay here with my mother, dear 'Quiou; I do not disturb her, for you see she is not busy, and she does not want to be alone either, for there are a great many persons with her. Therefore, I may stay here, too, may I not, dear mamma empress!"

"Yes, my son, stay here," said the empress, abstractedly, looking again at the door.

"I am not afraid of the enemy," cried the little king, proudly throwing back his head. "My papa will soon come and drive him away. But tell me, mamma, what is the name of the enemy who wants to rob us of our beautiful palace. What is his name?"

"Hush, Napoleon!" said the empress, almost indignantly; "what good would it do you to hear what you do not understand?"

"Oh, dear mamma," cried the child, with a triumphant air, "I can understand very well, for my papa has often played war on the floor with me, and we have built fortresses. And not long ago, papa emperor told me, too, that he was going to the army, and he spoke of his enemies. I remember them very well: they are the Emperor of Russia, who once kissed my papa's hand, and thanked God that papa emperor consented to be his friend; the King of Prussia, from whom my papa could have taken all his states; the crown prince of Sweden, who learned the art of war from my papa, and is a faithless servant; and last, the Emperor of Austria. But tell me, mamma, is not he your father? And did you not tell me that I ought to pray every night for my grandfather, the Emperor of Austria?"

"I did tell you so, Napoleon," whispered the empress, whose eyes filled with tears.

The boy looked down for a moment musingly; and then, lifting his large blue eyes to his mother, "Mamma," he said, "henceforth I shall never again pray for the Emperor of Austria, for he is now my papa's enemy, and, therefore, no longer my grandfather. No, no, I shall not pray for him, but only as my papa likes me to do." And the boy knelt down, lifting up his hands, and exclaiming in a loud voice, "Good God, I pray to Thee for France and for my father!"

Expressions of deep emotion were heard in the room. The empress covered her face with her handkerchief, and wept bitterly. The little king was still on his knees, with his eyes raised toward heaven. Suddenly the door at which the empress had looked so long and anxiously, opened. It was not King Joseph who entered, but the adjutant of General Clarke, the regent's minister of war. Approaching the empress, he begged leave to communicate a message from the minister.

"Speak," said Maria Louisa, hastily, "and loud enough for every one to hear the news."

"His excellency, the minister of war, has commissioned me to implore your majesty in his name to leave without a moment's delay. He believes that every minute increases the danger, and that an hour hence it might be impossible for you to get away, because your majesty would then run the risk of falling into the hands of roving bands of Cossacks. The Russian corps are already near, and we shall soon hear their cannon thunder at the very gates of Paris." *

"Well, then," said Maria Louisa, with quivering lips, "be it so! Let us set out."

All felt that the decisive hour was at hand. The empress quickly advanced a few steps. "Come!" she exclaimed, in feverish agitation. "Let us set out for Rambouillet!"

Suddenly her son grasped her hand and endeavored to draw her back. "Dear mamma," he cried, anxiously, "do not go! Rambouillet is an ugly old castle. Let us not go, but stay here!" †

"It cannot be, my son; we must go!"

But little Napoleon pushed back her hand with a gesture of indignation. "Well, then, mamma," he said, "go! I will not go. I will not leave

---

* Meneval, "Marie Louise," vol. II., p. 266.
† The little king's words.—Ibid.

my house! As papa is not here, I am the master! and I say I *will* not go!"[*]

The empress motioned to the equerry on service. "M. de Comisy," she ordered, "take the prince in your arms and carry him to the carriage."

"The prince! I am no prince, I am the King of Rome," cried the boy, in the most violent anger. "I will not go! I will not leave my house; I do not want you to betray my dear papa!"[†] The empress took no longer any notice of him; M. de Comisy lifted the crying, struggling boy into his arms. "'Quiou, dear 'Quiou!" cried the child, "oh, come to my assistance! I will not leave my house!"

"Sire," said Madame de Montesquiou, weeping, "we must leave: the emperor has ordered us to do so!"

"It is false!" cried the prince, bursting into a flood of tears, and still trying to disengage himself. "My papa never ordered any such thing, for he says that one ought never to flee from the enemy. I will not go, I will not flee!"

"Come, sire; come!" exclaimed M. de Comisy.

"I will not go!" said the boy, and clung to the door. But Madame de Montesquiou, vainly trying to comfort the prince by gentle words, disengaged his tiny hands, and M. de Comisy hurried on. The whole court, the whole travelling cortege thronged forward, following the empress and the King of Rome.

Soon the brilliant apartment was empty; but the deserted rooms echoed the distant cries of the little King of Rome. All his struggles were in vain. M. de Comisy was not allowed to have pity on him; the will of the empress had to be fulfilled.

At length the preparations were completed, **and all had** taken their seats. The large clock on the tower of the Tuileries struck eleven as the empress's carriage rolled slowly across the spacious court-yard. The crying of the little king, who sat by the side of his mother, was still

---

* Meneval, "Marie Louise."
† The king's words.—Vide "Mémoires du Duc de Rovigo," vol. vii., p. 5.

heard. With them were also the mistress of ceremonies, the Duchess de Montebello, and the governess. Nine other carriages followed, decorated with the imperial coat-of-arms, and numerous baggage-wagons, and the whole train of a brilliant court. The procession filled the whole length of the court-yard of the Tuileries.

When the carriage of the empress drove through the large iron enclosure, a small crowd of spectators stood near, and gazed in mournful silence. Not a hand was raised to salute the fugitives; not a voice shouted a farewell. The sad train passed along, while the people looked after it, as if the funeral procession of the empire. The imperial party disappeared among the trees of the *Champs Elysées*, and left Paris by the "Gate of Victory."

CHAPTER LI.

THE CAPITULATION OF PARIS.

THE roar of cannon, which continued all the day long of the 30th of March, began now to cease; but the great battle which the allies fought under the walls of Paris with the corps of Marmont and Mortier, was not finished. Before resorting to a bombardment, and an assault on the city, conciliation was once more to be tried. Delegates of the monarchs, therefore, repaired to the marshals, and requested them to consent to an honorable capitulation.

"This is another instance of our foolish generosity!" growled Blucher, leaning back in his carriage. "The whole rats'-nest ought to be demolished; Bonaparte and the French would then have to submit. But I see already how it will be. The peace will be unsatisfactory, and our demands will be as modest as possible, lest we incur the displeasure of the dear French.—Pipemaster, hand me a short pipe! I must smoke, **to** stifle my anger."

"Your excellency," said Christian, riding up to the carriage, "you have promised the surgeon general not to smoke much, and least of all a short pipe, because the hot smoke is injurious to the eyes. Your excellency has smoked six pipes to-day!"

"And it seems to me that is very little! What are six pipes for a general-in-chief, who has to reflect so much as I have to-day? Give me a pipe, Christian; it is bad enough that I have to sit in such a monkey-box of a carriage, instead of riding on horseback at the head of my troops."

"Nevertheless, every thing passed off very well," said Christian, calmly. "You shouted your orders out of the carriage like a madman, and the generals and adjutants heard and executed all as if you had been on horseback among them. In fact, it would have been only necessary for you to order, 'Forward!' It would have been just as well, for your hussars were intent on nothing else; and, like their field-marshal, they wished only to reach Paris."

"And now we have to wait here without firing a gun," replied Blucher. "Moreover, my eyes ache as if they were burning. The sun has been blazing all day, as though curious to see whether or not we should take Paris; he has poured his rays on me since daybreak, and I had no protection for my old eyes. On looking out of the carriage early this morning I lost my shade; the wind carried it off as though it were a kite. I have lost it, and, what is worse, I cannot even enter Paris, for we shall of course sign a capitulation."

"Here is the pipe, your excellency," said Christian, "and now, good-by, field-marshal; I have to attend to a little private matter."

He galloped off, and Blucher looked after him. "Happy fellow!" he said, sighing; "he can gallop as light as a bird, while I must sit here as a poor old prisoner!" At this moment his adjutant, Major von Nostiz, rode up to the field-marshal's carriage. "Well, Nostiz, tell me how things look in the outer world. What is the news?"

"Bad and good, your excellency," said Nostiz. "A murderous battle has taken place to-day, and we have sustained heavy losses. About eight thousand men were killed on our side, but in re-

turn we have gained a large number of trophies, field-pieces, caissons, and stands of colors."

"We ought to have taken all their colors!" cried Blucher, eagerly. "What say the monarchs now, Nostiz? Will they still leave the Parisians the choice to suffer a bombardment or not?"

"The negotiations are still pending."

"Are the monarchs themselves taking part in them? Do they condescend to negotiate in person?"

"No, your excellency. The monarchs have returned to their quarters; the King of Prussia has gone to the village of Pantin, the Emperor of Russia to Bondy, and their representatives have repaired to the suburb of La Chapelle, where they are treating with Marshals Mortier and Marmont and their two adjutants in regard to the capitulation of Paris."

"Would that their negotiations were unsuccessful—that we might have the pleasure of bombarding this infamous city which, for twenty years past, has brought so much misery on Europe!"

"There is some prospect of it," said Nostiz, smiling. "The allies have demanded that the French corps should surrender as prisoners of war. To this the marshals refused to accede, declaring that they would perish first in the streets, so the allies agreed to abandon this article. A discussion next rose as to the route by which the corps of Marmont and Mortier should retire, so as to be prevented from joining the approaching forces of the emperor, the allies insisting for that of Brittany, the French for any that they might choose. The marshals refused positively to agree to these demands."

"They did!" cried Blucher, in an angry voice. "Well, I am glad of it, for I see now that we shall have a bombardment. Let us immediately make all necessary dispositions for it, in order that when the fun commences we may be ready. Bring me my horse!" With the activity of a youth Blucher opened his carriage and vaulted on the horse, which the groom led close to the carriage. For a moment he reeled in the saddle; for he felt as if red-hot daggers were piercing his eyes, but he overcame his faintness and pain. "Where are the members of my staff, Nostiz?" he asked, eagerly.

"They are near, your excellency, at La Villette."

"Let us ride, then, to La Villette, and thence up the Montmartre. Nostiz, you will have immediately eighty or ninety pieces planted on the Montmartre, that, when the bombardment commences early in the morning, there may be no delay.* Make haste, Nostiz! There must be at least eighty pieces! We shall startle the Parisians out of their slumber," growled Blucher, riding along the road to La Villette, attended by his orderlies; "let them see that another state of affairs exists, and that they are no longer the masters of the world, and able to trample others in the dust!"

At La Villette, Blucher met the members of his staff, and, with Gneisenau and Muffling by his side, and followed by the other officers, rode up the heights of Montmartre. The sun had set, but his last beams still lingered in the evening clouds. The silence reigning around them after the uproar of the day, made upon their minds a solemn impression. At first the party engaged in an animated conversation, but it gradually ceased. Peaceful nature in this spring eventide contrasted the noise and bloodshed of the day with her own indifference, so that even Blucher himself was deeply moved.

They reached the crest of the Montmartre. Paris—the long-feared, but now vanquished Paris, which for centuries had not seen a conquering enemy near its walls—lay at their feet. The steeples of Notre-Dame, of St. Genevieve, the large cupola of the Hotel des Invalides, the countless spires proudly looming up, the vast pile of the Tuileries, the Louvre, the Palais-Royal, where for twenty years Napoleon had given laws to trembling Europe, were plainly discerned. And this great city, with its temples and palaces, was in the hands of the enemy. They were Prussian

generals who looked down from the heights of the Montmartre, and who for seven years had borne the disgrace of their country with sad yet courageous hearts; but this moment was a sufficient indemnity for the long years of wretchedness.

"This, then, is Paris," said Blucher, after a long pause, and his voice was gentle and tremulous. "This is Paris, for which I have longed during seven years—the city which I knew my eyes would see, that I might die in peace! Good God," he cried, lifting his blue eyes toward heaven, and taking off his cap, "I thank Thee for having permitted us to be here, for lending us Thy assistance in attaining our object, and hurling from the throne the man who has so long been a terror to humanity. I thank Thee for having called us, the men who saw the disastrous day of Jena, to participate in the day of liberation! Blessed spirit of our Queen Louisa! if thou, with thine heavenly eyes that wept so much on earth, now lookest down upon us, behold our hearts full of gratitude toward God, and of love for thee as when thou wast among us! Thou hast assisted us in gaining the victory; assist us now, too, in profiting by it in a manner worthy ourselves, and for the welfare of the fatherland!" He paused, and, shading his face with his cap, prayed in a low voice. The generals followed his example; removing their hats, they offered silent prayers of gratitude to God. "Now," cried Blucher, putting on his cap again, "we have paid homage to Heaven, let us think a little of ourselves. I am still in hope that there will be a bombardment, and that we shall send our balls to the Parisians for breakfast to-morrow. I will, therefore, remain on the Montmartre, and establish here my quarters for the night."

"Field-marshal!" shouted a voice at a distance. "Field-Marshal Blucher, where are you?"

"Here I am!" shouted Blucher.

"And here I am!" cried Hennemann, galloping up.

"Pipe-master, is it you?" asked Blucher, in amazement. "Well, what do you want, and where have you been so long?"

---

* Varnhagen von Ense, "Life of Blucher," p. 850.

"I have just brought an eye-shade for you, and here it is," said Christian, handing with profound gravity a lady's bonnet of green silk, with a broad green brim.

"A bonnet!" exclaimed Blucher, laughing. "What am I to do with it?"

"Put it on," said Christian, composedly. "We can cut off the crown, then it will be a good shade; your excellency will put it on, and wear your general's hat over it."

"That will do," said Blucher. "But tell me, my boy, where did you get it?"

"I saw this afternoon a lady with a green bonnet at a villa near which I passed, and when you told me you ought to have an eye-shade, I thought immediately of the bonnet. Well, I rode to the house, and knocked so long at the door that they opened it. There were none but women at the house, and they cried and wailed dreadfully on seeing me. Well, I told them at once that I would not hurt them, but was only desirous of getting the green bonnet. While the women were raising such a hue-and-cry, another door opened, and the lady who owned the house came in, with the bonnet on. Well, I went directly to her, made her an obeisance, and said, 'Madame, be so kind as to give me your green bonnet for my field-marshal, who has sore eyes.'"

"Well, and did she understand your good Mecklenburg German?" inquired Blucher, smiling.

"No, she did not understand me apparently, but I made myself understood, your excellency."

"Well, what did you do?"

"Oh, your excellency, I simply stepped near her, took hold of the large knot by which her bonnet was tied under her chin, loosened it, seized the bonnet by the brim, and took it very gently from her head. She cried a little, and fainted away—but that will not hurt a woman; I know she will soon be better. I secured my prize, and here I am, and here is your excellency's eye-shade."

"And a good one it is. I thank you, my boy; I will wear it in honor of you, for my eyes are aching dreadfully, and I have need of a shade. I

will raise this standard when we make our entrance into Paris, and I believe, pipe-master, the fair Parisians will rejoice at seeing me dressed in the latest Parisian fashion. But now, milliner, cut off the crown, else I cannot use it."

"I will do so at once," said Christian, taking a pair of scissors from his dressing-pouch, and transforming a lady's bonnet into an eye-shade.

A few hours afterward, all was quiet on the Montmartre, and on all the other heights around Paris. After the battle the armies needed sleep, and it was undisturbed, for there was no longer an enemy to dispute their possession of the French capital.

CHAPTER LII.

NIGHT AND MORNING NEAR PARIS.

So the allied armies encamped and rested round the bivouac-fires, while, at a house in the suburbs of La Chapelle, the plenipotentiaries of the sovereigns were still negotiating with the French marshals the terms on which the city was to be surrendered. But he who now rode along the road to Paris at a gallop in an open carriage knew no peace or rest. His quivering features were expressive of alarm; ruin sat enthroned on his forehead, covered with perspiration. By his side sat Caulaincourt; behind him, Berthier and Flahault. The carriage thundered along at the utmost speed. "Caulaincourt, I shall arrive at Paris in time," murmured the emperor; "we are already at Fromenteau; in an hour we shall be there. The watch-fires of the enemy are seen on the opposite bank of the Seine. Ah, I shall extinguish them; to-morrow night the enemy will not be so near.—But what is that? Do you hear nothing? Have the carriage stopped!"

Berthier shouted to the driver—the carriage stopped. They all heard a sort of hollow noise.

"It is a squad of cavalry riding along this road," whispered Caulaincourt.

"It is artillery," murmured Napoleon. "Forward! They can only be our own men. But why are they retreating from **Paris**? Forward!"

The carriage rolled on. And from the other side of the road a dark mass, with a rumbling noise, moved toward them. Napoleon was not mistaken, nor was Caulaincourt mistaken.

"Who is there?" shouted the emperor to the horsemen at the head of the column. "Halt!"

"It is the emperor!" cried a voice, in amazement, and a horseman dismounting in a moment approached the carriage.

"It is General Belliard," exclaimed the emperor, and alighted hastily from his carriage. "General, whither are you moving? What about **Paris?**"

"Sire, all is lost!" said Belliard, after a mournful pause.

"How so?" cried Napoleon, vehemently. "You see I am coming! I shall be in **Paris** in an hour. I will call out the National Guard, and put myself at the head of the troops."

"Sire, we are too weak; the enemy is five times stronger."

"But I am there, and my name will increase the strength of my army fivefold."

"Sire, it is too late."

"Too late! What do you mean?"

"Marmont and Mortier have capitulated; we are taking advantage of the night to evacuate Paris, while the marshals are still negotiating the terms of capitulation."

A single cry of anger burst from Napoleon's lips; then, as if crushed by the blow, his head dropped on his breast. Recovering himself in a moment, he said, imperiously: "General Belliard! return with your troops; I shall be there before you reach the city. Resuming hostilities, I will call upon all Paris to take up arms; the people love me, they will remain faithful; the majority of the working-men are composed of old soldiers. They know how to fight, and I will lead them. We shall fight as the Spaniards fought against us at Saragossa, defending with our blood the streets of our capital; detaining the enemy at least for a day, my army will arrive, and we shall be strong enough to give battle. I

must go to Paris; when I am not there, they do nothing but blunder! My brother Joseph is a pusillanimous and easily-disheartened man, and Minister Clarke is a blockhead. Marmont and Mortier are traitors deserving death, for they violated my express instructions. I asked them to hold out only two days, and the traitors capitulated before they had elapsed! Oh, I shall hold them responsible for it: I know how to punish traitors and poltroons!" He hurried on in a rapid step, General Belliard walking by his side, and Caulaincourt, Berthier, and Flahault following him. "I must go to Paris," cried the emperor, after a momentary pause. "Order my carriage!"

"Sire," said Belliard, solemnly, "it is no longer possible for your majesty to reach Paris. You would run the risk of falling into the hands of the vanguard of the allies. If your majesty were at Paris, it would be of no avail. The enemy is in possession of all the heights, and they can bombard the city without being interfered with by the exhausted troops of Mortier and Marmont. Sire, all is lost; there is no prospect which would justify us to hope for a favorable change."

"To Paris!" cried the emperor. "You say I can no longer enter the city. Well, then, I shall put myself at the head of the troops of Marshals Mortier and Marmont, and, while the allies are making their entrance into the city, resume the struggle."

"Sire," said Belliard, mournfully, "it is too late, the marshals have agreed to surrender Paris; it was only on this condition that our troops were allowed to move out. The capitulation cannot be broken."

"What do I care for the capitulation of traitorous marshals?" said the emperor, stamping; "my will alone reigns here, and my will is, that the troops face about and follow me.—Say, Hulin," said the emperor, turning toward the commander of Paris, who had just approached him, "are you not of my opinion? The troops should return to Paris?"

"No, sire," said General Hulin, sighing, "the capitulation has already been concluded, and it does not permit the soldiers to return on any pretext."

"Are you of the same opinion?" asked Napoleon, turning toward General Curial, who had just come up with a corps of infantry, and saluted the emperor.

"I am, sire," said Curial. "The capitulation has been concluded, and we are happy to have received permission for our troops, who are exhausted, to evacuate the city. We are already on the march in the direction of Fontainebleau. We have no hope of conquering, and we could only be involved in a last dreadful but useless carnage. Your majesty cannot desire that. Have pity on poor France, bleeding from a thousand wounds; you do not wish the enemy to bombard the heart of our country."

"And you?" asked Napoleon, turning his eyes, with an expression of agony, toward his attendants. "Caulaincourt, do you, too, share the views of these gentlemen?"

"Yes, sire," said Caulaincourt, with tears in his eyes. "It is too late to conquer; it only remains for us to save what we can."

"And you, Berthier and Flahault?"

"Sire, that is our opinion! It is too late; all is lost!"

Napoleon's sigh sounded like a death-rattle. "Well, then," he said, in a faint, hollow voice, "I will return to Fontainebleau."

Napoleon reëntered his carriage. When his three attendants had taken seats, he rose and called out in a commanding voice, "General Belliard!" The general approached the carriage hesitatingly; he was still afraid lest the emperor should change his mind.

"Belliard," said Napoleon, "dispatch immediately an orderly to Marshals Marmont and Mortier, and communicate to them that they march their troops to Essonne, ten leagues south of Paris; there they are to take a position, and await further orders.—To Fontainebleau!"

The carriage passed again along the road by which it had arrived, bearing away a wearied and despairing man, who a moment before was full of hope and energy. The clock of the village of Jarissy struck twelve, when he halted in front of the "Cour de France," and had the horses changed. "Caulaincourt," he said, hurriedly, "alight, take post-horses, and hasten to Paris! Penetrate to the headquarters of the Emperor Alexander! Prevent the capitulation—do so in my name; you have full powers! Negotiate, consent to any treaty that recognizes me as sovereign of France!" *

It was past midnight, and with a new day began a new era. The rising sun shone upon the brilliant array of the allies. The terms of the capitulation had been adjusted at two in the morning. It was stipulated that the marshals should evacuate Paris at seven on the same day; that the public arsenals and magazines be surrendered in the same state in which they were when the capitulation was concluded; that the National Guard, according to the pleasure of the allies, be either disbanded, or employed under their direction in the service of the city; that the wounded and stragglers, found after ten in the morning, be considered prisoners of war; and that Paris be recommended to the generosity of the sovereigns.†

It was now eight in the morning, and the corps of the allied troops that were to make their entrance into the city were in readiness. A staff, composed of hundreds of Austrian, Russian, Prussian, Wurtemberg, Bavarian, and Swedish generals, awaited the arrival of the Emperor of Russia and the King of Prussia, when the triumphal march into Paris would take place.

Overcoming his pain, and keeping erect by a violent effort, Field-Marshal Blucher had himself dressed by his servants. The toilet was finished, and, attired in his uniform, covered with glittering orders, he stepped from his bedroom, and sent for Christian. "Pipe-master," he said, "I am ready now, and believe I look quite imposing; but you must adjust the last ornament of my toilet. You captured it, and ought to add it to my uniform."

"What ornament, your excellency?"

---

* Beitzke, vol. III., p. 494.
† "Mémoires du Duc de Rovigo," vol. III.

"Well, the eye-shade, Christian. Come and adorn me!" He handed the crownless bonnet to Christian, and sat down on a chair. The article was carefully placed on the head of the field-marshal, so that his bald scalp protruded from the aperture of the shade like a full moon surrounded by a green halo. He then carefully put on it the field-marshal's hat, with its waving plumes and gold-lace.*

"Now I am ready," said Blucher, rising.

At this moment the door opened, and General Gneisenau, accompanied by Surgeon-General Voelzke, entered the room.

"What!" exclaimed Gneisenau, in amazement. "An hour ago I found you in bed, a prey to a raging fever, complaining of your eyes; and now you have not only risen, but are in full feather, and ready for the march into the city!"

"Why, yes, of course, I am," said Blucher, sullenly. "I must make my entry, I must keep my word, and get into Paris after aiding in getting him out of it."

"That is to say," cried Dr. Voelzke, "you intend to break your pledge, and prove faithless to your oath?"

"What oath?" asked Blucher, greatly surprised.

"Did you not solemnly pledge me your word four days ago, your excellency, to submit to my treatment for two weeks, and adhere to my instructions?"

"Yes, and I think I have kept my word. I have swallowed your medicines, pills, and powders, rubbed in your salves, and applied your plasters, in accordance with your directions, although I must say that all this did not help me any"

"But your eyes have not grown any worse, and they will soon improve, if you continue my treatment."

"Well, what do you want me to do, then?"

"You must stay here. You must not be six or eight hours on horseback; you must not expose yourself so long to the dust and sun."

"What! I am not to participate in the entrance of the monarchs into Paris?" cried Blucher, indignantly.

"I implore your excellency not to do so," said the physician, in an impressive tone. "Give yourself a few days' rest and recreation, and your eyes will get well; but if you expose yourself to-day I shall never again cross your threshold, for I do not care to be disgraced by the report that Field-Marshal Blucher lost his eyesight while under my care; and I tell you, you will be blind, and then I can do nothing for you."

"Stay here, your excellency," begged Gneisenau; "do not trifle with your dear eyes, destined to see still many beautiful things, and gladden the world by their heroic glances! What can a triumph of a few hours' duration be to you to whom every day will be a triumph, and whom delivered Germany awaits to greet with manifestations of love and gratitude?"

"Ah, it is not for the sake of the triumph that I wish to go," cried Blucher, morosely. "But I have sworn, for seven years, and it has been my only consolation, that, in spite of Bonaparte, I would make my triumphal entrance into Paris, as Bonaparte did into Berlin, and now you insist on my not fulfilling my oath!"

"You will nevertheless make your entrance into Paris," exclaimed Gneisenau; "though your person be absent, your name will float as our banner of victory over the monarchs, and all know full well that Blucher is *the* conqueror."

"Stay!" begged Voelzke; "think of the pain which you have already suffered, and of that you will suffer, and of which I give you sufficient warning."

"Yes, field-marshal," begged Hennemann, with tearful eyes, "pray do what the doctor says; do not hazard your sight; for, let me say, field-marshal, a blind man is like a pipe that will not draw; both of them will go out."

"Well, I do not care," cried Blucher, "I will stay. It will not hurt me. My task is performed, and it makes no difference to me how I enter Paris. I have my share of the victory, and no one can take it from me. *He* has been cast down, and none will deny that I assisted."

---

* Varnhagen, "Life of Blucher," p. 382.

"Well, I think I have also assisted a little in it," said Christian, solemnly; "for had I not always kept the pipes in so good a state, the field marshal would not have had such successful ideas, nor could he have so well said, 'Forward!'"

"You are right, pipe-master," said Blucher, pleasantly. "The pipe—but what is that? Was not that a gun, and there another? Have the negotiations miscarried, after all, and the bombardment commenced in earnest?"

"No, your excellency," said Gneisenau, smiling, "you must give up that hope! There are the guns which give the troops the signal that the monarchs have arrived, and that the march into the city is to commence."

"Well, good-by, then; make haste and leave!" cried Blucher, pushing Gneisenau and Voelzke toward the door.

They left, and the field-marshal was again alone with Christian Hennemann.

"Well," he said, "give me a pipe; while the others are making their entrance into Paris, I want you to afford me a little pleasure, too. Come here, therefore, and sing to me the Low-German song which you sang to me on the day when you arrived at Kunzendorf."

The reports of the artillery continued; the monarchs were entering Paris. The field-marshal in the mean time sat with the green bonnet on his head, puffing his pipe. No one was with him but Christian Hennemann, who sang in a loud voice, "*Spinn doch, spinn doch, mihn lütt lewes Döchting!*"

———+———

CHAPTER LIII.

NAPOLEON AT FONTAINEBLEAU.

NAPOLEON passed seven days of indescribable mental anguish at Fontainebleau. Adversity had befallen him, but he bore it with the semblance of calmness, uttering no complaint. His was still the cold, inscrutable face of the emperor, such as it had been on his triumphal entrance into Berlin and Madrid, after the victories of Austerlitz and Jena, in the days of Erfurt and Tilsit, at the conflagration of Moscow, at the Beresina, and at Leipsic. He gave no expression to his soul's agony. It was only in the dead of night that his faithful servants heard him sometimes sigh, pacing his room, restless and melancholy. He did not yet feel wholly discouraged; he still hoped. His bravest marshals were still with him; his Old Guard had not yet gone, and at Paris there were many devoted friends, because they owed to him honor and riches.

He was hopeful that Marmont's troops would arrive at Fontainebleau, when, concentrating all his corps, he would march with them and reconquer his capital. Engrossed with this idea, he was alone in his cabinet; bent over his maps, he examined the various positions of his troops, and considered when they might all reach him. But while he was thinking of war, his marshals were thinking of peace. They had withdrawn into one of the remote apartments of Fontainebleau for the purpose of holding a secret consultation. Ther were his old comrades Ney, Prince de la Moskwa; Macdonald, Duke de Tarento; Lefebvre, Duke de Dantzic; Oudinot, Duke de Reggio—all of them owing their glory to Napoleon: it was, therefore, pardonable if he confided in their gratitude—but gratitude to the fallen, who had nothing more to give, and whose misfortunes resembled an infectious disease, repelling even his dearest friends.

"He is lost," said Oudinot, in an undertone; "he is on the edge of the precipice, and those who abide by him will fall with him."

"We must, therefore, leave him," whispered Lefebvre. "We are unable to keep him back; prudence commands us to keep aloof."

"We have suffered and bled for him for years," said Macdonald; "it is time now for him to suffer and bleed for us. His death would be a relief."

"Yes," murmured Ney, "his death would give us a new life. But he will not die; his heart is made of bronze, and will not break."

"No, he will not die voluntarily," said Oudinot. The marshals paused and looked at each other with dark and significant glances. All seemed to read each other's souls, and to divine the sinister thoughts that began to find utterance.

"No, he will not die voluntarily," repeated Macdonald. "But the millions of soldiers that have fallen on the battle-fields have not died voluntarily, either: Napoleon drove them into the jaws of death. Now he is no longer any thing but a mere soldier; could we be blamed, if, in order to save France, we should drive him into the grave?"

"But how could we do it?" asked Lefebvre. "He has with him Caulaincourt, Berthier, and Maret, who would certainly be capable of showing, like Anthony, the blood-stained cloak of Cæsar to the people, and of bringing upon us a destiny such as befell Brutus and Cassius. I am not desirous of seeing my house set on fire, and of being compelled to flee."

"We ought not to imitate Cæsar's generals," said Ney, gloomily. "He has lived like a demi-god, and must die like a demi-god. Not a vestige of him must remain; he must, like Romulus, ascend to the gods."

"Let us consider what ought to be done," said Macdonald.

They whispered in low tones, so that they themselves scarcely heard each other. After a prolonged secret consultation, they seemed agreed as to what should be done, and as if there were now no longer any doubt or objection.

"Caulaincourt, Bertrand, and Maret, are alone to be feared," said Oudinot, loudly. "If they refuse to be silent, they must be silenced! And Berthier? what are we to do with Berthier?"

"We shall tell him all when it is over," responded Macdonald, with a shrug. "Berthier is not formidable; he has a heart of cotton, and a head of wind."

All laughed; Oudinot then said, in a grave and menacing voice: "It is time for us to come to a decision. We are already in April, and nothing decided; the Emperor of Russia is impatient, and the future King of France will never forgive us if we delay his return to Paris. Come, gentlemen, let us for the last time try the way of kindness and persuasion. Let us openly and honestly advise Napoleon to abdicate; he must make up his mind to do so, or—"

"Or we shall compel him," said Macdonald. "He has often enough compelled us to do what was repugnant to us. Come, gentlemen, let us go to the emperor." *

The emperor was still bending over his maps when the four marshals entered his cabinet. With a quick glance he read in their pale, sullen faces that they came to him, not as friends and servants, but as adversaries. "I am glad," he said calmly, "that you anticipate my request, and come to me when I intended to send for you. We must hold a council of war, marshals. I have determined to make a general assault upon the allies to-morrow, and I wished to assemble you here to lay the details of my plan before you. One of you may go and call Berthier, who should participate in our deliberations."

"Sire," said Ney, in a harsh tone, "before entering into deliberations on the war, we should first consider whether it is still desirable." Napoleon cast on him a glance which once would have frozen the marshal's blood, but which now made no impression on him. "I believe," added Ney, "that France can no longer bear the burden of war. She is exhausted, bleeding from many wounds, and would sink to certain ruin if she continue a useless struggle. Her finances cannot be restored, for the people are destitute. Our fields are uncultivated, our industry is paralyzed; our workshops and stores are closed, our commerce is prostrated, for France is destitute of money, credit, and laborers. What means has your majesty to shield her from the most terrible misfortunes?"

"I have but one—to attack the allies to-morrow, expelling those who have caused all the misfortunes of France."

"Sire, our country is tired of war," cried Ney; "she wants peace."

"Is that your opinion, marshals?" asked the emperor, hastily.

"Yes, sire, it is."

---

* "Memoirs of the Duchess d'Abrantes."

" **Well**, then," said Napoleon, after a moment's reflection, " do you know of any way of restoring peace ? "

The marshals were silent. Their lips seemed to shrink from uttering the thoughts of their souls; but the Prince de la Moskwa, Marshal Ney, overcame his timidity. " Sire," he remarked, " the allies say in their proclamation that it is not France against which they wage war."

" Not France, but myself ! " cried Napoleon. " Ah, you come to propose an abdication to me ? "

" We come to implore your majesty to make a last great sacrifice."

" Sire," exclaimed Oudinot, " let your heroic soul conquer itself, and restore peace to France."

" She will forever bless you," said Lefebvre.

" Restore to France the peace for which she has been vainly longing for twenty-five years ! " cried Macdonald.

Now that they had all spoken, there was an anxious, breathless pause. Suddenly Napoleon passed over to his desk. He cast a last glance, full of pride, contempt, and anger, on his four marshals; then, seating himself, he took up a pen with a firm hand, and wrote. **The** marshals stood in **silence, and looked** at him in an embarrassed manner. Laying aside the pen, and rising, he held up the paper on which he had written, and motioned to Marshal Ney. " Here, Prince de la Moskwa," said Napoleon, " read to the marshals what I have written."

Ney read in a tremulous voice: " ' The allied powers, having proclaimed that the Emperor Napoleon is the sole obstacle to the reëstablishment of peace in Europe, the Emperor Napoleon, faithful to his oath, declares that he is ready to descend from the throne, to quit France, and even life itself, for the good of the country, inseparable from the rights of his son, of the regency of the empress, and of the maintenance of the laws of the empire.' " *

" You have willed it so," said Napoleon, when Ney had finished. " Macdonald and Ney, with Caulaincourt, will immediately repair with this docu-

ment to Paris. On the way they will meet Mortier, and request him to accompany them. The four dukes will present my conditional abdication to the Emperor Alexander, and treat with him in regard to the future of my son and the regency of my consort."

On the 7th of April the Duke de Vicenza entered the emperor's cabinet, pale and with a mournful air.

" Caulaincourt," cried Napoleon, " you have **delivered** my abdication to Alexander ? "

" Yes, sire," said Caulaincourt, sadly. " Ah, sire, I bring bad news, which my lips almost refuse to utter ! "

" Speak, I am courageous enough to hear all; be, then, courageous enough to tell me all. I wish no concealment whatever—I desire to know **the** whole truth."

" Well, sire, all is lost. The Emperor Alexander has issued to-day a manifesto, which has been placarded over every part of Paris, to the effect that ' he would no longer treat with Bonaparte, nor with any member of his family.' "

" Ah, the perfidious wretch ! " murmured Napoleon, " he plighted me once eternal friendship and fidelity.—Proceed, Caulaincourt ! What says the so-called provisional government presided over by M. Talleyrand, the renegade priest, whom I made a man of distinction, whom I raised to the dignity of a prince, on whom I lavished honors, and who has now become the leader of the royalists? What say M. Talleyrand, and the provisional government, and the senate, who swore allegiance to me ? "

" Sire, the senate solemnly declared yesterday, the 6th of April, that the Emperor Napoleon has forfeited his throne, because, by abusing the powers conferred on him, by despotism, by trampling under foot the liberty of the press, by undertaking wars in violation of right, and by his openly manifested contempt of man and human law, he has rendered himself unworthy of the sovereignty of the nation. The senate, besides, have called back the Bourbons to the throne of France. In consequence of this declaration, the provisional government has proclaimed to-day that, till **the ar**

---

* Fain. "**Manuscrit** de 1814." p. 221.

rival of King Louis **XVIII.**, the administration is exclusively in their hands."

"Ah, the traitors!" cried Napoleon. "They have dared to proclaim such sentiments! to carry their impudence so far! See what venal creatures those men are! As long as fortune was faithful to me, they, who now call themselves the provisional government and senate, in the name of France, were my most sycophantic servants. A sign from me was an order for the senate, **who** always did more than was desired of them, **and not a whisper was heard against the** abuses **of power. Ah, they** charge me with despising **them—tell me,** Caulaincourt, will not the world see now whether or not I had reasons for my opinion?" *

"Sire, it is true, your majesty has met with many ingrates during **your career,** and will still meet with them," said Caulaincourt, sighing. "Perfidy seems to have become an epidemic."

"Ah, I see you have not yet told me **every** thing. Speak! **In the first place, what was the result of** your negotiations with the Emperor Alexander?"

"Sire, if your majesty agrees to renounce, for yourself and your heirs, the throne of France, the allied sovereigns offer Corsica or Elba as a sovereign principality, and France will pay **your** majesty an annual pension of two million **francs."**

"**I am** to renounce the throne, too, for my son —my dear little King of Rome?" cried Napoleon, mournfully. "No, never! I cannot deprive my son of his inheritance. This is too much. I will put myself at the head of my army and run the risk of any calamities, rather **than** submit to a humiliation worse than them all!"

"Your majesty has no army. Treason has infected your marshals."

"What do you mean? Ah, it is true, you come **alone!** Where are the marshals? Where is Ney? Where is Macdonald?"

"Sire, they have remained in Paris."

"Ah, I understand," exclaimed Napoleon, with

a scornful laugh; "they are waiting there for King Louis XVIII, in order to offer him their **services. But where is** Marmont? You know well that I am greatly attached to Marmont, and I long to see him. Why does he not come?"

"Sire, Marshal Marmont has passed over to the allies with a corps of ten thousand men."

"Marmont!" cried Napoleon, almost with a scream—"Marmont a traitor! That is false— that is impossible! Marmont cannot have betrayed me!"

"Sire, he did betray you. He marched the troops, notwithstanding their undisguised reluctance, to Versailles, in order there to join the allies, after receiving from them the solemn promise that the French soldiers should be treated as friends."

"Marmont has betrayed me!" murmured Napoleon. "Marmont, whom I loved as a son— who owes me all—who—" His voice faltered; his heart was rent, and, sinking on a chair, he buried his quivering face in his hands.

CHAPTER LIV.

A SOUL IN PURGATORY.

IT was the 11th of April. Napoleon, at Fontainebleau, sat at his desk and stared at the paper before him. It contained an absolute resignation of his throne for himself and his family. After signing this document, he was no more Emperor of France, nor his son King of Rome, nor his consort empress—perhaps, no longer even his wife. By signing this paper, he accepted all the conditions imposed on him by the allies; that is to say, he descended from the sovereignty of all his states and went to the little island of Elba, to live there a pensioner of **Europe**; his consort wore no longer, like him, the imperial title, but became Duchess of Parma; and the King of Rome became not the heir of his father, the Emperor of Elba, but the heir of his mother, the Duchess of Parma, and the title of "Duke de Reichstadt"

---

* Fain, "Manuscrit de 1814," p. 225.

was to be given him. He renounced not only France, but his wife and his son!

Napoleon was fondly and sincerely attached to Maria Louisa, and he loved the King of Rome with passionate tenderness. Before consenting, therefore, to affix his signature to this act of abdication, he wished to know whether Maria Louisa agreed to it, and whether she would not at least ask the allies, one of whom was her own father, to permit her to reside with her son and her husband on the island of Elba, sharing the emperor's exile. For some time he had not heard from his consort; he wrote to her every day, but for six days past no answers came. He did not, however, distrust **her**; he knew that Maria Louisa loved him. His heart longed for her and his child. He **had sent** Berthier to Orleans the day before with a letter for Maria Louisa. He was to tell him what his consort was thinking and wishing. If she was courageous enough to claim her rights, and desired to do so, Berthier was to convey her to the emperor, and, at Fontainebleau, Maria Louisa was to declare to her father that she insisted on her sacred right of staying with her husband. Napoleon expected this, and he was nervous and anxious, waiting for the return of his general, and in hope that Maria Louisa would accompany him.

He contemplated the paper, and, while reading the words of despair, he thought of the past—of the days when Europe had been at his feet, and when he himself showed no mercy. The door of the cabinet was softly opened, and the Duke de Bassano entered. "Maret," he exclaimed, "you come to inform me that Berthier has returned, do you not?"

"Yes, sire."

"And he—he is alone?"

"Yes, sire, he is alone."

Napoleon sighed. "Admit Berthier," he said, "but stay here."

Maret stepped to the door and opened it. The Prince of Neufchatel entered, mournful and silent. A single glance told Napoleon that his mission had failed.

"Well, Berthier, you have seen the empress?"

"I have, sire. I met the empress leaving Orleans."

"Ah, then, she is coming!" exclaimed Napoleon.

"No, sire. Prince Metternich had paid her a visit on the preceding day, and delivered to her autograph letters from her father the Emperor of Austria. He had asked his daughter to repair to Rambouillet, where he would meet her."

"And Louisa consented?"

"She did, sire. Her majesty told me with tears in her eyes that nothing remained for her but to submit to the will of her father, because only his intercession could secure her own future and that of her son. She deplored that she was not **at liberty to** come to Fontainebleau, but stated **she had** solemnly pledged her word to Prince Metternich, who, in the emperor's name, had required a pledge neither to see nor to correspond with your majesty."

"And she did not indignantly reject this base demand?" cried the emperor. "She did not remember that she is my wife, and that she plighted her faith to me?"

"**Sire, the empress said** that, for her son's **sake,** she was **allowed** now only to consider herself a princess of Austria, and the Austrian princesses were all educated in unconditional and unmurmuring obedience to the orders of the emperor their father.[*] Hence, she obeyed her father now, in order to enjoy at a later time the happiness of belonging to your majesty. For, as soon as her future was secured, as soon as the duchy of Parma was settled upon her, and her son declared its heir, nothing would prevent her from rejoining her beloved husband; and if your majesty agreed to accept the island of Elba, the empress would certainly soon repair thither. She proposed that, prohibited from directly corresponding with your majesty, you might have intercourse through your private secretaries; your majesty might have Baron Fain write to her all you wished her to **know,** and she would do the same through Baron de Meneval."

---

[*] Meneval, "Mémoires," etc. vol. II., p. 50.

"A genuine woman's stratagem," murmured Napoleon, gloomily, to himself. "She is destitute of courage, and does not love me enough to brave her father.—Berthier," he then asked aloud, "did you see my son?"

"No, sire, they would not let me see the prince; they feared lest it would excite him too much, and remind him of the past. For the King of Rome is constantly longing for his father."

"And his father cannot see him—cannot call him to his side! Oh, Berthier, this is painful, very painful!"

"But your majesty will soon be reunited with him," said Maret, feelingly. "Sign the act of abdication; go to Elba, sire, and no one can prevent the empress from coming to you with her son. She wishes and has a right to do so."

"Well, then, be it so," said the emperor, drawing a deep breath. "I will sign every thing. I will abdicate; I will sign this second treaty, which makes me Emperor of Elba! My wife and my son must be restored to me!" He quickly stepped to the desk, and signed the two papers with a steady hand.

"Well," he said, flinging the pen into a corner of the room, "now I am no longer Emperor of France, but at the same time no longer a prisoner at Fontainebleau. At Elba I shall be free, at least; I shall be surrounded by the brave soldiers of my Old Guard; I shall see again my wife and my son. That is to say," he gloomily murmured to himself, "if her father permits them to rejoin me; for without his permission she will not come. Louisa is a princess of Austria, and has, therefore, been brought up in obedience. Oh, how I longed for the consolation of her presence! She ought not to have left me alone in these days!" His lips murmured softly, "Josephine would not have done so! She would have gone with me into exile!" He sat a long time absorbed in his reflections, which whispered to him of the past, and of Josephine. He felt that they moved him too deeply, and, with an impetuous gesture, he jumped up, and, proudly throwing back his head, exclaimed: "Well, then,

I have submitted to my fate, and shall bear it manfully. We shall go to Elba, then! You will accompany me, my friends, and I shall not be alone? Maret and Berthier, you will not leave me, I hope?"

"Sire, I would follow your majesty to the end of the world!" said Maret, tenderly.

"I know of no more glorious destiny than to remain your majesty's faithful servant," exclaimed Berthier, emphatically. "I thank you for permitting me to go with you to Elba, and I joyfully accept this permission; but as I have to make some necessary preparations, I request two days' leave of absence of your majesty."

While Berthier was speaking, the emperor contemplated him with painful astonishment; now he quickly came near him, and, laying his hand on his shoulder, he fixed his keen eyes on him, as if he wished to read his most secret thoughts. "Berthier," he said, in a gentle, imploring voice, "you see how much I have need of consultation; how necessary it is for me to have true friends about me. You will, therefore, return to-morrow, will you not?"

"Sire, certainly," faltered Berthier.

Napoleon's eyes still rested on the pale, confused face of the prince. "Berthier," he said, after a pause, "if you wish to leave me, tell me so frankly and sincerely."

"I leave you!" exclaimed Berthier. "Your majesty knows well that I am devoted to you with immovable fidelity—that my heart can never forget you, and that I shall always be your obedient servant."

"Words, words!" said Napoleon, shaking his head. "Well, then, it is your will: go, therefore, to Paris. Attend to the affairs which you have more at heart than my wishes. Go, and—if you can, come back soon!"

Berthier wished to grasp the emperor's hand and press it to his lips, but he hastily withdrew it, and, lifting it up, pointed with an imperious glance at the door. Berthier bowed, and, walking backward, approached the door with bent head, and departed. The emperor looked after him long and gloomily; then he slowly turned his

"Josephine, I have wrung many tears from you, but Fate has avenged you."   p. 293.

head toward the Duke de Bassano. "Maret," he said, slowly, "Berthier will not come back."

"What, sire!" exclaimed Maret, in dismay. "Your majesty believes—"

"I know it," said Napoleon, slowly, "Berthier will **not** come back!" He threw himself into an easy-chair, at times heaving a sigh, out without uttering a single complaint; and thus he sat all day. From time to time the few faithful men who had remained with him dared to speak, but the emperor, starting from his meditations, only stared at them, and then slowly dropped his head again on his breast. At dinner-time Maret endeavored to induce him to go to the table; but he **only** responded by indignantly shaking his head, **and** waving him toward the door.

Evening had come, and the emperor still sat alone in his cabinet, motionless and sad. He did not hear the door behind him softly open; he did not see a dark, veiled female form that had slowly entered, and now, as if overwhelmed by grief, leaned against the wall. Her veil prevented her, perhaps, from seeing Napoleon; she threw it back, and now Josephine's pale, quivering face was seen. She fixed her eyes on him with an expression of boundless tenderness, and then lifted them to heaven with an imploring air, softly raising her arms, and her lips moving in inaudible prayer.

The emperor did not yet notice her. Josephine stepped noiselessly across the carpet, and laid her hand gently on his head. "Napoleon," she whispered, "Napoleon!"

He uttered a cry and jumped up. "Josephine," he exclaimed, "my Josephine! Oh, now I am no longer alone!" He clasped her with impassioned tenderness in his arms; he kissed her quivering lips, and held her streaming face between his hands, gazing at it with the tender expression of a lover. Encircling her with his arms, and no longer able to restrain his heart, he laid his head on her shoulder, and wept bitterly. Recovering, his face resumed its inscrutable expression. "Josephine," he said, "I have wrung many tears from you, but Fate has avenged you; I have wept, too; and what is worse than tears is that which is gnawing at my heart. I thank you, Josephine, for coming to me. All have deserted me!"

"I know it, Napoleon," whispered Josephine, smiling **amid** tears, "and that **is why** I am here. You will not go all alone to Elba; I shall go with you. No, Bonaparte, no! do not shake your head; do not reject me! I have a right to accompany you; for, whatever men may say, I was your wife and am your wife, and what God has joined together no man can sunder. My soul is one with yours. I love you to-day as tenderly as I did on the day when I stood with you before the altar and plighted my fidelity to you; **I love** you now even more intensely, for you are unfortunate, and have need of my love. Bid me, **therefore,** not go any more. *She* is not here, and her place by your side, which she **has** deserted, belongs to me!"

"No," said Napoleon, gravely, "let her absence remind her of her duty. I will not give my son's mother a pretext for staying away from me; she shall not say that she cannot rejoin me because I have yielded to another woman the place that belongs to her. No, Josephine, she must not be able to reproach me. I thank you for coming, but you have come to take leave of me. I have seen you—your faithful love has been a balm to my heart. Now, farewell!"

"Then, you bid me go already?" cried Josephine, reproachfully; "oh, Bonaparte, let me stay here at least till your departure. No one will betray to *her* that I am here."

"It would remain no secret, Josephine, and it would be used to excuse her, and to accuse me. Go, then, and take with you the consciousness that you have afforded me the last joy of my life."

"Oh, Bonaparte, you break my heart!" murmured Josephine, leaning her head on his shoulder. "I cannot leave you, I cannot bear to see you go alone into exile."

"Fate has decreed it, and so has the evil star **that** arose upon my path when I left you, Josephine! Let this be my farewell. Now, go!"

"No, Bonaparte," she cried, passionately;

"tell me not to go if you do not wish me to die! Your misfortunes have pierced my heart. My only hope of life is by your side, for **sorrow at** the remembrance of your misfortunes will **kill me**"

A strange smile played around the emperor's lips. "I do not pity those who die," he said; "death is a kind friend, and pray God that He may soon send this friend to me!" He kissed her forehead and conducted her gently to the door. **"Go, my Josephine,"** he said; "this is **the last sacrifice which** I shall ask of you!"

"I go!" she sighed. "Farewell, Bonaparte, farewell!" **She** fixed on him a look full of love and grief. "We shall never meet again!"

"Yes," he said, slowly and solemnly, lifting his hand toward heaven, "we shall meet again!"

"I shall await you there!" she said, with an expression of intense love and sorrow.

The door closed; Napoleon **was again alone; he stood in** the middle of the room, **as if still beholding her** pale, smiling face, **and hearing her sweet voice. "She** will await **me there!" he** murmured. "But why should she await **me?** Why should she die, and I live? And why must I live?" he asked, in a loud, and almost joyful tone. "Why shall I suffer **these** mean, cowardly creatures, who formerly lay **in** the dust before **me, now to** enjoy their triumph? Why must I **live?"** He sank into his chair, thinking of the **disgrace soon to be** brought **upon him,** remembering **that** each **of the allied sovereigns** would send **an envoy to Fontainebleau, and** that he was to be transported **to Elba—escorted, like a** caged lion, by Russian, **Prussian, and** Austrian **commissioners!** His heart **for** a moment grew **strong** in his anguish. **He** jumped up, rushed **to his** desk, pulled out the drawers, and opened **a secret** compartment. There lay **a small** black silken **bag.** Taking it out, he cut it open, and drew a **package** from it. "Ha!" **he** exclaimed, joyfully, **"now I** have the kind friend that will deliver **me! They want** to drag me through the country **as a** prisoner! **But** thou, **blessed poison, wilt release me!"**

In the night of the **13th** of April, Constant, Napoleon's valet de chambre, was awakened **by** an extraordinary groaning, proceeding from Napoleon's bedroom, whither Constant hastened. Yes, **it was** the emperor **who was** suffering. His face was deadly pale; his limbs **were** quivering; a paper lay on the floor in **front of** him; on the table by his side stood a glass, in which were still seen some drops of **a** whitish color. Constant rushed toward him. He gazed at his servant with fixed looks, and murmured, "I suffer dreadfully! Fire is consuming my bowels; but it does not kill me!"

Uttering a cry, and hastening from the room, Constant went for the domestic surgeon, Dr. Ivan, Maret, and Caulaincourt. They appeared in the utmost consternation, and surrounded the easy-chair on which the emperor still sat. Dr. Ivan felt his forehead, which was covered with clammy perspiration; and his pulse was feeble and sluggish, but still throbbing. He recognized his physician, and his livid lips murmured almost inaudibly, "Ivan, I have taken poison, that which you gave me one day in Russia; but it has lost its efficacy! It does not kill, while it causes me excruciating pain."

Ivan went weeping out of the room to prepare a remedy.

Napoleon turned his eyes with an expression of agony toward Maret and Caulaincourt, who were kneeling before him. "My friends," he said, "I sought death! But you see God did not will it! He commands me to live and suffer." [*]

On the morning after this night of terror, the emperor rose from his couch, and his face, which for the last few days had been so gloomy, assumed now a serene expression. "Providence has spared me for other purposes," he murmured to himself. "Well, then, I shall live! To the living belongs the future!" [†]

A week afterward, on the 20th of April, Napoleon left Fontainebleau for Elba. In the courtyard of the palace, the Old Guard was drawn up

---

[*] Constant's "Mémoires," vol. vi., p. 88. Fain, "Manuscrit."

[†] Bausset's "Mémoires," vol. ii., p. 244.

In the **splendor** of their arms, with their eagles and banners. **Near** the ranks of the soldiers, in front of **the** main portal, stood Bonaparte's travelling-carriage, and beside it the foreign commissioners. Before setting out, he wished to take leave of his faithful soldiers. Advancing into the midst of the Old Guard, he addressed them in a firm voice: "Soldiers of my Old Guard, I bid you adieu! During twenty years I have ever found you in the path of honor. In the last days, as in those of our prosperity, you have never ceased to be models of bravery and fidelity. With such men as you our cause could never have been lost; but the war would never end; it would have become a civil war, and France must daily **have been** more unhappy. I have, therefore, sacrificed all our interests to those of our country: I depart; but you remain to serve France Her happiness was my only thought; it will always be the object of my fervent wishes. Lament **not my** destiny: if I have consented to survive myself, it was because I might **contribute** to your **glory,** Adieu, my children! **I would I** could press **you** all to my heart; **but** I will, at least, press your eagle!" At these words, General Petit advanced with the eagle; Napoleon received the general in his arms, and, kissing the standard, he added: "I cannot embrace you all, but I do so in the person of your general! Adieu, once again, my old companions!"

The veteran soldiers had no reply but tears and sobs, and, stretching out their hands toward Napoleon, they implored him to stay. But the carriage rolled rapidly across the court-yard, bearing into exile, **or at best to the** sovereignty of an insignificant **island, a man who, in aiming at the empire of the world, had subdued almost all the** kingdoms of Europe.

THE END

LOUISA MÜHLBACH'S HISTORICAL NOVELS.

"We have on several occasions, in noticing the works of the great German authoress, Miss Mühlbach, expressed our admiration of them, but are now, after much careful reading of each volume as it has come from the press, almost constrained to pronounce them matchless; unrivaled in the whole domain of historical romance."—*Chicago Journal of Commerce.*

NAPOLEON AND THE QUEEN OF PRUSSIA. Illustrated. 8vo. Cloth, $1.00.

THE EMPRESS JOSEPHINE. Illustrated. 8vo. Cloth, $1.00.

NAPOLEON AND BLUCHER. Illustrated. 8vo. Cloth, $1.00.

QUEEN HORTENSE. Illustrated. 8vo. Cloth, $1.00.

MARIE ANTOINETTE AND HER SON. Illustrated. 8vo. Cloth, $1.00.

PRINCE EUGENE AND HIS TIMES. Illustrated. 8vo. Cloth, $1.00.

THE DAUGHTER OF AN EMPRESS. Illustrated. 8vo. Cloth, $1.00.

JOSEPH II AND HIS COURT. Illustrated. 8vo. Cloth, $1.00.

FREDERICK THE GREAT AND HIS COURT. Illustrated. 8vo. Cloth, $1.00.

FREDERICK THE GREAT AND HIS FAMILY. Illustrated. 8vo. Cloth, $1.00.

BERLIN AND SANS-SOUCI. Illustrated. 8vo. Cloth, $1.00.

GOETHE AND SCHILLER. Illustrated. 8vo. Cloth, $1.00.

MERCHANT OF BERLIN and **MARIA THERESA AND HER FIRE-MAN.** 8vo. Cloth, $1.00.

LOUISA OF PRUSSIA AND HER TIMES. Illustrated. 8vo. Cloth, $1.00.

OLD FRITZ AND THE NEW ERA. Illustrated. 8vo. Cloth, $1.00.

ANDREAS HOFER. Illustrated. 8vo. Cloth, $1.00.

MOHAMMED ALI AND HIS HOUSE. Illustrated. 8vo. Cloth, $1.00.

HENRY VIII AND CATHERINE PARR. Illustrated. 8vo. Cloth, $1.00.

⁂ Bound complete in 6 volumes, sold by set only, $12.00.

New York: D. APPLETON & CO., 1, 3, & 5 Bond Street.

RHODA BROUGHTON'S NOVELS.

"I love the romances of Miss Broughton; I think them much truer to Nature than Ouida's, and more impassioned and less preachy than George Eliot's. Miss Broughton's heroines are living beings, having not only flesh and blood, but also esprit and soul; in a word, they are real women—neither animals nor angels, but allied to both."—ANDRÉ THEURIET (the French Novelist).

COMETH UP AS A FLOWER. 8vo. Paper, 30 cents. 12mo. Cloth, $1.00.

NOT WISELY, BUT TOO WELL. 8vo. Paper, 30 cents. 12mo. Cloth, $1.00.

NANCY. 8vo. Paper, 50 cents. 12mo. Cloth, $1.00.

GOOD-BYE, SWEETHEART! 8vo. Paper, 30 cents. 12mo. Cloth, $1.00.

RED AS A ROSE IS SHE. 8vo. Paper, 30 cents. 12mo. Cloth, $1.00.

JOAN. 8vo. Paper, 50 cents.

BELINDA. 12mo. Cloth, $1.00.

SECOND THOUGHTS. 18mo. Paper, 50 cents; cloth, 75 cents.

A WIDOWER INDEED. By RHODA BROUGHTON and ELIZABETH BISLAND. 12mo. Paper, 50 cents; cloth, $1.00.

ROBERT BUCHANAN'S NOVELS.

MASTER OF THE MINE. 12mo. Paper, 25 cents.

MATT: A Tale of a Caravan. 12mo. Paper, 25 cents.

THE SHADOW OF THE SWORD. 8vo. Paper, 75 cents.

ANDRÉ THEURIET'S NOVELS.

GERARD'S MARRIAGE. 16mo. Paper, 25 cents; cloth, 60 cents.

THE GODSON OF A MARQUIS. 16mo. Paper, 25 cents; cloth, 60 cents.

YOUNG MAUGARS. 12mo. Paper, 25 cents; cloth, 60 cents.

RAYMONDE. 18mo. Paper, 30 cents.

ALL ALONE. 18mo. Paper, 25 cents.

ANTOINETTE. 18mo. Paper, 20 cents.

THE HOUSE OF THE TWO BARBELS. 18mo. Paper, 20 cents.

New York: D. APPLETON & CO., 1, 3, & 5 Bond Street.